Praise for the Cl[...]

'Archer is on top form'   *Daily Telegraph*

'I was touched and enthralled by this tale of how Harry from the Bristol backstreets rises from obscurity to high society . . . He's about to marry into the upper classes when tragedy strikes on the steps of the altar. I won't spoil it for you by revealing any more. Or the trademark twist, which is gasp-making'
                                                                    Daily Mail

'I enjoyed the book and marvelled at both its pace and the imaginative cliffhanger ending, whetting our appetite for volume two'   *Sunday Express*

'The ability to tell a story is a great – and unusual – gift . . . [it] is not something that can be taught or acquired. You have it or you don't . . . Jeffrey Archer is, first and foremost, a storyteller . . . You don't sell 250 million copies of your books (250 million!) if you can't keep an audience hooked – and that's what Archer does, book after book. Archer's audience will stick with him to the last. They want to know what happens next'
                                           Erica Wagner, Literary Editor, *The Times*

'I was reading the book on tour and found I was bunking off from my own signing sessions to get back to the story. Sitting in a Starbucks in Oxford, feverishly thumbing the pages to find out what dire machinations Hugo Barrington (a villain straight out of Victorian melodrama) would come up with next, I had to admit I was utterly hooked. It was an absurdly enjoyable read'
                                              Anthony Horowitz, *Telegraph*

'This is a cracker of a read. And quite "unputdownable". The whole thing about Jeffrey is that he has always had the knack of producing page-turners . . . This is a tale about love, treachery, deceit, decency and good triumphing over evil. It is quite captivating . . . and just as you sit on the end of your seat expecting all the loose ends to be tied into a neat little bow, Archer drops a bombshell in the last paragraph of the last chapter . . . If I was head of drama at the BBC I'd start planning the first season now'   Jerry Hayes, *Spectator*

Praise for Jeffrey Archer's novels

'If there was a Nobel prize for storytelling, Archer would win'
Daily Telegraph

'Probably the greatest storyteller of our age'   *Mail on Sunday*

'The man's a genius . . . the strength and excitement of the idea carries all before it'   *Evening Standard*

'A storyteller in the class of Alexandre Dumas' *Washington Post*

'Archer has a gift for storytelling that can only be described as genius'   *Daily Telegraph*

'Back on top form . . . Archer's imagination at its most sublime
. . . an entertaining, pacey page-turner'   *Sunday Times*

'Few are more famous than Archer for keeping the pages turning . . . an extravagant romp – possibly his best' *The Times*

THE CLIFTON CHRONICLES

VOLUMES ONE AND TWO

JEFFREY ARCHER, whose novels and short stories include *Kane and Abel*, *A Prisoner of Birth* and *Cat O' Nine Tales*, has topped the bestseller lists around the world, with sales of over 270 million copies.

He is the only author ever to have been a number one bestseller in fiction (eighteen times), short stories (four times) and non-fiction (*The Prison Diaries*).

The author is married to Dame Mary Archer, and they have two sons and two grandsons.

www.jeffreyarcher.com

Facebook.com/JeffreyArcherAuthor

@Jeffrey_Archer

ALSO BY JEFFREY ARCHER

THE CLIFTON CHRONICLES
Only Time Will Tell   The Sins of the Father
Best Kept Secret   Be Careful What You Wish For
Mightier than the Sword

NOVELS
Not a Penny More, Not a Penny Less
Shall We Tell the President?   Kane and Abel
The Prodigal Daughter   First Among Equals
A Matter of Honour   As the Crow Flies
Honour Among Thieves
The Fourth Estate   The Eleventh Commandment
Sons of Fortune   False Impression
The Gospel According to Judas
(with the assistance of Professor Francis J. Moloney)
A Prisoner of Birth   Paths of Glory

SHORT STORIES
A Quiver Full of Arrows   A Twist in the Tale
Twelve Red Herrings   The Collected Short Stories
To Cut a Long Story Short   Cat O' Nine Tales
And Thereby Hangs a Tale

PLAYS
Beyond Reasonable Doubt   Exclusive   The Accused

PRISON DIARIES
Volume One – Belmarsh: Hell
Volume Two – Wayland: Purgatory
Volume Three – North Sea Camp: Heaven

SCREENPLAYS
Mallory: Walking Off the Map   False Impression

JEFFREY ARCHER

THE CLIFTON CHRONICLES

VOLUMES ONE AND TWO

ONLY TIME WILL TELL

THE SINS OF THE FATHER

PAN BOOKS

Only Time Will Tell first published 2011 by Macmillan
First published in paperback 2011 by Pan Books

The Sins of the Father first published 2012 by Macmillan
First published in paperback 2012 by Pan Books

This omnibus edition first published 2015 by Pan Books
an imprint of Pan Macmillan, a division of Macmillan Publishers Limited
Pan Macmillan, 20 New Wharf Road, London N1 9RR
Basingstoke and Oxford
Associated companies throughout the world
www.panmacmillan.com

ISBN 978-1-5098-0177-0

1 3 5 7 9 8 6 4 2

A CIP catalogue record for this book is available from the British Library.

Typeset by SetSystems Ltd, Saffron Walden, Essex
Printed and bound by CPI Group (UK) Ltd, Croydon, CR0 4YY

Visit www.panmacmillan.com to read more about all our books
and to buy them. You will also find features, author interviews and
news of any author events, and you can sign up for e-newsletters
so that you're always first to hear about our new releases.

CONTENTS

ONLY TIME WILL TELL

ALAN QUILTER

1927–1998

My thanks go to the following people for their
invaluable advice and research:

John Anstee, Simon Bainbridge, John Cleverdon,
Eleanor Dryden, George Havens, Alison Prince,
Mari Roberts, Susan Watt, David Watts
and Peter Watts

THE BARRINGTONS

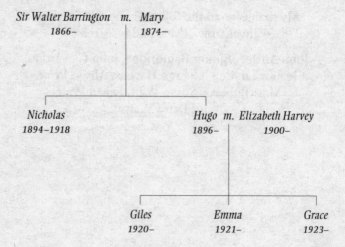

Sir Walter Barrington   m.   Mary
1866–   1874–

Nicholas   Hugo   m.   Elizabeth Harvey
1894–1918   1896–   1900–

Giles   Emma   Grace
1920–   1921–   1923–

THE CLIFTONS

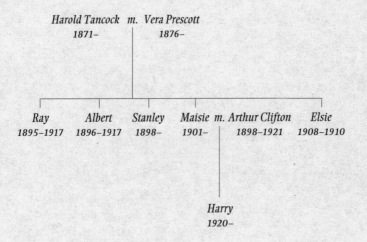

Harold Tancock m. Vera Prescott
1871–   1876–

Ray   Albert   Stanley   Maisie m. Arthur Clifton   Elsie
1895–1917   1896–1917   1898–   1901–   1898–1921   1908–1910

Harry
1920–

MAISIE CLIFTON

1919

PRELUDE

This story would never have been written if I hadn't become pregnant. Mind you, I had always planned to lose my virginity on the works outing to Weston-super-Mare, just not to that particular man.

Arthur Clifton was born in Still House Lane, just like me; even went to the same school, Merrywood Elementary, but as I was two years younger than him he didn't know I existed. All the girls in my class had a crush on him, and not just because he captained the school football team.

Although Arthur had never shown any interest in me while I was at school, that changed soon after he'd returned from the Western Front. I'm not even sure he realized who I was when he asked me for a dance that Saturday night at the Palais but, to be fair, I had to look twice before I recognized him because he'd grown a pencil moustache and had his hair slicked back like Ronald Colman. He didn't look at another girl that night, and after we'd danced the last waltz I knew it would only be a matter of time before he asked me to marry him.

Arthur held my hand as we walked back home, and when we reached my front door he tried to kiss me. I turned away. After all, the Reverend Watts had told me often enough that I had to stay pure until the day I was married, and Miss Monday, our choir mistress, warned me that men

3

only wanted one thing, and once they'd got it, they quickly lost interest. I often wondered if Miss Monday spoke from experience.

The following Saturday, Arthur invited me to the flicks to see Lillian Gish in *Broken Blossoms*, and although I allowed him to put an arm around my shoulder, I still didn't let him kiss me. He didn't make a fuss. Truth is, Arthur was rather shy.

The next Saturday I did allow him to kiss me, but when he tried to put a hand inside my blouse, I pushed him away. In fact I didn't let him do that until he'd proposed, bought a ring and the Reverend Watts had read the banns a second time.

My brother Stan told me that I was the last known virgin on our side of the River Avon, though I suspect most of his conquests were in his mind. Still, I decided the time had come, and when better than the works outing to Weston-super-Mare with the man I was going to marry in a few weeks' time?

However, as soon as Arthur and Stan got off the charabanc, they headed straight for the nearest pub. But I'd spent the past month planning for this moment, so when I got off the coach, like a good girl guide, I was prepared.

I was walking towards the pier feeling pretty fed up when I became aware someone was following me. I looked around and was surprised when I saw who it was. He caught up with me and asked if I was on my own.

'Yes,' I said, aware that by now Arthur would be on his third pint.

When he put a hand on my bum, I should have slapped his face, but for several reasons I didn't. To start with, I thought about the advantages of having sex with someone I wasn't likely to come across again. And I have to admit I was flattered by his advances.

By the time Arthur and Stan would have been downing

their eighth pints, he'd booked us into a guest house just off the seafront. They seemed to have a special rate for visitors who had no plans to spend the night. He started kissing me even before we'd reached the first landing, and once the bedroom door was closed he quickly undid the buttons of my blouse. It obviously wasn't his first time. In fact, I'm pretty sure I wasn't the first girl he'd had on a works outing. Otherwise, how did he know about the special rates?

I must confess I hadn't expected it to be all over quite so quickly. Once he'd climbed off me, I disappeared into the bathroom, while he sat on the end of the bed and lit up a fag. Perhaps it would be better the second time, I thought. But when I came back out, he was nowhere to be seen. I have to admit I was disappointed.

I might have felt more guilty about being unfaithful to Arthur if he hadn't been sick all over me on the journey back to Bristol.

The next day I told my mum what had happened, without letting on who the bloke was. After all, she hadn't met him, and was never likely to. Mum told me to keep my mouth shut as she didn't want to have to cancel the wedding, and even if I did turn out to be pregnant, no one would be any the wiser, as Arthur and I would be married by the time anyone noticed.

HARRY CLIFTON

1920–1933

1

I was told my father was killed in the war.

Whenever I questioned my mother about his death, she didn't say any more than that he'd served with the Royal Gloucestershire Regiment and had been killed fighting on the Western Front only days before the Armistice was signed. Grandma said my dad had been a brave man, and once when we were alone in the house she showed me his medals. My grandpa rarely offered an opinion on anything, but then he was deaf as a post so he might not have heard the question in the first place.

The only other man I can remember was my uncle Stan, who used to sit at the top of the table at breakfast time. When he left of a morning I would often follow him to the city docks, where he worked. Every day I spent at the dockyard was an adventure. Cargo ships coming from distant lands and unloading their wares: rice, sugar, bananas, jute and many other things I'd never heard of. Once the holds had been emptied, the dockers would load them with salt, apples, tin, even coal (my least favourite, because it was an obvious clue to what I'd been doing all day and annoyed my mother), before they set off again to I knew not where. I always wanted to help my uncle Stan unload whatever ship had docked that morning, but he just laughed, saying, 'All in good time, my lad.' It couldn't be soon enough for me, but, without any warning, school got in the way.

I was sent to Merrywood Elementary when I was six and I thought it was a complete waste of time. What was the point of school when I could learn all I needed to at the docks? I wouldn't have bothered to go back the following day if my mother hadn't dragged me to the front gates, deposited me and returned at four o'clock that afternoon to take me home.

I didn't realize Mum had other plans for my future, which didn't include joining Uncle Stan in the shipyard.

Once Mum had dropped me off each morning, I would hang around in the yard until she was out of sight, then slope off to the docks. I made sure I was always back at the school gates when she returned to pick me up in the afternoon. On the way home, I would tell her everything I'd done at school that day. I was good at making up stories, but it wasn't long before she discovered that was all they were: stories.

One or two other boys from my school also used to hang around the docks, but I kept my distance from them. They were older and bigger, and used to thump me if I got in their way. I also had to keep an eye out for Mr Haskins, the chief ganger, because if he ever found me loitering, to use his favourite word, he would send me off with a kick up the backside and the threat: 'If I see you loiterin' round here again, my lad, I'll report you to the headmaster.'

Occasionally Haskins decided he'd seen me once too often and I'd be reported to the headmaster, who would leather me before sending me back to my classroom. My form master, Mr Holcombe, never let on if I didn't show up for his class, but then he was a bit soft. Whenever my mum found out I'd been playing truant, she couldn't hide her anger and would stop my halfpenny-a-week pocket money. But despite the occasional punch from an older boy, regular leatherings from the headmaster and the loss of my pocket money, I still couldn't resist the draw of the docks.

I made only one real friend while I 'loitered' around the dockyard. His name was Old Jack Tar. Mr Tar lived in an abandoned railway carriage at the end of the sheds. Uncle Stan told me to keep away from Old Jack because he was a stupid, dirty old tramp. He didn't look that dirty to me, certainly not as dirty as Stan, and it wasn't long before I discovered he wasn't stupid either.

After lunch with my uncle Stan, one bite of his Marmite sandwich, his discarded apple core and a swig of beer, I would be back at school in time for a game of football; the only activity I considered it worth turning up for. After all, when I left school I was going to captain Bristol City, or build a ship that would sail around the world. If Mr Holcombe kept his mouth shut and the ganger didn't report me to the headmaster, I could go for days without being found out, and as long as I avoided the coal barges and was standing by the school gate at four o'clock every afternoon, my mother would never be any the wiser.

◄○►

Every other Saturday, Uncle Stan would take me to watch Bristol City at Ashton Gate. On Sunday mornings, Mum used to cart me off to Holy Nativity Church, something I couldn't find a way of getting out of. Once the Reverend Watts had given the final blessing, I would run all the way to the recreation ground and join my mates for a game of football before returning home in time for dinner.

By the time I was seven it was clear to anyone who knew anything about the game of football that I was never going to get into the school team, let alone captain Bristol City. But that was when I discovered that God had given me one small gift, and it wasn't in my feet.

To begin with, I didn't notice that anyone who sat near

me in church on a Sunday morning stopped singing whenever I opened my mouth. I wouldn't have given it a second thought if Mum hadn't suggested I join the choir. I laughed scornfully; after all, everyone knew the choir was only for girls and cissies. I would have dismissed the idea out of hand if the Reverend Watts hadn't told me that choirboys were paid a penny for funerals and tuppence for weddings; my first experience of bribery. But even after I'd reluctantly agreed to take a vocal test, the devil decided to place an obstacle in my path, in the form of Miss Eleanor E. Monday.

I would never have come across Miss Monday if she hadn't been the choir mistress at Holy Nativity. Although she was only five feet three, and looked as though a gust of wind might blow her away, no one tried to take the mickey. I have a feeling that even the devil would have been frightened of Miss Monday, because the Reverend Watts certainly was.

I agreed to take a vocal test, but not before my mum had handed over a month's pocket money in advance. The following Sunday I stood in line with a group of other lads and waited to be called.

'You will always be on time for choir practice,' Miss Monday announced, fixing a gimlet eye on me. I stared back defiantly. 'You will never speak, unless spoken to.' I somehow managed to remain silent. 'And during the service, you will concentrate at all times.' I reluctantly nodded. And then, God bless her, she gave me a way out. 'But most importantly,' she declared, placing her hands on her hips, 'within twelve weeks, you will be expected to pass a reading and writing test, so that I can be sure you are able to tackle a new anthem or an unfamiliar psalm.'

I was pleased to have fallen at the first hurdle. But as I was to discover, Miss Eleanor E. Monday didn't give up easily.

'What piece have you chosen to sing, child?' she asked me when I reached the front of the line.

'I haven't chosen anything,' I told her.

She opened a hymn book, handed it to me and sat down at the piano. I smiled at the thought that I might still be able to make the second half of our Sunday morning football game. She began to play a familiar tune, and when I saw my mother glaring at me from the front row of pews, I decided I'd better go through with it, just to keep her happy.

'*All things bright and beautiful, all creatures great and small. All things wise and wonderful...*' A smile had appeared on Miss Monday's face long before I reached '*the Lord God made them all*'.

'What's your name, child?' she asked.

'Harry Clifton, miss.'

'Harry Clifton, you will report for choir practice on Mondays, Wednesdays and Fridays at six o'clock sharp.' Turning to the boy standing behind me, she said, 'Next!'

I promised my mum I'd be on time for the first choir practice, even though I knew it would be my last, as Miss Monday would soon realize I couldn't read or write. And it would have been my last, if it hadn't been obvious to anyone listening that my singing voice was in a different class to that of any other boy in the choir. In fact, the moment I opened my mouth, everyone fell silent, and the looks of admiration, even awe, that I had desperately sought on the football field, were happening in church. Miss Monday pretended not to notice.

After she dismissed us, I didn't go home, but ran all the way to the docks so I could ask Mr Tar what I should do about the fact that I couldn't read or write. I listened carefully to the old man's advice, and the next day I went back to school and took my place in Mr Holcombe's class.

The schoolmaster couldn't hide his surprise when he saw me sitting in the front row, and was even more surprised when I paid close attention to the morning lesson for the first time.

Mr Holcombe began by teaching me the alphabet, and within days I could write out all twenty-six letters, if not always in the correct order. My mum would have helped me when I got home in the afternoon but, like the rest of my family, she also couldn't read or write.

Uncle Stan could just about scrawl his signature, and although he could tell the difference between a packet of Wills's Star and Wild Woodbines, I was fairly sure he couldn't actually read the labels. Despite his unhelpful mutterings, I set about writing the alphabet on any piece of scrap paper I could find. Uncle Stan didn't seem to notice that the torn-up newspaper in the privy was always covered in letters.

Once I'd mastered the alphabet, Mr Holcombe introduced me to a few simple words: 'dog', 'cat', 'mum' and 'dad'. That was when I first asked him about my dad, hoping that he might be able to tell me something about him. After all, he seemed to know everything. But he seemed puzzled that I knew so little about my own dad. A week later he wrote my first four-letter word on the blackboard, 'book', and then five, 'house', and six, 'school'. By the end of the month, I could write my first sentence, 'The quick brown fox jumps over the lazy dog', which, Mr Holcombe pointed out, contained every letter in the alphabet. I checked, and he turned out to be right.

By the end of term I could spell 'anthem', 'psalm' and even 'hymn', although Mr Holcombe kept reminding me I still dropped my aitches whenever I spoke. But then we broke up for the holidays and I began to worry I would never pass Miss Monday's demanding test without Mr

Holcombe's help. And that might have been the case, if Old Jack hadn't taken his place.

◄○►

I was half an hour early for choir practice on the Friday evening when I knew I would have to pass my second test if I hoped to continue as a member of the choir. I sat silently in the stalls, hoping Miss Monday would pick on someone else before she called on me.

I had already passed the first test with what Miss Monday had described as flying colours. We had all been asked to recite *The Lord's Prayer*. This was not a problem for me, because for as long as I could remember my mum knelt by my bed each night and repeated the familiar words before tucking me up. However, Miss Monday's next test was to prove far more demanding.

By this time, the end of our second month, we were expected to read a psalm out loud, in front of the rest of the choir. I chose Psalm 121, which I also knew off by heart, having sung it so often in the past. *I will lift up mine eyes unto the hills, from whence cometh my help.* I could only hope that my help cometh from the Lord. Although I was able to turn to the correct page in the psalm book, as I could now count from one to a hundred, I feared Miss Monday would realize that I was unable to follow every verse line by line. If she did, she didn't let on, because I remained in the choir stalls for another month while two other miscreants – her word, not that I knew what it meant until I asked Mr Holcombe the next day – were dispatched back to the congregation.

When the time came for me to take the third and final test, I was ready for it. Miss Monday asked those of us who remained to write out the Ten Commandments in the correct order without referring to the Book of Exodus.

15

The choir mistress turned a blind eye to the fact that I placed theft ahead of murder, couldn't spell 'adultery', and certainly didn't know what it meant. Only after two other miscreants were summarily dismissed for lesser offences did I realize just how exceptional my voice must be.

On the first Sunday of Advent, Miss Monday announced that she had selected three new trebles – or 'little angels', as the Reverend Watts was wont to describe us – to join her choir, the remainder having been rejected for committing such unforgivable sins as chattering during the sermon, sucking a gobstopper and, in the case of two boys, being caught playing conkers during the *Nunc Dimittis*.

The following Sunday, I dressed up in a long blue cassock with a ruffled white collar. I alone was allowed to wear a bronze medallion of the Virgin Mother around my neck, to show that I had been selected as the treble soloist. I would have proudly worn the medallion all the way back home, even to school the next morning, to show off to the rest of the lads, if only Miss Monday hadn't retrieved it at the end of each service.

On Sundays I was transported into another world, but I feared this state of delirium could not last for ever.

2

WHEN UNCLE STAN rose in the morning, he somehow managed to wake the entire household. No one complained, as he was the breadwinner in the family, and in any case he was cheaper and more reliable than an alarm clock.

The first noise Harry would hear was the bedroom door slamming. This would be followed by his uncle tramping along the creaky wooden landing, down the stairs and out of the house. Then another door would slam as he disappeared into the privy. If anyone was still asleep, the rush of water as Uncle Stan pulled the chain, followed by two more slammed doors before he returned to the bedroom, served to remind them that Stan expected his breakfast to be on the table by the time he walked into the kitchen. He only had a wash and a shave on Saturday evenings before going off to the Palais or the Odeon. He took a bath four times a year on quarter-day. No one was going to accuse Stan of wasting his hard-earned cash on soap.

Maisie, Harry's mum, would be next up, leaping out of bed moments after the first slammed door. There would be a bowl of porridge on the stove by the time Stan came out of the privy. Grandma followed shortly afterwards, and would join her daughter in the kitchen before Stan had taken his place at the head of the table. Harry had to be down within five minutes of the first slammed door if he hoped to get any breakfast. The last to arrive in the kitchen would be Grandpa, who was so deaf he often managed to sleep through Stan's early morning ritual. This daily routine in the Clifton household never varied. When you've only got one outside privy, one sink and one towel, order becomes a necessity.

By the time Harry was splashing his face with a trickle of cold water, his mother would be serving breakfast in the kitchen: two thickly sliced pieces of bread covered in lard for Stan, and four thin slices for the rest of the family, which she would toast if there was any coal left in the sack dumped outside the front door every Monday. Once Stan had finished his porridge, Harry would be allowed to lick the bowl.

A large brown pot of tea was always brewing on the hearth, which Grandma would pour into a variety of mugs through a silver-plated Victorian tea strainer she had inherited from her mother. While the other members of the family enjoyed a mug of unsweetened tea – sugar was only for high days and holidays – Stan would open his first bottle of beer, which he usually gulped down in one draught. He would then rise from the table and burp loudly before picking up his lunch box, which Grandma had prepared while he was having his breakfast: two Marmite sandwiches, a sausage, an apple, two more bottles of beer and a packet of five coffin nails. Once Stan had left for the docks, everyone began to talk at once.

Grandma always wanted to know who had visited the tea shop where her daughter worked as a waitress: what they ate, what they were wearing, where they sat; details of meals that were cooked on a stove in a room lit by electric light bulbs that didn't leave any candle wax, not to mention customers who sometimes left a thruppenny-bit tip, which Maisie had to split with the cook.

Maisie was more concerned to find out what Harry had done at school the previous day. She demanded a daily report, which didn't seem to interest Grandma, perhaps because she'd never been to school. Come to think of it, she'd never been to a tea shop either.

Grandpa rarely commented, because after four years of loading and unloading an artillery field gun, morning, noon and night, he was so deaf he had to satisfy himself with watching their lips move and nodding from time to time. This could give outsiders the impression he was stupid, which the rest of the family knew to their cost he wasn't.

The family's morning routine only varied at weekends. On Saturdays, Harry would follow his uncle out of the kitchen, always remaining a pace behind him as he walked to the docks. On Sunday, Harry's mum would accompany the boy to Holy Nativity Church, where, from the third row of the pews, she would bask in the glory of the choir's treble soloist.

But today was Saturday. During the twenty-minute walk to the docks, Harry never opened his mouth unless his uncle spoke. Whenever he did, it invariably turned out to be the same conversation they'd had the previous Saturday.

'When are you goin' to leave school and do a day's work, young'un?' was always Uncle Stan's opening salvo.

'Not allowed to leave until I'm fourteen,' Harry reminded him. 'It's the law.'

'A bloody stupid law, if you ask me. I'd packed up school and was workin' on the docks by the time I were twelve,' Stan would announce as if Harry had never heard this profound observation before. Harry didn't bother to respond, as he already knew what his uncle's next sentence would be. 'And what's more I'd signed up to join Kitchener's army before my seventeenth birthday.'

'Tell me about the war, Uncle Stan,' said Harry, aware that this would keep him occupied for several hundred yards.

'Me and your dad joined the Royal Gloucestershire Regiment on the same day,' Stan said, touching his cloth cap as if saluting a distant memory. 'After twelve weeks' basic training at Taunton Barracks, we was shipped off to Wipers to fight the Boche. Once we got there, we spent most of our time cooped up in rat-infested trenches waiting to be told by some toffee-nosed officer that when the bugle sounded, we was going over the top, bayonets fixed, rifles firing as we advanced towards the enemy lines.' This would be followed by a long pause, after which Stan would add, 'I was one of the lucky ones. Got back to Blighty all ship-shape and Bristol fashion.' Harry could have predicted his next sentence word for word, but remained silent. 'You just don't know how lucky you are, my lad. I lost two brothers, your uncle Ray and your uncle Bert, and your father not only lost a brother, but his father, your other grandad, what you never met. A proper man, who could down a pint of beer faster than any docker I've ever come across.'

If Stan had looked down, he would have seen the boy mouthing his words, but today, to Harry's surprise, Uncle Stan added a sentence he'd never uttered before. 'And your dad would still be alive today, if only management had listened to me.'

Harry was suddenly alert. His dad's death had always been the subject of whispered conversations and hushed tones. But Uncle Stan clammed up, as if he realized he'd gone too far. Maybe next week, thought Harry, catching his uncle up and keeping in step with him as if they were two soldiers on a parade ground.

'So who are City playin' this afternoon?' asked Stan, back on script.

'Charlton Athletic,' Harry replied.

'They're a load of old cobblers.'

'They trounced us last season,' Harry reminded his uncle.

'Bloody lucky, if you ask me,' said Stan, and didn't open his mouth again. When they reached the entrance to the dockyard, Stan clocked in before heading off to the pen where he was working with a gang of other dockers, none of whom could afford to be a minute late. Unemployment was at an all-time high and too many young men were standing outside the gates waiting to take their place.

Harry didn't follow his uncle, because he knew that if Mr Haskins caught him hanging around the sheds he would get a clip round the ear, followed by a boot up the backside from his uncle for annoying the ganger. Instead, he set off in the opposite direction.

Harry's first port of call every Saturday morning was Old Jack Tar, who lived in the railway carriage at the other end of the dockyard. He had never told Stan about his regular visits because his uncle had warned him to avoid the old man at all costs.

'Probably hasn't had a bath in years,' said a man who washed once a quarter, and then only after Harry's mother complained about the smell.

But curiosity had long ago got the better of Harry, and one morning he'd crept up to the railway carriage on his hands and knees, lifted himself up and peeped through a window. The old man was sitting in first class, reading a book.

Old Jack turned to face him and said, 'Come on in, lad.' Harry jumped down, and didn't stop running until he reached his front door.

The following Saturday, Harry once again crawled up to the carriage and peered inside. Old Jack seemed to be fast asleep, but then Harry heard him say, 'Why don't you come in, my boy? I'm not going to bite you.'

Harry turned the heavy brass handle and tentatively pulled open the carriage door, but he didn't step inside. He just stared at the man seated in the centre of the carriage. It was hard to tell how old he was because his face was covered in a well-groomed salt-and-pepper beard, which made him look like the sailor on the Players Please packet. But he looked at Harry with a warmth in his eyes that Uncle Stan had never managed.

'Are you Old Jack Tar?' Harry ventured.

'That's what they call me,' the old man replied.

'And is this where you live?' Harry asked, glancing around the carriage, his eyes settling on a stack of old newspapers piled high on the opposite seat.

'Yes,' he replied. 'It's been my home for these past twenty years. Why don't you close the door and take a seat, young man?'

Harry gave the offer some thought before he jumped back out of the carriage and once again ran away.

The following Saturday, Harry did close the door, but he kept hold of the handle, ready to bolt if the old man as much as twitched a muscle. They stared at each other for some time before Old Jack asked, 'What's your name?'

'Harry.'

'And where do you go to school?'

'I don't go to school.'

'Then what are you hoping to do with your life, young man?'

'Join my uncle on the docks, of course,' Harry replied.

'Why would you want to do that?' said the old man.

'Why not?' Harry bristled. 'Don't you think I'm good enough?'

'You're far too good,' replied Old Jack. 'When I was your age,' he continued, 'I wanted to join the army, and nothing my old man could say or do would dissuade me.' For the next hour Harry stood, mesmerized, while Old Jack Tar reminisced about the docks, the city of Bristol, and lands beyond the sea that he couldn't have been taught about in geography lessons.

The following Saturday, and for more Saturdays than he would remember, Harry continued to visit Old Jack Tar. But he never once told his uncle or his mother, for fear they would stop him going to see his first real friend.

◄o►

When Harry knocked on the door of the railway carriage that Saturday morning, Old Jack had clearly been waiting for him, because his usual Cox's Orange Pippin had been placed on the seat opposite. Harry picked it up, took a bite and sat down.

'Thank you, Mr Tar,' Harry said as he wiped some juice from his chin. He never asked where the apples came from; it just added to the mystery of the great man.

How different he was from Uncle Stan, who repeated the little he knew again and again, whereas Old Jack introduced Harry to new words, new experiences, even new worlds every week. He often wondered why Mr Tar wasn't a schoolmaster – he seemed to know even more than Miss Monday, and almost as much as Mr Holcombe. Harry was convinced that Mr Holcombe knew everything, because he never failed to answer any question Harry put to him. Old Jack smiled across at him, but didn't speak until Harry had finished his apple and thrown the core out of the window.

'What have you learnt at school this week,' the old man asked, 'that you didn't know a week ago?'

'Mr Holcombe told me there are other countries beyond the sea that are part of the British Empire, and they are all reigned over by the King.'

'He's quite right,' said Old Jack. 'Can you name any of those countries?'

'Australia. Canada. India.' He hesitated. 'And America.'

'No, not America,' said Old Jack. 'That used to be the case, but it isn't any more, thanks to a weak Prime Minister and a sick King.'

'Who was the King, and who was the Prime Minister?' demanded Harry angrily.

'King George III was on the throne in 1776,' said Old Jack, 'but to be fair, he was a sick man, while Lord North, his Prime Minister, simply ignored what was taking place in the colonies, and, sadly, in the end our own kith and kin took up arms against us.'

'But we must have beaten them?' said Harry.

'No, we didn't,' said Old Jack. 'Not only did they have right on their side – not that that's a prerequisite for victory—'

'What does prerequisite mean?'

'Required as a pre-condition,' said Old Jack, who then continued as if he hadn't been interrupted. 'But they were also led by a brilliant general.'

'What was his name?'

'George Washington.'

'You told me last week that Washington was the capital of America. Was he named after the city?'

'No, the city was named after him. It was built on an area of marshland known as Columbia, through which the Potomac River flows.'

'Is Bristol named after a man too?'

'No,' chuckled Old Jack, amused by how quickly Harry's inquisitive mind could switch from subject to subject. 'Bristol was originally called Brigstowe, which means the site of a bridge.'

'So when did it become Bristol?'

'Historians differ in their opinions,' said Old Jack, 'although Bristol Castle was built by Robert of Gloucester in 1109, when he saw the opportunity to trade wool with the Irish. After that, the city developed into a trading port. Since then it's been a centre of shipbuilding for hundreds of years, and grew even more quickly when the navy needed to expand in 1914.'

'My dad fought in the Great War,' said Harry with pride. 'Did you?'

For the first time, Old Jack hesitated before answering one of Harry's questions. He just sat there, not saying a word. 'I'm sorry, Mr Tar,' said Harry. 'I didn't mean to pry.'

'No, no,' said Old Jack. 'It's just that I haven't been asked that question for some years.' Without another word, he opened his hand to reveal a sixpence.

Harry took the little silver coin and bit it, something he'd seen his uncle do. 'Thank you,' he said before pocketing it.

'Go and buy yourself some fish and chips from the dockside café, but don't tell your uncle, because he'll only ask where you got the money.'

In truth, Harry had never told his uncle anything about Old Jack. He'd once heard Stan tell his mum, 'The loony ought to be locked up.' He'd asked Miss Monday what a loony was, because he couldn't find the word in the dictionary, and when she told him, he realized for the first time just how stupid his Uncle Stan must be.

'Not necessarily stupid,' Miss Monday counselled, 'simply ill-informed and therefore prejudiced. I have no doubt, Harry,' she added, 'that you'll meet many more such men during your lifetime, some of them in far more exalted positions than your uncle.'

3

MAISIE WAITED UNTIL she heard the front door slam and was confident that Stan was on his way to work before she announced, 'I've been offered a job as a waitress at the Royal Hotel.'

No one seated round the table responded, as conversations at breakfast were supposed to follow a regular pattern and not take anyone by surprise. Harry had a dozen questions he wanted to ask but waited for his grandma to speak first. She simply busied herself with pouring another cup of tea, as if she hadn't heard her daughter in the first place.

'Will someone please say something?' said Maisie.

'I didn't even realize you were looking for another job,' ventured Harry.

'I wasn't,' said Maisie. 'But last week a Mr Frampton, the manager of the Royal, dropped into Tilly's for coffee. He came back several times, and then he offered me a job!'

'I thought you were happy at the tea shop,' said Grandma, finally joining in. 'After all, Miss Tilly pays well, and the hours suit.'

'I am happy,' said Harry's mum, 'but Mr Frampton's offering me five pounds a week, and half of all the tips. I could be bringing home as much as six pounds

27

on a Friday.' Grandma sat there with her mouth wide open.

'Will you have to work nights?' asked Harry, once he'd finished licking Stan's porridge bowl.

'No, I won't,' Maisie said, ruffling her son's hair, 'and what's more I'll get one day off a fortnight.'

'Are your clothes posh enough for a grand hotel like the Royal?' asked Grandma.

'I'll be supplied with a uniform, and a fresh white apron every morning. The hotel even has its own laundry.'

'I don't doubt it,' said Grandma, 'but I can think of one problem we're all going to have to learn to live with.'

'And what's that, Mum?' asked Maisie.

'You could end up earnin' more than Stan, and he's not going to like that, not one little bit.'

'Then he'll just have to learn to live with it, won't he?' said Grandpa, offering an opinion for the first time in weeks.

—◦—

The extra money was going to come in useful, especially after what had happened at the Holy Nativity. Maisie had been about to leave the church after the service when Miss Monday walked purposefully down the aisle towards her.

'Can I have a private word with you, Mrs Clifton?' she asked, before turning and walking back down the aisle towards the vestry. Maisie chased after her like a child in the Pied Piper's wake. She feared the worst. What had Harry been up to this time?

Maisie followed the choir mistress into the vestry and felt her legs give way when she saw the Reverend

Watts, Mr Holcombe and another gentleman standing there. As Miss Monday closed the door quietly behind her, Maisie began to shake uncontrollably.

The Reverend Watts placed an arm around her shoulder. 'There's nothing for you to worry about, my dear,' he assured her. 'On the contrary, I hope you will feel we are the bearers of glad tidings,' he added, offering her a seat. Maisie sat down, but still couldn't stop shaking.

Once everyone was seated, Miss Monday took over. 'We wanted to talk to you about Harry, Mrs Clifton,' she began. Maisie pursed her lips; what could the boy possibly have done to bring three such important people together?

'I'll not beat about the bush,' the choir mistress continued. 'The music master at St Bede's has approached me and asked if Harry would consider entering his name for one of their choral scholarships.'

'But he's very happy at Holy Nativity,' said Maisie. 'In any case, where is St Bede's Church? I've never even heard of it.'

'St Bede's is not a church,' said Miss Monday. 'It's a choir school that supplies choristers for St Mary Redcliffe, which was famously described by Queen Elizabeth as the fairest and godliest church in all the land.'

'So would he have to leave his school, as well as the church?' asked Maisie in disbelief.

'Try to look upon it as an opportunity that might change his whole life, Mrs Clifton,' said Mr Holcombe, speaking for the first time.

'But wouldn't he have to mix with posh, clever boys?'

'I doubt if there will be many children at St Bede's cleverer than Harry,' said Mr Holcombe. 'He's the brightest lad I've ever taught. Although we get the occasional boy into the grammar school, none of our pupils has ever been offered the chance of a place at St Bede's before.'

'There's something else you need to know before you make up your mind,' said the Reverend Watts. Maisie looked even more anxious. 'Harry would have to leave home during term time, because St Bede's is a boarding school.'

'Then it's out of the question,' said Maisie. 'I couldn't afford it.'

'That shouldn't prove a problem,' said Miss Monday. 'If Harry is offered a scholarship, the school would not only waive any fees, but also award him a bursary of ten pounds a term.'

'But is this one of those schools where the fathers wear suits and ties, and the mothers don't work?' asked Maisie.

'It's worse than that,' said Miss Monday, trying to make light of it. 'The masters wear long black gowns and mortarboards on their heads.'

'Still,' said the Reverend Watts joining in, 'at least there would be no more leatherings for Harry. They're far more refined at St Bede's. They just cane the boys.'

Only Maisie didn't laugh. 'But why would he want to leave home?' she asked. 'He's settled at Merrywood Elementary, and he won't want to give up being senior chorister at Holy Nativity.'

'I must confess that my loss would be even greater than his,' said Miss Monday. 'But then, I'm sure our Lord would not want me to stand in the way of such a gifted child, simply because of my own selfish desires,' she added quietly.

'Even if I agree,' said Maisie, playing her last card, 'that doesn't mean Harry will.'

'I had a word with the boy last week,' admitted Mr

Holcombe. 'Of course he was apprehensive about such a challenge, but if I recall, his exact words were "I'd like to have a go, sir, but only if you think I'm good enough." But,' he added before Maisie could respond, 'he also made it clear that he wouldn't even consider the idea unless his mother agreed.'

◄o►

Harry was both terrified and excited by the thought of taking the entrance exam, but just as anxious about failing and letting so many people down as he was about succeeding and having to leave home.

During the following term, he never once missed a lesson at Merrywood, and when he returned home each evening, he went straight up to the bedroom he shared with Uncle Stan, where, with the aid of a candle, he studied for hours that until then he hadn't realized existed. There were even occasions when his mother found Harry sound asleep on the floor, open books scattered around him.

Every Saturday morning he continued to visit Old Jack, who seemed to know a great deal about St Bede's, and continued to teach Harry about so many other things, almost as if he knew where Mr Holcombe had left off.

On Saturday afternoons, much to the disgust of Uncle Stan, Harry no longer accompanied him to Ashton Gate to watch Bristol City, but returned to Merrywood, where Mr Holcombe gave him extra lessons. It would be years before Harry worked out that Mr Holcombe was also forgoing his regular visits to support the Robins, in order to teach him.

As the day of the examination drew nearer, Harry became even more frightened of failure than of the possibility of success.

On the appointed day, Mr Holcombe accompanied his star pupil to the Colston Hall, where the two-hour examination would take place. He left Harry at the entrance to the building, with the words, 'Don't forget to read each question twice before you even pick up your pen,' a piece of advice he'd repeated several times during the past week. Harry smiled nervously, and shook hands with Mr Holcombe as if they were old friends.

He entered the examination hall to find about sixty other boys standing around in small groups, chattering. It was clear to Harry that many of them already knew each other, while he didn't know anyone. Despite this, one or two of them stopped talking and glanced at him as he made his way to the front of the hall trying to look confident.

'Abbott, Barrington, Cabot, Clifton, Deakins, Fry . . .'

Harry took his place at a desk in the front row, and just moments before the clock struck ten, several masters in long black gowns and mortarboards swept in and placed examination papers on the desks in front of each candidate.

'Gentlemen,' said a master standing at the front of the hall, who had not taken part in the distribution of the papers, 'my name is Mr Frobisher, and I am your invigilator. You have two hours in which to answer one hundred questions. Good luck.'

A clock he couldn't see struck ten. All around him, pens dipped into inkwells and began to scratch furiously across paper, but Harry simply folded his arms, leant on the desk and read each question slowly. He was among the last to pick up his pen.

Harry couldn't know that Mr Holcombe was pacing up and down on the pavement outside, feeling far more nervous than his pupil. Or that his mother was glancing up at the clock in the foyer of the Royal Hotel every few minutes as she served morning coffee. Or that Miss Monday was kneeling in silent prayer before the altar at Holy Nativity.

Moments after the clock had struck twelve, the examination papers were gathered up and the boys were allowed to leave the hall, some laughing, some frowning, others thoughtful.

When Mr Holcombe first saw Harry, his heart sank. 'Was it that bad?' he asked.

Harry didn't reply until he was certain no other boy could overhear his words. 'Not at all what I expected,' he said.

'What do you mean?' asked Mr Holcombe anxiously.

'The questions were far too easy,' replied Harry.

Mr Holcombe felt that he had never been paid a greater compliment in his life.

◄○►

'Two suits, madam, grey. One blazer, navy. Five shirts, white. Five stiff collars, white. Six pairs of calf-length socks, grey. Six sets of undergarments, white. And one St Bede's tie.' The shop assistant checked the list carefully. 'I think that covers everything. Oh, no, the boy will also need a school cap.' He reached under the counter, opened a drawer and removed a red and black cap which he placed on Harry's head. 'A perfect fit,' he pronounced. Maisie smiled at her son with considerable pride. Harry looked every inch a St Bede's boy. 'That will be three pounds, ten shillings and six pence, madam.'

Maisie tried not to look too dismayed. 'Is it possible to purchase any of these items second-hand?' she whispered.

'No, madam, this is not a second-hand shop,' said the assistant, who had already decided that this customer would not be allowed to open an account.

Maisie opened her purse, handed over four pound notes and waited for the change. She was relieved that St Bede's had paid the first term's bursary in advance, especially as she still needed to buy two pairs of leather shoes, black with laces, two pairs of gym shoes, white with laces, and one pair of slippers, bedroom.

The assistant coughed. 'The boy will also need two pairs of pyjamas and a dressing gown.'

'Yes, of course,' said Maisie, hoping she had enough money left in her purse to cover the cost.

'And am I to understand that the boy is a choral scholar?' asked the assistant, looking more closely at his list.

'Yes, he is,' Maisie replied proudly.

'Then he'll also require one cassock, red, two sur-plices, white, and a St Bede's medallion.' Maisie wanted to run out of the shop. 'Those items will be supplied by the school when he attends his first choir practice,' the assistant added before handing over her change. 'Will you be requiring anything else, madam?'

'No, thank you,' said Harry, who picked up the two bags, grabbed his mother by the arm and led her quickly out of T.C. Marsh, Tailors of Distinction.

◄○►

Harry spent the Saturday morning before he was due to report to St Bede's with Old Jack.

'Are you nervous about going to a new school?' asked Old Jack.

'No, I'm not,' said Harry defiantly. Old Jack smiled. 'I'm terrified,' he admitted.

'So is every new bug, as you'll be called. Try to treat

the whole thing as if you're starting out on an adventure to a new world, where everyone begins as equals.'

'But the moment they hear me speak, they'll realize I'm not their equal.'

'Possibly, but the moment they hear you sing, they'll realize they're not *your* equal.'

'Most of them will have come from rich families, with servants.'

'That will only be a consolation for the more stupid ones,' said Old Jack.

'And some of them will have brothers at the school, and even fathers and grandfathers who were there before them.'

'Your father was a fine man,' said Old Jack, 'and none of them will have a better mother, of that I can assure you.'

'You knew my father?' said Harry, unable to mask his surprise.

'Knew would be an exaggeration,' said Old Jack, 'but I observed him from afar, as I have many others who have worked at the docks. He was a decent, courageous, God-fearing man.'

'But do you know how he died?' asked Harry, looking Old Jack in the eye, hoping he would at last get an honest reply to the question that had troubled him for so long.

'What have you been told?' asked Old Jack cautiously.

'That he was killed in the Great War. But as I was born in 1920, even I can work out that that can't be possible.'

Old Jack didn't speak for some time. Harry remained on the edge of his seat.

'He was certainly badly wounded in the war, but you're right, that was not the cause of his death.'

'Then how did he die?' asked Harry.

'If I knew, I'd tell you,' replied Old Jack. 'But there were so many rumours flying around at the time that I wasn't sure who to believe. However, there are several men, and three in particular, who undoubtedly know the truth about what happened that night.'

'My uncle Stan must be one of them,' said Harry, 'but who are the other two?'

Old Jack hesitated, before he replied, 'Phil Haskins and Mr Hugo.'

'Mr Haskins? The ganger?' said Harry. 'He wouldn't give me the time of day. And who's Mr Hugo?'

'Hugo Barrington, the son of Sir Walter Barrington.'

'The family who own the shipping line?'

'The same,' replied Old Jack, fearing he'd gone too far.

'And are they also decent, courageous, God-fearing men?'

'Sir Walter is among the finest men I've ever known.'

'But what about his son, Mr Hugo?'

'Not cut from the same cloth, I fear,' said Old Jack, without further explanation.

4

THE SMARTLY DRESSED BOY sat next to his mother on the back seat of the tram.

'This is our stop,' she said when the tram came to a halt. They got off, and began to walk slowly up the hill towards the school, going a little slower with each step.

Harry held on to his mother with one hand, while he clutched a battered suitcase with the other. Neither of them spoke as they watched several hansom cabs, as well as the occasional chauffeur-driven car, pull up outside the front gates of the school.

Fathers were shaking hands with their sons, while fur-draped mothers embraced their offspring before giving them a peck on the cheek, like a bird finally having to acknowledge her fledglings were about to fly the nest.

Harry didn't want his mother to kiss him in front of the other boys, so he let go of her hand when they were still fifty yards from the gate. Maisie, sensing his discomfort, bent down and kissed him quickly on the forehead. 'Good luck, Harry. Make us all proud of you.'

'Goodbye, Mum,' he said, fighting back the tears.

Maisie turned and began to walk back down the hill, tears flooding down her own cheeks.

Harry walked on, recalling his uncle's description of

going over the top at Ypres before charging towards the enemy lines. *Never look back, or you're a dead man.* Harry wanted to look back, but he knew if he did, he would not stop running until he was safely on the tram. He gritted his teeth and kept on walking.

'Did you have a good hols, old chap?' one of the boys was asking a friend.

'Topping,' the other replied. 'The pater took me to Lord's for the Varsity match.'

Was Lord's a church, Harry wondered, and if so, what sort of match could possibly take place in a church? He marched resolutely on through the school gates, coming to a halt when he recognized a man standing by the front door of the school holding a clipboard.

'And who are you, young man?' he asked, giving Harry a welcoming smile.

'Harry Clifton, sir,' he replied, removing his cap just as Mr Holcombe had instructed him to do whenever a master or a lady spoke to him.

'Clifton,' he said, running a finger down a long list of names. 'Ah, yes.' He placed a tick by Harry's name. 'First generation, choral scholar. Many congratulations, and welcome to St Bede's. I'm Mr Frobisher, your housemaster, and this is Frobisher House. If you leave your suitcase in the hall, a prefect will accompany you to the refectory where I'll be addressing all the new boys before supper.'

Harry had never had supper before. 'Tea' was always the last meal in the Clifton household, before being sent to bed the moment it was dark. Electricity hadn't yet reached Still House Lane, and there was rarely enough money over to spend on candles.

'Thank you, sir,' said Harry, before making his way through the front door and into a large, highly polished wood-panelled hall. He put his case down and stared up at a painting of an old man with grey hair and bushy white sideburns, dressed in a long black gown with a red hood draped around his shoulders.

'What's your name?' barked a voice from behind him.

'Clifton, sir,' said Harry, turning to see a tall boy wearing long trousers.

'You don't call me sir, Clifton. You call me Fisher. I'm a prefect, not a master.'

'Sorry, sir,' said Harry.

'Leave your case over there and follow me.'

Harry placed his second-hand, battered suitcase next to a row of leather trunks. His was the only one that didn't have a set of initials stamped on it. He followed the prefect down a long corridor that was lined with photographs of old school teams and display cabinets filled with silver cups, to remind the next generation of past glories. When they reached the refectory, Fisher said, 'You can sit anywhere you like, Clifton. Just be sure to stop talking the moment Mr Frobisher enters the refectory.'

Harry hesitated for some time before deciding which of the four long tables he would sit at. A number of boys were already milling around in clusters, talking quietly. Harry walked slowly to the far corner of the room and took a place at the end of the table. He looked up to see several boys pouring into the hall, looking just as perplexed as he felt. One of them came and sat next to Harry, while another sat opposite him. They continued chatting to each other as if he wasn't there.

Without warning, a bell rang and everyone stopped talking as Mr Frobisher entered the refectory. He took his place behind a lectern Harry hadn't noticed and tugged at the lapels of his gown.

'Welcome,' he began, doffing his mortarboard to the

assembled gathering, 'on this, the first day of your first term at St Bede's. In a few moments' time you will experience your first school meal, and I can promise you that it doesn't get any better.' One or two of the boys laughed nervously. 'Once you have finished supper, you will be taken up to your dormitories, where you will unpack. At eight o'clock, you will hear another bell. Actually it's the same bell, just being rung at a different time.' Harry smiled, although most of the boys hadn't caught Mr Frobisher's little joke.

'Thirty minutes later, the same bell will ring again, and you will then go to bed, but not before you've washed and brushed your teeth. You will then have thirty minutes to read before lights out, after which you will go to sleep. Any child caught talking after lights out will be punished by the duty prefect. You will not hear another bell,' continued Mr Frobisher, 'until six thirty tomorrow morning, when you will rise, wash and dress in time to report back to the refectory before seven. Any child who is late will forgo his breakfast.

'Morning assembly will be held at eight o'clock in the great hall, where the headmaster will address us. This will be followed by your first lesson at eight thirty. There will be three sixty-minute lessons during the morning, with ten-minute breaks between them, giving you time to change classrooms. This will be followed by lunch at twelve.

'In the afternoon there will only be two more lessons before games, when you will play football.' Harry smiled for a second time. 'This is compulsory for everyone who is not a member of the choir.' Harry frowned. No one had told him that choristers didn't get to play football. 'After games or choir practice, you will return to Frobisher House for supper, which will be followed by an hour of prep before you retire to bed, when once again you can read until lights out – but only if the book has been approved by Matron,' added Mr Frobisher. 'This must all sound very bemusing to you' – Harry made a mental note to look up the word in the dictionary Mr Holcombe had presented him with. Mr Frobisher once again tugged at the lapels of his gown before continuing. 'But don't worry, you'll soon get used to our traditions at St Bede's. That's all I'm going to say for the moment. I'll now leave you to enjoy your supper. Goodnight, boys.'

'Goodnight, sir,' some boys had the courage to reply as Mr Frobisher left the room.

Harry didn't move a muscle as several women in pinafores marched up and down the tables placing bowls of soup in front of each boy. He watched attentively as the boy opposite him picked up a strangely shaped spoon, dipped it into his soup and pushed it away from him before putting it to his mouth. Harry attempted to imitate the motion, but only ended up spilling several drops of soup on the table, and when he did manage to transfer what was left into his mouth, most of it dribbled down his chin. He wiped his mouth with his sleeve. This didn't attract much attention, but when he slurped loudly with each mouthful, several of the boys stopped eating and stared at him. Embarrassed, Harry placed the spoon back on the table and left his soup to go cold.

The second course was a fishcake, and Harry didn't move until he'd seen which fork the boy opposite him picked up. He was surprised to notice that the boy placed his knife and fork on the plate between each mouthful, while Harry clung on to his as firmly as if they were pitchforks.

A conversation struck up between the boy opposite him and the boy next to him, on the subject of riding to hounds. Harry didn't join in, partly because the nearest he'd been to sitting on a horse was a halfpenny ride on a donkey one afternoon on an outing to Weston-super-Mare.

Once the plates had been whisked away, they were replaced with puddings, or what his mum called treats, because he didn't get them often. Yet another spoon, yet another taste, yet another mistake. Harry didn't realize that a banana wasn't like an apple, so to the astonishment of all those around him, he tried to eat the skin. For the rest of the boys, their first lesson might well be tomorrow at 8.30 a.m., but Harry's was already taking place.

After supper had been cleared away, Fisher returned and, as duty prefect, led his charges up a wide wooden staircase to the dormitories on the first floor. Harry entered a room with thirty beds neatly lined up in three rows of ten. Each had a pillow, two sheets and two blankets. Harry had never had two of anything.

'This is the new bugs' dorm,' said Fisher with disdain. 'It's where you'll remain until you're civilized. You'll find your names in alphabetical order, at the foot of each bed.'

Harry was surprised to find his suitcase on the bed and wondered who'd put it there. The boy next to him was already unpacking.

'I'm Deakins,' he said, pushing his spectacles further up his nose so he could take a closer look at Harry.

'I'm Harry. I sat next to you during exams last summer. I couldn't believe you answered all the questions in just over an hour.'

Deakins blushed.

'That's why he's a scholar,' said the boy on the other side of Harry.

Harry swung around. 'Are you a scholar, too?' he asked.

'Good heavens, no,' said the boy as he continued to unpack. 'The only reason they let me into St Bede's was because my father and grandfather were here before me. I'm the third generation to go to the school. Was your father here by any chance?'

'No,' said Harry and Deakins in unison.

'Stop chattering!' shouted Fisher, 'and get on with unpacking your cases.'

Harry opened his suitcase and began taking his clothes out and placing them neatly in the two drawers next to his bed. His mother had put a bar of Fry's Five Boys chocolate in between his shirts. He hid it under the pillow.

A bell sounded. 'Time to get undressed!' declared Fisher. Harry had never undressed in front of another boy, let alone a room full of them. He faced the wall, took off his clothes slowly and quickly pulled on his pyjamas. Once he'd tied the cord of his dressing gown, he followed the other boys into the washroom. Once again, he watched carefully as they washed their faces with flannels before brushing their teeth. He didn't have a flannel or a toothbrush. The boy from the next bed rummaged around in his wash bag and handed him a brand new toothbrush and a tube of toothpaste. Harry didn't want to take them until the boy said, 'My mother always packs two of everything.'

'Thank you,' said Harry. Although he cleaned his teeth quickly, he was still among the last to return to the dormitory. He climbed into bed, two clean sheets, two blankets and a soft pillow. He had just looked across to see that Deakins was reading *Kennedy's Latin Primer* when the other boy said, 'This pillow is brick hard.'

'Would you like to swap with me?' Harry asked.

'I think you'll find they're all the same,' the boy said with a grin, 'but thanks.'

Harry took his bar of chocolate from under the pillow and broke it into three pieces. He handed one piece to Deakins, and another to the boy who'd given him the toothbrush and toothpaste.

'I see your mater's far more sensible than mine,' he said after taking a bite. Another bell. 'By the way, my name's Giles Barrington. What's yours?'

'Clifton. Harry Clifton.'

Harry didn't sleep for more than a few minutes at a time, and it wasn't just because his bed was so comfortable. Could it be possible that Giles was related to one of the three men who knew the truth about how his father had died? And if so, was he cut from the same cloth as his father, or his grandfather?

Suddenly Harry felt very lonely. He unscrewed the top of the toothpaste Barrington had given him and began to suck it until he fell asleep.

◄○►

When the now-familiar bell rang at 6.30 next morning, Harry climbed slowly out of bed, feeling sick. He followed Deakins into the washroom, to find Giles was testing the water. 'Do you think this place has ever heard of hot water?' he asked.

Harry was just about to reply when the prefect hollered, 'No talking in the washroom!'

'He's worse than a Prussian general,' said Barrington, clicking his heels. Harry burst out laughing.

'Who was that?' asked Fisher, glaring at the two boys.

'Me,' said Harry immediately.

'Name?'

'Clifton.'

'Open your mouth again, Clifton, and I'll slipper you.'

Harry had no idea what being slippered meant, but he had a feeling it wouldn't be pleasant. Once he'd brushed his teeth, he walked quickly back into the dorm and dressed without another word. Once he'd done up his tie – something else he hadn't quite mastered – he caught up with Barrington and Deakins as they made their way down the stairs to the refectory.

Nobody said a word, as they weren't sure if they were allowed to talk while they were on the staircase. When they sat down for breakfast in the refectory, Harry slipped in between his two new friends, and watched as bowls of porridge were placed in front of each boy. He was relieved to find there was only one spoon in front of him, so he couldn't make a mistake this time.

Harry gulped down his porridge so quickly it was as if he was afraid Uncle Stan would appear and snatch it away from him. He was the first to finish, and without a moment's thought he put his spoon down on the table, picked up his bowl and began to lick it. Several other boys stared at him in disbelief, some pointed, while others sniggered. He turned a bright shade of crimson and put the bowl back down. He would have burst into tears, if Barrington hadn't picked up his own bowl and begun licking it.

5

THE REVEREND SAMUEL OAKSHOTT MA (Oxon) stood, feet apart, at the centre of the stage. He peered benignly down on his flock, for that was certainly how the headmaster of St Bede's viewed the pupils.

Harry, seated in the front row, stared up at the frightening figure who towered above him. Dr Oakshott was well over six feet tall, and had a head of thick, greying hair and long bushy sideburns that made him look even more forbidding. His deep blue eyes pierced right through you and he never seemed to blink, while the criss-cross of lines on his forehead hinted at great wisdom. He cleared his throat before addressing the boys.

'Fellow Bedeans,' he began. 'We are once again gathered together at the beginning of a new school year, no doubt prepared to face whatever challenges should confront us. For the senior boys,' he turned his attention to the back of the hall, 'you don't have a moment to lose if you hope to be offered a place at the school of your first choice. Never settle for second best.

'For the middle school,' his eyes moved to the centre of the hall, 'this will be a time when we discover which of you is destined for greater things. When you return next year, will you be a prefect, a monitor, a house

46

captain or a captain of sport? Or will you simply be among the also-rans?' Several boys bowed their heads.

'Our next duty is to welcome the new boys, and do everything in our power to make them feel at home. They are being handed the baton for the first time as they begin life's long race. Should the pace prove to be too demanding, one or two of you may fall by the wayside,' he warned, staring down at the front three rows. 'St Bede's is not a school for the faint-hearted. So be sure never to forget the words of the great Cecil Rhodes: *If you are lucky enough to have been born an Englishman, you have drawn first prize in the lottery of life.*'

The assembled gathering burst into spontaneous applause as the headmaster left the stage, followed by a crocodile of masters whom he led down the centre aisle, out of the great hall and into the morning sunshine.

Harry, his spirits raised, was determined not to let the headmaster down. He followed the senior boys out of the hall, but the moment he stepped out into the quad, his exuberance was dampened. A posse of older boys were hanging around in one corner, hands in pockets to indicate they were prefects.

'There he is,' said one of them, pointing at Harry.

'So that's what a street urchin looks like,' said another.

A third, whom Harry recognized as Fisher, the prefect who had been on duty the previous night, added, 'He's an animal, and it's nothing less than our duty to see that he's returned to his natural habitat as quickly as possible.'

Giles Barrington ran after Harry. 'If you ignore them,' he said, 'they'll soon get bored and start picking on someone else.' Harry wasn't convinced, and ran ahead to the classroom where he waited for Barrington and Deakins to join him.

A moment later, Mr Frobisher entered the room. Harry's first thought was, does he also think I'm a street urchin, unworthy of a place at St Bede's?

'Good morning, boys,' said Mr Frobisher.

'Good morning, sir,' replied the boys as their form master took his place in front of the blackboard. 'Your first lesson this morning,' he said, 'will be history. As I am keen to get to know you, we will start with a simple test to discover how much you have already learnt, or perhaps how little. How many wives did Henry the Eighth have?'

Several hands shot up. 'Abbott,' he said, looking at a chart on his desk and pointing to a boy in the front row.

'Six, sir,' came back the immediate reply.

'Good, but can anyone name them?' Not quite as many hands were raised. 'Clifton?'

'Catherine of Aragon, Anne Boleyn, Jane Seymour, then another Anne I think,' he said before coming to a halt.

'Anne of Cleves. Can anyone name the missing two?' Only one hand remained in the air. 'Deakins,' said Frobisher after checking his chart.

'Catherine Howard and Catherine Parr. Anne of Cleves and Catherine Parr both outlived Henry.'

'Very good, Deakins. Now, let's turn the clock forward a couple of centuries. Who commanded our fleet at the Battle of Trafalgar?' Every hand in the room shot up. 'Matthews,' he said, nodding at a particularly insistent hand.

'Nelson, sir.'

'Correct. And who was Prime Minister at the time?'

'The Duke of Wellington, sir,' said Matthews, not sounding quite as confident.

'No,' said Mr Frobisher, 'it wasn't Wellington, although he was a contemporary of Nelson's.' He looked around the class, but only Clifton's and Deakins's hands were still raised. 'Deakins.'

'Pitt the Younger, 1783 to 1801, and 1804 to 1806.'

'Correct, Deakins. And when was the Iron Duke Prime Minister?'

'1828 to 1830, and again in 1834,' said Deakins.

'And can anyone tell me what his most famous victory was?'

Barrington's hand shot up for the first time. 'Waterloo, sir!' he shouted before Mr Frobisher had time to select anyone else.

'Yes, Barrington. And whom did Wellington defeat at Waterloo?'

Barrington remained silent.

'Napoleon,' whispered Harry.

'Napoleon, sir,' said Barrington confidently.

'Correct, Clifton,' said Frobisher, smiling. 'And was Napoleon also a Duke?'

'No, sir,' said Deakins, after no one else had attempted to answer the question. 'He founded the first French Empire, and appointed himself Emperor.'

Mr Frobisher was not surprised by Deakins's response, as he was an open scholar, but he was impressed by Clifton's knowledge. After all, he was a choral scholar, and over the years he had learnt that gifted choristers, like talented sportsmen, rarely excel outside their own field. Clifton was already proving an exception to that rule. Mr Frobisher would have liked to know who had taught the boy.

When the bell rang for the end of class, Mr Frobisher announced, 'Your next lesson will be geography with Mr Henderson, and he is not a master who likes to be kept waiting. I recommend that during the break you find out where his classroom is, and are seated in your places long before he enters the room.'

Harry stuck close to Giles, who seemed to know where everything was. As they strolled across the quad together, Harry became aware that some of the boys lowered their voices when they passed, and one or two even turned to stare at him.

Thanks to countless Saturday mornings spent with Old Jack, Harry held his own in the geography lesson, but in maths, the final class of the morning, no one came close to Deakins, and even the master had to keep his wits about him.

When the three of them sat down for lunch, Harry could feel a hundred eyes watching his every move. He pretended not to notice, and simply copied everything Giles did. 'It's nice to know there's something I can teach you,' Giles said as he peeled an apple with his knife.

Harry enjoyed his first chemistry lesson later that afternoon, especially when the master allowed him to light a Bunsen burner. But he didn't excel at nature studies, the final lesson of the day, because Harry was the only boy whose home didn't have a garden.

When the final bell sounded, the rest of the class went off for games, while Harry reported to the chapel for his first choir practice. Once again, he noticed everyone was staring at him, but this time it was for all the right reasons.

But no sooner had he walked out of the chapel than he was subjected to the same sotto voce jibes from boys who were making their way back from the playing fields.

'Isn't that our little street urchin?' said one.

'Pity he doesn't have a toothbrush,' said another.

'Sleeps down at the docks at night, I'm told,' said a third.

Deakins and Barrington were nowhere to be seen as

Harry hurried back to his house, avoiding any gatherings of boys on the way.

During supper, the gawping eyes were less obvious, but only because Giles had made it clear to everyone within earshot that Harry was his friend. But Giles was unable to help when they all went up to the dormitory after prep and found Fisher standing by the door, clearly waiting for Harry.

As the boys began to undress, Fisher announced in a loud voice, 'I'm sorry about the smell, gentlemen, but one of your form comes from a house without a bath.' One or two of the boys sniggered, hoping to ingratiate themselves with Fisher. Harry ignored him. 'Not only does this guttersnipe not have a bath, he doesn't even have a father.'

'My father was a good man who fought for his country in the war,' said Harry proudly.

'What makes you think I was talking about you, Clifton?' said Fisher. 'Unless of course you're also the boy whose mother works –' he paused – 'as a hotel waitress.'

'An hotel,' said Harry, correcting him.

Fisher grabbed a slipper. 'Don't you ever answer me back, Clifton,' he said angrily. 'Bend down and touch the end of your bed.' Harry obeyed, and Fisher administered six strokes with such ferocity that Giles had to turn away. Harry crept into bed, fighting to hold back the tears.

Before Fisher switched off the light, he added, 'I'll look forward to seeing you all again tomorrow night, when I will continue with my bedtime tale of the Cliftons of Still House Lane. Wait until you hear about Uncle Stan.'

The following night, Harry learnt for the first time

that his uncle had spent eighteen months in prison for burglary. This revelation was worse than being slippered. He crept into bed wondering if his father could still be alive but in jail, and that was the real reason no one at home ever talked about him.

Harry hardly slept for a third night running, and no amount of success in the classroom, or admiration in the chapel, could stop him continually thinking about the next inevitable encounter with Fisher. The slightest excuse, a drop of water spilt on the washroom floor, a pillow that wasn't straight, a sock that had fallen around his ankle, would ensure that Harry could expect six of the best from the duty prefect; a punishment that would be administered in front of the rest of the dorm, but not before Fisher had added another episode from the Clifton Chronicles. By the fifth night, Harry had had enough, and even Giles and Deakins could no longer console him.

During prep on Friday evening, while the other boys were turning the pages of their *Kennedy's Latin Primer*, Harry ignored Caesar and the Gauls and went over a plan that would ensure Fisher never bothered him again. By the time he climbed into bed that night, after Fisher had discovered a Fry's wrapper by his bed and slippered him once again, Harry's plan was in place. He lay awake long after lights out, and didn't stir until he was certain every boy was asleep.

Harry had no idea what time it was when he slipped out of bed. He dressed without making a sound, then crept between the beds until he reached the far side of the room. He pushed the window open, and the rush of cold air caused the boy in the nearest bed to turn over. Harry climbed out on to the fire escape and slowly closed the window before making his way down to the ground. He walked around the edge of the lawn, taking advantage of any shadows to avoid a full moon that seemed to beam down on him like a searchlight.

Harry was horrified to discover that the school gates were locked. He crept along the wall, searching for the slightest crack or indentation that would allow him to climb over the top and escape to freedom. At last he spotted a missing brick and was able to lever himself up until he was straddling the wall. He lowered himself down the other side, clinging on by the tips of his fingers, said a silent prayer, then let go. He landed on the ground in a heap, but didn't seem to have broken anything.

Once he'd recovered, he began to run down the road, slowly at first, but then he speeded up and didn't stop running until he reached the docks. The night shift was just coming off duty and Harry was relieved to find his uncle was not among them.

After the last docker had disappeared out of sight, he walked slowly along the quayside, past a line of moored ships that stretched as far as the eye could see. He noticed that one of the funnels proudly displayed the letter B, and thought about his friend who would be fast asleep. Would he ever . . . his thoughts were interrupted when he came to a halt outside Old Jack's railway carriage.

He wondered if the old man was also fast asleep. His question was answered when a voice said, 'Don't just stand there, Harry, come inside before you freeze to death.' Harry opened the carriage door to find Old Jack striking a match and trying to light a candle. Harry slumped into the seat opposite him. 'Have you run away?' asked Old Jack.

Harry was so taken aback by his direct question that he didn't answer immediately. 'Yes, I have,' he finally spluttered.

'And no doubt you've come to tell me why you've made this momentous decision.'

'I didn't make the decision,' said Harry. 'It was made for me.'

'By whom?'

'His name is Fisher.'

'A master or a boy?'

'My dormitory prefect,' said Harry, wincing. He then told Old Jack everything that had happened during his first week at St Bede's.

Once again, the old man took him by surprise. When Harry came to the end of his story, Jack said, 'I blame myself.'

'Why?' asked Harry. 'You couldn't have done more to help me.'

'Yes I could,' said Old Jack. 'I should have prepared you for a brand of snobbery that no other nation on earth can emulate. I should have spent more time on the significance of the old school tie, and less on geography and history. I had rather hoped things just might have changed after the war to end all wars, but they clearly haven't at St Bede's.' He fell into a thoughtful silence before finally asking, 'So what are you going to do next, my boy?'

'Run away to sea. I'll take any boat that will have me,' said Harry, trying to sound enthusiastic.

'What a good idea,' said Old Jack. 'Why not play straight into Fisher's hands?'

'What do you mean?'

'Just that nothing will please Fisher more than to be able to tell his friends that the street urchin had no guts, but then, what do you expect from the son of a docker whose mother is a waitress?'

'But Fisher's right. I'm not in his class.'

'No, Harry, the problem is that Fisher already real-izes he's not in your class, and never will be.'

'Are you saying I should go back to that horrible place?' said Harry.

'In the end, only you can make that decision,' said Old Jack, 'but if you run away every time you come up against the Fishers of this world, you'll end up like me, one of life's also-rans, to quote the headmaster.'

'But you're a great man,' said Harry.

'I might have been,' said Old Jack, 'if I hadn't run away the moment I came across my Fisher. But I settled for the easy way out, and only thought about myself.'

'But who else is there to think about?'

'Your mother for a start,' said Old Jack. 'Don't forget all the sacrifices she made to give you a better start in life than she ever dreamed was possible. And then there's Mr Holcombe, who when he discovers you've run away will only blame himself. And don't forget Miss Monday, who called in favours, twisted arms and spent countless hours to make sure you were good enough to win that choral scholarship. And when you come to weigh up the pros and cons, Harry, I suggest you place Fisher on one side of the scales and Barrington and Deakins on the other, because I suspect that Fisher will quickly fade into insignificance, while Barrington and Deakins will surely turn out to be close friends for the rest of your life. If you run away, they will be forced to listen to Fisher continually reminding them that you weren't the person they thought you were.'

Harry remained silent for some time. Finally, he rose slowly to his feet. 'Thank you, sir,' he said. Without another word he opened the carriage door and let himself out.

He walked slowly down the quayside, once again

staring up at the vast cargo ships, all of which would soon be departing for distant ports. He kept on walking until he reached the dockyard gates, where he broke into a run and headed back towards the city. By the time he reached the school gates they were already open, and the clock on the great hall was about to chime eight times.

Despite the telephone call, Mr Frobisher would have to walk across to the headmaster's house and report that one of his boys was missing. As he looked out of his study window, he caught a glimpse of Harry nipping in and out between the trees as he made his way cautiously towards the house. Harry tentatively opened the front door as the final chime rang out, and came face to face with his housemaster.

'Better hurry, Clifton,' Mr Frobisher said, 'or you'll miss breakfast.'

'Yes, sir,' said Harry, and ran down the corridor. He reached the dining room just before the doors were closed and slipped into place between Barrington and Deakins.

'For a moment I thought I'd be the only one licking my bowl this morning,' said Barrington. Harry burst out laughing.

He didn't come across Fisher that day, and was surprised to find that another prefect had replaced him on dorm duty that night. Harry slept for the first time that week.

6

THE ROLLS-ROYCE drove through the gates of the Manor House and up a long driveway lined with tall oaks, standing like sentinels. Harry had counted six gardeners even before he set eyes on the house.

During their time at St Bede's, Harry had picked up a little about how Giles lived when he returned home for the holidays, but nothing had prepared him for this. When he saw the house for the first time, his mouth opened, and stayed open.

'Early eighteenth century would be my guess,' said Deakins.

'Not bad,' said Giles, '1722, built by Vanbrugh. But I'll bet you can't tell me who designed the garden. I'll give you a clue: it's later than the house.'

'I've only ever heard of one landscape gardener,' said Harry, still staring at the house. 'Capability Brown.'

'That's exactly why we chose him,' said Giles, 'simply so that my friends would have heard of the fellow two hundred years later.'

Harry and Deakins laughed as the car came to a halt in front of a three-storey mansion built from golden Cotswold stone. Giles jumped out before the chauffeur had a chance to open the back door. He ran up the steps with his two friends following less certainly in his wake.

The front door was opened long before Giles reached the top step, and a tall man, elegantly dressed in a long black coat, pinstripe trousers and a black tie, gave a slight bow as the young master shot past him. 'Happy birthday, Mr Giles,' he said.

'Thank you, Jenkins. Come on, chaps!' shouted Giles as he disappeared into the house. The butler held open the door to allow Harry and Deakins to follow.

As soon as Harry stepped into the hall, he found himself transfixed by the portrait of an old man who appeared to be staring directly down at him. Giles had inherited the man's beak-like nose, fierce blue eyes and square jaw. Harry looked around at the other portraits that adorned the walls. The only oil paintings he'd seen before were in books: the *Mona Lisa*, the *Laughing Cavalier* and *Night Watch*. He was looking at a land-scape by an artist called Constable when a woman swept into the hall wearing what Harry could only have described as a ball gown.

'Happy birthday, my darling,' she said.

'Thank you, Mater,' said Giles, as she bent down to kiss him. It was the first time Harry had ever seen his friend look embarrassed. 'These are my two best friends, Harry and Deakins.' As Harry shook hands with a woman who wasn't much taller than he was, she gave him such a warm smile that he immediately felt at ease.

'Why don't we all go through to the drawing room,' she suggested, 'and have some tea?' She led the boys across the hall and into a large room that overlooked the front lawn.

When Harry entered, he didn't want to sit down but to look at the paintings that hung on every wall. However, Mrs Barrington was already ushering him towards the sofa. He sank down into the plush cushions and couldn't stop himself staring out of the bay window on to a finely cut lawn that was large enough to play a game of cricket on. Beyond the lawn, Harry could see a lake where contented mallards swam aimlessly around, clearly not worried about where their next meal would be coming from. Deakins sat himself down on the sofa next to Harry.

Neither of them spoke as another man, this one dressed in a short black jacket, entered the room, followed by a young woman in a smart blue uniform, not unlike the one his mother wore at the hotel. The maid carried a large silver tray which she placed on an oval table in front of Mrs Barrington.

'Indian or China?' Mrs Barrington asked, looking at Harry.

Harry wasn't sure what she meant.

'We'll all have Indian, thank you, Mother,' said Giles.

Harry thought Giles must have taught him every-thing there was to know about etiquette as practised in polite society, but Mrs Barrington had suddenly raised the bar to a new level.

Once the under-butler had poured three cups of tea, the maid placed them in front of the boys, along with a side plate. Harry stared at a mountain of sandwiches, not daring to touch. Giles took one and put it on his plate. His mother frowned. 'How many times have I told you, Giles, always to wait until your guests decide what they would like before you help yourself?'

Harry wanted to tell Mrs Barrington that Giles always took the lead, just so that he would know what to do and, more important, what not to do. Deakins selected a sandwich and put it on his plate. Harry did the same. Giles waited patiently until Deakins had picked up his sandwich and taken a bite.

'I do hope you like smoked salmon,' said Mrs Barrington.

'Spiffing,' said Giles, before his friends had a chance to admit that they had never tasted smoked salmon before. 'We only get fish paste sandwiches at school,' he added.

'So, tell me how you're all getting on at school,' said Mrs Barrington.

'Room for improvement, is how I think the Frob describes my efforts,' said Giles, as he took another sandwich. 'But Deakins is top of everything.'

'Except for English,' said Deakins, speaking for the first time, 'Harry pipped me in that subject by a couple of per cent.'

'And did you pip anyone in anything, Giles?' asked his mother.

'He came second in maths, Mrs Barrington,' said Harry, coming to Giles's rescue. 'He has a natural gift for figures.'

'Just like his grandfather,' said Mrs Barrington.

'That's a nice picture of you above the fireplace, Mrs Barrington,' said Deakins.

She smiled. 'It's not me, Deakins, it's my dear mother.' Deakins bowed his head before Mrs Barrington quickly added, 'But what a charming compliment. She was considered a great beauty in her day.'

'Who painted it?' asked Harry, coming to Deakins's rescue.

'László,' replied Mrs Barrington. 'Why do you ask?'

'Because I was wondering if the portrait of the gentleman in the hall might be by the same artist.'

'How very observant of you, Harry,' said Mrs Barrington. 'The painting you saw in the hall is of my father, and was indeed also painted by László.'

'What does your father do?' asked Harry.

'Harry never stops asking questions,' said Giles. 'One just has to get used to it.'

Mrs Barrington smiled. 'He imports wines to this country, in particular, sherries from Spain.'

'Just like Harvey's,' said Deakins, his mouth full of cucumber sandwich.

'Just like Harvey's,' repeated Mrs Barrington. Giles grinned. 'Do have another sandwich, Harry,' said Mrs Barrington, noticing that his eyes were fixed on the plate.

'Thank you,' said Harry, unable to choose between smoked salmon, cucumber, or egg and tomato. He settled for salmon, wondering what it would taste like.

'And how about you, Deakins?'

'Thank you, Mrs Barrington,' he said, and took another cucumber sandwich.

'I can't go on calling you Deakins,' said Giles's mother. 'It makes you sound like one of the servants. Do tell me your Christian name.'

Deakins bowed his head again. 'I prefer to be called Deakins,' he said.

'It's Al,' said Giles.

'Such a nice name,' said Mrs Barrington, 'although I expect your mother calls you Alan.'

'No she doesn't,' said Deakins, his head still bowed. The other two boys looked surprised by this revelation, but said nothing. 'My name's Algernon,' he finally spluttered.

Giles burst out laughing.

Mrs Barrington paid no attention to her son's outburst. 'Your mother must be an admirer of Oscar Wilde,' she said.

'Yes, she is,' said Deakins. 'But I wish she'd called me Jack, or even Ernest.'

'I wouldn't let it worry you,' said Mrs Barrington. 'After all, Giles suffers from a similar indignity.'

'Mother, you promised you wouldn't—'

'You must get him to tell you his middle name,' she said, ignoring the protest. When Giles didn't respond, Harry and Deakins looked at Mrs Barrington hopefully. 'Marmaduke,' she declared with a sigh. 'Like his father and grandfather before him.'

'If either of you tell anyone about this when we get back to school,' Giles said, looking at his two friends, 'I swear I'll kill you, and I mean, kill you.' Both boys laughed.

'Do you have a middle name, Harry?' asked Mrs Barrington.

Harry was about to reply when the drawing-room door flew open and a man who couldn't have been mistaken for a servant strode into the room carrying a large parcel. Harry looked up at a man who could only have been Mr Hugo. Giles leapt up and ran towards his father, who handed him the parcel and said, 'Happy birthday, my boy.'

'Thank you, Papa,' said Giles, and immediately began to untie the ribbon.

'Before you open your present, Giles,' said his mother, 'perhaps you should first introduce your guests to Papa.'

'Sorry, Papa. These are my two best friends, Deakins and Harry,' said Giles, placing the gift on the table. Harry noticed that Giles's father had the same athletic build and restless energy he'd assumed was uniquely his son's.

'Pleased to meet you, Deakins,' said Mr Barrington, shaking him by the hand. He then turned to Harry. 'Good afternoon, Clifton,' he added, before sitting down in the empty chair next to his wife. Harry was puzzled that Mr Barrington didn't shake hands with him. And how did he know his name was Clifton?

Once the under-butler had served Mr Barrington

with a cup of tea, Giles removed the wrapping from his present and let out a yelp of delight when he saw the Roberts radio. He pushed the plug into a wall socket and began to tune the radio to different stations. The boys applauded and laughed with each new sound that was emitted from the large wooden box.

'Giles tells me that he came second in mathematics this term,' said Mrs Barrington, turning to her husband.

'Which doesn't make up for him being bottom in almost every other subject,' he retorted. Giles tried not to look embarrassed, as he continued to search for another station on his radio.

'But you should have seen the goal he scored against Avonhurst,' said Harry. 'We're all expecting him to captain the eleven next year.'

'Goals aren't going to get him into Eton,' said Mr Barrington, not looking at Harry. 'It's time the boy buckled down and worked harder.'

No one spoke for some time, until Mrs Barrington broke the silence. 'Are you the Clifton who sings in the choir at St Mary Redcliffe?' she asked.

'Harry's the treble soloist,' said Giles. 'In fact, he's a choral scholar.'

Harry became aware that Giles's father was now staring at him.

'I thought I recognized you,' said Mrs Barrington. 'Giles's grandfather and I attended a performance of the Messiah at St Mary's, when the choir of St Bede's joined forces with Bristol Grammar School. Your *I Know That My Redeemer Liveth* was quite magnificent, Harry.'

'Thank you, Mrs Barrington,' said Harry, blushing.

'Are you hoping to go on to Bristol Grammar School after you leave St Bede's, Clifton?' asked Mr Barrington.

Clifton again, thought Harry. 'Only if I win a scholarship, sir,' he replied.

'But why is that important?' asked Mrs Barrington. 'Surely you will be offered a place, like any other boy?'

'Because my mother wouldn't be able to afford the fees, Mrs Barrington. She's a waitress at the Royal Hotel.'

'But wouldn't your father—'

'He's dead,' said Harry. 'He was killed in the war.' He watched carefully to see how Mr Barrington would react, but like a good poker player he gave nothing away.

'I'm sorry,' said Mrs Barrington. 'I didn't realize.'

The door opened behind Harry and the under-butler entered, carrying a two-tier birthday cake on a silver tray which he placed on the centre of the table. After Giles had succeeded in blowing out all twelve candles with one puff, everyone applauded.

'And when's your birthday, Clifton?' asked Mr Barrington.

'It was last month, sir,' Harry replied.

Mr Barrington looked away.

The under-butler removed the candles before handing the young master a large cake knife. Giles cut deep into the cake and placed five uneven slices on the tea plates the maid had laid out on the table.

Deakins devoured the lumps of icing that had fallen on to his plate before taking a bite of the cake. Harry followed Mrs Barrington's lead. He picked up the small silver fork by the side of his plate, using it to remove a tiny piece of his cake before placing it back on the plate.

Only Mr Barrington didn't touch his cake. Suddenly, without warning, he rose from his place and left without another word.

Giles's mother made no attempt to conceal her surprise at her husband's behaviour, but she said nothing. Harry never took his eyes off Mr Hugo as he left the room, while Deakins, having finished his cake, turned his attention back to the smoked salmon sandwiches, clearly oblivious to what was going on around him.

Once the door was closed, Mrs Barrington continued to chat as if nothing unusual had happened. 'I'm sure you'll win a scholarship to Bristol Grammar, Harry, especially considering everything Giles has told me about you. You're obviously a very clever boy, as well as a gifted singer.'

'Giles does have a tendency to exaggerate, Mrs Barrington,' said Harry. 'I can assure you only Deakins is certain of winning a scholarship.'

'But doesn't BGS offer grants for music scholars?' she asked.

'Not for trebles,' said Harry. 'They won't take the risk.'

'I'm not sure I understand,' said Mrs Barrington. 'Nothing can take away the years of choral training you've been put through.'

'True, but sadly no one can predict what will happen when your voice breaks. Some trebles end up as basses or baritones, and the really lucky ones become tenors, but there's no way of telling in advance.'

'Why not?' asked Deakins, taking an interest for the first time.

'There are plenty of treble soloists who can't even get a place in their local choir once their voice has broken. Ask Master Ernest Lough. Every household in England has heard him sing *Oh, for the wings of a dove*, but after his voice broke no one ever heard from him again.'

'You're just going to have to work harder,' said Deakins between mouthfuls. 'Don't forget the grammar school awards twelve scholarships every year, and I can only win one of them,' he added matter-of-factly.

'But that's the problem,' said Harry. 'If I'm going to

work any harder, I'll have to give up the choir, and without my bursary, I'd have to leave St Bede's, so . . .'

'You're between a rock and a hard place,' said Deakins.

Harry had never heard the expression before and decided to ask Deakins later what it meant.

'Well, one thing's for certain,' said Mrs Barrington, 'Giles isn't likely to win a scholarship to any school.'

'Maybe not,' said Harry. 'But Bristol Grammar isn't likely to turn down a left-handed batsman of his calibre.'

'Then we'll have to hope that Eton feels the same way,' said Mrs Barrington, 'because that's where his father wants him to go.'

'I don't want to go to Eton,' said Giles, putting down his fork. 'I want to go to BGS and be with my friends.'

'I'm sure you'll make a lot of new friends at Eton,' said his mother. 'And it would be a great disappointment to your father if you didn't follow in his footsteps.'

The under-butler coughed. Mrs Barrington looked out of the window to see a car drawing up at the bottom of the steps. 'I think the time has come for you all to return to school,' she said. 'I certainly don't want to be responsible for anyone being late for prep.'

Harry looked longingly at the large plate of sand-wiches and the half-finished birthday cake but reluc-tantly rose from his place and began to walk towards the door. He glanced back once and could have sworn he saw Deakins put a sandwich in his pocket. He took one last look out of the window and was surprised to notice, for the first time, a gangly young girl with long pigtails who was curled up in the corner reading a book.

'That's my frightful sister, Emma,' said Giles. 'She never stops reading. Just ignore her.' Harry smiled at Emma, but she didn't look up. Deakins didn't give her a second look.

Mrs Barrington accompanied the three boys to the front door, where she shook hands with Harry and Deakins. 'I do hope you'll both come again soon,' she said. 'You're such a good influence on Giles.'

'Thank you very much for having us to tea, Mrs Barrington,' Harry said. Deakins just nodded. Both boys looked away when she hugged her son and gave him a kiss.

As the chauffeur drove down the long driveway towards the gates, Harry looked out of the back window at the house. He didn't notice Emma staring out of the window at the disappearing car.

7

THE SCHOOL TUCK SHOP was open between four and six every Tuesday and Thursday afternoon.

Harry rarely visited the 'Emporium', as it was known by the boys, since he only had two shillings' pocket money a term, and he knew his mother wouldn't appreciate any little extras appearing on his end-of-term account. However, on Deakins's birthday, Harry made an exception to this rule, as he intended to purchase a one-penny bar of fudge for his friend.

Despite Harry's rare visits to the tuck shop, a bar of Fry's Five Boys chocolate could be found on his desk every Tuesday and Thursday evening. Although there was a school rule that no boy could spend more than sixpence a week in the tuck shop, Giles would also leave a packet of Liquorice Allsorts for Deakins, making it clear to his friends that he expected nothing in return.

When Harry arrived at the tuck shop that Tuesday, he joined a long queue of boys waiting to be served. His mouth watered as he stared at the neatly stacked rows of chocolate, fudge, jelly babies, liquorice and, the latest craze, Smiths potato crisps. He'd considered buying a packet for himself, but after a recent introduction to Mr Wilkins Micawber, he had been left in no doubt about the value of sixpence.

As Harry ogled the Emporium's treasures, he heard Giles's voice and noticed that he was a few places ahead of him in the queue. He was just about to hail his friend when he saw Giles remove a bar of chocolate from a shelf and slip it into his trouser pocket. A few moments later, a packet of chewing gum followed. When Giles reached the front of the queue, he placed on the counter a box of Liquorice Allsorts, 2d, and a bag of crisps, 1d, which Mr Swivals, the master in charge of the shop, entered neatly in his ledger against the name of Barrington. The two other items remained in Giles's pocket, unaccounted for.

Harry was horrified, and before Giles could turn round, he slipped out of the shop, not wanting his friend to spot him. Harry walked slowly around the school block, trying to work out why Giles would want to steal anything, when he could so obviously afford to pay. He assumed there had to be some simple explanation, although he couldn't imagine what it might be.

Harry went up to his study just before prep, to find the pilfered bar of chocolate on his desk, and Deakins tucking into a box of Liquorice Allsorts. He found it difficult to concentrate on the causes of the Industrial Revolution while he tried to decide what, if anything, he should do about his discovery.

By the end of prep, he'd made his decision. He placed the unopened bar of chocolate in the top drawer of his desk, having decided he would return it to the tuck shop on Thursday, without telling Giles.

Harry didn't sleep that night, and after breakfast he took Deakins to one side and explained why he hadn't been able to give him a birthday present. Deakins couldn't hide his disbelief.

'My dad's been having the same problem in his shop,' said Deakins. 'It's called shoplifting. The *Daily Mail* is blaming it on the Depression.'

'I don't think Giles's family will have been affected much by the Depression,' said Harry with some feeling.

Deakins nodded thoughtfully. 'Perhaps you should tell the Frob?'

'Sneak on my best friend?' said Harry. 'Never.'

'But if Giles is caught he could be expelled,' said Deakins. 'The least you can do is warn him you've found out what he's up to.'

'I'll think about it,' said Harry. 'But in the meantime I'm going to return anything Giles gives me to the tuck shop without letting him know.'

Deakins leant over. 'Could you take my stuff back as well?' he whispered. 'I never go to the tuck shop, so I wouldn't know what to do.'

Harry agreed to take on the responsibility, and after that he went to the tuck shop twice a week and placed Giles's unwanted gifts back on the shelves. He had concluded that Deakins was right and that he would have to confront his friend before he was caught, but decided to put it off until the end of term.

◄◦►

'Good shot, Barrington,' said Mr Frobisher as the ball crossed the boundary. A ripple of applause broke out around the ground. 'Mark my words, headmaster, Barrington will play for Eton against Harrow at Lord's.'

'Not if Giles has anything to do with it,' Harry whispered to Deakins.

'What are you doing for the summer hols, Harry?' asked Deakins, seemingly oblivious to all that was going on around him.

'I don't have any plans to visit Tuscany this year, if that's what you're asking,' Harry replied with a grin.

'I don't think Giles really wants to go either,' said

Deakins. 'After all, the Italians have never understood cricket.'

'Well, I'd be happy to change places with him,' said Harry. 'It doesn't bother me that Michelangelo, Da Vinci and Caravaggio were never introduced to the finer subtleties of leg break bowling, not to mention all that pasta he'll be expected to wade through.'

'So where are you going?' asked Deakins.

'A week on the Riviera of the West,' said Harry with bravado. 'The grand pier at Weston-super-Mare is usually the high spot, followed by fish and chips at Coffins café. Care to join me?'

'Can't spare the time,' said Deakins, who clearly thought Harry was being serious.

'And why's that?' asked Harry, playing along.

'Too much work to do.'

'You intend to go on working during the holidays?' asked Harry in disbelief.

'Work *is* a holiday for me,' said Deakins. 'I enjoy it every bit as much as Giles does his cricket, and you do your singing.'

'But where do you work?'

'In the municipal library, clot. They have everything I need.'

'Can I join you?' asked Harry, sounding just as serious. 'I need all the help I can get if I'm to have any chance of winning a scholarship to BGS.'

'Only if you agree to remain silent at all times,' said Deakins. Harry would have laughed, but he knew his friend didn't consider work a laughing matter.

'But I desperately need some help with my Latin grammar,' said Harry. 'I still don't understand the consecutive clause, let alone subjunctives, and if I don't manage a pass mark in the Latin paper, it's curtains, even if I do well in every other subject.'

'I'd be willing to help you with your Latin,' said Deakins, 'if you do me a favour in return.'

'Name it,' said Harry, 'though I can't believe you're hoping to perform a solo at this year's carol service.'

'Good shot, Barrington,' said Mr Frobisher again. Harry joined in the applause. 'That's his third half-century this season, headmaster,' added Mr Frobisher.

'Don't be frivolous, Harry,' said Deakins. 'The truth is, my dad needs someone to take over the morning paper round during the summer holidays, and I've suggested you. The pay is a shilling a week, and as long as you can report to the shop by six o'clock every morning, the position's yours.'

'Six o'clock?' said Harry scornfully. 'When you've got an uncle who wakes up the whole house at five, that's the least of your problems.'

'Then you'd be willing to take on the job?'

'Yes of course,' said Harry. 'But why don't you want it? A bob a week is not to be sniffed at.'

'Don't remind me,' said Deakins, 'but I can't ride a bicycle.'

'Oh hell,' said Harry. 'I don't even have a bicycle.'

'I didn't say I didn't *have* a bicycle,' sighed Deakins, 'I said I couldn't ride one.'

'Clifton,' said Mr Frobisher as the cricketers walked off the ground for tea, 'I'd like to see you in my study after prep.'

—◦—

Harry had always liked Mr Frobisher, who was one of the few masters who treated him as an equal. He also didn't appear to have any favourites, while some of the other beaks left him in no doubt that a docker's son should never have been allowed to enter the hallowed portals of St Bede's however good his voice was.

When the bell rang at the end of prep, Harry put down his pen and walked across the corridor to Mr Frobisher's study. He had no idea why his housemaster wanted to see him, and hadn't given the matter a great deal of thought.

Harry knocked on the study door.

'Come,' said the voice of a man who never wasted words. Harry opened the door and was surprised not to be greeted with the usual Frob smile.

Mr Frobisher stared up at Harry as he came to a halt in front of his desk. 'It has been brought to my attention, Clifton, that you have been stealing from the tuck shop.' Harry's mind went blank as he tried to think of a response that wouldn't condemn Giles. 'You were seen by a prefect, removing goods from the shelves,' continued Frobisher in the same uncompromising tone, 'and then slipping out of the shop before you reached the front of the queue.'

Harry wanted to say, 'Not removing, sir, returning,' but all he managed was, 'I have never taken anything from the tuck shop, sir.' Despite the fact that he was telling the truth, he could still feel his cheeks reddening.

'Then how do you explain your twice weekly visits to the Emporium, when there isn't a single entry against your name in Mr Swivals's ledger?'

Mr Frobisher waited patiently, but Harry knew if he told the truth, Giles would surely be expelled.

'And this bar of chocolate and packet of Liquorice Allsorts were found in the top drawer of your desk, not long after the tuck shop had closed.'

Harry looked down at the sweets, but still said nothing.

'I'm waiting for an explanation, Clifton,' said Mr Frobisher. After another long pause, he added, 'I am of course aware that you have far less pocket money than any other boy in your class, but that is no excuse for stealing.'

'I have never stolen anything in my life,' said Harry.

It was Mr Frobisher's turn to look dismayed. He rose from behind his desk. 'If that is the case, Clifton – and I want to believe you – you will report back to me after choir practice with a full explanation of how you came to be in possession of tuck you clearly didn't pay for. Should you fail to satisfy me, we will both be paying a visit to the headmaster, and I have no doubt what his recommendation will be.'

Harry left the room. The moment he closed the door behind him, he felt sick. He made his way back to his study, hoping Giles wouldn't be there. When he opened the door, the first thing he saw was another bar of chocolate on his desk.

Giles looked up. 'Are you feeling all right?' he asked when he saw Harry's flushed face. Harry didn't reply. He placed the bar of chocolate in a drawer and left for choir practice without saying a word to either of his friends. Giles's eyes never left him, and once the door was closed, he turned to Deakins and asked casually, 'What's his problem?' Deakins went on writing as if he hadn't heard the question. 'Didn't you hear me, cloth ears?' said Giles. 'Why's Harry in a sulk?'

'All I know is that he had an appointment to see the Frob.'

'Why?' asked Giles, sounding more interested.

'I've no idea,' said Deakins, who didn't stop writing.

Giles stood up and strolled across the room to Deakins's side. 'What aren't you telling me?' he demanded, grabbing him by the ear.

Deakins dropped his pen, nervously touched the bridge of his glasses and pushed them further up his nose, before he eventually squeaked, 'He's in some sort of trouble.'

'What sort of trouble?' asked Giles, twisting the ear.

'I think he might even be expelled,' whimpered Deakins.

Giles let go of his ear and burst out laughing. 'Harry, expelled?' he scoffed. 'The Pope's more likely to be defrocked.' He would have returned to his desk if he hadn't noticed beads of sweat appearing on Deakins's forehead. 'What for?' he asked more quietly.

'The Frob thinks he's been stealing from the tuck shop,' said Deakins.

If Deakins had looked up, he would have seen that Giles had turned ashen white. A moment later, he heard the door close. He picked up his pen and tried to concentrate, but for the first time in his life, he didn't finish his prep.

◄○►

When Harry came out of choir practice an hour later, he spotted Fisher leaning on the wall, unable to mask a smile. That was when he realized who must have reported him. He ignored Fisher and strolled back to his house as if he didn't have a care in the world, whereas in fact he felt like a man mounting the gallows, knowing that unless he ditched his closest friend, a stay of execution would not be possible. He hesitated before knocking on his housemaster's door.

The 'Come' was far gentler than it had been earlier that afternoon, but when Harry entered the room he was greeted with the same uncompromising stare. He bowed his head.

'I owe you a sincere apology, Clifton,' said Frobisher, rising from behind his desk. 'I now realize that you were not the culprit.'

Harry's heart was still beating fast, but his anxiety was now for Giles. 'Thank you, sir,' he said, his head still bowed. He had so many questions he would have liked to ask the Frob, but he knew none of them would be answered.

Mr Frobisher stepped out from behind his desk and shook hands with Harry, something he'd never done before. 'You'd better hurry, Clifton, if you hope to get any supper.'

When Harry came out of the Frob's study, he walked slowly towards the dining room. Fisher was standing by the door, a surprised look on his face. Harry walked straight past him and took his place on the end of the bench next to Deakins. The seat opposite him was empty.

8

GILES DIDN'T SHOW UP for supper, and his bed wasn't slept in that night. If St Bede's hadn't lost their annual fixture against Avonhurst by thirty-one runs, Harry suspected that not many boys or even masters would have noticed he was missing.

But, unfortunately for Giles, it was a home match, so everyone had an opinion on why the school's opening batsman had not taken his guard at the crease, not least Fisher, who was telling anyone who cared to listen that the wrong man had been rusticated.

—◦—

Harry hadn't been looking forward to the holidays; not just because he wondered if he'd ever see Giles again, but also because it meant returning to No. 27 Still House Lane and once again having to share a room with his uncle Stan, who more often than not returned home drunk.

After spending the evening going over old exam papers, Harry would climb into bed around ten. He quickly fell asleep, only to be woken sometime after midnight by his uncle, who was often so drunk he couldn't find his own bed. The sound of Stan trying to pee into a chamberpot, and not always hitting the target, was something that would remain etched in Harry's mind for the rest of his life.

Once Stan had collapsed on to his bed – he rarely bothered to get undressed – Harry would try to fall asleep a second time, often to be woken a few minutes later by loud drunken snores. He longed to be back at St Bede's, sharing a dormitory with twenty-nine other boys.

Harry still hoped that in an unguarded moment Stan might let slip some more details about his father's death, but most of the time he was too incoherent to answer even the simplest question. On one of the rare occasions when he was sober enough to speak, he told Harry to bugger off and warned him that if he raised the subject again, he'd thrash him.

The only good thing about sharing a room with Stan was that there was never any chance of his being late for his paper round.

Harry's days at Still House Lane fell into a well-ordered routine: up at five, one slice of toast for breakfast – he no longer licked his uncle's bowl – report to Mr Deakins at the newsagent's by six, stack the papers in the correct order, then deliver them. The whole exercise took about two hours, allowing him to be back home in time for a cup of tea with Mum before she went off to work. At around eight thirty Harry would set off for the library, where he would meet up with Deakins, who was always sitting on the top step waiting for someone to open the doors.

In the afternoon, Harry would report for choir practice at St Mary Redcliffe, as part of his obligation to St Bede's. He never considered it an obligation because he enjoyed singing so much. In fact, he'd more than once whispered, 'Please God, when my voice breaks, let me be a tenor, and I'll never ask for anything else.'

After he returned home for tea in the evening, Harry

would work at the kitchen table for a couple of hours before going to bed, dreading his uncle's return every bit as much as he had Fisher's in his first week at St Bede's. At least Fisher had departed for Colston's Grammar School, so Harry assumed their paths would never cross again.

＜◦►

Harry was looking forward to his final year at St Bede's, although he wasn't in any doubt just how much his life would change if he and his two friends ended up going their separate ways: Giles to he knew not where, Deakins to Bristol Grammar, while if he failed to win a scholarship to BGS, he might well have to return to Merrywood Elementary, and then, at the age of four-teen, leave school and look for a job. He tried not to think about the consequences of failure, despite Stan never missing an opportunity to remind him he could always find work at the docks.

'The boy should never have been allowed to go to that stuck-up school in the first place,' he regularly told Maisie once she'd placed his bowl of porridge in front of him. 'It's given him ideas above his station,' he added, as if Harry wasn't there. A view that Harry felt Fisher would have happily agreed with, but then he'd long ago come to the conclusion that Uncle Stan and Fisher had a lot in common.

'But surely Harry should be given the chance to better himself?' countered Maisie.

'Why?' said Stan. 'If the docks was good enough for me and his old man, why aren't they good enough for him?' he demanded with a finality that brooked no argument.

'Perhaps the boy's cleverer than both of us,' suggested Maisie.

This silenced Stan for a moment, but after another spoonful of porridge, he declared, 'Depends on what you mean by clever. After all, there's clever and then there's clever.' He took another spoonful, but added nothing more to this profound observation.

Harry would cut his slice of toast into four pieces as he listened to his uncle play the same record again and again every morning. He never spoke up for himself, as clearly Stan had already made up his mind on the subject of Harry's future and nothing was going to budge him. What Stan didn't realize was that his constant jibes only inspired Harry to work even harder.

'Can't hang around here all day,' would be Stan's final comment, especially if he felt he was losing the argument. 'Some of us have a job to do,' he added as he rose from the table. No one bothered to argue. 'And another thing,' he said as he opened the kitchen door. 'None of you've noticed the boy's gone soft. He doesn't even lick my porridge bowl no longer. God knows what they've been teachin' him at that school.' The door slammed behind him.

'Take no notice of your uncle,' said Harry's mother. 'He's just jealous. He doesn't like the fact that we're all so proud of you. And even he'll have to change his tune when you win that scholarship, just like your friend Deakins.'

'But that's the problem, Mum,' said Harry. 'I'm not like Deakins, and I'm beginning to wonder if it's all worth it.'

The rest of the family stared at Harry in silent disbelief, until Grandpa piped up for the first time in days. 'I wish I'd been given the chance to go to Bristol Grammar School.'

'Why's that, Grandpa?' shouted Harry.

'Because if I had, we wouldn't have had to live with your uncle Stan all these years.'

◄○►

Harry enjoyed his morning paper round, and not just because it got him out of the house. As the weeks went by, he came to know several of Mr Deakins's regulars, some of whom had heard him sing at St Mary's and would wave when he delivered their paper, while others offered him a cup of tea, even an apple. Mr Deakins had warned him that there were two dogs he should avoid on the round; within a fortnight, both of them were wagging their tails when he got off his bicycle.

Harry was delighted to discover that Mr Holcombe was one of Mr Deakins's regular customers, and they often had a word when he dropped off his copy of *The Times* each morning. His first teacher left Harry in no doubt that he didn't want to see him back at Merrywood, and added that if he needed any extra tuition, he was free most evenings.

When Harry returned to the newsagent's after his round, Mr Deakins would always slip a penny bar of Fry's chocolate into his satchel before sending him on his way. It reminded him of Giles. He often wondered what had become of his friend. Neither he nor Deakins had heard from Giles since the day Mr Frobisher had asked to see Harry after prep. Then, before he left the shop to go home, he always paused in front of the display cabinet to admire a watch he knew he'd never be able to afford. He didn't even bother to ask Mr Deakins how much it cost.

There were only two regular breaks in Harry's weekly routine. He would always try to spend Saturday morning with Old Jack, taking with him copies of all the previous week's *Times*, and on Sunday evenings, once he'd fulfilled his duties at St Mary's, he would rush across the city so he could be at Holy Nativity in time for Evensong.

A frail Miss Monday would beam with pride during the treble solo. She only hoped she would live long enough to see Harry go up to Cambridge. She had plans to tell him about the choir at King's College, but not until he'd won a place at Bristol Grammar.

◄○►

'Is Mr Frobisher going to make you a prefect?' asked Old Jack, even before Harry had sunk into his usual seat on the opposite side of the carriage.

'I've no idea,' replied Harry. 'Mind you, the Frob always says,' he added, tugging his lapels, *'Clifton, in life you get what you deserve, no more and certainly no less.'*

Old Jack chuckled, and just stopped himself saying, 'Not a bad imitation of the Frob.' He satisfied himself with, 'Then my bet is you're about to become a prefect.'

'I'd rather win a scholarship to BGS,' said Harry, suddenly sounding older than his years.

'And what about your friends, Barrington and Deakins?' Old Jack asked, trying to lighten the mood. 'Are they also destined for higher things?'

'They'll never make Deakins a prefect,' said Harry. 'He can't even take care of himself, let alone anyone else. In any case, he's hoping to be the library monitor, and as no one else wants the job, Mr Frobisher shouldn't lose too much sleep over that appointment.'

'And Barrington?'

'I'm not sure he'll be coming back next term,' said Harry wistfully. 'Even if he does, I'm fairly certain they won't make him a prefect.'

'Don't underestimate his father,' said Old Jack. 'That

man will undoubtedly have found a way to ensure that his son returns on the first day of term. And I wouldn't put money on his not being a prefect.'

'Let's hope you're right,' said Harry.

'And if I am, I presume he will then follow his father to Eton?'

'Not if he has any say in it. Giles would prefer to go to BGS with Deakins and me.'

'If he doesn't get into Eton, they're unlikely to offer him a place at the grammar school. Their entrance exam is one of the hardest in the country.'

'He told me he's got a plan.'

'It had better be a good one, if he hopes to fool his father as well as the examiners.'

Harry didn't comment.

'How's your mother?' asked Old Jack, changing the subject, as it was clear that the boy didn't want to go any further down that path.

'She's just been promoted. She's now in charge of all the waitresses in the Palm Court room, and reports directly to Mr Frampton, the hotel manager.'

'You must be very proud of her,' said Old Jack.

'Yes, I am, sir, and what's more, I'm going to prove it.'

'What do you have in mind?'

Harry let him in to his secret. The old man listened attentively, and nodded his approval from time to time. He could see one small problem, but it wasn't insurmountable.

—◦—

When Harry returned to the shop having completed his last paper round before going back to school, Mr Deakins gave him a shilling bonus. 'You're the best paper boy I've ever had,' he said.

'Thank you, sir,' said Harry, pocketing the money. 'Mr Deakins, can I ask you a question?'

'Yes, of course, Harry.'

Harry walked over to the cabinet, where two watches were displayed side by side on the top shelf. 'How much is that one?' he asked, pointing to the Ingersoll.

Mr Deakins smiled. He'd been waiting for Harry to ask that question for some weeks, and had his answer well prepared. 'Six shillings,' he said.

Harry couldn't believe it. He'd been sure that such a magnificent object would cost more than double that. But despite his having put aside half his earnings each week, even with Mr Deakins's bonus, he was still a shilling short.

'You do realize, Harry, that it's a lady's watch?' said Mr Deakins.

'Yes, I do, sir,' said Harry. 'I was hoping to give it to my mother.'

'Then you can have it for five shillings.'

Harry couldn't believe his luck.

'Thank you, sir,' he said as he handed over four shillings, one sixpence, one thruppence and three pennies, leaving him with empty pockets.

Mr Deakins took the watch out of the display cabinet, discreetly removed the sixteen-shilling price tag and then placed it in a smart box.

Harry left the shop whistling. Mr Deakins smiled and placed the ten-shilling note in the till, delighted that he'd fulfilled his part of the bargain.

9

THE BELL WENT.

'Time to get undressed,' said the duty prefect in the new boys' dorm on the first evening of term. They all looked so small and helpless, Harry thought. One or two of them were clearly fighting back tears, while others were looking around, uncertain what they should do next. One boy was facing the wall, shaking. Harry walked quickly across to him.

'What's your name?' Harry asked gently.

'Stevenson.'

'Well, I'm Clifton. Welcome to St Bede's.'

'And I'm Tewkesbury,' said a boy standing on the other side of Stevenson's bed.

'Welcome to St Bede's, Tewkesbury.'

'Thank you, Clifton. Actually, my father and grandfather were here, before they went on to Eton.'

'I don't doubt it,' said Harry. 'And I'll bet they captained Eton against Harrow at Lord's,' he added, immediately regretting his words.

'No, my father was a wet bob,' said Tewkesbury unperturbed, 'not a dry bob.'

'A wet bob?' said Harry.

'He captained Oxford against Cambridge in the boat race.'

Stevenson burst into tears.

'What's the matter?' asked Harry, sitting down on the bed beside him.

'My dad's a tram driver.'

Everyone else stopped unpacking and stared at Stevenson.

'Is that right?' said Harry. 'Then I'd better let you into a secret,' he added, loud enough to be sure that every boy in the dormitory could hear his words. 'I'm the son of a dock worker. I wouldn't be surprised to discover that you're the new choral scholar.'

'No,' said Stevenson, 'I'm an open scholar.'

'Many congratulations,' said Harry, shaking him by the hand. 'You follow in a long and noble tradition.'

'Thank you. But I have a problem,' the boy whispered.

'And what's that, Stevenson?'

'I don't have any toothpaste.'

'Don't worry about that, old chap,' said Tewkesbury, 'my mother always packs a spare one.'

Harry smiled as the bell rang again. 'Everyone into bed,' he said firmly as he walked across the dormitory towards the door.

He heard a voice whisper, 'Thank you for the toothpaste.'

'Think nothing of it, old chap.'

'Now,' said Harry as he flicked off the light, 'I don't want to hear another word from any of you until the bell goes at six thirty tomorrow morning.' He waited for a few moments before he heard someone whispering. 'I meant it – not another word.' He smiled as he walked down the staircase to join Deakins and Barrington in the senior prefects' study.

Harry had been surprised by two things when he arrived back at St Bede's on the first day of term. No sooner had he walked through the front door than Mr Frobisher took him to one side.

'Congratulations, Clifton,' he said softly. 'It won't be announced until assembly tomorrow morning, but you're to be the new school captain.'

'It should have been Giles,' said Harry without thinking.

'Barrington will be captain of games, and—'

Harry had leapt in the air the moment he heard the news that his friend would be returning to St Bede's. Old Jack had been right when he said Mr Hugo would find a way to make sure his son was back for the first day of term.

When Giles walked into the front hall a few moments later, the two boys shook hands, and Harry never once referred to the subject that must have been on both their minds.

'What are the new bugs like?' Giles asked as Harry entered the study.

'One of them reminds me of you,' said Harry.

'Tewkesbury, no doubt.'

'You know him?'

'No, but Papa was at Eton at the same time as his father.'

'I told him I was the son of a docker,' said Harry as he slumped into the only comfortable chair in the room.

'Did you now?' said Giles. 'And did he tell you he's the son of a cabinet minister?'

Harry said nothing.

'Are there any others I should keep an eye out for?' asked Giles.

'Stevenson,' said Harry. 'He's a cross between Deakins and me.'

'Then we'd better lock the fire-escape door before he makes a dash for it.'

Harry often thought about where he might be now if Old Jack hadn't talked him into returning to St Bede's that night.

'What's our first lesson tomorrow?' asked Harry, checking his timetable.

'Latin,' said Deakins. 'Which is why I'm guiding Giles through the first Punic war.'

'264 to 241 BC,' said Giles.

'I bet you're enjoying that,' said Harry.

'Yes, I am,' said Giles, 'and I just can't wait for the sequel, the second Punic war.'

'218 to 201 BC,' said Harry.

'It always amazes me how the Greeks and Romans seemed to know exactly when Christ would be born,' said Giles.

'Ho, ho, ho,' said Harry.

Deakins didn't laugh, but said, 'And finally, we will have to consider the third Punic War, 149 to 146 BC.'

'Do we really need to know about all three of them?' said Giles.

◄○►

St Mary Redcliffe was packed with town and gown who'd come to celebrate an Advent service of eight readings and eight carols. The choir made their entrance through the nave, and advanced slowly down the aisle singing *O Come All Ye Faithful*, then took their places in the choir stalls.

The headmaster read the first lesson. This was followed by *O Little Town of Bethlehem*. The service sheet indicated that the soloist for the third verse would be Master Harry Clifton.

How silently, how silently, the wondrous gift is given, while God ... Harry's mother sat proudly in the third row, while the old lady sitting next to her wanted to tell everyone in the congregation that they were listening to her grandson. The man seated on the other side of Maisie couldn't hear a word, but you would never have known that from the contented smile on his face. Uncle Stan was nowhere to be seen.

The captain of games read the second lesson, and when Giles returned to his place, Harry noticed that he was seated next to a distinguished-looking man with a head of silver hair, who he assumed must be Sir Walter Barrington. Giles had once told him that his grandfather lived in an even larger house than his, but Harry didn't think that could be possible. On the other side of Giles sat his mother and father. Mrs Barrington smiled across at him, but Mr Barrington didn't once look in his direction.

When the organ struck up the prelude for *We Three Kings*, the congregation rose and sang lustily. The next lesson was read by Mr Frobisher, after which came what Miss Monday anticipated would be the highlight of the service. The thousand-strong congregation didn't stir while Harry sang *Silent Night* with a clarity and confidence that caused even the headmaster to smile.

The library monitor read the next lesson. Harry had already coached him through St Mark's words several times. Deakins had tried to get out of the chore, as he described it to Giles, but Mr Frobisher had insisted; the fourth lesson was always read by the librarian. Deakins wasn't Giles, but he wasn't bad. Harry winked at him as he shuffled back to his seat next to his parents.

The choir then rose to sing *In Dulci Jubilo* while the congregation remained seated. Harry considered the carol to be among the most demanding in their repertoire, because of its unconventional harmonies.

Mr Holcombe closed his eyes so that he could hear the senior choral scholar more clearly. Harry was singing

Now let all hearts be singing when he thought he heard a slight, almost imperceptible, crack in the voice. He assumed Harry must have a cold. Miss Monday knew better. She'd heard those early signs so many times before. She prayed that she was mistaken, but knew her prayer would not be answered. Harry would get through the rest of the service with only a handful of people realizing what had happened, and he would even be able to carry on for a few more weeks, possibly months, but by Easter another child would be singing *Rejoice that the Lord has arisen.*

An old man who'd turned up only moments after the service had begun was among those who weren't in any doubt what had happened. Old Jack left just before the bishop gave his final blessing. He knew Harry wouldn't be able to visit him until the following Saturday, which would give him enough time to work out how to answer the inevitable question.

◄○►

'Might I have a private word with you, Clifton?' said Mr Frobisher as the bell sounded for the end of prep. 'Perhaps you'd join me in my study.' Harry would never forget the last time he'd heard those words.

When Harry closed the study door, his housemaster beckoned him towards a seat by the fire, something he had never done before. 'I just wanted to assure you, Harry' – another first – 'that the fact you are no longer able to sing in the choir will not affect your bursary. We at St Bede's are well aware that the contribution you have made to school life stretches far beyond the chapel.'

'Thank you, sir,' said Harry.

'However, we must now consider your future. The

music master tells me that it will be some time before your voice fully recovers, which I'm afraid means that we must be realistic about your chances of being offered a choral scholarship to Bristol Grammar School.'

'There is no chance,' said Harry calmly.

'I have to agree with you,' said Frobisher. 'I'm relieved to find you understand the situation. But,' he continued, 'I would be happy to enter your name for an open scholarship to BGS. However,' he added before Harry had time to respond, 'in the circumstances, you might consider that you'd have a better chance of being offered a bursary at, say, Colston's School, or King's College Gloucester, both of which have far less demanding entrance examinations.'

'No, thank you, sir,' said Harry. 'My first choice remains Bristol Grammar.' He'd said the same thing to Old Jack just as firmly the previous Saturday, when his mentor had mumbled something about not burning your boats.

'So be it,' said Mr Frobisher, who had not expected any other response, but had still felt it was nothing less than his duty to come up with an alternative. 'Now, let's turn this setback to our advantage.'

'How do you suggest I do that, sir?'

'Well, now that you've been released from daily choir practice, you will have more time to prepare for your entrance exam.'

'Yes, sir, but I still have my responsibilities as—'

'And I will do everything in my power to ensure that your duties as school captain are less onerous in future.'

'Thank you, sir.'

'By the way, Harry,' said Frobisher as he rose from his chair, 'I've just read your essay on Jane Austen, and I was fascinated by your suggestion that if Miss Austen had been able to go to university, she might never have written a novel, and even if she had, her work probably wouldn't have been so insightful.'

'Sometimes it's an advantage to be disadvantaged,' said Harry.

'That doesn't sound like Jane Austen,' said Mr Frobisher.

'It isn't,' replied Harry. 'But it was said by someone else who didn't go to university,' he added without explanation.

◄o►

Maisie glanced at her new watch and smiled. 'I'll have to leave now, Harry, if I'm not going to be late for work.'

'Of course, Mum,' said Harry, leaping up from the table. 'I'll walk with you to the tram stop.'

'Harry, have you thought about what you'll do if you don't win that scholarship?' said his mother, finally asking a question she'd been avoiding for weeks.

'Constantly,' said Harry as he opened the door for her. 'But I won't be given much choice in the matter. I'll just have to go back to Merrywood, and when I turn fourteen I'll leave and look for a job.'

10

'Do you feel ready to face the examiners, my boy?' asked Old Jack.

'As ready as I'm ever likely to be,' replied Harry. 'By the way, I took your advice, and checked over the examination papers for the past ten years. You were right, there's a definite pattern, with some of the same questions coming up at regular intervals.'

'Good. And how's your Latin coming on? We can't afford to fail that, however well we do in your other papers.'

Harry smiled when Old Jack said 'we'. 'Thanks to Deakins I managed 69 per cent in mocks last week, even if I did have Hannibal crossing the Andes.'

'Only about six thousand miles out,' chuckled Old Jack. 'So what do you think will be your biggest problem?'

'The forty boys from St Bede's who are also taking the exam, not to mention the two hundred and fifty from other schools.'

'Forget them,' said Old Jack. 'If you do what you're capable of, they won't be a problem.'

Harry remained silent.

'So, how's your voice coming along?' asked Old Jack, who always changed the subject whenever Harry fell silent.

'Nothing new to report,' said Harry. 'It could be weeks before I know if I'm a tenor, a baritone or a bass, and even then, there's no guarantee I'll be any good. One thing's for certain, BGS aren't going to offer me a choral scholarship while I'm like a horse with a broken leg.'

'Snap out of it,' said Old Jack. 'It's not that bad.'

'It's worse,' said Harry. 'If I was a horse, they'd shoot me and put me out of my misery.'

Old Jack laughed. 'So when are the exams?' he asked, even though he knew the answer.

'Thursday week. We start with general knowledge at nine o'clock, and there are five other papers during the day, ending with English at four.'

'It's good that you finish with your favourite subject,' said Jack.

'Let's hope so,' said Harry. 'But pray there's a question on Dickens, because there hasn't been one for the past three years, which is why I've been reading his books after lights out.'

'Wellington wrote in his memoirs,' said Old Jack, 'that the worst moment of any campaign is waiting for the sun to rise on the morning of battle.'

'I agree with the Iron Duke, which means I won't be getting much sleep for the next couple of weeks.'

'All the more reason not to come and see me next Saturday, Harry. You ought to be making better use of your time. In any case, if I remember correctly, it's your birthday.'

'How did you know that?'

'I confess that I didn't read it on the court page of

The Times. But as it fell on the same day last year, I took a gamble and bought a small gift for you.' He picked up a parcel wrapped in a page from one of last week's newspapers, and handed it to Harry.

'Thank you, sir,' said Harry as he untied the string. He removed the newspaper, opened the small dark blue box and stared in disbelief at the man's Ingersoll watch he'd last seen in the display cabinet at Mr Deakins's shop.

'Thank you,' Harry repeated as he strapped the watch on his wrist. He couldn't take his eyes off it for some time, and could only wonder how Old Jack could possibly afford six shillings.

◄○►

Harry was wide awake long before the sun rose on the morning of the exams. He skipped breakfast in favour of going over some old general knowledge papers, checking capitals against countries from Germany to Brazil, dates of prime ministers from Walpole to Lloyd George, and of monarchs from King Alfred to George V. An hour later he felt ready to face the examiner.

Once again, he was seated in the front row, between Barrington and Deakins. Was this the last time, he wondered. When the clock on the tower struck ten, several masters marched down the rows of desks handing out the general knowledge paper to forty nervous boys. Well, thirty-nine nervous boys, and Deakins.

Harry read through the questions slowly. When he reached number 100, he allowed a smile to cross his face. He picked up his pen, dipped the nib in the inkwell and began to write. Forty minutes later he was back at question 100. He glanced at his watch; he still had another ten minutes in which to double-check his answers. He stopped for a moment at question 34 and reconsidered his original answer. Was it Oliver Cromwell or Thomas Cromwell who was sent to the Tower of London for treason? He recalled the fate of Cardinal Wolsey, and selected the man who'd taken his place as Lord Chancellor.

When the clock began to strike again, Harry had reached question 92. He quickly looked over his last eight answers before his paper was snatched away, the ink still drying on his final answer, Charles Lindbergh.

During the twenty-minute break, Harry, Giles and Deakins walked slowly around the cricket field where Giles had scored a century only a week before.

'*Amo, amas, amat*,' said Deakins as he painstakingly took them through their conjugations without once referring to *Kennedy's Latin Primer*.

'*Amamus, amatis, amant*,' repeated Harry as they made their way back towards the examination hall.

When Harry handed in his Latin paper an hour later, he felt confident he'd scored more than the required 60 per cent, and even Giles looked pleased with himself. As the three of them strolled across to the refectory, Harry put an arm around Deakins's shoulder and said, 'Thanks, old chum.'

After Harry had read through the geography paper later that morning, he silently thanked his secret weapon. Old Jack had passed on so much knowledge over the years without ever making him feel that he'd been in a classroom.

Harry didn't pick up a knife or fork during lunch. Giles managed half a pork pie, while Deakins didn't stop eating.

History was the first paper that afternoon, and didn't cause him any anxiety. Henry VIII, Elizabeth, Raleigh, Drake, Napoleon, Nelson and Wellington all marched on to the battlefield, and Harry marched them back off again.

The mathematics paper was far easier than he had expected, and Giles even thought he might have scored another century.

During the final break, Harry returned to his study and glanced over an essay he'd written on *David Copperfield*, confident that he would excel in his favourite subject. He walked slowly back to the examination hall, repeating Mr Holcombe's favourite word again and again. Concentrate.

He stared down at the final paper of the day, to find that this year belonged to Thomas Hardy and Lewis Carroll. He'd read *The Mayor of Casterbridge* and *Alice's Adventures in Wonderland*, but the Mad Hatter, Michael Henchard and the Cheshire Cat were not as familiar to him as Peggotty, Dr Chillip and Barkis. His pen scratched slowly across the page, and when the clock chimed on the hour, he wasn't sure if he'd done enough. He walked out of the hall and into the afternoon sunshine, feeling a little depressed, although it was clear from the looks on the faces of his rivals that no one thought it had been an easy paper. That made him wonder if he was still in with a chance.

◄○►

There followed what Mr Holcombe had often described as the worst part of any exam, those days of endless waiting before the results were formally posted on the school notice board; a time when boys end up doing something they will later regret, almost as if they want to be rusticated rather than learn their fate. One boy was caught drinking cider behind the bicycle shed, another smoking a Woodbine in the lavatory, while a third was seen leaving the local cinema after lights out.

Giles was out for a duck the following Saturday, his first of the season. While Deakins returned to the library, Harry went on long walks, going over every answer in his head again and again. It didn't improve matters.

On Sunday afternoon, Giles had a long net; on Monday, Deakins reluctantly handed over his responsibilities to the new library monitor, and on Tuesday Harry read *Far from the Madding Crowd* and cursed out loud. On Wednesday night, Giles and Harry talked into the small hours, while Deakins slept soundly.

◄○►

Long before the clock on the tower struck ten that Thursday morning, forty boys were already roaming around the quad, hands in pockets, heads bowed as they waited for the headmaster to make his appearance. Although every one of them knew that Dr Oakshott wouldn't be a minute early or a minute late, by five to ten most eyes were staring across the quad waiting for the door of the headmaster's house to open. The rest were looking up at the clock on the great hall, willing the minute hand to move a little faster.

As the first chime sounded, the Reverend Samuel Oakshott opened his front door and stepped out on to the path. He was carrying a sheet of paper in one hand and four tin-tacks in the other. Not a man who left anything to chance. When he reached the end of the path, he opened the little wicket gate and walked across the quad at his usual pace, oblivious to all around him. The boys quickly stood aside, creating a corridor so the headmaster's progress would not be impeded. He came to a halt in front of the notice board as the tenth chime rang out. He posted the exam results on the board, and departed without a word.

Forty boys rushed forward, forming a scrum around the notice board. No one was surprised that Deakins headed the list, with 92 per cent, and had been awarded the Peloquin Scholarship to Bristol Grammar School. Giles leapt in the air, making no attempt to disguise his relief when he saw 64 per cent by his name.

They both turned to look for their friend. Harry was standing alone, far from the madding crowd.

MAISIE CLIFTON

1920–1936

11

When Arthur and me got married, the occasion couldn't have been described as pushing the boat out, but then, neither the Tancocks nor the Cliftons ever did have two brass farthings to rub together. The biggest expense turned out to be the choir, half a crown, and worth every penny. I'd always wanted to be a member of Miss Monday's choir, and although she told me my voice was good enough, I wasn't considered on account of the fact I couldn't read or write.

The reception, if you could call it that, was held at Arthur's parents' terraced house in Still House Lane: a barrel of beer, some peanut butter sandwiches and a dozen pork pies. My brother Stan even brought his own fish and chips. And to top it all, we had to leave early to catch the last bus to Weston-super-Mare for our honeymoon. Arthur booked us into a seafront guest house on the Friday evening, and as it rained for most of the weekend, we rarely left the bedroom.

It felt strange that the second time I had sex was also in Weston-super-Mare. I was shocked when I saw Arthur naked for the first time. A deep red, roughly stitched scar stretched tight across his stomach. Damn the Germans. He never said he'd been wounded during the war.

I wasn't surprised that Arthur became aroused the

moment I pulled off my slip, but I must admit I'd expected him to take his boots off before we made love.

We checked out of the guest house on Sunday afternoon and caught the last bus back to Bristol, as Arthur had to report to the dockyard by six o'clock on Monday morning.

After the wedding, Arthur moved into our house – just until we could afford a place of our own, he told my father, which usually meant until one of our parents passed away. In any case, both our families had lived on Still House Lane for as long as anyone could remember.

Arthur was delighted when I told him I was in the family way, because he wanted at least six babies. My worry was whether the first would be his, but, as only my mum and I knew the truth, there was no reason for Arthur to be suspicious.

Eight months later I gave birth to a boy, and thank God there was nothing to suggest that he wasn't Arthur's. We christened him Harold, which pleased my father, because it meant his name would survive for another generation.

From then on, I took it for granted that, like Mum and Gran, I would be stuck at home having a baby every other year. After all, Arthur came from a family of eight, and I was the fourth of five. But Harry turned out to be my only child.

◄o►

Arthur usually came straight home after work of an evening so he could spend some time with the baby before I put him to bed. When he didn't turn up that Friday night, I assumed he'd gone off to the pub with my brother. But when Stan staggered in just after midnight, blind drunk and flashing a wad of fivers, Arthur was nowhere to be seen. In fact, Stan gave me one of the fivers, which made me wonder if he'd robbed a bank. But when I asked him where Arthur was, he clammed up.

I didn't go to bed that night, just sat on the bottom step

MAISIE CLIFTON

of the stairs waiting for my husband to come home. Arthur had never stayed out all night from the day we was married.

Although Stan had sobered up by the time he came down to the kitchen the following morning, he didn't say a word during breakfast. When I asked him again where Arthur was, he claimed he hadn't seen him since they'd clocked off work the previous evening. It's not difficult to tell when Stan's lying, because he won't look you in the eye. I was about to press him further when I heard a loud banging on the front door. My first thought was that it must be Arthur, so I rushed to answer it.

When I opened the door, two policemen burst into the house, ran into the kitchen, grabbed Stan, handcuffed him and told him he was being arrested for burglary. Now I knew where the wad of fivers had come from.

'I didn't steal anything,' protested Stan. 'Mr Barrington gave me the money.'

'A likely story, Tancock,' said the first copper.

'But it's the God's honest truth, officer,' he was saying as they dragged him off to the nick. This time I knew Stan wasn't lying.

I left Harry with my mum and ran all the way to the dockyard, hoping to find that Arthur had reported for the morning shift and would be able to tell me why Stan had been arrested. I tried not to think about the possibility that Arthur might also be locked up.

The man on the gate told me he hadn't seen Arthur all morning. But after he checked the rota, he looked puzzled, because Arthur hadn't clocked off the night before. All he had to say was, 'Don't blame me. I wasn't on the gate last night.'

It was only later that I wondered why he'd used the word 'blame'.

I went into the dockyard and asked some of Arthur's mates, but they all parroted the same line. 'Haven't seen him since he clocked off last night.' Then they quickly walked away. I was about to go off to the nick to see if Arthur had been arrested as well, when I saw an old man going past, head bowed.

I chased after him, quite expecting him to tell me to bugger off or claim he didn't know what I was talking about. But when I approached, he stopped, took off his cap and said, 'Good morning.' I was surprised by his good manners, which gave me the confidence to ask him if he'd seen Arthur that morning.

'No,' he replied. 'I last saw him yesterday afternoon when he was on the late shift with your brother. Perhaps you should ask him.'

'I can't,' I said. 'He's been arrested and taken off to the nick.'

'What have they charged him with?' asked Old Jack, looking puzzled.

'I don't know,' I replied.

Old Jack shook his head. 'I can't help you, Mrs Clifton,' he said. 'But there are at least two people who know the whole story.' He nodded towards the large red-brick building that Arthur always called 'management'.

I shivered when I saw a policeman coming out of the front door of the building, and when I looked back, Old Jack had disappeared.

I thought about going into 'management', or Barrington House, to give it its proper name, but decided against it. After all, what would I say if I came face to face with Arthur's boss? In the end I began to walk aimlessly back home, trying to make sense of things.

◄◦►

I watched Hugo Barrington when he gave his evidence. The same self-confidence, the same arrogance, the same half-truths spouted convincingly to the jury, just as he'd whispered them to me in the privacy of the bedroom. When he stepped down from the witness box, I knew Stan didn't have a snowball's chance in hell of getting off.

In the judge's summing-up, he described my brother as a common thief, who had taken advantage of his position to rob his employer. He ended by saying he had no choice but to send him down for three years.

I had sat through every day of the trial, hoping to pick up some snippet of information that might give me a clue as to what had happened to Arthur that day. But by the time the judge finally declared, 'Court adjourned,' I was none the wiser, although I was in no doubt that my brother wasn't telling the whole story. It would be some time before I found out why.

The only other person who attended the court every day was Old Jack Tar, but we didn't speak. In fact, I might never have seen him again if it hadn't been for Harry.

◄○►

It was some time before I was able to accept that Arthur would never be coming home.

Stan had only been away for a few days before I discovered the true meaning of the words 'eke out'. With one of the two breadwinners in the family banged up, and the other God knows where, we soon found ourselves quite literally on the bread-line. Luckily there was an unwritten code that operated in Still House Lane: if someone was 'away on holiday', the neighbours did whatever they could to help support his family.

The Reverend Watts dropped in regularly, and even returned some of the coins we'd put in his collection plate over the years. Miss Monday appeared irregularly and dispensed far more than good advice, always leaving with an empty basket. But nothing could compensate me for the loss of a husband, an innocent brother locked up in jail, and a son who no longer had a father.

Harry had recently taken his first step, but I was already fearful of hearing his first word. Would he even remember who used to sit at the head of the table, and ask why he was no longer there? It was Grandpa who came up with a solution as to what we should say if Harry started to ask questions. We all made a pact to stick to the same story; after all, Harry was hardly likely to come across Old Jack.

But at that time the Tancock family's most pressing problem was how to keep the wolf from our door, or, more important, the rent collector and the bailiff. Once I'd spent Stan's five pounds, pawned my mum's silver-plated tea strainer, my engagement ring and finally my wedding ring, I feared it couldn't be long before we were evicted.

But that was delayed for a few weeks by another knock on the door. This time it wasn't the police, but a man called Mr Sparks, who told me he was Arthur's trade union representative, and that he'd come to see if I'd had any compensation from the company.

Once I'd settled Mr Sparks down in the kitchen and poured him a cup of tea, I told him, 'Not a brass farthing. They say he left without giving notice, so they aren't responsible for his actions. And I still don't know what really happened that day.'

'Neither do I,' said Mr Sparks. 'They've all clammed up, not just the management, but the workers as well. I can't get a word out of them. "More than my life's worth," one of them told me. But your husband's subs were fully paid up,' he added, 'so you're entitled to union compensation.'

I just stood there, with no idea what he was going on about.

Mr Sparks took a document out of his briefcase, placed it on the kitchen table and turned to the back page.

'Sign here,' he said placing a forefinger on the dotted line.

After I had put an X where he was pointing, he took an envelope out of his pocket. 'I'm sorry it's so little,' he said as he handed it to me.

I didn't open the envelope until he had finished his cup of tea and left.

Seven pounds, nine shillings and sixpence turned out to be the value they'd put on Arthur's life. I sat alone at the kitchen table, and I think that was the moment I knew I'd never see my husband again.

That afternoon I went back to the pawn shop and redeemed my wedding ring from Mr Cohen; it was the least I could do in memory of Arthur. The following morning I cleared the rent arrears, as well as the slate at the butcher, the baker and yes, the candlestick maker. There was just enough left over to buy some second-hand clothes from the church jumble sale, mostly for Harry.

But it was less than a month before the chalk was once again scratching across the slate at the butcher, the baker and the candlestick maker, and it wasn't long after that I had to return to the pawn shop and hand my wedding ring back to Mr Cohen.

When the rent collector came knocking on the door of number 27 and never received a reply, I suppose none of the family should have been surprised that the next caller would be the bailiff. That was when I decided the time had come for me to look for a job.

12

MAISIE'S ATTEMPTS to find a job didn't turn out to be easy, not least because the government had recently issued a directive to all employers advising them to take on men who had served in the armed forces before considering any other candidates. This was in keeping with Lloyd George's promise that Britain's soldiers would return home to a land fit for heroes.

Although women over thirty had been given the vote at the last election after their sterling service in munitions factories during the war, they were pushed to the back of the queue when it came to peacetime jobs. Maisie decided that her best chance of finding employment was to apply for jobs men wouldn't consider, either because they felt they were too demeaning, or the pay was derisory. With that in mind, Maisie stood in line outside W.D. & H.O. Wills, the city's largest employer. When she reached the front of the queue, she asked the supervisor, 'Is it true you're looking for packers in the cigarette factory?'

'Yes, but you're too young, luv,' he told her.

'I'm twenty-two.'

'You're too young,' he repeated. 'Come back in two or three years' time.'

Maisie was back at Still House Lane in time to share

a bowl of chicken broth and a slice of last week's bread with Harry and her mum.

The next day, she joined an even longer queue outside Harvey's, the wine merchants. When she reached the front, three hours later, she was told by a man wearing a starched white collar and a thin black tie that they were only taking on applicants with experience.

'So how do I get experience?' Maisie asked, trying not to sound desperate.

'By joining our apprentice scheme.'

'Then I'll join,' she told the starched collar.

'How old are you?'

'Twenty-two.'

'You're too old.'

Maisie repeated every word of the sixty-second interview to her mother over a thinner bowl of broth from the same pot along with a crust of bread from the same loaf.

'You could always try the docks,' her mother suggested.

'What do you have in mind, Mum? Should I sign up to be a stevedore?'

Maisie's mum didn't laugh, but then Maisie couldn't remember the last time she had. 'They've always got work for cleaners,' she said. 'And God knows that lot owe you.'

Maisie was up and dressed long before the sun had risen the following morning and, as there wasn't enough breakfast to go round, she set out hungry on the long walk to the docks.

When she arrived, Maisie told the man on the gate she was looking for a cleaning job.

'Report to Mrs Nettles,' he said, nodding in the direction of the large red-brick building she'd so nearly entered once before. 'She's in charge of hirin' and firin' cleaners.' He clearly didn't remember her from her previous visit.

Maisie walked uneasily towards the building, but came to a halt a few paces before she reached the front door. She stood and watched as a succession of smartly dressed men wearing hats and coats and carrying umbrellas made their way through the double doors.

Maisie remained rooted to the spot, shivering in the cold morning air as she tried to find enough courage to follow them inside. She was just about to turn away when she spotted an older woman in overalls entering another door, at the side of the building. Maisie chased after her.

'What do you want?' asked the woman suspiciously once Maisie had caught up with her.

'I'm lookin' for a job.'

'Good,' she said. 'We could do with some young 'uns. Report to Mrs Nettles,' she added, pointing towards a narrow door that might have been mistaken for a broom cupboard. Maisie walked boldly up to it and knocked.

'Come on in,' said a tired voice.

Maisie opened the door to find a woman of about her mother's age sitting on the only chair, surrounded by buckets, mops and several large bars of soap.

'I was told to report to you if I was lookin' for a job.'

'You was told right. That's if you're willing to work all the hours God gives, for damn all pay.'

'What are the hours, and what's the pay?' asked Maisie.

'You start at three in the morning, and you have to be off the premises by seven, before their nibs turns up, when they expect to find their offices spick and span. Or you can start at seven of an evening and work through till midnight, whichever suits you. Pay's the same whatever you decide, sixpence an hour.'

'I'll do both shifts,' said Maisie.

'Good,' the woman said, selecting a bucket and mop. 'I'll see you back here at seven this evenin', when I'll show you the ropes. My name's Vera Nettles. What's yours?'

'Maisie Clifton.'

Mrs Nettles dropped the bucket on the floor and propped the mop back up against the wall. She walked across to the door and opened it. 'There's no work for you here, Mrs Clifton,' she said.

—◄○►—

Over the next month, Maisie tried to get a job in a shoe shop, but the manager didn't feel he could employ someone with holes in her shoes; a milliner's, where the interview was terminated the moment they discovered she couldn't add up; and a flower shop, which wouldn't consider taking on anyone who didn't have their own garden. Grandpa's allotment didn't count. In desperation, she applied for a job as a barmaid in a local pub, but the landlord said, 'Sorry, luv, but your tits aren't big enough.'

The following Sunday at Holy Nativity, Maisie knelt and asked God to give her a helping hand.

That hand turned out to be Miss Monday's, who told Maisie she had a friend who owned a tea shop on Broad Street and was looking for a waitress.

'But I don't have any experience,' said Maisie.

'That may well prove to be an advantage,' said Miss Monday. 'Miss Tilly is most particular, and prefers to train her staff in her own way.'

'Perhaps she'll think I'm too old, or too young.'

'You are neither too old nor too young,' said Miss Monday. 'And be assured, I wouldn't recommend you if I didn't think you were up to it. But I must warn you,

Maisie, that Miss Tilly is a stickler for time-keeping. Be at the tea shop before eight o'clock tomorrow. If you're late, that will not only be the first impression you make, but also the last.'

Maisie was standing outside Tilly's Tea Shop at six o'clock the following morning, and didn't budge for the next two hours. At five minutes to eight a plump, middle-aged, smartly dressed woman, with her hair arranged in a neat bun and a pair of half-moon spectacles propped on the end of her nose, turned the 'closed' sign on the door to 'open', to allow a frozen Maisie to step inside.

'You've got the job, Mrs Clifton,' were her new boss's first words.

◄○►

Harry was left in the care of his grandmother whenever Maisie went to work. Although she was only paid nine pence an hour, she was allowed to keep half her tips, so that at the end of a good week she could take home as much as three pounds. There was also an unexpected bonus. Once the 'open' sign had been turned back to 'closed' at six o'clock in the evening, Miss Tilly would allow Maisie to take home any food that was left over. The word 'stale' was never allowed to cross a customer's lips.

After six months, Miss Tilly was so pleased with Maisie's progress that she put her in charge of her own station of eight tables, and after another six months, several regulars would insist that Maisie served them. Miss Tilly solved the problem by increasing Maisie's allocation of tables to twelve, and raising her pay to a shilling an hour. With two pay packets coming in each week, Maisie was once again able to wear both her engagement ring and her wedding ring, and the silver-plated tea strainer was back in its place.

—◄o►—

If Maisie was honest about it, Stan being released from prison for good behaviour after only eighteen months turned out to be a bit of a mixed blessing.

Harry, now aged three and a half, had to move back into his mother's room, and Maisie tried not to think about just how peaceful it had been while Stan was away.

Maisie was surprised when Stan got his old job back at the docks as if nothing had happened. This only convinced her that he knew far more about Arthur's disappearance than he let on, however much she pressed him. On one occasion when she became a little too persistent, he belted her one. Although, the following morning, Miss Tilly pretended not to notice the black eye, one or two of the customers did, so Maisie never raised the subject with her brother again. But whenever Harry asked him about his father, Stan stuck to the family line and said, 'Your old man was killed in the war. I was standin' by his side when the bullet hit him.'

—◄o►—

Maisie spent as much of her spare time with Harry as she could. She assumed that once he was old enough to attend Merrywood Elementary School, her life would become a lot easier. But taking Harry to school in the morning meant the added expense of a tram ride to make sure she was not late for work. She would then take a break in the afternoon so she could pick him up from school. Once Maisie had given him his tea, she would leave him in the care of his grandma and return to work.

Harry had only been at school for a few days when Maisie noticed some cane marks on his backside while she was giving him his weekly bath.

'Who did that?' she demanded.

'The headmaster.'

'Why?'

'Can't tell you, Mum.'

When Maisie saw six new red stripes even before the previous ones had faded, she questioned Harry again, but still he didn't let on. The third time the marks appeared, she put on her coat and set off for Merrywood Elementary with the intention of giving his teacher a piece of her mind.

Mr Holcombe wasn't at all what Maisie had expected. To start with, he couldn't have been much older than she was, and he stood up when she entered the room – not at all like the teachers she remembered from her days at Merrywood.

'Why is my son being caned by the headmaster?' she demanded, even before Mr Holcombe had a chance to offer her a seat.

'Because he keeps playing truant, Mrs Clifton. He disappears soon after morning assembly, and gets back in time for football in the afternoon.'

'So where is he spending the day?'

'At the docks would be my guess,' said Mr Holcombe. 'Perhaps you might be able to tell me why.'

'Because his uncle works there, and he's always telling Harry that school is a waste of time because sooner or later he'll end up joining him at Barrington's.'

'I hope not,' said Mr Holcombe.

'Why do you say that?' asked Maisie. 'It was good enough for his father.'

'That may well be, but it won't be good enough for Harry.'

'What do you mean?' Maisie asked indignantly.

'Harry is bright, Mrs Clifton. Very bright. If only I could persuade him to attend class more regularly, there's no saying what he might achieve.'

Maisie suddenly wondered if she would ever find out which of the two men was Harry's father.

'Some clever children don't discover how bright they are until after they've left school,' continued Mr Holcombe, 'and then spend the rest of their lives regretting the wasted years. I want to make sure Harry does not fall into that category.'

'What would you like me to do?' asked Maisie, finally sitting down.

'Encourage him to stay at school, and not slope off to the docks every day. Tell him how proud you'd be if he did well in class, and not only on the football field – which, just in case you didn't realize, Mrs Clifton, isn't his forte.'

'His forte?'

'I do apologize. But even Harry must have worked out by now that he's never going to make the school XI, let alone play for Bristol City.'

'I'll do anything I can to help,' promised Maisie.

'Thank you, Mrs Clifton,' said Mr Holcombe as Maisie rose to leave. 'If you felt able to encourage him, I've no doubt it will be far more effective in the long term than the headmaster's cane.'

From that day, Maisie began to take a far greater interest in what Harry got up to at school. She enjoyed listening to his stories about Mr Holcombe and what he'd taught him that day, and as the stripes didn't reappear, she assumed he must have stopped playing truant. And then one night just before going to bed, she checked on the sleeping child and found that the stripes were back, redder and deeper than before. She didn't need to go and see Mr Holcombe, because he called in at the tea shop the following day.

'He managed to come to my class for a whole month,' said Mr Holcombe, 'and then he disappeared again.'

'But I don't know what more I can do,' said Maisie helplessly. 'I've already stopped his pocket money, and told him not to expect another penny from me unless he stays at school. The truth is, his uncle Stan has far more influence over him than I do.'

'More's the pity,' said Mr Holcombe. 'But I may have found a solution to our problem, Mrs Clifton. However, it has no chance of succeeding without your full cooperation.'

◄o►

Maisie assumed that although she was only twenty-six, she would never marry again. After all, widows with a child in tow were not much of a catch when there were so many single women available. The fact that she always wore her engagement and wedding rings probably cut down the number of propositions she received at the tea shop, although one or two still tried it on. She didn't include dear old Mr Craddick, who just liked to hold her hand.

Mr Atkins was one of Miss Tilly's regulars, and he liked to sit at one of the tables where Maisie was serving. He dropped in most mornings, always ordering a black coffee and a piece of fruit cake. To Maisie's surprise, after he'd paid his bill one morning, he invited her to the cinema.

'Greta Garbo in *Flesh and the Devil*,' he said, trying to make it sound more tempting.

This wasn't the first time one of the customers had

asked Maisie out, but it was the first time someone young and good-looking had shown any interest.

In the past, her stock response had succeeded in putting off the most persistent of suitors. 'How kind of you, Mr Atkins, but I like to spend any spare time I have with my son.'

'Surely you could make an exception for just one evening?' he said, not giving up quite as easily as the others.

Maisie glanced quickly at his left hand: no sign of a wedding ring, or, even more damning, a pale circle revealing that one had been removed.

She heard herself saying, 'How kind of you, Mr Atkins,' and agreed to meet him on Thursday evening, after she'd put Harry to bed.

'Call me Eddie,' he said, leaving a sixpenny tip.

Maisie was impressed when Eddie turned up in a Flatnose Morris to drive her to the cinema. And to her surprise, all he got up to while they sat together in the back row was to watch the film. She wouldn't have complained if he had put an arm around her shoulder. In fact, she was considering how far she would let him go on their first date.

After the curtain came down, the organ lit up and they all rose to sing the National Anthem.

'Care for a drink?' asked Eddie as they made their way out of the cinema.

'I ought to be getting home before the trams pack up for the night.'

'You don't have to worry about the last tram, Maisie, when you're with Eddie Atkins.'

'All right then, just a quick one,' she said as he guided her across the road to the Red Bull.

'So what do you do, Eddie?' Maisie asked as he

placed a half pint of orange squash on the table in front of her.

'I'm in the entertainment business,' he said, without going into any detail. Instead, he switched the subject back to Maisie. 'I don't have to ask what you do.'

After a second orange juice, he looked at his watch and said, 'I've got an early start tomorrow, so I'd better get you home.'

On the way back to Still House Lane, Maisie chatted about Harry, and how she was hoping he would join the choir at Holy Nativity. Eddie seemed genuinely interested, and when he brought the car to a halt outside No. 27, she waited for him to kiss her. But he just jumped out, opened the car door for her and accompanied Maisie to her front door.

Maisie sat at the kitchen table and told her mother everything that had happened, or not happened, that night. All Grandma had to say was, 'What's his game?'

13

WHEN MAISIE SAW Mr Holcombe walk into Holy Nativity accompanied by a smartly dressed man, she assumed that Harry must be in trouble again. She was surprised, because there hadn't been any red marks for over a year.

She braced herself as Mr Holcombe headed towards her, but the moment he saw Maisie he simply gave her a shy smile before he and his companion slipped into the third pew on the other side of the aisle.

From time to time, Maisie glanced across to look at them, but she didn't recognize the other man, who was considerably older than Mr Holcombe. She wondered if he might be the headmaster of Merrywood Elementary.

When the choir rose to sing the first anthem, Miss Monday glanced in the direction of the two men, before nodding to the organist to show that she was ready.

Maisie felt that Harry excelled himself that morning, but she was surprised when a few minutes later he rose to sing a second solo, and even more surprised when he performed a third. Everyone knew that Miss Monday never did anything unless there was a reason, but it still wasn't clear to Maisie what that reason might be.

After the Reverend Watts had blessed his flock at the end of the service, Maisie remained in her place and waited for Harry to appear, hoping he'd be able to tell her why he'd been asked to sing three solos. As she chatted anxiously to her mother, her eyes never left Mr Holcombe, who was introducing the older man to Miss Monday and the Reverend Watts.

A moment later, the Reverend Watts led the two men into the vestry. Miss Monday marched down the aisle towards Maisie, a resolute look on her face, which every parishioner knew meant she was on a mission. 'Can I have a private word with you, Mrs Clifton?' she asked.

She didn't give Maisie a chance to reply, but simply turned and walked back down the aisle towards the vestry.

‐<o>‐

Eddie Atkins hadn't shown his face in Tilly's for over a month, but then one morning he reappeared and took his usual seat at one of Maisie's tables. When she came over to serve him, he gave her a huge smile, as if he'd never been away.

'Good morning, Mr Atkins,' Maisie said as she opened her notepad. 'What can I get for you?'

'My usual,' said Eddie.

'It's been so long, Mr Atkins,' said Maisie. 'You'll have to remind me.'

'I'm sorry I haven't been in touch, Maisie,' said Eddie, 'but I had to go to America at rather short notice, and I only got back last night.'

She wanted to believe him. Maisie had already admitted to her mother that she was a little disappointed she hadn't heard from Eddie after he'd taken her to the cinema. She'd enjoyed his company and felt the evening had gone rather well.

Another man had started visiting the tea shop regularly, and like Eddie he would only sit at one of Maisie's tables. Although she couldn't help noticing that he was showing considerable interest in her, she didn't give him any encouragement, because not only was he middle-aged but he was also wearing a wedding ring. He had a detached air about him, like a solicitor who is studying a client, and whenever he spoke to her he sounded a little pompous. Maisie could hear her mother asking, 'What's his game?' But perhaps she'd misunderstood his intentions, because he never once tried to strike up a conversation with her.

Even Maisie couldn't resist a grin when, a week later, both of her suitors dropped in for a coffee on the same morning, and both asked if they could meet up with her later.

Eddie was first, and he got straight to the point. 'Why don't I pick you up after work this evening, Maisie? There's something I'm rather keen to show you.'

Maisie wanted to tell him she already had a date, just to make him realize she wasn't available whenever it suited him, but when she returned to his table a few minutes later with his bill, she found herself saying, 'I'll see you after work then, Eddie.'

She still had a smile on her face when the other customer said, 'I wonder if I might have a word with you, Mrs Clifton?'

Maisie wondered how he knew her name.

'Wouldn't you prefer to speak to the manageress, Mr . . . ?'

'Frampton,' he replied. 'No, thank you, it's you I was hoping to speak to. Might I suggest we meet at the Royal Hotel during your afternoon break? It shouldn't take more than fifteen minutes of your time.'

'Talk about buses never turning up when you need one,' Maisie said to Miss Tilly, 'and then two arrive at once.' Miss Tilly told Maisie she thought she recognized Mr Frampton, but couldn't place him.

When Maisie presented Mr Frampton with his bill, she emphasized that she could only spare fifteen minutes because she had to be on time to pick up her son from school at four o'clock. He nodded as if that was something else he was aware of.

◄o►

Was it really in Harry's best interests to apply for a scholarship to St Bede's?

Maisie wasn't sure who to discuss the problem with. Stan was bound to be against the idea, and wasn't likely to consider the other side of the argument. Miss Tilly was too close a friend of Miss Monday's to give a dispassionate view, and the Reverend Watts had already advised her to seek the Lord's guidance, which hadn't proved particularly reliable in the past. Mr Frobisher had seemed such a nice man, but he'd made it clear that only she could make the final decision. Mr Holcombe hadn't left her in any doubt how he felt.

Maisie didn't give Mr Frampton another thought until she'd finished serving her last customer. She then exchanged a pinafore for her old coat.

Miss Tilly watched through the window as Maisie set off in the direction of the Royal Hotel. She felt a little anxious, but wasn't sure why.

Although Maisie had never been in the Royal before, she knew it had the reputation of being one of the best-run hotels in the West Country, and the chance to see it from the inside was one of the reasons she'd agreed to see Mr Frampton.

She stood on the opposite pavement and watched as customers pushed their way through the revolving doors. She'd never seen anything quite like them, and only when she felt confident she'd got the hang of how they worked did she cross the road and step inside. She pushed a little too hard and found herself propelled into the foyer more quickly than she'd anticipated.

Maisie looked around and spotted Mr Frampton sitting alone in a quiet alcove in the corner of the foyer. She walked across to join him. He immediately rose from his place, shook hands with her, and waited until she had taken the seat opposite him.

'Can I order you a coffee, Mrs Clifton?' he asked, and before she could reply he added, 'I should warn you, it's not in the same class as Tilly's.'

'No, thank you, Mr Frampton,' said Maisie, whose only interest was to find out why he wanted to see her.

Mr Frampton took his time lighting a cigarette, then inhaled deeply. 'Mrs Clifton,' he began as he placed the cigarette on the ashtray, 'you cannot have failed to notice that I have recently become a regular customer at Tilly's.' Maisie nodded. 'I have to confess that my only reason for visiting the café was you.' Maisie had her well-prepared 'amorous suitor' line ready for just as soon as he stopped talking. 'In all the years I've been in the hotel trade,' he continued, 'I've never seen anyone do their job more efficiently than you. I only wish that every waitress in this hotel was of your calibre.'

'I've been well trained,' said Maisie.

'So have the other four waitresses in that tea shop, but none of them has your flair.'

'I'm flattered, Mr Frampton. But why are you telling—'

'I am the general manager of this hotel,' he said, 'and I'd like you to take charge of our coffee room, which is known as the Palm Court. As you can see –' he waved a hand expansively – 'we have about a hundred covers, but less than a third of the places are regularly occupied. That's not exactly a worthwhile return on the company's investment. No doubt that would change if you were to take over. I believe I can make it worth your while.'

Maisie didn't interrupt him.

'I can't see why your hours should differ greatly from those of your current employment. I'd be willing to pay you five pounds a week, and all the tips earned by the waitresses in the Palm Court would be split fifty-fifty with you. If you were able to build up the clientele, that could prove very remunerative. And then I—'

'But I couldn't think of leaving Miss Tilly,' interrupted Maisie. 'She's been so good to me over the past six years.'

'I fully appreciate your feelings, Mrs Clifton. Indeed, I would have been disappointed if that had not been your immediate response. Loyalty is a trait I greatly admire. However, you must not only consider your own future, but also your son's, should he take up the offer of a choral scholarship to St Bede's.'

Maisie was speechless.

◄○►

When Maisie finished work that evening, she found Eddie sitting in his car outside the tea shop waiting for her. She noticed that he didn't jump out to open the passenger door this time.

'So, where are you taking me?' she asked as she climbed in beside him.

'It's a surprise,' said Eddie as he pressed the starter, 'but I don't think you'll be disappointed.'

He pushed the gear lever into first, and headed towards a part of the city that Maisie hadn't visited before. A few minutes later, he drove into a side alley and came to a halt outside a large oak door below a neon sign that announced in glowing red letters, EDDIE'S NIGHTCLUB.

'This is yours?' asked Maisie.

'Every square inch,' said Eddie proudly. 'Come inside and see for yourself.' He leapt out of the car, opened the front door and led Maisie inside. 'This used to be a granary,' he explained as he took her down a narrow wooden staircase. 'But now that ships can no longer sail this far up the river, the company's had to move, so I was able to pick up their lease for a very reasonable price.'

Maisie entered a large, dimly lit room. It was some time before her eyes had adjusted well enough to take it all in. There were half a dozen men sitting on high leather stools drinking at the bar, and almost as many waitresses fluttering around them. The wall behind the bar consisted of a vast mirror, giving the impression the room was far larger than it actually was. At the centre was a dance floor, surrounded by plush velvet banquettes that would just about seat two people. At the far end was a small stage with a piano, double bass, a set of drums and several music stands.

Eddie took a seat at the bar. Looking around the room he said, 'This is why I've been spending so much time in America. Speakeasies like this are springing up all over New York and Chicago, and they're making a fortune.' He lit a cigar. 'And I promise you, there won't be anything else like this in Bristol, that's for sure.'

'That's for sure,' Maisie repeated as she joined him at the bar, but didn't attempt to climb up on to one of the high stools.

'What's your poison, doll?' said Eddie, in what he imagined to be an American accent.

'I don't drink,' Maisie reminded him.

'That's one of the reasons I chose you.'

'Chose me?'

'Sure. You'd be the ideal person to take charge of the cocktail waitresses. Not only would I pay you six pounds a week, but if the place takes off, the tips alone would be more than you could ever hope to earn at Tilly's.'

'And would I be expected to dress like that?' asked Maisie, pointing to one of the waitresses who was wearing an off-the-shoulder red blouse and a tight-fitting black skirt that barely covered her knees. It amused Maisie that they were the same colours as the St Bede's uniform.

'Why not? You're a great-lookin' broad, and the punters will pay good money to be served by someone like you. You'll get the odd proposition, of course, but I feel sure you can handle that.'

'What's the point of a dance floor if it's a men-only club?'

'Another idea I picked up from the States,' said Eddie. 'If you want to dance with one of the cocktail waitresses, it'll cost you.'

'And what else does that cost include?'

'That's up to them,' said Eddie with a shrug of the shoulders. 'So long as it doesn't take place on the premises, nothing to do with me,' he added, laughing a little too loudly. Maisie didn't laugh. 'So what do you think?' he asked.

'I think I'd better be getting home,' said Maisie. 'I didn't have time to let Harry know I'd be late.'

'Whatever you say, honey,' said Eddie. He draped an arm around her shoulder and led her out of the bar and back up the stairs.

As he drove her to Still House Lane, he told Maisie about his plans for the future. 'I've already got my eye on a second site,' he said excitedly, 'so the sky's the limit.'

'The sky's the limit,' Maisie repeated, as they drew up outside No. 27.

Maisie jumped out of the car and walked quickly to the front door.

'So will you need a few days to think it over?' said Eddie, chasing after her.

'No, thank you, Eddie,' said Maisie without hesitation. 'I've already made up my mind,' she added, taking a key out of her handbag.

Eddie grinned and put an arm around her. 'I didn't think it would be a difficult decision for you to make.'

Maisie removed the arm, smiled sweetly and said, 'It's kind of you to consider me, honey, but I think I'll stick to serving coffee.' She opened her front door before adding, 'But thanks for asking.'

'Anything you say, doll, but if you change your mind, my door is always open.'

Maisie closed the door behind her.

14

MAISIE FINALLY SETTLED ON the one person she felt she could seek advice from. She decided to turn up at the docks unannounced and hope he'd be around when she knocked on his door.

She didn't tell either Stan or Harry who she was visiting. One of them would try to stop her, while the other would feel she'd betrayed a confidence.

Maisie waited until her day off, and once she had dropped Harry at school, she took a tram to the dockyard. She had chosen her time carefully: late morning, when he was still likely to be in his office, while Stan would be fully occupied loading or unloading cargo at the other end of the dock.

Maisie told the man on the gate that she'd come to apply for a job as a cleaner. He pointed indifferently towards the red-brick building and still didn't remember her.

As she walked towards Barrington House, Maisie looked up at the windows on the fifth floor and wondered which office was his. She recalled her encounter with Mrs Nettles, and the way she had been shown the door the moment she mentioned her name. Now Maisie not only had a job she enjoyed and where she was respected, but she'd had two other offers in the past few days. She didn't give Mrs Nettles another thought as she walked straight past the building and continued along the quayside.

Maisie didn't slacken her pace until she could see his home. She found it hard to believe that anyone could possibly live in a railway carriage, and began to wonder if she'd made a dreadful mistake. Had Harry's stories of a dining room, a bedroom and even a library, been exaggerated? 'You can't stop now you've come this far, Maisie Clifton,' she told herself, and knocked boldly on the carriage door.

'Come in, Mrs Clifton,' said a gentle voice.

Maisie opened the door to find an old man sitting in a comfortable seat, with books and other possessions scattered around him. She was surprised how clean the carriage was, and realized that, despite Stan's claims, it was she, and not Old Jack, who lived in third class. Stan had perpetuated a myth that had been ignored when viewed through the eyes of an unprejudiced child.

Old Jack immediately rose from his place and beckoned her towards the seat opposite. 'You'll have come to see me about young Harry, no doubt.'

'Yes, Mr Tar,' she replied.

'Let me guess,' he said. 'You can't make up your mind whether he should go to St Bede's, or remain at Merrywood Elementary.'

'How could you possibly know that?' asked Maisie.

'Because I've been considering the same problem for the past month,' said Old Jack.

'So what do you think he should do?'

'I think that despite the many difficulties he will undoubtedly face at St Bede's, if he doesn't take this opportunity, he could well spend the rest of his life regretting it.'

'Perhaps he won't win a scholarship and the decision will be taken out of our hands.'

'The decision was taken out of our hands,' said Old Jack, 'the moment Mr Frobisher heard young Harry sing. But I have a feeling that wasn't the only reason you came to see me.'

Maisie was beginning to understand why Harry admired this man so much. 'You're quite right, Mr Tar, I need your advice on another matter.'

'Your son calls me Jack, except when he's cross with me, then he calls me Old Jack.'

Maisie smiled. 'I've been worried that even if he did win a scholarship, I wasn't earning enough for Harry to have all the little extras that the other boys at a school like St Bede's take for granted. But fortunately I've just been offered another job, which would mean more money.'

'And you're worried about how Miss Tilly will react when you tell her you're thinking of leaving?'

'You know Miss Tilly?'

'No, but Harry has spoken of her many times. She's clearly from the same mould as Miss Monday, and let me assure you, that's a limited edition. There's no need for you to concern yourself.'

'I don't understand,' said Maisie.

'Allow me to explain,' said Old Jack. 'Miss Monday has already invested a great deal of her time and expertise in making sure that Harry not only wins a scholarship to St Bede's but, far more important, goes on to prove himself worthy of it. My bet is that she will have discussed every possible eventuality with her closest friend, who just happens to be Miss Tilly. So when you tell her about the new job, you may well find it doesn't come as a complete surprise.'

'Thank you, Jack,' said Maisie. 'How lucky Harry is to have you as a friend. The father he never knew,' she said softly.

'That is the nicest compliment I've received for a good many years,' said Old Jack. 'I'm only sorry that he lost his father in such tragic circumstances.'

'Do you know how my husband died?'

'Yes, I do,' replied Old Jack. Aware that he should never had raised the subject, he quickly added, 'But only because Harry told me.'

'What did he tell you?' asked Maisie anxiously.

'That his father was killed in the war.'

'But you know that's not true,' said Maisie.

'Yes, I do,' said Old Jack. 'And I suspect Harry also knows his father couldn't have died in the war.'

'Then why doesn't he say so?'

'He probably thinks there's something you don't want to tell him.'

'But I don't know the truth myself,' admitted Maisie.

Old Jack didn't comment.

Maisie walked slowly home; one question answered, another still unresolved. Even so, she wasn't in any doubt that Old Jack could be added to the list of people who knew the truth about what had happened to her husband.

Old Jack turned out to be right about Miss Tilly, because when Maisie told her about Mr Frampton's offer, she couldn't have been more supportive and understanding.

'We'll all miss you,' she said, 'and frankly the Royal is lucky to have you.'

'How can I begin to thank you for all you've done for me over the years?' said Maisie.

'It's Harry who should be thanking you,' said Miss

Tilly, 'and I suspect it will only be a matter of time before he realizes that.'

◄o►

Maisie started her new job a month later, and it didn't take her long to discover why the Palm Court was never more than a third full.

The waitresses regarded their work simply as a job, unlike Miss Tilly, who considered it to be a vocation. They never bothered to remember the customers' names, or their favourite tables. Worse, the coffee was often cold by the time it was served, and the cakes were left to go stale until someone bought them. Maisie wasn't surprised they didn't get any tips; they didn't deserve them.

After another month, she began to realize just how much Miss Tilly had taught her.

After three months, Maisie had replaced five of the seven waitresses, without having to recruit anyone from Tilly's. She had also ordered smart new uniforms for all her staff, along with new plates, cups and saucers and, even more important, changed her coffee supplier and her cake-maker. That was something she was willing to steal from Miss Tilly.

'You're costing me a lot of money, Maisie,' said Mr Frampton when another stack of bills landed on his desk. 'Try not to forget what I said about return on investment.'

'Give me another six months, Mr Frampton, and you'll see the results.'

Although Maisie worked night and day, she always found time to drop Harry off at school in the morning and pick him up in the afternoon. But she warned Mr Frampton that there would be one day when she wouldn't be on time for work.

When she told him why, he gave her the whole day off.

◄o►

Just before they left the house, Maisie checked herself in the mirror. She was dressed in her Sunday best but not going to church. She smiled down at her son, who looked so smart in his new red and black school uniform. Even so, she felt a little self-conscious as they waited at the tram stop.

'Two to Park Street,' she told the clippie when the No. 11 pulled away. She was unable to hide her pride when she noticed him taking a closer look at Harry. It only convinced Maisie that she had made the right decision.

When they reached their stop, Harry refused to let his mum carry his suitcase. Maisie held on to his hand as they walked slowly up the hill towards the school, not sure which one of them was more nervous. She couldn't take her eyes off the hansom cabs and chauffeur-driven cars that were dropping off other boys for their first day of term. She only hoped that Harry would be able to find at least one friend among them. After all, some of the nannies were better dressed than she was.

Harry began to slow down as they got nearer the school gates. Maisie could sense his discomfort – or was it just fear of the unknown?

'I'll leave you now,' she said, and bent down to kiss him. 'Good luck, Harry. Make us all proud of you.'

'Goodbye, Mum.'

As she watched him walk away, Maisie noticed that someone else appeared to be taking an interest in Harry Clifton.

15

MAISIE WOULD NEVER FORGET the first time she had to turn away a customer.

'I'm sure there will be a table available in a few minutes, sir.'

She prided herself on the fact that once a customer had paid the bill, her staff could clear the table, replace the cloth and have it re-laid and ready for the next guest within five minutes.

The Palm Court quickly became so popular that Maisie had to keep a couple of tables permanently reserved, just in case one of her regulars turned up un-expectedly.

She was a little embarrassed that some of her old customers from Tilly's had begun to migrate to the Palm Court, not least dear old Mr Craddick, who remembered Harry from his paper round. She considered it an even greater compliment when Miss Tilly herself began to drop in for a morning coffee.

'Just checking on the opposition,' she said. 'By the way, Maisie, this coffee is superb.'

'So it should be,' Maisie replied. 'It's yours.'

Eddie Atkins also came in from time to time, and if the size of his cigars, not to mention his waistline, was anything to go by, the sky must still have been the limit.

Although he was friendly, he never asked Maisie out, but he did regularly remind her that his door was always open.

Not that Maisie didn't have a string of admirers she occasionally allowed to take her out in the evening, maybe to dinner at a fashionable restaurant, sometimes a visit to the Old Vic or the cinema, especially if a Greta Garbo film was playing. But when they parted at the end of the evening, she allowed none of them more than a peck on the cheek before returning home. At least, not until she met Patrick Casey, who proved that the charm of the Irish was not just a cliché.

When Patrick first walked into the Palm Court, hers wasn't the only head that turned to take a closer look. He was a shade over six foot, with wavy dark hair and the build of an athlete. That would have been enough for most women, but it was the smile that captivated Maisie, as, she suspected, it had many others.

Patrick told her he was in finance, but then Eddie had said he was in the entertainment business. His work brought him to Bristol once or twice a month, when Maisie would allow him to take her to dinner, the theatre or the cinema, and occasionally she even broke her golden rule, and didn't take the last tram back to Still House Lane.

She wouldn't have been surprised to discover that Patrick had a wife and half a dozen offspring back at home in Cork, although he swore, hand on heart, that he was a bachelor.

◄o►

Whenever Mr Holcombe dropped into the Palm Court, Maisie would guide him to a table in the far corner of the room that was partly obscured by a large pillar and was shunned by her regulars. But its privacy allowed her to bring him up to date on how Harry was getting on.

Today, he seemed more interested in the future than the past, and asked, 'Have you decided what Harry will do once he leaves St Bede's?'

'I haven't given it much thought,' Maisie admitted. 'After all, it's not for some time.'

'It's soon enough,' said Mr Holcombe, 'and I can't believe you'll want him to return to Merrywood Elementary.'

'No, I don't,' said Maisie firmly, 'but what choice is there?'

'Harry says he'd like to go to Bristol Grammar School, but if he fails to win a scholarship, he's worried that you won't be able to afford the fees.'

'That won't be a problem,' Maisie assured him. 'With my present pay, combined with the tips, no one need know his mother is a waitress.'

'Some waitress,' said Mr Holcombe, looking around the packed room. 'I'm only surprised you haven't opened your own place.'

Maisie laughed, and didn't give it another thought until she had an unexpected visit from Miss Tilly.

—◦—

Maisie attended Matins at St Mary Redcliffe every Sunday so she could hear her son sing. Miss Monday had warned her that it wouldn't be much longer before Harry's voice broke, and she mustn't assume that a few weeks later he'd be singing tenor solos.

Maisie tried to concentrate on the canon's sermon that Sunday morning but found her mind drifting. She glanced across the aisle to see Mr and Mrs Barrington sitting with their son Giles and two young girls who she assumed must be their daughters, but whose names she didn't know. Maisie had been surprised when Harry told her that Giles Barrington was his closest friend. Nothing more than a coincidence of the alphabet had put them together in the first place, he'd said. She hoped it would never become necessary for her to tell him that Giles might be more than just a good friend.

◄○►

Maisie often wished she could do more to help Harry with his efforts to win a scholarship to Bristol Grammar School. Although Miss Tilly had taught her how to read a menu, add and subtract, and even write a few simple words, just the thought of what Harry must be putting himself through filled her with trepidation.

Miss Monday boosted Maisie's confidence by continually reminding her that Harry would never have got this far if she hadn't been willing to make so many sacrifices. 'And in any case,' she added, 'you're every bit as clever as Harry, you just haven't been given the same opportunities.'

Mr Holcombe kept her informed on what he described as 'the timing', and, as the date of the examination drew nearer, Maisie became just as nervous as the candidate. She realized the truth of one of Old Jack's remarks, that often the onlooker suffers even more than the participant.

The Palm Court room was now packed every day, but it didn't stop Maisie from initiating even more changes in a decade the press were describing as the 'frivolous thirties'.

In the morning, she had started offering her customers a variety of biscuits to go with their coffee, and in the afternoon, her tea menu was proving just as popular, especially after Harry told her that Mrs Barrington had given him the choice of Indian or China tea.

However, Mr Frampton vetoed the suggestion that smoked salmon sandwiches should appear on the menu.

Every Sunday, Maisie would kneel on her little cushion; her one prayer was to the point. 'Please God make sure Harry wins a scholarship. If he does, I'll never ask you for anything again.'

With a week to go to the exams, Maisie found she couldn't sleep, and lay awake wondering how Harry was coping. So many customers wanted to pass on their best wishes to him, some because they had heard him singing in the church choir, others because he'd delivered their morning papers, or simply because their own children had been, were, or would at some time in the future be going though the same experience. It seemed to Maisie that half of Bristol was taking the exam.

On the morning of the examination, Maisie placed several regulars at the wrong table, gave Mr Craddick coffee instead of his usual hot chocolate, and even presented two customers with someone else's bill. No one complained.

Harry told her he thought he'd done quite well, but he couldn't be certain if he'd done well enough. He mentioned someone called Thomas Hardy, but Maisie wasn't sure if he was a friend or one of the masters.

◄o►

When the long-case clock in the Palm Court room struck ten on that Thursday morning, Maisie knew the head-master would be posting the exam results on the school notice board. But it was another twenty-two minutes before Mr Holcombe walked into the room and headed straight for his usual table behind the pillar. Maisie could not tell how Harry had done from the expression on the schoolmaster's face. She quickly crossed the room to join him and, for the first time in four years, sat down in the seat opposite a customer, although 'collapsed' might be a more accurate description.

'Harry has passed with distinction,' said Mr Holcombe, 'but I'm afraid he just missed out on a scholarship.'

'What does that mean?' Maisie asked, trying to stop her hands from trembling.

'The top twelve candidates had marks of 80 per cent or above, and were all awarded open scholarships. In fact, Harry's friend Deakins came top, with 92 per cent. Harry achieved a very commendable 78 per cent, and came seventeenth out of three hundred. Mr Frobisher told me his English paper let him down.'

'He should have read Hardy instead of Dickens,' said a woman who'd never read a book.

'Harry will still be offered a place at BGS,' said Mr Holcombe, 'but he won't receive the annual hundred pounds a year scholar's grant.'

Maisie rose from her place. 'Then I'll just have to work three shifts instead of two, won't I? Because he's not going back to Merrywood Elementary, Mr Holcombe, I can tell you that.'

◄○►

Over the next few days, Maisie was surprised by how many regulars offered their congratulations on Harry's magnificent achievement. She also discovered that one or two of her customers had children who had failed to pass the exam, in one case by a single percentage point. They would have to settle for their second choice. It made Maisie all the more determined that nothing would stop Harry reporting to Bristol Grammar School on the first day of term.

One strange thing she noticed during the next week was that her tips doubled. Dear old Mr Craddick slipped her a five-pound note, saying, 'For Harry. May he prove worthy of his mother.'

When the thin white envelope dropped through the letterbox in Still House Lane, an event in itself, Harry opened the letter and read it to his mother. 'Clifton, H.' had been offered a place in the A stream for the Michaelmas term starting on September 15th. When he came to the last paragraph, which asked Mrs Clifton to write and confirm whether the candidate wished to accept or reject the offer, he looked nervously at her.

'You must write back straight away, accepting the offer!' she said.

Harry threw his arms around her and whispered, 'I only wish my father was alive.'

Perhaps he is, thought Maisie.

—<o>—

A few days later, a second letter landed on the doormat. This one detailed a long list of items that had to be purchased before the first day of term. Maisie noticed that Harry seemed to require two of everything, in some cases three or more, and in one case, six: socks, grey calf length, plus garters.

'Pity you can't borrow a pair of my suspenders,' she said. Harry blushed.

A third letter invited new pupils to select three extra-curricular activities from a list ranging from the car club to the Officer Training Corps – some of which involved an added charge of five pounds per activity. Harry chose the choir, for which there was no extra charge, as well as the theatre club and the Arts Appreciation Society. The latter included a proviso that any visits to galleries outside Bristol would incur an extra cost.

Maisie wished there were a few more Mr Craddicks around, but she never allowed Harry to suspect there was any reason for concern, even though Mr Holcombe reminded her that her boy would be at Bristol Grammar School for the next five years. The first member of the family not to leave school before the age of fourteen, she told him.

Maisie braced herself for another visit to T.C. Marsh, Tailors of Distinction.

By the time Harry was fully kitted out and ready for the first day of term, Maisie had once again begun to walk to and from work, saving five pence a week on tram fares, or as she told her mother, 'A pound a year, enough to pay for a new suit for Harry.'

—◄o►—

Parents, Maisie had learnt over the years, may be considered an unfortunate necessity by their offspring, but more often than not they are also an embarrassment.

On her first speech day at St Bede's, Maisie had been the only mother not wearing a hat. After that, she had bought one from a second-hand shop and, however out of fashion it would become, it was going to have to last until Harry left Bristol Grammar School.

Harry had agreed that she should accompany him to school on the first day of term, but Maisie had already decided that he was old enough to catch a tram home in the evening. Her main anxiety was not about how Harry would get to and from school, but what to do with him in the evenings, now he was a day boy and would no longer be sleeping at school during term. She had no doubt that if he went back to sharing a room with his uncle Stan, it could only end in tears. She tried to put the problem out of her mind as she prepared for Harry's first day in his new school.

Hat in place, best, and only, overcoat recently cleaned, sensible black shoes with the only pair of silk stockings she possessed, Maisie felt ready to face the other parents. When she came down the stairs, Harry was already waiting for her by the door. He looked so smart in his new uniform of claret and black that she would have liked to parade him up and down Still House Lane so the neighbours would know that someone from the street was going to Bristol Grammar School.

As they had on his first day at St Bede's, they caught the tram, but Harry asked Maisie if they could get off one stop before University Road. She was no longer allowed to hold his hand, although she did straighten his cap and tie more than once.

When Maisie first saw the noisy gathering of young men crowded around the school gates, she said, 'I'd better be off or I'll be late for work,' which puzzled Harry, because he knew Mr Frampton had given her the day off.

She gave her son a quick hug, but kept a wary eye on him as he made his way up the hill. The first person to greet him was Giles Barrington. Maisie was surprised to see him, as Harry had told her he would probably be going to Eton. They shook hands like a couple of grown men who had just closed an important deal.

Maisie could see Mr and Mrs Barrington standing at the back of the crowd. Was he making sure he avoided her? A few minutes later, Mr and Mrs Deakins joined them, accompanied by the Peloquin Memorial scholar. More handshakes, left-handed in Mr Deakins's case.

As the parents began to take leave of their children, Maisie watched Mr Barrington as he shook hands first with his son and then with Deakins, but turned away when Harry offered his hand. Mrs Barrington looked embarrassed, and Maisie wondered if she might later ask why Hugo had ignored Giles's closest friend. If she did, Maisie felt certain he would not tell her the real reason. Maisie feared it couldn't be long before Harry asked why Mr Barrington always snubbed him. As long as only three people knew the truth, she couldn't think of any reason why Harry would ever find out.

16

MISS TILLY HAD BECOME such a regular at the Palm Court that she even had her own table.

She would usually arrive around four o'clock, and order a cup of tea (Earl Grey) and a cucumber sandwich. She always declined to take anything from the large assortment of cream cakes, jam tarts and chocolate éclairs, but would occasionally allow herself a buttered scone. When she popped by just before five one evening, unusually late for her, Maisie was relieved that her usual table was free.

'I wonder if I might sit somewhere a little more discreet today, Maisie. I need to have a quiet word with you.'

'Of course, Miss Tilly,' said Maisie, and led her to Mr Holcombe's preferred table behind the pillar at the far end of the room. 'I'm off in ten minutes,' Maisie told her. 'I'll join you then.'

When her deputy Susan arrived to take over, Maisie explained that she would be joining Miss Tilly for a few minutes, but didn't expect to be served.

'Is the old duck unhappy about something?' Susan asked.

'That old duck taught me everything I know,' said Maisie with a grin.

When five o'clock struck, Maisie walked across the

room and took the seat opposite Miss Tilly. She rarely sat down with a customer, and on the few occasions she did, she had never felt at ease.

'Would you care for some tea, Maisie?'

'No, thank you, Miss Tilly.'

'I quite understand. I'll try not to keep you too long, but before I tell you my real purpose for wanting to see you, may I ask how Harry is getting on?'

'I wish he'd stop growing,' said Maisie. 'I seem to be letting down his trousers every few weeks. At this rate his long trousers will be short trousers before the end of the year.'

Miss Tilly laughed. 'What about his work?'

'His end-of-term report said – ' Maisie paused, trying to recall the exact words – ' "A most satisfactory start. Very promising." He came top in English.'

'Somewhat ironic,' said Miss Tilly. 'If I remember correctly, that was the subject that let him down in the entrance exam.'

Maisie nodded, and tried not to think about the financial consequences of Harry not having read enough Thomas Hardy.

'You must be very proud of him,' said Miss Tilly. 'And when I went to St Mary's on Sunday, I was delighted to see that he's back in the choir.'

'Yes, but he now has to be satisfied with a place in the back row with the other baritones. His days as a soloist are over. But he's joined the theatre club, and because there are no girls at BGS, he's playing Ursula in the school play.'

'*Much Ado About Nothing*,' said Miss Tilly. 'Still, I mustn't waste any more of your time, so I'll come to the reason I wanted to see you.' She took a sip of tea, as if she wanted to compose herself before she spoke again, and then it all came out in a rush.

'I'll be sixty next month, my dear, and for some time I have been considering retiring.'

It had never crossed Maisie's mind that Miss Tilly wouldn't go on for ever.

'Miss Monday and I have been thinking about moving down to Cornwall. We have our eye on a little cottage by the sea.'

You mustn't leave Bristol, Maisie wanted to say. I love you both, and if you go, who will I turn to for advice?

'Matters came to a head last month,' continued Miss Tilly, 'when a local businessman made me an offer for the tea shop. It seems he wants to add it to his growing empire. And although I don't care for the idea of Tilly's being part of a chain, his offer was far too tempting to turn down out of hand.' Maisie only had one question, but she didn't interrupt while Miss Tilly was in full flow. 'Since then, I've been giving the matter a great deal of thought, and I decided that if you were able to come up with the same amount he has offered, I would rather you took over the business than I hand it over to a stranger.'

'How much did he offer?'

'Five hundred pounds.'

Maisie sighed. 'I'm flattered you even thought of me,' she said at last, 'but the truth is, I don't have five hundred pennies to my name, let alone five hundred pounds.'

'I was afraid you might say that,' said Miss Tilly. 'But if you could find a backer, I feel sure they would consider the business a good investment. After all, I made a profit of one hundred and twelve pounds and ten shillings last year, which didn't include my salary. I would have let you have it for less than five hundred pounds, but we've found a delightful little cottage in St

Mawes, and the owners won't consider a penny less than three hundred. Miss Monday and I could just about survive on our savings for a year or two, but as neither of us has a pension to fall back on, the extra two hundred pounds will make all the difference.'

Maisie was just about to tell Miss Tilly how sorry she was but it was out of the question, when Patrick Casey strolled into the room and sat down at his usual table.

<o>

It wasn't until after they'd made love that Maisie told Patrick about Miss Tilly's offer. He sat up in bed, lit a cigarette and inhaled deeply.

'Raising that amount of capital shouldn't prove too difficult. After all, it's hardly Brunel trying to raise the money to build Clifton Suspension Bridge.'

'No, but it is Mrs Clifton trying to raise five hundred pounds when she hasn't got two halfpennies to rub together.'

'True, but you'd be able to show a cash flow and a proven income stream, not to mention the tea shop's goodwill. Mind you, I'll need to look at the books for the past five years and make sure you've been told the whole story.'

'Miss Tilly would never try to deceive anyone.'

'You'll also have to check that there isn't a rent review due in the near future,' Patrick said, ignoring her protestations, 'and double-check that her accountant hasn't come up with penalty clauses the moment you start making a profit.'

'Miss Tilly wouldn't do something like that,' said Maisie.

'You're so trusting, Maisie. What you have to re- member is, this won't be in the hands of Miss Tilly, but a lawyer who feels he's got to earn his fee, and an accountant looking for a pay-day in case you don't retain him.'

'You've clearly never met Miss Tilly.'

'Your faith in the old lady is touching, Maisie, but my job is to protect people like you, and a hundred and twelve pounds ten shillings profit a year wouldn't be enough for you to live on, remembering you'll be expected to make regular repayments to your investor.'

'Miss Tilly assured me that the profit didn't include her salary.'

'That might well be the case, but you don't know what that salary is. You'll need at least another two hundred and fifty pounds a year if you're to survive, otherwise not only will you be out of pocket, but Harry will be out of the grammar school.'

'I can't wait for you to meet Miss Tilly.'

'And what about tips? At the Royal you get 50 per cent of all the tips, which comes to at least another two hundred pounds a year, which at the moment isn't taxed, although I've no doubt some future government will catch on to that.'

'Perhaps I should tell Miss Tilly that it's too great a risk. After all, as you keep reminding me, I have a guaranteed income at the Royal, with no risks attached.'

'True, but if Miss Tilly is half as good as you say she is, this could be an opportunity that might not arise again.'

'Make your mind up, Patrick,' said Maisie, trying not to sound exasperated.

'I will, the moment I've seen the books.'

'You will, the moment you meet Miss Tilly,' Maisie said, 'because then you'll understand the real meaning of goodwill.'

'I can't wait to meet this paragon of virtue.'

'Does that mean you'll represent me?'

'Yes,' he said, stubbing out his cigarette.

'And how much will you be charging this penniless widow, Mr Casey?'

'Turn the light out.'

◄○►

'Are you sure this is a risk worth taking,' asked Mr Frampton, 'when you have so much to lose?'

'My financial adviser thinks so,' replied Maisie. 'He's assured me that not only do all the figures add up, but once I've paid off the loan, I should be showing a profit within five years.'

'But those are the years Harry will be at Bristol Grammar.'

'I'm well aware of that, Mr Frampton, but Mr Casey has secured a substantial salary for me as part of the bargain, and after I've split the tips with my staff, I should be earning roughly the same amount I'm currently taking home. More important, in five years' time I'll own a real asset, and from then on, all the profits will be mine,' she said, trying to recall Patrick's exact words.

'It's clear to me that you've made up your mind,' said Mr Frampton. 'But let me warn you, Maisie, there's a great deal of difference between being an employee, when you know you'll be taking home a wage packet every week, and being an employer, when it will be your responsibility to put your money into several wage packets every Friday night. Frankly, Maisie, you are the best at what you do, but are you really sure you want to switch from being a player to joining the management?'

'Mr Casey will be there to advise me.'

'Casey's a capable fellow, I'll give you that, but he also has to look after more important clients right across the country. It will be you who has to run the business from day to day. If anything were to go wrong, he won't always be around to hold your hand.'

'But I may not be given an opportunity like this again in my lifetime.' Another of Patrick's pronouncements.

'So be it, Maisie,' said Frampton. 'And don't be in any doubt how much we'll all miss you at the Royal. The only reason you're not irreplaceable is because you trained your deputy so well.'

'Susan won't let you down, Mr Frampton.'

'I'm sure she won't. But she'll never be Maisie Clifton. Let me be the first to wish you every success in your new venture, and if things don't work out as planned, there will always be a job for you here at the Royal.'

Mr Frampton rose from behind his desk and shook hands with Maisie, just as he'd done six years before.

17

A MONTH LATER, Maisie signed six documents in the presence of Mr Prendergast, the manager of the National Provincial Bank on Corn Street. But not until Patrick had taken her through each page, line by line, now happy to admit how wrong he'd been to doubt Miss Tilly. If everyone behaved as honourably as she did, he told her, he'd be out of a job.

Maisie handed Miss Tilly a cheque for £500 on March 19th, 1934, receiving a huge hug and a tea shop in return. A week later, Miss Tilly and Miss Monday left for Cornwall.

When Maisie opened her doors for business the following day, she retained the name 'Tilly's'. Patrick had advised her never to underestimate the goodwill of Tilly's name above the door ('founded in 1898') and that she should not even think of changing it until Miss Tilly was of blessed memory and perhaps not even then. 'Regulars don't like change, especially sudden ones, so don't rush them into anything.'

Maisie did, however, spot a few changes that could be made without offending any of the regulars. She felt a new set of tablecloths wouldn't go amiss, and the chairs and even the tables were beginning to look, well, quaint. And hadn't Miss Tilly noticed the carpet was wearing a bit thin?

'Pace yourself,' Patrick warned her on one of his monthly visits. 'Remember that it's far easier to spend money than to earn it, and don't be surprised if a few of the old biddies disappear and you don't make quite as much as you'd anticipated in the first few months.'

Patrick turned out to be right. The number of covers dropped in the first month, and then again in the second, proving just how popular Miss Tilly had been. Had they fallen again in the third, Patrick would have been advising Maisie about cash flow and overdraft limits, but it bottomed – another of Patrick's expressions – and even began to climb the following month, though not sharply.

◄o►

At the end of her first year, Maisie had broken even, but she hadn't made enough to pay back any of the bank's loan.

'Don't fret, my dear,' Miss Tilly told her on one of her rare visits to Bristol. 'It was years before I made a profit.' Maisie didn't have years.

The second year began well, with some of her regulars from the Palm Court returning to their old stamping ground. Eddie Atkins had put on so much weight, and his cigars were so much larger, that Maisie could only assume the entertainment business was thriving. Mr Craddick appeared at eleven o'clock every morning, dressed in a raincoat, umbrella in hand, whatever the weather. Mr Holcombe dropped in from time to time, always wanting updates on how Harry was getting on, and she never allowed him to pay the bill. Patrick's first stop whenever he returned to Bristol was always Tilly's.

During her second year, Maisie had to replace one supplier who didn't seem to know the difference between fresh and stale, and one waitress who wasn't convinced that the customer was always right. Several young women applied for the job, as it was becoming more acceptable for women to go to work. Maisie settled on a young lady called Karen, who had a mop of curly fair hair, big blue eyes and what the fashion magazines were describing as an hourglass figure. Maisie had a feeling that Karen might attract some new customers who were a little younger than most of her regulars.

Selecting a new cake supplier proved a more difficult task. And although several companies tendered for the contract, Maisie was very demanding. However, when Bob Burrows of Burrows' Bakery (founded 1935) turned up on her doorstep and told her that Tilly's would be his first customer, she put him on a month's trial.

Bob turned out to be hard-working and reliable, and even more important, his goods were always so fresh and tempting that her customers would often say, 'Well, perhaps just one more.' His cream buns and fruit scones were particularly popular, but it was his chocolate brownies, the new fad, that seemed to disappear from the cakestand long before midday. Although Maisie regularly pressed him, Bob kept telling her that he just couldn't make any more.

One morning, after Bob had dropped off his wares, Maisie thought he looked a little forlorn, so she sat him down and poured him a cup of coffee. He confessed to her that he was suffering from the same cash-flow problems she'd experienced in her first year. But he was confident things would soon look up as he'd recently been taken on by two new shops, although he stressed how much he owed to Maisie for giving him his first break.

As the weeks passed, these morning coffee breaks became something of a ritual. Even so, Maisie couldn't have been more surprised when Bob asked her out on a date, as she considered theirs to be a professional relationship. He had bought tickets for *Glamorous Night*, a new musical that was playing at the Hippodrome, which Maisie had hoped Patrick might take her to. She thanked Bob, but said she didn't want to spoil their relationship. She would have liked to add that there were already two men in her life, a fifteen-year-old who was worrying about his acne, and an Irishman who only visited Bristol once a month and didn't seem to realize she was in love with him.

Bob didn't take no for an answer, and a month later Maisie was even more embarrassed when he presented her with a marcasite brooch. She kissed him on the cheek, and wondered how he'd found out it was her birthday. That evening she placed the brooch in a drawer, and might have forgotten all about it if other gifts hadn't followed at regular intervals.

Patrick seemed amused by his rival's persistence, and over dinner one night he reminded Maisie that she was a good-looking woman with prospects.

Maisie didn't laugh. 'It's got to stop,' she said.

'Then why don't you find another supplier?'

'Because good ones are a lot harder to find than lovers. In any case, Bob's reliable, his cakes are the best in town and his prices are lower than any of his competitors.'

'And he's in love with you,' said Patrick.

'Don't tease, Patrick. It's got to stop.'

'I'll tell you something far more important that's got to stop,' said Patrick, bending down and opening his briefcase.

'May I remind you,' said Maisie, 'that we're meant

to be having a romantic candlelit dinner together, not talking business.'

'I'm afraid this can't wait,' he said, placing a sheaf of papers on the table. 'These are your accounts for the past three months, and they don't make happy reading.'

'But I thought you said things have been looking up.'

'So they have. You've even managed to keep your outgoings within the limit recommended by the bank, but, inexplicably, your income has dropped during the same period.'

'How's that possible?' said Maisie. 'We did a record number of covers last month.'

'That's why I decided to check carefully through all your bills and receipts for the past month. They just don't add up. I've come to the sad conclusion, Maisie, that one of your waitresses must have her hand in the till. It's common enough in the catering trade; it usually turns out to be the barman or the head waiter but once it starts, there's no way of stopping it until you find the person responsible and sack them. If you don't identify the culprit fairly soon, you're going to have another year without showing a profit, and you won't be able to pay back one penny of the bank loan, let alone start reducing your overdraft.'

'What do you advise?'

'You'll have to keep a closer eye on all your staff in future, until one of them gives herself away.'

'How will I know which one it is?'

'There are several signs to look out for,' said Patrick. 'Someone who's living beyond their means, perhaps wearing a new coat or an expensive piece of jewellery, or taking a holiday they wouldn't normally be able to afford. She'll probably tell you she's got a new boyfriend, but—'

'Oh, hell,' said Maisie. 'I think I know who it might be.'

'Who?'

'Karen. She's only been with me a few months, and recently she's been going up to London on her weekends off. Last Monday she turned up at work wearing a new scarf and a pair of leather gloves that made me feel quite envious.'

'Don't jump to any conclusions,' said Patrick, 'but keep a close eye on her. Either she's pocketing the tips or she's got her hands in the till, or both. And one thing I can promise you, it won't stop. In most cases the thief becomes more and more confident until they're finally caught. You need to stop it, and stop it quickly, before she puts you out of business.'

◄○►

Maisie hated having to spy on her staff. After all, she'd chosen most of the younger ones herself, while the older ones had been at Tilly's for years.

She kept an especially close eye on Karen, but there weren't any obvious signs that she was stealing. But then, as Patrick had warned her, thieves are more cunning than honest people, and there was no way Maisie could keep an eye on her all the time.

And then the problem solved itself. Karen handed in her notice, announcing that she was engaged and would be joining her fiancé in London at the end of the month. Maisie thought her engagement ring was quite exquisite, although she could only wonder who'd paid for it. But she dismissed the thought, relieved she would now have one less problem to worry about.

But when Patrick returned to Bristol a few weeks later, he warned Maisie that her monthly income had dropped again, so it couldn't have been Karen.

'Is it time to call in the police?' Maisie asked.

'Not yet. The last thing you need are any false accusations or rumours that will only cause ill-feeling among your staff. The police may well flush out the thief, but before they do you could lose some of your best staff, who won't like being under suspicion. And you can also be sure that some of the customers will find out, and you don't need that.'

'How much longer can I afford to go on like this?'

'Let's give it another month. If we haven't found out who it is by then, you'll have to call in the police.' He gave her a huge smile. 'Now let's stop talking business and try to remember that we're meant to be celebrating your birthday.'

'That was two months ago,' she said. 'And if it hadn't been for Bob, you wouldn't even have known.'

Patrick opened his briefcase once again, but this time he produced a royal blue box with Swan's familiar logo on it. He passed it across to Maisie, who took her time opening it, to find a pair of black leather gloves and a woollen scarf in the traditional Burberry pattern.

'So you're the one who's been robbing me blind,' said Maisie as she threw her arms around him.

Patrick didn't respond.

'What's the matter?' asked Maisie.

'I have another piece of news.' Maisie looked into his eyes, and wondered what else could possibly be going wrong at Tilly's. 'I've been promoted. I'm to be the new deputy manager of our head office in Dublin. I'll be tied to my desk most of the time, so somebody else will be taking my place over here. I will still be able to visit you, but not that often.'

Maisie lay in his arms and cried all night. She had thought she wouldn't want to get married again, until the man she loved was no longer available.

She turned up late for work the following morning to find Bob waiting on the doorstep. Once she'd opened the front door, he began to unload the morning delivery from his van.

'I'll be with you in a moment,' said Maisie as she disappeared into the staff washroom.

She'd said her last goodbyes to Patrick as he boarded a train at Temple Meads, when she'd burst into tears again. She must have looked a sight and didn't want the regulars to think anything was wrong. 'Never bring your personal problems to work,' Miss Tilly had often reminded her staff. 'The customers have enough problems of their own without having to worry about yours.'

Maisie looked in the mirror: her make-up was a mess. 'Damn,' she said out loud when she realized she'd left her handbag on the counter. As she walked back into the shop to retrieve it, she suddenly felt sick. Bob was standing with his back to her, one hand in the till. She watched as he stuffed a handful of notes and coins into a trouser pocket, closed the till quietly and then went back to his van to pick up another tray of cakes.

Maisie knew exactly what Patrick would have advised. She walked into the café and stood by the till as Bob strolled back through the door. He was not carrying a tray, but a small red leather box. He gave her a huge smile and fell on one knee.

'You will leave the premises right now, Bob Burrows,' Maisie said, in a tone that surprised even her. 'If I ever see you anywhere near my tea shop again, I will call the police.'

She expected a stream of explanations or expletives, but Bob simply stood up, put the money he'd stolen back on the counter and left without a word. Maisie collapsed on to the nearest chair just as the first member of staff arrived.

'Good morning, Mrs Clifton. Nice weather for the time of year.'

18

WHENEVER A THIN BROWN envelope dropped through the letterbox at No. 27, Maisie assumed it was from Bristol Grammar School, and would probably be another bill for Harry's tuition fees, plus any 'extras', as the Bristol Municipal Charities liked to describe them.

She always called into the bank on the way home to deposit the day's takings in the business account and her share of the tips in a separate account, described as 'Harry's', hoping that at the end of each quarter she would have enough to cover the next bill from BGS.

Maisie ripped open the envelope, and, although she couldn't read every word of the letter, recognized the signature and, above it, the figures £37 10s. It was going to be a close-run thing, but after Mr Holcombe had read Harry's latest report to her, she had to agree with him: it was proving to be a good investment.

'Mind you,' Mr Holcombe had warned her, 'the outgoings aren't going to be any less when the time comes for him to leave school.'

'Why not?' Maisie asked. 'He shouldn't find it hard to get a job after all that education, and then he can start paying his own bills.'

Mr Holcombe shook his head sadly, as if one of his less attentive pupils had failed to grasp a point. 'I'm rather hoping that when he leaves Bristol, he'll want to go up to Oxford and read English.'

'And how long will that take?' asked Maisie.

'Three, possibly four years.'

'He should have read an awful lot of English by then.'

'Certainly enough to get a job.'

Maisie laughed. 'Perhaps he'll end up a schoolmaster like you.'

'He's not like me,' said Mr Holcombe. 'If I had to guess, he'll end up as a writer.'

'Can you make a living as a writer?'

'Certainly, if you're successful. But if that doesn't work out, you could be right – he might end up a schoolmaster like me.'

'I'd like that,' Maisie said, missing the irony.

She placed the envelope in her bag. When she called into the bank after work that afternoon, she would have to make sure there was at least £37 10s in Harry's account before she could consider writing out a cheque for the full amount. Only the bank makes money when you're overdrawn, Patrick had told her. The school had occasionally given her two or three weeks' grace in the past, but Patrick had explained that, like the tea shop, they would also have to balance their books at the end of each term.

Maisie didn't have long to wait for her tram, and once she had taken her seat, her thoughts returned to Patrick. She would never admit to anyone, even her mother, how much she missed him.

Her thoughts were interrupted by a fire engine overtaking the tram. Some of the passengers stared out of the window to follow its progress. Once it was out of sight, Maisie turned her attention to Tilly's. Since she'd sacked Bob Burrows, the bank manager had reported that the tea shop had begun to make a steady profit each month, and might even break Miss Tilly's record of £112 10s by the end of the year, which would allow Maisie to start paying back some of the £500 loan. There might even be enough left over to buy a new pair of shoes for Harry.

Maisie got off the tram at the end of Victoria Street. As she made her way across Bedminster Bridge, she checked her watch, his first present, and once again thought about her son. Seven thirty-two: she would have more than enough time to open the tea shop and be ready to serve her first customer by eight. It always pleased her to find a little queue waiting on the pavement as she turned the 'closed' sign to 'open'.

Just before she reached the High Street, another fire engine shot past, and she could now see a plume of black smoke rising high into the sky. But it wasn't until she turned into Broad Street that her heart began to beat faster. The three fire engines and a police car were parked in a semi-circle outside Tilly's.

Maisie began to run.

'No, no, it can't be Tilly's,' she shouted, and then she spotted several members of her staff standing in a group on the other side of the road. One of them was crying. Maisie was only a few yards from where the front door used to be when a policeman stepped in her path and prevented her from going any further.

'But I'm the owner!' she protested as she stared in disbelief at the smoking embers of what had once been the most popular tea shop in the city. Her eyes watered and she began to cough as the thick black smoke enveloped her. She stared at the charred remains of the once gleaming counter, while a layer of ash covered the floor where the chairs and tables with their spotless white tablecloths had stood when she'd locked up the previous evening.

'I'm very sorry, madam,' said the policeman, 'but for your own safety I must ask you to join your staff on the other side of the road.'

Maisie turned her back on Tilly's and reluctantly began to cross the road. Before she reached the other side, she saw him standing on the edge of the crowd. The moment their eyes met, he turned and walked away.

━◇━

Detective Inspector Blakemore opened his notebook and looked across the table at the suspect.

'Can you tell me where you were at around three o'clock this morning, Mrs Clifton?'

'I was at home in bed,' Maisie replied.

'Is there anyone who can verify that?'

'If by that, Detective Inspector, you mean was anyone in bed with me at the time, the answer is no. Why do you ask?'

The policeman made a note, which gave him a little more time to think. Then he said, 'I'm trying to find out if anyone else was involved.'

'Involved in what?' asked Maisie.

'Arson,' he replied, watching her carefully.

'But who would want to burn down Tilly's?' Maisie demanded.

'I was rather hoping you might be able to assist me on that point,' said Blakemore. He paused, hoping Mrs Clifton would add something that she would later regret. But she said nothing.

Detective Inspector Blakemore couldn't make up his mind if Mrs Clifton was a very cool customer, or simply naive. He knew one person who would be able to answer that question.

◄○►

Mr Frampton rose from behind his desk, shook hands with Maisie and motioned her towards a chair.

'I was so sorry to hear about the fire at Tilly's,' he said. 'Thank God no one was hurt.' Maisie hadn't been thanking God a lot lately. 'I do hope the building and contents were comprehensively insured,' he added.

'Oh, yes,' said Maisie. 'Thanks to Mr Casey it was well covered, but unfortunately the insurance company is refusing to pay out a penny until the police can confirm that I was not involved.'

'I can't believe the police think you're a suspect,' said Frampton.

'With my financial problems,' said Maisie, 'who can blame them?'

'It will only be a matter of time before they work out that's a ridiculous suggestion.'

'I don't have any time,' said Maisie. 'Which is why I've come to see you. I've got to find a job, and when we last met in this room, I recall you saying that if I ever wanted to come back to the Royal . . .'

'And I meant it,' interrupted Mr Frampton. 'But I can't give you your old position back, because Susan's doing an excellent job, and I've recently taken on three of Tilly's staff, so I don't have any vacancies in the Palm Court. The only position I have available at the moment is hardly worthy—'

'I'll consider anything, Mr Frampton,' said Maisie, 'and I mean anything.'

'Some of our customers have been telling us that they would like something to eat after the hotel restaurant has closed for the night,' said Mr Frampton.

'I've been considering introducing a limited service of coffee and sandwiches after ten o'clock, which would be available until the breakfast room opens at six a.m. I could only offer you three pounds a week to begin with, although of course all the tips would be yours. Naturally I'd understand if you felt—'

'I'll take it.'

'When would you be able to start?'

'Tonight.'

<o>

When the next brown envelope landed on the mat at No. 27, Maisie stuffed it in her bag, unopened, and wondered how long it would be before she received a second, perhaps a third, and then finally a thick white envelope containing a letter not from the bursar, but the headmaster, requesting that Mrs Clifton withdraw her son from the school at the end of term. She dreaded the moment when Harry would have to read that letter to her.

In September Harry was expecting to enter the sixth form, and he couldn't hide the excitement in his eyes whenever he talked about 'going up' to Oxford and reading English at the feet of Alan Quilter, one of the most prominent scholars of the day. Maisie couldn't bear the thought of having to tell him that would no longer be possible.

Her first few nights at the Royal had been very quiet, and things didn't get much busier during the following month. She hated being idle, and when the cleaning staff arrived at five in the morning they would often discover there was nothing for them to do in the Palm Court room. Even on her busiest night Maisie didn't have more than half a dozen customers, and several of those had been turfed out of the hotel bar just after midnight and seemed more interested in propositioning her than in ordering coffee and a ham sandwich.

Most of her customers were commercial travellers who only booked in for one night, so her chances of building up a regular clientele didn't look promising, and the tips were certainly not going to take care of the brown envelope that remained unopened in her handbag.

Maisie knew that if Harry was to remain at Bristol Grammar School and have the slightest chance of going up to Oxford, there was only one person she could turn to for help. She would beg if necessary.

19

'WHAT MAKES YOU THINK Mr Hugo would be willing to help?' asked Old Jack, leaning back in his seat. 'He's never shown any sign of caring about Harry in the past. On the contrary . . .'

'Because if there's one person on earth who ought to feel some responsibility for Harry's future, it's that man.' Maisie immediately regretted her words.

Old Jack was silent for a moment before he asked, 'Is there something you're not telling me, Maisie?'

'No,' she replied, a little too quickly. She hated lying, especially to Old Jack, but she was determined that this was one secret she would take to her grave.

'Have you given any thought to when and where you will confront Mr Hugo?'

'I know exactly what I'm going to do. He rarely leaves his office before six in the evening, and by then most of the other staff in the building have already left for the night. I know his office is on the fifth floor, I know it's the third door on the left. I know—'

'But do you know about Miss Potts?' interrupted Old Jack. 'Even if you did manage to get past reception and somehow made it to the fifth floor unnoticed, there's no way of avoiding her.'

'Miss Potts? I've never heard of her.'

'She's been Mr Hugo's private secretary for the past fifteen years. I can tell you from personal experience, you don't need a guard dog if you've got Miss Potts as a secretary.'

'Then I'll just have to wait until she goes home.'

'Miss Potts never goes home before the boss, and she's always behind her desk thirty minutes before he arrives in the morning.'

'But I'll have even less chance of getting into the Manor House,' said Maisie, 'where they have a guard dog too. He's called Jenkins.'

'Then you'll have to find a time and place when Mr Hugo will be on his own, can't escape and can't rely on Miss Potts or Jenkins to come to his rescue.'

'Is there such a time and place?' asked Maisie.

'Oh yes,' said Old Jack. 'But you'll have to get your timing right.'

<o>

Maisie waited until it was dark before she slipped out of Old Jack's railway carriage. She tiptoed across the gravel path, eased open the back door, climbed in, and shut it behind her. Resigned to a long wait, she settled herself down on the comfortable leather seat. She had a clear view of the building through a side window. Maisie waited patiently for each light to go out. Old Jack had warned her that his would be among the last.

She used the time to go over the questions she planned to ask him. Questions she'd rehearsed for several days before trying them out on Old Jack that afternoon. He'd made several suggestions, which she'd happily agreed to.

Just after six, a Rolls-Royce drew up and parked outside the front of the building. A chauffeur got out and stationed himself alongside. A few moments later

Sir Walter Barrington, the chairman of the company, marched out of the front door, climbed into the back of the car and was whisked away.

More and more lights went out, until finally only one was still aglow, like a single star on the top of a Christmas tree. Suddenly Maisie heard feet crunching across the gravel. She slipped off the seat and crouched down on the floor. She could hear two men, deep in conversation, heading towards her. Her plan didn't include two men, and she was about to leap out of the other side and try to disappear into the night when they came to a halt.

'. . . But despite that,' said a voice she recognized, 'I'd be obliged if my involvement could remain strictly between the two of us.'

'Of course, sir, you can rely on me,' said another voice she'd heard before, although she couldn't remember where.

'Let's keep in touch, old fellow,' said the first voice. 'I have no doubt I'll be calling on the bank's services again.'

Maisie heard one set of footsteps moving away. She froze when the car door opened.

He got in, took his place behind the wheel and pulled the door closed. Doesn't have a chauffeur, prefers to drive the Bugatti himself, fancies himself behind the wheel – all priceless pieces of information supplied by Old Jack.

He switched on the ignition and the vehicle shuddered into life. He revved the engine several times before crunching the gear lever into first. The man on the gate saluted as Mr Barrington drove out on to the main road and headed towards the city, just as he did every night, on his way back to the Manor House.

'Don't let him know you're in the back until he's

reached the city centre,' Old Jack had advised. 'He won't risk stopping there, because he'll be afraid someone might see you together and recognize him. But once he reaches the outskirts of the city, he won't hesitate to chuck you out. You'll have ten to fifteen minutes at most.'

'That's all I'll need,' Maisie had told him.

Maisie waited until he'd driven past the cathedral and across College Green, which was always busy at that time of night. But just as she was about to sit up and tap him on the shoulder, the car began to slow down and then came to a halt. The door opened, he got out, the door closed. Maisie peered between the front seats and was horrified to see that he had parked outside the Royal Hotel.

A dozen thoughts flashed through her mind. Should she jump out before it was too late? Why was he visiting the Royal? Was it a coincidence that it was on her day off? How long did he plan to be there? She decided to stay put, fearing she would be spotted if she got out in such a public place. Besides, this could well be her last chance to confront him face to face before the bill had to be paid.

The answer to one of her questions turned out to be twenty minutes, but long before he got back into the driver's seat and drove off, Maisie was in a cold sweat. She had no idea her heart could beat that fast. She waited until he had gone about half a mile before she sat up and tapped him on the shoulder.

He looked shocked as he turned round, which was followed by a look of recognition, and then realization. 'What do you want?' he demanded, recovering slightly.

'I have a feeling you know exactly what I want,' said Maisie. 'My only interest is Harry, and making sure his school fees are paid for the next two years.'

'Give me one good reason why I should pay your son's school fees.'

'Because he's your son,' Maisie replied calmly.

'And what makes you so sure of that?'

'I watched you when you first saw him at St Bede's,' said Maisie, 'and every Sunday at St Mary's when he sang in the choir. I saw the look in your eyes then, and I saw it again when you refused to shake hands with him on the first day of term.'

'That's not proof,' said Barrington, sounding a little more confident. 'It's nothing more than a woman's intuition.'

'Then perhaps the time has come to let another woman know what you get up to on a works outing.'

'What makes you think she'd believe you?'

'Nothing more than a woman's intuition,' said Maisie. This silenced him, and gave her the confidence to continue. 'Mrs Barrington might also be interested to know why you went to so much trouble to have my brother arrested the day after Arthur disappeared.'

'A coincidence, nothing more.'

'And is it also just a coincidence that my husband has never been seen since?'

'I had nothing to do with Clifton's death!' shouted Barrington as he swerved across the road, narrowly missing an oncoming vehicle.

Maisie sat bolt upright, stunned by what she'd heard. 'So it was you who was responsible for my husband's death.'

'You have no proof of that,' he said defiantly.

'I don't need any more proof. But in spite of all the damage you've done to my family over the years, I'll still give you an easy way out. You take care of Harry's education while he's still at Bristol Grammar School, and I won't bother you again.'

It was some time before Barrington responded. He eventually said, 'I'll need a few days to work out the best way to handle the payments.'

'The company's charitable trust could easily take care of such a small amount,' said Maisie. 'After all, your father is chairman of the governors.'

This time he didn't have a ready response. Was he wondering how she'd come across that piece of information? He wasn't the first person to underestimate Old Jack. Maisie opened her handbag, pulled out the thin brown envelope and placed it on the seat beside him.

The car swung into an unlit alley. Barrington jumped out and opened the back door. Maisie stepped out, feeling that the confrontation couldn't have gone much better. As her feet touched the ground, he grabbed her by the shoulders and shook her violently.

'Now you listen to me, Maisie Clifton, and listen carefully,' he said, a look of fury in his eyes. 'If you ever threaten me again, I'll not only see that your brother is sacked, but I'll make sure he never works in this city again. And if you're ever foolish enough to even hint to my wife that I'm that boy's father, I'll have you arrested, and it won't be a prison you'll end up in, but a mental asylum.'

He let go of her, clenched a fist and then punched her full in the face. She collapsed on to the ground and curled up into a ball, expecting him to kick her again and again. When nothing happened, she looked up to see him standing over her. He was tearing the thin brown envelope into little pieces and scattering them like confetti over a bride.

Without another word, he jumped back into the car and sped away.

—◦—

When the white envelope came through the letterbox, Maisie knew she was beaten. She would have to tell Harry the truth when he got back from school that afternoon. But first she had to drop into the bank, deposit her meagre tips from the previous evening, and tell Mr Prendergast there would be no more bills from BGS, as her son would be leaving at the end of term.

She decided to walk to the bank and save a penny on the tram fare. On the way, she thought about all the people she'd let down. Would Miss Tilly and Miss Monday ever forgive her? Several of her staff, particularly some of the older ones, hadn't been able to find another job. Then there were her parents, who had always watched over Harry so that she could go to work; Old Jack, who couldn't have done more to help her son; and most of all, Harry himself, who in the words of Mr Holcombe, was about to be crowned with the laurels of victory.

When she reached the bank, she joined the longest queue, as she was in no hurry to be served.

'Good morning, Mrs Clifton,' said the teller cheerfully when she eventually reached the front of the line.

'Good morning,' Maisie replied before placing four shillings and sixpence on the counter.

The teller checked the amount carefully, then placed the coins in different trays below the counter. He next wrote out a slip to confirm the sum Mrs Clifton had deposited, and handed it to her. Maisie stood to one side to allow the next customer to take her place while she put the slip in her bag.

'Mrs Clifton,' said the teller.

'Yes?' she said, looking back up.

'The manager was hoping to have a word with you.'

'I quite understand,' she said. Maisie didn't need him to tell her there wasn't enough money in her account to cover the latest invoice from the school. In fact, it would be a relief to let Mr Prendergast know there would be no further bills for extra-curricular activities.

The young man led her silently across the banking hall and down a long corridor. When he reached the manager's office, he knocked gently on the door, opened it and said, 'Mrs Clifton, sir.'

'Ah, yes,' said Mr Prendergast. 'I do need to have a word with you, Mrs Clifton. Please come in.' Where had she heard that voice before?

'Mrs Clifton,' he continued once she was seated, 'I am sorry to have to inform you that we have been unable to honour your most recent cheque for thirty-seven pounds ten shillings, made payable to Bristol Municipal Charities. Were you to present it again, I fear there are still insufficient funds in your account to cover the full amount. Unless, of course, you anticipate depositing any further funds in the near future?'

'No,' said Maisie, taking the white envelope from her bag and placing it on the desk in front of him. 'Perhaps you would be kind enough to let the BMC know that, given time, I will pay off any other expenses that have arisen during Harry's last term.'

'I'm very sorry, Mrs Clifton,' said Mr Prendergast. 'I only wish I could help in some way.' He picked up the white envelope. 'May I open this?' he asked.

'Yes, of course,' said Maisie, who until that moment had tried to avoid finding out just how much she still owed the school.

Mr Prendergast picked up a thin silver paperknife from his desk and slit open the envelope. He extracted a cheque from the Bristol and West of England Insurance Company to the value of six hundred pounds, made payable to Mrs Maisie Clifton.

HUGO BARRINGTON

1921–1936

20

I wouldn't even have remembered her name, if she hadn't later accused me of killing her husband.

It all began when my father insisted I accompany the workers on their annual outing to Weston-super-Mare. 'Good for their morale to see the chairman's son taking an interest,' he said.

I wasn't convinced, and quite frankly considered the whole exercise a waste of time, but once my father has made up his mind about anything, there is no point arguing. And it would have been a waste of time if Maisie – such a common name – hadn't come along for the ride. Even I was surprised to find how eager she was to jump into bed with the boss's son. I assumed that once we were back in Bristol, I'd never hear from her again. Perhaps I wouldn't have, if she hadn't married Arthur Clifton.

◄○►

I was sitting at my desk going over the tender for the *Maple Leaf*, checking and rechecking the figures, hoping to find some way the company might save a little money, but however hard I tried, the bottom line didn't make good reading. It didn't help that it had been my decision to tender for the contract.

My opposite number at Myson had driven a hard bargain, and after several delays I hadn't budgeted for, we were running five months behind schedule, with penalty clauses that would be triggered should we fail to complete the build by December 15th. What had originally looked like a dream contract that would show a handsome profit, was turning into a nightmare, where we would wake up on December 15th with heavy losses.

My father had been against Barrington's taking on the contract in the first place and had made his views clear. 'We should stick to what we're good at,' he repeated from the chair at every board meeting. 'For the past hundred years, Barrington's Shipping Line has transported goods to and from the far corners of the earth, leaving our rivals in Belfast, Liverpool and Newcastle to build ships.'

I knew I wouldn't be able to sway him, so I spent my time trying to persuade the younger members of the board that we had missed out on several opportunities in recent years, while others had snapped up lucrative contracts that could easily have come our way. I finally convinced them, by a slim majority, to dip a toe in the water and sign up with Myson to build them a cargo vessel to add to their fast-growing fleet.

'If we do a good job and deliver the *Maple Leaf* on time,' I told the board, 'more contracts are sure to follow.'

'Let's hope we don't live to regret it,' was my father's only comment after he'd lost the vote at the board meeting.

I was already regretting it. Although the Barrington Line was predicting record profits for 1921, it was beginning to look as if its new subsidiary, Barrington Shipbuilding, would be the only red entry on the annual balance sheet. Some members of the board were already distancing themselves from the decision, while reminding everyone that they had voted with my father.

I had only recently been appointed managing director of the company and I could just imagine what was being said behind my back. 'Chip off the old block' clearly wasn't on anyone's lips. One director had already resigned and couldn't have made his views more clear when he departed, warning my father, 'The boy lacks judgement. Be careful he doesn't end up bankrupting the company.'

But I hadn't given up. I remained convinced that as long as we finished the job on time, we could still break even, and possibly make a small profit. So much depended on what happened during the next few weeks. I'd already given the order to work round the clock in three eight-hour shifts, and promised the workforce handsome bonuses if they managed to complete the contract on time. After all, there were enough men hanging around outside the gates, desperate for work.

<o>

I was just about to tell my secretary I was going home, when he burst into my office unannounced.

He was a short, squat man, with heavy shoulders and bulging muscles, the build of a stevedore. My first thought was to wonder how he had managed to get past Miss Potts, who followed in his wake looking unusually flustered. 'I couldn't stop him,' she said, stating the obvious. 'Shall I call the watchman?'

I looked into the man's eyes and said, 'No.'

Miss Potts remained by the door while we sized each other up, like a mongoose and a snake, each wondering who would strike first. Then the man reluctantly removed his cap and started jabbering. It was some time before I could understand what he was saying.

'My best mate's goin' to die! Arthur Clifton's goin' to die unless you do somethin' about it.'

I told him to calm down and explain what the problem was, when my works manager came charging into the room.

'I'm sorry you've been troubled by Tancock, sir,' he said

once he'd caught his breath, 'but I can assure you it's all under control. Nothin' for you to worry about.'

'What is all under control?' I asked.

'Tancock here claims that his mate Clifton was workin' inside the hull when the shift changed, and the new shift somehow managed to seal him inside.'

'Come and see for yourself!' shouted Tancock. 'You can hear him tappin'!'

'Could that be possible, Haskins?' I asked.

'Anything's possible, sir, but it's more likely Clifton's buggered off for the day and is already in the pub.'

'Then why hasn't he signed off at the gate?' demanded Tancock.

'Nothing unusual in that, sir,' said Haskins, not looking at him. 'Signin' on's what matters, not signin' off.'

'If you don't come and see for yourself,' said Tancock, 'you'll go to your grave with his blood on your hands.' This outburst silenced even Haskins.

'Miss Potts, I'm going down to number one dock,' I said. 'I shouldn't be too long.'

The squat little man ran out of my office without another word.

'Haskins, join me in my car,' I said. 'We can discuss what ought to be done on the way.'

'Nothin' needs to be done, sir,' he insisted. 'It's all stuff and nonsense.'

It wasn't until we were alone in the car that I put it bluntly to my ganger. 'Is there any chance that Clifton really might be sealed up in the hull?'

'No chance, sir,' said Haskins firmly. 'I'm only sorry to be wastin' your time.'

'But the man seems pretty certain,' I said.

'Like he's always certain about what'll win the three thirty at Chepstow.'

I didn't laugh.

'Clifton's shift ended at six,' Haskins continued, taking on a more serious tone. 'He must've known that the welders would be moving in and would expect to finish the job before the next shift reported for duty at two in the mornin'.'

'What was Clifton doing down in the hull in the first place?'

'Making the final checks before the welders got to work.'

'Is it possible he didn't realize his shift had ended?'

'You can hear the end-of-shift horn in the middle of Bristol,' said Haskins as we drove past Tancock, who was running like a man possessed.

'Even if you were deep inside the hull?'

'I suppose it's just possible he might not have heard it if he was in the double bottom, but I've never come across a docker who didn't know what time his shift ends.'

'As long as he has a watch,' I said, looking to see if Haskins was wearing one. He wasn't. 'If Clifton really is still down there, do we have the equipment to get him out?'

'We've got enough acetylene torches to burn through the hull and remove a complete section. Problem is, it'd take hours, and if Clifton's down there, there wouldn't be much chance of him still bein' alive by the time we reached him. On top of that, it would take the men another fortnight, perhaps longer, to replace the whole section. And as you keep remindin' me, guv, you've got everyone on bonuses to save time, not waste it.'

The night shift was well into its second hour by the time I brought my car to a halt by the side of the ship. There must have been over a hundred men on board, working flat out, hammering, welding and sealing in the rivets. As I climbed the gangway, I could see Tancock running towards the ship. When he caught up with me a few moments later he had to bend double, his hands on his thighs, while he recovered.

'So, what do you expect me to do, Tancock?' I asked once he'd caught his breath.

'Stop them all workin', guv, just for a few minutes, then you'll hear him tappin'.'

I nodded my approval.

Haskins shrugged his shoulders, clearly unable to believe I would even consider giving such an order. It took him several minutes to get everyone to down tools and for the workers to fall silent. Every man on the ship, as well as the dockside, stood still and listened intently, but other than the occasional squawk from a passing gull or a smoker's cough, I heard nothing.

'Like I said, sir, it's been a waste of everyone's time,' said Haskins. 'By now Clifton will be suppin' his third pint at the Pig and Whistle.'

Someone dropped a hammer, and the sound echoed around the docks. Then for a moment, just a moment, I thought I heard a different sound, regular and soft.

'That's him!' shouted Tancock.

And then, as suddenly as it had started, the noise stopped.

'Did anyone else hear anything?' I shouted.

'I didn't hear nothin',' said Haskins, looking around at the men, almost daring them to defy him.

Some of them stared back at him, while one or two picked up their hammers menacingly, as if they were waiting for someone to lead them over the top.

I felt like a captain who was being given one last chance to quell a mutiny. Either way I couldn't win. If I told the men to go back to work, the rumours would spread until every man in the dockyard believed I was personally responsible for Clifton's death. It would be weeks, months, possibly even years before I could recover my authority. But if I gave the order to break open the hull, any hope of making a profit on the contract would be scuppered, and with it my chances of ever becoming chairman of the board. I just stood there, hoping the continued silence would convince the men that

Tancock was wrong. As each second of silence passed, my confidence grew.

'It seems no one heard nothin', sir,' Haskins said a few moments later. 'Can I have your permission to put the men back to work?'

They didn't move a muscle, just continued to glare defiantly at me. Haskins stared back at them, and one or two eventually lowered their eyes.

I turned to the ganger and gave the order to get back to work. In the moment's silence that followed, I could have sworn I heard a tap. I glanced at Tancock, but then the sound was drowned out by a thousand other noises as the men went resentfully back to work.

'Tancock, why don't you bugger off down the pub and see if your mate's there,' said Haskins. 'And when you find him, give him a tickin' off for wastin' everybody's time.'

'And if he isn't,' I said, 'call by his house and ask his wife if she's seen him.' I realized my mistake the moment I'd spoken, and quickly added, 'That is, assuming he has a wife.'

'Yes, guv, he does,' said Tancock. 'She's my sister.'

'If you still can't find him, report back to me.'

'It'll be too late by then,' said Tancock as he turned and walked off, his shoulders slumped.

'I'll be in my office should you need me, Haskins,' I said, before walking down the gangway. I drove back to Barrington House, hoping never to see Tancock again.

I returned to my desk, but was unable to concentrate on the letters Miss Potts had left for me to sign. I could still hear that tapping in my head, repeating itself again and again, like a popular melody that plays continually in your mind and even stops you from sleeping. I knew that if Clifton didn't report for work the next morning, I would never be rid of it.

During the next hour, I began to feel more confident that

Tancock must have found his mate and would now be regretting making such a fool of himself.

It was one of the rare occasions when Miss Potts left the office before me, and I was just locking the top drawer of my desk before going home, when I heard footsteps running up the stairs. It could only be one man.

I looked up, and the man I'd hoped never to see again was standing in the doorway, pent-up fury blazing in his eyes.

'You killed my best mate, you bastard,' he said, shaking a fist. 'You may as well have murdered him with your bare hands!'

'Now, steady on, Tancock, old chap,' I said. 'For all we know, Clifton may still be alive.'

'He's gone to his grave just so you could finish your bloody job on time. No man will ever sail on that ship once they find out the truth.'

'Men die in shipbuilding accidents every day,' I said lamely.

Tancock took a pace towards me. He was so angry that for a moment I thought he was going to hit me, but he just stood there, feet apart, fists clenched, glaring at me. 'When I've told the police what I know, you'll have to admit you could've saved his life with a single word. But because you were only interested in how much money you would make, I'm going to make sure that no man on these docks will ever work for you again.'

I knew if the police did become involved, half of Bristol would think Clifton was still inside that hull and the union would demand it was opened up. If that happened, I wasn't in any doubt what they'd find.

I rose slowly from my chair and walked across to the safe on the far side of the room. I entered the code, turned the key, pulled open the door and extracted a thick white envelope before returning to my desk. I picked up a silver letter opener, slit open the envelope and took out a five-pound note. I even wondered whether Tancock had ever seen one before. I placed it on the blotting pad in front of him and watched his piggy eyes grow larger by the second.

'Nothing is going to bring back your friend,' I said, placing a second note on top of the first. His eyes never left the money. 'And anyway, who knows, he might just have done a bunk for a few days. That wouldn't be considered unusual in his line of work.' I placed a third note on top of the second. 'And when he comes back, your mates will never let you forget it.' A fourth note was followed by a fifth. 'And you wouldn't want to be charged with wasting the police's time, would you? That's a serious offence for which you can go to jail.' Two more notes. 'And of course you'd also lose your job.' He looked up at me, his anger visibly turning to fear. Three more notes. 'I could hardly be expected to employ a man who was accusing me of murder.' I placed the last two notes on top of the pile. The envelope was empty.

Tancock turned away. I took out my wallet and added one more five-pound note, three pounds and ten shillings to the pile: £68 10s in all. His eyes returned to the notes. 'There's plenty more where that came from,' I said, hoping I sounded convincing.

Tancock walked slowly towards my desk and, without looking at me, gathered up the notes, stuffed them into his pocket and left without a word.

I went to the window and watched as he walked out of the building and headed slowly for the dock gate.

I left the safe wide open, scattered some of its contents on the floor, dropped the empty envelope on my desk and left my office without locking up. I was the last person to leave the building.

21

'DETECTIVE INSPECTOR BLAKEMORE, sir,' said Miss Potts, then stood aside to allow the policeman to enter the managing director's office.

Hugo Barrington studied the inspector carefully as he entered the room. He couldn't have been much more than the regulation minimum height of five feet nine inches, and he was a few pounds overweight, but still looked fit. He was carrying a raincoat that had probably been bought when he was still a constable, and wore a brown felt hat of a more recent vintage, indicating that he hadn't been an inspector all that long.

The two men shook hands, and once he was seated, Blakemore took a notebook and pen out of an inside jacket pocket. 'As you know, sir, I am following up enquiries concerning an alleged theft that took place on these premises last night.' Barrington didn't like the word 'alleged'. 'Could I begin by asking when you first discovered that the money was missing?'

'Yes, of course, inspector,' said Barrington, trying to sound as helpful as possible. 'I arrived at the docks around seven o'clock this morning and drove straight to the sheds to check how the night shift had got on.'

'Is that something you do every morning?'

'No, only from time to time,' said Hugo, puzzled by the question.

'And how long did you spend there?'

'Twenty, perhaps thirty minutes. Then I came up to my office.'

'So you would have been in your office at around seven twenty, seven thirty at the latest.'

'Yes, that sounds about right.'

'And was your secretary already here by then?'

'Yes, she was. I rarely manage to get in before her. She's a formidable lady,' he added with a smile.

'Quite,' said the detective inspector. 'So it was Miss Potts who told you the safe had been broken into?'

'Yes. She said that when she came in this morning, she'd found the safe door open and some of its contents scattered on the floor, so she immediately rang the police.'

'She didn't ring you first, sir?'

'No, inspector. I would have been in my car on the way to work at that time.'

'So, you say your secretary arrived before you this morning. And did you leave before her last night, sir?'

'I don't recall,' said Barrington. 'But it would be most unusual for me to leave after her.'

'Yes, Miss Potts has confirmed that,' said the detective inspector. 'But she also said – ' he glanced down at his notebook – ' "I left before Mr Barrington last night, as a problem had arisen which needed his attention." ' Blakemore looked up. 'Are you able to tell me what that problem was, sir?'

'When you run a company as large as this,' said Hugo, 'problems arise all the time.'

'So you don't remember what particular problem arose yesterday evening?'

'No, inspector, I do not.'

'When you arrived in your office this morning and found the safe door open, what was the first thing you did?'

'I checked to see what was missing.'

'And what did you discover?'

'All my cash had been taken.'

'How can you be sure it had *all* been taken?'

'Because I found this open envelope on my desk,' Hugo said, handing it over.

'And how much should there have been in the envelope, sir?'

'Sixty-eight pounds and ten shillings.'

'You seem very certain of that.'

'Yes, I am,' said Hugo. 'Why should that surprise you?'

'It's simply that Miss Potts told me there was only sixty pounds in the safe, all in five-pound notes. Perhaps you could tell me, sir, where the other eight pounds and ten shillings came from?'

Hugo didn't answer immediately. 'I do sometimes keep a little loose change in my desk drawer, inspector,' he said finally.

'That's quite a large sum to describe as "a little loose change". However, allow me to return to the safe for a moment. When you entered your office this morning, the first thing you noticed was that the safe door was open.'

'That is correct, inspector.'

'Do you have a key for the safe?'

'Yes, of course.'

'Are you the only person who knows the code and is in possession of a key, sir?'

'No, Miss Potts also has access to the safe.'

'Can you confirm that the safe was locked when you went home last night?'

'Yes, it always is.'

'Then we must assume that the burglary was carried out by a professional.'

'What makes you say that, inspector?' asked Barrington.

'But if he was a professional,' said Blakemore, ignoring the question, 'what puzzles me is why he left the safe door open.'

'I'm not sure I'm following you, inspector.'

'I'll explain, sir. Professional burglars tend to leave everything just as they found it, so that their crime won't be found out immediately. It allows them more time to dispose of the stolen goods.'

'More time,' repeated Hugo.

'A professional would have closed the safe door and taken the envelope with him, making it more likely that it would be some time before you discovered anything was missing. In my experience, some people don't open their safes for days, even weeks. Only an amateur would have left your office in such disarray.'

'Then perhaps it was an amateur?'

'Then how did he manage to open the safe, sir?'

'Maybe he somehow got hold of Miss Potts's key?'

'And the code as well? But Miss Potts assures me that she takes her safe key home every night, as I understand you do, sir.' Hugo said nothing. 'May I be allowed to look inside the safe?'

'Yes, of course.'

'What is that?' asked the inspector, pointing to a tin box on the bottom shelf of the safe.

'It's my coin collection, inspector. A hobby of mine.'

'Would you be kind enough to open it, sir?'

'Is that really necessary?' asked Hugo impatiently.

'Yes, I'm afraid it is, sir.'

Hugo reluctantly opened the box, to reveal a hoard of gold coins he had collected over many years.

'Now, here's another mystery,' said the inspector. 'Our thief takes sixty pounds from the safe, and eight pounds ten shillings from your desk drawer, but leaves behind a box of gold coins that must be worth considerably more. And then there's the problem of the envelope.'

'The envelope?' said Hugo.

'Yes, sir, the envelope you say contained the money.'

'But I found it on my desk this morning.'

'I don't doubt that, sir, but you will notice that it has been slit neatly open.'

'Probably with my letter opener,' said Hugo, holding it up triumphantly.

'Quite possibly, sir, but in my experience, burglars have a tendency to rip open envelopes, not slit them neatly with a letter opener as if they already knew what was inside.'

'But Miss Potts told me that you'd found the thief,' said Hugo, trying not to sound exasperated.

'No, sir. We have found the money, but I'm not convinced that we've found the guilty party.'

'But you found some of the money in his possession?'

'Yes, we did, sir.'

'Then what more do you want?'

'To be certain we've got the right man.'

'And who is the man you've charged?'

'I didn't say I'd charged him, sir,' said the inspector as he turned a page in his notebook. 'A Mr Stanley Tancock, who turns out to be one of your stevedores. Name ring a bell, sir?'

'Can't say it does,' said Hugo. 'But if he works in the yard, he would certainly have known where my office was.'

'I am in no doubt, sir, that Tancock knew where your office was, because he says he came to see you around seven yesterday evening to tell you that his brother-in-law, a Mr Arthur Clifton, was trapped in the hull of a ship being built in the yard, and if you didn't give the order to get him out, he would die.'

'Ah, yes, I remember now. I did go over to the yard yesterday afternoon as my ganger will confirm, but it turned out to be a false alarm and a waste of everyone's time. Clearly he just wanted to find out where the safe was, so he could come back later and rob me.'

'He admits that he came back to your office a second time,' said Blakemore, turning another page of his notes, 'when he claims you offered him sixty-eight pounds and ten shillings if he would keep his mouth shut about Clifton.'

'I've never heard such an outrageous suggestion.'

'Then let us consider the alternative for a moment, sir. Let us suppose that Tancock did come back to your office with the intention of robbing you some time between seven o'clock and seven thirty yesterday evening. Having somehow managed to get into the building unobserved he reaches the fifth floor, makes his way to your office, and with either your key or Miss Potts's unlocks the safe, enters the code, removes the envelope, slits it neatly open and takes out the money, but doesn't bother with a box of gold coins. He leaves the safe door open, spreads some of its contents on the floor and places the neatly opened envelope on your desk, and then, like the Scarlet Pimpernel, disappears into thin air.'

'It needn't have been between seven and seven thirty in the evening,' said Hugo defiantly. 'It could have been any time before eight this morning.'

'I think not, sir,' said Blakemore. 'You see, Tancock has an alibi between eight and eleven o'clock last night.'

'No doubt this so-called "alibi" is some mate of his,' said Barrington.

'Thirty-one of them, at the last count,' said the detective inspector. 'It seems that having stolen your money, he turned up at the Pig and Whistle public house at around eight o'clock, and not only were the drinks on him, but he also cleared his slate. He paid the landlord with a new five-pound note, which I have in my possession.'

The detective removed his wallet, took out the note and placed it on Barrington's desk.

'The landlord also added that Tancock left the pub at around eleven, and was so drunk that two of his friends had to accompany him to his home in Still House Lane, where we found him this morning. I am bound to say, sir, that if it was Tancock who robbed you, we have a master criminal on our hands and I'd be proud to be the man who puts him behind bars. Which I suspect is exactly what you had in mind, sir,' he added, looking directly at Barrington, 'when you *gave* him the money.'

'And why on earth would I do that?' said Hugo, trying to keep his voice even.

'Because if Stanley Tancock was arrested and sent to jail, no one would take his story about Arthur Clifton seriously. Incidentally, Clifton hasn't been seen since yesterday afternoon. So I shall be recommending to my superiors that the hull be opened up without further delay so that we can discover if it was a false alarm and Tancock was wasting everyone's time.'

◄○►

Hugo Barrington checked in the mirror and straightened his bow tie. He hadn't told his father about the Arthur Clifton incident or the visit from Detective Inspector Blakemore. The less the old man knew the better. All he'd said was that some money had been stolen from his office and one of the stevedores had been arrested.

Once he'd put on his dinner jacket, Hugo sat on the end of the bed and waited for his wife to finish dressing. He hated being late, but he knew that no amount of badgering would make Elizabeth move any faster. He'd checked on Giles and his baby sister Emma, who were both fast asleep.

Hugo had wanted two sons, an heir and a spare. Emma was an inconvenience, which meant he'd have to try again. His father had been a second child and lost his older brother fighting the Boers in South Africa. Hugo's older brother had been killed at Ypres, along with half his regiment. So, in time, Hugo could expect to succeed his father as chairman of the company and, when his father died, to inherit the title and the family fortune.

So he and Elizabeth would have to try again. Not that making love to his wife was a pleasure any more. In fact, he couldn't remember if it ever had been. Recently he'd been looking for distractions elsewhere.

'Yours is a marriage made in heaven,' his mother used to say. His father was more practical. He had felt that bringing together his elder son and the only daughter of Lord Harvey was more of a merger than a marriage. When Hugo's brother was killed on the Western Front, his fiancée was passed on to Hugo. No longer a merger, more of a takeover. Hugo wasn't surprised to discover on his wedding night that Elizabeth was a virgin; his second virgin, in fact.

Elizabeth finally emerged from the dressing room, apologizing, as she always did, for keeping him waiting. The journey from the Manor House to Barrington Hall was only a couple of miles, and all the land in between the two houses belonged to the family. By the time Hugo and Elizabeth entered his parents' drawing room at a few minutes past eight, Lord Harvey was already on his second sherry. Hugo glanced around the room at the other guests. There was only one couple he didn't recognize.

His father immediately took him across and introduced him to Colonel Danvers, the recently appointed chief constable of the county. Hugo decided not to mention his meeting that morning with Detective Inspector Blakemore to the colonel, but just before they sat down for dinner, he took his father on one side to bring him up to date on the theft, never once mentioning the name of Arthur Clifton.

Over a dinner of game soup, succulent lamb and green beans, followed by crème brûlée, the conversation ranged from the Prince of Wales's visit to Cardiff and his less than helpful remarks about sympathizing with the mine workers, to Lloyd George's latest import tariffs and the effect they would have on the shipping industry, and George Bernard Shaw's *Heartbreak House*, which had recently opened to mixed reviews at the Old Vic Theatre, before returning to the Prince of Wales and the vexed question of how to find him a suitable wife.

When the servants had cleared the table after dessert, the ladies retired to the drawing room to enjoy coffee, while the butler offered the gentlemen brandy or port.

'Shipped by me and imported by you,' said Sir Walter, raising a glass to Lord Harvey while the butler circled the table offering cigars to the guests. Once Lord Harvey's Romeo y Julieta had been lit to his satisfaction, he turned to his son-in-law and said, 'Your father tells me that some blighter broke into your office and stole a large amount of cash.'

'Yes, that's correct,' Hugo replied. 'But I'm pleased to say they've caught the thief. Sadly he turned out to be one of our stevedores.'

'Is that right, Danvers?' asked Sir Walter. 'You've caught the man?'

'I did hear something about it,' responded the chief constable, 'but I wasn't told that anybody had been charged yet.'

'Why not?' demanded Lord Harvey.

'Because the man is saying that I *gave* him the money,' Hugo interjected. 'In fact, when the detective inspector questioned me this morning, I began to wonder which one of us was the criminal, and which the injured party.'

'I'm sorry to hear you feel that way,' said Colonel Danvers. 'May I ask who the officer in charge of the investigation was?'

'Detective Inspector Blakemore,' said Hugo, before adding, 'I got the impression he might have a grudge against our family.'

'When you employ as many people as we do,' said Sir Walter, placing his glass back on the table, 'there's bound to be the odd person who bears a grudge.'

'I must admit,' said Danvers, 'that Blakemore's not known for his tact. But I'll look into the matter, and if I feel he's overstepped the mark I'll assign someone else to the case.'

22

SCHOOLDAYS ARE THE happiest days of your life, claimed R.C. Sherriff, but that had not been Hugo Barrington's experience. Although he had a feeling that Giles would, as his father put it, 'make a better fist of things'.

Hugo tried to forget what had happened on his first day at school, some twenty-four years ago. He'd been driven to St Bede's in a hansom carriage, accompanied by his father, mother and elder brother Nicholas, who had just been appointed school captain. Hugo had burst into tears when another new bug had innocently asked, 'Is it true your grandfather was a docker?' Sir Walter was proud his father had 'pulled himself up by his bootstraps', but with eight-year-olds, first impressions stick. 'Grandpa was a docker! Grandpa was a docker! Cry baby! Cry baby!' chanted the rest of the dorm.

Today his son Giles would be driven to St Bede's in Sir Walter Barrington's Rolls-Royce. Hugo had wanted to take his son to school in his own car, but his father wouldn't hear of it. 'Three generations of Barringtons have been educated at St Bede's and Eton. My heir must arrive in style.'

Hugo didn't point out to his father that Giles hadn't, as yet, been offered a place at Eton, and that it was even possible the boy might have ideas of his own as to where he would like to be educated. 'Heaven forbid,' he could hear his father saying. 'Ideas smack of rebellion and rebellions must be put down.'

Giles hadn't spoken since they'd left the house, although his mother hadn't stopped fussing over her only son for the past hour. Emma had started to sob when she was told she couldn't accompany them, while Grace – another girl; he wouldn't bother to try again – just clung on to Nanny's hand and waved from the top step as they drove away.

Hugo had other things than the family's female line on his mind as the car manoeuvred its way slowly through the country lanes towards the city. Was he about to see Harry Clifton for the first time? Would he recognize him as the other son he'd wanted but would never have, or would he be left in no doubt the moment he saw the boy that he couldn't be his kinsman?

Hugo would have to be careful to avoid Clifton's mother. Would he even recognize her? He'd recently discovered that she was working as a waitress in the Palm Court room at the Royal Hotel, which he used to frequent whenever he had business meetings in the city. Now he would have to confine himself to the occasional visit in the evening, and then only if he was certain she'd left for the day.

Maisie's brother, Stan Tancock, had been released from prison after serving eighteen months of his three-year sentence. Hugo never did find out what had happened to Detective Inspector Blakemore but he never saw the man again following his father's dinner party. A young detective sergeant gave evidence at Tancock's trial, and he clearly wasn't in any doubt who the guilty party was.

Once Tancock was safely behind bars, speculation

about what had happened to Arthur Clifton quickly dried up. In a business where death is commonplace, Arthur Clifton became just another statistic. However, when Lady Harvey launched the *Maple Leaf* six months later, Hugo couldn't help thinking that *Davy Jones's Locker* would have been a more appropriate name for the vessel.

When the final figures were presented to the board, Barrington's ended up showing a loss of £13,712 on the project. Hugo didn't suggest that they tender for any more shipbuilding contracts in the future, and Sir Walter never referred to the subject again. In the years that followed, Barrington's returned to its traditional business as a shipping line, and continued to go from strength to strength.

After Stan had been carted off to the local prison, Hugo had assumed that would be the last he heard of him. But shortly before Tancock was due to be released, the deputy governor of HMP Bristol rang Miss Potts and asked for an appointment. When they met, the deputy governor pleaded with Barrington to give Tancock his old job back, otherwise he would have little hope of ever being employed again. At first, Hugo was delighted to hear this piece of news, but after giving the matter some thought, changed his mind and dispatched Phil Haskins, his chief ganger, to visit Tancock in prison and tell him he could have his job back on one condition: he was never to mention the name of Arthur Clifton again. If he did, he could collect his cards and look for work elsewhere. Tancock had accepted the offer gratefully, and as the years passed it became clear that he had kept his side of the bargain.

The Rolls-Royce drew up outside the front gate of St Bede's and the chauffeur leapt out to open the back door. Several pairs of eyes turned to look in their direction, some with admiration, others with envy.

Giles clearly didn't enjoy the attention and quickly walked away, disowning the chauffeur as well as his parents. His mother chased after him, bent down and pulled his socks up, before giving his fingernails one last inspection. Hugo spent his time looking into the faces of countless children, wondering if he would instantly recognize someone he'd never seen before.

And then he saw a boy walking up the hill, unaccompanied by a mother or father. He looked past the boy to see a woman watching him, a woman he could never forget. Both of them must have been wondering if he had one son or two reporting for their first day at St Bede's.

◄○►

When Giles caught chicken pox and had to spend a few days in the sanatorium, his father realized this might be his chance to prove that Harry Clifton wasn't his son. He didn't tell Elizabeth he was going to visit Giles while he was in the san, as he didn't want her around when he asked Matron a seemingly innocuous question.

Once he'd dealt with the morning post, Hugo told Miss Potts that he would be popping into St Bede's to see his son and she shouldn't expect him back for at least a couple of hours. He drove into the city and parked outside Frobisher House. He remembered only too well where the san was, as he'd had to visit it regularly when he was at St Bede's.

Giles was sitting up in bed having his temperature taken when his father strode into the room. The boy's face lit up the moment he saw him.

Matron was standing by the bed, checking her

patient's temperature. 'Down to ninety-nine. We'll have you back in time for the first lesson on Monday morning, young man,' she declared as she shook the thermometer. 'I'll leave you now, Mr Barrington, so you can spend a little time with your son.'

'Thank you, Matron,' said Hugo. 'I wonder if I might have a word with you before I leave?'

'Of course, Mr Barrington. You'll find me in my office.'

'You don't look too bad to me, Giles,' said Hugo once Matron had left the room.

'I'm fine, Papa. In fact, I was rather hoping Matron would let me out on Saturday morning so I can play football.'

'I'll have a word with her before I go.'

'Thank you, Papa.'

'So, how's the work coming along?'

'Not bad,' said Giles. 'But that's only because I share a study with the two brightest boys in my class.'

'And who are they?' asked his father, dreading the reply.

'There's Deakins, he's the cleverest boy in the school. In fact, the other boys won't even talk to him because they think he's a swot. But my best friend is Harry Clifton. He's very clever too, but not as clever as Deakins. You've probably heard him singing in the choir. I know you'll like him.'

'But isn't Clifton the son of a stevedore?' Hugo said.

'Yes, and just like Grandpa he doesn't hide the fact. But how did you know that, Papa?'

'I think Clifton used to work for the company,' Hugo said, immediately regretting his words.

'It must have been before your time, Papa,' said Giles, 'because his father was killed in the war.'

'Who told you that?' said Hugo.

'Harry's mother. She's a waitress at the Royal Hotel. We went to tea there on his birthday.'

Hugo would have liked to have asked when Clifton's birthday was, but feared it might be one question too many. Instead, he said, 'Your mother sends her love. I think she and Emma plan to visit you later this week.'

'Yuk. That's all I need,' said Giles. 'Chicken pox and a visit from my dreadful sister.'

'She's not that bad,' said his father, laughing.

'She's worse,' said Giles. 'And Grace doesn't look as if she's going to be any better. Do they have to come on holiday with us, Papa?'

'Yes, of course they do.'

'I was wondering if Harry Clifton could join us in Tuscany this summer. He's never been abroad.'

'No,' said Hugo a little too firmly. 'Holidays are strictly for the family, not to be shared with strangers.'

'But he's not a stranger,' said Giles. 'He's my best friend.'

'No,' Hugo repeated, 'and that's an end of the matter.' Giles looked disappointed. 'So what would you like for your birthday, my boy?' Hugo asked, quickly changing the subject.

'The latest radio,' said Giles without hesitation. 'It's called a Roberts Reliable.'

'Are you allowed to have radios at school?'

'Yes,' said Giles, 'but you can only play them at weekends. If you're caught listening after lights out or during the week, they get confiscated.'

'I'll see what I can do. Will you be coming home on your birthday?'

'Yes, but only for tea. I have to be back at school in time for prep.'

'Then I'll try and drop in,' said Hugo. 'I'll be off now. I want a word with Matron before I leave.'

'Don't forget to ask her if she'll let me out on Saturday morning,' Giles reminded him as his father left the room to carry out the real purpose of his visit.

'I'm so glad you were able to drop by, Mr Barrington. It will perk Giles up no end,' said Matron as he walked into her office. 'But as you can see, he's almost fully recovered.'

'Yes, and he's hoping you'll let him out on Saturday morning so he can play in a football match.'

'I'm sure that will be possible,' said Matron. 'But you said there was something else you wanted to talk about?'

'Yes, Matron. As you know, Giles is colour-blind. I just wanted to ask if it was causing him any difficulties.'

'Not that I'm aware of,' said Matron. 'If it is, it certainly doesn't stop him hitting a red ball across a green field until it reaches a white boundary.'

Barrington laughed before he delivered his next well-prepared line. 'When I was at St Bede's, I used to be teased because I was the only boy who suffered from colour-blindness.'

'Let me assure you,' said Matron, 'no one teases Giles. And in any case, his best friend is also colourblind.'

◄○►

Hugo drove back to his office thinking that something had to be done before the situation got out of control. He decided to have another word with Colonel Danvers.

Once he was back behind his desk, he told Miss Potts he didn't want to be disturbed. He waited until she'd closed the door before he picked up the telephone. A few moments later the chief constable was on the line.

'It's Hugo Barrington, Colonel.'

'How are you, my boy?' asked the chief constable.

'I'm well, sir. I was wondering if you could advise me on a private matter.'

'Fire away, old fellow.'

'I'm looking for a new head of security, and I wondered if you might be able to point me in the right direction.'

'As a matter of fact I do know a man who might fit the bill, but I'm not sure if he's still available. I'll find out and give you a call back.'

The chief constable was as good as his word, and phoned back the following morning. 'The man I had in mind has a part-time job at the moment, but he's looking for something more permanent.'

'What can you tell me about him?' asked Hugo.

'He was being groomed for higher things in the force, but he had to leave when he was badly injured trying to apprehend a robber during a raid on the Midland Bank. You probably remember the story. It even hit the national press. In my opinion, he'd be the ideal candidate to head your security team, and frankly you'd be lucky to get him. If you're still interested, I could drop you a line with his details.'

◄○►

Barrington rang Derek Mitchell from his home, as he didn't want Miss Potts to find out what he was up to. He agreed to meet the former policeman at the Royal Hotel at six o'clock on Monday evening, after Mrs Clifton would have left for the day and the Palm Court would be empty.

Hugo arrived a few minutes early and headed straight for a table at the far end of the room that he wouldn't normally have considered. He took a seat behind the pillar, where he knew his meeting with

Mitchell would not be seen or overheard. While he waited, he went over a list of questions in his mind that needed answering if he was going to put his trust in a complete stranger.

At three minutes to six, a tall, well-built man of military bearing pushed his way through the revolving doors. His dark navy blazer, grey flannels, short hair and highly polished shoes all suggested a life of discipline.

Hugo stood and raised a hand as if he was summoning a waiter. Mitchell walked slowly across the room, making no attempt to disguise a slight limp, an injury which, according to Danvers, was the reason Mitchell had been invalided out of the police service.

Hugo recalled the last occasion he'd come face to face with a police officer, but this time he would be asking the questions.

'Good evening, sir.'

'Good evening, Mitchell,' said Hugo as they shook hands. Once Mitchell had sat down, Hugo took a closer look at his broken nose and cauliflower ears, and also recalled from Colonel Danvers's notes that he used to play in the second row for Bristol.

'Let me say from the outset, Mitchell,' said Hugo, not wasting any time, 'that what I want to discuss with you is of a highly confidential nature, and must be kept strictly between the two of us.' Mitchell nodded. 'It is so confidential, in fact, that even Colonel Danvers has no idea of the real reason I needed to see you, as I am certainly not looking for someone to head up my security operation.'

Mitchell's face remained inscrutable as he waited to hear what Hugo had in mind.

'I am looking for someone to act as a private detective. His sole purpose will be to report to me each month on the activities of a woman who lives in this city, and in fact works in this hotel.'

'I understand, sir.'

'I want to know everything she gets up to, whether professional or personal, however insignificant it might seem. She must never, I repeat, never, become aware of your interest in her. So before I reveal her name, do you consider yourself capable of carrying out such an assignment?'

'These things are never easy,' said Mitchell, 'but they're not impossible. As a young detective sergeant, I worked on an undercover operation which resulted in a particularly loathsome individual ending up behind bars for sixteen years. If he were to walk into this hotel now, I'm confident he wouldn't recognize me.'

Hugo smiled for the first time. 'Before I go any further,' he continued, 'I need to know if you would be willing to take on such an assignment?'

'That would depend on several things, sir.'

'Such as?'

'Would it be a full-time position, because I currently have a night security job, working for a bank.'

'Hand in your notice tomorrow,' said Hugo. 'I don't want you to be working for anyone else.'

'And what are the hours?'

'At your discretion.'

'And my salary?'

'I will pay you eight pounds a week, a month in advance, and will also cover any legitimate expenses.'

Mitchell nodded. 'May I suggest you make any payments in cash, sir, so that nothing can be traced back to you?'

'That seems sensible,' said Hugo, who'd already made that decision.

'And would you want the monthly reports to be in writing, or in person?'

'In person. I want as little committed to paper as possible.'

'Then we should always meet at a different location and never on the same day of the week. That way it would be unlikely that anyone would come across us more than once.'

'I have no problem with that,' said Hugo.

'When would you want me to start, sir?'

'You started half an hour ago,' said Barrington. He removed a slip of paper and an envelope containing £32 from an inside pocket and handed them to Mitchell.

Mitchell studied the name and address written on the piece of paper for a few moments before handing it back to his new boss. 'I'll also need your private number, sir, and details of when and where you can be contacted.'

'At my office any evening between five and six,' said Hugo. 'You must never contact me at home unless it's an emergency,' he added as he took out a pen.

'Just tell me the numbers, sir, don't write them down.'

23

'WERE YOU THINKING OF attending Master Giles's birthday party?' asked Miss Potts.

Hugo looked at his diary. *Giles, 12th birthday, 3 p.m., Manor House* was written in bold letters at the top of the page.

'Do I have time to pick up a present on the way home?'

Miss Potts left the room, and returned a moment later carrying a large parcel wrapped in shiny red paper and tied with a ribbon.

'What's inside?' asked Hugo.

'The latest Roberts radio; the one he asked for when you visited him in the san last month.'

'Thank you, Miss Potts,' said Hugo. He checked his watch. 'I'd better leave now if I'm going to be in time to see him cut the cake.'

Miss Potts placed a thick file in his briefcase and before he could ask, she said, 'Your background notes for tomorrow morning's board meeting. You can go over them after Master Giles has returned to St Bede's. That way there will be no need for you to come back this evening.'

'Thank you, Miss Potts,' said Hugo. 'You think of everything.'

As he drove through the city on his way home, Hugo couldn't help noticing how many more cars there seemed to be on the highway than there had been a year ago. Pedestrians were becoming more wary of casually crossing the road since the government had increased the speed limit to 30 miles per hour. A horse reared up as Hugo shot past a hansom cab. He wondered how much longer they could hope to survive now that the city council had authorized its first taxi cab.

Once he had driven out of the city, Hugo sped up, not wanting to be late for his son's party. How quickly the boy was growing. He was already taller than his mother. Would he end up taller than his father?

When Giles left St Bede's and took up his place at Eton in a year's time, Hugo felt confident that his friendship with the Clifton boy would soon be forgotten, although he realized there were other difficulties that needed to be addressed before then.

He slowed down as he passed through the gates of his estate. He always enjoyed the long drive through the avenue of oaks up to the Manor House. Jenkins was standing on the top step as Hugo got out of the car. He held open the front door and said, 'Mrs Barrington is in the drawing room sir, with Master Giles and two of his school friends.'

As he walked into the hall, Emma came running down the stairs and threw her arms around her father.

'What's in the parcel?' she demanded.

'A birthday present for your brother.'

'Yes, but what is it?'

'You'll have to wait and see, young lady,' said her father with a smile before he handed his briefcase to the butler. 'Would you put that in my study, Jenkins,' he said as Emma grabbed him by the hand and began to tug him towards the drawing room.

Hugo's smile evaporated the moment he opened the door and saw who was sitting on the sofa.

Giles leapt up and ran towards his father, who handed him the parcel and said, 'Happy birthday, my boy.'

'Thank you, Papa,' he said, before introducing his friends.

Hugo shook Deakins's hand, but when Harry offered his, he just said, 'Good afternoon, Clifton,' and sat down in his favourite chair.

Hugo watched with interest as Giles undid the ribbon on his parcel and they both saw the present for the first time. Even his son's unbridled delight with his new radio didn't bring a smile to Hugo's lips. He had a question that he needed to ask Clifton, but it mustn't appear as if the boy's reply was of any significance.

He remained silent while the three boys took turns tuning into the two stations and listening intently to the strange voices and music that came out of the speaker. This was regularly followed by laughter or applause.

Mrs Barrington chatted to Harry about a recent concert of the *Messiah* she'd attended, adding how much she'd enjoyed his rendition of *I Know That My Redeemer Liveth*.

'Thank you, Mrs Barrington,' said Harry.

'Are you hoping to go on to Bristol Grammar School after you leave St Bede's, Clifton?' asked Hugo, spotting an opening.

'Only if I win a scholarship, sir,' he replied.

'But why is that important?' asked Mrs Barrington. 'Surely you will be offered a place, like any other boy?'

'Because my mother wouldn't be able to afford the fees, Mrs Barrington. She's a waitress at the Royal Hotel.'

'But wouldn't your father—'

'He's dead,' said Harry. 'He was killed in the war.'

'I'm sorry,' said Mrs Barrington. 'I didn't realize.'

At that moment the door opened and the under-butler entered the room carrying a large cake on a silver tray. After Giles had succeeded in blowing out all twelve candles with one puff, everyone applauded.

'And when's your birthday, Clifton?' asked Hugo.

'It was last month, sir,' Harry replied.

After Giles had cut the cake, Hugo stood up and left the room without another word.

He went straight to his study, but found he couldn't concentrate on his papers for the next day's board meeting. Clifton's reply meant he would have to seek advice from a lawyer who specialized in the law of heredity.

After an hour or so he heard voices in the hall, then the front door closing and the sound of a car driving away. A few minutes later there was a knock on his study door, and Elizabeth walked in.

'What made you leave us so abruptly?' she asked. 'And why didn't you come and say goodbye, when you must have known Giles and his guests were leaving?'

'I have a very tricky board meeting tomorrow morn-ing,' he said without looking up.

'That's no reason not to say goodbye to your son, especially on his birthday.'

'I've got a lot on my mind,' he said, still looking down at his notes.

'Surely nothing is so important that you need to be rude to guests. You were more offhand with Harry Clifton than you would be with one of the servants.'

Hugo looked up for the first time. 'That's possibly because I consider Clifton inferior to our servants.' Eliza-beth looked shocked. 'Did you know that his father was a dock labourer and his mother is a waitress? I'm not sure that's the sort of boy Giles should be mixing with.'

'Giles clearly thinks otherwise, and whatever his background, Harry's a charming boy. I can't understand why you're so against him. You didn't treat Deakins that way, and his father's a newsagent.'

'He's also an open scholar.'

'And Harry is the school's prize choral scholar, as every church-going citizen in Bristol knows. Next time you come across him, I hope you'll be a little more civil.' Without another word, Elizabeth left the room, closing the door firmly behind her.

◄○►

Sir Walter Barrington remained in his place at the head of the boardroom table as his son entered the room.

'I'm becoming increasingly concerned about the government's proposed legislation on import tariffs,' said Hugo as he took a seat on the right of his father, 'and the effect it might have on our balance sheet.'

'That's why we have a lawyer on the board,' said Sir Walter, 'so that he can advise us on such matters.'

'But I've calculated that it could cost us twenty thousand pounds a year if it becomes law. Don't you think we ought to seek a second opinion?'

'I suppose I could have a word with Sir James Amhurst when I'm next in London.'

'I'm travelling up to London on Tuesday for the Association of British Ship Owners' annual dinner,' said Hugo. 'As he's the industry's legal adviser, perhaps I should have a word with him.'

'Only if you're convinced it's necessary,' said Sir Walter. 'And don't forget that Amhurst charges by the hour, even at dinner.'

◄○►

The Association of British Ship Owners' dinner was held at the Grosvenor House, and was attended by over a thousand members and their guests.

Hugo had earlier phoned the association's secretary and asked if he could be seated next to Sir James Amhurst. The secretary raised an eyebrow, but agreed to rearrange the guests on the top table. After all, old Joshua Barrington had been a founder member of the association.

After the Bishop of Newcastle had said grace, Hugo made no attempt to interrupt the eminent silk while he was deep in conversation with the man on his right. However, when the lawyer finally turned his attention to the stranger they'd put on his left, Hugo didn't waste any time in getting to the point.

'My father, Sir Walter Barrington,' he began, capturing his quarry's attention, 'is rather concerned about the import tariff bill that is going through the House of Commons, and the effects it might have on the industry. He wonders if he could consult you on the subject when he's next in London.'

'By all means, dear boy,' said Sir James. 'Just ask his secretary to give my clerk a call and I'll make sure I'm free when he's next in town.'

'Thank you, sir,' said Hugo. 'On a lighter note, I wondered if you'd ever read anything by Agatha Christie?'

'Can't say I have,' said Sir James. 'Is she any good?'

'I'm much enjoying her latest book, *Where There's a Will*,' said Hugo, 'but I'm not sure if the plot would stand up in a court of law.'

'What's the lady suggesting?' asked Amhurst as a sliver of over-cooked beef served on a cold plate was placed in front of him.

'According to Miss Christie, the eldest son of an

hereditary knight automatically inherits his father's title, even if the child is illegitimate.'

'Ah, now that is indeed an interesting legal conundrum,' said Sir James. 'In fact, the Law Lords have quite recently reviewed such a case. Benson *v*. Carstairs, if I remember correctly. It's often referred to by the press as "the bastard's amendment".'

'And what conclusion did their lordships come to?' asked Hugo, trying not to sound too interested.

'If no loophole could be found in the original will, they came out in favour of the first born, even if the young man in question was illegitimate.' Another answer Hugo hadn't wanted to hear. 'However,' Sir James continued, 'their lordships decided to cover their backsides, and added a codicil that each case should be treated on its own merits, and then only after it had been reviewed by the Garter King of Arms. Typical of the Law Lords,' he added before picking up his knife and fork and attacking the beef. 'Too frightened to set a precedent, but quite happy to pass the buck.'

When Sir James returned his attention to the man on his right, Hugo thought about the implications of Harry Clifton discovering that he might have the right to inherit not only the Barrington shipping line, but also the family estate. Having to admit he had sired an illegitimate son would be bad enough, but the idea of Harry Clifton inheriting the family title after his death and becoming Sir Harry did not bear thinking about. He would be willing to do anything in his power to make sure that wouldn't be the outcome.

24

HUGO BARRINGTON was having breakfast when he read the letter from the headmaster of St Bede's, outlining the details of an appeal the school was launching to raise a thousand pounds to build a new cricket pavilion for the First XI. He opened his cheque book and had written the figures '100' when he was distracted by the sound of a car coming to a halt on the gravel outside.

Hugo walked across to the window to see who could possibly be visiting him so early on a Saturday morning. He was puzzled when he saw his son step out of the back of a taxi carrying a suitcase, as he'd been looking forward to watching him open the batting for the school that afternoon in the final match of the season against Avonhurst.

Jenkins appeared just in time to open the front door as Giles reached the top step. 'Good morning, Master Giles,' he said, as if he'd been expecting him.

Hugo walked quickly out of the breakfast room to find his son standing in the hall, head bowed, suitcase by his side. 'What are you doing at home?' he asked. 'Isn't there another week to go before the end of term?'

'I've been rusticated,' said Giles simply.

'Rusticated?' repeated his father. 'And what have you done to merit that, may I ask?'

Giles looked up at Jenkins, who stood silently by the front door. 'I'll take Master Giles's suitcase up to his bedroom,' the butler said, before picking up the bag and proceeding slowly up the stairs.

'Follow me,' said Hugo once the butler was out of sight.

Neither of them spoke again until Hugo had closed the study door behind him. 'What have you done to cause the school to take such a drastic measure?' demanded his father as he sank back into his chair.

'I was caught stealing from the tuck shop,' said Giles, who had been left standing in the middle of the room.

'Is there some simple explanation? A misunderstanding, perhaps?'

'No, there isn't, sir,' said Giles, fighting back tears.

'Do you have anything to say in your defence?'

'No, sir.' Giles hesitated. 'Except . . .'

'Except what?'

'I always gave the sweets away, Papa. I never kept them for myself.'

'To Clifton, no doubt.'

'And to Deakins as well,' said Giles.

'Was it Clifton who put you up to it in the first place?'

'No, it was not,' responded Giles firmly. 'In fact, once he found out what I'd been up to, Harry always took the sweets I gave him and Deakins back to the tuck shop. He even took the blame when Mr Frobisher accused him of stealing them.'

A long silence followed before his father said, 'So you've been rusticated, not actually expelled?'

Giles nodded.

'Do you think they will allow you to go back next term?'

'I doubt it,' said Giles.

'What makes you so sure of that?'

'Because I've never seen the headmaster so angry.'

'Not half as angry as your mother will be when she finds out.'

'Please don't tell her, Papa,' pleaded Giles, bursting into tears.

'And how do you expect me to explain to her why you're home a week early and might not even be returning to St Bede's next term?'

Giles made no attempt to respond, but continued to sob quietly.

'And Heaven knows what your grandparents will say,' his father added, 'when I have to tell them why you won't be going to Eton after all.'

Another long silence followed.

'Go to your room, and don't even think about coming back down until I say so.'

'Yes, sir,' said Giles. He turned to leave.

'And whatever you do, don't discuss this with anyone, especially not in front of the servants.'

'Yes, Papa,' said Giles, who ran out of the room, nearly colliding with Jenkins as he shot past him on the stairs.

Hugo leant forward in his chair, trying to think if there might be some way to turn the situation around before he had to face an inevitable call from the headmaster. He placed his elbows on the desk and his head in his hands, but it was some time before his eyes focused on the cheque.

A smile crossed his lips as he added an extra nought before signing it.

25

MITCHELL WAS SEATED in the far corner of the waiting room, reading the *Bristol Evening Post* when Hugo walked across and sat down beside him. It was so draughty that Hugo kept his hands in his pockets.

'The subject,' said Mitchell, still looking at his newspaper, 'is trying to raise five hundred pounds for a business venture.'

'What sort of business venture could she possibly be interested in?'

'Tilly's tea shop,' replied Mitchell. 'It seems the subject worked there before she moved to the Palm Court room at the Royal. Miss Tilly has recently had an offer of five hundred pounds for the business from a Mr Edward Atkins. Miss Tilly doesn't care for Atkins and has made it clear to the subject that if she were able to raise the same amount, she would prefer her to take over the business.'

'Where could she possibly hope to get hold of that much money?'

'Perhaps from someone who wished to have financial control over her, which might at a later date prove advantageous?'

Hugo remained silent. Mitchell's eyes never left his paper.

'Has she approached anyone to try and raise the money?' Hugo eventually asked.

'She's currently taking advice from a Mr Patrick Casey, who represents Dillon and Co., a finance company based in Dublin. They specialize in raising loans for private clients.'

'How do I get in touch with Casey?'

'I wouldn't advise that,' said Mitchell.

'Why not?'

'He visits Bristol about once a month, and always stays at the Royal.'

'We wouldn't have to meet at the Royal.'

'He has struck up a close personal relationship with the subject. Whenever he's in town he takes her to dinner or the theatre, and recently she's been seen returning with him to the hotel, where they spend the night together in room 371.'

'Fascinating,' said Hugo. 'Anything else?'

'It may also interest you to know that the subject banks with the National Provincial, 49 Corn Street. The manager is a Mr Prendergast. Her current account is showing a balance of twelve pounds and nine shillings.'

Hugo would like to have asked how Mitchell had come across that particular piece of information, but satisfied himself with saying, 'Excellent. The moment you come up with anything else, however insignificant, ring me.' He took a bulky envelope from his overcoat pocket and slipped it across to Mitchell.

'The train now arriving at platform nine is the seven twenty-two from Taunton.'

Mitchell pocketed the envelope, folded his newspaper and walked out of the waiting room. He'd never once looked at his employer.

◄○►

Hugo had been unable to hide his anger when he discovered the real reason Giles had failed to be offered a place at Eton. He'd phoned the headmaster, who refused to take his calls, his prospective housemaster, who sympathized but offered no hope of redemption, and even the provost, who said he'd call back, but didn't. Although Elizabeth and the girls had no idea what had caused Hugo to so regularly lose his temper of late, and for no apparent reason, they continued to bear the brunt of Giles's misdemeanours with equanimity.

Hugo reluctantly accompanied Giles to Bristol Grammar School on his first day of term, although he wouldn't allow either Emma or Grace to join them, despite Emma bursting into tears and sulking.

When Hugo brought the car to a halt in College Street, the first person he saw standing outside the school gates was Harry Clifton. Even before he pulled on the brake, Giles had leapt out and run across to greet his friend.

Hugo avoided mingling with the other parents, whom Elizabeth seemed quite happy to chat to, and when he inadvertently came across Clifton, he made a point of not shaking hands with him.

On the journey back to the Manor House, Elizabeth asked her husband why he treated Giles's best friend with such disdain. Hugo reminded his wife that their son should have gone to Eton, where he would have mixed with other gentlemen and not with the sons of local tradesmen and, in Clifton's case, far worse. Elizabeth retreated into the comparative safety of silence, as she had so often done recently.

26

'LOCAL TEA SHOP burnt to the ground! Arson suspected!' hollered the paperboy standing on the corner of the Broad.

Hugo threw on the brakes, leapt out of his car and handed the lad a ha'penny. He began reading the front page as he walked back to his car.

> Tilly's Tea Shop, a Bristol landmark, much frequented by local citizens, was razed to the ground in the early hours of the morning. Police have arrested a local man in his early thirties and charged him with arson. Miss Tilly, who now lives in Cornwall . . .

Hugo smiled when he saw the photograph of Maisie Clifton and her staff standing on the pavement, grimly surveying the burnt-out remains of Tilly's. The gods were clearly on his side.

He climbed back into his car, placed the newspaper on the passenger seat and continued on his journey to Bristol Zoo. He would need to make an early appointment to see Mr Prendergast.

Mitchell had advised him that if he hoped to keep the fact that he was the subject's backer confidential, any meetings with Prendergast should be held in Barrington's offices, and preferably after Miss Potts had gone home for the night. Hugo didn't attempt to explain to Mitchell that he wasn't sure if Miss Potts did go home at night. He was looking forward to the meeting with Prendergast, when he would administer the last rites, but there was someone else he needed to see before he could do that.

─◆─

Mitchell was feeding Rosie when he arrived.

Hugo walked slowly across, leant on the railing and pretended to take an interest in the Indian elephant that Bristol Zoo had recently acquired from the United Provinces, and was already attracting a large number of visitors. Mitchell tossed up a lump of bread, which Rosie caught in her trunk and transferred to her mouth in one fluid movement.

'The subject has returned to work at the Royal Hotel,' said Mitchell as if he was addressing the elephant. 'She's doing the late shift in the Palm Court from ten at night until six the following morning. She's paid three pounds a week, plus whatever she can make in tips, which, as there are so few customers at that time of night, doesn't add up to much.' He threw another crust at the elephant, and continued, 'A Bob Burrows has been arrested and charged with arson. Burrows was her patisserie supplier before the subject sacked him. He's made a full confession, even admitting that he had planned to propose to the subject and had purchased an engagement ring, but she'd spurned him; or at least that's his story.'

A smile crossed Hugo's lips. 'And who's in charge of the case?' he asked.

'A Detective Inspector Blakemore,' said Mitchell. Hugo's smile was replaced by a frown. 'Although Blakemore initially thought the subject might be an accomplice of Burrows,' continued Mitchell, 'he has since informed the Bristol and West of England Insurance Company that she is no longer a suspect.'

'That's a pity,' said Hugo, the frown still in place.

'Not necessarily,' said Mitchell. 'The insurance company will be issuing Mrs Clifton with a cheque for six hundred pounds in full and final settlement of her claim.' Hugo smiled.

'I wonder if she's told her son,' said Hugo, almost to himself.

If Mitchell heard the comment, he ignored it. 'The only other piece of information that might be of some interest to you,' he continued, 'is that Mr Patrick Casey booked into the Royal Hotel on Friday night, and took the subject to the Plimsoll Line for dinner. They returned to the hotel afterwards, when she accompanied him to his room, No. 371, and didn't leave until just after seven o'clock the following morning.'

A long silence followed, always the sign that Mitchell had come to the end of his monthly report. Hugo removed an envelope from an inside pocket and slipped it to Mitchell, who didn't acknowledge the transaction as he threw his last piece of bread to a contented Rosie.

◄○►

'Mr Prendergast to see you,' said Miss Potts, standing aside to allow the banker to enter the managing director's office.

'It's good of you to come all this way,' said Hugo. 'I'm sure you'll appreciate why I didn't want to discuss such a highly confidential matter at the bank.'

'I quite understand,' said Prendergast, who had opened his Gladstone bag and extracted a thick file even before he'd sat down. He passed a single sheet of paper across the desk to Mr Barrington.

Hugo checked the bottom line, before settling back in his chair.

'Just to recap, if I may,' said Prendergast. 'You put up a capital sum of five hundred pounds, which allowed Mrs Clifton to purchase the business known as Tilly's, a tea shop on Broad Street. The agreed contract was for the full amount, plus compound interest at five per cent per annum, to be paid back to the principal within a period of five years.

'Although Tilly's managed to declare a small trading profit in Mrs Clifton's first year and again in her second, there was never a large enough surplus for her either to pay the interest or to return any part of the capital sum, so at the time of the fire, Mrs Clifton owed you £572 16 shillings. To this sum I must add bank charges of £20, making a grand total of £592 16 shillings. This, of course, will be well covered by the insurance payout, which means that while your investment is secure, Mrs Clifton will be left with virtually nothing.'

'How unfortunate,' said Hugo. 'May I ask why the final sum doesn't appear to include any charge for services rendered by Mr Casey?' he added after studying the figures more closely.

'Because Mr Casey has informed the bank that he will not be submitting any bills for his services.'

Hugo frowned. 'At least that is one piece of good news for the poor woman.'

'Indeed. None the less, I fear she will no longer be able to cover her son's fees at Bristol Grammar School for next term.'

'How sad,' said Hugo. 'So will the boy have to be removed?'

'I'm sorry to say that's the inevitable conclusion,' said Mr Prendergast. 'It is a great shame, because she dotes on the child, and I believe she would sacrifice almost anything to keep him there.'

'A great shame,' repeated Hugo as he closed the file and rose from his chair. 'I won't keep you any longer, Mr Prendergast,' he added. 'I have an appointment in the city in about half an hour. Perhaps I can give you a lift?'

'That is most kind of you, Mr Barrington, but it won't be necessary. I drove myself over here.'

'What do you drive?' Hugo asked as he picked up his briefcase and headed towards the door.

'A Morris Oxford,' said Prendergast, quickly stuffing some papers back into his Gladstone bag and following Hugo out of the office.

'The people's car,' said Hugo. 'I'm told that, like you, Mr Prendergast, it's very reliable.' Both men laughed as they walked down the stairs together. 'Sad business, Mrs Clifton,' said Hugo as they stepped out of the building. 'But then, I'm not altogether sure I approve of women getting involved in business. It's not the natural way of things.'

'I quite agree,' said Prendergast, as the two men came to a halt by Barrington's car. 'Mind you,' he added, 'you could not have done more for the poor woman.'

'It's kind of you to say so, Prendergast,' said Hugo. 'But despite that, I'd be obliged if my involvement could remain strictly between the two of us.'

'Of course, sir,' said Prendergast as the two men shook hands, 'you can rely on me.'

'Let's keep in touch, old fellow,' said Hugo as he climbed into his car. 'I have no doubt I'll be calling on the bank's services again.' Prendergast smiled.

As Hugo drove towards the city, his thoughts

returned to Maisie Clifton. He had dealt her a blow from which she was unlikely to recover, but he now intended to deliver the knock-out punch.

He drove into Bristol wondering where she was at that moment. Probably sitting her son down to explain to him why he would have to leave BGS at the end of the summer term. Had she even for one fleeting moment imagined that Harry might be able to continue his studies as if nothing had happened? Hugo decided that he wouldn't raise the subject with Giles until the boy told him the sad news that his friend Harry would not be returning to BGS to join him in the sixth form.

Even the thought of his own son having to go to Bristol Grammar School still made him pulse with anger, but he had never let Elizabeth or his father know the real reason Giles had failed to get a place at Eton.

Once he'd driven past the cathedral, he continued across College Green before turning into the entrance of the Royal Hotel. He was a few minutes early for his appointment, but he was confident the manager would not keep him waiting. He pushed his way through the revolving doors and strolled across the lobby, not needing to be told where Mr Frampton's office was.

The manager's secretary leapt up the moment Hugo entered the room. 'I'll let Mr Frampton know you're here,' she said, almost running into the adjoining office. The manager appeared a moment later.

'What a pleasure to see you, Mr Barrington,' he said, ushering him into his office. 'I do hope you and Mrs Barrington are both well.' Hugo nodded and took a seat opposite the hotel manager, but didn't shake hands.

'When you asked to see me, I took the liberty of checking over the arrangements for your company's annual dinner,' said Frampton. 'Just over three hundred guests will be attending, I understand?'

'I have no interest how many guests are attending,' said Hugo. 'That isn't the reason I came to see you, Frampton. I wish to discuss a private matter that I find most distasteful.'

'I'm very sorry to hear that,' said Frampton, sitting bolt upright.

'One of our non-executive directors was staying at the hotel on Thursday night, and the following day he made a most serious allegation that I feel it is my duty to bring to your attention.'

'Yes, of course,' said Frampton, rubbing his sweating palms on his trousers. 'The last thing we would want to do is annoy one of our most valued customers.'

'I'm glad to hear it,' said Hugo. 'The gentleman in question checked into the hotel after the restaurant had closed and went into the Palm Court in the hope of being provided with some light refreshment.'

'A service I myself instituted,' said Frampton, allowing himself a strained smile.

'He gave his order to a young lady who appeared to be in charge,' continued Hugo, ignoring the comment.

'Yes, that would be our Mrs Clifton.'

'I've no idea who it was,' said Hugo. 'However, as she was serving him with a cup of coffee and some sandwiches, another gentleman entered the Palm Court, made an order and asked if it could be sent up to his room. The only thing my friend recalls about the man was that he had a slight Irish accent. My friend then signed his bill and retired for the night. He rose early the following morning, as he wished to have breakfast and go over his papers before the board meeting. When he came out of his room he observed the same woman, still dressed in her hotel uniform, leaving room 371. She then walked to the end of the corridor, climbed through the window and out on to the fire escape.'

'I'm absolutely appalled, sir. I . . .'

'The board member concerned has requested that whenever he comes to Bristol in the future, he should be booked into another hotel. Now, I don't wish to appear prudish, Frampton, but the Royal has always been somewhere I've been happy to bring my wife and children.'

'Be assured, Mr Barrington, the person concerned will be dismissed immediately, and not supplied with a reference. May I add how grateful I am that you have brought this matter to my attention.'

Hugo rose from his place. 'Of course, I wouldn't want any reference made to me or the company should you feel it necessary to dismiss the lady in question.'

'You can be assured of my discretion,' said Frampton.

Hugo smiled for the first time. 'On a happier note, may I say how much we're all looking forward to the annual dinner, which no doubt will be up to your usual high standard. Next year we'll be celebrating the company's centenary, so I feel sure my father will want to push the boat out.' Both men laughed a little too loudly.

'You can rely on us, Mr Barrington,' said Frampton as he followed his client out of the office.

'And one more thing, Frampton,' said Hugo, as they walked across the foyer. 'I'd rather you didn't say anything to Sir Walter about this. My father can be a little old-fashioned when it comes to such matters, so I think it's best kept between ourselves.'

'I couldn't agree more, Mr Barrington,' said Frampton. 'You can be assured I shall deal with the matter personally.'

As Hugo pushed his way back through the revolving doors, he couldn't help wondering just how many hours Mitchell must have spent at the Royal before he was able to supply him with such a priceless piece of information.

He jumped back into his car, switched on the engine and continued on his journey home. He was still thinking about Maisie Clifton when he felt a tap on his shoulder. He experienced a moment of blind panic as he turned around and saw who was sitting on the back seat. He even wondered if somehow she'd found out about his meeting with Frampton.

'What do you want?' he demanded, not slowing down for fear that someone might see them together.

As he listened to her demands, he could only wonder how she was so well informed. Once she'd finished, he readily agreed to her terms, knowing that it would be the easiest way of getting her out of the car.

Mrs Clifton placed a thin brown envelope on the passenger seat next to him. 'I'll wait to hear from you,' she said.

Hugo put the envelope in an inside pocket. He only slowed down when he came to an unlit alley, but didn't stop until he was certain no one else could see them. He leapt out of the car and opened the back door. When he saw the look on her face, it was clear she felt she'd more than achieved her purpose.

Hugo allowed her a moment of triumph, before he grabbed her by the shoulders and shook her as if he was trying to remove an obstinate apple from a tree. Once he'd left her in no doubt what would happen if she ever bothered him again, he punched her in the face with all his strength. She collapsed to the ground curled up into a ball, and didn't stop shaking. Hugo thought about kicking her in the stomach but didn't want to risk being witnessed by a passer-by. He drove away without giving her another thought.

OLD JACK TAR

1925–1936

27

On a balmy Thursday afternoon in the Northern Transvaal, I killed eleven men, and a grateful nation awarded me the Victoria Cross for service above and beyond the call of duty. I haven't had a peaceful night's sleep since.

If I'd killed one Englishman in my homeland, a judge would have sentenced me to hang by the neck until I was dead. Instead, I have been sentenced to life imprisonment, because I still see the faces of those eleven wretched young men every day, like an image on a coin that never fades. I've often considered suicide, but that would be the coward's way out.

In the citation, gazetted in *The Times*, it was stated that my actions had been responsible for saving the lives of two officers, five non-commissioned officers and seventeen private soldiers of the Royal Gloucesters. One of those officers, Lieutenant Walter Barrington, has made it possible for me to serve my sentence with some dignity.

Within weeks of the action I was shipped back to England, and a few months later I was honourably discharged following what would now be described as a mental breakdown. After six months in an army hospital, I was released back into the world. I changed my name, avoided my home town of Wells in Somerset, and set off for Bristol. Unlike the prodigal son, I refused to travel a few miles into the next county where I would have been able to enjoy the tranquillity of my father's home.

During the day, I would roam the streets of Bristol, rummaging around in dustbins for scraps, while at night my bedroom was a park, my resting place a bench, my blanket a newspaper, my morning call the first bird to announce a new dawn. When it was too cold or wet, I retreated to the waiting room of a local railway station, where I slept below the bench and rose before the first train shunted in the next morning. As the nights became longer, I signed up as a non-paying guest of the Salvation Army on Little George Street, where kind ladies supplied me with thick bread and thin soup before I fell asleep on a horse-hair mattress below a single blanket. Luxury.

As the years passed I hoped that my former com-panions-in-arms and brother officers would assume I was dead. I had no desire for them to find out that this was the prison I'd chosen to carry out my life sentence in. And it might have stayed thus, had a Rolls-Royce not screeched to a halt in the middle of the road. The back door swung open and out leapt a man I hadn't seen for years.

'Captain Tarrant!' he cried as he advanced towards me. I looked away, hoping he'd think he'd made a mistake. But I remembered only too well that Walter Barrington was not a man who suffered from self-doubt. He grabbed me by the shoulders and stared at me for some time before he said, 'How can this be possible, old fellow?'

The more I tried to convince him I did not need his help, the more determined he became to be my saviour. I finally gave in, but not before he had agreed to my terms and conditions.

At first he begged me to join him and his wife at the Manor House, but I'd survived too long without a roof over my head to regard such comfort as anything other than a burden. He even offered me a seat on the board of the shipping company that bore his name.

'What use could I possibly be to you?' I asked.

'Your very presence, Jack, would be an inspiration to us all.'

I thanked him, but explained that I had not yet completed my sentence for the murder of eleven men. Still he didn't give in.

I finally agreed to take the job of night watchman at the docks, with three pounds a week pay and accommodation provided: an abandoned Pullman railway carriage now became my prison cell. I suppose I might have continued my life sentence until the day I died, had I not come into contact with Master Harry Clifton.

Harry would claim, years later, that I had shaped his whole life. In truth, it was he who saved mine.

The first time I came across young Harry, he couldn't have been more than four or five. 'Come on in, lad,' I called to him when I spotted him crawling towards the carriage on his hands and knees. But he immediately leapt up and ran away.

The following Saturday he got as far as looking in through the window. I tried again. 'Why don't you come in, my boy? I'm not going to bite you,' I said, trying to reassure him. This time he took up my offer and opened the door, but after exchanging a few words, he ran away again. Was I that frightening a figure?

The next Saturday, he not only opened the door, but stood, feet apart, in the doorway, staring at me defiantly. We chatted for over an hour, about everything from Bristol City FC to why snakes shed their skins and who built Clifton Suspension Bridge, before he said, 'I'll have to be off now, Mr Tar, my mum's expecting me home for tea.' This time he walked away, but looked back several times.

After that, Harry came to visit me every Saturday until he went to Merrywood Elementary School, when he started turning up most mornings. It took me some time to convince the boy that he should stay at school and learn to read and write. Frankly I wouldn't have managed even that without the help of Miss Monday, Mr Holcombe and Harry's spirited mother. It took a formidable team to get Harry Clifton to realize his potential, and I knew we had succeeded when once again he could only find the time to visit me on Saturday mornings because he was preparing to enter for a choral scholarship to St Bede's.

Once Harry had started at his new school, I didn't expect to see him again until the Christmas holidays. But to my surprise, I found him standing outside my door just before eleven o'clock on the first Friday night of term.

He told me he'd left St Bede's because a prefect was bullying him – damned if I can recall the cad's name – and he was going to run away to sea. If he had, I suspect the boy would have ended up an admiral. But happily he listened to my advice and was back at school in time for breakfast the following morning.

Because he always used to come to the docks with Stan Tancock, it was some time before I realized Harry was Arthur Clifton's boy. He once asked me if I'd known his father, and I told him yes, and that he was a good and decent man with a fine war record. He then asked me if I knew how he died. I said I didn't. The only time I ever lied to the boy. It was not for me to ignore the wishes of his mother.

◄O►

I was standing on the dockside when the shift changed. No one ever gave me a second glance, almost as if I wasn't there, and I knew that some of them thought I wasn't *all* there. I did nothing to dispel this, as it allowed me to serve my sentence in anonymity.

Arthur Clifton had been a good ganger, one of the best, and he took his job seriously, unlike his best mate, Stan Tancock, whose first port of call on the way home was always the Pig and Whistle. That was on the nights he managed to get home.

I watched Clifton as he disappeared inside the hull of the *Maple Leaf* to make some final checks before the welders moved in to seal the double bottom. It was the raucous sound of the shift horn that must have distracted everyone; one shift coming off, another coming on, and the welders needed to get started promptly if they were going to finish the job by the end of their shift and earn their bonus. No one gave a second thought to whether Clifton had climbed back out of the double bottom, myself included.

We all assumed that he must have heard the blast on the horn and was among the hundreds of dockers trooping through the gates, making their way home. Unlike his brother-in-law, Clifton rarely stopped for a pint at the Pig and Whistle, preferring to go straight to Still House Lane and be with his wife and child. In those days, I didn't know his wife or child, and perhaps I never would have if Arthur Clifton had returned home that night.

The second shift was working flat out when I heard Tancock shouting at the top of his voice. I saw him pointing to the ship's hull. But Haskins, the chief ganger, simply brushed him aside as if he were a tiresome wasp.

Once Tancock realized he was getting nowhere with Haskins, he charged down the gangway and began to run along the quayside in the direction of Barrington House. When Haskins realized where Tancock was headed, he chased after him and had nearly caught up with him by the time he barged through the swing doors into the shipping line's headquarters.

To my surprise, a few minutes later Tancock came running back out of the building, and I was even more surprised when Haskins and the managing director followed close behind. I couldn't imagine what would have convinced Mr Hugo to leave his office after such a brief conversation with Stan Tancock.

I found out the reason soon enough, because the moment Mr Hugo arrived on the dock, he gave orders for the entire shift to lay down their tools, stop working and remain silent, as if it were Remembrance Sunday. And indeed, a minute later, Haskins ordered them all back to work.

That was when it first occurred to me that Arthur Clifton might still be inside the double bottom. But surely no man could be so callous as to walk away if he'd thought, even for a moment, that someone might be trapped alive in a steel grave of their own making.

When the welders went back to work, Mr Hugo spoke to Tancock again before Tancock trooped off through the dock-yard gates and out of sight. I looked back to see if Haskins was pursuing him again, but he was clearly more interested in pushing his men to their limits to recover lost time, like a galley master driving his slaves. A moment later, Mr Hugo walked down the gangway, climbed back into his car and drove off to Barrington House.

The next time I looked out of my carriage window I saw Tancock running back through the gates and once again charging towards Barrington House. This time he didn't reappear for at least half an hour, and when he did, he was no longer red-cheeked and pulsating with rage, but appeared far calmer. I decided he must have found Clifton and was simply letting Mr Hugo know.

I looked up at Mr Hugo's office and saw him standing by the window watching Tancock as he left the yard. He didn't move away from the window until he was out of sight. A few minutes later Mr Hugo came out of the building, walked across to his car and drove away.

I wouldn't have given the matter another thought if Arthur Clifton had clocked in for the morning shift, but he didn't, nor did he ever again.

The following morning, a Detective Inspector Blakemore paid me a visit in my carriage. You can often judge the character of a person by the way he treats his fellow men. Blakemore was one of those rare people who could see beyond his nose.

'You say that you saw Stanley Tancock leaving Barrington House between seven and seven thirty yesterday evening?'

'Yes, I did,' I told him.

'Did he appear to be in a hurry, or anxious, or attempting to slip away unnoticed?'

'On the contrary,' I said. 'I remember thinking at the time he looked remarkably carefree given the circumstances.'

'Given the circumstances?' repeated Blakemore.

'Only an hour or so earlier, he'd been protesting that his mate Arthur Clifton was trapped in the double bottom of the *Maple Leaf*, and they were doing nothing to help him.'

Blakemore wrote down my words in his notebook.

'Do you have any idea where Tancock went after that?'

'No,' I replied. 'When I last saw him he was walking out of the gates with an arm around one of his mates.'

'Thank you, sir,' said the detective inspector. 'That's been most helpful.' It had been a long time since anyone had called me sir. 'Would you be willing, at your own convenience, to come down to the station and make a written statement?'

'I'd prefer not to, inspector,' I told him, 'for personal reasons. But I'd be quite happy to write out a statement that you could collect at any time that suits you.'

'That's good of you, sir.'

The detective inspector opened his briefcase, dug out a

police statement sheet and handed it to me. He then raised his hat and said, 'Thank you, sir, I'll be in touch.' But I never saw him again.

Six weeks later, Stan Tancock was sentenced to three years' imprisonment for theft, with Mr Hugo acting as the prosecution's principal witness. I attended every day of the trial, and there wasn't any doubt in my mind which one of them was the guilty party.

28

'TRY NOT TO FORGET that you saved my life.'

'I've spent the last twenty-six years trying to forget,' Old Jack reminded him.

'But you were also responsible for saving the lives of twenty-four of your fellow West Countrymen. You remain a hero in this city and you seem to be totally unaware of the fact. So I'm bound to ask, Jack, how much longer you intend to go on torturing yourself?'

'Until I can no longer see the eleven men I killed as clearly as I can see you now.'

'But you were doing no more than your duty,' protested Sir Walter.

'That's how I saw it at the time,' admitted Jack.

'So what changed?'

'If I could answer that question,' replied Jack, 'we wouldn't be having this conversation.'

'But you're still capable of doing so much for your fellow men. Take that young friend of yours, for example. You tell me he keeps playing truant, but if he was to discover that you are Captain Jack Tarrant of the Royal Gloucestershire Regiment, winner of the Victoria Cross, don't you think he might listen to you with even more respect?'

'He might also run away again,' replied Jack. 'In any case, I have other plans for young Harry Clifton.'

'Clifton, Clifton . . .' said Sir Walter. 'Why is that name familiar?'

'Harry's father was trapped in the double bottom of the *Maple Leaf*, and no one came to his—'

'That's not what I heard,' said Sir Walter, his tone changing. 'I was told that Clifton left his wife because she was, not to put too fine a point on it, a loose woman.'

'Then you were misled,' said Jack, 'because I can tell you that Mrs Clifton is a delightful and intelligent woman, and any man who was lucky enough to be married to her would never want to leave her.'

Sir Walter looked genuinely shocked, and it was some time before he spoke again. 'Surely you don't believe that cock and bull story about Clifton being trapped in the double bottom?' he asked quietly.

'I'm afraid I do, Walter. You see, I witnessed the whole episode.'

'Then why didn't you say something about it at the time?'

'I did. When I was interviewed by Detective Inspector Blakemore the following day, I told him everything I'd seen, and at his request I made a written statement.'

'Then why wasn't your statement produced in evidence at Tancock's trial?' asked Sir Walter.

'Because I never saw Blakemore again. And when I turned up at the police station, I was told he was no longer in charge of the case and his replacement refused to see me.'

'I had Blakemore taken off the case,' said Sir Walter. 'The damn man was as good as accusing Hugo of giving the money to Tancock, so there wouldn't be an investigation into the Clifton affair.' Old Jack remained silent.

'Let's not talk of this any more,' said Sir Walter. 'I know my son is far from perfect, but I refuse to believe—'

'Or perhaps you don't want to believe,' said Old Jack.

'Jack, whose side are you on?'

'On the side of justice. As you used to be when we first met.'

'And I still am,' said Sir Walter. But he fell silent for some time before adding, 'I want you to make me a promise, Jack. If you ever find out anything about Hugo that you believe would harm the family's reputation, you won't hesitate to tell me.'

'You have my word on it.'

'And you have my word, old friend, that I would not hesitate to hand Hugo over to the police if I thought for one moment that he had broken the law.'

'Let's hope nothing else arises that would make that necessary,' said Old Jack.

'I agree, old friend. Let's talk of more palatable things. Is there anything you are in need of at the moment? I could still . . .'

'Do you have any old clothes that are surplus to requirements?'

Sir Walter raised an eyebrow. 'Dare I ask?'

'No, you daren't,' said Old Jack. 'But I have to visit a particular gentleman, and I'll need to be appropriately dressed.'

◄○►

Old Jack had grown so thin over the years that Sir Walter's clothes hung off him like flax on a distaff, and, like Sir Andrew Aguecheek, he was several inches taller than his old friend, so he had to let down the turn-ups on the trousers and even then they barely reached his ankles. But he felt that the tweed suit, checked shirt and

243

striped tie would serve its purpose for this particular meeting.

As Jack walked out of the dockyard for the first time in years, a few familiar faces turned to give the smartly dressed stranger a second look.

When the school bell rang at four o'clock, Old Jack stepped back into the shadows while the noisy, boisterous nippers poured out through the gates of Merrywood Elementary as if they were escaping from prison.

Mrs Clifton had been waiting there for the past ten minutes, and when Harry saw his mum, he reluctantly allowed her to take him by the hand. A damn fine-looking woman, Old Jack thought as he watched the two of them walking away, Harry, as always, jumping up and down, endlessly chattering, displaying as much energy as Stephenson's *Rocket*.

Old Jack waited until they were out of sight before he crossed the road and walked into the school yard. If he'd been dressed in his old clothes, he would have been stopped by someone in authority long before he reached the front door. He looked up and down the corridor, and spotted a master coming towards him.

'I'm sorry to trouble you,' said Old Jack, 'but I'm looking for Mr Holcombe.'

'Third door on the left, old fellow,' the man said, pointing down the corridor.

When Old Jack came to a halt outside Mr Holcombe's classroom he gave a gentle tap on the door.

'Come in.'

Old Jack opened the door to find a young man, his long black gown covered in chalk dust, seated at a table in front of rows of empty desks, marking exercise books. 'I'm sorry to disturb you,' said Old Jack, 'I'm looking for Mr Holcombe.'

'Then you need look no further,' said the schoolmaster, putting down his pen.

'My name is Tar,' he said as he stepped forward, 'but my friends call me Jack.'

Holcombe's face lit up. 'I do believe you're the man Harry Clifton goes off to visit most mornings.'

'I fear I am,' admitted Old Jack. 'I apologize.'

'No need,' said Holcombe. 'I only wish I had the same influence over him that you do.'

'That's why I came to see you, Mr Holcombe. I'm convinced that Harry's an exceptional child and should be given every chance to make the best of his talents.'

'I couldn't agree with you more,' said Holcombe. 'And I suspect he has one talent even you don't know about.'

'And what might that be?'

'He has the voice of an angel.'

'Harry's no angel,' said Old Jack with a grin.

'I quite agree, but it may turn out to be our best chance of breaking down his defences.'

'What do you have in mind?' asked Old Jack.

'There's a possibility he might just be tempted to join the choir at Holy Nativity. So if you were able to convince him to come to school more often, I know I can teach him to read and write.'

'Why's that so important for a church choir?'

'It's compulsory at Holy Nativity, and Miss Monday, the choir mistress, refuses to make any exceptions to the rule.'

'Then I'll just have to make sure the boy attends your lessons, won't I?' said Old Jack.

'You could do more than that. On the days he doesn't come to school, you could teach him yourself.'

'But I'm not qualified to teach anyone.'

'Harry Clifton is not impressed by qualifications, and we both know that he listens to you. Perhaps we could work as a team.'

'But if Harry were to find out what we were up to, neither of us would ever see him again.'

'How well you know him,' said the schoolmaster with a sigh. 'We'll just have to make sure he doesn't find out.'

'That may prove something of a challenge,' said Old Jack, 'but I'm willing to give it a try.'

'Thank you, sir,' said Mr Holcombe. The schoolmaster paused before adding, 'I wonder if I might be allowed to shake hands with you.' Old Jack looked surprised as the schoolmaster thrust out his hand. Old Jack shook it warmly. 'And may I say it has been an honour to meet you, Captain Tarrant.'

Old Jack looked horrified. 'How could you possibly . . .'

'My father has a picture of you that still hangs on the wall in our front room.'

'But why?' asked Old Jack.

'You saved his life, sir.'

◨

Harry's visits to Old Jack became less frequent during the next few weeks, until the only time they met was on a Saturday morning. Old Jack knew that Mr Holcombe must have succeeded in his plan when Harry asked him if he would come to Holy Nativity the following Sunday to hear him sing.

On Sunday morning, Old Jack rose early, used Sir Walter's private cloakroom on the fifth floor of Barrington House to have a shower, a recent invention, and even trimmed his beard, before putting on the other suit Sir Walter had given him.

Arriving at Holy Nativity just before the service

began, he slipped into the back row and took a seat at the end of the pew. He spotted Mrs Clifton in the third row, sitting between what could only have been her mother and father. As for Miss Monday, he could have picked her out in a congregation of a thousand.

Mr Holcombe had not been exaggerating about the quality of Harry's voice. It was as good as anything he could remember from his days at Wells Cathedral. As soon as the boy opened his mouth to sing *Lead Me, Lord*, Old Jack was left in no doubt that his protégé had an exceptional gift.

Once the Reverend Watts had given his final blessing, Old Jack slipped back out of the church and quickly made his way to the docks. He would have to wait until the following Saturday before he could tell the boy how much he'd enjoyed his singing.

As he walked back, Old Jack recalled Sir Walter's reproach. 'You could do so much more for Harry if you would only give up this self-denial.' He thought carefully about Sir Walter's words but he wasn't yet ready to remove the shackles of guilt. He did, however, know a man who could change Harry's life, a man who had been with him on that dreadful day, a man he hadn't spoken to for more than twenty-five years. A man who taught at a school that supplied St Mary Redcliffe with choristers. Unfortunately Merrywood Elementary was not a natural recruiting ground for its annual choral scholarship, so the man would have to be guided in the right direction.

Old Jack's only fear was that Lieutenant Frobisher might not remember him.

29

OLD JACK WAITED until Hugo had left Barrington House, but it was another half an hour before the lights finally went out in Miss Potts's room.

Jack stepped out of the railway carriage and began to walk slowly towards Barrington House, aware that he had only half an hour before the cleaning ladies came on duty. He slipped into the unlit building and climbed the stairs to the fifth floor; after twenty-five years of Sir Walter turning a blind eye, like a cat he could find his way to the door marked 'Managing Director' in the dark.

He sat down at Hugo's desk. He switched on the light; if anyone noticed it was on, they would simply assume Miss Potts was working late. He thumbed through the telephone directory until he came to the 'St's: Andrew's, Bartholomew's, Beatrice's, Bede's.

He picked up a telephone for the first time in his life, not quite sure what to do next. A voice came on the line. 'Number please?'

'TEM 8612,' said Jack, his forefinger resting just below the number.

'Thank you, sir.' As he waited, Old Jack became more nervous by the minute. What would he say if someone else came on the line? He'd just put the phone down. He took a piece of paper out of his pocket, unfolded it and laid it out on the desk in front of him. Next, he heard a ringing tone, followed by a click, then a man's voice. 'Frobisher House.'

'Is that Noel Frobisher?' he asked, recalling the tradition that each house at St Bede's was named after the housemaster of the day. He looked down at his script; each line had been carefully prepared and endlessly rehearsed.

'Speaking,' said Frobisher, clearly surprised to hear a voice he didn't recognize addressing him by his Christian name. A long silence followed. 'Is there anyone there?' Frobisher asked, sounding a little irritated.

'Yes, it's Captain Jack Tarrant.'

There was an even longer silence, before Frobisher eventually said, 'Good evening, sir.'

'Forgive me for calling at this late hour, old fellow, but I need to seek your advice.'

'Not at all, sir. It's a great privilege to speak to you after all these years.'

'Kind of you to say so,' said Old Jack. 'I'll try not to waste too much of your time, but I need to know if St Bede's still supplies St Mary Redcliffe with trebles for its choir?'

'We do indeed, sir. Despite so many changes in this modern world, that's one tradition that remains constant.'

'And in my day,' said Old Jack, 'the school awarded a choral scholarship each year to a treble who showed exceptional talent.'

'We still do, sir. In fact, we will be considering applications for the position in the next few weeks.'

'From any school in the county?'

'Yes, from any school that can produce a treble of outstanding quality. But they must also have a solid academic grounding.'

'Well, if that's the case,' said Old Jack, 'I would like to submit a candidate for your consideration.'

'Of course, sir. Which school is the boy attending at the moment?'

'Merrywood Elementary.'

Another long silence followed. 'I have to admit that it would be the first time we've had an applicant from that particular school. Do you by any chance know the name of its music master?'

'It doesn't have a music master,' said Old Jack, 'but you should get in touch with the boy's teacher, Mr Holcombe, who will introduce you to his choir mistress.'

'May I ask the boy's name?' said Frobisher.

'Harry Clifton. If you want to hear him sing, I recommend you attend Matins at Holy Nativity Church this Sunday.'

'Will you be there, sir?'

'No,' said Old Jack.

'How do I get in touch with you once I've heard the boy sing?' asked Frobisher.

'You don't,' said Old Jack firmly, and put the phone down. As he folded up his script and placed it back in his pocket, he could have sworn he heard footsteps crunching across the gravel outside. He quickly switched off the light, slipped out of Mr Hugo's office and into the corridor.

He heard a door open, and voices on the stairs. The last thing he needed was to be found on the fifth floor, which was strictly out of bounds to anyone other than the company's executives and Miss Potts. He wouldn't want to embarrass Sir Walter.

He began to walk quickly down the stairs. He'd reached the third floor when he saw Mrs Nettles heading towards him, a mop in one hand, a bucket in the other, a woman he didn't recognize by her side.

'Good evening, Mrs Nettles,' said Old Jack. 'And what a fine evening it is to be doing my rounds.'

'Evenin', Old Jack,' she replied as she ambled past him. Once he had turned the corner, he stopped and listened attentively. 'That's Old Jack,' he heard Mrs Nettles say. 'The so-called night watchman. He's completely crackers, but quite harmless. So if you come across him, just ignore him . . .' Old Jack chuckled as her voice faded with each step she took.

As he strolled back towards the railway carriage, he wondered how long it would be before Harry came to seek his advice on whether he should enter his name for a choral scholarship to St Bede's.

30

HARRY KNOCKED ON the carriage door, strolled in and took the seat opposite Old Jack in first class.

During term time at St Bede's, Harry had only been able to see Old Jack regularly on Saturday mornings. Jack had returned the compliment by attending Matins at St Mary Redcliffe, where from the back pew he enjoyed watching Mr Frobisher and Mr Holcombe beam with pride at his protégé.

In the school holidays, Old Jack could never be sure exactly when Harry was going to turn up because he treated the railway carriage like a second home. Whenever he returned to St Bede's at the beginning of a new term, Old Jack missed the boy's company. He was touched when Mrs Clifton described him as the father Harry never had. In truth, Harry was the son he'd always wanted.

'Finished your paper round early?' said Old Jack, rubbing his eyes and blinking, when Harry strolled into the carriage that Saturday morning.

'No, you just dozed off, old man,' said Harry, passing him a copy of the previous day's *Times*.

'And you're getting cheekier by the day, young man,' Old Jack said with a grin. 'So, how's the paper round working out?'

'Good. I think I'm going to be able to save enough money to buy my mum a watch.'

'A sensible present, considering your mother's new job. But can you afford it?'

'I've already saved four shillings,' said Harry. 'I reckon I'll have about six by the end of the holidays.'

'Have you chosen the watch you want?'

'Yes. It's in Mr Deakins's display cabinet, but it won't be there for much longer,' said Harry, grinning.

Deakins. A name Old Jack could never forget. 'How much is it?' he asked.

'No idea,' said Harry. 'I'm not going to ask Mr Deakins until the day before I go back to school.'

Old Jack wasn't sure how to tell the boy that six shillings wasn't going to be enough to buy a watch, so he changed the subject. 'I hope the paper round isn't stopping you from studying. I'm sure I don't have to remind you that the exams are getting closer by the day.'

'You're worse than the Frob,' said Harry, 'but you'll be pleased to learn that I'm spending two hours every morning in the library with Deakins, and another two most afternoons.'

'*Most* afternoons?'

'Well, Giles and I do occasionally go to the flicks, and as Gloucestershire are playing Yorkshire at the county ground next week, it will be a chance to see Herbert Sutcliffe batting.'

'You'll miss Giles when he goes to Eton,' said Old Jack.

'He's still working on his father to let him join me and Deakins at BGS.'

'Deakins and me,' said Old Jack. 'And be warned, if Mr Hugo has made up his mind, it will take more than Giles to shift him.'

'Mr Barrington doesn't like me,' said Harry, taking Old Jack by surprise.

'What makes you say that?'

'He treats me differently from the other boys at St Bede's. It's as if I'm not good enough to be a friend of his son.'

'You're going to have to face that problem all your life, Harry,' said Old Jack. 'The English are the biggest snobs on earth, and most of the time without reason. The lesser the talent, the bigger the snob, in my experience. It's the only way the so-called upper classes can hope to survive. Be warned, my boy, they don't care for upstarts like you who barge into their club without an invitation.'

'But you don't treat me like that,' said Harry.

'That's because I'm not upper class,' said Old Jack, laughing.

'Perhaps not, but my mum says you're first class,' said Harry, 'so that's what I want to be.'

It didn't help that Old Jack couldn't tell Harry the real reason Mr Hugo was always so off-hand. He sometimes wished he hadn't been in the wrong place at the wrong time, and witnessed what had really happened the day the boy's father died.

'Have you fallen asleep again, old man?' said Harry. 'Because I can't hang around chatting to you all day. I promised my mum I'd meet her at Clarks in the Broad because she wants to buy me a new pair of shoes. Not that I can see what's wrong with the pair I've got.'

'Special lady, your mum,' said Old Jack.

'That's why I'm buying her a watch,' said Harry.

◄○►

The bell above the door rang as he entered the shop. Old Jack hoped that enough time had passed to ensure that Private Deakins wouldn't remember him.

'Good morning, sir. How can I help you?'

Old Jack couldn't fail to recognize Mr Deakins immediately. He smiled and walked across to the display cabinet and studied the two watches on the top shelf. 'I just need to know the price of this Ingersoll.'

'The lady's or the gentleman's model, sir?' asked Mr Deakins, coming out from behind the counter.

'The lady's,' said Old Jack.

Deakins unlocked the cabinet with his one hand, deftly removed the watch from its stand, checked the label and said, 'Sixteen shillings, sir.'

'Good,' said Old Jack, and placed a ten-bob note on the counter. Mr Deakins looked even more puzzled. 'When Harry Clifton asks you how much the watch is, Mr Deakins, please tell him it's six shillings, because that's how much he will have saved by the time he stops working for you, and I know he's hoping to buy it as a present for his mother.'

'You must be Old Jack,' said Deakins. 'He'll be so touched that you . . .'

'But you won't ever tell him,' said Old Jack, looking Mr Deakins in the eye. 'I want him to believe that the price of the watch is six shillings.'

'I understand,' said Mr Deakins, placing the watch back on the stand.

'And how much is the man's watch?'

'One pound.'

'Would you allow me to put down another ten bob as a deposit, and then give you half a crown a week for the next month until I've paid off the full amount?'

'That is quite acceptable, sir. But wouldn't you like to try it on first?'

'No, thank you,' said Old Jack. 'It's not for me. I'm going to give it to Harry when he wins a scholarship to Bristol Grammar School.'

'I had the same thought,' said Mr Deakins, 'should my son Algy be fortunate enough to win one.'

'Then you'd better order another one pretty quickly,' said Old Jack, 'because Harry tells me your son's a racing certainty.'

Mr Deakins laughed, and took a closer look at Old Jack. 'Have we met before, sir?'

'I don't think so,' said Old Jack, and left the shop without another word.

31

IF MUHAMMAD WON'T COME to the mountain ...
Old Jack smiled to himself as he rose to greet Mr
Holcombe and offered him a seat.

'Would you care to join me in the buffet car for a
cup of tea?' Old Jack asked. 'Mrs Clifton was kind
enough to supply me with a quite excellent packet of
Earl Grey.'

'No, thank you sir,' said Holcombe, 'I've only just
had breakfast.'

'So, the boy just missed out on a scholarship,' said
Old Jack, assuming that was what the schoolmaster had
come to see him about.

'Failed is how Harry looks upon it,' said Holcombe,
'despite coming seventeenth out of three hundred, and
being offered a place in the school's A stream this
September.'

'But will he be able to accept the offer? It will place
an extra financial burden on his mother.'

'As long as there are no unexpected bombshells, she
should be able to get Harry through the next five years.'

'Even so, Harry won't be able to afford the little
extras most of the other boys will take for granted.'

'Possibly, but I have managed to cover some of his
sundry expenses from the school's list, so he'll be able

to consider at least two of the three extra-curricular activities he's keen to sign up for.'

'Let me guess,' said Old Jack. 'The choir, the theatre club and . . . ?'

'Art appreciation,' said Holcombe. 'Miss Monday and Miss Tilly are taking responsibility for any trips the choir might make, I'm covering the theatre club and . . .'

'So I get art appreciation,' said Old Jack. 'His new passion. I can still hold my own with Harry when it comes to Rembrandt and Vermeer, even this new chap, Matisse. Now he's trying to get me interested in a Spaniard called Picasso, but I can't see it myself.'

'I've never heard of him,' admitted Holcombe.

'And I doubt if you ever will,' said Old Jack, 'but don't tell Harry I said so.' He picked up a small tin box, opened it, and took out three notes and almost all the coins he possessed.

'No, no,' said Holcombe, 'that isn't the reason I came to see you. In fact, I plan to visit Mr Craddick later this afternoon, and I'm confident he'll—'

'I think you'll find that I take precedence over Mr Craddick,' said Old Jack, handing across the money.

'That's very generous of you.'

'Money well spent,' said Old Jack, 'even if it is the widow's mite. At least my father would approve,' he added as an afterthought.

'Your father?' repeated Holcombe.

'He's the resident canon at Wells Cathedral.'

'I had no idea,' said Holcombe. 'So at least you're able to visit him from time to time.'

'Sadly not. I fear I am a modern prodigal son,' said Old Jack. Not wishing to go any further down that road, he said, 'So tell me, young man, why did you want to see me?'

'I can't remember the last occasion anyone called me "young man".'

'Just be grateful that anyone still does,' said Old Jack.

Holcombe laughed. 'I've got a couple of tickets for the school play, *Julius Caesar*. As Harry is performing, I thought you might like to join me for the opening night.'

'I knew he was auditioning,' said Old Jack. 'What part did he get?'

'He's playing Cinna,' said Holcombe.

'Then we'll know him by his gait.'

Holcombe bowed low. 'Does that mean you'll join me?'.

'I fear not,' said Old Jack, raising a hand. 'It's extremely kind of you to think of me, Holcombe, but I'm not yet ready for a live performance, even as just a member of the audience.'

◄○►

Old Jack was disappointed to miss Harry's performance in the school play and had to be satisfied with being told the boy's version of how he had performed. The following year, when Holcombe suggested that perhaps Old Jack should attend because Harry's roles were getting bigger, he nearly gave in, but it wasn't until Harry played Puck, a year later, that he finally allowed the dream a reality.

Although he was still fearful of large crowds, Old Jack had decided that he would slip into the back of the school hall, where no one would see him or, even worse, recognize him.

It was while he was trimming his beard in the fifth-floor washroom of Barrington House that he noticed the screaming headline in a copy of the local rag that someone had left behind. *Tilly's tea shop burnt to the ground. Arson suspected.* When he saw the photograph below it, he felt sick; Mrs Clifton was standing on the pavement surrounded by her staff, surveying the burnt-out remains of the shop. *Turn to page 11 for full story.* Old Jack obeyed the instruction, but there was no page 11.

He quickly left the washroom, hoping to find the missing page on Miss Potts's desk. He wasn't surprised to find that her desk was clear and her wastepaper basket had been emptied. He tentatively opened the door to the managing director's office, looked inside and spotted the missing page laid out on Mr Hugo's desk. He sat down in the high-backed leather chair and began to read.

Jack's immediate reaction once he'd finished was to wonder if Harry would have to leave school.

The report noted that unless the insurance company paid the full amount on her premium, Mrs Clifton would be facing bankruptcy. The reporter went on to say that a spokesman for the Bristol and West of England had made it clear that the company wouldn't be paying out a brass farthing until the police had eliminated all suspects from their enquiries. What else could possibly go wrong for the poor woman, Old Jack wondered.

The reporter had been careful not to refer to Maisie by name, but Old Jack wasn't in any doubt why her photograph was so prominently displayed on the front page. He continued to read the article. When he discovered that Detective Inspector Blakemore was in charge of the case, he felt a little more hopeful. It wouldn't take that particular gentleman long to work out that Mrs Clifton built things up; she didn't burn them down.

As Old Jack placed the newspaper back on Mr Hugo's desk, he noticed a letter for the first time. He would have ignored it, none of his business, if he hadn't seen the name 'Mrs Clifton' in the first paragraph.

He began to read the letter, and found it hard to believe it was Hugo Barrington who had put up the five hundred pounds that had made it possible for Mrs Clifton to purchase Tilly's. Why would he want to help Maisie, he wondered. Was it possible he felt some remorse about the death of her husband? Or did he feel ashamed that he had sent an innocent man to prison for a crime he had not committed? Certainly he had given Tancock his old job back the moment he was released. Old Jack began to wonder if he should perhaps give Hugo the benefit of the doubt. He recalled Sir Walter's words: 'He's not all bad, you know.'

He read the letter once again. It was from Mr Prendergast, the manager of the National Provincial Bank, who wrote that he had been pressing the insurance company to fulfil its contractual obligations and recompense Mrs Clifton for the full value of the policy, which was £600. Mrs Clifton, Prendergast pointed out, was the innocent party, and Detective Inspector Blakemore had recently informed the bank that she no longer played any part in his enquiries.

In the final paragraph of his letter, Prendergast suggested that he and Barrington should meet in the near future to resolve the matter, so that Mrs Clifton could receive the full amount she was entitled to. Old Jack looked up when the little clock on the desk chimed seven times.

He switched off the light, ran into the corridor and down the stairs. He didn't want to be late for Harry's performance.

32

WHEN OLD JACK got home later that night, he picked up a copy of *The Times* Harry had left for him earlier in the week. He never bothered with the personal ads on the front page as he didn't need a new bowler hat, a pair of suspenders or a first edition of *Wuthering Heights*.

He turned the page to find a photo of King Edward VIII, enjoying a yachting holiday in the Mediterranean. Standing by his side was an American woman called Mrs Simpson. The report was couched in ambiguous terms, but even the Thunderer was finding it hard to support the young King in his desire to marry a divorced woman. It made Old Jack sad, because he admired Edward, especially after his visit to the Welsh miners when he had so clearly been affected by their plight. But as his old nanny used to say, there'll be tears before bedtime.

Old Jack then spent some considerable time reading a report on the Tariff Reform Bill, which had just passed its second reading in the House, despite the firebrand Winston Churchill declaring that it was neither 'fish nor fowl', and no one would benefit from it, including the government, when it came to an election. He couldn't wait to hear Sir Walter's unexpurgated views on that particular subject.

He turned a page to learn that the British Broadcasting Corporation had made its first television broadcast from Alexandra Palace. This was a concept he couldn't begin to comprehend. How could a picture be beamed into your home? He didn't even have a radio, and had absolutely no desire to own a television.

He moved on to the sports pages, to find a photograph of an elegantly dressed Fred Perry under the headline, *Three times Wimbledon champion tipped to win the American Open*. The tennis correspondent went on to suggest that some of the foreign competitors might be wearing shorts at Forest Hills, something else Jack couldn't come to terms with.

As he did whenever he read *The Times*, Old Jack saved the obituaries till last. He'd reached that age when men younger than himself were dying, and not just in wars.

When he turned the page, the colour drained from his face, and he experienced an overwhelming sadness. He took his time reading the obituary of the Reverend Thomas Alexander Tarrant, Resident Canon of Wells Cathedral, described in the headline as a godly man. When Old Jack had finished reading his father's obituary, he felt ashamed.

◄o►

'Seven pounds four shillings?' repeated Old Jack. 'But I thought you got a cheque for six hundred pounds from the Bristol and West of England Insurance Company, "in full and final settlement", if I recall the exact words.'

'I did,' said Maisie, 'but by the time I'd paid back the original loan, the compound interest on that loan, as well as bank charges, I ended up with seven pounds and four shillings.'

'I'm so naive,' said Old Jack. 'And to think that for a

moment, just a moment, I actually thought Barrington was trying to be helpful.'

'You're not half as naive as me,' said Maisie. 'Because if I had thought, even for one moment, that man was involved, I would never have taken a penny of his money, and because I did, I've lost everything. Even my job at the hotel.'

'But why?' asked Old Jack. 'Mr Frampton always said you were irreplaceable.'

'Well, it seems I'm not any more. When I asked him why he'd sacked me, he refused to give a reason, other than to say he'd received a complaint about me from an "unimpeachable source". It can't be a coincidence that I was sacked the day after that "unimpeachable source" dropped into the Royal Hotel for a chat with the manager.'

'Did you see Barrington going into the hotel?' asked Old Jack.

'No, I didn't, but I saw him coming out. Don't forget, I was hiding in the back of his car, waiting for him.'

'Of course,' said Old Jack. 'So what happened when you confronted him about Harry?'

'While we were in the car,' said Maisie, 'he virtually admitted to being responsible for Arthur's death.'

'He finally came clean after all these years?' said Old Jack in disbelief.

'Not exactly,' said Maisie. 'More a slip of the tongue, but when I left the envelope with the invoice for next term's fees on the front seat of his car, he put it in his pocket and said he'd see what he could do to help.'

'And you fell for it?'

'Hook, line and sinker,' admitted Maisie, 'because when he stopped the car he even got out to open the back door for me. But the moment I stepped out, he knocked me to the ground, tore up the bill and drove off.'

'Is that how you got the black eye?'

Maisie nodded. 'And he also warned me he'd have me committed to a mental asylum if I even thought about contacting his wife.'

'That's nothing more than a bluff,' said Old Jack, 'because even he couldn't get away with that.'

'You may be right,' said Maisie, 'but it's not a risk I'm willing to take.'

'And if you did tell Mrs Barrington that her husband was responsible for Arthur's death,' said Old Jack, 'all he'd have to do is let her know you're Stan Tancock's sister, and she'd dismiss it out of hand.'

'Possibly,' said Maisie. 'But she wouldn't dismiss it out of hand if I told her her husband might be Harry's father . . .'

Old Jack was stunned into silence as he tried to take in the implications of Maisie's words. 'I'm not only naive,' he eventually managed, 'but I'm also bone stupid. Hugo Barrington won't care if his wife does or doesn't believe he was involved in your husband's death. His greatest fear is Harry ever finding out that he might be his father . . .'

'But I would never tell Harry,' said Maisie. 'The last thing I'd want is for him to spend the rest of his life wondering who his father is.'

'That is precisely what Barrington is banking on. And now he's broken you, he'll be hell-bent on destroying Harry.'

'But why?' asked Maisie. 'Harry's never done him any harm.'

'Of course he hasn't, but if Harry were able to prove that he is Hugo Barrington's eldest son, he might just be in line to inherit not only the title, but everything that goes with it, and at the same time, Giles would end up with nothing.'

It was Maisie's turn to be speechless.

'So, now we've discovered the real reason Barrington is so keen to have Harry thrown out of the grammar school, perhaps the time has come for me to pay a visit to Sir Walter, and tell him some unpalatable truths about his son.'

'No, please don't do that,' begged Maisie.

'Why not? It might be our one chance of keeping Harry at BGS.'

'Possibly, but it would also guarantee that my brother Stan would get the sack, and God knows what else Barrington is capable of.'

Old Jack didn't reply for some time. Then he said, 'If you won't allow me to tell Sir Walter the truth, I'll have to start crawling around in the sewer that Hugo Barrington currently occupies.'

33

'YOU WANT WHAT?' asked Miss Potts, not sure she'd heard him correctly.

'A private meeting with Mr Hugo,' said Old Jack.

'And am I permitted to enquire what the purpose of this meeting might be?' she said, making no attempt to hide the sarcasm in her voice.

'His son's future.'

'Wait here for a moment. I'll see if Mr Barrington is willing to see you.'

Miss Potts knocked gently on the managing director's door and disappeared inside. She returned a moment later with a surprised look on her face.

'Mr Barrington will see you now,' she said, holding open the door.

Old Jack couldn't resist a smile as he strolled past her. Hugo Barrington looked up from behind his desk. He didn't offer the old man a seat, and made no attempt to shake hands with him.

'What possible interest can you have in Giles's future?' asked Barrington.

'None,' admitted Old Jack. 'It's your other son whose future I'm interested in.'

'What the hell are you talking about?' said Barrington, a little too loudly.

'If you didn't know who I was talking about, you wouldn't have agreed to see me,' replied Old Jack contemptuously.

The colour drained from Barrington's face. Old Jack even wondered if he was going to faint. 'What do you want from me?' he finally said.

'All your life you've been a trader,' said Old Jack. 'I am in possession of something you'll want to trade.'

'And what could that possibly be?'

'The day after Arthur Clifton mysteriously disappeared and Stan Tancock was arrested for a crime he didn't commit, I was asked by Detective Inspector Blakemore to make a statement of everything I'd witnessed that evening. Because you had Blakemore taken off the case, that statement remains in my possession. I have a feeling it would make very interesting reading if it were to fall into the wrong hands.'

'I think you'll find that's blackmail,' said Barrington, spitting out the words, 'for which you can go to prison for a very long time.'

'Some might consider it nothing more than a matter of civic duty for such a document to enter the public domain.'

'And who do you imagine would be interested in the ravings of an old man? Certainly not the press, once my lawyers have explained the libel laws to them. And as the police closed the file some years ago, I can't see the chief constable going to the trouble and expense of reopening it on the word of an old man who might be considered at best eccentric and at worst mad. So I'm bound to ask, who else do you have in mind to share your preposterous allegations with?'

'Your father,' said Old Jack, bluffing, but then Barrington didn't know about his promise to Maisie.

Barrington slumped back in his chair, only too aware of the influence Old Jack had with his father, even if he had never understood why. 'How much do you expect me to pay for this document?'

'Three hundred pounds.'

'That's daylight robbery!'

'It's no more and no less than the amount required to cover the fees and any little extras that will allow Harry Clifton to remain at Bristol Grammar School for the next two years.'

'Why don't I just pay his fees at the beginning of each term, as I do for my own son?'

'Because you would stop paying one of your sons' fees the moment you got your hands on my statement.'

'You'll have to take cash,' said Barrington, taking a key from his pocket.

'No, thank you,' said Old Jack. 'I remember only too well what happened to Stan Tancock after you'd handed him your thirty pieces of silver. And I have no desire to spend the next three years in prison for a crime I didn't commit.'

'Then I'll have to call the bank if I'm to write out a cheque for such a large amount.'

'Be my guest,' said Old Jack, gesturing towards the phone on Barrington's desk.

Barrington hesitated for a moment before picking up the handset. He waited for a voice to come on the line. 'TEM 3731,' he said.

Another wait, before another voice said, 'Yes?'

'Is that you, Prendergast?'

'No, sir,' said the voice.

'Good, you're just the man I need to speak to,' Barrington replied. 'I'll be sending a Mr Tar around to see you in the next hour, with a cheque for three hundred pounds made payable to Bristol Municipal Charities. Would you see that it's processed immediately, and make sure you phone me straight back.'

'If you want me to ring you back, just say "Yes, that's right," and I'll call in a couple of minutes,' the voice said.

'Yes, that's right,' said Barrington, and put the phone down.

He opened the drawer of his desk, took out a cheque book and wrote the words *Pay Bristol Municipal Charities* and, on a separate line, *Three hundred pounds*. He then signed the cheque and passed it to Old Jack, who studied it carefully and nodded.

'I'll just put it in an envelope,' said Barrington. He pressed the buzzer under his desk. Old Jack glanced at Miss Potts as she entered the room.

'Yes, sir?'

'Mr Tar is leaving to go to the bank,' said Barrington, placing the cheque in the envelope. He sealed it and addressed it to Mr Prendergast, adding the word PRIVATE in bold letters, then handed it to Old Jack.

'Thank you,' said Jack. 'I'll deliver the document to you personally as soon as I get back.'

Barrington nodded, just as the phone on his desk began to ring. He waited for Old Jack to leave the room before he picked it up.

Old Jack decided to take the tram into Bristol, feeling that the expense was justified on such a special occasion. When he walked into the bank twenty minutes later, he told the young man on the reception that he had a letter for Mr Prendergast. The receptionist didn't seem particularly impressed, until Old Jack added, 'It's from Mr Hugo Barrington.'

The young man immediately deserted his post, led Old Jack across the banking hall and down a long corridor to the manager's office. He knocked on the door, opened it and announced, 'This gentleman has a letter from Mr Barrington, sir.'

Mr Prendergast leapt up from behind his desk, shook hands with the old man and ushered him to a seat on the other side of the desk. Old Jack handed the envelope to Prendergast, with the words, 'Mr Barrington asked me to give this to you personally.'

'Yes, of course,' said Prendergast, who immediately recognized the familiar hand of one of his most valued customers. He slit open the envelope and extracted a cheque. He looked at it for a moment, before saying, 'There must be some mistake.'

'There's no mistake,' said Old Jack. 'Mr Barrington would like the full amount to be paid to Bristol Municipal Charities at your earliest convenience, as he instructed you over the phone only half an hour ago.'

'But I haven't spoken to Mr Barrington this morning,' said Prendergast, passing the cheque back to Old Jack.

Old Jack stared in disbelief at a blank cheque. It only took him a few moments to realize that Barrington must have switched the cheques when Miss Potts entered the room. The true genius of his action was to address the envelope to Mr Prendergast and mark it private, thus ensuring it wouldn't be opened until it had been handed to the manager. But the one mystery Jack couldn't fathom was: who had been on the other end of the phone?

Old Jack hurried out of the office without saying another word to Prendergast. He crossed the banking hall and ran out into the street. He only had to wait a few minutes for a tram to the docks. He couldn't have been away for much more than an hour by the time he walked back through the gates and into the dockyard.

A man he didn't recognize was striding towards him. He had a military air about him and Old Jack wondered if the limp had been caused by an injury he'd suffered in the Great War.

Old Jack hurried past him and on down the quayside. He was relieved to see that the carriage door was closed, and when he opened it he was even more pleased to find that everything was just as he'd left it. He sank to his knees and lifted the corner of the carpet, but the police statement was no longer there. Detective Inspector Blakemore would have described the theft as the work of a professional.

34

OLD JACK TOOK his place in the fifth row of the congregation, hoping no one would recognize him. The cathedral was so packed that people who had been unable to find a seat in the side chapels stood in the aisles and were crammed in at the back.

The Bishop of Bath and Wells brought tears to Old Jack's eyes when he talked about his father's unquestioning faith in God, and how, since the premature death of his wife, the canon had devoted himself to serving the community, 'The proof of which,' proclaimed the Bishop, raising his arms to acknowledge the vast congregation, 'can be seen by the number of those present, who have come to honour him from so many walks of life, and to pay their respects.

'And although the man knew no vanity, he could not hide a certain pride in his only son, Jack, whose selfless courage, bravery and willingness to sacrifice his own life in South Africa during the Boer War saved so many of his comrades, and led to him being awarded the Victoria Cross.' He paused, looked down into the fifth row and said, 'And how delighted I am to see him in the congregation today.'

Several people began looking around for a man they had never seen before. Jack bowed his head in shame.

At the end of the service, many members of the congregation came up to tell Captain Tarrant how much they had admired his father. The words 'dedication', 'selflessness', 'generosity' and 'love' fell from everyone's lips.

Jack felt proud of being his father's son, while at the same time ashamed that he had excluded him from his life, in the same way as he had the rest of his fellow men.

As he was leaving, he thought he recognized an elderly gentleman standing by the great gates, clearly waiting to speak to him. The man stepped forward and raised his hat. 'Captain Tarrant?' he enquired with a voice that suggested authority.

Jack returned the compliment. 'Yes, sir?'

'My name is Edwin Trent. I had the privilege of being your father's solicitor, and, I'd like to think, one of his oldest and closest friends.'

Jack shook him warmly by the hand. 'I remember you well, sir. You taught me a love of Trollope and an appreciation of the finer points of spin bowling.'

'It's kind of you to remember,' Trent chuckled. 'I wonder if I might accompany you on your way back to the station?'

'Of course, sir.'

'As you know,' said Trent as they began walking towards the town, 'your father was resident canon of this cathedral for the past nine years. You'll also know that he cared nothing for worldly goods, and shared even the little he had with those less fortunate than himself. If he were to be canonized, he would surely be the patron saint of vagabonds.'

Old Jack smiled. He recalled going to school one morning without breakfast because three tramps were sleeping in the hallway and, to quote his mother, they had eaten them out of house and home.

'So when his will comes to be read,' continued Trent, 'it will show that just as he entered this world with nothing, he has also left it with nothing – other than a thousand friends, that is, which he would have considered a veritable fortune. Before he died, he entrusted me with one small task should you attend his funeral, namely that of handing you the last letter he ever wrote.' He extracted an envelope from an inside pocket of his overcoat and handed it to Old Jack, raised his hat once more and said, 'I have carried out his request, and am proud to have met his son once again.'

'I am obliged, sir. I only wish that I hadn't made it necessary for him to have to write in the first place.' Jack raised his hat and the two men parted.

Old Jack decided that he would not read his father's letter until he was on the train, and had begun the journey back to Bristol. As the engine shunted out of the station, billowing clouds of grey smoke, Jack settled back in a third-class compartment. As a child, he remembered asking his father why he always travelled third class, to which he had replied, 'Because there isn't a fourth class.' It was ironic that, for the past thirty years, Jack had been living in first class.

He took his time unsealing the envelope, and even after he had extracted the letter, he left it folded while he continued to think about his father. No son could have asked for a better mentor or friend. When he looked back on his life, all his actions, judgements and decisions were nothing more than pale imitations of his father's.

When he finally unfolded the letter, another flood of memories came rushing back the moment he saw the familiar bold, copperplate hand in jet-black ink. He began to read.

The Close
Wells Cathedral
Wells, Somerset

26th August, 1936

My beloved son,

If you were kind enough to attend my funeral, you must now be reading this letter. Allow me to begin by thanking you for being among the congregation.

Old Jack raised his head and looked out at the passing countryside. He felt guilty once again for treating his father in such an inconsiderate and thoughtless manner, and now it was too late to ask for his forgiveness. His eyes returned to the letter.

When you were awarded the Victoria Cross, I was the proudest father in England, and your citation still hangs above my desk to this very day. But then, as the years passed, my happiness turned to sorrow, and I asked our Lord what I had done that I should be so punished by losing not only your dear mother, but also you, my only child.

I accept that you must have had some noble purpose for turning your head and your heart against this world, but I wish you had shared your reason for so doing with me. But, should you read this letter, perhaps you might grant me one last wish.

Old Jack removed the handkerchief from his top pocket and wiped his eyes before he was able to continue reading.

*God gave you the remarkable gift of leadership and
the ability to inspire your fellow men, so I beg you
not to go to your grave knowing that when the time
comes for you to face your maker, you will, as in the
parable Matthew 25, v14–30, have to confess that
you buried the one talent He gave you.*

*Rather, use that gift for the benefit of your
fellow men, so that when your time comes, as it
surely must, and those same men attend your
funeral, the Victoria Cross will not be the only thing
they remember when they hear the name Jack
Tarrant.*

Your loving father

'Are you all right, my luv?' asked a lady who had
moved from the other side of the carriage to sit next to
Old Jack.

'Yes, thank you,' he said, the tears streaming down
his face. 'It's just that I was released from prison today.'

GILES BARRINGTON

1936–1938

35

I was thrilled when I saw Harry walk through the school gates on the first day of term. I'd spent the summer hols at our villa in Tuscany, so I wasn't in Bristol when Tilly's was burnt to the ground and didn't find out about it until I returned to England the weekend before term began. I had wanted Harry to join us in Italy, but my father wouldn't hear of it.

I've never met anyone who didn't like Harry, with the exception of my father, who won't even allow his name to be mentioned in the house. I once asked Mama if she could explain why he felt so strongly, but she didn't seem to know any more than I did.

I didn't press the point with my old man, as I've never exactly covered myself in glory in his eyes. I nearly got myself expelled from my prep school for stealing – heaven knows how he managed to fix that – and after that I let him down by failing to get into Eton. I told Papa when I came out of the exam that I couldn't have tried harder, which was the truth. Well, half the truth. I would have got away with it if my co-conspirator had only kept his mouth shut. At least it taught me a simple lesson: if you make a deal with a fool, don't be surprised when they act foolishly.

My co-conspirator was the Earl of Bridport's son, Percy. He was facing an even greater dilemma than I was, because seven generations of Bridports had been educated at Eton, and it was looking as if young Percy was going to ruin that rather fine batting average.

Eton has been known to bend the rules when it comes to members of the aristocracy and will occasionally allow a stupid boy to darken its doors, which is why I selected Percy for my little subterfuge in the first place. It was after I overheard the Frob saying to another beak, 'If Bridport was any brighter, he'd be a half-wit,' that I knew I didn't need to look any further for my accomplice.

Percy was as desperate to be offered a place at Eton as I was to be rejected, so I saw this as no more than an opportunity for both of us to achieve our purpose.

I didn't discuss my plan with Harry or Deakins. Harry would undoubtedly have disapproved, he's such a morally upright fellow, and Deakins wouldn't have been able to understand why anyone would want to fail an exam.

On the day before the examination was due to take place my father drove me to Eton in his swish new Bugatti, which could do a hundred miles an hour, and once we hit the A4 he proved it. We spent the night at the Swann Arms, the same hotel in which he had stayed over twenty years before when he took the entrance exam. Over dinner, Papa didn't leave me in any doubt how keen he was that I should go to Eton and I nearly had a change of heart at the last moment, but I had given my word to Percy Bridport, and felt I couldn't let him down.

Percy and I had shaken hands on the deal back at St Bede's, agreeing that when we entered the examination hall, we would give the recorder the other's name. I rather enjoyed being addressed as 'my lord' by all and sundry, even if it was only for a few hours.

The examination papers were not as demanding as the ones I'd sat a fortnight earlier for Bristol Grammar, and I felt I'd done more than enough to ensure that Percy would be returning to Eton in September. However, they were difficult enough for me to feel confident that his lordship would not let me down.

Once we'd handed in our papers and reverted to our true personas, I went off to tea with my pa, in Windsor. When he asked me how it had gone, I told him I'd done the best I possibly could. He seemed satisfied by this, and even began to relax, which only made me feel more guilty. I didn't enjoy the journey back to Bristol, and felt even worse when I got home and my mother asked me the same question.

Ten days later, I received an *I'm sorry to have to inform you* letter from Eton. I had only managed 32 per cent. Percy scored 56 per cent and was offered a place for the Michaelmas term, which delighted his father and was met with incredulity by the Frob.

Everything would have worked out just fine, if Percy hadn't told a friend how he'd managed to get into Eton. The friend told another friend, who told another friend, who told Percy's father. The Earl of Bridport MC, being an honourable man, immediately informed the headmaster of Eton. This resulted in Percy being expelled before he'd even set foot in the place. If it hadn't been for a personal intervention by the Frob, I might have suffered the same fate at Bristol Grammar.

My father tried to convince the headmaster of Eton that it was simply a clerical error, and that, as I'd actually scored 56 per cent in the exam, I should be reinstated in Bridport's place. This piece of logic was rejected by return of post, as Eton wasn't in need of a new cricket pavilion. I duly reported to Bristol Grammar School on the first day of term.

─◄o►─

During my first year, I restored my reputation somewhat by scoring three centuries for the Colts and ended the season being awarded my colours. Harry played Ursula in *Much Ado*

About Nothing, and Deakins was Deakins, so no one was surprised when he won the First Form prize.

During my second year, I became more aware of the financial constraints Harry's mother must be experiencing when I noticed that he was wearing his shoes with the laces undone, and he admitted they were pinching because they were so tight.

So when Tilly's was burnt to the ground only weeks before we were expected to enter the sixth form, I was not altogether surprised to learn that Harry thought he might not be able to stay on at the school. I thought about asking my father if he might be able to help, but Mama told me I would be wasting my time. That's why I was so delighted when I saw him walking through the school gates on the first day of term.

He told me that his mother had begun a new job at the Royal Hotel, working nights, and it was proving to be far more lucrative than she had originally thought possible.

During the next summer hols I would, once again, have liked to invite Harry to join the family in Tuscany, but I knew my father would not consider the idea. But as the Arts Appreciation Society, of which Harry was now secretary, was planning a trip to Rome, we agreed to meet up there, even if it did mean I would have to visit the Villa Borghese.

◄○►

Although we were living in a little bubble of our own down in the West Country, it would have been impossible not to be aware of what was taking place on the continent.

The rise of the Nazis in Germany, and the Fascists in Italy, didn't seem to be affecting the average Englishman, who was still enjoying a pint of cider and a cheese sandwich at his local on a Saturday, before watching, or in my case playing, cricket on the village green in the afternoon. For years this blissful state of affairs had been able to continue because another war with Germany didn't bear thinking about. Our fathers had fought in the war to end all wars, but now the unmentionable seemed to be on everyone's lips.

Harry told me in no uncertain terms that if war was declared, he wouldn't be going to university but would join up immediately, just as his father and uncle had done some twenty years before. My father had 'missed out', as he put it, because unfortunately he was colour-blind, and those in authority thought he'd serve the war effort better by remaining at his post, playing an important role in the docks. Though I've never been quite sure exactly what that important role was.

◄o►

In our final year at BGS, both Harry and I decided to enter our names for Oxford; Deakins had already been offered an open scholarship to Balliol College. I wanted to go to the House, but was informed most politely by the entrance tutor that Christ Church rarely took grammar school boys, so I settled for Brasenose, which had once been described by Bertie Wooster as a college 'where brains are neither here nor there'.

As Brasenose was also the college with the most cricket blues, and I had scored three centuries in my final year as captain of BGS, one of them at Lord's for a Public Schools XI, I felt I must be in with a chance. In fact, my form master, Dr Paget, told me that when I went for my interview they would probably throw a cricket ball at me as I entered the room. If I caught it, I would be offered a place. If I caught it one-handed, a scholarship. This turned out to be apocryphal. However, I'm bound to admit that during drinks with the college principal, he asked me more questions about Hutton than Horace.

There were other highs and lows during my last two years at school: Jesse Owens winning four gold medals at the Olympic Games in Berlin, right under Hitler's nose, was a definite high, while the abdication of Edward VIII because he wished to marry an American divorcee was an undoubted low.

The nation seemed to be divided on whether the King should have abdicated, as were Harry and I. I failed to understand how a man born to be King could be willing to sacrifice the throne to marry a divorced woman. Harry was far more sympathetic to the King's plight, saying that we couldn't begin to understand what the poor man was going through until we fell in love ourselves. I dismissed this as codswallop, until that trip to Rome that was to change both our lives.

36

IF GILES IMAGINED he'd worked hard during his final days at St Bede's, in those last two years at Bristol Grammar School both he and Harry became acquainted with hours only Deakins was familiar with.

Dr Paget, their sixth-form master, told them in no uncertain terms that if they hoped to be offered a place at Oxford or Cambridge, they would have to forget any other activities, as they would need to spend every waking moment preparing for the entrance exams.

Giles was hoping to captain the school's First XI in his final year, while Harry was keen to land the lead in the school play. Dr Paget raised an eyebrow when he heard this, even though *Romeo and Juliet* was the set text for Oxford that year. 'Just be sure you don't sign up for anything else,' he said firmly.

Harry reluctantly resigned from the choir, which gave him two more free evenings a week to study. However, there was one activity no pupil could exempt himself from: every Tuesday and Thursday, at four o'clock, all the boys had to be standing to attention on the parade ground, fully kitted out and ready for inspection as members of the Officer Training Corps.

'Can't allow the Hitler Youth to imagine that if

Germany is foolish enough to declare war on us a second time, we won't be ready for them,' bellowed the RSM.

Every time ex-Regimental Sergeant Major Roberts delivered these words, it sent a shiver through the ranks of schoolboys, who realized as each day passed that it was becoming more and more likely they would be serving on the front line as junior officers in some foreign field, rather than going up to university as under-graduates.

Harry took the RSM's words to heart and was quickly promoted to cadet officer. Giles took them less seriously, knowing that if he was called up, he could, like his father, take the easy way out and remind them of his colour-blindness to avoid coming face to face with the enemy.

Deakins showed little interest in the whole process, declaring with a certainty that brooked no argument, 'You don't need to know how to strip a Bren gun when you're in the intelligence corps.'

By the time the long summer nights began to draw to a close, they were all ready for a holiday before they would return for their final year, at the end of which they would have to face the examiners once again. Within a week of term ending, all three of them had left for their summer break: Giles to join his family at their villa in Tuscany, Harry to Rome with the school's Arts Appreciation Society, while Deakins entombed himself in Bristol Central library, avoiding contact with any other human beings, despite the fact that he'd already been offered a place at Oxford.

◄o►

Over the years, Giles had come to accept that if he wanted to see Harry during the holidays, he had to make sure his father didn't find out what he was up to, otherwise the best-laid schemes of mice and . . . But in order to achieve this, he often had to get his sister Emma to join in the subterfuge, and she never failed to extract her pound of flesh before agreeing to become his accomplice.

'If you take the lead over dinner tonight, I'll follow up,' said Giles once he'd outlined his latest scheme to her.

'Sounds like the natural order of things,' said Emma scornfully.

After the first course had been served, Emma innocently asked her mother if she could possibly take her to the Villa Borghese the following day, as it had been recommended as a must by her art mistress. She was well aware that Mama had already made other plans.

'I'm so sorry, darling,' she said, 'but your father and I are going to lunch with the Hendersons in Arezzo tomorrow. You're most welcome to join us.'

'There's nothing to stop Giles taking you into Rome,' interjected his father from the other end of the table.

'Do I have to?' said Giles, who had just been about to make the same suggestion.

'Yes, you do,' replied his father firmly.

'But what's the point, Pa? By the time we get there, we'll have to turn round and come back. It's hardly worth it.'

'Not if you were to spend the night at the Plaza Hotel. I'll call them first thing in the morning, and book a couple of rooms.'

'Are you sure they're grown up enough for that?' asked Mrs Barrington, sounding a little anxious.

'Giles will be eighteen in a few weeks. It's time he grew up and took some responsibility.' Giles bowed his head as if he had given in meekly.

The following morning, a taxi drove him and Emma

to the local station just in time to catch the early morning train to Rome.

'Be sure to take care of your sister,' were his father's last words before they left the villa.

'I will,' promised Giles as the car drove off.

Several men rose to offer Emma their seat as she entered the carriage, while Giles was left standing for the entire journey. On arrival in Rome, they took a taxi to the Via del Corso, and once they'd booked into their hotel they continued on to the Villa Borghese. Giles was struck by how many young men not much older than himself were in uniform, while almost every pillar and lamp-post they passed displayed a poster of Mussolini.

Once the taxi had dropped them off, they made their way up through the gardens, passing more men in uniform and even more posters of 'Il Duce' before they finally reached the palatial Villa Borghese.

Harry had written to tell Giles they would be setting out on their official tour at ten o'clock. He checked his watch – a few minutes past eleven, with luck the tour would be nearly over. He bought two tickets, handed one to Emma, bounded up the steps to the galleria and went in search of the school party. Emma took her time admiring the Bernini statues that dominated the first four rooms, but then she wasn't in a hurry. Giles went from gallery to gallery until he spotted a group of young men dressed in dark claret jackets and black flannel trousers, who were crowded around a small portrait of an elderly man dressed in a cream silk cassock with a white mitre on his head.

'There they are,' he said, but Emma was nowhere to be seen. Not giving his sister another thought, he headed over to the attentive group. The moment he saw her, he quite forgot the reason he had come to Rome.

'Caravaggio was commissioned to paint this portrait of Pope Paul V in 1605,' she said, with a slight accent. 'You will notice that it was not finished, and that is because the artist had to flee from Rome.'

'Why, miss?' demanded a young boy in the front row, who was clearly determined to take Deakins's place at some time in the future.

'Because he became involved in a drunken brawl, during which he ended up killing a man.'

'Did they arrest him?' asked the same boy.

'No,' said the tour guide, 'Caravaggio always managed to move on to the next city before the forces of justice could catch up with him, but in the end the Holy Father decided to grant him a pardon.'

'Why?' demanded the same boy.

'Because he wanted Caravaggio to carry out several more commissions for him. Some of them are among the seventeen works that can still be seen in Rome today.'

At that moment, Harry spotted Giles gazing in awe in the direction of the painting. He left the group and walked across to join him. 'How long have you been standing there?' he asked.

'Long enough to fall in love,' said Giles, his eyes still fixed on the tour guide.

Harry laughed when he realized it wasn't the painting Giles was staring at, but the elegant, self-assured young woman who was addressing the boys. 'I think she's a bit out of your age group,' said Harry, 'and I suspect even your price range.'

'I'm willing to take that risk,' said Giles as the guide led her little group into the next room. Giles followed obediently and positioned himself so he had a clear view of her, while the rest of the group studied a statue of

Paolina Borghese by Canova, 'arguably the greatest sculptor of all time', she said. Giles wasn't going to disagree with her.

'Well, that brings us to the end of our tour,' she announced. 'But if you have any more questions I will be here for a few more minutes, so don't hesitate to ask.'

Giles didn't hesitate.

Harry watched in amusement as his friend strode up to the young Italian woman and began chatting to her as if they were old friends. Even the little boy from the front row didn't dare to interrupt him. Giles rejoined Harry a few minutes later, a large grin plastered across his face.

'She's agreed to have dinner with me tonight.'

'I don't believe you,' said Harry.

'But a problem has arisen,' he added, ignoring his friend's Doubting Thomas look.

'More than one, I suspect.'

'. . . which can be overcome with your assistance.'

'You need a chaperone to accompany you,' suggested Harry, 'just in case things get out of hand.'

'No, you ass. I want you to take care of my sister while Caterina introduces me to Rome's night-life.'

'Not a hope,' said Harry. 'I didn't come all the way to Rome just to act as your babysitter.'

'But you're my best friend,' pleaded Giles. 'If you won't help me, who else can I turn to?'

'Why don't you try Paolina Borghese? I doubt if she has any plans for tonight.'

'All you have to do is take her out for dinner, and make sure she's in bed by ten.'

'Forgive me for mentioning it, Giles, but I thought you'd come to Rome to have dinner with me?'

'I'll give you a thousand lira if you take her off my

hands. And we can still have breakfast at my hotel in the morning.'

'I'm not that easily bribed.'

'And,' said Giles, playing his trump card, 'I'll also give you my recording of Caruso singing *La Bohème*.'

Harry turned to find a young girl standing by his side.

'By the way,' said Giles, 'this is my sister, Emma.'

'Hello,' said Harry. Turning back to Giles, he said, 'You've got yourself a deal.'

<o>

Harry joined Giles for breakfast at the Palace Hotel the following morning, when his friend greeted him with the same immodest smile he always wore just after he'd scored a century.

'So, how was Caterina?' Harry asked, not wanting to hear his reply.

'Beyond my wildest dreams.'

Harry was about to question him more closely when a waiter appeared by his side. '*Cappuccino, per favore.*' Then he asked, 'So how far did she let you go?'

'All the way,' said Giles.

Harry's mouth fell open, but no words came out. 'Did you . . .'

'Did I what?'

'Did you . . .' Harry tried again.

'Yes?'

'See her naked?'

'Yes, of course.'

'The whole body?'

'Naturally,' said Giles as a cup of coffee was placed in front of Harry.

'The bottom half as well as the top?'

'Everything,' said Giles. 'And I mean everything.'

'Did you touch her breasts?'

'I licked her nipples actually,' said Giles, taking a sip of coffee.

'You did what?'

'You heard me,' said Giles.

'But did you, I mean, did you . . .'

'Yes, I did.'

'How many times?'

'I lost count,' said Giles. 'She was insatiable. Seven, perhaps eight. She just wouldn't let me get to sleep. I'd still be there now if she hadn't had to be at the Vatican museum at ten this morning to lecture the next bunch of brats.'

'But what if she gets pregnant?' said Harry.

'Don't be so naive, Harry. Try to remember she's an Italian.' After another sip of coffee, he asked, 'So, how did my sister behave herself?'

'The food was excellent, and you owe me your Caruso recording.'

'That bad? Well, we can't all be winners.'

Neither of them had noticed Emma enter the room until she was standing by their side. Harry leapt up and offered her his seat. 'Sorry to leave you,' he said, 'but I have to be at the Vatican museum by ten.'

'Give Caterina my love!' shouted Giles as Harry almost ran out of the breakfast room.

Giles waited until Harry was out of sight before he asked his sister, 'So, how did last night go?'

'Could have been worse,' she said, picking up a croissant. 'A bit serious, isn't he?'

'You should meet Deakins.'

Emma laughed. 'Well, at least the food was good. But don't forget, I now own your gramophone.'

37

GILES LATER DESCRIBED IT as the most memorable night of his life – for all the wrong reasons.

The annual play is one of the major events in the Bristol Grammar School calendar, not least because the city boasts a fine theatre tradition, and 1937 was to prove a vintage year.

The school, like so many others in the country, performed one of Shakespeare's set texts for the year. The choice had been between *Romeo and Juliet* and *A Midsummer Night's Dream*. Dr Paget chose the tragedy rather than the comedy, not least because he had a Romeo and he didn't have a Bottom.

For the first time in the school's history, the young ladies of Red Maids' on the other side of the city were invited to audition for the girls' parts, but not before several discussions had taken place with Miss Webb, the headmistress, who had insisted on a set of ground rules that would have impressed a mother superior.

The play was to be performed on three consecutive evenings in the last week of term. As always, the Saturday night was sold out first, because former pupils and the parents of the cast wished to attend the closing night.

Giles was standing anxiously in the foyer checking

his watch every few moments as he waited impatiently for his parents and younger sister to arrive. He hoped that Harry would give another fine performance, and his father would finally come round to accepting him.

The critic from the *Bristol Evening World* had described Harry's performance as 'mature beyond his years', but he had saved the highest praise for Juliet, reporting that he had not seen the death scene performed more movingly even at Stratford.

Giles shook hands with Mr Frobisher as he walked into the foyer. His old housemaster introduced his guest, a Mr Holcombe, before they went through to the great hall to take their seats.

A murmur rippled around the audience when Captain Tarrant walked down the centre aisle and took his place in the front row. His recent appointment as a governor of the school had been met with universal approval. As he leant across to have a word with the chairman of the governors, he spotted Maisie Clifton sitting just a few rows behind. He gave her a warm smile, but didn't recognize the man she was sitting with. The next surprise came when he studied the cast list.

The headmaster and Mrs Barton were among the last members of the audience to enter the great hall. They took their places in the front row alongside Sir Walter Barrington and Captain Tarrant.

Giles was becoming more nervous with each passing minute. He was beginning to wonder if his parents would turn up before the curtain rose.

'I'm so sorry, Giles,' said his mother when they finally appeared. 'It's my fault, I lost track of time,' she added as she and Grace hurried into the hall. His father followed a yard behind and raised his eyebrows when he saw his son. Giles didn't hand him a programme as he wanted it to be a surprise, although he had shared the news with his mother who, like him, hoped her husband would finally treat Harry as if he were a friend of the family, and not an outsider.

The curtain rose only moments after the Barringtons had taken their seats, and a hush of anticipation descended on the packed audience.

When Harry made his first entrance, Giles glanced in his father's direction. As there didn't appear to be any immediate reaction, he began to relax for the first time that evening. But this happy state of affairs only lasted until the ballroom scene, when Romeo, and Hugo, saw Juliet for the first time.

Some people in the seats near the Barringtons became irritated by a restless man who was spoiling their enjoyment of the play with his loud whispering and demands to see a programme. They became even more annoyed after Romeo said, 'Is she not Capulet's daughter?' at which point Hugo Barrington stood up and barged along the row, not caring whose feet he trod on. He then marched down the centre aisle, pushed his way through the swing doors and disappeared into the night. It was some time before Romeo fully regained his composure.

Sir Walter tried to give the impression he hadn't noticed what was going on behind him, and although Captain Tarrant frowned, his eyes never left the stage. Had he turned round, he would have seen Mrs Clifton was ignoring Barrington's unscripted exit as she concentrated on every word the two young lovers had to say.

During the interval, Giles went in search of his father but couldn't find him. He checked the car park, but there was no sign of the Bugatti. When he returned to the foyer, he saw his grandfather bending down and whispering in his mother's ear.

'Has Hugo gone completely mad?' asked Sir Walter.

'No, he's sane enough,' said Elizabeth, making no attempt to hide her anger.

'Then what in heaven's name does he think he's up to?'

'I have no idea.'

'Could it possibly have something to do with the Clifton boy?'

She would have replied if Jack Tarrant hadn't walked across to join them.

'Your daughter has a remarkable talent, Elizabeth,' he said after kissing her hand, 'as well as the advantage of inheriting your beauty.'

'And you're an old flatterer, Jack,' she said, before adding, 'I don't think you've met my son, Giles.'

'Good evening, sir,' said Giles. 'It's a great honour to meet you. May I congratulate you on your recent appointment.'

'Thank you, young man,' said Tarrant. 'And how do you feel about your friend's performance?'

'Remarkable, but did you know—'

'Good evening, Mrs Barrington.'

'Good evening, headmaster.'

'I must be joining a long queue of those who wish to add their . . .'

Giles watched as Captain Tarrant slipped away to join Harry's mother, and wondered how they knew each other.

'How lovely to see you, Captain Tarrant.'

'And you, Mrs Clifton, and how glamorous you're looking tonight. If Cary Grant had known that such beauty existed in Bristol, he would never have deserted us for Hollywood.' He then lowered his voice. 'Did you have any idea that Emma Barrington was playing Juliet?'

'No, Harry didn't mention it to me,' said Maisie. 'But then, why should he?'

'Let's hope that the affection they are displaying for one another on stage is nothing more than good acting, because if it's how they really feel about each other, we may have an even bigger problem on our hands.' He looked around to make sure no one was eavesdropping on their conversation. 'I presume you still haven't said anything to Harry?'

'Not a word,' said Maisie. 'And from Barrington's ill-mannered behaviour it seems he was also taken by surprise.'

'Good evening, Captain Tarrant,' said Miss Monday, touching Jack's arm. Miss Tilly was by her side. 'How good of you to come all the way down from London to see your protégé.'

'My dear Miss Monday,' said Tarrant, 'Harry's every bit as much your protégé and he'll be so pleased that you travelled all the way up from Cornwall to see his performance.' Miss Monday beamed, as a bell sounded to indicate the audience should return to their seats.

Once everyone had settled back in their places, the curtain rose for the second half, although one seat in the sixth row remained conspicuously empty. The death scene brought tears to the eyes of some who had never shed a tear in public, while Miss Monday hadn't wept that much since Harry's voice had broken.

The moment the final curtain fell, the audience rose as one. Harry and Emma were greeted by a storm of applause as they walked to the front of the stage, holding hands, and grown men, who rarely showed their feelings, cheered.

When they turned to bow to each other, Mrs Barrington smiled, and blushed. 'Good heavens, they weren't acting,' she said, loud enough for Giles to hear. The same thought had also crossed the minds of Maisie Clifton and Jack Tarrant long before the actors took their final bow.

Mrs Barrington, Giles and Grace went backstage to find Romeo and Juliet still holding hands as people queued up to lavish praise on them.

'You were great,' said Giles, slapping his friend on the back.

'I was all right,' said Harry, 'but Emma was magnificent.'

'So when did all this happen?' he whispered.

'It began in Rome,' admitted Harry with an impish grin.

'And to think I sacrificed my Caruso recording, not to mention my gramophone, to bring you two together.'

'As well as paying for our first dinner date.'

'Where's Papa?' asked Emma, looking around.

Grace was about to tell her sister what had happened when Captain Tarrant appeared.

'Congratulations, my boy,' he said. 'You were quite splendid.'

'Thank you sir,' said Harry, 'but I don't think you've met the real star of the show.'

'No, but let me assure you, young lady, if I was forty years younger, I'd see off any of my rivals.'

'You don't have any rivals for my affection,' said Emma. 'Harry never stops telling me how much you've done for him.'

'That's a two-way street,' said Jack as Harry spotted his mother and threw his arms around her.

'I'm so proud of you,' said Maisie.

'Thank you, Mum. But let me introduce you to Emma Barrington,' he said, placing an arm around Emma's waist.

'Now I know why your son is so good-looking,' said

Emma as she shook Harry's mother by the hand. 'May I introduce my mother,' she added.

It was a meeting Maisie had thought about for many years, but this was not a scenario that had ever crossed her mind. She was apprehensive as she shook hands with Elizabeth Barrington, but was greeted with such a friendly smile that it quickly became clear she was unaware of any possible connection between them.

'And this is Mr Atkins,' said Maisie, introducing the man who had been sitting beside her during the performance.

Harry had never come across Mr Atkins before. Looking at his mother's fur coat, he wondered if Atkins was the reason he now had three pairs of shoes.

He was about to speak to Mr Atkins, when he was interrupted by Dr Paget, who was keen to introduce him to Professor Henry Wyld. Harry recognized the name at once.

'I hear that you're hoping to come up to Oxford to read English,' said Wyld.

'Only if I can be taught by you, sir.'

'I see that Romeo's charm has not been left behind on the stage.'

'And this is Emma Barrington, sir.'

Oxford's Merton Professor of English Language and Literature gave a slight bow. 'You were quite magnificent, young lady.'

'Thank you, sir,' said Emma. 'I am also hoping to be taught by you,' she added. 'I've applied to Somerville for next year.'

Jack Tarrant glanced at Mrs Clifton, and couldn't miss the unmasked horror in her eyes.

'Grandfather,' said Giles as the chairman of the governors joined them. 'I don't think you know my friend, Harry Clifton.'

Sir Walter shook Harry warmly by the hand, before throwing his arms around his granddaughter. 'You two made an old man proud,' he said.

It was becoming painfully clear to Jack and Maisie that the two 'star-crossed lovers' had no idea of the problems they had set in motion.

◄○►

Sir Walter ordered his chauffeur to drive Mrs Barrington and the children back to the Manor House. Despite Emma's triumph, her mother made no attempt to hide her feelings as the car made its way towards Chew Valley. As they drove through the gates and up to the house, Giles noticed that some lights were still on in the drawing room.

Once the chauffeur had dropped them off, Elizabeth told Giles, Emma and Grace to go to bed, in a tone of voice none of them had heard for many years, while she headed for the drawing room. Giles and Emma reluctantly climbed the wide staircase but sat down on the top step the moment their mother was out of sight, while Grace obediently went to her room. Giles even wondered if his mother had left the door open on purpose.

When Elizabeth entered the room, her husband didn't bother to stand up. She noticed a half empty bottle of whisky and a tumbler on the table by his side.

'No doubt you have some explanation for your unforgivable behaviour?'

'I don't have to explain anything I do to you.'

'Emma somehow managed to rise above your appalling behaviour tonight.'

Barrington poured himself another tumbler of whisky and took a gulp. 'I have arranged for Emma to be removed from Red Maids immediately. Next term she will be enrolled at a school far enough away to ensure she never sees that boy again.'

On the stairs, Emma burst into tears. Giles wrapped an arm around her.

'What can Harry Clifton possibly have done to make you behave in such a shameful way?'

'It's none of your business.'

'Of course it's my business,' said Elizabeth, trying to remain calm. 'We are discussing our daughter and your son's closest friend. If Emma has fallen in love with Harry, and I suspect she has, I can't think of a nicer or more decent young man for her to lose her heart to.'

'Harry Clifton is the son of a whore. That's why her husband left her. And I repeat, Emma will never be allowed to come in contact with the little bastard again.'

'I'm going to bed before I lose my temper,' said Elizabeth. 'Don't even think of joining me in your present state.'

'I wasn't thinking of joining you in any state,' said Barrington, pouring himself another whisky. 'You haven't given me any pleasure in the bedroom for as long as I can remember.'

Emma leapt up and ran to her room, locking the door behind her. Giles didn't move.

'You are obviously drunk,' said Elizabeth. 'We'll discuss this in the morning, when you're sober.'

'There will be nothing to discuss in the morning,' slurred Barrington as his wife left the room. A moment later his head fell back on the cushion and he began to snore.

―◦―

When Jenkins pulled back the shutters in the drawing room just before eight the following morning he showed no surprise when he found his master slumped in an armchair, sound asleep and still wearing his dinner jacket.

The morning sunlight caused Barrington to stir. He blinked, and peered at the butler before he checked his watch.

'There will be a car coming to pick up Miss Emma in about an hour's time, Jenkins, so be sure she's packed and ready.'

'Miss Emma is not here, sir.'

'What? Then where is she?' demanded Barrington as he tried to stand up, but wobbled unsteadily for a moment before falling back into the chair.

'I have no idea, sir. She and Mrs Barrington left the house just after midnight.'

38

'WHERE DO YOU THINK they've gone?' asked Harry, once Giles had described what happened after he had arrived back at the Manor House.

'I've no idea,' said Giles. 'I was asleep when they left the house. All I could get out of Jenkins was that a taxi had taken them to the station just after midnight.'

'And you say your father was drunk when you returned home last night?'

'As a skunk, and he hadn't sobered up by the time I came down for breakfast this morning. He was shouting and screaming at anyone who crossed his path. He even tried to blame me for everything. That was when I decided to go and stay with my grandparents.'

'Do you think your grandfather might know where they are?'

'I don't think so, although he didn't seem that surprised when I told him what had happened. Grandma said I could stay with them for as long as I wanted to.'

'They can't be in Bristol,' said Harry, 'if the taxi took them to the station.'

'They could be anywhere by now,' said Giles.

Neither of them spoke again for some time, until Harry suggested, 'Your villa in Tuscany perhaps?'

'Unlikely,' said Giles. 'That's the first place Papa would think of, so they wouldn't be safe there for long.'

'So it has to be somewhere your father would think twice about before going after them.' Both boys fell silent again, until Harry said, 'I can think of someone who might know where they are.'

'And who's that?'

'Old Jack,' said Harry, who still couldn't quite bring himself to call him Captain Tarrant. 'I know he's become a friend of your mother's, and she certainly trusts him.'

'Do you know where he might be at the moment?'

'Anyone who reads *The Times* knows that,' said Harry scornfully.

Giles punched his friend on the arm. 'So where is he, clever clogs?'

'He'll be at his office in London. Soho Square, if I remember correctly.'

'I've always wanted an excuse to spend a day in London,' said Giles. 'It's just a pity I've left all my money back at the house.'

'Not a problem,' said Harry. 'I'm flush. That Atkins fellow gave me a fiver, although he did say I was to spend it on books.'

'Don't worry,' said Giles, 'I can think of an alternative plan.'

'Like what?' asked Harry, looking hopeful.

'We can just sit around and wait for Emma to write to you.'

It was Harry's turn to punch his friend. 'OK,' he said. 'But we'd better get going before anyone finds out what we're up to.'

◄○►

'I'm not in the habit of travelling third class,' said Giles as the train pulled out of Temple Meads.

'Well, you'd better get used to it while I'm paying,' said Harry.

'So tell me, Harry, what's your friend Captain Tarrant up to? I know the government has appointed him Director of the Citizens Displacement Unit, which sounds pretty impressive, but I'm not sure what he actually does.'

'What it says,' said Harry. 'He's responsible for finding accommodation for refugees, in particular those families who are escaping the tyranny of Nazi Germany. He says he's carrying on his father's work.'

'Class act, your friend Captain Tarrant.'

'You don't know the half of it,' said Harry.

'Tickets, please.'

The two boys spent most of the journey trying to work out where Emma and Mrs Barrington could possibly be, but by the time the train pulled into Paddington Station, they still hadn't come to any firm conclusions.

They took the tube to Leicester Square, emerged into the sunlight and went in search of Soho Square. As they made their way through the West End, Giles became so distracted by the bright neon lights and shop windows full of goods he'd never seen before that Harry occasionally had to remind him why they'd actually come to London.

When they reached Soho Square, neither of them could have missed the steady flow of bedraggled men, women and children, heads bowed, shuffling in and out of a vast building on the far side of the square.

The two young men dressed in blazers, grey flannels and ties looked strangely incongruous as they entered the building and followed the arrows directing them to the third floor. Several of the refugees stood to one side to allow them to pass, assuming they must be there on official business.

Giles and Harry joined the long queue outside the director's office, and might have been there for the rest of the day if a secretary had not come out and spotted them. She walked straight up to Harry and asked if he had come to see Captain Tarrant.

'Yes,' said Harry. 'He's an old friend.'

'I know,' said the woman. 'I recognized you immediately.'

'How?' asked Harry.

'He has a photograph of you on his desk,' she said. 'Follow me. Captain Tarrant will be delighted to see you.'

Old Jack's face lit up when the two boys – he should stop thinking of them as boys, they were now young men – walked into his office. 'It's good to see you both,' he said, jumping up from behind his desk to greet them. 'So who are you running away from this time?' he added with a smile.

'My father,' said Giles quietly.

Old Jack crossed the room, closed the door and sat the two young men down on an uncomfortable sofa. He drew up a chair and listened carefully as they told him everything that had happened since they'd seen him at the play the previous evening.

'I saw your father leave the theatre, of course,' said Old Jack, 'but it would never have crossed my mind he could treat your mother and sister quite so appallingly.'

'Do you have any idea where they might be, sir?' asked Giles.

'No. But if I had to guess, I'd say they were staying with your grandfather.'

'No, sir, I spent the morning with Grandpa, and even he doesn't know where they are.'

'I didn't say which grandfather,' said Jack.

'Lord Harvey?' said Harry.

'That would be my bet,' said Jack. 'They'd feel safe with him, and confident that Barrington would think twice before going after them.'

'But Grandpa has at least three homes that I'm aware of,' said Giles. 'So I wouldn't know where to begin looking.'

'How stupid of me,' said Harry. 'I know exactly where he is.'

'You do?' said Giles. 'Where?'

'At his country estate in Scotland.'

'You sound very certain,' said Jack.

'Only because last week he dropped Emma a line to explain why he wouldn't be able to attend the school play. It seems he always spends December and January in Scotland. But I'm damned if I can remember the address.'

'Mulgelrie Castle, near Mulgelrie, Highlands,' said Giles.

'Most impressive,' said Jack.

'Not really, sir. It's just years of Mama making me write thank-you letters to all my relations on Boxing Day. But as I've never been to Scotland, I haven't got a clue where it is.'

Old Jack got up and removed a large atlas from the bookshelf behind his desk. He looked up Mulgelrie in the index, flicked over several pages and then laid it on the desk in front of him. Running a finger from London to Scotland, he said, 'You'll have to take the overnight sleeper to Edinburgh, and then change to a local train for Mulgelrie.'

'I don't think we've got enough money left for that,' said Harry, checking his wallet.

'Then I'll have to issue you both with rail warrants, won't I?' said Jack. He opened his desk drawer, pulled out a large buff-coloured pad and tore off two forms.

He filled them in, signed and stamped them. 'After all,' he added, 'you are clearly stateless refugees in search of a home.'

'Thank you, sir,' said Giles.

'One last word of advice,' said Old Jack as he rose from behind his desk. 'Hugo Barrington is not a man who likes to be crossed, and while I'm fairly confident he won't do anything to annoy Lord Harvey, that doesn't necessarily apply to you, Harry. So be on your guard until you're safely inside Mulgelrie Castle. Should you at any time come across a man with a limp,' he added, 'be wary of him. He works for Giles's father. He's clever and resourceful, but more important, he has no allegiance to anyone except his paymaster.'

39

GILES AND HARRY were directed to another third-class carriage, but they were both so tired that despite the frequent opening and closing of carriage doors during the night, the clattering of the wheels over points and the regular blast of the train's whistle, they slept soundly.

Giles woke with a start as the train pulled into Newcastle a few minutes before six. He looked out of the window to be greeted by a dull grey day and the sight of lines of soldiers waiting to board the train. A sergeant saluted a second lieutenant who didn't look much older than Giles and asked, 'Permission to board the train, sir?' The young man returned his salute and replied in a softer voice, 'Carry on, sergeant,' and the soldiers began to file on to the train.

The ever-present threat of war, and the question of whether he and Harry would be in uniform before they had the chance to go up to Oxford, was never far from Giles's mind. His uncle Nicholas, whom he'd never met, an officer just like the young man on the platform, had led a platoon of soldiers and been cut down at Ypres. Giles wondered what would be the names of the battle-fields that would be commemorated with poppies every year if there was to be another Great War to end all wars.

His thoughts were interrupted when he noticed a passing reflection in the carriage window. He swung round, but the figure was no longer there. Had Captain Tarrant's warning caused him to overreact, or was it just a coincidence?

Giles looked across at Harry, who was still sound asleep, but then he probably hadn't slept for the past two nights. As the train shunted into Berwick-on-Tweed, Giles noticed the same man walking past their compartment. Just a glance, and he was gone; no longer a coincidence. Was he checking to see which station they got off at?

Harry finally woke, blinked and stretched his arms. 'I'm starving,' he said.

Giles leant over and whispered, 'I think there's someone on this train who's following us.'

'What makes you say that?' asked Harry, suddenly wide awake.

'I've seen the same man pass our carriage once too often.'

'Tickets please!'

Giles and Harry handed their warrants to the ticket collector. 'How long does this train stop at each station?' he asked once the man had clipped them.

'Now, that all depends on whether we're runnin' on time or not,' he replied a little wearily, 'but never less than four minutes is the company regulation.'

'What is the next station?' asked Giles.

'Dunbar. We should be there in about thirty minutes. But you've both got warrants for Mulgelrie,' he added before moving on to the next compartment.

'What was all that about?' asked Harry.

'I'm trying to find out if we're being followed,' said Giles, 'and the next part of my plan will involve you.'

'What role will I be playing this time?' said Harry, sitting on the edge of his seat.

'Certainly not Romeo,' said Giles. 'When the train stops at Dunbar, I want you to get off while I watch if anyone follows you. Once you're on the platform, walk quickly towards the ticket barrier, then turn back, go into the waiting room and buy a cup of tea. Don't forget you've only got four minutes to be back on board before the train sets off again. And whatever you do, don't look back, or he'll know we're on to him.'

'But if there is someone following us, surely he'll be more interested in you than me?'

'I don't think so,' said Giles, 'and certainly not if Captain Tarrant is right, because I have a feeling your friend knows more than he's willing to admit.'

'That doesn't exactly fill me with confidence,' said Harry.

Half an hour later, the train shuddered to a halt in Dunbar. Harry opened the carriage door, stepped out on to the platform and headed for the exit.

Giles caught no more than a glimpse of the man as he hurried after Harry.

'Got you,' Giles said, then leant back and closed his eyes, confident that once the man realized Harry had only got off to buy a cup of tea, he would look in his direction just to make sure he hadn't also left the carriage.

Giles opened his eyes again when Harry returned to the compartment holding a bar of chocolate.

'Well,' said Harry, 'did you spot anyone?'

'Sure did,' said Giles. 'In fact, he's just getting back on the train.'

'What does he look like?' asked Harry, trying not to sound anxious.

'I only caught a glimpse of him,' said Giles, 'but I'd say he's around forty, a little over six foot, smartly dressed, with very short hair. The one thing you can't miss is his limp.'

'So now we know what we're up against, Sherlock, what next?'

'First, Watson, it's important to remember that we have several things going for us.'

'I can't think of one,' said Harry.

'Well, for a start, we know we're being followed, but he doesn't know we know. We also know where we're going, which he clearly doesn't. We're also fit, and less than half his age. And with that limp, he won't be able to move all that quickly.'

'You're rather good at this,' said Harry.

'I do have a built-in advantage,' said Giles. 'I am my father's son.'

—◦—

By the time the train pulled into Edinburgh Waverley, Giles had gone over his plan with Harry a dozen times. They stepped out of the carriage and walked slowly down the platform towards the barrier.

'Don't even think about looking back,' said Giles as he produced his rail warrant, then headed towards a line of taxis.

'The Royal Hotel,' said Giles to the cabbie. 'And can you let me know if another taxi follows us?' he added before joining Harry in the back.

'Right you are,' said the cabbie, as he eased off the rank and joined the traffic.

'How do you know there's a Royal Hotel in Edinburgh?' asked Harry.

'There's a Royal Hotel in every city,' said Giles.

A few minutes later the cabbie said, 'I cannae be sure, but the next cab off the rank isn't far behind us.'

'Good,' said Giles. 'How much is the fare to the Royal?'

'Two shillings, sir.'

'I'll give you four if you can lose him.'

The driver immediately put his foot down on the accelerator, causing both of his passengers to be thrown back into their seats. Giles recovered quickly and looked through the back window to see the taxi behind them had also speeded up. They had gained sixty or seventy yards, but Giles realized that advantage wouldn't last for long.

'Cabbie, take the next turning on the left and then slow down for a moment. After we jump out, I want you to continue on to the Royal and don't stop until you reach the hotel.' An outstretched arm appeared. Harry placed two florins into the palm.

'When I jump out,' said Giles, 'just follow me, and then do exactly as I do.' Harry nodded.

The taxi swung round the corner and slowed down for a moment just as Giles opened the door. He leapt out on to the pavement, toppled over, quickly picked himself up, then dashed into the nearest shop, throwing himself on the floor. Harry followed only seconds later, slammed the door behind him and was lying by his friend's side just as the second cab shot around the corner.

'Can I help you, sir?' asked a sales assistant, hands on hips, looking down at the two young men lying prostrate on the ground.

'You already have,' said Giles, rising to his feet and giving her a warm smile. He brushed himself down, said 'Thank you,' and left the shop without another word.

When Harry stood up, he came face to face with a slim-waisted mannequin wearing only a corset. He turned bright red, ran out of the shop and joined Giles on the pavement.

'I don't expect the man with the limp will be booking into the Royal for the night,' said Giles, 'so we'd better get moving.'

'Agreed,' said Harry as Giles flagged down another cab. 'Waverley station,' he said before climbing into the back.

'Where did you learn how to do all that?' asked Harry in admiration, as they headed back in the direction of the station.

'You know, Harry, you should read a little less Joseph Conrad and a little more John Buchan if you want to know how to travel in Scotland while being pursued by a fiendish foe.'

The journey to Mulgelrie was considerably slower and far less exciting than the one to Edinburgh had been, and there was certainly no sign of any man with a limp. When the engine finally dragged its four carriages and two passengers into the little station, the sun had already disappeared behind the highest mountain. The station master was standing by the exit waiting to check their tickets when they got off the last train that day.

'Any hope of getting a taxi?' Giles asked as they handed over their warrants.

'No, sir,' replied the station master. 'Jock goes home for tea around six o'clock, and he'll nae be back for another hour.'

Giles thought twice about explaining the logic of Jock's actions to the station master, before he asked, 'Then perhaps you'd be kind enough to tell us how we can get to Mulgelrie Castle.'

'You'll have to walk,' said the station master helpfully.

'And which direction might it be?' asked Giles, trying not to sound exasperated.

'It's about three miles up yonder,' the man said, pointing up the hill. 'You cannae miss it.'

'Up yonder' turned out to be the only accurate piece of information the station master had offered, because after the two of them had been walking for over an hour, it was pitch black and there was still no sign of any castle.

Giles was beginning to wonder if they were going to have to spend their first night in the Highlands sleeping in a field with only a flock of sheep to keep them company, when Harry shouted, 'There it is!'

Giles stared through the misty gloom and although he still couldn't quite make out the outline of a castle, his spirits were lifted by flickering lights coming from several windows. They trudged on until they reached a massive pair of wrought-iron gates which had not been locked. As they made their way up the long driveway Giles could hear barking, but he couldn't see any dogs. After about another mile they came to a bridge spanning a moat, and on the far side, a heavy oak door that didn't look as if it welcomed strangers.

'Leave the talking to me,' said Giles as they staggered across the bridge and came to a halt outside the door.

Giles banged three times with the side of his fist, and within moments the door was pulled open to reveal a giant of a man dressed in a kilt with a dark lovat jacket, white shirt and white bow tie.

The head steward looked down on the weary, bedraggled objects that stood in front of him. 'Good evening, Mr Giles,' he said, although Giles had never set eyes on the man before. 'His lordship has been expecting you for some time, and wondered if you would care to join him for dinner?'

40

```
GILES AND HARRY CLIFTON ON THEIR WAY

   TO MULGELRIE -(STOP)- SHOULD ARRIVE

AROUND SIX -(STOP)-
```

LORD HARVEY handed the telegram to Giles and chuckled. 'Sent by our mutual friend, Captain Tarrant. He only turned out to be wrong about what time you'd arrive.'

'We had to walk all the way from the station,' protested Giles between mouthfuls.

'Yes, I did consider sending the car to meet you off the last train,' said Lord Harvey, 'but there's nothing like a bracing Highland walk to work up a good appetite.'

Harry smiled. He'd hardly spoken since they'd come down for dinner, and as Emma had been placed at the far end of the table he had to satisfy himself with the occasional wistful gaze, wondering if they'd ever be left alone together.

The first course was a thick Highland broth, which Harry finished a little too quickly, but when Giles was served a second helping, he also allowed his bowl to be refilled. Harry would have asked for a third helping if everyone else hadn't continued making polite conversation while they waited for him and Giles to finish so that the main course could be served.

'There's no need for either of you to be anxious about anyone wondering where you are,' said Lord Harvey, 'because I've already sent telegrams to Sir Walter and to Mrs Clifton, to assure them you are both safe and well. I didn't bother to get in touch with your father, Giles,' he added without further comment. Giles glanced across the table to see his mother purse her lips.

Moments later the dining room doors swung open and several liveried servants entered and whisked away the soup bowls. Three more servants followed, carrying silver salvers on which rested what looked to Harry like six small chickens.

'I do hope you like grouse, Mr Clifton,' said Lord Harvey, the first person ever to call him Mr, as a bird was placed in front of him. 'I shot these myself.'

Harry couldn't think of an appropriate response. He watched as Giles picked up his knife and fork and began to slice tiny pieces off the bird, bringing back memories of their first meal together at St Bede's. By the time the plates were cleared, Harry had only managed about three morsels and wondered how old he would have to be before he could say, 'No, thank you, I'd prefer another bowl of soup.'

Things improved a little when a large plate of different fruits, some of which Harry had never seen before, was placed in the centre of the table. He would have liked to ask his host their names and the countries they originated from, but memories of his first banana came to mind, when he had definitely slipped. He satisfied himself with following Giles's lead, watching carefully to see which had to be peeled, which had to be cut and which you could simply take a bite out of.

When he'd finished, a servant appeared and placed a bowl of water by the side of his plate. He was just about to pick it up and drink it, when he saw Lady Harvey place her fingers in hers and moments later a servant passed her a linen napkin so she could dry her hands. Harry dipped his fingers in the water and, like magic, a napkin immediately appeared.

After dinner, the ladies retired to the drawing room. Harry wanted to join them so he could at last catch up with Emma and tell her everything that had happened since she'd poisoned herself. But no sooner had she left the room than Lord Harvey sat back down, a sign for the under-butler to offer his lordship a cigar while another servant poured him a large glass of Cognac.

Once he'd taken a sip, he nodded and glasses were placed in front of Giles and Harry. The butler closed the humidor, before filling their glasses with brandy.

'Well,' said Lord Harvey after two or three luxuriant puffs. 'Am I to understand that you are both hoping to go up to Oxford?'

'Harry's a safe bet,' said Giles. 'But I'll need to score a couple of centuries during the summer, and preferably one at Lord's if the examiners are going to overlook my more obvious deficiencies.'

'Giles is being modest, sir,' said Harry. 'He has just as good a chance of being offered a place as I do. After all, he's not only the captain of cricket, he's also school captain.'

'Well, if you are successful, I can assure you that you'll experience three of the happiest years of your life. That's assuming Herr Hitler isn't foolish enough to insist on a replay of the last war in the vain hope that he'll be able to reverse the result.'

The three of them raised their glasses and Harry took his first sip of brandy. He didn't like the taste and was wondering if it would be thought discourteous if he didn't finish it, when Lord Harvey came to his rescue.

'Perhaps it's time for us to join the ladies,' he said, draining his glass. He put his cigar in an ashtray, rose from his place and marched out of the dining room, not waiting for a second opinion. The two young men followed him across the hall and into the drawing room.

Lord Harvey took the seat next to Elizabeth, while Giles winked at Harry and went across to join his grandmother. Harry sat next to Emma on the sofa.

'How gallant of you to come all this way, Harry,' she said, touching his hand.

'I'm so sorry about what happened after the play. I only hope I wasn't responsible for causing the problem in the first place.'

'How could you possibly be responsible, Harry? You've never done anything that could have caused my father to speak to Mama that way.'

'But it's no secret that your father doesn't think we should be together, even on stage.'

'Let's talk about it tomorrow morning,' Emma whispered. 'We can go for a long walk in the hills and be on our own, with only the Highland cattle to overhear us.'

'I'll look forward to that,' said Harry. He would have liked to hold her hand, but there were too many eyes continually glancing in their direction.

'You two young men must be very tired after such an exhausting journey,' said Lady Harvey. 'Why don't you both go off to bed, and we'll see you at breakfast in the morning.'

Harry didn't want to go to bed; he wanted to stay with Emma and try to find out if she'd discovered why her father was so opposed to them being together. But Giles rose immediately, kissed his grandmother and mother on the cheek and said goodnight, leaving Harry with no choice but to join him. He leaned across and kissed Emma on the cheek, thanked his host for a wonderful evening and followed Giles out of the room.

As they walked down the hall, Harry paused to admire a painting of a bowl of fruit by an artist called Peploe when Emma came dashing out of the drawing room, threw her arms around his neck and kissed him gently on the lips.

Giles continued up the stairs as if he hadn't noticed, while Harry kept his eyes on the drawing-room door. Emma broke away when she heard it opening behind her.

'Good night, good night, parting is such sweet sorrow,' she whispered.

'That I shall say good night till it be morrow,' Harry replied.

◄o►

'Where are you two off to?' asked Elizabeth Barrington as she came out of the breakfast room.

'We're going to climb Crag Cowen,' said Emma. 'Don't wait up, because you may never see us again.'

Her mother laughed. 'Then make sure you wrap up well, because even the sheep catch cold in the Highlands.' She waited until Harry had closed the door behind them before she added, 'Giles, your grandfather wishes to see us in his study at ten o'clock.' It sounded to Giles more like a command than a request.

'Yes, Mother,' he said, before looking through the window and watching Harry and Emma walking down the path towards Crag Cowen. They'd only gone a few yards before Emma took Harry's hand. Giles smiled as they turned the corner and disappeared behind a row of pines.

When the clock in the hall began to strike, Giles had to walk quickly along the corridor to make sure he reached his grandfather's study before the tenth chime. His grandparents and his mother stopped talking the moment he entered the room. They had clearly been waiting for him.

'Have a seat, dear boy,' said his grandfather.

'Thank you, sir,' Giles replied, and sat down on a chair between his mother and his grandmother.

'I suppose this would best be described as a council of war,' said Lord Harvey, looking up from his high-backed leather chair as if he was addressing a board meeting. 'I'll try to bring everyone up to date before we decide what the best course of action should be.' Giles was flattered that his grandfather now considered him to be a full member of the family board.

'I telephoned Walter last night. He was just as appalled by Hugo's conduct at the play as I was when Elizabeth told me about it, although I had to fill him in on what happened when she returned to the Manor House.' Giles's mother bowed her head, but didn't interrupt. 'I went on to tell him that I'd had a long talk with my daughter, and that we felt there were only two possible courses of action.'

Giles sat back in his chair, but didn't relax.

'I left Walter in no doubt that if Elizabeth were even to consider returning to the Manor House, it would be necessary for Hugo to make several concessions. First, he must apologize unequivocally for his appalling behaviour.'

Giles's grandmother nodded in agreement.

'Second, he will never again, and I repeated, never again, suggest that Emma should be taken out of her school, and he will in future fully support her efforts to gain a place at Oxford. God knows it's hard enough for a young man to make the grade nowadays, but it's damn nigh impossible for a woman.

'My third and most important demand, and on this I was quite adamant, is that he explain to us all why he continues to treat Harry Clifton so appallingly. I suspect it might have something to do with Harry's uncle stealing from Hugo. The sins of the father are one thing, but an uncle ... I refuse to accept, as he has so often claimed to Elizabeth, that he considers Clifton unworthy to mix with his children simply because his father was a docker and his mother is a waitress. Perhaps Hugo has forgotten that my grandfather was a jobbing clerk in a firm of wine merchants, while his own grandfather left school at the age of twelve and started out as a docker like young Clifton's father, and just in case anyone has forgotten, I'm the first Lord Harvey in this family, and you don't get much more nouveau than that.'

Giles wanted to cheer.

'Now, none of us can have failed to notice,' continued Lord Harvey, 'how Emma and Harry feel about each other, which is hardly surprising as they are two exceptional young people. If, in the fullness of time, their relationship blossoms, no one would be more delighted than Victoria and I. On that subject, Walter was in full agreement with me.'

Giles smiled. He liked the idea of Harry becoming a member of the family, even though he didn't believe his father would ever accept it.

'I told Walter,' continued his grandfather, 'that if Hugo felt unable to abide by these terms, Elizabeth would be left with no choice but to institute divorce proceedings immediately. I would also have to resign from the board of Barrington's, and make public my reasons for doing so.'

Giles was saddened by this, as he knew there had never been a divorce in either family.

'Walter kindly agreed to get back to me in the next few days, after he's had a chance to talk things over with his son, but he did tell me that Hugo has already promised to stop drinking, and that he appears to be genuinely contrite. Let me finish by reminding you that this is a family matter and should not in any circumstances be discussed with outsiders. We must hope that this proves to be nothing more than an unfortunate incident that will soon be forgotten.'

The following morning, Giles's father telephoned and asked to speak to him. He apologized profusely, saying how sorry he was to have blamed Giles for something that was entirely his own fault. He begged Giles to do everything in his power to convince his mother and Emma to return to Gloucestershire so they could all spend Christmas together at the Manor House. He also hoped that, as his father-in-law had suggested, the incident would be quickly forgotten. He made no mention of Harry Clifton.

41

ONCE THEY'D DISEMBARKED from the train at Temple Meads, Giles and his mother waited in the car while Emma said goodbye to Harry.

'They've just spent the last nine days together,' said Giles. 'Have they forgotten that they'll be seeing each other again tomorrow?'

'And probably the next day,' said Giles's mother. 'But try not to forget, unlikely though it might seem, that it could even happen to you one day.'

Emma eventually joined them, but when they drove off she continued to look out of the back window and didn't stop waving until Harry was out of sight.

Giles was keen to get home and finally discover what it was that Harry could have done to make his father treat him so cruelly over the years. Surely it couldn't be worse than stealing from the tuck shop or deliberately failing your exams. He'd considered a dozen possibilities but none of them made any sense. Now, at last, he hoped he was going to find out the truth. He glanced across at his mother. Although she rarely displayed her emotions, she was clearly becoming more and more agitated as they approached Chew Valley.

Giles's father was standing on the top step waiting to greet them when the car drew up outside the house; no sign of Jenkins. He apologized immediately to Elizabeth and then the children, before telling them how much he'd missed them.

'Tea is set up in the drawing room,' he said. 'Please join me there as soon as you're ready.'

Giles was the first back downstairs and he sat uneasily in a chair opposite his father. While they waited for his mother and Emma to join them, his father confined himself to asking Giles how he'd enjoyed Scotland, and to explain that Nanny had taken Grace into Bristol to buy her school uniform. At no time did he mention Harry. When Giles's mother and sister entered the room a few minutes later, his father immediately stood up. Once they were seated, he poured them all a cup of tea. He clearly didn't want any servants to overhear what he was about to reveal.

Once everyone had settled, Giles's father sat on the edge of his seat and began to speak softly.

'Let me begin by saying to all three of you how unacceptable my behaviour was on the night of what everyone has described as Emma's great triumph. That your father was not there for the curtain call was bad enough, Emma,' he said, looking directly at his daughter, 'but the way I treated your mother when you returned home that night was quite unforgivable, and I realize it may take some time before such a deep wound can be healed.'

Hugo Barrington placed his head in his hands and Giles noticed that he was trembling. He eventually steadied himself.

'You have all, for different reasons, asked to know why I have treated Harry Clifton so badly over the years. It is true that I cannot bear to be in his presence, but the fault is entirely of my own making. When you learn the reason, you might begin to understand, and possibly even sympathize.'

Giles glanced at his mother, who was sitting stiffly in her chair. There was no way of telling how she felt.

'Many years ago,' continued Barrington, 'when I first became managing director of the company, I convinced the board that we should branch out into shipbuilding, despite my father's reservations. I signed a contract with a Canadian company to build a merchant ship called the *Maple Leaf*. That not only turned out to be a financial disaster for the company, but a personal catastrophe for me, from which I have never fully recovered and doubt if I ever will. Allow me to explain.

'One afternoon a docker burst into my office insisting that his work mate was trapped inside the hull of the *Maple Leaf* and if I didn't give the order to break it open, his life would be lost. Naturally I went down to the dock immediately and the ganger assured me there was absolutely no truth in the story. However, I insisted the men down tools so that we could listen for any sound coming from inside the hull. I waited for some considerable time, but as there was no sound, I gave the order for them to return to work, as we were already several weeks behind schedule.

'I assumed the docker in question would sign on for his usual shift the following day. But not only did he not turn up, he was never seen again. The possibility of his death has been on my conscience ever since.' He paused, raised his head and said, 'That man's name was Arthur Clifton, and Harry is his only son.'

Emma began to sob.

'I want you to imagine, if you possibly can, what I go through whenever I see that young man, and how he would feel were he ever to find out that I might have been responsible for his father's death. That Harry Clifton has become Giles's closest friend, and fallen in love with my daughter, is the stuff of a Greek tragedy.'

Once again, he buried his head in his hands and didn't speak for some time. When he finally looked up, he said, 'If you wish to ask me any questions, I will do my best to answer them.'

Giles waited for his mother to speak first. 'Were you responsible for sending an innocent man to jail for a crime he did not commit?' Elizabeth asked quietly.

'No, my dear,' said Barrington. 'I hope you know me well enough to realize I am not capable of such a thing. Stan Tancock was a common thief, who broke into my office and robbed me. Because he was Arthur Clifton's brother-in-law, and for no other reason, I gave him back his job the day he was released from prison.' Elizabeth smiled for the first time.

'Father, I wonder if I might be allowed to ask a question,' said Giles.

'Yes, of course.'

'Did you have Harry and me followed when we travelled up to Scotland?'

'Yes, I did, Giles. I was desperate to find out where your mother and Emma were so I could apologize to them for my disgraceful behaviour. Please try to forgive me.'

Everyone turned their attention to Emma, who hadn't yet spoken. When she did, her words took them all by surprise. 'You'll have to tell Harry everything you've told us,' she whispered, 'and if he is willing to forgive you, you must then welcome him into our family.'

'I would be delighted to welcome him into the family, my darling, although it would be understandable if he never wanted to speak to me again. But I cannot tell him the truth about what happened to his father.'

'Why not?' demanded Emma.

'Because Harry's mother has made it clear that she

does not want him ever to find out how his father died, as he has been brought up to believe he was a brave man who was killed in the war. Up until this moment, I have kept my promise never to reveal to anyone what took place on that dreadful day.'

Elizabeth Barrington rose, walked across to her husband and kissed him gently. Barrington broke down and sobbed. A moment later Giles joined his parents and placed an arm around his father's shoulders.

Emma didn't move.

42

'HAS YOUR MOTHER always been that good-looking?'
said Giles. 'Or am I just getting older?'

'I've no idea,' said Harry. 'All I can say is that *your*
mother always looks so elegant.'

'Much as I love the dear creature, she looks positively prehistoric compared to yours,' said Giles as Elizabeth Barrington, parasol in one hand and handbag in
the other, bore down upon them.

Giles, like every other boy, had been dreading what
outfit his mother might turn up in. As for the selection
of hats, it was worse than Ascot, with every mother and
daughter trying to outdo each other.

Harry looked more carefully at his mother, who was
chatting to Dr Paget. He had to admit that she was
attracting more attention than most of the other
mothers, which he found a little embarrassing. But he
was pleased that she no longer appeared to be burdened
by financial worries, and assumed the man standing on
her right had something to do with that.

However grateful he was to Mr Atkins, he didn't
care for the idea of him becoming his stepfather. Mr
Barrington may in the past have been over-zealous about
his daughter, but Harry could not deny that he felt just
as protective when it came to his mother.

She had recently told him that Mr Frampton was so pleased with her work at the hotel that he had promoted her to night supervisor and given her another pay rise. And certainly Harry no longer had to wait for his trousers to be too short before they were replaced. But even he had been surprised when she hadn't commented about the cost of his travelling to Rome with the Arts Appreciation Society.

'How nice to see you, Harry, on your day of triumph,' said Mrs Barrington. 'Two prizes, if I remember correctly. I'm only sorry that Emma can't be with us to share in your glory, but as Miss Webb pointed out, her gels cannot be expected to take the morning off for someone else's speech day, even if her brother is the school captain.'

Mr Barrington came across to join them, and Giles watched his father carefully as he shook hands with Harry. There was still a distinct lack of warmth on his father's part, although no one could deny that he was making every effort to conceal it.

'So, when are you expecting to hear from Oxford, Harry?' asked Barrington.

'Some time next week, sir.'

'I'm confident they'll offer you a place, although I suspect it will be a close-run thing for Giles.'

'Don't forget he's also had his moment of glory,' said Harry.

'I don't recall that,' said Mrs Barrington.

'I think Harry's referring to the century I scored at Lord's, Mama.'

'Admirable though that might be, for the life of me I can't see how it will help you get into Oxford,' said his father.

'Normally I would agree with you, Papa,' said Giles, 'were it not for the fact that the Professor of History was sitting next to the President of the MCC at the time.'

The laughter that followed was drowned out by the sound of bells. The boys began to move rapidly in the direction of the great hall, with their parents following dutifully a few paces behind them.

Giles and Harry took their places among the prefects and prize-winners in the front three rows.

'Do you recall our first day at St Bede's?' said Harry, 'when we all sat in the front row, quite terrified of Dr Oakshott?'

'I was never terrified of the Shot,' said Giles.

'No, of course you weren't,' said Harry.

'But I do remember when we came down for breakfast on the first morning that you licked your porridge bowl.'

'And I remember you swore you'd never mention it again,' whispered Harry.

'And I promise I never will again,' replied Giles not whispering. 'What was the name of that frightful bully who slippered you on our first night?'

'Fisher,' said Harry. 'And it was the second night.'

'Wonder what he's up to now?'

'He's probably running a Nazi youth camp.'

'Then that's a good enough reason to go to war,' said Giles as everyone in the hall rose to welcome the chairman of the governors and his board.

The crocodile of smartly dressed men made their way slowly down the aisle and up on to the stage. The last person to take his seat was Mr Barton, the headmaster, but not before he'd ushered the guest of honour into the centre chair in the front row.

Once everyone had settled, the headmaster rose to welcome the parents and guests, before delivering the school's annual report. He began by describing 1938 as a vintage year, and for the next twenty minutes he elaborated on this claim, giving details of the school's academic and sporting achievements. He ended by inviting the Right Honourable Winston Churchill MP, Chancellor of Bristol University and Member of Parliament for Epping, to address the school and present the prizes.

Mr Churchill rose slowly from his place and stared down at the audience for some time before he began.

'Some guests of honour begin their speeches by telling their audience that they never won any prizes when they were at school, in fact they were always bottom of the class. I cannot make such a claim: although I certainly never won a prize, at least I was never bottom of the class – I was second to bottom.' The boys roared and cheered, while the masters smiled. Only Deakins remained unmoved.

The moment the laughter had subsided, Churchill scowled. 'Our nation today faces another of those great moments in history, when the British people may once again be asked to decide the fate of the free world. Many of you present in this great hall . . .' He lowered his voice and concentrated his attention on the rows of boys seated in front of him, not once looking in the direction of their parents.

'Those of us who lived through the Great War will never forget the tragic loss of life our nation suffered, and the effect it has had on an entire generation. Of the twenty boys in my class at Harrow who went on to serve in the front line, only three of them lived long enough to cast a vote. I only hope that whoever delivers this speech in twenty years' time will not need to refer to that barbaric and unnecessary waste of life as the *First* World War. With that single hope, I wish you all long, happy and successful lives.'

Giles was among the first to rise and give the guest

of honour a standing ovation as he returned to his seat. He felt that if Britain were left with no choice but to go to war, this was the one man who should take over from Neville Chamberlain and become Prime Minister. When everyone had resumed their places some minutes later, the headmaster invited Mr Churchill to present the prizes.

Giles and Harry cheered when Mr Barton not only announced that Deakins was scholar of the year but added, 'This morning I received a telegram from the Master of Balliol College, Oxford, to say that Deakins has been awarded the senior classics scholarship. I might add,' continued Mr Barton, 'that he is the first boy to achieve this distinction in the school's four-hundred-year history.'

Giles and Harry were on their feet immediately, as a gangly, six-foot-two-inch boy with pebble glasses, wearing a suit that hung on him as if it had never left its coathanger, made his way slowly up on to the stage. Mr Deakins wanted to leap up and take a photograph of his son being presented with his prize by Mr Churchill, but didn't do so, for fear it might be frowned upon.

Harry received a warm reception when he was awarded the English prize, as well as the school reading prize. The headmaster added, 'None of us will ever forget his performance as Romeo. Let us all hope that Harry will be among those who receive a telegram next week offering them a place at Oxford.'

When Mr Churchill presented Harry with his prize, he whispered, 'I never went to university. I only wish I had. Let's hope you receive that telegram, Clifton. Good luck.'

'Thank you, sir,' said Harry.

But the biggest cheer of the day was reserved for Giles Barrington when he went up to receive the headmaster's prize for captain of the school and captain of cricket. To the guest of honour's surprise, the chairman of the governors leapt up from his place and shook hands with Giles before he reached Mr Churchill.

'My grandson, sir,' Sir Walter explained with considerable pride.

Churchill smiled, gripped Giles by the hand and, looking up at him, said, 'Be sure you serve your country with the same distinction with which you have clearly served your school.'

That was the moment when Giles knew exactly what he would do if Britain went to war.

Once the ceremony was over, the boys, parents and masters rose as one to sing *Carmen Bristoliense*.

Sit clarior, sit dignior, quotquot labuntur menses:
Sit primus nobis hic decor, Sumus Bristolienses.

Once the last chorus had rung out, the headmaster led the guest of honour and his staff off the stage, out of the great hall and into the afternoon sunshine. Moments later, everyone else poured out on to the lawn to join them for tea. Three boys in particular were surrounded by well-wishers, as well as by a bevy of sisters who thought Giles was 'just cute'.

'This is the proudest day of my life,' said Harry's mother as she embraced him.

'I know how you feel, Mrs Clifton,' said Old Jack, shaking Harry by the hand. 'I only wish Miss Monday had lived long enough to see you today, because I don't doubt it would have also been the happiest day of her life.'

Mr Holcombe stood to one side and waited patiently to add his congratulations. Harry introduced him to Captain Tarrant, unaware that they were old friends.

When the band had stopped playing, and the captains and the kings had departed, Giles, Harry and Deakins sat alone on the grass and reminisced about things past, no longer schoolboys.

43

A TELEGRAM WAS DELIVERED to Harry's study by a junior boy on Thursday afternoon. Giles and Deakins waited patiently for him to open it, but instead he handed the little brown envelope to Giles.

'Passing the buck again,' said Giles as he ripped it open. He couldn't hide his surprise when he read the contents.

'You failed,' said Giles, sounding shocked. Harry collapsed back into his chair. 'To win a scholarship. However,' Giles added, reading the telegram aloud, *'We are delighted to offer you an exhibition to Brasenose College, Oxford. Many congratulations. Details to follow in the next few days. W.T.S. Stallybrass, Principal.* Not bad, but you're clearly not in Deakins's class.'

'And which class are you in?' said Harry, immediately regretting his words.

'One scholar, one exhibitionist—'

'Exhibitioner,' corrected Deakins.

'And one commoner,' said Giles, ignoring his friend. 'Has a nice ring about it.'

Eleven other telegrams were delivered to successful applicants from Bristol Grammar School that day, but none was addressed to Giles Barrington.

'You should let your mother know,' said Giles as they

walked into the hall for supper. 'She probably hasn't slept all week worrying about it.'

Harry looked at his watch. 'It's too late, she'll already have left for work. I won't be able to tell her until tomorrow morning.'

'Why don't we go and surprise her at the hotel?' said Giles.

'I can't do that. She'd think it unprofessional to interrupt her while she's at work, and I don't feel I can make an exception, even for this,' he said, waving the telegram triumphantly.

'But don't you think she has a right to know?' said Giles. 'After all, she's sacrificed everything to make it possible for you. Frankly, if they offered me a place at Oxford, I'd interrupt Mama even if she was addressing the Mothers' Union. Don't you agree, Deakins?'

Deakins removed his glasses and began to polish them with a handkerchief, always a sign that he was deep in thought. 'I'd ask Paget's opinion, and if he raises no objection—'

'Good idea,' said Giles. 'Let's go and see the Page.'

'Are you coming, Deakins?' asked Harry, but then noticed that Deakins's glasses had been returned to the end of his nose, a sign that he had been transported to another world.

'Many congratulations,' said Dr Paget once he'd read the telegram. 'And well deserved, if I may say so.'

'Thank you, sir,' said Harry. 'I wondered if it would be possible for me to go to the Royal Hotel so I can tell my mother the news?'

'I can't see any reason why not, Clifton.'

'Can I trot along with him?' asked Giles innocently.

Paget hesitated. 'Yes, you can, Barrington. But don't even think about having a drink or smoking while you're in the hotel.'

'Not even one glass of champagne, sir?'

'No, Barrington, not even a glass of cider,' said Paget firmly.

As the two young men strolled out of the school gates, they passed a lamp lighter who was standing on his bicycle, stretching up to light a street lamp. They chatted about the summer hols, when Harry would be joining Giles's family in Tuscany for the first time, and agreed they would have to be back in time to see the Australians when they played against Gloucestershire at the county ground. They discussed the possibility, or, according to Harry, the probability, of war being declared now that everyone had been issued with a gas mask. But neither of them touched on another subject that was on both of their minds: would Giles be joining Harry and Deakins at Oxford in September?

As they approached the hotel, Harry had second thoughts about interrupting his mother while she was at work, but Giles had already barged through the revolving doors and was standing in the foyer waiting for him.

'It will only take a couple of minutes,' said Giles when Harry joined him. 'Just tell her the good news and we can go straight back to school.' Harry nodded.

Giles asked the doorman where the Palm Court was, and he directed them to a raised area at the far end of the foyer. After climbing the half dozen steps, Giles walked up to the desk and, keeping his voice low, asked the receptionist, 'Can we have a quick word with Mrs Clifton?'

'Mrs Clifton?' asked the girl. 'Has she made a reservation?' She ran her finger down a list of bookings.

'No, she works here,' said Giles.

'Oh, I'm new here,' said the girl, 'but I'll just ask one of the waitresses. They're bound to know.'

'Thank you.'

Harry remained on the bottom step, his eyes searching the room for his mother.

'Hattie,' the receptionist asked a passing waitress, 'does a Mrs Clifton work here?'

'Not any longer she doesn't,' came back the immediate reply. 'She left a couple of years ago. Haven't heard a dicky-bird from her since.'

'There must be some mistake,' said Harry, bounding up the steps to join his friend.

'Do you have any idea where we might find her?' asked Giles, keeping his voice low.

'No,' said Hattie. 'But you could have a word with Doug, the night porter. He's been here for ever.'

'Thank you,' said Giles and, turning to Harry, added, 'There's bound to be a simple explanation, but if you'd prefer to leave it . . .'

'No, let's find out if Doug knows where she is.'

Giles walked slowly across to the porter's desk, giving Harry enough time to change his mind, but he didn't say a word. 'Are you Doug?' he asked a man dressed in a faded blue frockcoat with buttons that no longer shone.

'I am, sir,' he replied. 'How can I help you?'

'We're looking for Mrs Clifton.'

'Maisie don't work here any longer, sir. She must have left at least a couple of years back.'

'Do you know where she is working now?'

'I've no idea, sir.'

Giles took out his purse, extracted half a crown and placed it on the counter. The porter eyed it for some time before he spoke again. 'It's just possible you'll find her at Eddie's Nightclub.'

'Eddie Atkins?' enquired Harry.

'I believe that's correct, sir.'

'Well, that explains it,' said Harry. 'And where is Eddie's Nightclub?'

'Welsh Back, sir,' replied the porter as he pocketed the half a crown.

Harry left the hotel without another word and jumped into the back of a waiting cab. Giles got in beside him. 'Don't you think we should get back to school?' said Giles, looking at his watch. 'You can always tell your mother in the morning.'

Harry shook his head. 'It was you who said you'd interrupt your mother even if she was addressing the Mothers' Union,' Harry reminded him. 'Eddie's Nightclub, Welsh Back, please, cabbie,' he said firmly.

Harry didn't speak during the short journey. When the cab turned into a dark alley and came to a halt outside Eddie's, he got out and walked towards the entrance.

Harry banged firmly on the door. A shutter slid open and a pair of eyes stared at the two young men. 'The entrance fee is five shillings each,' said a voice behind the eyes. Giles pushed a ten-shilling note through the hole. The door swung open immediately.

The two of them made their way down a dimly lit staircase to the basement. Giles saw her first and quickly turned to leave, but it was too late. Harry was staring, transfixed, at a row of girls seated on stools at the bar, some chatting to men, others on their own. One of them, wearing a white see-through blouse, a short black leather skirt and black stockings, approached them and said, 'Can I help you, gents?'

Harry ignored her. His eyes had settled on a woman at the far end of the bar who was listening intently to an older man who had his hand on her thigh. The girl looked to see who he was staring at. 'I must say, you know class when you see it,' she said. 'Mind you, Maisie can be choosy, and I have to warn you, she doesn't come cheap.'

Harry turned and bolted back up the steps, pulled open the door and ran out on to the street, with Giles chasing after him. Once Harry was on the pavement, he fell to his knees and was violently sick. Giles knelt and put his arm around his friend, trying to comfort him.

A man who had been standing in the shadows on the other side of the road limped away.

EMMA BARRINGTON

1932–1939

44

I'll never forget the first time I saw him.

He came to tea at the Manor House to celebrate my brother's twelfth birthday. He was so quiet and reserved that I wondered how he could possibly be Giles's best friend. The other one, Deakins, was really strange. He never stopped eating and hardly said a word all afternoon.

And then Harry spoke, a soft, gentle voice that made you want to listen. The birthday party had apparently been going swimmingly until my father burst into the room, and then he hardly spoke again. I'd never known my father to be so off-hand with anyone, and I couldn't understand why he should behave in that way towards a complete stranger. But even more inexplicable was Papa's reaction when he asked Harry when his birthday was. How could such an innocuous question bring on such an extreme reaction? A moment later my father got up and left the room, without even saying goodbye to Giles and his guests. I could see that Mama was embarrassed by his behaviour, although she poured another cup of tea and pretended not to notice.

A few minutes later, my brother and his two friends left to go back to school. He turned and smiled at me before leaving, but just like my mother, I pretended not to notice. But when the front door closed I stood by the drawing-room window and watched as the car disappeared down the driveway and out of sight. I thought I saw him looking out of the back window, but I couldn't be sure.

After they had left, Mama went straight to my father's study and I could hear raised voices, which had recently become more and more common. When she came back out, she smiled at me as if nothing unusual had happened.

'What's the name of Giles's best friend?' I asked.

'Harry Clifton,' she replied.

◄○►

The next time I saw Harry Clifton was at the Advent carol service at St Mary Redcliffe. He sang *O Little Town of Bethlehem*, and my best friend, Jessica Braithwaite, accused me of swooning as if he was the new Bing Crosby. I didn't bother to deny it. I saw him chatting to Giles after the service and I would have liked to congratulate him, but Papa seemed to be in a hurry to get home. As we left, I saw his nanny giving him a huge hug.

I was also at St Mary Redcliffe the evening his voice broke, but at the time I didn't understand why so many heads were turning and some members of the congregation began to whisper among themselves. All I know is that I never heard him sing again.

When Giles was driven to the grammar school on his first day, I begged my mother to let me go along, but only because I wanted to meet Harry. But my father wouldn't hear of it, and despite my bursting into controlled tears, they still left me standing on the top step with my younger sister Grace. I knew Papa was cross about Giles not being offered a place at Eton, something I still don't understand, because a lot of boys more stupid than my brother passed the exam. Mama didn't seem to mind which school Giles went to, whereas I was delighted he was going to Bristol Grammar, because it meant I'd have a better chance of seeing Harry again.

In fact I must have seen him at least a dozen times during the next three years, but he was never able to recall any of those occasions, until we met up in Rome.

The family were all staying at our villa in Tuscany that summer when Giles took me to one side and said he needed to ask my advice. He only ever did that when he wanted something. But this time it turned out to be something I wanted just as much as he did.

'So what are you expecting me to do this time?' I asked.

'I need an excuse to go into Rome tomorrow,' he said, 'because I'm meant to be meeting up with Harry.'

'Harry who?' I said, feigning indifference.

'Harry Clifton, stupid. He's on a school trip to Rome and I promised to get away and spend the day with him.' He didn't need to spell out that Papa wouldn't have approved. 'All you have to do,' he continued, 'is ask Mama if she could take you to Rome for the day.'

'But she'll need to know why I want to go into Rome.'

'Tell her you've always wanted to visit the Villa Borghese.'

'Why the Villa Borghese?'

'Because that's where Harry will be at ten o'clock tomorrow morning.'

'But what happens if Mama agrees to take me? Then you'll be stymied.'

'She won't. They're having lunch with the Hendersons in Arezzo tomorrow, so I'll volunteer to be your chaperone.'

'And what do I get in exchange?' I demanded, as I didn't want Giles to know how keen I was to see Harry.

'My gramophone,' he said.

'For keeps, or just to borrow?'

Giles didn't speak for some time. 'For ever,' he said reluctantly.

'Hand it over now,' I said, 'or you can forget it.' To my surprise he did.

I was even more amazed when, the next day, my mother fell for his little ploy. Giles didn't even have to offer to act as my chaperone; Papa insisted that he accompany me. My deceitful brother made a show of protesting, but finally gave in.

I rose early the following morning and spent some considerable time thinking about what I should wear. It would have to be fairly conservative if my mother wasn't to become suspicious, but on the other hand I wanted to make sure Harry noticed me.

While we were on the train to Rome, I disappeared into the lavatory and put on a pair of mother's silk stockings and just a touch of lipstick, not enough for Giles to notice.

Once we'd checked into our hotel, Giles wanted to leave immediately for the Villa Borghese. So did I.

As we walked through the gardens and up towards the villa, a soldier turned to look at me. It was the first time that had happened, and I could feel my cheeks reddening.

No sooner had we entered the gallery than Giles went off in search of Harry. I hung back, pretending to take a great deal of interest in the paintings and statues. I needed to make an entrance.

When I eventually caught up with them, I found Harry chatting to my brother, although Giles wasn't even pretending to listen to him as he was clearly besotted by the tour guide. If he'd asked me, I could have told him he didn't have a chance. But older brothers rarely listen to their sisters when it comes to women; I would have advised him to comment on her shoes, which made me quite envious. Men think the Italians are only famous for designing cars. One exception to this rule is Captain Tarrant, who knows exactly how to treat a lady. My brother could learn a lot from him. Giles simply regarded me as his gauche little sister, not that he would have known what the word gauche meant.

I picked my moment, then strolled across and waited

for Giles to introduce us. Imagine my surprise when Harry invited me to join him for dinner that night. My only thought was that I hadn't packed a suitable evening dress. Over dinner, I discovered that my brother had paid Harry a thousand lira to take me off his hands, but he had refused until Giles also agreed to part with his Caruso recording. I told Harry he'd got the records and I'd got the gramophone. He didn't catch on.

As we crossed the road on the way back to the hotel, he held my hand for the first time, and when we reached the other side, I didn't let go. I could tell it was the first time Harry had held a girl's hand, because he was so nervous he was sweating.

I tried to make it easy for him to kiss me when we got back to my hotel, but he just shook hands and said good night as if we were old chums. I hinted that perhaps we might bump into each other again once we were back in Bristol. This time he responded more positively, and even suggested the most romantic location for our next date: the city's central library. He explained that it was somewhere Giles would never come across us. I happily agreed.

It was just after ten when Harry left and I went up to my room. A few minutes later I heard Giles unlocking his bedroom door. I had to smile. His evening with Caterina can't have been worth a Caruso recording and a gramophone.

When the family returned to Chew Valley a couple of weeks later, there were three letters waiting for me on the hall table, each with the same handwriting on the envelope. If my father noticed, he said nothing.

During the next month, Harry and I spent many happy hours together in the city library without anyone becoming suspicious, not least because he'd discovered a room where no one was likely to find us, even Deakins.

Once term began and we weren't able to see each other

as often, I quickly became aware just how much I missed Harry. We wrote every other day, and tried to grab a few hours together at the weekends. And that's how it might have continued, had it not been for the unwitting intervention of Dr Paget.

Over coffee at Carwardine's one Saturday morning, Harry, who had become quite bold, told me that his English master had persuaded Miss Webb to allow her girls to take part in the Bristol Grammar School play that year. By the time the auditions were held three weeks later, I knew the part of Juliet by heart. Poor innocent Dr Paget couldn't believe his luck.

Rehearsals meant not only that the two of us could be together for three afternoons a week, but that we were allowed to play the parts of young lovers. By the time the curtain went up on the first night, we were no longer acting.

The first two performances went so well that I couldn't wait for my parents to attend the closing night, although I didn't tell my father I was playing Juliet as I wanted it to be a surprise. It wasn't long after my first entrance that I became distracted by someone noisily leaving the auditorium. But Dr Paget had told us on several occasions never to look into the audience, it broke the spell, so I had no idea who had left so publicly. I prayed it wasn't my father, but when he didn't come backstage after the performance I realized my prayer had not been answered. What made it worse was my certainty that his little outburst was aimed at Harry, although I still didn't know why.

When we returned home that night, Giles and I sat on the stairs and listened to my parents having another row. But it was different this time, because I'd never heard my father be so unkind to Mama. When I could bear it no longer, I went to my room and locked myself in.

I was lying on my bed, thinking about Harry, when I

heard a gentle knock on the door. When I opened it, my mother made no attempt to hide the fact that she'd been crying, and told me to pack a small suitcase because we would be leaving shortly. A taxi drove us to the station and we arrived just in time to catch the milk train to London. During the journey, I wrote to Harry to let him know what had happened and where he could get in touch with me. I posted the letter in a box on King's Cross station before we boarded another train for Edinburgh.

Imagine my surprise when the following evening Harry and my brother turned up at Mulgelrie Castle, just in time for dinner. We spent an unexpected and glorious nine days in Scotland together. I didn't ever want to return to Chew Valley, even though my father had rung and apologized unreservedly for the way he'd behaved on the night of the play.

But I knew that eventually we would have to go home. I promised Harry on one of our long morning walks that I would try to find out the reason for my father's continued hostility towards him.

When we arrived back at the Manor House, Papa could not have been more conciliatory. He tried to explain why he had treated Harry so badly over the years, and my mother and Giles seemed to accept his explanation. But I wasn't convinced he had told us the whole story.

What made things even more difficult for me was that he forbade me to tell Harry the truth about how his father had died, as his mother was adamant that it should remain a family secret. I had a feeling that Mrs Clifton knew the real reason my father didn't approve of Harry and me being together, although I would have liked to tell them both that nothing and no one could keep us apart. However, it all came to a head in a way I could never have predicted.

I was just as impatient as Harry to find out if he'd been

offered a place at Oxford, and we arranged to meet outside the library on the morning after he received the telegram letting him know the result.

I was a few minutes late that Friday morning, and when I saw him sitting on the top step, head in hands, I knew he must have failed.

45

HARRY LEAPT UP and threw his arms around Emma the moment he saw her. He continued to cling to her, something he'd never done in public before, which confirmed her belief that it could only be bad news.

Without a word passing between them, he took her by the hand, led her into the building, down a circular wooden staircase and along a narrow brick corridor until he came to a door marked 'Antiquities'. He peered inside to make sure that no one else had discovered their hiding place.

The two of them sat opposite each other at a small table where they had spent so many hours studying during the past year. Harry was trembling, and not because of the chill in the windowless room that was lined on all sides by shelves of leather-bound books covered in dust, some of which looked as if they hadn't been opened for years. In time they would become antiquities in their own right.

It was some time before Harry spoke.

'Do you think there is anything I could say or do that would stop you loving me?'

'No, my darling,' said Emma, 'absolutely nothing.'

'I've found out why your father has been so determined to keep us apart.'

'I already know,' said Emma, bowing her head slightly, 'and I promise you it makes no difference.'

'How can you possibly know?' said Harry.

'My father told us the day we returned from Scotland, but he swore us to secrecy.'

'He told you my mother was a prostitute?'

Emma was stunned. It was some time before she recovered enough to speak. 'No, he did not,' she said vehemently. 'How could you say anything so cruel?'

'Because it's the truth,' said Harry. 'My mother hasn't been working at the Royal Hotel for the past two years, as I thought, but at a nightclub called Eddie's.'

'That doesn't make her a prostitute,' said Emma.

'The man sitting at the bar with a glass of whisky in one hand and the other on her thigh wasn't hoping for stimulating conversation.'

Emma leant across the table and touched Harry gently on the cheek. 'I'm so sorry, my darling,' she said, 'but it makes no difference to how I feel about you, and it never will.'

Harry managed a weak smile, but Emma remained silent, knowing it could only be a few moments before he asked her the inevitable question.

'If that wasn't the secret your father asked you to keep,' he said, suddenly serious again, 'what did he tell you?'

It was Emma's turn to hold her head in her hands, aware that he'd left her with no choice but to tell him the truth. Like her mother, she was no good at dissembling.

'What did he tell you?' Harry repeated, more emphatically.

Emma held on to the edge of the table as she tried to steady herself. Finally she summoned up the strength to look at Harry. Although he was only a few feet away, he could not have been more distant. 'I need to ask you the same question you asked me,' said Emma. 'Is there anything I could say or do that would stop you loving me?'

Harry leant across and took her hand. 'Of course not,' he said.

'Your father wasn't killed in the war,' she said softly. 'And my father was probably responsible for his death.' She gripped his hand firmly before revealing everything her father had told them the day they returned from Scotland.

When she'd finished, Harry looked dazed and was unable to speak. He tried to stand up but his legs gave way beneath him, like a boxer who'd taken one punch too many, and he fell back into his chair.

'I've known for some time that my father couldn't have died in the war,' Harry said quietly, 'but what I still don't understand is why my mother didn't simply tell me the truth.'

'And now you do know the truth,' said Emma, trying to hold back the tears, 'I would understand if you wanted to break off our relationship after what my father has put your family through.'

'It's not your fault,' said Harry, 'but I'll never forgive him.' He paused before adding, 'And I won't be able to face him once he finds out the truth about my mother.'

'He need never find out,' said Emma, taking him by the hand again. 'It will always be a secret between us.'

'That's not possible any longer,' said Harry.

'Why not?'

'Because Giles saw the man who followed us to Edinburgh standing in a doorway opposite Eddie's Nightclub.'

'Then it's my father who's prostituted himself,' said Emma, 'because not only did he lie to us yet again, but he's already gone back on his word.'

'How?'

'He promised Giles that man would never follow him again.'

'That man wasn't interested in Giles,' said Harry. 'I think he was following my mother.'

'But why?'

'Because if he was able to prove how my mother earned her living, he must have hoped it would convince you to give me up.'

'How little he knows his own daughter,' said Emma, 'because I'm now even more determined that nothing will keep us apart. And he certainly can't stop me admiring your mother even more than I did before.'

'How can you say that?' said Harry.

'She works as a waitress to support her family, ends up owning Tilly's, and when it's burnt to the ground she's accused of arson, but holds her head high, knowing she is innocent. She finds herself another job at the Royal Hotel, and when she's sacked, she still refuses to give up. She receives a cheque for six hundred pounds, and for a moment believes all her problems are solved, only to discover she's in fact penniless just at the time when she needs money to make sure you can stay at school. In desperation, she then turns to . . .'

'But I wouldn't have wanted her to . . .'

'She would have known that, Harry, but she still felt it was a sacrifice worth making.'

Another long silence followed. 'Oh my God,' said Harry. 'How can I ever have thought badly of her.' He looked up at Emma. 'I need you to do something for me.'

'Anything.'

'Can you go and see my mother? Use any excuse, but try to find out if she saw me in that dreadful place last night.'

'How will I know, if she isn't willing to admit it?'

'You'll know,' said Harry quietly.

'But if your mother did see you, she's bound to ask me what you were doing there.'

'I was looking for her.'

'But why?'

'To tell her that I've been offered a place at Oxford.'

—◁○▷—

Emma slipped into a pew at the back of Holy Nativity and waited for the service to end. She could see Mrs Clifton sitting in the third row, next to an old lady. Harry had seemed a little less tense when they'd met again earlier that morning. He'd been very clear what he needed to find out, and she promised not to stray beyond her remit. They had rehearsed every possible scenario several times, until she was word perfect.

After the elderly priest had given the final blessing, Emma stepped out into the centre of the aisle and waited, so Mrs Clifton couldn't possibly miss her. When Maisie saw Emma, she couldn't hide a look of surprise, but it was quickly replaced by a welcoming smile. She walked quickly towards her and introduced the old lady who was with her. 'Mum, this is Emma Barrington, she's a friend of Harry's.'

The old lady gave Emma a toothy grin. 'There's a great deal of difference between being his friend and being his girlfriend. Which are you?' she demanded.

Mrs Clifton laughed, but it was clear to Emma that she was just as interested to hear her reply.

'I'm his girlfriend,' said Emma proudly.

The old lady delivered another toothy grin, but Maisie didn't smile.

'Well, that's all right then, isn't it?' Harry's grand-mother said, before adding, 'I can't stand around here all day chatting, I've got dinner to make.' She began to walk away, but then turned back and asked, 'Would you like to join us for dinner, young lady?'

This was a question that Harry had anticipated, and for which he'd even scripted a reply. 'That's very kind of you,' said Emma, 'but my parents will be expecting me.'

'Quite right too,' said the old lady. 'You should always respect your parents' wishes. I'll see you later, Maisie.'

'May I walk with you, Mrs Clifton?' asked Emma as they stepped out of the church.

'Yes, of course, my dear.'

'Harry asked me to come and see you, because he knew you'd want to know that he's been offered a place at Oxford.'

'Oh, that's wonderful news,' said Maisie, throwing her arms around Emma. She suddenly released her, and asked, 'But why didn't he come and tell me himself?'

Another scripted reply. 'He's stuck in detention,' said Emma, hoping she didn't sound over-rehearsed, 'writing out passages from Shelley. I'm afraid my brother's to blame. You see, after he heard the good news, he smuggled a bottle of champagne into school, and they were caught celebrating in his study last night.'

'Is that so wicked?' asked Maisie, grinning.

'Dr Paget seemed to think so. Harry's dreadfully sorry.'

Maisie laughed so uproariously that Emma had no doubt she'd no idea her son had visited the club last night. She would have liked to ask one more question that still puzzled her, but Harry couldn't have been more emphatic: 'If my mother doesn't want me to know how my father died, so be it.'

'I'm sorry you can't stay to lunch,' said Maisie, 'because there was something I wanted to tell you. Perhaps another time.'

46

HARRY SPENT THE FOLLOWING week waiting for another bombshell to drop. When it did, he cheered out loud.

Giles received a telegram on the last day of term telling him he'd been offered a place at Brasenose College, Oxford, to read History.

'By the skin of his teeth,' was the expression Dr Paget used when he informed the headmaster.

Two months later, one scholar, one exhibitioner and one commoner arrived in the ancient university city, by different modes of transport, to begin their three-year undergraduate courses.

Harry signed up for the dramatic society and the officer training corps, Giles for the union and the cricket club, while Deakins settled himself down in the bowels of the Bodleian library, and, like a mole, was rarely seen above ground. But then, he had already decided that Oxford was where he was going to spend the rest of his life.

Harry couldn't be so sure how he would be spending the rest of his life, while the Prime Minister continued to fly back and forth to Germany, finally returning to Heston airport with a smile on his face, waving a piece of paper and telling people what they wanted to hear.

Harry wasn't in any doubt that Britain was on the brink of war. When Emma asked him why he was so convinced, he replied, 'Haven't you noticed that Herr Hitler never bothers to visit us? We are always the importunate suitor, and in the end we will be spurned.' Emma ignored his opinion, but then, like Mr Chamberlain, she didn't want to believe he might be right.

Emma wrote to Harry twice a week, sometimes three times, despite the fact that she was working flat out preparing for her own entrance exams to Oxford.

◄○►

When Harry returned to Bristol for the Christmas vacation, the two of them spent as much time together as possible, although Harry made sure he kept out of the way of Mr Barrington.

Emma turned down the chance to spend her holiday with the rest of the family in Tuscany, not hiding the fact from her father that she'd rather be with Harry.

As her entrance exam drew nearer, the number of hours Emma spent in the Antiquities room would have impressed even Deakins, but then Harry was coming to the conclusion that she was about to impress the examiners just as much as his reclusive friend had done the year before. Whenever he suggested this to Emma, she would remind him that there were twenty male students at Oxford for every female.

'You could always go to Cambridge,' Giles foolishly suggested.

'Where they're even more prehistoric,' Emma responded. 'They still don't award degrees to women.'

Emma's greatest fear was not that she wouldn't be offered a place at Oxford, but that by the time she took it up, war would have been declared, and Harry would have signed up and departed for some foreign field that was not forever England. All her life she had been continually reminded of the Great War by the number of women who still wore black every day, in memory of their husbands, lovers, brothers and sons who had never returned from the Front, in what nobody was any longer calling the war to end all wars.

She had pleaded with Harry not to volunteer if war was declared, but at least to wait until he was called up. But after Hitler had marched into Czechoslovakia and annexed the Sudetenland, Harry never wavered in his belief that war with Germany was inevitable, and that the moment it was declared, he would be in uniform the following day.

When Harry invited Emma to join him for the Commem Ball at the end of his first year, she resolved not to discuss the possibility of war. She also made another decision.

—◦—

Emma travelled up to Oxford on the morning of the ball and checked into the Randolph Hotel. She spent the rest of the day being shown around Somerville, the Ashmolean and the Bodleian by Harry, who was confident she would be joining him as an undergraduate in a few months' time.

Emma returned to the hotel, giving herself plenty of time to prepare for the ball. Harry had arranged to pick her up at eight.

He strolled through the front door of the hotel a few minutes before the appointed hour. He was dressed in a fashionable midnight blue dinner jacket which his mother had given him for his nineteenth birthday. He called Emma's room from the front desk to tell her he was downstairs and would wait for her in the foyer.

'I'll be straight down,' she promised.

As the minutes passed, Harry began to pace around the foyer, wondering what Emma meant by 'straight down'. But Giles had often told him that she'd learnt how to tell the time from her mother.

And then he saw her, standing at the top of the staircase. He didn't move as she walked slowly down, her strapless turquoise silk dress emphasizing her graceful figure. Every other young man in the foyer looked as if he'd be happy to change places with Harry.

'Wow,' he said as she reached the bottom step. 'Who needs Vivien Leigh? By the way, I love the shoes.' Emma felt the first part of her plan was falling into place.

They walked out of the hotel and strolled arm in arm towards Radcliffe Square. As they entered the gates of Harry's college, the sun began to dip behind the Bodleian. No one entering Brasenose that evening would have thought that Britain was only a few weeks away from a war in which over half the young men who danced the night away would never graduate.

But nothing could have been further from the thoughts of the gay young couples dancing to the music of Cole Porter and Jerome Kern. While several hundred undergraduates and their guests consumed crates of champagne and ate their way through a mountain of smoked salmon, Harry rarely let Emma out of his sight, fearful that some ungallant soul might attempt to steal her away.

Giles drank a little too much champagne, ate far too many oysters and didn't dance with the same girl twice the entire evening.

At two o'clock in the morning, the Billy Cotton Dance Band struck up the last waltz. Harry and Emma clung to each other as they swayed to the rhythm of the orchestra.

When the conductor finally raised his baton for the National Anthem, Emma couldn't help noticing that all the young men around her, whatever state of inebriation they were in, stood rigidly to attention as they sang 'God Save the King'.

Harry and Emma walked slowly back to the Randolph chatting about nothing of any consequence, just not wanting the evening to end.

'Well, at least you'll be back in a fortnight's time to sit your entrance exam,' said Harry as they climbed the steps to the hotel, 'so it won't be too long before I see you again.'

'True,' said Emma, 'but there'll be no time for any distractions until I've completed the last paper. Once that's out of the way, we can spend the rest of the weekend together.'

Harry was about to kiss her goodnight, when she whispered, 'Would you like to come up to my room? I've got a present for you. I wouldn't want you to think I'd forgotten your birthday.'

Harry looked surprised, as did the hall porter when the young couple walked up the staircase together hand in hand. When they reached Emma's room, she fumbled nervously with the key before finally pushing open the door.

'I'll just be a moment,' she said as she disappeared into the bathroom.

Harry sat down in the only chair in the room and tried to think of what he'd most like for his birthday. When the bathroom door opened, Emma was framed in the half light. The elegant strapless gown had been replaced by a hotel towel.

Harry could hear his heart beating as she walked slowly towards him.

'I think you're a little overdressed, my darling,' Emma said, as she slipped off his jacket and let it fall to the floor. Next she undid his bow tie before unbuttoning his shirt, and both joined the jacket. Two shoes and two socks followed, before she slowly pulled down his trousers. She was about to remove the one remaining obstacle in her path, when he gathered her up in his arms and carried her across the bedroom.

As he dumped her unceremoniously on to the bed, the towel fell to the floor. Emma had often imagined this moment since they'd returned from Rome, and assumed that her first attempts at making love would be awkward and clumsy. But Harry was gentle and considerate, although he was clearly every bit as nervous as she was. After they'd made love, she lay in his arms, not wanting to fall asleep.

'Did you like your birthday present?' she asked.

'Yes I did,' said Harry. 'But I hope it's not going to be another year before I can unwrap the next one. That reminds me, I've got a present for you too.'

'But it's not my birthday.'

'It's not a birthday present.'

He jumped out of bed, picked his trousers up off the floor and rummaged around in the pockets until he came across a small leather box. He returned to the bedside, fell to one knee and said, 'Emma, my darling, will you marry me?'

'You look quite ridiculous down there,' said Emma, frowning. 'Get back into bed before you freeze to death.'

'Not until you've answered my question.'

'Don't be silly, Harry. I decided that we were going

to be married the day you came to the Manor House for
Giles's twelfth birthday.'

Harry burst out laughing as he placed the ring on
the third finger of her left hand.

'I'm sorry it's such a small diamond,' he said.

'It's as big as the Ritz,' she said as he climbed back
into bed. 'And as you seem to have everything so well
organized,' she teased, 'what date have you chosen for
our wedding?'

'Saturday, July the twenty-ninth, at three o'clock.'

'Why then?'

'It's the last day of term, and in any case, we can't
book the university church after I've gone down.'

Emma sat up, grabbed the pencil and pad from the
bedside table and started to write.

'What are you doing?' asked Harry.

'I'm working on the guest list. If we've only got seven
weeks . . .'

'That can wait,' said Harry, taking her back in his
arms. 'I feel another birthday coming on.'

—◇—

'She's too young to be thinking about marriage,' said
Emma's father, as if she wasn't in the room.

'She's the same age I was when you proposed to
me,' Elizabeth reminded him.

'But you weren't about to sit the most important
exam of your life, just weeks before the wedding.'

'That's exactly why I've taken over all the arrangements,' said Elizabeth. 'That way Emma won't have any
distractions until her exams are over.'

'Surely it would be better to put the wedding off for
a few months. After all, what's the hurry?'

'What a good idea, Daddy,' said Emma, speaking for

the first time. 'Perhaps we could also ask Herr Hitler if he'd be kind enough to put off the war for a few months, because your daughter wants to get married.'

'And what does Mrs Clifton think about all of this?' her father asked, ignoring his daughter's comment.

'Why should she be anything other than delighted by the news?' Elizabeth asked him. He didn't respond.

◄o►

An announcement of the forthcoming marriage between Emma Grace Barrington and Harold Arthur Clifton was published in *The Times* ten days later. The first banns were read from the pulpit of St Mary's by the Reverend Styler on the following Sunday and over three hundred invitations were sent out during the next week. No one was surprised when Harry asked Giles to be his best man, with Captain Tarrant and Deakins as the principal ushers.

But Harry was shocked when he received a letter from Old Jack, declining his kind invitation because he couldn't leave his post in the current circumstances. Harry wrote back, begging him to reconsider and at least attend the wedding, even if he felt unable to take on the task of being an usher. Old Jack's reply left Harry even more confused: 'I feel my presence might turn out to be an embarrassment.'

'What is he talking about?' said Harry. 'Surely he knows that we'd all be honoured if he came.'

'He's almost as bad as my father,' said Emma. 'He's refusing to give me away, and says he's not even sure he'll come.'

'But you told me he'd promised to be more supportive in the future.'

'Yes, but that all changed the moment he heard we were engaged.'

'I can't pretend that my mother sounded all that enthusiastic when I told her the news either,' Harry admitted.

◄◊►

Emma didn't see Harry again until she returned to Oxford to sit her exams, and even then not until she'd completed the final paper. When she came out of the examination hall, her fiancé was waiting on the top step, a bottle of champagne in one hand and two glasses in the other.

'So, how do you think you got on?' he asked as he filled her glass.

'I don't know,' sighed Emma, as dozens of other girls poured out of the examination hall. 'I didn't realize what I was up against until I saw that lot.'

'Well, at least you've got something to distract you while you wait for the results.'

'Just three weeks to go,' Emma reminded him. 'That's more than enough time for you to change your mind.'

'If you don't win a scholarship, I may have to reconsider my position. After all, I can't be seen associating with a commoner.'

'And if I do win a scholarship, I may have to reconsider my position and look for another scholar.'

'Deakins is still available,' said Harry as he topped up her glass.

'It will be too late by then,' said Emma.

'Why?'

'Because the results are due to be announced on the morning of our wedding.'

Emma and Harry spent most of the weekend locked away in her little hotel room, endlessly going over the wedding arrangements when they weren't making love. By Sunday night, Emma had come to one conclusion.

'Mama has been quite magnificent,' she said, 'which is more than I can say for my father.'

'Do you think he'll even turn up?'

'Oh yes. Mama's talked him into coming, but he's still refusing to give me away. What's the latest on Old Jack?'

'He hasn't even replied to my last letter,' said Harry.

47

'HAVE YOU PUT ON a little weight, darling?' asked Emma's mother as she tried to fasten the last clasp on the back of her daughter's wedding dress.

'I don't think so,' replied Emma, looking at herself critically in the full-length mirror.

'Stunning,' was Elizabeth's verdict as she stood back to admire the bride's outfit.

They had travelled to London several times to have the dress fitted by Madame Renée, the proprietor of a small, fashionable boutique in Mayfair, thought to be patronized by Queen Mary and Queen Elizabeth. Madame Renée had personally supervised each fitting, and the Victorian embroidered lace around the neck and hem, something old, blended quite naturally with the silk bodice and empire bell skirt that was proving so fashionable that year, something new. The little cream tear-drop hat, Madame Renée had assured them, was what women of fashion would be wearing next year. The only comment Emma's father made on the subject came when he saw the bill.

Elizabeth Barrington glanced at her watch. Nineteen minutes to three. 'No need to rush,' she told Emma when there was a knock on the door. She was sure she'd hung the Do Not Disturb sign on the doorknob and told the chauffeur not to expect them before three. At the rehearsal the previous day, the journey from the hotel to the church had taken seven minutes. Elizabeth intended Emma to be fashionably late. 'Keep them waiting for a few minutes, but don't give them any cause for concern.' A second knock.

'I'll get it,' Elizabeth said, and went to the door. A young porter in a smart red uniform handed her a telegram, the eleventh that day. She was about to close the door when he said, 'I was told to inform you, madam, that this one is important.'

Elizabeth's first thought was to wonder who could possibly have cancelled at the last moment. She only hoped it wouldn't mean reorganizing the top table at the reception. She tore open the telegram and read the contents.

'Who's it from?' asked Emma, adjusting the angle of her hat by another inch and wondering if it was perhaps a little too risqué.

Elizabeth handed her the telegram. Once Emma had read it, she burst into tears.

'Many congratulations, darling,' said her mother, taking a handkerchief out of her handbag and beginning to dry her daughter's tears. 'I'd hug you, but I don't want to crease your dress.'

Once Elizabeth was satisfied that Emma was ready, she spent a moment checking her own outfit in the mirror. Madame Renée had pronounced, 'You mustn't outdo your daughter on her big day, but at the same time, you can't afford to go unnoticed.' Elizabeth particularly liked the Norman Hartnell hat, even if it was not what the young were calling 'chic'.

'Time to leave,' she declared after one more look at her watch. Emma smiled as she glanced at the going-away outfit she would change into once the reception was over, when she and Harry would travel up to Scotland for their honeymoon. Lord Harvey had offered them Mulgelrie Castle for a fortnight, with the promise that no other member of the family would be allowed within ten miles of the estate during that time and, perhaps more important, Harry could ask for three portions of Highland broth every night, without a suggestion of grouse to follow.

Emma followed her mother out of the suite and along the corridor. By the time she reached the top of the staircase, she felt sure her legs were about to give way. As she descended the stairs, other guests stood aside so that nothing would impede her progress.

A porter held open the front door of the hotel for her, while Sir Walter's chauffeur stood by the back door of the Rolls so the bride could join her grandfather. As Emma sat down beside him, carefully arranging her dress, Sir Walter placed his monocle in his right eye and declared, 'You look quite beautiful, young lady. Harry is indeed a most fortunate man.'

'Thank you, Grandpa,' she said, kissing him on the cheek. She glanced out of the rear window to see her mother climbing into a second Rolls-Royce, and a moment later the two cars moved off to join the afternoon traffic as they began their sedate journey to the university church of St Mary's.

'Is Daddy at the church?' asked Emma, trying not to sound anxious.

'Among the first to arrive,' said her grandfather. 'I do believe he's already regretting allowing me the privilege of giving you away.'

'And Harry?'

'Never seen him so nervous. But Giles seems to have everything under control, which must be a first. I know he's spent the last month preparing his best man's speech.'

'We're both lucky to have the same best friend,' said Emma. 'You know, Grandpa, I once read that every bride has second thoughts on the morning of her wedding.'

'That's natural enough, my dear.'

'But I've never had a second thought about Harry,' said Emma, as they came to a halt outside the university church. 'I know we'll spend the rest of our lives together.'

She waited for her grandfather to step out of the car before she gathered up her dress and joined him on the pavement.

Her mother rushed forward to check Emma's outfit one last time before she would allow her to enter the church. Elizabeth handed her a small bouquet of pale pink roses as the two bridesmaids, Emma's younger sister Grace and her school friend Jessica, gathered up the end of the train.

'You next, Grace,' said her mother, bending down to unruffle her bridesmaid's dress.

'I hope not,' said Grace, loud enough for her mother to hear.

Elizabeth stepped back and nodded. Two sidesmen pulled open the heavy doors, the sign for the organist to strike up Wagner's *Wedding March*, and the congregation to rise and welcome the bride.

As Emma stepped into the church, she was taken by surprise to see how many people had travelled to Oxford to share in her happiness. She walked slowly down the aisle on her grandfather's arm, the guests turning to smile at her as she made her way towards the altar.

She noticed Mr Frobisher sitting next to Mr Holcombe

on the right-hand side of the aisle. Miss Tilly, who was wearing quite a daring hat, must have come all the way from Cornwall, while Dr Paget gave her the warmest of smiles. But nothing compared with the smile that appeared on her own face when she spotted Captain Tarrant, head bowed, wearing a morning suit that didn't quite fit. Harry would be so pleased he had decided to come after all. In the front row sat Mrs Clifton, who had clearly spent some time selecting her outfit because she looked so fashionable. A smile crossed Emma's lips, but she was surprised and disappointed that her future mother-in-law didn't turn to look at her as she passed.

And then she saw Harry, standing on the altar steps next to her brother as they waited for the bride. Emma continued up the aisle on the arm of one grandfather, while the other stood bolt upright in the front row, next to her father, who she thought looked a little melancholy. Perhaps he really was regretting his decision not to give her away.

Sir Walter stood to one side as Emma climbed the four steps to join her future husband. She leaned over and whispered, 'I nearly had a change of heart.' Harry tried not to grin as he waited for the punch line. 'After all, scholars of this university cannot be seen to marry beneath themselves.'

'I'm so proud of you, my darling,' he said. 'Many congratulations.'

Giles bowed low in genuine respect, and Chinese whispers broke out among the congregation as the news spread from row to row.

The music stopped, and the college chaplain raised his hands and said, '*Dearly beloved, we are gathered together here in the sight of God, and in the face of this congregation, to join together this Man and this Woman, in holy matrimony . . .*'

Emma suddenly felt nervous. She had learnt all the responses by heart but now she couldn't recall one of them.

'*First it was ordained for the procreation of children . . .*'

Emma tried to concentrate on the chaplain's words, but she couldn't wait to escape and be alone with Harry. Perhaps they should have gone up to Scotland the night before and eloped at Gretna Green; so much more convenient for Mulgelrie Castle, she'd pointed out to Harry.

'*Into which holy estate these two persons present come now to be joined. Therefore if any man can show any just cause why they may not lawfully be joined together, let him now speak, or else hereafter for ever hold his peace . . .*'

The chaplain paused, to allow a diplomatic period of time to pass before he pronounced the words, *I require and charge you both*, when a clear voice declared, 'I object!'

Emma and Harry both swung round to see who could possibly have uttered two such damning words.

The chaplain looked up in disbelief, wondering for a moment if he had misheard, but all over the church, heads were turning as the congregation tried to discover who had made the unexpected intervention. The chaplain had never experienced such a turn of events before, and tried desperately to recall what he was expected to do in the circumstances.

Emma buried her head in Harry's shoulder, while he searched among the chattering congregation, trying to find out who it was who had caused such consternation. He assumed it must be Emma's father, but when he looked down at the front row he saw Hugo Barrington, white as a sheet, was also trying to see who had brought the ceremony to a premature halt.

The Reverend Styler had to raise his voice to be heard above the growing clamour. 'Would the gentleman who has objected to this marriage taking place please make himself known.'

A tall, upright figure stepped out into the aisle. Every eye remained fixed on Captain Jack Tarrant as he made his way up to the altar before coming to a halt in front of the chaplain. Emma clung on to Harry, fearful he was about to be prised away from her.

'Am I to understand, sir,' said the chaplain, 'that you feel this marriage should not be allowed to proceed?'

'That is correct, sir,' said Old Jack quietly.

'Then I must ask you, the bride and groom and the members of their immediate family to join me in the vestry.' Raising his voice, he added, 'The congregation should remain in their places until I have considered the objection, and made my decision known.'

Those who had been bidden were led by the chaplain into the vestry, followed by Harry and Emma. Not one of them spoke, although the congregation continued to whisper noisily among themselves.

Once the two families had crammed themselves into the tiny vestry, the Reverend Styler closed the door.

'Captain Tarrant,' he began, 'I must tell you that I alone am vested by law with the authority to decide whether this marriage should continue. Naturally I shall not come to any decision until I have heard your objections.'

The only person in that overcrowded room who appeared calm was Old Jack. 'Thank you, chaplain,' he began. 'Firstly, I must apologize to you all, and in particular to Emma and Harry, for my intervention. I have spent the past few weeks wrestling with my conscience before coming to this unhappy decision. I could have taken the easy way out and simply found some excuse for not attending this ceremony today. I have remained silent until now in the hope that in time any objection would prove irrelevant. But sadly that has not proved to be the case, for Harry and Emma's love for each other has in fact grown over the years, and not diminished, which is why it has become impossible for me to remain silent any longer.'

Everyone was so gripped by Old Jack's words that only Elizabeth Barrington noticed her husband slip quietly out of the back door of the vestry.

'Thank you, Captain Tarrant,' said the Reverend Styler. 'While I accept your intervention in good faith, I need to know what specific charges you bring against these two young people.'

'I bring no charge against Harry or Emma, both of whom I love and admire, and believe to be as much in the dark as the rest of you. No, my charge is against Hugo Barrington, who has known for many years that there is a possibility that he is the father of both of these unfortunate children.'

A gasp went around the room as everyone tried to grasp the enormity of this statement. The chaplain said nothing until he was able to regain their attention. 'Is there anyone present who can verify or refute Captain Tarrant's claim?'

'This can't possibly be true,' said Emma, still clinging on to Harry. 'There must be some mistake. Surely my father can't . . .'

That was the moment everyone became aware that the father of the bride was no longer among them. The chaplain turned his attention to Mrs Clifton, who was quietly sobbing.

'I can't deny Captain Tarrant's fears,' she said haltingly. It was some time before she continued. 'I confess I did have a relationship with Mr Barrington on one occasion.' She paused again. 'Only once, but, unfortunately, it was just a few weeks before I married my husband –' she raised her head slowly – 'so I have no way of knowing who Harry's father is.'

'I should point out to you all,' said Old Jack, 'that Hugo Barrington threatened Mrs Clifton on more than one occasion, should she ever reveal his dreadful secret.'

'Mrs Clifton, may I be allowed to ask you a question?' said Sir Walter gently.

Maisie nodded, although her head remained bowed.

'Did your late husband suffer from colourblindness?'

'Not that I'm aware of,' she said, barely loudly enough to be heard.

Sir Walter turned to Harry. 'But I believe you do, my boy?'

'Yes I do, sir,' said Harry without hesitation. 'Why is that of any importance?'

'Because I am also colour-blind,' said Sir Walter. 'As are my son and grandson. It is a hereditary trait that has troubled our family for several generations.'

Harry took Emma in his arms. 'I swear to you, my darling, I didn't know anything about this.'

'Of course you didn't,' said Elizabeth Barrington, speaking for the first time. 'The only man who knew was my husband, and he didn't have the courage to come forward and admit it. If he had, none of this need ever have happened. Father,' she said, turning to Lord Harvey, 'can I ask you to explain to our guests why the ceremony will not be continuing.'

Lord Harvey nodded. 'Leave it to me, old gal,' he said, touching her gently on the arm. 'But what are you going to do?'

'I'm going take my daughter as far away from this place as possible.'

'I don't want to go as far away as possible,' Emma said, 'unless it's with Harry.'

'I fear your father has left us with no choice,' said Elizabeth, taking her gently by the arm. But Emma continued to cling on to Harry until he whispered, 'I'm afraid your mother's right, my darling. But one thing your father will never be able to do is stop me loving you, and if it takes the rest of my life, I'll prove he's not my father.'

'Perhaps you'd prefer to leave by the rear entrance, Mrs Barrington,' suggested the chaplain. Emma reluctantly released Harry and allowed her mother to take her away.

The chaplain led them out of the vestry and down a narrow corridor to a door that he was surprised to find unlocked. 'May God go with you, my children,' he said before letting them out.

Elizabeth accompanied her daughter around the outside of the church to the waiting Rolls-Royces. She ignored those members of the congregation who had strayed outside for some fresh air or to smoke a cigarette and now made no attempt to conceal their curiosity when they spotted the two women climbing unceremoniously into the back of the limousine.

Elizabeth had opened the door of the first Rolls and bundled her daughter into the back seat before the chauffeur spotted them. He had stationed himself by the great door as he hadn't expected the bride and groom to appear for at least another half an hour, when a peal of bells would announce the marriage of Mr and Mrs Harry Clifton to the world. The moment the chauffeur heard the door slam, he stubbed out his cigarette, ran across to the car and jumped behind the wheel.

'Take us back to the hotel,' Elizabeth said.

Neither of them spoke again until they had reached

the safety of their room. Emma lay sobbing on the bed while Elizabeth stroked her hair, the way she had when she was a child.

'What am I going to do?' cried Emma. 'I can't suddenly stop loving Harry.'

'I'm sure you never will,' said her mother, 'but fate has decreed that you cannot be together until it can be proved who Harry's father is.' She continued to stroke her daughter's hair, and thought she might even have fallen asleep, until Emma quietly added, 'What will I tell my child when they ask who their father is?'

HARRY CLIFTON

1939–1940

48

The thing I remember most after Emma and her mother had left the church was how calm everyone appeared to be. No hysterics, no one fainted, there weren't even any raised voices. A visitor might have been forgiven for not realizing how many people's lives had just been irreparably damaged, even ruined. How very British, stiff upper lip and all that; no one willing to admit that their personal life had been shattered in the space of a single hour. Well, I have to admit, mine had.

I had stood in numbed silence as the different actors played out their roles. Old Jack had done no more or less than what he considered his duty, though the pallor of his skin and the deeply etched lines on his face suggested otherwise. He could have taken the easy way out and simply declined our invitation to the wedding, but Victoria Cross winners don't walk away.

Elizabeth Barrington was cast from that metal which, when put to the test, proved she was the equal of any man: a veritable Portia, who sadly hadn't married a Brutus.

As I looked around the vestry waiting for the chaplain to return, I felt saddest for Sir Walter, who had walked his granddaughter down the aisle, and had not gained a grandson, but rather lost a son, who, as Old Jack had warned me so many years ago, 'was not cut from the same cloth' as his father.

My dear mother was fearful to respond when I tried to take her in my arms and reassure her of my love. She clearly believed she alone was to blame for everything that had taken place that day.

And Giles, he became a man when his father crept out of the vestry to hide under some slimy stone, leaving the responsibility for his actions to others. In time, many of those present would become aware that what had taken place that day was every bit as devastating for Giles as for Emma.

Finally, Lord Harvey. He was an example to us all of how to behave in a crisis. Once the chaplain had returned and explained the legal implications of consanguinity to us, we agreed among ourselves that Lord Harvey should address the waiting congregation on behalf of both families.

'I would like Harry to stand on my right,' he said, 'as I wish everyone present to be left in no doubt, as my daughter Elizabeth made abundantly clear, that no blame rests on his shoulders.

'Mrs Clifton,' he said, turning to my mother, 'I hope you will be kind enough to stand on my left. Your courage in adversity has been an example to us all, and to one of us in particular.

'I hope that Captain Tarrant will stand by Harry's side: only a fool blames the messenger. Giles should take his place beside him. Sir Walter, perhaps you would stand next to Mrs Clifton, while the rest of the family take their places behind us. Let me make it clear to you all,' he continued, 'that I only have one purpose in this tragic business, namely to ensure that everyone gathered in this church today will be in no doubt of our resolve in this matter, so that no one will ever say we were a divided house.'

Without another word, he led his small flock out of the vestry.

When the chattering congregation saw us filing back into the church, Lord Harvey didn't need to call for silence. Each one of us took our allocated place on the altar steps as if we were about to pose for a family photograph that would later find its way into a wedding album.

'Friends, if I may be so bold,' began Lord Harvey, 'I have been asked to let you know on behalf of our two families that sadly the marriage between my granddaughter, Emma Barrington, and Mr Harry Clifton will not be taking place today, or for that matter on any other day.' Those last four words had a finality about them that was chilling when you were the only person present who still clung on to a vestige of hope that this might one day be resolved. 'I must apologize to you all,' he continued, 'if you have been inconvenienced in any way for that was surely not our purpose. May I conclude by thanking you for your presence here today, and wish you all a safe journey home.'

I wasn't sure what would happen next, but one or two members of the congregation rose from their places and began to make their way slowly out of the church; within moments the trickle turned into a steady stream, until finally those of us standing on the altar steps were the only ones remaining.

Lord Harvey thanked the chaplain, and warmly shook hands with me before accompanying his wife down the aisle and out of the church.

My mother turned to me and tried to speak, but was overcome by her emotions. Old Jack came to our rescue, taking her gently by the arm and leading her away, while Sir Walter took Grace and Jessica under his wing. Not a day mothers or bridesmaids would want to recall for the rest of their lives.

Giles and I were the last to leave. He had entered the church as my best man, and now he left it wondering if he was my half-brother. Some people stand by you in your darkest hour, while others walk away; only a select few march towards you and become even closer friends.

Once we had bidden farewell to the Reverend Styler, who seemed unable to find the words to express how sorry he felt, Giles and I trudged wearily across the cobbled stones of the quad and back to our college. Not a word passed between us as we climbed the wooden staircase to my rooms and sank into old leather chairs and young maudlin silence.

We sat alone as day turned slowly into night. Sparse conversation that had no sequence, no meaning, no logic. When the first long shadows appeared, those heralds of darkness that so often loosen the tongue, Giles asked me a question I hadn't thought about for years.

'Do you remember the first time you and Deakins visited the Manor House?'

'How could I forget? It was your twelfth birthday, and your father refused to shake hands with me.'

'Have you ever wondered why?'

'I think we found out the reason today,' I said, trying not to sound too insensitive.

'No, we didn't,' said Giles quietly. 'What we found out today was the possibility that Emma might be your half-sister. I now realize the reason my father kept his affair with your mother secret for so many years was because he was far more worried you might find out you were his son.'

'I don't understand the difference,' I said, staring at him.

'Then it's important for you to recall the only question my father asked on that occasion.'

'He asked when my birthday was.'

'That's right, and when he discovered you were a few

weeks older than me, he left the room without another word. And later, when we had to leave to go back to school, he didn't come out of his study to say goodbye, even though it was my birthday. It wasn't until today that I realized the significance of his actions.'

'How can that minor incident still be of any significance after all these years?' I asked.

'Because that was the moment my father realized you might be his first born, and that when he dies it could be you, not me, who inherits the family title, the business, and all his worldly goods.'

'But surely your father can leave his possessions to whomever he pleases, and that certainly wouldn't be me.'

'I wish it was that simple,' said Giles, 'but as my grandpa so regularly reminds me, his father, Sir Joshua Barrington, was knighted by Queen Victoria in 1877 for services to the shipping industry. In his will, he stated that all his titles, deeds and possessions were to be left to the first-born surviving son, in perpetuity.'

'But I have no interest in claiming what clearly is not mine,' I said, trying to reassure him.

'I'm sure you don't,' said Giles, 'but you may have no choice in the matter, because in the fullness of time, the law will require you to take your place as head of the Barrington family.'

—◆—

Giles left me just after midnight to drive to Gloucestershire. He promised to find out if Emma was willing to see me, as we'd parted without even saying goodbye, and said he would return to Oxford the moment he had any news.

I didn't sleep that night. So many thoughts were racing through my mind, and for a moment, just a moment, I even contemplated suicide. But I didn't need Old Jack to remind me that that was the coward's way out.

I didn't leave my rooms for the next three days. I didn't respond to gentle knocks on the door. I didn't answer the telephone when it rang. I didn't open the letters that were pushed under the door. It may have been inconsiderate of me not to respond to those who had only kindness in their hearts, but sometimes an abundance of sympathy can be more overwhelming than solitude.

Giles returned to Oxford on the fourth day. He didn't need to speak for me to realize his news wasn't going to give me succour. It turned out to be far worse than I had even anticipated. Emma and her mother had left for Mulgelrie Castle, where we had meant to be spending our honeymoon, with no relations to be allowed within ten miles. Mrs Barrington had instructed her solicitors to begin divorce proceedings, but they were unable to serve any papers on her husband as no one had seen him since he'd crept unnoticed out of the vestry. Lord Harvey and Old Jack had both resigned from the board of Barrington's, but out of respect for Sir Walter neither had made their reasons for doing so public – not that that would stop the rumour-mongers having a field day. My mother had left Eddie's Nightclub and taken a job as a waitress in the dining room of the Grand Hotel.

'What about Emma?' I said. 'Did you ask her . . .'

'I didn't have a chance to speak to her,' said Giles. 'They'd left for Scotland before I arrived. But she'd left a letter for you on the hall table.' I could feel my heart beating faster as he handed me an envelope bearing her familiar handwriting. 'If you feel like a little supper later, I'll be in my rooms.'

'Thank you,' I said, inadequately.

I sat in my chair by the window overlooking Cobb's quad, not wanting to open a letter that I knew wouldn't offer me a glimmer of hope. I finally tore open the envelope and extracted three pages written in Emma's neat hand. Even then, it was some time before I could read her words.

The Manor House
Chew Valley
Gloucestershire

July 29th, 1939

My Darling Harry,

It's the middle of the night, and I am sitting in my bedroom writing to the only man I will ever love.

Deep hatred for my father, whom I can never forgive, has been replaced by a sudden calm, so I must write these words before bitter recrimination returns to remind me of just how much that treacherous man has denied us both.

I only wish we'd been allowed to part as lovers, and not as strangers in a crowded room, the fates having decided we should never say the words 'until death do us part', although I am certain I will go to my grave only having loved one man.

I will never be satisfied with just the memory of your love, for while there is the slightest hope that Arthur Clifton was your father, be assured, my darling, that I will remain constant.

Mama is convinced that given enough time, the memory of you, like the evening sun, will fade, and then finally disappear, before heralding a new dawn. Does she not recall telling me on the day of my wedding that our love for each other was so pure, so simple and so rare, that it would unquestionably withstand the test of time, which Mama confessed she could only envy, as she had never experienced such happiness.

But until I can be your wife, my darling, I am

resolved that we must remain apart, unless, and until such time, it can be shown that we can be legally bound. No other man can hope to take your place and, if necessary, I will remain single, rather than settle for some counterfeit.

I wonder if the day will dawn when I do not reach out, expecting to find you by my side, and if it will ever be possible to fall asleep without whispering your name.

I would happily sacrifice the rest of my life to spend another year like the one we have just shared together, and no law made by God or man can change that. I still pray that the day will come when we can be joined together in the sight of that same God and those same men, but until then, my darling, I will always be your loving wife in all but name,

Emma

49

WHEN HARRY FINALLY summoned up the strength to open the countless letters that littered the floor, he came across one from Old Jack's secretary in London.

> *Soho Square*
> *London*
>
> *Wednesday, August 2nd, 1939*
>
> *Dear Mr Clifton,*
>
> *You may not receive this letter until you've returned from your honeymoon in Scotland, but I wondered if Captain Tarrant stayed on in Oxford after the wedding. He didn't return to the office on Monday morning, and he hasn't been seen since, so I wondered if you had any idea where I might contact him.*
>
> *I look forward to hearing from you.*
> *Yours sincerely,*
>
> *Phyllis Watson*

Old Jack had clearly forgotten to let Miss Watson know he was going down to Bristol to spend a few days

with Sir Walter, to make it clear that, although he had
caused the wedding to be abandoned and had resigned
from the board of Barrington's, he remained a close
friend of the chairman's. As there wasn't a second letter
from Miss Watson among his pile of unopened mail,
Harry assumed that Old Jack must have returned to
Soho Square and be back behind his desk.

Harry spent the morning answering every one of the
letters he'd left unopened; so many kind people offering
sympathy – it wasn't their fault they reminded him of
his unhappiness. Suddenly Harry decided he had to be
as far away from Oxford as possible. He picked up the
phone and told the operator he wanted to make a long-
distance call to London. Half an hour later, she called
back to tell him the number was continually engaged.
Next, he tried Sir Walter at Barrington Hall, but the
number just rang and rang. Frustrated by his failure to
contact either of them, Harry decided to follow one of
Old Jack's maxims: *Get off your backside and do something positive.*

He grabbed the suitcase he had packed for his
honeymoon in Scotland, walked across to the lodge and
told the porter he was going up to London and wouldn't
be returning until the first day of term. 'Should Giles
Barrington ask where I am,' he added, 'please tell him
I've gone to work for Old Jack.'

'Old Jack,' repeated the porter, writing the name
down on a slip of paper.

On the train journey to Paddington, Harry read in
The Times about the latest communiqués that were
bouncing back and forth between the Foreign Office
in London and the Reich Ministry in Berlin. He was
beginning to think that Mr Chamberlain was the only
person who still believed in the possibility of peace in
our time. *The Times* was predicting that Britain would

be at war within days and that the Prime Minister couldn't hope to survive in office if the Germans defied his ultimatum and marched into Poland.

The Thunderer went on to suggest that in that eventuality, a coalition government would have to be formed, led by the Foreign Secretary, Lord Halifax (a safe pair of hands), and not Winston Churchill (unpredictable and irascible). Despite the paper's obvious distaste for Churchill, Harry didn't believe that Britain needed a 'safe pair of hands' at this particular moment in history, but someone who was not frightened to bully a bully.

When Harry stepped off the train at Paddington, he was met by a wave of different coloured uniforms coming at him from every direction. He'd already decided which service he would join the moment war was declared. A morbid thought crossed his mind as he boarded a bus for Piccadilly Circus: if he was killed while serving his country, it would solve all the Barrington family's problems – except one.

When the bus reached Piccadilly, Harry jumped off and began to weave his way through the clowns that made up the West End circus, through theatre land and on past exclusive restaurants and overpriced nightclubs, which appeared determined to ignore any suggestion of war. The queue of displaced immigrants trooping in and out of the building in Soho Square appeared even longer and more bedraggled than on Harry's first visit. Once again, as he climbed the stairs to the third floor, several of the refugees stood aside, assuming he must be a member of staff. He hoped he would be within the hour.

When he reached the third floor, he headed straight for Miss Watson's office. He found her filling in forms, issuing rail warrants, arranging accommodation and handing out small amounts of cash to desperate people. Her face lit up when she saw Harry. 'Do tell me Captain Tarrant's with you,' were her first words.

'No, he isn't,' said Harry. 'I assumed he'd returned to London, which is why I'm here. I was wondering if you might be able to use an extra pair of hands.'

'That's very kind of you, Harry,' she said, 'but the most useful thing you could do for me right now is to find Captain Tarrant. This place is bursting at the seams without him.'

'The last I heard he was staying with Sir Walter Barrington at his home in Gloucester,' said Harry, 'but that was at least a fortnight ago.'

'We haven't set eyes on him since the day he went to Oxford for your wedding,' said Miss Watson as she tried to comfort two more immigrants who couldn't speak a word of English.

'Has anyone phoned his flat to see if he's there?' asked Harry.

'He doesn't have a phone,' said Miss Watson, 'and I've hardly been to my own home for the past two weeks,' she added, nodding in the direction of a queue that stretched as far as the eye could see.

'Why don't I start there, and report back to you?'

'Would you?' said Miss Watson as two little girls began sobbing. 'Don't cry, everything's going to be all right,' she reassured the children as she knelt and placed an arm round them.

'Where does he live?' asked Harry.

'Number twenty-three, Prince Edward Mansions, Lambeth Walk. Take the number eleven bus to Lambeth, then you'll have to ask for directions. And thank you, Harry.'

Harry turned and headed towards the stairs. Something wasn't right, he thought. Old Jack would never have deserted his post without giving Miss Watson a reason.

'I forgot to ask,' Miss Watson shouted after him, 'how was your honeymoon?'

Harry felt he was far enough away not to have heard her.

Back at Piccadilly Circus he boarded a double-decker bus overcrowded with soldiers. It drove down Whitehall, which was full of officers, and on through Parliament Square, where a vast crowd of onlookers was waiting for any snippets of information that might come out of the House of Commons. The bus continued its journey across Lambeth Bridge, and Harry got off when it reached Albert Embankment.

A paperboy who was shouting *'Britain Awaits Hitler's Response'* told Harry to take the second on the left, then the third on the right, and added for good measure, 'I thought everyone knew where Lambeth Walk was.'

Harry began to run like a man being pursued and he didn't stop until he came to a block of flats that was so dilapidated he could only wonder which Prince Edward it had been named after. He pushed open a door that wouldn't survive much longer on those hinges and walked quickly up a flight of stairs, stepping nimbly between piles of rubbish that hadn't been cleared for days.

When he reached the second floor, he stopped outside No. 23 and knocked firmly on the door, but there was no reply. He knocked again, louder, but still no one responded. He ran back down the stairs in search of someone who worked in the building, and when he reached the basement he found an old man slumped in an even older chair, smoking a roll-up and flicking through the pages of the *Daily Mirror*.

'Have you seen Captain Tarrant recently?' Harry asked sharply.

'Not for the past couple of weeks, sir,' said the man, leaping to his feet and almost standing to attention when he heard Harry's accent.

'Do you have a master key that will open his flat?' asked Harry.

'I do, sir, but I'm not allowed to use it except in emergencies.'

'I can assure you this is an emergency,' said Harry, who turned and bounded back up the stairs, not waiting for his reply.

The man followed, if not quite as quickly. Once he'd caught up, he opened the door. Harry moved quickly from room to room, but there was no sign of Old Jack. The last door he came to was closed. He knocked quietly, fearing the worst. When there was no reply, he cautiously went in, to find a neatly made bed and no sign of anyone. He must still be with Sir Walter, was Harry's first thought.

He thanked the porter, walked back down the stairs and out on to the street as he tried to gather his thoughts. He hailed a passing taxi, not wanting to waste any more time on buses in a city that did not know him.

'Paddington Station. I'm in a hurry.'

'Everyone seems to be in a hurry today,' said the cabbie as he moved off.

Twenty minutes later Harry was standing on platform 6, but it was another fifty minutes before the train would depart for Temple Meads. He used the time to grab a sandwich and a cup of tea – 'Only got cheese, sir.' – and to phone Miss Watson to let her know that Old Jack hadn't been back to his flat. If it was possible, she sounded even more harassed than when he had left her. 'I'm on my way to Bristol,' he told her. 'I'll ring you as soon as I catch up with him.'

As the train made its way out of the capital, through

the smog-filled back streets of the city and into the clean air of the countryside, Harry decided he had no choice but to go straight to Sir Walter's office at the dockyard, even if it meant running into Hugo Barrington. Finding Old Jack surely outweighed any other consideration.

Once the train shunted into Temple Meads, Harry knew the two buses he needed to catch without having to ask the paperboy who was standing on the corner bellowing *'Britain Awaits Hitler's Response'* at the top of his voice. Same headline, but this time a Bristolian accent. Thirty minutes later, Harry was at the dockyard gates.

'Can I help you?' asked a guard who didn't recognize him.

'I have an appointment with Sir Walter,' said Harry, hoping this would not be questioned.

'Of course, sir. Do you know the way to his office?'

'Yes, thank you,' said Harry. He started walking slowly towards a building he'd never entered before. He began to think about what he would do if he came face to face with Hugo Barrington before he reached Sir Walter's office.

He was pleased to see the chairman's Rolls-Royce parked in its usual place, and even more relieved that there was no sign of Hugo Barrington's Bugatti. He was just about to enter Barrington House when he glanced at the railway carriage in the distance. Was it just possible? He changed direction and walked towards the Pullman *wagon lit*, as Old Jack was wont to describe it after a second glass of whisky.

When Harry reached the carriage he knocked gently on the glass pane as if it were a grand home. A butler did not appear, so he opened the door and climbed in. He walked along the corridor to first class, and there he was, sitting in his usual seat.

It was the first time Harry had ever seen Old Jack wearing his Victoria Cross.

Harry took the seat opposite his friend and recalled the first time he'd sat there. He must have been about five and his feet hadn't reached the ground. Then he thought of the time he'd run away from St Bede's, and the shrewd old gentleman had persuaded him to be back in time for breakfast. He recalled when Old Jack had come to hear him sing a solo in the church, the time his voice had broken. Old Jack had dismissed this as a minor setback. Then there was the day he learnt he'd failed to win a scholarship to Bristol Grammar School, a major setback. Despite his failure, Old Jack had presented him with the Ingersoll watch he was still wearing today. It must have cost him every penny he possessed. In Harry's last year at school, Old Jack had travelled down from London to see him playing Romeo, and Harry had introduced him to Emma for the first time. And he would never forget his final speech day, when Jack had sat on stage as a governor of his old school and watched Harry being awarded the English prize.

And now, Harry would never be able to thank him for so many acts of friendship over the years that couldn't be repaid. He stared at a man he'd loved and had assumed would never die. As they sat there together in first class, the sun went down on his young life.

50

HARRY WATCHED AS the stretcher was placed in the ambulance. A heart attack, the doctor had said, before the ambulance drove away.

Harry didn't need to go and tell Sir Walter that Old Jack was dead, because when he woke the following morning, the chairman of Barrington's was sitting by his side.

'He told me he no longer had any reason to live,' were Sir Walter's first words. 'We have both lost a close and dear friend.'

Harry's response took Sir Walter by surprise. 'What will you do with this carriage, now that Old Jack is no longer around?'

'No one will be allowed anywhere near it, as long as I'm chairman,' said Sir Walter. 'It harbours too many personal memories for me.'

'Me too,' said Harry. 'I spent more time here when I was a boy than I did in my own home.'

'Or in the classroom for that matter,' said Sir Walter with a wry smile. 'I used to watch you from my office window. I thought what an impressive child you must be if Old Jack was willing to spend so much time with you.'

Harry smiled when he remembered how Old Jack

had come up with a reason why he should go back to school and learn to read and write.

'What will you do now, Harry? Return to Oxford and continue with your studies?'

'No, sir. I fear that we'll be at war by . . .'

'By the end of the month would be my guess,' said Sir Walter.

'Then I'll leave Oxford immediately and join the navy. I've already told my college supervisor, Mr Bainbridge, that that's what I plan to do. He assured me I can return and continue with my studies as soon as the war is over.'

'Typical of Oxford,' said Sir Walter, 'they always take the long view. So will you go to Dartmouth and train as a naval officer?'

'No, sir, I've been around ships all my life. In any case, Old Jack started out as a private soldier and managed to work his way up through the ranks, so why shouldn't I?'

'Why not indeed?' said Sir Walter. 'In fact, that was one of the reasons he was always considered to be a class above the rest of us who served with him.'

'I had no idea you'd served together.'

'Oh yes, I served with Captain Tarrant in South Africa,' said Sir Walter. 'I was one of the twenty-four men whose lives he saved on the day he was awarded the Victoria Cross.'

'That explains so much that I've never really understood,' said Harry. He then surprised Sir Walter a second time. 'Do I know any of the others, sir?'

'The Frob,' said Sir Walter. 'But in those days he was Lieutenant Frobisher. Corporal Holcombe, Mr Holcombe's father. And young Private Deakins.'

'Deakins's father?' said Harry.

'Yes. Sprogg, as we used to call him. A fine young soldier. He never said much, but he turned out to be very brave. Lost an arm on that dreadful day.'

The two men fell silent, each lost in his own thoughts of Old Jack, before Sir Walter asked, 'So if you're not going to Dartmouth, my boy, may I ask how you plan to win the war single-handed?'

'I'll serve on any ship that will take me, sir, as long as they're willing to go in search of His Britannic Majesty's enemies.'

'Then it's possible I may be able to help.'

'That's kind of you, sir, but I want to join a war ship, not a passenger liner or a cargo vessel.'

Sir Walter smiled again. 'And so you will, dear boy. Don't forget, I'm kept informed about every ship that comes in and out of these docks and I know most of their captains. Come to think of it, I knew most of their fathers when they were captains. Why don't we go up to my office and see what ships are due in and out of the port in the next few days, and, more important, find out if any of them might be willing to take you on?'

'That's very decent of you, sir, but would it be all right if I visited my mother first? I might not have the chance to see her again for some time.'

'Only right and proper, my boy,' said Sir Walter. 'And once you've been to see your mother, why don't you drop into my office later this afternoon? That should give me enough time to check on the latest shipping lists.'

'Thank you, sir. I'll return as soon as I've told my mother what I plan to do.'

'When you come back, just tell the man on the gate you've got an appointment with the chairman, then you shouldn't have any trouble getting past security.'

'Thank you, sir,' said Harry, masking a smile.

'And do pass on my kindest regards to your dear mother. A remarkable woman.'

Harry was reminded why Sir Walter was Old Jack's closest friend.

◄○►

Harry walked into the Grand Hotel, a magnificent Victorian building in the centre of the city, and asked the doorman the way to the dining room. He walked across the lobby and was surprised to find a small queue at the maître d's desk, waiting to be allocated tables. He joined the back of the queue, recalling how his mother had always disapproved of him dropping in to see her at Tilly's or the Royal Hotel during working hours.

While Harry waited, he looked around the dining room, which was full of chattering people, none of whom looked as if they were anticipating a food shortage, or thinking of enlisting in the armed forces should the country go to war. Food was being whisked in and out of the swing doors on heavily laden silver trays, while a man in a chef's outfit was wheeling a trolley from table to table, slicing off slivers of beef, while another followed in his wake carrying a gravy boat.

Harry could see no sign of his mother. He was even beginning to wonder if Giles had only told him what he wanted to hear, when suddenly she burst through the swing doors, three plates balanced on her arms. She placed them in front of her customers so deftly they hardly noticed she was there, then returned to the kitchen. She was back a moment later, carrying three vegetable dishes. By the time Harry had reached the front of the queue he'd been reminded of who had given him his boundless energy, uncritical enthusiasm and a spirit that didn't contemplate defeat. How would he ever be able to repay this remarkable woman for all the sacrifices she had made—

'I'm sorry to have kept you waiting, sir,' said the maître d', interrupting his thoughts, 'but I don't have a table available at the moment. If you'd care to come back in about twenty minutes?'

Harry didn't tell him he didn't actually want a table, and not just because his mother was one of the waitresses, but because he wouldn't have been able to afford anything on the menu other than perhaps the gravy.

'I'll come back later,' he said, trying to sound disappointed. About ten years later, he thought, by which time he suspected his mother would probably be the maître d'. He left the hotel with a smile on his face and took a bus back to the docks.

—<o>—

He was ushered straight through to Sir Walter's office by his secretary and found the chairman leaning on his desk, peering down at the port schedules, timetables and ocean charts that covered every inch of its surface.

'Have a seat, dear boy,' said Sir Walter, before fixing his monocle in his right eye and looking sternly at Harry. 'I've had a little time to think about our conversation this morning,' he continued, sounding very serious, 'and before we go any further, I need to be convinced that you're making the right decision.'

'I'm absolutely certain,' said Harry without hesitation.

'That may be, but I'm equally certain that Jack would have advised you to return to Oxford and wait until you were called up.'

'He may well have done so, sir, but he wouldn't have taken his own advice.'

'How well you knew him,' said Sir Walter. 'Indeed,

that's exactly what I expected you to say. Let me tell you what I've come up with so far,' he continued, returning his attention to the papers that covered his desk. 'The good news is that the Royal Navy battleship HMS *Resolution* is due to dock at Bristol in about a month's time, when it will refuel before awaiting further orders.'

'A month?' said Harry, making no attempt to hide his frustration.

'Patience, boy,' said Sir Walter. 'The reason I chose the *Resolution* is because the captain is an old friend, and I'm confident I can get you on board as a deckhand, as long as the other part of my plan works out.'

'But would the captain of the *Resolution* consider taking on someone with no seafaring experience?'

'Probably not, but if everything else falls into place, by the time you board the *Resolution* you will be an old sea dog.'

Recalling one of Old Jack's favourite homilies, *I find I don't learn a lot while I'm talking*, Harry decided to stop interrupting and start listening.

'Now,' Sir Walter continued, 'I've identified three ships that are due to leave Bristol in the next twenty-four hours and are expected to return within three to four weeks, which will give you more than enough time to sign up as a deckhand on the *Resolution*.'

Harry wanted to interrupt, but didn't.

'Let's begin with my first choice. The *Devonian* is bound for Cuba, with a manifest of cotton dresses, potatoes and Raleigh Lenton bicycles, and is due to return to Bristol in four weeks' time with a cargo of tobacco, sugar and bananas.

'The second ship on my shortlist is the SS *Kansas Star*, a passenger vessel that will be sailing to New York on the first tide tomorrow. It has been requisitioned by the United States government to transport American nationals back home before Britain finds itself at war with Germany.

'The third is an empty oil tanker, the SS *Princess Beatrice*, which is on its way back to Amsterdam to refuel and will return to Bristol with a full load before the end of the month. All three skippers are painfully aware that they need to be safely back in port as quickly as possible, because if war is declared, the two merchant vessels will be considered fair game by the Germans, while only the *Kansas Star* will be safe from the German U-boats skulking around the Atlantic just waiting for the order to sink anything flying a red or blue ensign.'

'What crew are these ships in need of?' asked Harry. 'I'm not exactly over-qualified.'

Sir Walter searched around his desk again, before extracting another sheet of paper. 'The *Princess Beatrice* is short of a deckhand, the *Kansas Star* is looking for someone to work in the kitchens, which usually means as a washer-upper or a waiter, while the *Devonian* needs a fourth officer.'

'So that one can be removed from the shortlist.'

'Funnily enough,' said Sir Walter, 'that's the position I consider you best qualified for. The *Devonian* has a crew of thirty-seven, and rarely goes to sea with a trainee officer, so no one would expect you to be anything other than a novice.'

'But why would the captain consider me?'

'Because I told him you were my grandson.'

51

HARRY WALKED ALONG the dock towards the *Devonian*. The small suitcase he was carrying made him feel like a schoolboy on his first day of term. What would the headmaster be like? Would he sleep in a bed next to a Giles or a Deakins? Would he come across an Old Jack? Would there be a Fisher on board?

Although Sir Walter had offered to accompany him and introduce him to the captain, Harry had felt that would not be the best way to endear himself to his new shipmates.

He stopped for a moment and looked closely at the ancient vessel on which he would be spending the next month. Sir Walter had told him that the *Devonian* had been built in 1913, when the oceans were still dominated by sail and a motorized cargo vessel would have been thought the latest thing. But now, twenty-six years later, it wouldn't be too long before she was decommissioned and taken to that area of the docks where old ships are broken up and their parts sold for scrap.

Sir Walter had also hinted that as Captain Havens only had one more year to serve before he retired, the owners might decide to scrap him at the same time as his ship.

The *Devonian*'s Articles of Agreement showed a

crew of thirty-seven, but as on so many cargo ships, that number wasn't quite accurate: a cook and a washer-up picked up in Hong Kong didn't appear on the payroll, nor did the occasional deckhand or two who was fleeing the law and had no desire to return to his homeland.

Harry made his way slowly up the gangway. Once he'd stepped on deck, he didn't move until he'd received permission to board. After all his years of hanging around the docks, he was well aware of ship's protocol. He looked up at the bridge and assumed the man he saw giving orders must be Captain Havens. Sir Walter had told him the senior officer on a cargo vessel was in fact a master mariner but should always be addressed on board as captain. Captain Havens was a shade under six foot, and looked nearer fifty than sixty. He was stockily built, with a weathered, tanned face and a dark neatly trimmed beard that, as he was going bald, made him look like George V.

When he spotted Harry waiting at the top of the gangway, the captain gave a crisp order to the officer standing next to him on the bridge, before making his way down on to the deck.

'I'm Captain Havens,' he said briskly. 'You must be Harry Clifton.' He shook Harry warmly by the hand. 'Welcome aboard the *Devonian*. You come highly recommended.'

'I should point out, sir,' began Harry, 'that this is my first—'

'I'm aware of that,' said Havens, lowering his voice, 'but I'd keep it to yourself if you don't want your time on board to be a living hell. And whatever you do, don't mention you were at Oxford, because most of this lot,' he said, indicating the seamen working on the deck, 'will think it's just the name of another ship. Follow me. I'll show you the fourth officer's quarters.'

Harry followed in the captain's wake, aware that a dozen suspicious eyes were watching his every move.

'There are two other officers on my ship,' said the captain once Harry had caught up with him. 'Jim Patterson, the senior engineer, spends most of his life down below in the boiler room, so you'll only see him at mealtimes, and sometimes not even then. He's served with me for the past fourteen years, and frankly I doubt if this old lady would still make it halfway across the Channel, let alone the Atlantic, if he wasn't down there to coax her along. My third officer, Tom Bradshaw, is on the bridge. He's only been with me for three years, so he's not yet earned his ticket. He keeps himself to himself, but whoever trained him knew what they were doing, because he's a damn fine officer.'

Havens began to disappear down a narrow stairwell that led to the deck below. 'That's my cabin,' he said as he continued down the corridor, 'and that's Mr Patterson's.' He came to a halt in front of what appeared to be a broom cupboard. 'This is your cabin.' He pushed the door open but it only moved a few inches before it banged against a narrow wooden bed. 'I won't come in as there isn't room for both of us. You'll find some clothes on the bed. Once you've changed, join me on the bridge. We'll be setting sail within the hour. Leaving the harbour will probably be the most interesting part of the voyage until we dock in Cuba.'

Harry squeezed through the half-open door and had to close it behind him to allow enough room to change his clothes. He checked the gear that had been left, neatly folded, on his bunk: two thick blue sweaters, two white shirts, two pairs of blue trousers, three pairs of blue woollen socks and a pair of canvas shoes with thick rubber soles. It really was like being back at school. Every item had one thing in common: they all looked as if they'd been worn by several other people before Harry. He quickly changed into his seaman's gear, then unpacked his suitcase.

As there was only one drawer, Harry placed the little suitcase, full of his civilian clothes, under the bed – the only thing in the cabin that fitted perfectly. He opened the door, squeezed back into the corridor and went in search of the stairwell. Once he'd located it, he emerged back on deck. Several more pairs of suspicious eyes followed his progress.

'Mr Clifton,' said the captain as Harry stepped on to the bridge for the first time, 'this is Tom Bradshaw, the third officer, who will be taking the ship out of the harbour as soon as we've been given clearance by the port authority. By the way, Mr Bradshaw,' said Havens, 'one of our tasks on this voyage will be to teach this young pup everything we know, so that when we return to Bristol in a month's time the crew of HMS *Resolution* will mistake him for an old sea dog.'

If Mr Bradshaw commented, his words were drowned by two long blasts on a siren, a sound Harry had heard many times over the years, indicating that the two tug boats were in place and waiting to escort the *Devonian* out of the harbour. The captain pressed some tobacco into his well-worn briar pipe, while Mr Bradshaw acknowledged the signal with two blasts of the ship's horn, to confirm that the *Devonian* was ready to depart.

'Prepare to cast off, Mr Bradshaw,' said Captain Havens, striking a match.

Mr Bradshaw removed the cover from a brass voice-pipe Harry hadn't noticed until that moment. 'All engines slow ahead, Mr Patterson. The tug boats are in place and ready to escort us out of harbour,' he added, revealing a slight American accent.

'All engines slow ahead, Mr Bradshaw,' came back a voice from the boiler room.

Harry looked down over the side of the bridge and watched as the crew carried out their allotted tasks. Four men, two at the bow and two at the stern, were unwinding thick ropes from the capstans on the dock. Another two were hauling up the gangway. 'Keep your eye on the pilot,' said the captain between puffs on his pipe. 'It's his responsibility to guide us out of the harbour and safely into the Channel. Once he's done that, Mr Bradshaw will take over. If you turn out to be any good, Mr Clifton, you may be allowed to take his place in about a year's time, but not until I've retired and Mr Bradshaw has taken over command.' As Bradshaw didn't give even the flicker of a smile, Harry remained silent and continued to watch everything going on around him. 'No one is allowed to take my girl out at night,' continued Captain Havens, 'unless I'm sure he won't take any liberties with her.' Again, Bradshaw didn't smile, but then he may have heard the comment before.

Harry found himself fascinated by how smoothly the whole operation was carried out. The *Devonian* eased away from the quayside and, with the help of the two tug boats, nosed her way slowly out of the docks, along the River Avon and under the suspension bridge.

'Do you know who built that bridge, Mr Clifton?' the captain asked, taking his pipe out of his mouth.

'Isambard Kingdom Brunel, sir,' said Harry.

'And why did he never live to see it opened?'

'Because the local council ran out of money, and he died before the bridge was completed.'

The captain scowled. 'Next you'll be telling me it's named after you,' he said, putting his pipe back in his mouth. He didn't speak again until the tug boats had reached Barry Island, when they gave two more long blasts, released their lines and headed back to port.

The *Devonian* may have been an old lady, but it soon became clear to Harry that Captain Havens and his crew knew exactly how to handle her.

'Take over, Mr Bradshaw,' said the captain, as another pair of eyes appeared on the bridge, their owner carrying two mugs of hot tea. 'There will be three officers on the bridge during this crossing, Lu, so be sure that Mr Clifton also gets a mug of tea.' The Chinaman nodded and disappeared below deck.

Once the harbour lights had disappeared over the horizon, the waves became larger and larger, causing the ship to roll from side to side. Havens and Bradshaw stood, feet apart, appearing to be glued to the deck, while Harry found himself regularly having to cling on to something to make sure he didn't fall over. When the Chinaman reappeared with a third mug of tea, Harry chose not to mention to the captain that it was cold, and that his mother usually added a lump of sugar.

Just as Harry was beginning to feel a little more confident, almost enjoying the experience, the captain said, 'Not much more you can do tonight, Mr Clifton. Why don't you go below and try to catch some shut-eye. Be back on the bridge by seven twenty to take over the breakfast watch.' Harry was about to protest, when a smile appeared on Mr Bradshaw's face for the first time.

'Goodnight, sir,' said Harry before making his way down the steps and on to the deck. He wobbled slowly towards the narrow stairwell, feeling with every step he took that he was being watched by even more eyes. One voice said, loud enough for him to hear, 'He must be a passenger.'

'No, he's an officer,' said a second voice.

'What's the difference?' Several men laughed.

Once he was back in his cabin, he undressed and climbed on to the thin wooden bunk. He tried to find a comfortable position without falling out or rolling into the wall as the ship swayed from side to side as well as lurching up and down. He didn't even have a wash basin to be sick in, or a porthole to be sick out of.

As he lay awake, his thoughts turned to Emma. He wondered if she was still in Scotland or had returned to the Manor House, or perhaps she'd already taken up residence at Oxford. Would Giles be wondering where he was, or had Sir Walter told him he'd gone to sea and would be joining the *Resolution* the moment he landed back in Bristol? And would his mother be wondering where he could be? Perhaps he should have broken her golden rule and interrupted her at work. Finally, he thought about Old Jack, and suddenly felt guilty when he realized he wouldn't be back in time for his funeral.

What Harry couldn't know was that his own funeral would take place before Old Jack's.

52

HARRY WAS WOKEN BY the sound of four bells. He leapt up, hitting his head on the ceiling, threw on his clothes, squeezed into the corridor, shot up the stairwell, ran across the deck and bounded up the steps on to the bridge.

'Sorry I'm late, sir, I must have overslept.'

'You don't have to call me sir when we're on our own,' said Bradshaw, 'the name's Tom. And as a matter of fact, you're over an hour early. The skipper obviously forgot to tell you it's seven bells for the breakfast watch, and four for the six o'clock watch. But as you're here, why don't you take over the wheel while I take a leak.' The shock for Harry was to realize that Bradshaw wasn't joking. 'Just be sure the arrow on the compass is always pointing sou'-sou'-west, then you can't go far wrong,' he added, his American accent sounding more pronounced.

Harry took the wheel with both hands and stared intently at the little black arrow as he tried to keep the ship ploughing through the waves in a straight line. When he looked back at the wake, he saw that the neat straight line Bradshaw had achieved with such apparent ease had been replaced by the sort of curves more associated with Mae West. Although Bradshaw was only away for a few minutes, Harry had rarely been more pleased to see anyone when he returned.

Bradshaw took over and the uninterrupted straight line quickly reappeared, although he only had one hand on the wheel.

'Remember, you're handling a lady,' said Bradshaw. 'You don't cling on to her, but gently caress her. If you can manage that, she'll stay on the straight and narrow. Now try again, while I plot our seven bells position on the daily chart.'

When one bell rang twenty-five minutes later and the captain appeared on the bridge to relieve Bradshaw, Harry's line in the ocean may not have been entirely straight, but at least it no longer appeared as if the ship was being steered by a drunken sailor.

‑‹ο›‑

At breakfast, Harry was introduced to a man who could only have been first engineer.

Jim Patterson's ghostly complexion made him look as if he'd spent most of his life below decks, and his paunch suggested he spent the rest of the time eating. Unlike Bradshaw, he never stopped talking, and it quickly became clear to Harry that he and the skipper were old friends.

The Chinaman appeared, carrying three plates that could have been cleaner. Harry avoided the greasy bacon and fried tomatoes in favour of a piece of burnt toast and an apple.

'Why don't you spend the rest of the morning finding your way around the ship, Mr Clifton,' suggested the captain after the plates had been cleared away. 'You could even join Mr Patterson in the engine room and see how many minutes you survive down there.' Patterson burst out laughing, grabbed the last two pieces of toast and said, 'If you think these are burnt, wait until you've spent a few minutes with me.'

—◦—

Like a cat that has been left alone in a new house, Harry began stalking around the outside of the deck as he tried to become familiar with his new kingdom.

He knew the ship was 475 feet long with a 56-foot beam and its top speed was fifteen knots, but he'd had no idea there would be so many nooks and crannies that undoubtedly served some purpose which, given time, he would learn. Harry also noticed there wasn't any part of the deck the captain couldn't keep a watchful eye on from the bridge, so there was no chance of escape for an idle seaman.

Harry took the stairwell down to the middle deck. The aft section consisted of the officers' quarters, amidships was the galley, and forward was a large open area of slung hammocks. How anyone could possibly sleep in one of those was beyond him. Then he noticed half a dozen sailors, who must have come off the dog watch, swaying gently from side to side with the rhythm of the ship and sleeping contentedly.

A narrow steel stairwell led down to the lower deck, where the wooden crates that held the 144 Raleigh bicycles, a thousand cotton dresses and two tons of potatoes were all safely secured, and wouldn't be opened until after the ship docked in Cuba.

Finally, he descended a narrow ladder that led to the boiler room, and Mr Patterson's domain. He heaved open the heavy metal hatch and, like Shadrach, Meshach and Abednego, marched boldly into the fiery furnace. He stood and watched as half a dozen squat, muscle-bound men, their vests soiled with black dust, sweat pouring down their backs, shovelled coal into two gaping mouths that needed to be fed more than four meals a day.

As Captain Havens had predicted, it was only a few minutes before Harry had to stagger back into the corridor, sweating and gasping for breath. It was some time before he recovered enough to make his way back up on to the deck, where he fell on his knees and gulped in the fresh air. He could only wonder how those men could survive in such conditions and be expected to carry out three two-hour shifts a day, seven days a week.

Once Harry had recovered, he made his way back up to the bridge, armed with a hundred questions, from which star in the Plough points to the North Star, to how many nautical miles the ship could average per day, to how many tons of coal were required for ... The captain happily answered them all, without once appearing exasperated by the young fourth officer's unquenchable thirst for knowledge. In fact, Captain Havens remarked to Mr Bradshaw during Harry's break that what impressed him most about the lad was that he never asked the same question twice.

◄○►

During the next few days, Harry learnt how to check the compass against the dotted line on the chart, how to gauge wind direction by watching seagulls, and how to take the ship through the trough of a wave and still maintain a constant course. By the end of the first week, he was allowed to take over the wheel whenever an officer took a meal break. By night, the captain taught him the names of the stars, which, he pointed out, were every bit as reliable as a compass, but he confessed his knowledge was limited to the northern hemisphere as the *Devonian* had never crossed the equator in all her twenty-six years on the high seas.

After ten days at sea, the captain was almost hoping for a storm, not only to stop the endless questions but also to see if there was anything that could throw this young man off his stride. Jim Patterson had already warned him that Mr Clifton had survived for an hour in the boiler room that morning and was determined to complete a full shift before they docked in Cuba.

'At least you're spared his endless questions down there,' remarked the captain.

'This week,' responded the chief engineer.

Captain Havens wondered if a time would come when he learnt something from his fourth officer. It happened on the twelfth day of the voyage, just after Harry had completed his first two-hour shift in the boiler room.

'Did you know that Mr Patterson collects stamps, sir?' Harry asked.

'Yes, I did,' replied the captain confidently.

'And that his collection now numbers over four thousand, including an unperforated Penny Black and a South African triangular Cape of Good Hope?'

'Yes, I did,' repeated the captain.

'And that the collection is now worth more than his home in Mablethorpe?'

'It's only a cottage, damn it,' said the captain, trying to hold his own, and before Harry could ask his next question, he added, 'I'd be more interested if you could find out as much about Tom Bradshaw as you seem to have wormed out of my chief engineer. Because frankly, Harry, I know more about you after twelve days than I do about my third officer after three years, and until now, I'd never thought of Americans as being a reserved race.'

The more Harry thought about the captain's observation, the more he realized just how little he too knew about Tom, despite having spent many hours with him on the bridge. He had no idea if the man had any brothers or sisters, what his father did for a living, where his parents lived, or whether he even had a girlfriend. And only his accent gave away the fact that he was an American, because Harry didn't know which town, or even state, he hailed from.

Seven bells rang. 'Would you take over the wheel, Mr Clifton,' said the captain, 'while I join Mr Patterson and Mr Bradshaw for dinner? Don't hesitate to let me know if you spot anything,' he added as he left the bridge, 'especially if it's bigger than we are.'

'Aye aye, sir,' said Harry, delighted to be left in charge, even if it was only for forty minutes, although those forty minutes were being extended each day.

◄o►

It was when Harry asked him how many more days it would be before they reached Cuba that Captain Havens realized the precocious youth was already bored. He was beginning to feel some sympathy for the captain of HMS *Resolution*, who had no idea what he was letting himself in for.

Harry had recently been taking over the wheel after dinner so that the other officers could enjoy a few hands of gin rummy before returning to the bridge. And whenever the Chinaman took up Harry's mug of tea now, it was always piping hot, with the requested one lump of sugar.

Mr Patterson was heard to remark to the captain one evening that should Mr Clifton decide to take over the ship before they got back to Bristol, he wasn't sure who he'd side with.

'Are you thinking of inciting a mutiny, Jim?' asked Havens as he poured his chief engineer another tot of rum.

'No, but I must warn you, skipper, that the young turk has already reorganized the shifts in the boiler room. So I know whose side my lads would be on.'

'Then the least we can do,' said Havens, pouring himself a glass of rum, 'is order the flag officer to send a message to the *Resolution*, warning them what they'll be up against.'

'But we don't have a flag officer,' said Patterson.

'Then we'll have to clap the lad in irons,' said the captain.

'Good idea, skipper. It's just a shame we don't have any irons.'

'More's the pity. Remind me to pick some up as soon as we get back to Bristol.'

'But you seem to have forgotten Clifton's leaving us to join the *Resolution* the moment we dock,' Patterson said.

The captain swallowed a mouthful of rum before repeating, 'More's the pity.'

53

HARRY REPORTED TO the bridge a few minutes before seven bells to relieve Mr Bradshaw, so he could go below and join the captain for dinner.

The length of time Tom left him in charge of the bridge was becoming longer and longer with each watch, but Harry never complained, because he enjoyed the illusion that for an hour a day the ship was under his command.

He checked the arrow on the compass and steered the course that had been set by the captain. He had even been entrusted with entering their position on the chart and writing up the daily log before he came off duty.

As Harry stood alone on the bridge, a full moon, a calm sea, and a thousand miles of ocean ahead of him, his thoughts drifted back to England. He wondered what Emma was doing at that moment.

Emma was sitting in her room at Somerville College, Oxford, tuning her radio to the Home Service so she could hear Mr Neville Chamberlain address the nation.

'This is the BBC in London. You will now hear a statement from the Prime Minister.'

'I am speaking to you from the Cabinet room, Ten Downing Street. This morning the British Ambassador

in Berlin handed the German government a final note, stating that unless we heard from them by eleven o'clock, that they were prepared at once to withdraw their troops from Poland, a state of war would exist between us. I have to tell you now, that no such undertaking has been received, and that consequently, this country is at war with Germany.'

But as the *Devonian*'s radio was unable to pick up the BBC, everyone on board went about their business as if it was a normal day.

Harry was still thinking about Emma when the first one shot past the bow. He wasn't sure what he should do. He was loath to disturb the captain during dinner for fear of being reprimanded for wasting his time. Harry was wide awake when he saw the second one, and this time he had no doubt what it was. Harry watched as the long, slender, shiny object slithered below the surface towards the bow of the ship. He instinctively swung the wheel to starboard but the ship veered to port. It wasn't quite what he'd intended, but the mistake gave him enough time to raise the alarm because the object shot past the bow, missing the ship by several yards.

This time he didn't hesitate and jammed the palm of his hand on the klaxon, which immediately emitted a loud blast. Moments later Mr Bradshaw appeared on deck and began racing towards the bridge, closely followed by the captain, pulling on his jacket.

One by one, the rest of the crew came rushing out of the bowels of the ship and headed straight for their stations, assuming it must be an unscheduled fire drill.

'What's the problem, Mr Clifton?' asked Captain Havens calmly as he stepped on to the bridge.

'I think I saw a torpedo, sir, but as I've never seen one before, I can't be sure.'

'Could it have been a dolphin enjoying our leftovers?' suggested the captain.

'No, sir, it wasn't a dolphin.'

'I've never seen a torpedo either,' Havens admitted as he took over the wheel. 'Which direction was it coming from?'

'Nor'-nor'-east.'

'Mr Bradshaw,' said the captain, 'all crew to emergency stations and prepare to lower the lifeboats on my command.'

'Aye aye, sir,' said Bradshaw, who slid down the railings on to the deck and immediately began to organize the crew.

'Mr Clifton, keep your eyes peeled and tell me the moment you spot anything.'

Harry grabbed the binoculars and began a slow sweep of the ocean. At the same time, the captain bellowed down the voicepipe, 'All engines reverse, Mr Patterson, all engines reverse, and stand by for further orders.'

'Aye aye, sir,' said a startled chief engineer, who hadn't heard that order since 1918.

'Another one,' said Harry. 'Nor'-nor'-east, coming directly towards us.'

'I see it,' said the captain. He swung the wheel to the left and the torpedo missed them by only a few feet. He knew he was unlikely to pull off that trick again.

'You were right, Mr Clifton. That wasn't a dolphin,' said Havens matter-of-factly. Under his breath he added, 'We must be at war. The enemy has torpedoes, and all I've got is a hundred and forty-four Raleigh bicycles, a few sacks of potatoes and some cotton dresses.' Harry kept his eyes peeled.

The captain remained so calm that Harry felt almost

no sense of danger. 'Number four coming directly at us, sir,' he said. 'Nor'-nor'-east again.'

Havens gamely tried to manoeuvre the old lady one more time, but she didn't respond quickly enough to his unwelcome advances and the torpedo ripped into the ship's bow. A few minutes later Mr Patterson reported that a fire had broken out below the waterline and that his men were finding it impossible to douse the flames with the ship's primitive foam hoses. The captain didn't need to be told that he was facing a hopeless task.

'Mr Bradshaw, prepare to abandon ship. All crew to stand by the lifeboats and await further orders.'

'Aye aye, sir,' shouted Bradshaw from the deck.

Havens bellowed down the voicepipe. 'Mr Patterson, get yourself and your men out of there immediately, and I mean immediately, and report to the lifeboats.'

'We're on our way, skipper.'

'Another one, sir,' said Harry. 'Nor'-nor'-west, heading towards the starboard side, amidships.'

The captain swung the wheel once again, but he knew this time he would not be able to ride the punch. Seconds later, the torpedo ripped into the ship, which began to list to one side.

'Abandon ship!' shouted Havens, reaching for the tannoy. 'Abandon ship!' he repeated several times, before he turned to Harry who was still scanning the sea through his binoculars.

'Make your way to the nearest lifeboat, Mr Clifton, and sharpish. There's no point in anyone remaining on the bridge.'

'Aye aye, sir,' said Harry.

'Captain,' came a voice from the engine room, 'number four hold is jammed. I'm trapped below deck along with five of my men.'

'We're on our way, Mr Patterson. We'll have you out of there in no time. Change of plan, Mr Clifton. Follow me.' The captain shot down the stairs, his feet barely touching the steps, with Harry just inches behind him.

'Mr Bradshaw,' shouted the captain as he dodged in and out of the oil-fed, lapping flames, which had reached the upper deck, 'get the men into the lifeboats sharpish and abandon ship.'

'Aye aye, sir,' said Bradshaw, who was clinging on to the ship's railings.

'I need an oar. And make sure you have one lifeboat on standby ready to take Mr Patterson and his men from the boiler room.'

Bradshaw grabbed an oar from one of the lifeboats and, with the help of another seaman, managed to pass it to the captain. Harry and the skipper took one end each and stumbled along the deck towards number four hold. Harry was puzzled what use an oar could possibly be against torpedoes, but this wasn't the time to be asking questions.

The captain charged on, past the Chinaman, who was on his knees, head bowed, praying to his God.

'Get yourself into the lifeboat, now, you stupid bugger!' shouted Havens. Mr Lu rose unsteadily to his feet, but didn't move. As Harry staggered past, he shoved the man in the direction of the third officer, causing Mr Lu to topple forwards and almost fall into Mr Bradshaw's arms.

When the captain reached the hatch above number four hold, he wedged the thin end of the oar into an arched hook, jumped up and threw all his weight on to the blade. Harry quickly joined him and together they managed to lever up the massive iron plate until there was a gap of about a foot.

'You pull the men out, Mr Clifton, while I try to

keep the hatch open,' said Havens, as two hands appeared through the gap.

Harry let go of the oar, fell to his knees and crawled towards the open hatch. As he grabbed the man's shoulders, a wave of water swept over him and into the hold. He yanked the seaman out and shouted at him to report straight to the lifeboats. The second man was more agile and managed to pull himself out without Harry's assistance, while the third was in such a blind panic that he shot through the hole and banged his head on the hatch lid before staggering off after his shipmates. The next two followed in quick succession and scrambled on their hands and knees in the direction of the last remaining lifeboat. Harry waited for the chief engineer to appear, but there was no sign of him. The ship lurched further over and Harry had to cling to the deck to stop himself falling head-first into the hold.

He peered down into the darkness and spotted an outstretched hand. He put his head through the hole and leaned down as far as he could without falling in, but couldn't quite reach the second officer's fingers. Mr Patterson tried several times to jump up, but with each attempt his efforts were hampered as more water poured in on top of him. Captain Havens could see what the problem was but couldn't come to their assistance, because if he let go of the oar the hatch lid would come crashing down on Harry.

Patterson, who was now up to his knees in water, shouted, 'For God's sake you two, get yourselves into the lifeboats before it's too late!'

'Not a chance,' said the captain. 'Mr Clifton, get yourself down there and push the bastard up, then you can follow.'

Harry didn't hesitate. He lowered himself backwards, feet first, into the hold, gripping on to the ledge with his fingertips. Finally he let go and dropped into the darkness. The sloshing, oily, freezing water broke his fall and once he'd regained his balance he gripped the sides, lowered himself down into the water and said, 'Climb on to my shoulders, sir, and you should be able to reach.'

The chief engineer obeyed the fourth officer, but when he stretched up, he was still a few inches short of the deck. Harry used every ounce of strength in his body to push Patterson further up until he was able to reach the rim of the hatch and cling on by the tips of his fingers. Water was now pouring into the hold, as the ship listed further and further over. Harry placed a hand under each of Mr Patterson's buttocks and began to press like a weightlifter until the chief engineer's head appeared above the deck.

'Good to see you, Jim,' grunted the captain, as he continued to place every ounce of his weight on to the oar.

'You too, Arnold,' replied the chief engineer, as he pulled himself slowly out of the hold.

It was at that moment the last torpedo hit the sinking ship. The oar snapped in half and the iron hatch lid came crashing down on the chief engineer. Like the axe of a medieval executioner, with one slice it cleanly severed his head and slammed shut. Patterson's body fell back into the hold, landing in the water next to Harry.

Harry thanked God he couldn't see Mr Patterson in the darkness that now surrounded him. At least the water had stopped flooding in, even if it meant there was now no escape.

As the *Devonian* began to keel over, Harry assumed the captain must also have been killed or he surely would have been banging on the hatch trying to find some way of getting him out. As he slumped down into the water, Harry thought how ironic it was that he should go to his grave like his father, entombed in the hollow bottom of a ship. He clung to the side of the hold in one final effort to cheat death. As he waited for the water to rise inch by inch above his shoulders, his neck, his head, myriad faces flashed before him. Strange thoughts take over when you know you only have a few moments left to live.

At least his death would solve problems for so many people he loved. Emma would be released from her pledge to forsake all others for the rest of her days. Sir Walter would no longer have to worry about the implications of his father's will. In time, Giles would inherit the family title and all his father's worldly goods. Even Hugo Barrington might survive now that it would no longer be necessary for him to prove he wasn't Harry's father. Only his dear mother . . .

Suddenly there was an almighty explosion. The *Devonian* split in two and seconds later both halves reared up like a startled horse, before the broken ship unceremoniously sank to the bottom of the ocean.

The captain of the U-boat watched through his periscope until the *Devonian* had disappeared below the waves, leaving in its wake a thousand brightly coloured cotton dresses and countless bodies bobbing up and down in the sea, surrounded by potatoes.

54

'CAN YOU TELL ME your name?' Harry looked up at the nurse but couldn't move his lips. 'Can you hear me?' she asked. Another American accent.

Harry managed a faint nod, and she smiled. He heard a door opening and although he couldn't see who had entered the sick bay, the nurse left him immediately, so it had to be someone in authority. Even if he couldn't see them, he could hear what they were saying. It made him feel like an eavesdropper.

'Good evening, Nurse Craven,' said an older man's voice.

'Good evening, Dr Wallace,' she replied.

'How are our two patients?'

'One's showing definite signs of improvement. The other's still unconscious.'

So at least two of us survived, thought Harry. He wanted to cheer but, although his lips moved, no words came out.

'And we still have no idea who they are?'

'No, but Captain Parker came in earlier to see how they were, and when I showed him what was left of their uniforms, he wasn't in much doubt they were both officers.'

Harry's heart leapt at the thought that Captain

Havens might have survived. He heard the doctor walk over to the other bed but he couldn't turn his head to see who was lying there. A few moments later, he heard, 'Poor devil, I'll be surprised if he survives the night.'

Then you obviously don't know Captain Havens, Harry wanted to tell him, because you won't kill him off that easily.

The doctor returned to Harry's bedside and began to examine him. Harry could just make out a middle-aged man with a serious, thoughtful face. Once Dr Wallace had finished his examination, he turned away and whispered to the nurse, 'I feel a lot more hopeful about this one, although the odds are still no better than fifty-fifty after what he's been through. Keep fighting, young man,' he said, turning to face Harry, though he couldn't be sure if the patient could hear him. 'We're going to do everything in our power to keep you alive.' Harry wanted to thank him, but all he could manage was another slight nod, before the doctor walked away. 'If either of them should die during the night,' he heard the doctor whisper to the nurse, 'are you familiar with the correct procedure?'

'Yes, doctor. The captain is to be informed immediately, and the body is to be taken down to the morgue.' Harry wanted to ask how many of his shipmates were already there.

'And I'd also like to be kept informed,' added Wallace, 'even if I've turned in for the night.'

'Of course, doctor. Can I ask what the captain has decided to do with those poor devils who were already dead when we pulled them out of the water?'

'He's given an order that as they were all sailors, they are to be buried at sea, at first light tomorrow morning.'

'Why so early?'

'He doesn't want the passengers to realize just how many lives were lost last night,' the doctor added as he walked away. Harry heard a door open. 'Goodnight, nurse.'

'Goodnight, doctor,' the nurse replied, and the door closed.

Nurse Craven walked back and sat down by Harry's bedside. 'I don't give a damn about the odds,' she said. 'You're going to live.'

Harry looked up at a nurse who was hidden behind her starched white uniform and white cap, but even so, he couldn't miss the burning conviction in her eyes.

◄○►

When Harry next woke, the room was in darkness apart from a glimmer of light in the far corner, probably from another room. His first thought was of Captain Havens, fighting for his life in the next bed. He prayed that he would survive and they'd be able to return to England together, when the captain would retire and Harry could sign up with any Royal Navy vessel Sir Walter could get him on.

His thoughts turned to Emma once again, and how his death would have solved so many problems for the Barrington family, that would now return to haunt them.

Harry heard the door open again and someone with an unfamiliar step walked into the sick bay. Although he couldn't see who it was, the sound of their shoes suggested two things: it was a man, and he knew where he was going. Another door opened on the far side of the room and the light became brighter.

'Hi, Kristin,' said a man's voice.

'Hello, Richard,' came back the nurse's reply. 'You're late,' she said, teasing, not angry.

'Sorry, honey. All the officers had to remain on the

bridge until the search for survivors was finally abandoned.'

The door closed, and the light softened once more. Harry had no way of knowing how much time had passed before the door opened again – half an hour, an hour perhaps – and he heard their voices.

'Your tie's not straight,' said the nurse.

'That won't do,' the man replied. 'Someone might figure out what we've been up to.' She laughed as he began walking towards the door. Suddenly he stopped. 'Who are these two?'

'Mr A and Mr B. The only survivors from last night's rescue operation.'

I'm Mr C, Harry wanted to tell her as they walked towards his bed. Harry closed his eyes; he didn't want them to think he'd been listening to their conversation. She took his pulse.

'I think Mr B is getting stronger by the hour. You know, I can't bear the thought of not saving at least one of them.' She left Harry and walked over to the other bed.

Harry opened his eyes and turned his head slightly to see a tall young man in a smart white dress uniform with gold epaulettes. Without warning, Nurse Craven began to sob. The young man placed an arm gently around her shoulder and tried to comfort her. No, no, Harry wanted to shout, Captain Havens can't die. We're going back to England together.

'What's the procedure in these circumstances?' asked the young officer, sounding rather formal.

'I have to inform the captain immediately, and then wake Dr Wallace. Once all the papers have been signed and clearance has been authorized, the body will be taken down to the morgue and prepared for tomorrow's burial service.'

No, no, no, Harry shouted, but neither of them heard him.

'I pray to whatever God,' continued the nurse, 'that America doesn't become involved in this war.'

'That's never going to happen, honey,' said the young officer. 'Roosevelt's far too canny to get himself involved in another European war.'

'That's what the politicians said last time,' Kristin reminded him.

'Hey, what's brought this on?' He sounded concerned.

'Mr A was about the same age as you,' she said. 'Perhaps he also had a fiancée back home.'

Harry realized that it wasn't Captain Havens in the next bed, but Tom Bradshaw. That was when he made the decision.

◄o►

When Harry woke again, he could hear voices coming from the next room. Moments later, Dr Wallace and Nurse Craven walked into the sick bay.

'It must have been heart-wrenching,' said the nurse.

'It wasn't at all pleasant,' admitted the doctor. 'Somehow it was made worse because they all went to their graves nameless, although I had to agree with the captain, that's the way a sailor would have wanted to be buried.'

'Any news from the other ship?' asked the nurse.

'Yes, they've done a little better than us. Eleven dead, but three survivors: a Chinaman and two Englishmen.'

Harry wondered if it was possible that one of the Englishmen might be Captain Havens.

The doctor bent down and unbuttoned Harry's pyjama top. He placed a cold stethoscope on several parts of his chest and listened carefully. Then the nurse placed a thermometer in Harry's mouth.

'His temperature is well down, doctor,' said the nurse after she had checked the vein of mercury.

'Excellent. You might try giving him some thin soup.'

'Yes, of course. Will you need my help with any of the passengers?'

'No, thank you, nurse, your most important job is to make sure this one survives. I'll see you in a couple of hours.'

Once the door had closed, the nurse returned to Harry's bedside. She sat down and smiled. 'Can you see me?' she asked. Harry nodded. 'Can you tell me your name?'

'Tom Bradshaw,' he replied.

55

'TOM,' SAID DR WALLACE once he'd completed his examination of Harry, 'I wonder if you can tell me the name of your fellow officer who died last night. I'd like to write to his mother, or his wife if he had one.'

'His name was Harry Clifton,' said Harry, his voice barely audible. 'He wasn't married, but I know his mother quite well. I'd planned to write to her myself.'

'That's good of you,' said Wallace, 'but I'd still like to send her a letter. Do you have her address?'

'Yes, I do,' said Harry. 'But it might be kinder if she heard from me first, and not from a complete stranger,' he suggested.

'If you think so,' said Wallace, not sounding at all sure.

'Yes, I do,' said Harry, a little more firmly this time. 'You can always post my letter when the *Kansas Star* returns to Bristol. That's assuming the captain is still planning to sail back to England, now we're at war with Germany.'

'*We* are not at war with Germany,' said Wallace.

'No, of course we're not,' said Harry, quickly correcting himself. 'And let's hope it never comes to that.'

'Agreed,' said Wallace, 'but that won't stop the *Kansas Star* making the return journey. There are still hundreds of Americans stranded in England, with no other way of getting home.'

'Isn't that a bit of a risk?' asked Harry. 'Especially considering what we've just been through.'

'No, I don't think so,' said Wallace. 'The last thing the Germans will want to do is sink an American passenger ship, which would be sure to drag us into the conflict. I suggest you get some sleep, Tom, because I'm hoping that tomorrow the nurse will be able to take you for a turn around the deck. Only one lap to begin with,' he emphasized.

Harry closed his eyes but made no attempt to sleep as he began to think about the decision he'd made, and how many lives it would affect. By taking Tom Bradshaw's identity, he had allowed himself a little breathing space to consider his future. Once they learnt that Harry Clifton had been killed at sea, Sir Walter and the rest of the Barrington family would be released from any obligations they might have felt bound by, and Emma would be free to begin a new life. A decision he felt Old Jack would have approved of, although the full implications hadn't yet sunk in.

However, the resurrection of Tom Bradshaw would undoubtedly create its own problems, and he would have to remain constantly on his guard. It didn't help that he knew almost nothing about Bradshaw, so that whenever Nurse Craven asked him about his past, he either had to make something up or change the subject.

Bradshaw had proved very adept at deflecting any questions he didn't wish to answer, and had clearly been a loner. He hadn't set foot in his own country for at least three years, possibly more, so his family would have no way of knowing of his imminent return. As soon as the *Kansas Star* arrived in New York, Harry planned to sail back to England on the first available ship.

His greatest dilemma was how to prevent his mother from being put through any unnecessary suffering by thinking she'd lost her only son. Dr Wallace had gone some way to solving that particular problem when he promised to post a letter to Maisie the moment he arrived back in England. But Harry still had to write that letter.

He had spent hours going over the text in his mind, so that by the time he'd recovered enough to commit his thoughts to paper, he almost knew the script by heart.

New York,
September 8th, 1939

My dearest mother,

I have done everything in my power to make sure you receive this letter before anyone can tell you I was killed at sea.

As the date on this letter shows, I did not die when the Devonian *was sunk on September 4th. In fact, I was plucked out of the sea by an American ship and am very much alive. However, an opportunity arose for me to assume another man's identity, and I did so, in the hope it would release both you and the Barrington family from the many problems I seem to have unwittingly caused over the years.*

It is important that you realize my love for Emma has in no way diminished; far from it. But I do not feel I have the right to expect her to spend the rest of her life clinging on to the vain hope that at some time in the future I might be able to prove that Arthur Clifton and not Hugo Barrington was

my father. This way, she can at least consider a
future with someone else. I envy that man.

I plan to return to England in the near future.
Should you receive any communication from a Tom
Bradshaw, it will be from me.

I will be in touch with you the moment I set foot
in England, but in the meantime, I must beg you to
keep my secret as steadfastly as you kept your own
for so many years.

Your loving son,

Harry

He read the letter several times before placing it in
an envelope marked 'Strictly private and confidential'.
He addressed it to Mrs Arthur Clifton, 27 Still House
Lane, Bristol.

The following morning, he handed the letter over to
Dr Wallace.

—◁◦▷—

'Do you think you're ready to try a short walk around
the deck?' asked Kristin.

'Sure am,' Harry replied, trying out one of the
expressions he'd heard her boyfriend use, although he
still found it unnatural to add the word 'honey'.

During those long hours he'd spent in bed, Harry
had listened carefully to Dr Wallace, and whenever he
was alone, he tried to imitate his accent, which he'd
heard Kristin describe to Richard as east coast. Harry
was thankful for the hours he'd spent with Dr Paget
learning voice skills that he'd assumed would only be of
use on stage. He was on stage. However, he still had the
problem of how to deal with Kristin's innocent curiosity
about his family background and upbringing.

He was assisted by a novel by Horatio Alger and another by Thornton Wilder, the only two books that had been left behind in the sick bay. From these he was able to conjure up a fictional family who hailed from Bridgeport, Connecticut. They consisted of a father who was a small-town bank manager with Connecticut Trust and Savings, a mother who was a dutiful home-maker and had once come second in the town's annual beauty pageant, and an older sister, Sally, who was happily married to Jake, who ran the local hardware store. He smiled to himself when he recalled Dr Paget's remark that, with his imagination, he was more likely to end up a writer than an actor.

Harry placed his feet tentatively on the floor and, with Kristin's help, pulled himself slowly up. Once he'd put on a dressing gown, he took her by the arm and made his way unsteadily towards the door, up a flight of steps and out on to the deck.

'How long is it since you've been home?' asked Kristin as they began their slow progress around the deck.

Harry always tried to stick to the little he actually knew about Bradshaw, adding a few snippets from the life of his fictitious family. 'Just over three years,' he said. 'My family never complain, because they knew I wanted to go to sea from an early age.'

'But how did you come to be serving on a British ship?'

Damn good question, thought Harry. He only wished he knew the answer. He stumbled, to give himself a little more time to come up with a convincing reply. Kristin bent down to assist him.

'I'm fine,' he said, once he'd taken Kristin's arm again. Then he began to sneeze repeatedly.

'Perhaps it's time to take you back to the ward,' suggested Kristin. 'We can't afford to have you catching a cold. We can always try again tomorrow.'

'Whatever you say,' said Harry, relieved she didn't ask any more questions.

After she'd tucked him up like a mother putting a young child to bed, he quickly fell into a deep sleep.

━◆━

Harry managed eleven laps of the deck the day before the *Kansas Star* sailed into New York Harbour. Although he couldn't admit it to anyone, he was quite excited about the prospect of seeing America for the first time.

'Will you be going straight back to Bridgeport once we've docked?' asked Kristin during his final lap. 'Or are you planning to stay in New York?'

'Haven't given it a lot of thought,' said Harry, who had in fact given it a great deal of thought. 'I suppose it will depend on what time we dock,' he added, as he tried to anticipate her next question.

'It's just that, if you'd like to spend the night at Richard's apartment on the East-side, that would be swell.'

'Oh, I wouldn't want to put him to any trouble.'

Kristin laughed. 'You know, Tom, there are times when you sound more like an Englishman than an American.'

'I guess after all those years serving on British ships you're bound to eventually get corrupted by the limeys.'

'Is that also the reason you felt unable to share your problem with us?' Harry came to a sudden halt: a stumble or a sneeze wasn't going to rescue him this time. 'If you'd been just a little more frank in the first place, we'd have been happy to sort out the problem.

But, given the circumstances, we had no choice but to inform Captain Parker and leave him to decide what should be done.'

Harry collapsed into the nearest deckchair, but as Kristin made no attempt to come to his rescue, he knew he was beaten. 'It's far more complicated than you realize,' he began. 'But I can explain why I didn't want to involve anyone else.'

'No need to,' said Kristin. 'The captain's already come to our rescue. But he did want to ask how you intended to deal with the bigger problem.'

Harry bowed his head. 'I'm willing to answer any questions the captain might have,' he said, feeling almost a sense of relief that he'd been found out.

'Like the rest of us, he wanted to know how you're going to get off the ship when you don't have any clothes, or a dime to your name?'

Harry smiled. 'I figured New Yorkers might consider a *Kansas Star* dressing gown to be pretty nifty.'

'Frankly, not too many New Yorkers would notice even if you did walk down Fifth Avenue in a robe,' said Kristin. 'And the ones that did would probably think it was the latest fashion. But just in case they don't, Richard's come up with a couple of white shirts and a sports jacket. Pity he's so much taller than you, otherwise he'd have been able to supply a pair of pants as well. Dr Wallace can spare a pair of brown wingtips, a pair of socks and a tie. That still leaves us with the problem of the pants, but the captain has a pair of Bermuda shorts that no longer fit him.' Harry burst out laughing. 'We hope you won't be offended, Tom, but we also held a little collection among the crew,' she added, passing him a thick envelope. 'I think you'll find there's more than enough to get you to Connecticut.'

'How do I begin to thank you?' said Harry.

442

'No need to, Tom. We're all so pleased you survived. I only wish we could have saved your friend Harry Clifton as well. Still, you'll be glad to hear that Captain Parker has instructed Dr Wallace to deliver your letter to his mother personally.'

56

HARRY WAS AMONG the first on deck that morning, some two hours before the *Kansas Star* was due to sail into New York Harbour. It was another forty minutes before the sun joined him, by which time he'd worked out exactly how he was going to spend his first day in America.

He had already said farewell to Dr Wallace, after trying, inadequately, to thank him for all he'd done. Wallace assured him that he would post his letter to Mrs Clifton just as soon as he arrived in Bristol, and had reluctantly accepted that it might not be wise to visit her, after Harry had hinted that she was of a nervous disposition.

Harry was touched when Captain Parker called into the sick bay to deliver a pair of Bermuda shorts and wish him luck. After he had returned to the bridge, Kristin said firmly, 'It's time for you to go to bed, Tom. You'll need all your strength if you're going to travel to Connecticut tomorrow.' Tom Bradshaw would have liked to spend a day or two with Richard and Kristin in Manhattan, but Harry Clifton couldn't afford to waste any time now that Britain had declared war on Germany.

'When you wake up in the morning,' continued Kristin, 'try to get up on to the passenger deck before first light, then you can watch the sun rising as we sail into New York. I know you'll have seen it many times before, Tom, but it never fails to excite me.'

'Me too,' said Harry.

'And once we've docked,' continued Kristin, 'why don't you wait for Richard and me to come off duty and then we can disembark together?'

◄O►

Dressed in Richard's sports jacket and shirt, a little too large, the captain's Bermuda shorts, a little too long, and the doctor's shoes and socks, a little too tight, Harry couldn't wait to go ashore.

The ship's purser had telegraphed ahead to advise the New York Immigration Department that they had an extra passenger on board, an American citizen called Tom Bradshaw. The NYID had telegraphed back to say that Mr Bradshaw should make himself known to one of the immigration officials and they would take it from there.

Once Richard had dropped him off at Grand Central, Harry planned to hang around in the station for a little while before heading back to the docks, where he intended to report straight to the union office and find out which ships were due to sail for England. It didn't matter which port they were heading for, as long as it wasn't Bristol.

Once he had identified a suitable vessel, he would sign up for any job on offer. He didn't care if he worked on the bridge or in the boiler room, scrubbed the decks or peeled potatoes, just as long as he got back to England. If there turned out to be no jobs available, he would book the cheapest passage home. He'd already checked the contents of the bulky white envelope Kristin had given him and there was more than enough to pay for a berth that couldn't be smaller than the broom cupboard he'd slept in on the *Devonian*.

It saddened Harry that when he returned to England he wouldn't be able to contact any of his old friends, and he'd have to be cautious even when he got in touch with his mother. But the moment he stepped ashore, his only purpose would be to join one of His Majesty's war ships and enlist in the fight against the King's enemies, even though he knew that whenever that ship returned to port he would have to remain on board, like a criminal on the run.

Harry's thoughts were interrupted by a lady. He gazed in admiration when he first saw the Statue of Liberty looming up in front of him through the early-morning mist. He had seen photographs of the iconic landmark but they had not given a true sense of her size as she towered above the *Kansas Star*, welcoming visitors, immigrants and her fellow countrymen to the United States.

As the ship continued on its way towards the harbour, Harry leant over the railings and looked towards Manhattan, disappointed that the skyscrapers didn't appear to be any taller than some of the buildings he remembered in Bristol. But then, as each minute passed, they grew and grew until they appeared to soar up into the heavens and he had to shade his eyes from the sun as he stared up at them.

A New York Port Authority tug boat came out to join them and guided the *Kansas Star* safely to its berth on number seven dock. When Harry saw the cheering crowds, he began to feel apprehensive for the first time, even though the young man who was sailing into New York that morning was far older than the fourth officer who'd left Bristol only three weeks earlier.

'Smile, Tom.'

Harry turned to see Richard looking down into a Kodak Brownie Box camera. He was peering at an upside-down image of Tom, with the Manhattan skyline as a backdrop.

'You'll be one passenger I sure won't forget in a hurry,' said Kristin, as she walked across to join him so that Richard could take a second photograph of them together. She had exchanged her nurse's uniform for a smart polka-dot dress, white belt and white shoes.

'Nor me you,' said Harry, hoping that neither of them could sense how nervous he was.

'Time for us to go ashore,' said Richard, closing the shutter of his camera.

The three of them took the wide staircase down to the lower deck, where several passengers were already streaming off the ship to be reunited with relieved relatives and anxious friends. As they made their way down the gangway, Harry's spirits were lifted by how many of the ship's passengers and crew wanted to shake him by the hand and wish him luck.

Once they'd stepped on to the dockside, Harry, Richard and Kristin headed towards immigration, where they joined one of four long queues. Harry's eyes darted about in every direction, and he wanted to ask so many questions, but any one of them would have revealed that this was the first time he'd set foot in America.

The first thing that struck him was the patchwork quilt of different colours that made up the American people. He'd only ever seen one black man in Bristol, and remembered stopping to stare at him. Old Jack had told him it was both rude and inconsiderate, adding, 'How would you feel if everyone stopped to stare at you just because you were white?' But it was the noise, the bustle and the sheer pace of everything around him that most caught Harry's imagination and made Bristol seem as if it were languishing in a bygone age.

He was already beginning to wish that he'd accepted Richard's offer to stay with him overnight and perhaps spend a few days in a city he was finding so exciting even before he'd left the dockside.

'Why don't I go through first?' said Richard, as they reached the head of the queue. 'Then I can pick up my car and meet you both outside the terminal.'

'Good idea,' said Kristin.

'Next!' shouted an immigration officer.

Richard walked up to the desk and handed over his passport to the official, who glanced briefly at the photo before stamping it. 'Welcome home, Lieutenant Tibbet.'

'Next!'

Harry stepped forward, uncomfortably aware that he had no passport, no identification and someone else's name.

'My name's Tom Bradshaw,' he said with a confidence he didn't feel. 'I think the purser of the SS *Kansas Star* telegraphed ahead to warn that I would be coming ashore.'

The immigration officer looked closely at Harry, then picked up a sheet of paper and began to study a long list of names. Finally he put a tick by one before turning round and nodding. For the first time, Harry noticed two men standing on the other side of the barrier, wearing identical grey suits and grey hats. One of them gave him a smile.

The immigration officer stamped a piece of paper and handed it to Harry. 'Welcome back, Mr Bradshaw. It's been a long time.'

'Sure has,' said Harry.

'Next!'

'I'll wait for you,' said Harry as Kristin made her way to the desk.

'I'll only be a moment,' she promised.

Harry passed through the barrier and entered the United States of America for the first time.

The two men in grey suits stepped forward. One of them said, 'Good morning, sir. Are you Mr Thomas Bradshaw?'

'That's me,' said Harry.

The words were hardly out of his mouth before the other man grabbed him and pinned his arms behind his back, while the first man handcuffed him. It all happened so quickly that Harry didn't even have time to protest.

He remained outwardly calm, as he had already considered the possibility that someone might work out that he wasn't Tom Bradshaw, but in fact an Englishman called Harry Clifton. Even so, he had assumed that the worst they could do was serve him with a deportation order and have him shipped back to Britain. And as that was exactly what he'd planned to do anyway, he didn't put up a fight.

Harry spotted two cars waiting by the sidewalk. The first was a black police car, with its back door being held open by another unsmiling man in a grey suit. The second was a red sports car, with Richard sitting on the bonnet, smiling.

The moment Richard saw that Tom had been hand-cuffed and was being led away, he leapt up and began to run towards him. At the same time, one of the police officers began to read Mr Bradshaw his rights, while the other continued to grip Harry firmly by the elbow.

'What the hell do you think you're doing?' demanded Richard, the moment he'd caught up with them.

Neither officer made any attempt to answer his question, as they marched Tom towards the waiting car.

Richard matched them stride for stride, and was amazed by how calm Tom appeared to be, almost as if he wasn't surprised to have been arrested. Despite this, he was determined to assist his friend, even though the two officers continued to ignore him. Just as they reached the police car, Richard leapt in front of the two detectives and blocked their path.

'What are you charging Mr Bradshaw with?' he said firmly.

The senior detective came to a halt, looked Richard in the eye, and said, 'First degree murder.'

THE SINS OF THE FATHER

SIR TOMMY MACPHERSON

CBE, MC**, TD, DL

Chevalier de la Légion d'Honneur,
Croix de Guerre with 2 Palms and a Star,
Medaglia d'Argento and Resistance Medal, Italy,
Kt of St Mary of Bethlehem

My thanks go to the following people for their
invaluable advice and research:

Simon Bainbridge, Eleanor Dryden,
Dr Robert Lyman FRHistS, Alison Prince,
Mari Roberts and Susan Watt

THE BARRINGTONS

Sir Walter Barrington 1866– m. Mary Barrington 1874–

Phyllis 1875– —— Andrew Harvey 1868– m. Leticia 1878–

Nicholas 1894–1918

Hugo 1896– m. Elizabeth Harvey 1900–

Giles 1920–   Emma 1921–   Grace 1923–

THE CLIFTONS

Harold Tancock 1871– m. Vera Prescott 1876–

Ray 1895–1917 Albert 1896–1917 Stanley 1898– Maisie 1901– m. Arthur Clifton 1898–1921 Elsie 1908–1910

Harry 1920–

Sebastian 1940–

'For I the Lord thy God am a jealous God, and visit the sins of the fathers upon the children unto the third and fourth generation . . .'

Book of Common Prayer

HARRY CLIFTON

1939–1941

1

'My name is Harry Clifton.'

'Sure, and I'm Babe Ruth,' said Detective Kolowski as he lit a cigarette.

'No,' said Harry, 'you don't understand, there's been a terrible mistake. I'm Harry Clifton, an Englishman from Bristol. I served on the same ship as Tom Bradshaw.'

'Save it for your lawyer,' said the detective, exhaling deeply and filling the small cell with a cloud of smoke.

'I don't have a lawyer,' protested Harry.

'If I was in the trouble you're in, kid, I'd consider having Sefton Jelks on my side to be about my only hope.'

'Who's Sefton Jelks?'

'You may not have heard of the sharpest lawyer in New York,' said the detective as he blew out another plume of smoke, 'but he has an appointment to see you at nine o'clock tomorrow morning, and Jelks don't leave his office unless his bill has been paid in advance.'

'But—' began Harry, as Kolowski banged the palm of his hand on the cell door.

'So when Jelks turns up tomorrow morning,'

3

Kolowski continued, ignoring Harry's interruption, 'you'd better come up with a more convincing story than we've arrested the wrong man. You told the immigration officer that you were Tom Bradshaw, and if it was good enough for him, it's going to be good enough for the judge.'

The cell door swung open, but not before the detective had exhaled another plume of smoke that made Harry cough. Kolowski stepped out into the corridor without another word and slammed the door behind him. Harry collapsed on to a bunk that was attached to the wall and rested his head on a brick-hard pillow. He looked up at the ceiling and began to think about how he'd ended up in a police cell on the other side of the world on a murder charge.

—<o>—

The door opened long before the morning light could creep through the bars of the window and into the cell. Despite the early hour, Harry was wide awake.

A warder strolled in carrying a tray of food that the Salvation Army wouldn't have considered offering a penniless hobo. Once he'd placed the tray on the little wooden table, he left without a word.

Harry took one look at the food before beginning to pace up and down. With each step, he grew more confident that once he explained to Mr Jelks the reason he'd exchanged his name with Tom Bradshaw, the matter would quickly be sorted out. Surely the worst punishment they could exact would be to deport him, and as he'd always intended to return to England and join the navy, it all fitted in with his original plan.

At 8.55 a.m., Harry was sitting on the end of the

bunk, impatient for Mr Jelks to appear. The massive iron door didn't swing open until twelve minutes past nine. Harry leapt up as a prison guard stood to one side and allowed a tall, elegant man with silver grey hair to enter. Harry thought he must have been about the same age as Grandpa. Mr Jelks wore a dark blue pinstripe, double-breasted suit, a white shirt and a striped tie. The weary look on his face suggested that little would surprise him.

'Good morning,' he said, giving Harry a faint smile. 'My name is Sefton Jelks. I am the senior partner of Jelks, Myers and Abernathy, and my clients, Mr and Mrs Bradshaw, have asked me to represent you in your upcoming trial.'

Harry offered Jelks the only chair in his cell, as if he was an old friend who had dropped in to his study at Oxford for a cup of tea. He perched on the bunk and watched the lawyer as he opened his briefcase, extracted a yellow pad and placed it on the table.

Jelks took a pen from an inside pocket and said, 'Perhaps you might begin by telling me who you are, as we both know you're not Lieutenant Bradshaw.'

If the lawyer was surprised by Harry's story he showed no sign of it. Head bowed, he wrote copious notes on his yellow pad while Harry explained how he'd ended up spending the night in jail. Once he'd finished, Harry assumed his problems must surely be over, as he had such a senior lawyer on his side – that was, until he heard Jelks's first question.

'You say that you wrote a letter to your mother while you were on board the *Kansas Star*, explaining why you had assumed Tom Bradshaw's identity?'

'That's correct, sir. I didn't want my mother to suffer

5

unnecessarily, but at the same time I needed her to understand why I'd made such a drastic decision.'

'Yes, I can understand why you might have considered that changing your identity would solve all your immediate problems, while not appreciating that it could involve you in a series of even more complicated ones,' said Jelks. His next question surprised Harry even more. 'Do you recall the contents of that letter?'

'Of course. I wrote and rewrote it so many times I could reproduce it almost verbatim.'

'Then allow me to test your memory,' Jelks said and, without another word, tore off a sheet from his yellow pad and handed it and his fountain pen to Harry.

Harry spent some time recalling the exact words, before he set about rewriting the letter.

My dearest mother,

I have done everything in my power to make sure you receive this letter before anyone can tell you that I died at sea. As the date on this letter shows, I did not perish when the Devonian *was sunk on September 4th. In fact, I was plucked out of the sea by a sailor from an American ship and thanks to him, I'm still very much alive. However, an unexpected opportunity arose for me to assume another man's identity, and I did so willingly, in the hope it would release Emma from the many problems I seem to have unwittingly caused her and her family over the years.*

It is important that you realize my love for Emma has in no way diminished; far from it. I cannot believe I shall ever experience such love

*again. But I do not feel I have the right to expect
her to spend the rest of her life clinging on to the
vain hope that at some time in the future I might
be able to prove that Hugo Barrington is not my
father, and that I am, in fact, the son of Arthur
Clifton. At least this way, she can consider a future
with someone else. I envy that man.*

*I plan to return to England on the first available
ship, so should you receive any communication
from a Tom Bradshaw, you can assume it's me.
I'll be in touch with you the moment I set foot in
Bristol, but in the meantime, I must beg you to keep
my secret as steadfastly as you kept your own for so
many years.*

Your loving son,

Harry

When Jelks had finished reading the letter, he once
again took Harry by surprise. 'Did you post the letter
yourself, Mr Clifton,' he asked, 'or did you give that
responsibility to someone else?'

For the first time Harry felt suspicious, and decided
not to mention that he'd asked Dr Wallace to deliver
the letter to his mother when he returned to Bristol in
a fortnight's time. He feared that Jelks might persuade
Dr Wallace to hand over the letter and then his mother
would have no way of knowing he was still alive.

'I posted the letter when I came ashore,' he said.

The elderly lawyer took his time before he responded. 'Do you have any proof that you are Harry
Clifton, and not Thomas Bradshaw?'

'No, sir, I do not,' said Harry without hesitation,

painfully aware that no one on board the *Kansas Star* had any reason to believe he wasn't Tom Bradshaw, and the only people who could verify his story were on the other side of the ocean, more than three thousand miles away, and it would not be long before they were all informed that Harry Clifton had been buried at sea.

'Then I may be able to assist you, Mr Clifton. That's assuming you still wish Miss Emma Barrington to believe you are dead. If you do,' said Jelks, an insincere smile on his face, 'I may be able to offer a solution to your problem.'

'A solution?' said Harry, looking hopeful for the first time.

'But only if you felt able to retain the persona of Thomas Bradshaw.'

Harry remained silent.

'The district attorney's office has accepted that the charge against Bradshaw is at best circumstantial, and the only real evidence they are clinging on to is that he left the country the day after the murder had been committed. Aware of the weakness of their case, they have agreed to drop the charge of murder if you felt able to plead guilty to the lesser charge of desertion while serving in the armed forces.'

'But why would I agree to that?' asked Harry.

'I can think of three good reasons,' replied Jelks. 'Firstly, if you don't, you're likely to end up spending six years in prison for entering the United States on false pretences. Secondly, you would retain your anonymity, so the Barrington family would have no reason to believe you are still alive. And thirdly, the Bradshaws are willing to pay you ten thousand dollars if you take their son's place.'

Harry realized immediately that this would be an opportunity to repay his mother for all the sacrifices she'd made for him over the years. Such a large sum of money would transform her life, making it possible for her to escape the two-up two-down in Still House Lane, along with the weekly knock on the door from the rent collector. She might even consider giving up her job as a waitress at the Grand Hotel and start living an easier life, although Harry thought that was unlikely. But before he agreed to fall in with Jelks's plans, he had some questions of his own.

'Why would the Bradshaws be willing to go through with such a deception, when they must now know that their son was killed at sea?'

'Mrs Bradshaw is desperate to have Thomas's name cleared. She will never accept that one of her sons might have killed the other.'

'So is that what Tom is accused of – murdering his brother?'

'Yes, but as I said, the evidence is flimsy and circumstantial, and certainly wouldn't stand up in court, which is why the DA's office is willing to drop the charge, but only if we agree to plead guilty to the lesser charge of desertion.'

'And how long might my sentence be, if I agreed to that?'

'The DA has agreed to recommend to the judge that you're sentenced to one year, so with good behaviour you could be free in six months; quite an improvement on the six years you can expect if you go on insisting that you're Harry Clifton.'

'But the moment I walk into the courtroom, someone's bound to realize that I'm not Bradshaw.'

'Unlikely,' said Jelks. 'The Bradshaws hail from Seattle, on the west coast, and although they're well off, they rarely visit New York. Thomas joined the navy when he was seventeen, and as you know to your cost, he hasn't set foot in America for the past four years. And if you plead guilty, you'll only be in the courtroom for twenty minutes.'

'But when I open my mouth, won't everyone know I'm not an American?'

'That's why you won't be opening your mouth, Mr Clifton.' The urbane lawyer seemed to have an answer for everything. Harry tried another ploy.

'In England, murder trials are always packed with journalists, and the public queue up outside the courtroom from the early hours in the hope of getting a glimpse of the defendant.'

'Mr Clifton, there are fourteen murder trials currently taking place in New York, including the notorious "scissors stabber". I doubt if even a cub reporter will be assigned to this case.'

'I need some time to think about it.'

Jelks glanced at his watch. 'We're due in front of Judge Atkins at noon, so you have just over an hour to make up your mind, Mr Clifton.' He called for a guard to open the cell door. 'Should you decide not to avail yourself of my services I wish you luck, because we will not be meeting again,' he added before he left the cell.

Harry sat on the end of the bunk, considering Sefton Jelks's offer. Although he didn't doubt that the silver-haired counsel had his own agenda, six months sounded a lot more palatable than six years, and who else could he turn to, other than this seasoned lawyer? Harry wished he could drop into Sir Walter Barrington's office for a few moments and seek his advice.

◄◦►

An hour later, Harry, dressed in a dark blue suit, cream shirt, starched collar and a striped tie, was handcuffed, marched from his cell to a prison vehicle and driven to the courthouse under armed guard.

'No one must believe you're capable of murder,' Jelks had pronounced after a tailor had visited Harry's cell with half a dozen suits, shirts and a selection of ties for him to consider.

'I'm not,' Harry reminded him.

Harry was reunited with Jelks in the corridor. The lawyer gave him that same smile before pushing his way through the swing doors and walking down the centre aisle, not stopping until he reached the two vacant seats at counsel's table.

Once Harry had settled into his place and his hand-cuffs had been removed, he looked around the almost empty courtroom. Jelks had been right about that. Few members of the public, and certainly no press, seemed interested in the case. For them, it must have been just another domestic murder, where the defendant was likely to be acquitted; no 'Cain and Abel' headlines while there was no possibility of the electric chair in court number four.

As the first chime rang out to announce midday, a door opened on the far side of the room and Judge Atkins appeared. He walked slowly across the court, climbed the steps and took his place behind a desk on the raised dais. He then nodded in the direction of the DA, as if he knew exactly what he was about to say.

A young lawyer rose from behind the prosecutor's desk and explained that the state would be dropping the murder charge, but would be pursuing Thomas Bradshaw on a charge of desertion from the US Navy. The judge nodded, and turned his attention to Mr Jelks, who rose on cue.

'And on the second charge, of desertion, how does your client plead?'

'Guilty,' said Jelks. 'I hope your honour will be lenient with my client on this occasion, as I don't need to remind you, sir, that this is his first offence, and before this uncharacteristic lapse he had an unblemished record.'

Judge Atkins scowled. 'Mr Jelks,' he said, 'some may consider that for an officer to desert his post while serving his country is a crime every bit as heinous as murder. I'm sure I don't have to remind *you* that until recently such an offence would have resulted in your client facing a firing squad.'

Harry felt sick as he looked up at Jelks, who didn't take his eyes off the judge.

'With that in mind,' continued Atkins, 'I sentence Lieutenant Thomas Bradshaw to six years in jail.' He banged his gavel and said, 'Next case,' before Harry had a chance to protest.

'You told me—' began Harry, but Jelks had already turned his back on his former client and was walking away. Harry was about to chase after him, when the two guards grabbed him by the arms, thrust them behind his back and quickly handcuffed the convicted criminal, before marching him across the courtroom towards a door Harry hadn't noticed before.

He looked back to see Sefton Jelks shaking hands

with a middle-aged man who was clearly congratulating him on a job well done. Where had Harry seen that face before? And then he realized – it had to be Tom Bradshaw's father.

2

HARRY WAS MARCHED unceremoniously down a long, dimly lit corridor and out of an unmarked door into a barren courtyard.

In the middle of the yard stood a yellow bus that displayed neither number nor any hint of its destination. A muscle-bound conductor clutching a rifle stood by the door, and nodded to indicate that Harry should climb on board. His guards gave him a helping hand, just in case he was having second thoughts.

Harry took a seat and stared sullenly out of the window as a trickle of convicted prisoners were led up to the bus, some with their heads bowed, while others, who had clearly trodden this path before, adopted a jaunty swagger. He assumed it wouldn't be long before the bus set off for its destination, wherever that might be, but he was about to learn his first painful lesson as a prisoner: once you've been convicted, no one is in any hurry.

Harry thought about asking one of the guards where they were going, but neither of them looked like helpful tour guides. He turned anxiously when a body slumped into the seat next to him. He didn't want to stare at his new companion, but as the man introduced himself immediately, Harry took a closer look at him.

'My name's Pat Quinn,' he announced with a slight Irish accent.

'Tom Bradshaw,' said Harry, who would have shaken hands with his new companion if they hadn't both been handcuffed.

Quinn didn't look like a criminal. His feet barely touched the ground, so he couldn't have been an inch over five feet, and whereas most of the other prisoners on the bus were either muscle-bound or simply over-weight, Quinn looked as if a gust of wind would blow him away. His thinning red hair was beginning to grey, although he couldn't have been a day over forty.

'You're a first-timer?' said Quinn confidently.

'Is it that obvious?' asked Harry.

'It's written all over your face.'

'What's written all over my face?'

'You haven't got a clue what's going to happen next.'

'So *you're* obviously not a first-timer?'

'This is the eleventh time I've been on this bus, or it could be the twelfth.'

Harry laughed for the first time in days.

'What are you in for?' Quinn asked him.

'Desertion,' Harry replied, without elaboration.

'Never heard of that one before,' said Quinn. 'I've deserted three wives, but they never put me in the slammer for it.'

'I didn't desert a wife,' said Harry, thinking about Emma. 'I deserted the Royal Navy— I mean the navy.'

'How long did you get for that?'

'Six years.'

Quinn whistled through his two remaining teeth. 'Sounds a bit rough. Who was the judge?'

'Atkins,' said Harry with feeling.

'Arnie Atkins? You got the wrong judge. If you're ever on trial again, make sure you pick the right judge.'

'I didn't know you could pick your judge.'

'You can't,' said Quinn, 'but there are ways of avoiding the worst ones.' Harry looked more closely at his companion, but didn't interrupt. 'There are seven judges who work the circuit, and you need to avoid two of them at all costs. One is Arnie Atkins. He's short on humour and long on sentencing.'

'But how could I have avoided him?' asked Harry.

'Atkins has presided over court four for the past eleven years, so if I'm heading in that direction, I have an epileptic fit and the guards take me off to see the court doctor.'

'You're an epileptic?'

'No,' said Quinn, 'you're not paying attention.' He sounded exasperated, and Harry fell silent. 'By the time I've staged a recovery, they will have allocated my case to another court.'

Harry laughed for the second time. 'And you get away with it?'

'No, not always, but if I end up with a couple of rookie guards, I'm in with a chance, though it's getting more difficult to pull the same stunt again and again. I didn't need to bother this time because I was taken straight to court two, which is Judge Regan's territory. He's Irish – like me, just in case you hadn't noticed – so he's more likely to give a fellow countryman a minimum sentence.'

'What was your offence?' asked Harry.

'I'm a pickpocket,' Quinn announced, as if he were an architect or a doctor. 'I specialize in race meetings in the summer and boxing halls in the winter. It's always easier if the marks are standing up,' he explained. 'But my luck's been running short recently because too many stewards recognize me, so I've had to work the subway and the bus depots, where the pickings are slim and you're more likely to be caught.'

Harry had so much he wanted to ask his new tutor and, like an enthusiastic student, he concentrated on the questions that would help him pass the entrance exam, rather pleased that Quinn hadn't questioned his accent.

'Do you know where we're going?' he asked.

'Lavenham or Pierpoint,' said Quinn. 'All depends on whether we come off the highway at exit twelve or fourteen.'

'Have you been to either of them before?'

'Both, several times,' said Quinn matter-of-factly. 'And before you ask, if there was a tourist guide to prisons, Lavenham would get one star and Pierpoint would be closed down.'

'Why don't we just ask the guard which one we're going to?' said Harry, who wanted to be put out of his misery.

'Because he'd tell us the wrong one, just to piss us off. If it's Lavenham, the only thing you need to worry about is which block they put you on. As you're a first-timer you'll probably end up on A block, where life is a lot easier. The old-timers, like me, are usually sent to D block, where there's no one under thirty and no one with a record for violence, so it's the ideal set-up if you just want to keep your head down and do your time.

Try to avoid B and C block – they're both full of hopheads and psychos.'

'What do I have to do to make sure I end up on A block?'

'Tell the reception officer you're a devout Christian, don't smoke and don't drink.'

'I didn't know you were allowed to drink in prison,' said Harry.

'You aren't, you stupid fucker,' said Quinn, 'but if you can supply the greenbacks,' he added, rubbing a thumb against the tip of his index finger, 'the guards suddenly become barmen. Even Prohibition didn't slow them down.'

'What's the most important thing for me to watch out for on my first day?'

'Make sure you get the right job.'

'What's the choice?'

'Cleaning, kitchen, hospital, laundry, library, gardening and the chapel.'

'What do I have to do to get in the library?'

'Tell 'em you can read.'

'What do you tell them?' asked Harry.

'That I trained as a chef.'

'That must have been interesting.'

'You still haven't caught on, have you?' said Quinn. 'I never trained as a chef, but it means I'm always put in the kitchen, which is the best job in any prison.'

'Why's that?'

'You're let out of your cell before breakfast, and you don't go back to it until after dinner. It's warm, and you have the best choice of food. Ah, we're going to Lavenham,' said Quinn as the bus turned off the highway at exit 12. 'That's good, 'cause now I won't have to answer any dumb questions about Pierpoint.'

'Anything else I ought to know about Lavenham?' asked Harry, unperturbed by Quinn's sarcasm, as he suspected that the old-timer was enjoying delivering a master class to such a willing pupil.

'Too much to tell you,' he sighed. 'Just remember to stick close by me once we've been registered.'

'But won't they automatically send you to D block?'

'Not if Mr Mason's on duty,' Quinn said without explanation.

Harry managed several more questions before the bus finally drew up outside the prison. In fact, he felt he'd learnt more from Quinn in a couple of hours than he'd managed in a dozen tutorials at Oxford.

'Stick with me,' repeated Quinn as the massive gates swung open. The bus moved slowly forward and on to a desolate piece of scrubland that had never seen a gardener. It stopped in front of a vast brick building that displayed rows of small, filthy windows, some with eyes staring out of them.

Harry watched as a dozen guards formed a corridor that led all the way to the entrance of the prison. Two armed with rifles had planted themselves on either side of the bus door.

'Leave the bus in twos,' one of them announced gruffly, 'with a five-minute interval between each pair. No one moves an inch unless I say so.'

Harry and Quinn remained on the bus for another hour. When they were finally ushered off, Harry looked up at the high walls topped with barbed wire that surrounded the entire prison and thought even the world record holder for the pole vault wouldn't have been able to escape from Lavenham.

Harry followed Quinn into the building, where they came to a halt in front of an officer who was seated behind a table and wearing a well-worn shiny blue uniform with buttons that didn't shine. He looked as if he'd already served a life sentence as he studied the list of names on his clipboard. He smiled when he saw the next prisoner.

'Welcome back, Quinn,' he said. 'You won't find much has changed since you were last here.'

Quinn grinned. 'It's good to see you too, Mr Mason. Perhaps you'd be kind enough to ask one of the bellhops to take my luggage up to my usual room.'

'Don't push your luck, Quinn,' said Mason, 'otherwise I might be tempted to tell the new doc you're not an epileptic.'

'But, Mr Mason, I've got a medical certificate to prove it.'

'From the same source as your chef's certificate no doubt,' said Mason, turning his attention to Harry. 'And who are you?'

'This is my buddy, Tom Bradshaw. He doesn't smoke, drink, swear or spit,' said Quinn before Harry had a chance to speak.

'Welcome to Lavenham, Bradshaw,' said Mason.

'Captain Bradshaw actually,' said Quinn.

'It used to be Lieutenant,' said Harry. 'I was never a captain.' Quinn looked disappointed with his protégé.

'A first-timer?' asked Mason, taking a closer look at Harry.

'Yes, sir.'

'I'll put you on A block. After you've showered and collected your prison clothes from the store, Mr Hessler will take you to cell number three-two-seven.' Mason checked his clipboard before turning to a young officer who was standing behind him, a truncheon swinging from his right hand.

'Any hope of joining my friend?' asked Quinn once Harry had signed the register. 'After all, Lieutenant Bradshaw might need a batman.'

'You're the last person he needs,' said Mason. Harry was about to speak as the pickpocket bent down, removed a folded dollar bill from inside his sock and slipped it into Mason's top pocket in the blink of an eye. 'Quinn will also be in cell three-two-seven,' said Mason to the junior officer. If Hessler had witnessed the exchange, he didn't comment. 'You two, follow me,' was all he said.

Quinn chased after Harry before Mason could change his mind.

The two new prisoners were marched down a long green brick corridor until Hessler stopped outside a small shower room that had two narrow wooden benches fixed to the wall, littered with discarded towels.

'Strip,' said Hessler, 'and take a shower.'

Harry slowly removed the tailored suit, smart cream shirt, stiff collar and striped tie that Mr Jelks had been so keen for him to wear in court to impress the judge. The trouble was, he'd picked the wrong judge.

Quinn was already under the shower before Harry had unlaced his shoes. He turned on the tap and a trickle of water reluctantly dripped down on to his balding head. He then picked up a sliver of soap from the floor and began to wash. Harry stepped under the cold water of the only other shower, and a moment later Quinn passed him what was left of the soap.

'Remind me to speak to the management about the facilities,' said Quinn as he picked up a damp towel, not much bigger than a dishcloth, and attempted to dry himself.

Hessler's lips remained pursed. 'Get dressed and follow me,' he said, before Harry had finished soaping himself.

Once again Hessler marched off down the corridor at a brisk pace, with a half-dressed, still wet Harry chasing after him. They didn't stop until they came to a double door marked STORES. Hessler rapped firmly and a moment later it was pulled open to reveal a world-weary officer, elbows on the counter, smoking a rolled cigarette. The officer smiled when he saw Quinn.

'I'm not sure we've got your last lot back from the laundry yet, Quinn,' he said.

'Then I'll need a new set of everything, Mr Newbold,' said Quinn, who bent down and removed something from inside his other sock, and once again it disappeared without trace. 'My requirements are simple,' he added. 'One blanket, two cotton sheets, one pillow, one pillowcase . . .' The officer selected each item from the shelves behind him, before placing them in a neat pile on the counter. '. . . Two shirts, three pairs of socks, six pairs of pants, two towels, one bowl, one plate, one knife, fork and spoon, one razor, one toothbrush and one tube of toothpaste – I prefer Colgate.'

Newbold made no comment as Quinn's pile grew larger and larger. 'Will there be anything else?' he eventually asked, as if Quinn were a valued customer who was likely to return.

'Yes, my friend Lieutenant Bradshaw will require the same order, and as he is an officer and a gentleman, be sure that he gets only the best.'

To Harry's surprise, Newbold began to build another pile, seeming to take his time selecting each item, and all because of the prisoner who'd sat next to him on the bus.

'Follow me,' said Hessler when Newbold had completed his task. Harry and Pat grabbed their piles of clothes and charged off down the corridor. There were several stops on the way, as a duty officer had to unlock and lock barred gates as they came nearer to the cells. When they eventually stepped on to the wing, they were greeted by the noise of a thousand prisoners.

Quinn said, 'I see we're on the top floor, Mr Hessler, but I won't be taking the elevator, as I need the exercise.' The officer ignored him and continued past the shouting prisoners.

'I thought you said this was the quiet wing,' said Harry.

'It's clear Mr Hessler is not one of the more popular officers,' whispered Quinn, just before the three of them reached cell 327. Hessler unlocked the heavy iron door and pulled it open to allow the new con and the old con to enter the home Harry had a lease on for the next six years.

Harry heard the door slam behind him. He looked around the cell, and noticed there was no handle on the inside of the door. Two bunks, one on top of the other, a steel washbasin attached to the wall, a wooden table, also attached to the wall, and a wooden chair. His eyes finally settled on a steel bowl under the lower bunk. He thought he was going to be sick.

'You get the top bunk,' said Quinn, interrupting his thoughts, 'on account of you being a first-timer. If I get out before you, you'll move down to the bottom one, and your new cellmate will get the top. Prison etiquette,' he explained.

Harry stood on the bottom bunk and slowly made up his bed, then climbed up, lay down and placed his head on the thin, hard pillow, painfully aware that it might be some time before he managed a night's sleep. 'Can I ask you one more question?' he said to Quinn.

'Yes, but don't speak again until lights on tomorrow morning.' Harry recalled Fisher saying almost the same words on his first night at St Bede's.

'It's obvious you've been able to smuggle in a considerable amount of cash, so why didn't the guards confiscate it as soon as you got off the bus?'

'Because if they did,' said Quinn, 'no con would ever bring in any money again, and the whole system would break down.'

3

HARRY LAY ON the top bunk and stared at the one-coated white ceiling that he could touch by reaching up with his fingers. The mattress was lumpy and the pillow so hard that he could only manage to sleep for a few minutes at a time.

His thoughts turned to Sefton Jelks and how easily he had been duped by the old advocate. Get my son off the murder charge, that's all I care about, he could hear Tom Bradshaw's father telling Jelks. Harry tried not to think about the next six years, which Mr Bradshaw didn't care about. Had it been worth $10,000?

He dismissed his lawyer and thought about Emma. He missed her so much, and wanted to write and tell her he was still alive, but he knew he couldn't. He wondered what she would be doing on an autumn day in Oxford. How was her work progressing as she began her freshman year? Was she being courted by another man?

And what of her brother, Giles, his closest friend? Now that Britain was at war, had Giles left Oxford and signed up to fight the Germans? If he had, Harry prayed that he was still alive. He thumped the side of the bunk with a clenched fist, angry that he was not being allowed to play his part. Quinn didn't speak, assuming that Harry was suffering 'first-night-itis'.

And what of Hugo Barrington? Had anyone seen him since he disappeared on the day Harry should have married his daughter? Would he find a way of creeping back into favour, when everyone believed Harry was dead? He dismissed Barrington from his mind, still unwilling to accept the possibility that the man might be his father.

When his thoughts turned to his mother, Harry smiled, hoping that she would make good use of the $10,000 Jelks had promised to send her once he'd agreed to take the place of Tom Bradshaw. With over £2,000 in the bank, Harry hoped she would give up her job as a waitress at the Grand Hotel and buy that little house in the country she'd always talked about; that was the only good thing that would come out of this whole charade.

And what of Sir Walter Barrington, who had always treated him like a grandchild? If Hugo was Harry's father, then Sir Walter *was* his grandfather. If that turned out to be the case, Harry would be in line to inherit the Barrington estate and the family title, and would in time become Sir Harry Barrington. But not only did Harry want his friend Giles, Hugo Barrington's legitimate son, to inherit the title, even more important, he was desperate to *prove* that his real father was Arthur Clifton. That would still give him an outside chance of being able to marry his beloved Emma. Harry tried to forget where he'd be spending the next six years.

◄○►

At seven o'clock a siren sounded to wake those prisoners who had served long enough to enjoy a night's sleep. You're not in prison when you're asleep, were the last words Quinn had muttered before falling into a deep slumber, then snoring. It didn't bother Harry. As a snorer, his uncle Stan was in a different class.

Harry had made up his mind about several things during his long, sleepless night. To help pass the numbing cruelty of wasted time, 'Tom' would be a model prisoner, in the hope that his sentence would be reduced for good behaviour. He would get a job in the library, and write a diary about what had happened before he was sentenced, and everything that took place while he was behind bars. He would keep himself fit, so that if war was still raging in Europe, he would be ready to sign up the moment he was released.

Quinn was already dressed by the time Harry climbed down from the top bunk.

'What now?' asked Harry, sounding like a new boy on his first day of term.

'Breakfast,' said Quinn. 'Get dressed, grab your plate and mug, and make sure you're ready when the screw unlocks the door. If you're a few seconds late, some officers get a kick out of slamming the door in your face.' Harry began to pull on his trousers. 'And don't talk on your way down to the canteen,' added Quinn. 'It draws attention to yourself, which annoys the old-timers. In fact, don't talk to anyone you don't know until your second year.'

Harry would have laughed, but he wasn't sure if Quinn was joking. He heard a key turning in the lock, and the cell door swung open. Quinn shot through like a greyhound out of the slips, with his cellmate only a stride behind. They joined a long line of silent prisoners who were making their way across the landing past the open doors of empty cells, before walking down a spiral staircase to the ground floor, where they would join their fellow inmates for breakfast.

The line came to a halt long before they reached the canteen. Harry watched the servers in their short white coats, standing behind the hotplate. A guard carrying a truncheon and wearing a long white coat was keeping an eye on them, making sure no one got an extra portion.

'How nice to see you again, Mr Siddell,' Pat said quietly to the guard once they reached the front of the queue. The two men shook hands as if they were old friends. This time Harry couldn't see any money changing hands, but a curt nod from Mr Siddell indicated that a deal had been struck.

Quinn moved along the line as his tin plate was filled with a fried egg with a solid yolk, a pile of potatoes more black than white and the regulation two slices of stale bread. Harry caught up with him as he was having his mug half filled with coffee. The servers looked puzzled when Harry thanked them one by one, as if he were a guest at a vicarage tea party.

'Damn,' he said when the last server offered him coffee. 'I left my mug in the cell.'

The server filled Quinn's mug to the brim. 'Don't forget next time,' said Harry's cellmate.

'No talking in line!' yelled Hessler, slamming his truncheon into a gloved hand. Quinn led Harry to the end of a long table and sat on the bench opposite him. Harry was so hungry he devoured every morsel on his plate, including the greasiest egg he'd ever tasted. He even considered licking his plate, and then he recalled his friend Giles, on another first day.

When Harry and Pat had finished their five-minute breakfast, they were marched back up the spiral staircase to the top floor. Once their cell door had been slammed shut, Quinn washed his plate and mug, and placed them neatly under his bunk.

'When you live in an eight by four for years on end, you make use of every inch of space,' he explained. Harry followed his lead, and could only wonder how long it would be before he was able to teach Quinn something.

'What next?' asked Harry.

'Work allocation,' said Quinn. 'I'll be joining Siddell in the kitchen, but we've still got to make sure they put you in the library. And that'll depend on which officer is on duty. Trouble is, I'm running out of cash.' Quinn had hardly got the words out of his mouth before the door was pulled open again and Hessler was silhouetted in the doorway, the truncheon thumping into his gloved hand.

'Quinn,' he said, 'report to the kitchen immediately. Bradshaw, go to station nine and join the other wing cleaners.'

'I was hoping to work in the library, Mr—'

'I don't give a fuck what you were hoping, Bradshaw,' said Hessler. 'As wing officer, I make the rules around here. You can go to the library on Tuesdays, Thursdays and Sundays between six and seven, like any other inmate. Is that clear enough for you?' Harry nodded. 'You're not an officer any longer, Bradshaw, just a con, like everyone else in this place. And don't waste your time thinking you can bribe me,' he added, before marching off to the next cell.

'Hessler's one of the few officers you can't bribe,' whispered Quinn. 'Your only hope now is Mr Swanson, the prison warden. Just remember that he considers himself a bit of an intellectual, which probably means he can manage joined-up writing. He's also a Fundamental Baptist. Hallelujah!'

'When will I get the chance to see him?' asked Harry.

'Could be any time. Just be sure to let him know you want to work in the library, because each new prisoner only gets five minutes of his time.'

Harry slumped down on the wooden chair and placed his head in his hands. If it wasn't for the $10,000 Jelks had promised to send to his mother, he'd use his five minutes to tell the warden the truth about how he'd ended up in Lavenham.

'Meantime, I'll do what I can to get you into the kitchen,' added Quinn. 'It may not be what you hoped for, but it's sure better than being a wing cleaner.'

'Thanks,' said Harry. Quinn scurried off to the kitchens, not needing directions. Harry took the stairs back down to the ground floor and went in search of station nine.

Twelve men, all first-timers, stood in a huddle and waited for instructions. Initiative was frowned on in Lavenham – it smacked of rebellion, or the suggestion that a prisoner just might be cleverer than an officer.

'Pick up a bucket, fill it with water, and get yourself a mop,' said Hessler. He smiled at Harry as he ticked off his name on yet another clipboard. 'As you were last down, Bradshaw, you'll be working in the shit house for the next month.'

'But I wasn't the last down,' protested Harry.

'I think you were,' said Hessler, the smile not leaving his face.

Harry filled his bucket with cold water and grabbed a mop. He didn't need to be told in which direction to go, he could smell the latrines from a dozen paces. He began retching before he'd even entered the large square room with thirty holes in the ground. He held his nose, but he had to continually leave the room to gasp for air. Hessler stood some way off, laughing.

'You'll get used to it, Bradshaw,' he said, 'in time.'

Harry regretted having eaten such a large breakfast, which he brought up within minutes. It must have been about an hour later that he heard another officer bellowing his name. 'Bradshaw!'

Harry staggered out of the latrines, white as a sheet. 'That's me,' he said.

'The warden wants to see you, so let's get movin'.'

Harry was able to breathe more deeply with each step he took, and by the time he'd reached the warden's office, he felt almost human.

'Wait there until you're called for,' said the officer.

Harry took a spare seat between two other prisoners, who quickly turned away. He couldn't blame them. He tried to gather his thoughts as each new prisoner went in and out of the warden's office. Quinn was right, the interviews lasted for about five minutes, some even less. Harry couldn't afford to waste one second of his allotted time.

'Bradshaw,' said the officer, and opened the door.

He stood aside as Harry entered the warden's office. Harry decided not to get too close to Mr Swanson, and remained several paces from his large leather-topped desk. Although the warden was seated, Harry could see that he was unable to do up the middle button of his sports jacket. His hair had been dyed black in an attempt to make him look younger, but it only made him look slightly ridiculous. What did Brutus say of Caesar's vanity? Offer him garlands, and praise him as if he were a god, and that will be his downfall.

Swanson opened Bradshaw's file and studied it for a few moments before looking up at Harry.

'I see you were sentenced to six years for desertion. Haven't come across that one before,' he admitted.

'Yes, sir,' said Harry, not wanting to waste any of his precious time.

'Don't bother telling me you're innocent,' Swanson continued, 'because only one in a thousand is, so the odds are stacked against you.' Harry had to smile. 'But if you keep your nose clean' – Harry thought about the latrines – 'and don't cause any trouble, I can't see why you would have to serve the full six years.'

'Thank you, sir.'

'Do you have any special interests?' Swanson asked, looking as if he wasn't at all interested if Harry did.

'Reading, art appreciation and choral singing, sir.'

The warden gave Harry a disbelieving look, not sure if he was trying to get a rise out of him. He pointed to a sign hanging on the wall behind his desk and asked, 'Can you tell me the next line, Bradshaw?'

Harry studied the embroidered sampler: *I will lift up mine eyes unto the hills*. He gave silent thanks to Miss Eleanor E. Monday, and the hours he'd spent at her choir practices. 'From whence cometh my help, sayeth the Lord. Psalm one hundred and twenty-one.'

The warden smiled. 'Tell me, Bradshaw, who are your favourite authors?'

'Shakespeare, Dickens, Austen, Trollope and Thomas Hardy.'

'None of our own countrymen good enough?'

Harry wanted to curse out loud, having made such an obvious blunder. He glanced across at the warden's half-filled bookshelf. 'Of course,' he said. 'I consider F. Scott Fitzgerald, Hemingway and O. Henry to be anyone's equal, and I believe Steinbeck is America's finest modern writer.' He hoped he'd pronounced the name correctly. He'd make sure he had read *Of Mice and Men* before he came across the warden again.

The smile returned to Swanson's lips. 'What job has Mr Hessler allocated to you?' he asked.

'Wing cleaner, although I'd like to work in the library, sir.'

'Would you indeed?' said the warden. 'Then I'll have to see if there's a vacancy.' He made a note on the pad in front of him.

'Thank you, sir.'

'If there is, you'll be informed later today,' said the warden as he closed the file.

'Thank you, sir,' repeated Harry. He left quickly, aware that he'd taken longer than his allotted five minutes.

Once he was out in the corridor, the duty officer escorted him back to the wing. Harry was thankful that Hessler was nowhere to be seen, and that the cleaners had moved on to the second floor by the time he rejoined them.

Long before the siren sounded for lunch, Harry was exhausted. He joined the line for the hotplate, and found Quinn already ensconced behind the counter, serving his fellow inmates. Large portions of potato and over-cooked meat were dropped on to Harry's plate. He sat alone at the long table and picked at his food. He feared that if Hessler were to reappear that afternoon, he would be dispatched back to the latrines, and so would his lunch.

Hessler was not on duty when Harry reported back to work, and a different officer put another first-timer on the latrines. Harry spent the afternoon sweeping corridors and emptying trash cans. His only thought was whether the warden had given an order to reallocate him to the library. If he hadn't, Harry would have to hope for a job in the kitchen.

When Quinn returned to their cell after dinner, the expression on his face left Harry in no doubt that he wouldn't be joining his friend.

'There was one place available for a washer-up.'

'I'll take it,' said Harry.

'But when Mr Siddell put your name forward, Hessler vetoed it. Said you'd have to do at least three months as a wing cleaner before he'd consider a transfer to kitchen duty.'

'What is it with that man?' asked Harry desperately.

'Rumour has it he signed up to be a naval officer, but failed the board exam and had to settle for the prison service. So Lieutenant Bradshaw has to suffer the consequences.'

4

HARRY SPENT the next twenty-nine days cleaning the latrines on A block, and it wasn't until another first-timer appeared on the wing that Hessler finally released him from his duties and began to make someone else's life hell.

'Damn man's a psycho,' said Quinn. 'Siddell's still willing to offer you a job in the kitchen, but Hessler's vetoed it.' Harry didn't comment. 'But the news isn't all bad,' Quinn suggested, 'because I've just heard that Andy Savatori, the deputy librarian, has been granted parole. He's due to be released next month and, even better, no one else seems to want his job.'

'Deakins would,' said Harry under his breath. 'So what do I have to do, to make sure I get it?'

'Nothing. In fact, try to give the impression you're not that interested, and keep out of Hessler's way, because we know the warden's on your side.'

The next month dragged on, each day seeming longer than the one before. Harry visited the library every Tuesday, Thursday and Sunday between six and seven, but Max Lloyd, the senior librarian, gave him no reason to believe he was being considered for the post.

Savatori, his deputy, remained tight-lipped, although he clearly knew something.

'I don't think Lloyd wants me to be his deputy,' said Harry after lights out one evening.

'Lloyd won't have a say about it,' said Quinn. 'That's the warden's decision.'

But Harry wasn't convinced. 'I suspect Hessler and Lloyd are working together to make sure I don't get the job.'

'You're becoming para— what's the word?' said Quinn.

'Paranoid.'

'Yeah, that's what you're becoming, not that I'm sure what it means.'

'Suffering from unfounded suspicions,' said Harry.

'Couldn't have put it better myself!'

Harry wasn't convinced that his suspicions were unfounded and, a week later, Savatori took him to one side and confirmed his worst fears.

'Hessler's put up three cons for the warden's consideration, and your name isn't on the list.'

'Then that's that,' said Harry, thumping the side of his leg. 'I'm going to be a wing cleaner for the rest of my days.'

'Not necessarily,' said Savatori. 'Come and see me the day before I'm due to be discharged.'

'But by then it will be too late.'

'I don't think so,' said Savatori, without explanation. 'Meanwhile, study every page of this very carefully.' He handed Harry a heavy, leather-bound tome that rarely left the library.

◄○►

Harry sat on the top bunk and opened the cover of the 273-page prison handbook. Before he'd reached page 6, he began to make notes. Long before he'd started reading the book a second time, a plan had begun to form in his mind.

He knew his timing would be critical, and both acts would have to be rehearsed, particularly as he would be on stage when the curtain went up. He accepted that he couldn't go ahead with his plan until after Savatori had been released, even though a new deputy librarian had already been appointed.

When Harry carried out a dress rehearsal in the privacy of their cell, Quinn told him that he was not only paranoid, but crazy, because, he assured him, his second performance would be in solitary.

–◦–

The warden made his monthly rounds of each block on a Monday morning, so Harry knew that he'd have to wait for three weeks after Savatori had been discharged, before he would reappear on A block. Swanson always took the same route, and prisoners knew that if they valued their skin, they disappeared out of sight the moment he came into view.

When Swanson stepped on to the top floor of A block that Monday morning, Harry was waiting to greet him, mop in hand. Hessler slipped in behind the warden, and waved his truncheon to indicate that if Bradshaw valued his life, he should step aside. Harry didn't budge, leaving the warden with no choice but to stop in his tracks.

'Good morning, warden,' said Harry, as if they bumped into each other regularly.

Swanson was surprised to come face to face with a prisoner on his rounds, and even more surprised when one spoke to him. He looked more closely at Harry. 'Bradshaw, isn't it?'

'You have a good memory, sir.'

'I also remember your interest in literature. I was surprised when you turned down the job as deputy librarian.'

'I was never offered the job,' said Harry. 'If I had been, I would have accepted it with alacrity,' he added, which clearly took the warden by surprise.

Turning to Hessler, Swanson said, 'You told me Bradshaw didn't want the job.'

Harry jumped in before Hessler could reply. 'Probably my fault, sir. I didn't realize I had to apply for the position.'

'I see,' said the warden. 'Well, that would explain it. And I can tell you, Bradshaw, that the new man doesn't know the difference between Plato and Pluto.' Harry burst out laughing. Hessler remained tight-lipped.

'A good analogy, sir,' said Harry as the warden attempted to move on. But Harry hadn't finished. He thought Hessler would explode when he removed an envelope from his jacket and handed it to the warden.

'What's this?' Swanson asked suspiciously.

'An official request to address the board when they make their quarterly visit to the prison next Tuesday, which is my prerogative under statute thirty-two of the penal code. I've sent a copy of the request to my lawyer, Mr Sefton Jelks.' For the first time, the warden looked anxious. Hessler could barely contain himself.

'Will you be making a complaint?' asked the warden cautiously.

Harry stared directly at Hessler before replying, 'Under statute one-one-six, it is my right not to disclose to any member of the prison staff why I wish to address the board, as I'm sure you're aware, warden.'

'Yes, of course, Bradshaw,' said the warden, sounding flustered.

'But it is my intention, among other things, to inform the board of the importance you place on including literature and religion as part of our daily lives.' Harry stood aside to allow the warden to continue on his way.

'Thank you, Bradshaw,' he said. 'That's good of you.'

'I'll be seeing you later, Bradshaw,' hissed Hessler under his breath.

'I'll look forward to that,' said Harry, loud enough for Mr Swanson to hear.

—◆—

Harry's confrontation with the warden was the main topic of conversation among the prisoners in the dinner queue, and when Quinn returned from the kitchen later that evening, he warned Harry that the rumour on the block was that once lights were out, Hessler was likely to kill him.

'I don't think so,' said Harry calmly. 'You see, the problem with being a bully is that on the flipside of that particular coin, you'll find the imprint of a coward.'

Quinn didn't look convinced.

Harry didn't have long to wait to prove his point, because within moments of lights out, the cell door swung open and Hessler strolled in, swinging his truncheon.

'Quinn, out,' he said, not taking his eyes off Harry. Once the Irishman had scurried on to the landing,

Hessler closed the cell door and said, 'I've been looking forward to this all day, Bradshaw. You're about to discover how many bones you've got in your body.'

'I don't think so, Mr Hessler,' said Harry, not flinching.

'And what do you think will save you?' asked Hessler, advancing. 'The warden isn't around to rescue you this time.'

'I don't need the warden,' said Harry. 'Not while you're being considered for promotion,' he added, meeting Hessler's stare. 'I'm reliably informed that you'll be appearing before the board next Tuesday afternoon at two o'clock.'

'So what?' said Hessler, now less than a foot away.

'You've clearly forgotten that *I'll* be addressing the board at ten o'clock that morning. One or two of them may be curious to find out how so many of my bones came to be broken after I dared to speak to the warden.' Hessler slammed his truncheon down on the side of the bunk, only inches from Harry's face, but Harry didn't flinch.

'Of course,' Harry continued, 'it's possible that you want to remain a wing officer for the rest of your life, but somehow I doubt it, because even you can't be so stupid as to ruin your one chance of promotion.' Hessler raised his truncheon once again, but hesitated when Harry took a thick exercise book from under his pillow.

'I've made a comprehensive list of the regulations you've broken over the past month, Mr Hessler, some of them several times. I'm confident that the board will find it interesting reading. This evening I'll be adding two more indiscretions: being alone in a cell with a prisoner while the cell door is closed, statute four-one-nine, and making physical threats when that prisoner has no way of defending himself, statute five-one-two.' Hessler took a pace back. 'But I'm confident that what will most influence the board when they come to consider your promotion, will be the question of why you had to leave the navy at such short notice.' The blood drained from Hessler's face. 'It certainly wasn't because you failed the exam when you applied to be an officer.'

'Who squealed?' said Hessler, his words barely a whisper.

'One of your former shipmates, who unfortunately ended up in here. You made sure he kept his mouth shut by giving him the job as deputy librarian. I expect nothing less.'

Harry handed his past month's work to Hessler, pausing to allow this latest piece of information to sink in before adding, 'I'll keep my mouth shut until the day I'm released – unless, of course, you give me some reason not to. And if you ever lay as much as a finger on me, I'll have you thrown out of the prison service even quicker than you were drummed out of the navy. Do I make myself clear?' Hessler nodded, but didn't speak. 'Also, should you decide to pick on any other unfortunate first-timers, all bets are off. Now get out of my cell.'

5

WHEN LLOYD STOOD to greet him at nine o'clock on his first morning as deputy librarian, Harry realized that he'd only ever seen the man sitting down. Lloyd was taller than he'd expected, well over six feet. Despite the unhealthy prison food he had a spare frame, and was one of the few prisoners who shaved every morning. With his swept-back, jet-black hair, he resembled an ageing matinee idol, rather than a man who was serving five years for fraud. Quinn didn't know the details of his crime, which meant that nobody other than the warden knew the full story. And the rule in jail was simple: if a prisoner didn't volunteer what he was in for, you didn't ask.

Lloyd took Harry through the daily routine, which the new deputy librarian had mastered by the time they went down for supper that evening. During the next few days he continued to quiz Lloyd with questions about matters like collecting overdue books, fines, and inviting prisoners to donate their own books to the library when they were released, which Lloyd hadn't even considered. Most of Lloyd's answers were mono-syllabic, so Harry finally allowed him to return to a resting position at his desk, well hidden behind a copy of the *New York Times*.

Although there were nearly a thousand prisoners locked up in Lavenham, fewer than one in ten of them could read and write, and not all of those who could bothered to visit the library on a Tuesday, Thursday or Sunday.

Harry soon discovered that Max Lloyd was both lazy and devious. He didn't seem to mind how many initiatives his new deputy came up with, as long as it didn't involve him in any extra work.

Lloyd's main task seemed to be to keep a pot of coffee on the go, just in case an officer dropped by. Once the warden's copy of the previous day's *New York Times* had been delivered to the library, Lloyd settled down at his desk for the rest of the morning. He first turned to the book review section, and when he finished perusing it, he turned his attention to the classified ads, followed by the news, and finally sports. After lunch he would make a start on the crossword puzzle, which Harry would complete the following morning.

By the time Harry got the newspaper, it was already two days out of date. He always began with the international news pages, as he wanted to find out how the war in Europe was progressing. That was how he learned about the invasion of France, and that Neville Chamberlain had resigned as Prime Minister, and Winston Churchill had succeeded him. Not everyone's first choice, although Harry would never forget the speech Churchill had made when he presented the prizes at Bristol Grammar School. He wasn't in any doubt that Britain was being led by the right man. Time and again Harry cursed the fact that he was a deputy librarian in an American prison, and not an officer in the Royal Navy.

During the last hour of the day, when even Harry couldn't find anything new to do, he brought his diary up to date.

—◀○▶—

It took Harry just over a month to reorganize all the books into their correct categories: first fiction, then non-fiction. During the second month, he broke them down into even smaller classifications, so that prisoners didn't have to waste time searching for the only three books on woodwork that were on the shelves. He explained to Lloyd that when it came to non-fiction, the category was more important than the author's name. Lloyd shrugged.

On Sunday mornings, Harry would push the library cart around the four blocks, retrieving overdue books from prisoners, some of which hadn't been returned for more than a year. He had expected a few of the old-timers on D block to be resentful, even to take offence at the intrusion, but they all wanted to meet the man who'd got Hessler transferred to Pierpoint.

After his interview with the board, Hessler had been offered a senior post at Pierpoint, and he accepted the promotion as it was nearer his home town. While Harry never suggested he'd had anything to do with Hessler's transfer, that wasn't the story Quinn peddled from ear to ear until it became legend.

During his trips around the blocks in search of missing books, Harry often picked up anecdotes that he would record in his diary that evening.

The warden occasionally dropped into the library, not least because when Harry had appeared before the board, he'd described Mr Swanson's attitude to the education of inmates as bold, imaginative and far-seeing. Harry couldn't believe how much undeserved flattery the warden was quite happy to soak up.

After his first three months, loans were up by 14 per cent. When Harry asked the warden if he could instigate a reading class in the evenings, Swanson hesitated for a moment, but gave in when Harry repeated the words *bold, imaginative* and *far-seeing*.

Only three prisoners attended Harry's first class, and one of them was Pat Quinn, who could already read and write. But by the end of the following month the class had grown to sixteen, even if several of them would have done almost anything to get out of their cells for an hour in the evening. But Harry managed to notch up one or two notable successes among the younger prisoners, and was continually reminded that just because you hadn't gone to the 'right' school, or hadn't gone to school at all, it didn't mean you were stupid – or the other way round, Quinn reminded him.

Despite all the extra activity Harry had initiated, he found he was still left with time on his hands, so he set himself the task of reading two new books a week. Once he'd conquered the few American classics in the library, he turned his attention to crime, by far the most popular category with his fellow inmates, taking up seven of the library's nineteen shelves.

Harry had always enjoyed Conan Doyle, and he was looking forward to turning his attention to his American rivals. He began with *The Bigger They Come* by Erle

Stanley Gardner, before moving on to Raymond Chandler's *The Big Sleep*. He felt a little guilty about enjoying them so much. What would Mr Holcombe think?

During the last hour before the library closed, Harry would continue to bring his diary up to date. He was taken by surprise one evening when Lloyd, having finished the paper, asked if he could read it. Harry knew that Lloyd had been a literary agent in New York on the outside, which was how he'd landed the job in the library. He sometimes dropped the names of authors he'd represented, most of whom Harry had never heard of. Lloyd only spoke about how he'd ended up in Lavenham on one occasion, watching the door to make sure no one overheard.

'A bit of bad luck,' Lloyd explained. 'In good faith I invested some of my clients' money on the Stock Exchange, and when things didn't go quite according to plan, I was left carrying the bag.'

When Harry repeated the story to Quinn that night, he raised his eyes to the heavens.

'More likely he spent the money on slow nags and fast dames.'

'Then why go into such detail,' asked Harry, 'when he's never mentioned the reason he's in here to anyone else?'

'You're so naïve sometimes,' said Quinn. 'With you as the messenger, Lloyd knows there's a far better chance of the rest of us believing his story. Just be sure you never make a deal with that man, because he's got six fingers on each hand' – a pickpocket's expression that Harry recorded in his diary that night. But he didn't take much notice of Quinn's advice, partly because he couldn't imagine any circumstances in which

46

he would make a deal with Max Lloyd, other than about whose turn it was to pour the coffee when the warden dropped in.

—◁o▷—

By the end of his first year at Lavenham, Harry had filled three exercise books with his observations on prison life, and could only wonder how many more pages of this daily chronicle he'd manage before he completed his sentence.

He was surprised by how enthusiastic Lloyd was, always wanting to read the next instalment. He even suggested he might be allowed to show Harry's work to a publisher. Harry laughed.

'I can't imagine anyone would be interested in my ramblings.'

'You'd be surprised,' said Lloyd.

EMMA BARRINGTON

1939–1941

6

'SEBASTIAN ARTHUR CLIFTON,' said Emma, handing
the sleeping child to his grandmother.

Maisie beamed as she took her grandson in her arms
for the first time.

'They wouldn't let me come and see you before I
was packed off to Scotland,' said Emma, making no
attempt to hide her scorn. 'That's why I called you the
moment I got back to Bristol.'

'That was kind of you,' said Maisie, as she stared
intently at the little boy, trying to convince herself that
Sebastian had inherited her husband's fair hair and clear
blue eyes.

Emma sat at the kitchen table, smiled and sipped
her tea: Earl Grey, how typical of Maisie to remember.
And cucumber and salmon sandwiches, Harry's favourite, which must have emptied her ration book. As she
looked around the room, her eyes settled on the mantelpiece, where she spotted a sepia photograph of a
private soldier from the first war. How Emma wished
she could see the shade of his hair, hidden under the
helmet, or even the colour of his eyes. Were they blue,
like Harry's, or brown, like hers? Arthur Clifton cut a

dashing figure in his army uniform. The square jaw and the determined looked showed Emma that he'd been proud to serve his country. Her gaze moved on to a more recent photo of Harry singing in the St Bede's school choir, just before his voice broke, and next to that, propped against the wall, was an envelope displaying Harry's unmistakable hand. She assumed it was the last letter he had written to his mother before he died. She wondered if Maisie would allow her to read it. She stood up and walked across to the mantelpiece, and was surprised to find that the envelope hadn't been opened.

'I was so sorry to hear you had to leave Oxford,' Maisie ventured, when she saw Emma staring at the envelope.

'Given the choice of continuing with my degree or having Harry's child, there was no contest,' said Emma, her eyes still fixed on the letter.

'And Sir Walter tells me that your brother Giles joined the Wessex regiment, but has sadly been—'

'I see you had a letter from Harry,' interrupted Emma, unable to contain herself.

'No, it's not from Harry,' said Maisie. 'It's from a Lieutenant Thomas Bradshaw who served with him on the SS *Devonian*.'

'What does Lieutenant Bradshaw have to say?' asked Emma, aware that the envelope hadn't been opened.

'I've no idea,' said Maisie. 'A Dr Wallace delivered it to me, and said it was a letter of condolence. I didn't feel I needed any more reminders of Harry's death, so I never opened it.'

'But isn't it possible that it might throw some light on what happened on the *Devonian*?'

'I doubt it,' Maisie replied, 'after all, they'd only known each other for a few days.'

'Would you like me to read the letter to you, Mrs Clifton?' Emma asked, aware that Maisie might be embarrassed by having to admit she couldn't read.

'No, thank you, my dear,' Maisie replied. 'After all, it's not going to bring Harry back, is it?'

'I agree,' said Emma, 'but perhaps you would allow me to read it for my own peace of mind,' she said.

'With the Germans targeting the docks at night,' said Maisie, 'I hope Barrington's hasn't been too badly affected.'

'We've escaped a direct hit,' said Emma, reluctantly accepting that she wasn't going to be allowed to read the letter. 'Mind you, I doubt even the Germans would dare to drop a bomb on Gramps.'

Maisie laughed, and for a moment Emma considered snatching the envelope from the mantelpiece and ripping it open before Maisie could stop her. But Harry would never have approved of that. If Maisie were to leave the room, even for a moment, Emma would use the steaming kettle to unseal the envelope, check the signature and make sure it was back in its place before she returned.

But it was almost as if Maisie could read her thoughts, because she remained by the mantelpiece and didn't budge.

'Gramps tells me congratulations are in order,' said Emma, still refusing to give up.

Maisie blushed, and began to chat about her new appointment at the Grand Hotel. Emma's eyes remained on the envelope. She carefully checked the

M, the C, the S, the H and the L in the address, knowing that she would have to keep the image of those letters in her mind's eye, like a photograph, until she returned to the Manor House. When Maisie handed little Sebastian back to her, explaining that sadly she had to get back to work, Emma reluctantly stood up, but not before she had given the envelope one last look.

On the way back to the Manor House, Emma tried to keep the image of the handwriting in her mind, thankful that Sebastian had fallen into a deep sleep. As soon as the car came to a halt on the gravel outside the front steps, Hudson opened the back door to allow Emma to get out and carry her son into the house. She took him straight up to the nursery, where Nanny Barrington was waiting for them. To Nanny's surprise, Emma kissed him on the forehead and left without a word.

Once she was in her own room, Emma unlocked the centre drawer of her writing desk and pulled out a stack of letters that Harry had written to her over the years.

The first thing she checked was the capital H of Harry's signature, so plain and bold, just like the H in Still House Lane on Maisie's unopened envelope. This gave her confidence to carry on with the quest. She next searched for a capital C, and eventually found one on a Christmas card, with the bonus of the capital M of Merry: the same M and the same C as Mrs Clifton on the envelope. Harry must surely be alive, she kept repeating out loud. Finding a Bristol was easy, but England was more difficult, until she came across a letter he'd written to her from Italy when they were both still at school. It took her over an hour to neatly cut out the thirty-nine letters and two numbers, before she was able to reproduce the address on the envelope.

> *Mrs M. Clifton*
> *27 Still House Lane*
> *Bristol*
> *England*

Emma collapsed exhausted on to her bed. She had no idea who Thomas Bradshaw was, but one thing was certain: the unopened letter propped on Maisie's mantelpiece had been written by Harry, and for some reason, best known to himself, he didn't want her to know he was still alive. She wondered if he would have thought differently had he known she was pregnant with his child, before he set off on that fateful voyage.

Emma was desperate to share the news that Harry might not be dead with her mother, Gramps, Grace and of course Maisie, but she realized she would have to remain silent until she had more conclusive proof than an unopened letter. A plan began to form in her mind.

◄○►

Emma didn't go down for dinner that evening, but remained in her room and continued to try to fathom out why Harry would want everyone except his mother to believe he'd died that night.

When she climbed into bed just before midnight, she could only assume that it must have been for what he considered a matter of honour. Perhaps he imagined, poor, foolish, disillusioned man, that it would release her from any obligation she might feel towards him. Didn't he realize that from the first moment she'd set eyes on him, at her brother's birthday party when she was only ten years old, there was never going to be another man in her life?

Emma's family had been delighted when she and Harry became engaged eight years later, with the exception of her father, who had for so long been living a lie – a lie that wasn't exposed until the day of their wedding. The two of them were standing at the altar, about to take their vows, when Old Jack had brought the ceremony to an unrehearsed and unexpected close. The revelation that Emma's father might also be Harry's father didn't stop her loving Harry, and it never would. No one was surprised that Harry behaved like a gentleman, while Emma's father had remained true to his character, and behaved like a cad. One stood and faced the music, while the other slunk out of the back door of the vestry and hadn't been seen since.

Harry had made it clear, long before he asked Emma to be his wife, that if war was declared he wouldn't hesitate to leave Oxford and join the Royal Navy. He was a stubborn man at the best of times, and these were the worst of times. Emma realized there was no point in trying to dissuade him, as nothing she could say or do would have changed his mind. He had also warned her that he would not consider returning to Oxford until the Germans had surrendered.

Emma had also left Oxford early, but unlike Harry, she hadn't been given a choice. For her there would be no chance of returning. Pregnancy was frowned upon at Somerville, and even more so when you weren't married to the father. The decision must have broken her mother's heart. Elizabeth Barrington had so wanted her daughter to achieve the academic accolades that she had been denied for no other reason than her sex. A rare glimmer of light appeared on the horizon a year later, when Emma's younger sister Grace won an open scholarship to Girton College, Cambridge, and from the day she'd arrived in that seat of learning she had outshone the brightest men.

Once it became obvious that Emma was pregnant, she was whisked off to her grandfather's estate in Scotland, to give birth to Harry's child. Barringtons don't produce illegitimate offspring, at least not in Bristol. Sebastian was crawling around the castle before the prodigal daughter was allowed to return to the Manor House. Elizabeth had wanted them to remain at Mulgelrie until the war was over, but Emma had had more than enough of being hidden away in a remote Scottish castle.

One of the first people she visited after returning to the West Country was her grandfather, Sir Walter Barrington. It had been he who had told her that Harry had joined the crew of the SS *Devonian*, and planned to return to Bristol within the month, as he intended to sign up as an ordinary seaman on HMS *Resolution*. Harry never returned, and six weeks went by before she learned that her lover had been buried at sea.

Sir Walter had taken it upon himself to visit each member of the family one by one, to inform them of the tragic news. He'd begun with Mrs Clifton, although he knew she had already heard what had happened from Dr Wallace, who had passed on Thomas Bradshaw's letter. He next travelled up to Scotland to break the news to Emma. Sir Walter was surprised that his granddaughter didn't shed a tear, but then Emma simply refused to accept that Harry was dead.

Once he'd returned to Bristol, Sir Walter visited Giles and told him the news. Harry's closest friend had sunk into a desolate silence, and there was nothing any of the family could say or do to console him. When Lord and Lady Harvey heard the news of Harry's death, they were stoical. A week later, when the family attended Captain Jack Tarrant's memorial service at Bristol Grammar School, Lord Harvey remarked that he was glad Old Jack had never found out what had happened to his protégé.

The only person in the family Sir Walter refused to visit was his son, Hugo. He made an excuse about not knowing how to get in touch with him, but when Emma returned to Bristol he admitted to her that even if he had known, he wouldn't have bothered, and added that her father was probably the one person who would be pleased that Harry was dead. Emma said nothing, but didn't doubt that he was right.

For several days after her visit to Maisie in Still House Lane, Emma had spent hours alone in her room endlessly considering what she might do with her new-found knowledge. She concluded that there was no way she could hope to discover the contents of the letter that had rested on the mantelpiece for more than a year, without harming her relationship with Maisie. However, Emma resolved not only to prove to the whole world that Harry was still alive, but to find him, wherever he might be. With that in mind, she made another appointment to see her grandfather. After all, Sir Walter Barrington was the only person other than Maisie who'd met Dr Wallace, so he must surely be her best chance of unravelling the mystery of exactly who Thomas Bradshaw was.

7

ONE THING Emma's grandfather had instilled in her from an early age was never to be late for an appointment. It gives the wrong impression, he told her; that is, if you want to be taken seriously.

With that in mind, Emma left the Manor House at 9.25 that morning, and was driven through the gates of Barrington's shipyard at exactly eight minutes to ten. The car parked outside Barrington House at six minutes to ten. By the time she stepped out of the lift on the fifth floor and walked down the corridor to the chairman's office, it was two minutes to ten.

Sir Walter's secretary, Miss Beale, opened the door of his office as the clock on his mantelpiece began to chime ten. The chairman smiled, rose from behind his desk and walked across the room to greet Emma with a kiss on both cheeks.

'And how is my favourite granddaughter?' he asked as he guided her to a comfortable chair by the fire.

'Grace is just fine, Gramps,' said Emma. 'Doing brilliantly at Cambridge, I'm told, and sends her love.'

'Don't get cheeky with me, young lady,' he said,

returning her smile. 'And Sebastian, my favourite great-grandson, how's he coming along?'

'Your only great-grandson,' Emma reminded him as she settled back into a deep leather chair.

'As you haven't brought him with you, I assume you have something serious to discuss.'

The small talk had already been dispensed with. Emma knew that Sir Walter would have allocated a certain amount of time for the meeting. Miss Beale had once told her that visitors were granted fifteen minutes, thirty minutes or an hour, depending on how important he considered they were. Family were not exempt from this rule, except on Sunday. Emma had a number of questions she needed answered, so hoped he'd allotted her at least half an hour.

She sat back and tried to relax, because she didn't want Gramps to work out the real reason she wanted to see him.

'Do you remember when you kindly travelled up to Scotland,' she began, 'to let me know that Harry had been killed at sea? I'm afraid I was in such a state of shock that I didn't take it all in, so I hoped you might tell me a little more about the last few days of his life.'

'Of course, my dear,' said Sir Walter sympathetically. 'Let's hope my memory is up to it. Is there anything in particular you want to know?'

'You told me that Harry signed up as the fourth officer on the *Devonian* after he'd come down from Oxford.'

'That's right. It was my old friend Captain Havens who made it possible, and he was among the few survivors of the tragedy. When I visited him recently, he could not have spoken more warmly of Harry. He described him as a courageous young man, who not only saved his life after the ship had been hit by a torpedo, but sacrificed his own when he attempted to rescue the chief engineer.'

'Was Captain Havens also picked up by the *Kansas Star*?'

'No, by another ship that was in the vicinity, so sadly he never saw Harry again.'

'So he didn't witness Harry being buried at sea?'

'No. The only officer from the *Devonian* who was with Harry when he died was an American, called Lieutenant Thomas Bradshaw.'

'You told me that a Dr Wallace delivered a letter from Lieutenant Bradshaw to Mrs Clifton.'

'That's correct. Dr Wallace was the chief medical officer on the *Kansas Star*. He assured me that he and his team did everything in their power to save Harry's life.'

'Did Bradshaw write to you as well?'

'No, only to the next of kin, if I recall Dr Wallace's words.'

'Then don't you find it strange that he didn't write to me?'

Sir Walter fell silent for some time. 'You know, I've never really given it any thought. Perhaps Harry never mentioned you to Bradshaw. You know how secretive he could be.'

Emma had often thought about it, but moved quickly on. 'Did you read the letter he sent to Mrs Clifton?'

'No, I didn't. But I saw it on the mantelpiece when I visited her the following day.'

'Do you think Dr Wallace had any idea what Bradshaw had written in that letter?'

'Yes. He told me it was a letter of condolence from a fellow officer who had served with Harry on the *Devonian*.'

'If only I could meet Lieutenant Bradshaw,' said Emma, fishing.

'I don't know how you'll manage that, my dear,' said Sir Walter, 'unless Wallace kept in touch with him.'

'Do you have an address for Dr Wallace?'

'Only care of the *Kansas Star*.'

'But surely they must have stopped sailing to Bristol when war was declared.'

'Not as long as there are Americans stranded in England who are willing to pay through the nose to get home.'

'Isn't that taking an unnecessary risk, with so many German U-boats patrolling the Atlantic?'

'Not while America remains neutral,' said Sir Walter. 'The last thing Hitler wants is to start a war with the Yanks simply because one of his U-boats sank an American passenger ship.'

'Do you know if the *Kansas Star* is expected to return to Bristol in the near future?'

'No, but I can easily find out.' The old man heaved himself out of his chair and walked slowly across to his desk. He began to flick through page after page of the monthly timetable of dockings.

'Ah, here it is,' he eventually said. 'She's due out of New York in four weeks' time, and is expected in Bristol on the fifteenth of November. If you're hoping to get in touch with anyone on board, be warned, she won't be hanging around for long, as it's the one place she'll be vulnerable to attack.'

'Will I be allowed on board?'

'Not unless you're a crew member or looking for a job, and frankly I can't see you as either a deckhand or a cocktail waitress.'

'So how can I get to see Dr Wallace?'

'You'll just have to wait on the dockside in the hope that he'll come ashore. Almost everyone does after a week-long voyage. So if he's on the ship, I'm sure you'll catch him. But don't forget, Emma, it's more than a year since Harry died, so Wallace may no longer be the ship's medical officer.' Emma bit her lip. 'But if you'd like me to arrange a private meeting with the captain, I'd be happy—'

'No, no,' said Emma quickly, 'it's not that important.'

'If you change your mind—' began Sir Walter, suddenly realizing just how important Emma considered it to be.

'No, thank you, Gramps,' she said as she rose from her place. 'Thank you for giving me so much of your time.'

'Not nearly enough,' said the old man. 'I only wish you'd drop in more often. And make sure you bring Sebastian with you next time,' he added as he accompanied her to the door.

Sir Walter was no longer in any doubt why his granddaughter had come to see him.

◄○►

In the car on the way back to the Manor House, one sentence remained etched in Emma's mind. She played the words over and over, like a gramophone needle stuck in a groove.

Once she had returned home, she joined Sebastian in the nursery. He had to be coaxed off his rocking horse, but not before a few tears had been shed. After lunch he curled up like a satisfied cat, and fell into a deep sleep. Nanny put him to bed while Emma rang for the chauffeur.

'I'd like to be driven back into Bristol, Hudson.'

'Anywhere in particular, miss?'

'The Grand Hotel.'

—◦—

'You want me to do what?' said Maisie.

'Take me on as a waitress.'

'But why?'

'I'd prefer not to tell you.'

'Do you have any idea how hard the work is?'

'No,' admitted Emma, 'but I won't let you down.'

'And when do you want to start?'

'Tomorrow.'

'Tomorrow?'

'Yes.'

'For how long?'

'One month.'

'Now let me try and get this straight,' said Maisie. 'You want me to train you as a waitress, starting tomorrow, and you'll be leaving in a month's time, but you won't tell me why?'

'That's about it.'

'Are you expecting to be paid?'

'No,' said Emma.

'Well, that's a relief.'

'So when do I start?'

'Six o'clock tomorrow morning.'

'Six o'clock?' repeated Emma in disbelief.

'This may come as a surprise, Emma, but I have

customers who need to be fed by seven, and at work by
eight, so you'll have to make sure you're at your station
by six – every morning.'

'My station?'

'I'll explain if you turn up before six.'

◄○►

Emma wasn't late for work once in the next twenty-
eight days, possibly because Jenkins tapped on her door
at 4.30 every morning, and Hudson dropped her off
a hundred yards from the staff entrance of the Grand
Hotel by 5.45.

Miss Dickens, as she was known by the rest of the
staff, took advantage of her acting skills to make sure
that no one worked out that she was a Barrington.

Mrs Clifton showed Emma no favours when she
spilt some soup over a regular customer, and even less
when she dropped a stack of plates that shattered in the
middle of the dining room. The cost would normally
have been deducted from her pay packet, if she'd had
one. And it was some time before Emma got the knack
of using her shoulder to barge through the swing doors
that led in and out of the kitchen without colliding with
another waitress coming from the opposite direction.

Despite this, Maisie quickly discovered that she only
had to tell Emma something once, and she never forgot
it. She was also impressed by how quickly Emma could ·
turn a table round, although she'd never laid one before
in her life. And while most trainees took several weeks
to master the skill of silver service, some never managing it, Emma didn't need any further supervision by
the end of her second week.

By the end of her third, Maisie wished she wasn't

leaving, and by the end of the fourth, so did several regulars, who were insisting that only Miss Dickens must serve them.

Maisie was becoming anxious about how she was going to explain to the hotel manager that Miss Dickens had given in her notice after only a month.

'You can tell Mr Hurst that I've been offered a better job, with more pay,' said Emma as she began folding up her uniform.

'He's not going to be pleased,' said Maisie. 'It might have been easier if you'd turned out to be useless, or at least been late a few times.' Emma laughed, and placed her little white cap neatly on top of her clothes for the last time.

'Is there anything else I can do for you, Miss Dickens?' asked Maisie.

'Yes please,' said Emma. 'I need a reference.'

'Applying for another unpaid job, are you?'

'Something like that,' replied Emma, feeling a little guilty that she wasn't able to take Harry's mother into her confidence.

'Then I'll dictate a reference, you write it, and I'll sign it,' she said, passing Emma a sheet of the hotel's headed notepaper. 'To whom it may concern,' Maisie began. 'During the short time—'

'Could I possibly leave out "short"?' asked Emma.

Maisie smiled.

'During the time Miss Dickens has been with us at the Grand' – Emma wrote 'Miss Barrington', but didn't tell her – 'she has proved hard-working, efficient and popular with both the customers and staff. Her skills as a waitress are impressive, and her ability to learn on the job convinces me that any establishment would be fortunate to have her as a member of their staff. We will be sorry to lose her, and should she ever want to return to this hotel, we would welcome her back.'

Emma smiled as she handed the sheet of paper back. Maisie scribbled her signature above the words *Restaurant Manageress*.

'Thank you,' said Emma, wrapping her arms around her.

'I have no idea what you're up to, my dear,' said Maisie, once Emma had released her, 'but whatever it is, I wish you luck.'

Emma wanted to tell her, I'm going in search of your son, and I won't return until I've found him.

8

EMMA HAD BEEN standing on the dockside for over an hour when she spotted the *Kansas Star* nosing its way into port, but it was another hour before the ship finally docked.

During that time, Emma thought about the decision she'd made, and was already beginning to wonder if she had the courage to go through with it. She tried to dismiss from her thoughts the sinking of the *Athenia* a few months before, and the possibility of never even making it to New York.

She had written a long letter to her mother, trying to explain why she'd be away for a couple of weeks – three at the most – and only hoped she would understand. But she couldn't write a letter to Sebastian to let him know that she was going in search of his father, and was already missing him. She kept trying to convince herself that she was doing it as much for her son as for herself.

Sir Walter had once again offered to introduce her to the captain of the *Kansas Star*, but Emma had politely declined, as it didn't fit in with her plan to remain anonymous. He'd also given her a vague description of Dr Wallace, and certainly no one who looked remotely like that had disembarked from the ship that morning. However, Sir Walter was able to pass on two other valuable pieces of information. The *Kansas Star* would be departing on the last tide that evening. And the purser could usually be found in his office between the hours of two and five every afternoon, completing embarkation forms. More important, he was responsible for the employment of non-crew members of staff.

Emma had written to her grandfather the day before to thank him for his help, but she still didn't let him know what she was up to, although she had a feeling he'd worked it out.

After the clock on Barrington House had struck twice, and there was still no sign of Dr Wallace, Emma picked up her small suitcase and decided the time had come to walk the gangplank. When she stepped nervously on to the deck, she asked the first person she saw in uniform the way to the purser's office, and was told lower deck aft.

She spotted a passenger disappearing down a wide staircase, and followed her to what she assumed must be the lower deck, but as she had no idea where aft was, she joined a queue at the information desk.

Behind the counter stood two girls, dressed in dark blue uniforms and white blouses. They were attempting to answer every passenger's query while keeping smiles etched on their faces.

'How can I help you, miss?' one of them asked when Emma eventually reached the front of the queue. The girl clearly assumed she was a passenger, and in fact Emma had considered paying for her passage to New York, but had decided she was more likely to find out what she needed to know if she signed on as a member of the crew.

'Where will I find the purser's office?' she asked.

'Second door on the right down that companionway,' replied the girl. 'You can't miss it.'

Emma followed her pointing finger, and when she reached a door marked *Purser* she took a deep breath and knocked.

'Come in.'

Emma opened the door and stepped inside to find a smartly dressed officer seated behind a desk that was strewn with forms. He wore a crisp, open-necked white shirt which had two gold epaulettes on each shoulder.

'How can I help you?' he asked in an accent she'd never heard before, and could hardly decipher.

'I'm looking for a job as a waitress, sir,' said Emma, hoping she sounded like one of the maids at the Manor House.

'Sorry,' he said, looking back down. 'Don't need any more waitresses. The only available position is on the information desk.'

'I'd be happy to work there,' said Emma, reverting to her normal voice.

The purser gave her a closer look. 'The pay's not good,' he warned her, 'and the hours are worse.'

'I'm used to that,' said Emma.

'And I can't offer you a permanent position,' continued the purser, 'because one of my girls is on shore leave in New York, and will be rejoining the ship after this crossing.'

'That's not a problem,' said Emma without explanation.

The purser still didn't look convinced. 'Can you read and write?'

Emma would like to have told him that she'd won a scholarship to Oxford, but simply said, 'Yes, sir.'

Without another word, he pulled open a drawer and extracted a long form, passed her a fountain pen and said, 'Fill this in.' As Emma began to answer the questions, he added, 'And I'll also need to see a reference.'

Once Emma had completed the form, she opened her bag and handed over Maisie's letter of recommendation.

'Very impressive,' he said. 'But are you sure you're suited to being a receptionist?'

'It was going to be my next job at the Grand,' Emma said. 'All part of my training to be a manageress.'

'Then why give up that opportunity to join us?'

'I have a great-aunt who lives in New York, and my mother wants me to stay with her until the war is over.'

This time the purser did look convinced, as it wasn't the first time someone had wanted to work their passage in order to get away from England. 'Then let's get you started,' he said, jumping up. He marched out of the office and led her on the short journey back to the information desk.

'Peggy, I've found someone to replace Dana on this voyage, so you better get her started straight away.'

'Thank God for that,' said Peggy, lifting a flap so Emma could join her behind the counter. 'What's your name?' she asked in the same almost impenetrable accent. For the first time Emma understood what Bernard Shaw had meant when he suggested that the

English and the Americans were divided by a common language.

'Emma Barrington.'

'Well, Emma, this is my assistant, Trudy. As we're so busy, perhaps you could just observe for now, and we'll try to fill you in as we go along.'

Emma took a pace back and watched as the two girls handled everything that was thrown at them, while somehow managing to keep smiling.

Within an hour, Emma knew at what time and where passengers should report for lifeboat drill, which deck the grill room was on, how far out to sea they had to be before passengers could order a drink, where they might find a partner for a round of bridge after dinner, and how to get to the upper deck if you wanted to watch the sunset.

For the next hour, Emma listened to most of the same questions being asked again and again, and during the third, she took a step forward and began to respond to the passengers' queries herself, only occasionally needing to refer to the other two girls.

Peggy was impressed, and when the queue had dwindled to a few latecomers, she said to Emma, 'Time to show you your quarters and grab some supper while the passengers are having a pre-dinner drink.' She turned to Trudy and added, 'I'll be back around seven to relieve you,' then lifted the flap and stepped out from behind the desk. Trudy nodded as another passenger came forward.

'Can you tell me if we have to dress for dinner tonight?'

'Not on the first night, sir,' came back the firm reply, 'but every other night.'

Peggy never stopped chatting as she led Emma down a long corridor, arriving at the top of some roped-off steps with a sign declaring in bold red letters, CREW ONLY.

'This leads to our quarters,' she explained as she unhooked the rope. 'You're going to have to share a cabin with me,' Peggy added as they walked down, 'because Dana's bunk is the only one available at the moment.'

'That's fine,' said Emma.

Down, down and down they went, the stairwells becoming more cramped with each deck. Peggy only stopped talking when a crew member stood aside to let them pass. Occasionally she would reward them with a warm smile. Emma had never come across anyone like Peggy in her life: so fiercely independent, yet somehow she managed to remain feminine, with her bobbed fair hair, skirt that only just fell below the knees, and tight jacket that left you in no doubt how good her figure was.

'This is our cabin,' she said finally. 'It's where you'll be sleeping for the next week. I hope you weren't expecting anything palatial.'

Emma entered a cabin that was smaller than any room at the Manor House, including the broom cupboard.

'Ghastly, isn't it?' said Peggy. 'In fact, this old tub has only one thing going for it.' Emma didn't need to ask what that might be, because Peggy was only too happy to answer her own questions, as well as Emma's. 'The male to female ratio is better than almost anywhere else on earth,' said Peggy, laughing, before she added, 'That's Dana's bunk, and this is mine. As you can see, there isn't enough room for two people in here at the same time, unless one of them is in bed. I'll leave you to get unpacked, and come back in half an hour to take you down to the staff canteen for supper.'

Emma wondered how they could go any further down, but Peggy had disappeared before she could ask. She sat on her bunk in a daze. How could she get Peggy to answer all of her questions if she never stopped talking? Or might that turn out to be an advantage; would she, given time, reveal everything Emma needed to know? She had a whole week to find out, so felt she could afford to be patient. She began to stuff her few possessions into a drawer that Dana had made no attempt to empty.

Two long blasts on the ship's horn, and a moment later she felt a little shudder. Although there was no porthole to look through, she could feel that they were on the move. She sat back down on her bunk and tried to convince herself she'd made the right decision. Although she planned to return to Bristol within a month, she was already missing Sebastian.

She began to look more carefully at what would be her residence for the next week. On each side of the cabin a narrow bunk was attached to the wall, whose dimensions assumed that any occupant would be below average height. She lay down and tested a mattress that didn't give, because it hadn't any springs, and rested her head on a pillow that was filled with foam rubber, not feathers. There was a small washbasin with two taps, both of which delivered the same trickle of tepid water.

She put on Dana's uniform, and tried not to laugh. When Peggy returned, she did laugh. Dana must have been at least three inches shorter and certainly three sizes larger than Emma. 'Be thankful it's only for a week,' said Peggy as she led Emma off for supper.

They descended even further into the bowels of the ship to join the other members of the crew. Several young men and one or two older ones invited Peggy to join them at their table. She favoured a tall young man who, she told Emma, was an engineer. Emma wondered if that explained why it wasn't only his hair that was covered in oil. The three of them joined the queue at the hotplate. The engineer filled his plate with almost everything on offer. Peggy managed about half, while Emma, feeling a little queasy, satisfied herself with a biscuit and an apple.

After supper, Peggy and Emma returned to the information desk to relieve Trudy. As the passengers' dinner was served at eight, few of them appeared at the desk, other than those who needed to ask for directions to the dining room.

During the next hour, Emma learnt a great deal more about Peggy than she did about the SS *Kansas Star*. When they came to the end of their shift at ten o'clock, they pulled down the grille and Peggy led her new companion back towards the lower deck staircase.

'Do you want to join us for a drink in the staff canteen?' she asked.

'No, thank you,' said Emma. 'I'm exhausted.'

'Do you think you can find your way back to the cabin?'

'Lower deck seven, room one-one-three. If I'm not in bed by the time you get back, send out a search party.'

As soon as Emma had entered her cabin, she quickly undressed, washed and slipped under the single sheet and blanket provided. She lay on the bunk trying to settle, her knees almost tucked under her chin, while the irregular bobbing of the vessel meant that she couldn't remain in the same position for more than a few moments. Her last thoughts before she drifted into a fitful sleep were of Sebastian.

Emma woke with a start. It was so dark she had no way of checking the time on her watch. At first she assumed the swaying was caused by the movement of the ship, until her eyes focused and she was able to make out two bodies in the bunk on the other side of the cabin, moving rhythmically up and down. One of the bodies had legs that stretched far beyond the end of the bunk and were braced against the wall; it had to be the engineer. Emma wanted to laugh, but she just lay very still until Peggy let out a long sigh and the movement stopped. A few moments later, the feet attached to the long legs touched the floor and began to wriggle into some old overalls. Not long afterwards, the cabin door opened and closed quietly. Emma fell into a deep sleep.

9

WHEN EMMA WOKE the following morning, Peggy was already up and dressed.

'I'm off for breakfast,' she announced. 'I'll see you at the desk later. By the way, we're expected on duty at eight.'

The moment the door closed, Emma jumped out of bed, and after she'd washed slowly and dressed quickly, she realized there wouldn't be any time for breakfast if she hoped to be behind the information desk on time.

Once she'd reported for work, Emma quickly discovered that Peggy took her job very seriously and put herself out to assist any passenger who needed her help. During their morning coffee break Emma said, 'One of the passengers asked me about doctor's surgery hours.'

'Seven to eleven in the morning,' replied Peggy, 'four to six in the afternoon. In case of an emergency, dial one-one-one on the nearest telephone.'

'And the doctor's name?'

'Parkinson. Dr Parkinson. He's the one man every girl on board has a crush on.'

'Oh – one of the passengers thought it was a Dr Wallace.'

'No, Wally retired about six months ago. Sweet old thing.'

Emma asked no more questions during the break, just drank coffee.

'Why don't you spend the rest of the morning finding your way around, so you know where you're sending everyone,' Peggy suggested once they'd reported back to the desk. She handed Emma a guide to the ship. 'See you for lunch.'

With the guidebook open, Emma began her quest on the upper deck: the dining rooms, the bars, the card room, a library, and even a ballroom with a resident jazz band. She only stopped to take a closer look when she came across the infirmary on lower deck two, tentatively opening the double doors and poking her head inside. Two neatly made, unoccupied beds stood against the wall on the far side of the room. Had Harry slept in one and Lieutenant Bradshaw in the other?

'Can I help you?' said a voice.

Emma swung round to see a tall man in a long white coat. She immediately understood why Peggy had a crush on him.

'I've just started on the information desk,' she blurted out, 'and I'm meant to be finding out where everything is.'

'I'm Simon Parkinson,' he said, giving her a friendly smile. 'Now you've found out where I am, you're most welcome to drop in at any time.'

'Thank you,' said Emma. She quickly stepped back into the corridor, closed the door behind her and hurried away. She couldn't remember the last time someone had flirted with her, but she wished it had been Dr Wallace. She spent the rest of the morning exploring each deck until she felt she'd mastered the ship's layout and would be able to tell any passenger where everything was with more confidence.

She was looking forward to spending the afternoon testing out her new skills, but Peggy asked her to go over the passenger files in the same way she'd studied the ship. Emma sat alone in the back office, learning about people she would never see again in her life.

In the evening she made an attempt to eat supper, beans on toast and a glass of lemonade, but she was back in her cabin soon afterwards, hoping to catch some sleep in case the engineer returned.

When the door opened, the light in the corridor woke her. Emma couldn't make out who it was that entered the cabin, but it certainly wasn't the engineer, because his feet didn't reach the wall. She lay awake for forty minutes, and didn't get back to sleep until the door had opened and closed again.

—◦—

Emma quickly became accustomed to the routine of the daily work followed by the nocturnal visits. These visits didn't vary greatly, only the men, although on one occasion the amorous visitor headed for Emma's bunk and not Peggy's.

'Wrong girl,' said Emma firmly.

'Sorry,' came back the reply, before he changed direction. Peggy must have assumed she had fallen asleep, because after the couple had made love, Emma could hear every word of their whispered conversation.

'Do you think your friend's available?'

'Why, have you taken a shine to her?' giggled Peggy.

'No, not me, but I know someone who'd like to be the first man to unbutton Dana's uniform.'

'Not a hope. She's got a boyfriend back home in Bristol, and I'm told even Dr Parkinson didn't make an impression on her.'

'Pity,' said the voice.

◄○►

Peggy and Trudy often talked about the morning that nine sailors from the *Devonian* had been buried at sea before breakfast. With some subtle prompts, Emma was able to gain information that neither her grandfather nor Maisie could possibly have known. But with only three days left before they reached New York, she was no nearer to discovering if it was Harry or Lieutenant Bradshaw who'd survived.

On the fifth day, Emma took charge of the desk for the first time, and there were no surprises. The surprise came on the fifth night.

When the cabin door opened at whatever hour it was, a man once again headed for Emma's bunk, but this time when she said, 'Wrong girl,' firmly, he left immediately. She lay awake wondering who it could possibly have been.

On the sixth day, Emma learnt nothing new about Harry or Tom Bradshaw, and was beginning to fear that she might arrive in New York without any leads to follow up. It was during dinner that night that she decided to ask Peggy about 'the one that survived'.

'I only met Tom Bradshaw once,' said Peggy, 'when he was roaming around the deck with his nurse. Well, come to think of it, he wasn't exactly roaming, because the poor man was on crutches.'

'Did you speak to him?' asked Emma.

'No, he seemed very shy. In any case, Kristin didn't let him out of her sight.'

'Kristin?'

'She was the hospital nurse at the time, worked alongside Dr Wallace. Between them, they undoubtedly saved Tom Bradshaw's life.'

'So you never saw him again?'

'Only when we docked in New York, and I spotted him going ashore with Kristin.'

'He left the ship with Kristin?' said Emma anxiously. 'Was Dr Wallace with them?'

'No, just Kristin and her boyfriend Richard.'

'Richard?' said Emma, sounding relieved.

'Yes, Richard something. I can't remember his surname. He was the third officer. Not long afterwards he married Kristin, and we never saw either of them again.'

'Was he a good-looking man?' asked Emma.

'Tom or Richard?' asked Peggy.

'Can I get you a drink, Peg?' asked a young man Emma had never seen before, but had a feeling she would be seeing in profile later that night.

Emma was right, and she didn't sleep before, during or after the visit, as she had something else on her mind.

—◦—

The following morning, for the first time on the voyage, Emma was standing behind the information desk waiting for Peggy to appear.

'Shall I prepare the passenger list for disembarkation?' she asked when Peggy finally arrived and lifted the counter flap.

'You're the first person I've ever known to volunteer for that job,' said Peggy, 'but be my guest. Someone has to make sure it's up to date in case immigration decides to double-check any of the passengers' details once we've docked in New York.'

Emma went straight through to the back office. Putting aside the current passenger list, she turned her attention to the files of past crew members, which she found in a separate cabinet that looked as if it hadn't been opened for some time.

She began a slow, meticulous search for the names Kristin and Richard. Kristin proved easy, because there was only one person with that name, and she'd worked as a senior staff nurse on the *Kansas Star* from 1936 to 1939. However, there were several Richards, Dicks and Dickies, but the address of one of them, Lieutenant Richard Tibbet, was in the same Manhattan apartment building as Miss Kristin Craven.

Emma made a note of the address.

10

'WELCOME TO the United States, Miss Barrington.'

'Thank you,' said Emma.

'How long do you plan to be in the United States?' asked the immigration officer as he checked her passport.

'A week, two at the most,' said Emma. 'I'm visiting my great-aunt, and then I'll be returning to England.' It was true that Emma had a great-aunt who lived in New York, Lord Harvey's sister, but she had no intention of visiting her, not least because she didn't want the rest of the family to find out what she was up to.

'Your great-aunt's address?'

'Sixty-fourth and Park.'

The immigration officer made a note, stamped Emma's passport and handed it back to her.

'Enjoy your stay in the Big Apple, Miss Barrington.'

Once Emma had passed through immigration, she joined a long queue of passengers from the *Kansas Star*. It was another twenty minutes before she climbed into the back of a yellow cab.

'I require a small, sensibly priced hotel, located near Merton Street in Manhattan,' she told the driver.

'You wanna run that past me again, lady?' said the cabbie, the stub of an unlit cigar protruding from the corner of his mouth.

As Emma had found it difficult to understand a word he said, she assumed he was having the same problem. 'I'm looking for a small, inexpensive hotel near Merton Street, on Manhattan Island,' she said, slowly enunciating each word.

'Merton Street,' repeated the driver, as if it was the only thing he'd understood.

'That's right,' said Emma.

'Why didn't you say so the first time?'

The driver took off, and didn't speak again until he'd dropped his fare outside a red-brick building that flew a flag proclaiming *The Mayflower Hotel*.

'That'll be forty cents,' said the cabbie, the cigar bobbing up and down with each word.

Emma paid the fare from the wage packet she'd earned while on the ship. Once she'd checked into the hotel, she took the lift to the fourth floor and went straight to her room. The first thing she did was to get undressed and run herself a hot bath.

When she reluctantly climbed out, she dried herself with a large fluffy towel, dressed in what she considered a demure frock and made her way back down to the ground floor. She felt almost human.

Emma found a quiet table in the corner of the hotel coffee shop and ordered a cup of tea – they hadn't heard of Earl Grey – and a club sandwich, something she'd never heard of. While she waited to be served, she began to write out a long list of questions on a paper napkin, hoping there would be someone living at 46 Merton Street who was willing to answer them.

Once she'd signed the check, another new word, Emma asked the receptionist for directions to Merton Street. Three blocks north, two blocks west, she was told. She hadn't realized that every New Yorker possessed a built-in compass.

Emma enjoyed the walk, stopping several times to admire windows filled with merchandise she had never seen in Bristol. She arrived outside a high-rise apartment block just after midday, unsure what she would do if Mrs Tibbet wasn't at home.

A smartly dressed doorman saluted and opened the door for her. 'Can I help you?'

'I've come to see Mrs Tibbet,' Emma said, trying to sound as if she was expected.

'Apartment thirty-one, on the third floor,' he said, touching the rim of his cap.

It was true, an English accent did appear to open doors.

As the elevator made its way slowly up to the third floor, Emma rehearsed some lines she hoped would open another door. When the elevator stopped, she pulled back the grille, stepped out into the corridor and went in search of number 31. There was a tiny circle of glass set in the middle of the Tibbets' door, which reminded Emma of a Cyclops eye. She couldn't see in, but she assumed the occupants could see out. A more familiar buzzer was on the wall beside the door. She pressed it and waited. It was some time before the door eventually opened, but only a few inches, revealing a brass chain. Two eyes peered out at her.

'What do you want?' asked a voice that she could at least understand.

'I'm sorry to bother you, Mrs Tibbet,' said Emma,

'but you may be my last chance.' The eyes looked suspicious. 'You see, I'm desperately trying to find Tom.'

'Tom?' repeated the voice.

'Tom Bradshaw. He's the father of my child,' said Emma, playing her last door-opening card.

The door closed, the chain was removed and the door opened once again to reveal a young woman carrying a baby in her arms.

'I'm sorry about that,' she said, 'but Richard doesn't like me opening the door to strangers. Please come in.' She led Emma through to the living room. 'Have a seat while I put Jake back in his cot.'

Emma sat down and glanced around the room. There were several photographs of Kristin with a young naval officer who she assumed must be her husband, Richard.

Kristin returned a few minutes later carrying a tray of coffee. 'Black or white?'

'White please,' said Emma, who'd never drunk coffee in England, but was quickly learning that Americans don't drink tea, even in the morning.

'Sugar?' enquired Kristin after she'd poured two coffees.

'No, thank you.'

'So, is Tom your husband?' asked Kristin as she sat down opposite Emma.

'No, I'm his fiancée. To be fair, he had no idea I was pregnant.'

'How did you find me?' asked Kristin, still sounding a little apprehensive.

'The purser on the *Kansas Star* said you and Richard were among the last people to see Tom.'

'That's true. We were with him until he was arrested a few moments after he stepped on shore.'

'Arrested?' said Emma in disbelief. 'What could he possibly have done to get himself arrested?'

'He was accused of murdering his brother,' said Kristin. 'But surely you knew that?'

Emma burst into tears, her hopes shattered by the realization that it must have been Bradshaw who'd survived, and not Harry. If Harry had been accused of murdering Bradshaw's brother, it would have been so easy for him to prove they'd arrested the wrong man.

If only she'd ripped open the letter on Maisie's mantelpiece, she would have discovered the truth and not put herself through this ordeal. She wept, accepting for the first time that Harry was dead.

GILES BARRINGTON

1939–1941

11

WHEN SIR WALTER BARRINGTON visited his grandson to tell him the terrible news that Harry Clifton had been killed at sea, Giles felt numb, as if he'd lost a limb. In fact, he would have been happy to lose a limb if it would have brought Harry back. The two of them had been inseparable since childhood, and Giles had always assumed they would both score one of life's centuries. Harry's pointless, unnecessary death made Giles even more determined not to make the same mistake himself.

Giles was in the drawing room listening to Mr Churchill on the radio when Emma asked, 'Do you have any plans to join up?'

'Yes, I shan't be returning to Oxford. I intend to sign up immediately.'

His mother was clearly surprised, but told him that she understood. Emma gave him a huge hug, and said, 'Harry would be proud of you.' Grace, who rarely displayed any emotion, burst into tears.

Giles drove into Bristol the following morning and parked his yellow MG ostentatiously outside the front door of the recruiting office. He marched in with what he hoped was resolution written across his face. A sergeant major from the Gloucesters – Captain Jack Tarrant's old regiment – stood smartly to attention the moment he saw young Mr Barrington. He handed Giles a form which he dutifully filled in, and an hour later he was invited to step behind a curtain and be examined by an army doctor.

The doctor placed a tick in every box after he'd thoroughly checked this latest recruit – ears, nose, throat, chest and limbs – before finally testing his eyesight. Giles stood behind a white line and recited the letters and numbers on demand; after all, he could dispatch a leather ball coming straight at him at ninety miles an hour, to the most distant boundary. He was confident he would pass with flying colours, until the doctor asked him if he was aware of any hereditary ailments or diseases in his family. Giles replied truth-fully, 'Both my father and grandfather are colour-blind.'

The doctor carried out a further series of tests, and Giles noticed that the ums and ahs turned into tut-tuts.

'I'm sorry to have to tell you, Mr Barrington,' he said when he came to the end of his examination, 'that given your family's medical history, I will not be able to recommend you for active service. But of course, there's nothing to stop you joining up and doing a desk job.'

'Can't you just tick the relevant box, doctor, and forget I ever raised the damn subject?' said Giles, trying to sound desperate.

The doctor ignored his protest, and in the final box on the form he wrote 'C3': unfit for active service.

Giles was back at the Manor House in time for lunch. His mother, Elizabeth, didn't comment on the fact that he drank almost a bottle of wine. He told everyone who asked, and several who didn't, that he'd been rejected by the Gloucesters because he suffered from colour-blindness.

'It didn't stop Grandfather fighting the Boers,' Grace reminded him after he'd been served with a second helping of pudding.

'They probably had no idea the condition existed back then,' said Giles, trying to make light of her barb.

Emma followed up with a punch below the belt. 'You never intended to sign up in the first place, did you?' she said, looking her brother in the eye. Giles was staring down at his shoes when she delivered the knockout blow. 'Pity your friend from the docks isn't here to remind you that he was also colour-blind.'

When Giles's mother heard the news she was clearly relieved, but didn't comment. Grace didn't speak to her brother again before she returned to Cambridge.

◄○►

Giles drove back to Oxford the following day trying to convince himself that everyone would accept the reason he'd been unable to sign up and intended to continue his life as an undergraduate. When he strolled through the college gates, he found that the quad resembled a recruiting centre rather than a university, with young men in uniform outnumbering those wearing subfusc. In Giles's opinion, the only good thing to come out of all this was that for the first time in history there were as many women as men up at the university. Unfortunately, most of them were only willing to be seen on the arm of someone in uniform.

Giles's old school friend Deakins was one of the few undergraduates who didn't seem uncomfortable about not signing up. Mind you, there wouldn't have been much point in Deakins taking a medical. It would have been one of the rare exams in which he failed to get a tick in any box. But then he suddenly disappeared, to somewhere called Bletchley Park. No one could tell Giles what they got up to there, except it was all 'hush-hush', and Deakins warned Giles that he wouldn't be able to visit him at any time, under any circumstances.

As the months passed, Giles began to spend more time alone in the pub than in the crowded lecture theatre, while Oxford began to fill up with servicemen returning from the front, some with one arm, others with one leg, a few who were blind, and they were just in his college. He tried to carry on as if he hadn't noticed, but the truth was, by the end of term, he began to feel more and more out of place.

—◦—

Giles drove up to Scotland at the end of term to attend the christening of Sebastian Arthur Clifton. Only the immediate family and one or two close friends were invited to the ceremony that took place in the chapel at Mulgelrie Castle. Emma and Giles's father was not among them.

Giles was surprised and delighted when Emma asked him to be a godfather, although he was somewhat taken aback when she admitted that the only reason she'd even considered him was that, despite everything, she had no doubt he would have been Harry's first choice.

As he was going down to breakfast the following morning, Giles noticed a light coming from his grand-father's study. As he passed the door on his way to the dining room, Giles heard his name come up in conversation. He stopped in his tracks, and took a step nearer to the half-open door. He froze in horror when he heard Sir Walter saying, 'It pains me to have to say this, but like father, like son.'

'I agree,' replied Lord Harvey. 'And I'd always thought so highly of the boy, which makes the whole damn business all the more distasteful.'

'No one,' said Sir Walter, 'could have been prouder than I was, as chairman of the governors, when Giles was appointed head boy of Bristol Grammar School.'

'I'd assumed,' said Lord Harvey, 'that he would put those remarkable talents of leadership and courage he displayed so often on the playing field to good use on the battlefield.'

'The only good thing to come out of all this,' suggested Sir Walter, 'is that I no longer believe that Harry Clifton could possibly be Hugo's son.'

Giles strode across the hallway, past the breakfast room and out of the front door. He climbed into his car and began the long journey back to the West Country.

The following morning, he parked the car outside a recruiting office. Once again he stood in line, not for the Gloucesters this time, but on the other side of the Avon, where the Wessex regiment were signing up new recruits.

After he'd filled in the form, he was put through another rigorous medical. This time when the doctor asked him, 'Are you aware of any hereditary ailments or diseases in your family that might prevent you from carrying out active service?' he replied, 'No, sir.'

12

AT NOON the following day, Giles left one world and entered another.

Thirty-six raw recruits, with nothing in common other than the fact that they had signed up to take the King's shilling, clambered aboard a train with a corporal acting as their nanny. As the train pulled out of the station, Giles stared through the grimy third-class window and was certain of only one thing: they were heading south. But not until the train shunted into Lympstone four hours later did he realize just how far south.

During the journey, Giles remained silent, and listened attentively to all those men around him who would be his companions for the next twelve weeks. A bus driver from Filton, a policeman from Long Ashton, a butcher from Broad Street, a builder from Nailsea and a farmer from Winscombe.

Once they disembarked from the train, the corporal ferried them on to a waiting bus.

'Where are we going?' asked the butcher.

'You'll find out soon enough, laddie,' replied the corporal, revealing his birthplace.

For an hour the bus trundled across Dartmoor until there was no sign of houses or people, just the occasional hawk flying overheard in search of prey.

They eventually stopped outside a desolate group of buildings, displaying a weathered sign that announced *Ypres Barracks: Training camp for the Wessex Regiment*. It didn't lift Giles's spirits. A soldier marched out of the gatehouse and raised the barrier to allow the bus to continue for another hundred yards before coming to a halt in the middle of a parade ground. A solitary figure stood waiting for them to disembark.

When Giles climbed off the bus, he came face to face with a giant of a man, barrel-chested and dressed in a khaki uniform, who looked as if he had been planted on the parade ground. There were three rows of medals on his chest and a pace stick under his left arm, but what struck Giles most about him was the knife-edge crease in his trousers and the fact that his boots were so highly polished he could see his reflection in them.

'Good afternoon, gentlemen,' the man said in a voice that boomed around the parade ground; not someone who would find any use for a megaphone, thought Giles. 'My name is Sergeant Major Dawson – sir, to you. It's my responsibility to turn you from a shambolic rabble into a fighting force in just twelve weeks. By then, you will be able to call yourselves members of the Wessex, the finest regiment of the line. For the next twelve weeks I will be your mother, your father and your sweetheart and, let me assure you, I only have one purpose in life, and that is to make sure that when you meet your first German, you'll be able to kill him before he kills you. That process will begin at five tomorrow morning.' A groan went up which the sergeant major ignored. 'Until then, I'll leave Corporal McCloud to take you to the canteen, before you settle into your barracks. Be sure to get a good night's rest, because you'll need every ounce of energy you possess when we meet again. Carry on, corporal.'

Giles sat down in front of a fishcake whose ingredients had never seen salt water, and after one sip of lukewarm brown water, posing as tea, he put his mug back on the table.

'If you're not going to eat your fishcake, can I have it?' asked the young man sitting next to him. Giles nodded, and they swapped plates. He didn't speak again until he'd devoured Giles's offering.

'I know your mum,' the man said.

Giles gave him a closer look, wondering how that could be possible.

'We supply the meat for the Manor House and Barrington Hall,' the man continued. 'I like your mum,' he said. 'Very nice lady. I'm Bates, by the way, Terry Bates.' He shook Giles firmly by the hand. 'Never thought I'd end up sitting next to you.'

'Right, chaps, let's be 'avin' you,' said the corporal. The new recruits leapt up from the benches and followed the corporal out of the canteen and across the parade ground to a Nissen hut with MARNE painted on the door. Another Wessex battle honour, the corporal explained before opening the door to reveal their new home.

Thirty-six beds, eighteen on each side, had been crammed into a space no larger than the dining room at Barrington Hall. Giles had been placed between Atkinson and Bates. Not unlike prep school, he thought, though he did come across one or two differences during the next few days.

'Right, chaps, time to get undressed and have a kip.'

Long before the last man had climbed into bed, the corporal switched off the lights and bellowed, 'Make sure you get some shut-eye. You've got a busy day ahead of you tomorrow.' It wouldn't have surprised Giles if, like Fisher, his old school prefect, he'd added, 'No talking after lights out.'

As promised, the lights came back on at five o'clock the following morning; not that Giles had a chance to look at his watch after Sergeant Major Dawson entered the hut and bellowed, 'The last man with both feet on the ground will be first to be bayoneted by a Kraut!'

A large number of feet quickly hit the floor as the sergeant major marched down the centre of the hut, his pace stick banging the end of any bed whose incumbent still didn't have both feet on the ground.

'Now listen, and listen carefully,' he continued. 'I'm going to give you four minutes to wash and shave, four minutes to make your bed, four minutes to get dressed and eight minutes to have breakfast. Twenty minutes in all. I don't recommend any talking, on account of the fact you can't afford to waste the time, and in any case, I'm the only one who's allowed to talk. Is that understood?'

'It most certainly is,' said Giles, which was followed by a ripple of surprised laughter.

A moment later the sergeant major was standing in front of him. 'Whenever you open your mouth, sonny,' he barked, placing his pace stick on Giles's shoulder, 'all I want to hear is yes, sir, no, sir, three bags full, sir. Is that clear?'

'Yes, sir,' said Giles.

'I don't think I heard you, sonny.'

'Yes, sir!' shouted Giles.

'That's better. Now get yourself in the washroom, you horrible little man, before I put you on jankers.'

Giles had no idea what jankers was, but it didn't sound enticing.

Bates was already on his way out of the washroom when Giles walked in. By the time he'd shaved, Bates had made his bed, dressed and was on his way to the canteen. When Giles eventually caught up with him, he took a seat on the bench opposite.

'How do you manage it?' asked Giles in admiration.

'Manage what?' asked Bates.

'To be so wide awake, when the rest of us are still half asleep.'

'Simple really. I'm a butcher, like me dad. Up every mornin' at four, and off to the market. If I want the best cuts I have to be waitin' for them the moment they're delivered from the docks or the station. Only have to be a few minutes late, and I'm gettin' second best. Half an hour late, and it's scrag-ends, and your mum wouldn't thank me for that, would she?'

Giles laughed as Bates leapt up and began heading back to the barracks, only to discover that the sergeant major hadn't allowed any time for cleaning teeth.

Most of the morning was spent fitting up the 'sprogs', as they were referred to, with uniforms, one or two of which looked as if they'd had a previous owner. Berets, belts, boots, tin hats, blanco, Brasso and boot polish followed. Once they had been kitted out, the recruits were taken on to the parade ground for their first drill session. Having served, if somewhat inattentively, in the school's Combined Cadet Force, Giles started with a slight advantage, but he had a feeling it wouldn't be too long before Terry Bates caught up with him.

At twelve, they were marched off to the canteen. Giles was so hungry he ate almost everything on offer. After lunch, they returned to the barracks and changed into their gym kit before being herded across to the gymnasium. Giles silently thanked his prep school PT instructor for having taught him how to climb a rope, how to balance on a beam and how to use the wall bars for stretching. He couldn't help noticing that Bates shadowed his every move.

The afternoon ended with a five-mile run across the Devon moors. Only eight of the thirty-six raw recruits came back through the barracks gates at the same time as their gym instructor. One even managed to get lost and a search party had to be sent out to look for him. Tea was followed by what the sergeant major described as recreation, which for most of the lads turned out to be collapsing on their bunks and falling into a deep sleep.

◄○►

At five the following morning, the door to the barracks flew open once again, and this time several pairs of feet were already on the ground before the sergeant major had switched the lights on. Breakfast was followed by another hour of marching on the parade ground, and by now almost everyone was in step. The new recruits then sat in a circle on the grass and learnt how to strip, clean, load and fire a rifle. The corporal pulled a 4 by 2 through the barrel in one clean movement, reminding them that the bullet doesn't know which side it's on, so give it every chance to leave the barrel from the front and kill the enemy, and not backfire and kill you.

The afternoon was spent on the rifle range, where the instructors taught each recruit to nestle the butt of the rifle firmly into their shoulder, line up the foresight and rearsight with the centre circle of the target, and squeeze the trigger gently, never snatch at it. This time Giles thanked his grandfather for the hours spent on his grouse moor that ensured he kept hitting the bullseye.

The day ended with another five-mile run, tea and recreation, followed by lights out at ten. Most of the men had collapsed on their beds long before that, wishing the sun would fail to rise the next morning, or at least that the sergeant major would die in his sleep. They didn't get lucky. The first week felt like a month to Giles, but by the end of the second he was beginning to master the routine, although he never once got to the washroom ahead of Bates.

Although he didn't enjoy basic training any more than the next man, Giles did relish the challenge of competition. But he had to admit that as each day went by, he was finding it more and more difficult to shake off the butcher from Broad Street. Bates was able to match him punch for punch in the boxing ring, trade bullseyes on the rifle range, and when they started wearing heavy boots and having to carry a rifle on the five-mile run, the man who for years had been hauling carcasses of beef around on his shoulder, morning, noon and night, suddenly became a lot harder to beat.

◄○►

At the end of the sixth week, no one was surprised that it was Barrington and Bates who were selected for promotion to lance corporal, and each given a section of their own.

No sooner had they sewn on their stripes than the two sections they led became deadly rivals; not just on the parade ground or in the gymnasium, but whenever they went out on night ops or were involved in field exercises and troop movements. At the end of each day, like a couple of schoolboys, Giles and Bates would both declare themselves the winner. Often the sergeant major would have to prise them apart.

As they approached the day of the passing-out parade, Giles could sense the pride in both sections, who'd begun to believe they might just be worthy of calling themselves Wessexions by the time they passed out; although the sergeant major repeatedly warned them that it wouldn't be long before they had to take part in a real battle, against a real enemy with real bullets. He also reminded them that he wouldn't be around to hold their hands. For the first time Giles accepted that he was going to miss the damn man.

'Bring 'em on,' was all Bates had to say on the subject.

When they finally passed out on the Friday of the twelfth week, Giles assumed that he would be returning to Bristol with the other lads, to enjoy a weekend's leave before reporting to the regimental depot the following Monday. But when he walked off the parade ground that afternoon, the sergeant major took him to one side.

'Corporal Barrington, you're to report to Major Radcliffe immediately.'

Giles would have asked why, but he knew he wouldn't get an answer.

He marched across the parade ground and knocked on the office door of the adjutant, a man he'd only ever seen at a distance.

'Enter,' said a voice. Giles walked in, stood to attention and saluted. 'Barrington,' Major Radcliffe said after he'd returned the salute, 'I have some good news for you. You've been accepted for officer training school.'

Giles didn't even realize he was being considered for a commission.

'You'll have to travel straight to Mons tomorrow morning, where you will begin an induction course on Monday. Many congratulations, and good luck.'

'Thank you, sir,' said Giles, before asking, 'Will Bates be joining me?'

'Bates?' said Major Radcliffe. 'Do you mean Corporal Bates?'

'Yes, sir.'

'Good heavens, no,' replied the adjutant. 'He's not officer material.'

Giles could only hope that the Germans were just as short-sighted when it came to selecting their officers.

—◇—

When Giles reported to the Mons Officer Cadet Training Unit in Aldershot the following afternoon, he was unprepared for how quickly his life would change again. It took him some time to get used to corporals, sergeants, even the sergeant major calling him 'sir'.

He slept in a single room where the door didn't fly open at five in the morning with an NCO banging the end of his bed with a stick, demanding he place both feet on the ground. The door only opened when Giles chose to open it. He had breakfast in the mess with a group of young men who didn't need to be taught how to hold a knife and fork, although one or two of them looked as if they would never learn how to handle a rifle, let alone fire it in anger. But in a few weeks' time these same men would be in the front line, leading inexperienced volunteers whose lives would depend on their judgement.

Giles joined these men in a classroom where they were taught military history, geography, map reading, battle tactics, German and the art of leadership. If he'd learnt one thing from the butcher from Broad Street, it was that the art of leadership couldn't be taught.

Eight weeks later, the same young men stood on a passing-out parade and were awarded the King's Commission. They were presented with two crowned pips, one for each shoulder, a brown leather officer's cane and a letter of congratulations from a grateful King.

All Giles wanted to do was to rejoin his regiment and team up with his old comrades, but he knew that wouldn't be possible, because when he walked off the parade ground that Friday afternoon, the corporals, the sergeants and, yes, even the sergeant major saluted him.

Sixty young second lieutenants left Aldershot that afternoon for every corner of the land, to spend a weekend with their families, some of them for the last time.

◄○►

Giles spent most of Saturday jumping on and off trains, as he made his way back to the West Country. He arrived at the Manor House just in time to join his mother for dinner.

When she first saw the young lieutenant standing in the hallway, Elizabeth made no attempt to hide her pride.

Giles was disappointed that neither Emma nor Grace was at home to see him in uniform. His mother explained that Grace, who was in her second term at Cambridge, rarely came home, even during the vacation.

Over a one-course meal served by Jenkins – several of the staff were now serving on the frontline, not at the dinner table, his mother explained – Giles told his mother about what they'd got up to in training camp on Dartmoor. When she heard about Terry Bates she sighed, 'Bates and Son, they used to be the best butchers in Bristol.'

'Used to be?'

'Every shop in Broad Street was razed to the ground, so we've been deprived of Bates the butcher. Those Germans have a lot to answer for.'

Giles frowned. 'And Emma?' he asked.

'Couldn't be better . . . except – '

'Except?' repeated Giles. It was some time before his mother quietly added, 'How much more convenient it would have been if Emma had produced a daughter, rather than a son.'

'Why is that important?' asked Giles, as he refilled his glass.

His mother bowed her head, but said nothing.

'Oh God,' said Giles, as the significance of her words sank in. 'I had assumed that when Harry died, I would inherit—'

'I'm afraid you can't assume anything, darling,' said his mother, looking up. 'That is, not until it can be established that your father is not also Harry's father. Until then, under the terms of your great-grandfather's will, it will be Sebastian who eventually inherits the title.'

Giles hardly spoke again during the meal while he tried to take in the significance of his mother's words. Once coffee had been served, his mother said she felt tired and went to bed.

When Giles climbed the stairs to his room a few moments later, he couldn't resist dropping into the nursery to see his godson. He sat alone with the heir to the Barrington title. Sebastian gurgled in blissful sleep, clearly untroubled by war, and certainly not giving a thought to his grandfather's will, or the significance of the words, *and all that therein is.*

The following day Giles joined his grandfathers for lunch at the Savage Club. It was a very different atmosphere from the weekend they'd shared five months earlier at Mulgelrie Castle. The only thing the two old men seemed keen to find out was where his regiment would be posted.

'I've no idea,' replied Giles, who would like to have known himself; but he would have given the same response even if he had been briefed, despite the fact that these two venerable old gentlemen were Boer War veterans.

◄○►

Lieutenant Barrington rose early on the Monday morning and, after breakfast with his mother, was driven by Hudson to the headquarters of the 1st Wessex regiment.

He was held up by a steady stream of armoured vehicles and lorries filled with troops pouring out of the main gate. He got out of the car and walked to the guard house.

'Good morning, sir,' said a corporal, after giving him a crisp salute; something Giles still hadn't got used to. 'The adjutant has requested that you report to his office as soon as you arrive.'

'I'd be happy to do so, corporal,' said Giles, returning his salute, 'if I knew where Major Radcliffe's office was.'

'Far side of the square, sir, green door. You can't miss it.'

Giles marched across the square, returning several more salutes before he reached the adjutant's office.

Major Radcliffe looked up from behind his desk as Giles entered the room.

'Ah, Barrington, old chap. Good to see you again,' he said. 'We weren't certain if you'd make it in time.'

'In time for what, sir?' asked Giles.

'The regiment's been posted abroad, and the colonel felt you should be given the opportunity of joining us, or staying behind and waiting for the next shindig.'

'Where are we going, sir?'

'Haven't a clue, old chap; way above my rank. But I can tell you one thing for certain, it will be a damn sight closer to the Germans than Bristol.'

HARRY CLIFTON

1941

13

HARRY WOULD NEVER FORGET the day Lloyd was released from Lavenham and, although he wasn't disappointed to see him go, he was surprised by Max's parting words.

'Would you do me a favour, Tom?' Lloyd said as they shook hands for the last time. 'I'm enjoying your diaries so much, I'd like to go on reading them. If you'd send them to this address,' he said, handing Harry a card as if he were already on the outside, 'I'll return them to you within a week.'

Harry was flattered, and agreed to send Max each exercise book once he'd completed it.

The following morning Harry took his place behind the librarian's desk, but didn't consider reading the previous day's newspaper before he'd completed his duties. He continued to update his diaries every evening, and whenever he came to the end of a notebook, he would post his latest efforts to Max Lloyd. He was relieved, and a little surprised, when they were always returned, as promised.

As the months passed, Harry began to accept the fact that prison life was mostly routine and mundane, so when the warden charged into the library one morning brandishing his copy of the *New York Times* he was taken by surprise. Harry put down the stack of books he had been replacing on the shelves.

'Do we have a map of the United States?' Swanson demanded.

'Yes, of course,' Harry replied. He walked quickly over to the reference section and extracted a copy of *Hubert's Map of America*. 'Anywhere in particular, warden?' he asked.

'Pearl Harbor.'

For the next twenty-four hours, there was only one subject on everyone's lips, prisoners and guards alike. When would America enter the war?

Swanson returned to the library the following morning.

'President Roosevelt has just announced on the radio that the United States has declared war on Japan.'

'That's all very well,' said Harry, 'but when will the Americans help us defeat Hitler?'

Harry regretted the word 'us' the moment he'd uttered it. He looked up to find Swanson staring at him quizzically, and quickly returned to shelving the previous day's books.

Harry found out the answer some weeks later, when Winston Churchill boarded the *Duke of York* and sailed to Washington to conduct discussions with the President. By the time the Prime Minister had arrived back in Britain, Roosevelt had agreed that the United States would turn their attention to the war in Europe, and the task of defeating Nazi Germany.

Harry filled page after page of his diary with the

reaction of his fellow prisoners to the news that their country was at war. He concluded that most of them fell into one of two distinct categories, the cowards and the heroes: those who were relieved to be safely locked up in jail, and only hoped the hostilities would be over long before they were released, and those who couldn't wait to get out and take on an enemy they hated even more than the prison guards. When Harry asked his cellmate which category he fell into, Quinn replied, 'Have you ever met an Irishman who didn't relish a scrap?'

For his part, Harry became even more frustrated, convinced that now the Americans had entered the war, it would be over long before he'd been given the chance to play his part. For the first time since being locked up, he thought about trying to escape.

◄○►

Harry had just finished reading a book review in the *New York Times* when an officer marched into the library and said, 'The warden wants to see you in his office immediately, Bradshaw.'

Harry wasn't surprised, although after glancing once again at the advertisement at the bottom of the page, he still wondered how Lloyd imagined he would get away with it. He folded the paper neatly, placed it back in the rack, and followed the officer out of the room.

'Any idea why he wants to see me, Mr Joyce?' Harry asked as they walked across the yard.

'Don't ask me,' said Joyce, not attempting to hide his sarcasm. 'I've never been one of the warden's confidants.'

Harry didn't speak again until they were standing outside the warden's office. Joyce gave a quiet tap on the door.

'Enter,' said an unmistakable voice. Joyce opened the door, and Harry walked into the room. He was surprised to find another man he'd never seen before seated opposite the warden. The man was wearing an army officer's uniform, and looked as smart as Harry felt unkempt. He never took his eyes off the prisoner.

The warden rose from behind his desk. 'Good morning, Tom.' It was the first time Swanson had addressed him by his Christian name. 'This is Colonel Cleverdon, of the Fifth Texas Rangers.'

'Good morning, sir,' said Harry.

Cleverdon stood up and shook hands with Harry; another first.

'Have a seat, Tom,' said Swanson. 'The colonel has a proposition he wants to put to you.'

Harry sat down.

'It's good to meet you, Bradshaw,' began Colonel Cleverdon as he sat back down. 'I'm the commanding officer of the Rangers.' Harry gave him a quizzical look. 'You won't find us listed in any recruitment manuals. I train groups of soldiers who will be dropped behind enemy lines with the purpose of causing as much mayhem for the enemy as possible, so the infantry will have a better chance to do their job. Nobody knows yet where or when our troops will be landing in Europe, but I'll be among the first to be told, as my boys will be parachuted into the target area a few days before the invasion.'

Harry was sitting on the edge of his seat.

'But before that balloon goes up, I'll be putting together a small specialist unit to prepare for any eventuality. This unit will consist of three groups, each comprising ten men: one captain, one staff sergeant, two corporals and six private soldiers. During the past few weeks I've been in touch with several prison wardens to ask if they had any exceptional men, who they felt might be suited for such an operation. Your name was one of the two put forward by Mr Swanson. Once I checked your record, from when you served in the navy, I had to agree with the warden that you'd be better off in uniform rather than wasting your time in here.'

Harry turned to the warden. 'Thank you, sir, but may I ask who the other person is?'

'Quinn,' said Swanson. 'The two of you have caused me so many problems during the past couple of years, I thought it was the Germans' turn to be subjected to your special brand of subterfuge.' Harry smiled.

'If you decide to join us, Bradshaw,' continued the colonel, 'you will begin an eight-week basic training course immediately, followed by a further six weeks with special operations. Before I go any further, I need to know if the idea appeals to you.'

'When do I start?' said Harry.

The colonel smiled. 'My car's outside in the yard, and I left the engine running.'

'I've already arranged for your civilian clothes to be collected from the stores,' said the warden. 'Obviously we need to keep the reason you've left at such short notice between ourselves. Should anyone ask, I'll say you and Quinn have been transferred to another prison.'

The colonel nodded. 'Any questions, Bradshaw?'

'Has Quinn agreed to join you?' asked Harry.

'He's sitting in the back seat of my car, probably wondering what's taking you so long.'

'But you do know the reason I'm in prison, colonel?'

'Desertion,' said Colonel Cleverdon. 'So I'll have to keep a close eye on you, won't I?' Both men laughed. 'You'll be joining my group as a private soldier, but I can assure you, your past record won't hinder your chances of promotion. However, while we're on that subject, Bradshaw, a change of name might be appropriate, given the circumstances. We wouldn't want some smart-ass in records to get their hands on your navy files and start asking embarrassing questions. Any ideas?'

'Harry Clifton, sir,' he said a little too quickly.

The warden smiled. 'I've always wondered what your real name was.'

EMMA BARRINGTON

1941

14

EMMA WANTED TO LEAVE Kristin's apartment as soon as possible, escape from New York and return to England. Once she was back in Bristol she could grieve alone and devote her life to bringing up Harry's son. But escape wasn't proving to be that easy.

'I'm so sorry,' said Kristin, placing an arm around Emma's shoulders. 'I had no idea you didn't know what had happened to Tom.'

Emma smiled weakly.

'I want you to know,' continued Kristin, 'that Richard and I never doubted even for a moment that he was innocent. The man I nursed back to life wasn't capable of murder.'

'Thank you,' said Emma.

'I have some photographs of Tom while he was with us on the *Kansas Star*. Would you like to see them?' asked Kristin.

Emma nodded politely, although she had no interest in seeing any photographs of Lieutenant Thomas Bradshaw. She decided that once Kristin had left the room, she would quietly slip out of the apartment and return to her hotel. She had no desire to continue making such a fool of herself in front of a complete stranger.

As soon as Kristin went out, Emma jumped up. As she did so, she knocked her cup off the table and on to the floor, spilling some coffee on the carpet. She fell to her knees and began weeping again, just as Kristin came back into the room, clutching a handful of photographs.

When she saw Emma on her knees in tears, she tried to comfort her. 'Please don't worry about the carpet, it's not important. Here, why don't you look at these, while I find something to clear it up?' She handed the photographs to Emma and quickly left the room again.

Emma accepted she could no longer make good her escape, so she returned to her chair and reluctantly began to look at the photos of Tom Bradshaw.

'Oh my God,' she said out loud. She stared in disbelief at a picture of Harry standing on the deck of a ship with the Statue of Liberty in the background, and then at another with the skyscrapers of Manhattan as the backdrop. Tears came to her eyes once again, even if she was unable to explain how it was possible. She waited impatiently for Kristin to return. It wasn't long before the conscientious housewife reappeared, knelt down and began to remove the small brown stain with a damp cloth.

'Do you know what happened to Tom after he was arrested?' Emma asked anxiously.

'Didn't anyone tell you?' asked Kristin, looking up. 'Apparently there wasn't enough evidence to try him for murder, and Jelks got him off. He was charged with desertion from the navy, pleaded guilty, and was sentenced to six years.'

Emma just didn't understand how Harry could have ended up in jail for a crime he obviously hadn't committed. 'Did the trial take place in New York?'

'Yes,' Kristin replied. 'As his lawyer was Sefton Jelks, Richard and I assumed he wasn't in need of any financial help.'

'I'm not sure I understand.'

'Sefton Jelks is the senior partner of one of New York's most prestigious law practices, so at least Tom was being well represented. When he came to see us about Tom, he seemed genuinely concerned. I know he also visited Dr Wallace and the ship's captain, and he assured all of us that Tom was innocent.'

'Do you know which prison they sent him to?' Emma asked quietly.

'Lavenham, in upstate New York. Richard and I tried to visit him, but Mr Jelks told us he didn't want to see anyone.'

'You've been so kind,' said Emma. 'Perhaps I can ask one more small favour before I leave. May I be allowed to keep one of these photographs?'

'Keep them all. Richard took dozens, he always does. Photography is his hobby.'

'I don't want to waste any more of your time,' said Emma, rising unsteadily to her feet.

'You're not wasting my time,' Kristin replied. 'What happened to Tom never made sense to either of us. When you see him, please pass on our best wishes,' she said as they walked out of the room. 'And if he'd like us to visit him, we'd be happy to.'

'Thank you,' said Emma as the chain was removed once again. As Kristin opened the door she said, 'We both realized Tom was desperately in love, but he didn't tell us you were English.'

15

EMMA SWITCHED ON the bedside light and once again studied the photographs of Harry standing on the deck of the *Kansas Star*. He looked so happy, so relaxed, and clearly unaware what awaited him when he stepped ashore.

She drifted in and out of sleep as she tried to work out why Harry would be willing to face a murder trial, and would plead guilty to desertion from a navy he'd never signed up for. She concluded that only Sefton Jelks could provide the answers. The first thing she needed to do was make an appointment to see him.

She glanced again at the bedside clock: 3.21. She got out of bed, put on a dressing gown, sat down at the little table and filled several sheets of hotel stationery with notes in preparation for her meeting with Sefton Jelks. It felt like prepping for an exam.

At six, she showered and dressed, then went downstairs to breakfast. A copy of the *New York Times* had been left on her table and she quickly turned the pages, only stopping to read one article. The Americans were becoming pessimistic about Britain being able to survive a German invasion, which was looking increasingly likely. Above a photograph of Winston Churchill standing on the white cliffs of Dover staring defiantly out across the Channel, his trademark cigar in place, was the headline, 'We will fight them on the beaches'.

Emma felt guilty about being away from her homeland. She must find Harry, get him released from prison and together they would return to Bristol.

The hotel receptionist looked up Jelks, Myers & Abernathy in the Manhattan telephone directory, wrote out an address on Wall Street and handed it to Emma.

The cab dropped her outside a vast steel and glass building that stretched high into the sky. She pushed through the revolving doors and checked a large board on the wall that listed the names of every firm on the forty-eight floors. Jelks, Myers & Abernathy was located on floors 20, 21 and 22; all enquiries at reception on the twentieth floor.

Emma joined a horde of grey-flannel-suited men who filled the first available elevator. When she stepped out on the twentieth floor, she was greeted by the sight of three smart women dressed in open-neck white blouses and black skirts, who sat behind a reception desk, something else she hadn't seen in Bristol. She marched confidently up to the desk. 'I'd like to see Mr Jelks.'

'Do you have an appointment?' the receptionist asked politely.

'No,' admitted Emma, who'd only ever dealt with a local solicitor, who was always available whenever a member of the Barrington family dropped in.

The receptionist looked surprised. Clients didn't just turn up at the front desk hoping to see the senior partner; they either wrote, or their secretary phoned to make an appointment in Mr Jelks's crowded diary. 'If I could take your name, I'll have a word with his assistant.'

'Emma Barrington.'

'Please have a seat, Miss Barrington. Someone will be with you shortly.'

Emma sat alone in a little alcove. 'Shortly' turned out to be more than half an hour, when another grey-suited man appeared carrying a yellow pad.

'My name is Samuel Anscott,' he said, offering his hand. 'I understand that you wish to see the senior partner.'

'That is correct.'

'I'm his legal assistant,' said Anscott as he took the seat opposite her. 'Mr Jelks has asked me to find out why you want to see him.'

'It's a private matter,' said Emma.

'I'm afraid he won't agree to see you unless I'm able to tell him what it's about.'

Emma pursed her lips. 'I'm a friend of Harry Clifton.'

She watched Anscott closely, but it was obvious that the name meant nothing to him, although he did make a note of it on his yellow pad.

'I have reason to believe that Harry Clifton was arrested for the murder of Adam Bradshaw, and that Mr Jelks represented him.'

This time the name did register, and the pen moved more swiftly across the pad.

'I wish to see Mr Jelks, in order to find out how a lawyer of his standing could have allowed my fiancé to take Thomas Bradshaw's place.'

A deep frown appeared on the young man's face. He clearly wasn't used to anyone referring to his boss in this way. 'I have no idea what you're talking about, Miss Barrington,' he said, which Emma suspected was true. 'But I will brief Mr Jelks, and come back to you. Perhaps you could give me a contact address.'

'I'm staying at the Mayflower Hotel,' said Emma, 'and I'm available to see Mr Jelks at any time.'

Anscott made another note on his pad, stood up, gave a curt nod, but this time didn't offer to shake hands. Emma felt confident that she wouldn't have to wait long before the senior partner agreed to see her.

She took a taxi back to the Mayflower Hotel, and could hear the phone ringing in her room even before she'd opened the door. She ran across the room, but by the time she picked up the receiver, the line had gone dead.

She sat down at the desk and began to write to her mother to say she'd arrived safely although she didn't mention the fact that she was now convinced Harry was alive. Emma would only do that when she'd seen him in the flesh. She was on the third page of the letter when the phone rang again. She picked it up.

'Good afternoon, Miss Barrington.'

'Good afternoon, Mr Anscott,' she said, not needing to be told who it was.

'I've spoken to Mr Jelks concerning your request for a meeting, but I'm afraid he's unable to see you, because it would create a conflict of interest with another client he represents. He is sorry not to be more helpful.'

The line went dead.

Emma remained at the desk, stunned, still clutching the phone, the words 'conflict of interest' ringing in her ears. Was there really another client and, if so, who could it be? Or was that just an excuse not to see her? She placed the receiver back in its cradle and sat still for some time, wondering what her grandfather would have done in these circumstances. She recalled one of his favourite maxims: there's more than one way to skin a cat.

Emma opened the desk drawer, thankful to find a fresh supply of stationery, and made a list of people who might be able to fill in some of the gaps created by Mr Jelks's supposed conflict of interest. She then went downstairs to reception, knowing that she was going to be fully occupied for the next few days. The receptionist tried to hide her surprise when the softly spoken young lady from England asked for the address of a courthouse, a police station and a prison.

Before she left the Mayflower, Emma dropped into the hotel's shop and purchased a yellow pad of her own. She walked out on to the pavement and hailed another cab.

It dropped her in a very different part of town to the one Mr Jelks inhabited. As she climbed the courthouse steps, Emma thought about Harry, and how he must have felt when he'd entered that same building, in very different circumstances. She asked the guard on the door where the reference library was, in the hope of finding out what those circumstances were.

'If you mean the records room, miss, it's in the basement,' the guard said.

After walking down two flights of stairs, Emma asked a clerk behind the counter if she could see the records for the case of the State of New York *v.* Bradshaw. The clerk handed her a form to fill in, which included the question, *Are you a student?* to which she answered yes. A few minutes later Emma was handed three large box files.

'We close in a couple hours,' she was warned. 'When the bell goes, you must return the records to this desk immediately.'

Once Emma had read a few pages of documents, she couldn't understand why the State hadn't proceeded with Tom Bradshaw's trial for murder, when they seemed to have such a strong case against him. The brothers had been sharing a hotel room; the whiskey decanter had Tom's bloody fingerprints all over it, and there was no suggestion anyone else had entered the room before Adam's body had been found lying in a pool of blood. But, worse, why had Tom fled the scene of the crime, and why had the state attorney settled for a guilty plea on the lesser charge of desertion? Even more puzzling was how Harry had ever become involved in the first place. Might the letter on Maisie's mantelpiece contain the answers to all these questions, or was it simply that Jelks knew something he didn't want her to find out?

Her thoughts were interrupted by a clanging bell, demanding that she return the files to the desk. Some questions had been answered, but far more remained unanswered. Emma made a note of two names she hoped could supply most of those answers, but would *they* also claim a conflict of interest?

She emerged from the courthouse just after five, clutching several more sheets of paper covered in her neat long-hand. She grabbed something called a Hershey's Bar and a Coke from a street vendor, before she hailed another cab and asked the driver to take her to the 24th precinct police station. She ate and drank on the move, something her mother would never have approved of.

On arrival at the police station, Emma asked to speak to either Detective Kolowski or Detective Ryan.

'They're both on nights this week,' she was told by the desk sergeant, 'so won't be back on duty until ten.'

Emma thanked him and decided to return to the hotel and have supper before going back to the 24th precinct at ten.

After a Caesar salad and her first knickerbocker glory, Emma returned to her room on the fourth floor. She lay down on the bed and thought about what she needed to ask Kolowski or Ryan, assuming either of them agreed to see her. Did Lieutenant Bradshaw have an American accent . . . ?

Emma fell into a deep sleep, to be jolted back to consciousness by the unfamiliar sound of a police siren blaring from the street below. Now she understood why the rooms on the upper floors were more expensive. She checked her watch. It was 1.15.

'Damn,' she cursed as she leapt off the bed, ran to the bathroom, soaked a flannel under the cold tap and covered her face. She quickly left the room and took the lift to the ground floor. When she stepped out of the hotel, she was surprised to find the street was just as busy, and the pavement every bit as crowded, as it had been at midday.

She hailed another cab and asked the driver to take her back to the 24th precinct. The New York cabbies were beginning to understand her, or was she beginning to understand them?

She climbed the steps to the police station a few

minutes before two. Another desk sergeant asked her to take a seat, and promised to let Kolowski or Ryan know she was waiting in reception.

Emma settled down for a long wait, but to her surprise, a couple of minutes later she heard the desk sergeant say, 'Hey, Karl, there's some lady sitting over there who says she wants to see you.' He gestured in Emma's direction.

Detective Kolowski, a coffee in one hand, a cigarette in the other, walked across and gave Emma a half smile. She wondered how quickly that smile would disappear when he discovered why she wanted to see him.

'How can I help you, ma'am?' he asked.

'My name is Emma Barrington,' she said, exaggerating her English accent, 'and I need to seek your advice on a private matter.'

'Then let's go to my office, Miss Barrington,' Kolowski said, and began to walk down a corridor until he came to a door which he kicked open with the heel of his shoe. 'Have a seat,' he said, pointing to the only other chair in the room. 'Can I get you a coffee?' he asked as Emma sat down.

'No, thank you.'

'A wise decision, ma'am,' he said as he placed his mug on the table, lit his cigarette and sat down. 'So, how can I help?'

'I understand that you were one of the detectives who arrested my fiancé.'

'What's his name?'

'Thomas Bradshaw.'

She was right. The look, the voice, the demeanour, everything about him changed. 'Yes, I was. And I can tell you, ma'am, it was an open and shut case until Sefton Jelks became involved.'

'But the case never came to trial,' Emma reminded him.

'Only because Bradshaw had Jelks as his lawyer. If that guy had defended Pontius Pilate, he would have convinced the jury that he was simply assisting a young carpenter who wanted to buy some nails for a cross he was working on.'

'Are you suggesting that Jelks—'

'No,' said Kolowski sarcastically before Emma could finish her sentence. 'I always thought it was a coincidence that the DA was coming up for re-election that year, and some of Jelks's clients were among his biggest campaign contributors. Anyway,' he continued after exhaling a long cloud of smoke, 'Bradshaw ended up getting six years for desertion, when the precinct's sweepstakes had him down for eighteen months – two years tops.'

'What are you suggesting?' asked Emma.

'That the judge accepted Bradshaw was guilty –' Kolowski paused and blew out another cloud of smoke before adding – 'of murder.'

'I agree with you and the judge,' said Emma. 'Tom Bradshaw probably was guilty of murder.' Kolowski looked surprised. 'But did the man you arrested ever tell you that you'd made a mistake, and that he wasn't Tom Bradshaw, but Harry Clifton?'

The detective gave Emma a closer look, and thought for a moment. 'He did say something like that early on, but Jelks must have told him that it wouldn't fly, because he never mentioned it again.'

'Would you be interested, Mr Kolowski, if I was able to prove that it would fly?'

'No, ma'am,' said Kolowski firmly. 'That case was closed a long time ago. Your fiancé is doin' six years for a crime he pleaded guilty to, and I've got too much work on my desk – ' he placed a hand on a stack of files – 'to be reopening old wounds. Now, unless you got anything else I can help you with . . .'

'Will they allow me to visit Tom at Lavenham?'

'I can't see why not,' said Kolowski. 'Write to the warden. He'll send you a visiting order. After you've filled it in and sent it back, they'll give you a date. It shouldn't take more than six to eight weeks.'

'But I haven't got six weeks,' protested Emma. 'I need to return to England in a couple of weeks' time. Isn't there anything I can do to speed up the process?'

'That's only possible on compassionate grounds,' said the detective, 'and that's limited to wives and parents.'

'What about the mother of the prisoner's child?' countered Emma.

'In New York, ma'am, that gives you the same rights as a wife, as long as you can prove it.'

Emma produced two photos from her handbag, one of Sebastian and one of Harry standing on the deck of the *Kansas Star*.

'That's good enough for me,' said Kolowski handing back the picture of Harry without commenting. 'If you promise to leave me in peace I'll speak to the warden and see if anything can be done.'

'Thank you,' said Emma.

'How do I reach you?'

'I'm staying at the Mayflower Hotel.'

'I'll be in touch,' said Kolowski, making a note. 'But I don't want you to be in any doubt, ma'am, that Tom Bradshaw killed his brother. I'm sure of it.'

'And I don't want you to be in any doubt, officer, that the man locked up in Lavenham is not Tom Bradshaw. I'm sure of that.' Emma placed the photographs back in her bag and rose to leave.

A frown appeared on the detective's face as she walked out of the room.

Emma returned to her hotel, undressed and went straight back to bed. She lay awake wondering if Kolowski might be having second thoughts about whether he'd arrested the right man. She still couldn't work out why Jelks had allowed Harry to be sentenced to six years, when it would have been so easy for him to prove that Harry wasn't Tom Bradshaw.

She finally fell asleep, grateful not to be woken by any nocturnal visitors.

◄○►

The phone rang when she was in the bathroom, but by the time she'd picked it up, there was only a dial tone.

The second call came just as she was closing the door of her room on her way down to breakfast. She dashed back inside and grabbed the phone, to hear a voice she recognized on the other end of the line.

'Good morning, Officer Kolowski,' she replied.

'The news isn't good,' said the detective, who didn't deal in small talk. She collapsed on to the bed, fearing the worst. 'I spoke to the warden of Lavenham just before I came off duty, and he told me that Bradshaw has made it clear he doesn't want any visitors, no exceptions. It seems that Mr Jelks has issued an order that he's not even to be informed when someone asks to see him.'

'Couldn't you try to get a message to him somehow?' begged Emma. 'I'm sure that if he knew it was me—'

'Not a hope, lady,' said Kolowski. 'You have no idea how far Jelks's tentacles reach.'

'He can overrule a prison warden?'

'A prison warden is small fry. The DA and half the judges in New York are under his thumb. Just don't tell anyone I said so.'

The line went dead.

Emma didn't know how much time had passed before she heard a knock on the door. Who could it possibly be? The door opened and a friendly face peered in.

'Can I clean the room, miss?' asked a woman pushing a trolley.

'I'll only be a couple of minutes,' said Emma. She checked her watch and was surprised to find it was ten past ten. She needed to clear her head before she could consider her next move, and decided to take a long walk in Central Park.

She strolled around the park before making a decision. The time had come to visit her great-aunt and seek her advice about what she should do next.

Emma headed off in the direction of 64th and Park, and was so deep in thought about how she was going to explain to Great-aunt Phyllis why she hadn't visited her earlier, that what she saw didn't fully register. She stopped, turned and retraced her steps, checking every window until she reached Doubleday's. A pyramid of books dominated the centre window, alongside a photograph of a man with slicked-back black hair and a pencil moustache. He was smiling out at her.

THE DIARY OF A CONVICT:
My time at Lavenham maximum security prison
by
Max Lloyd

The author of the runaway bestseller
will be signing books in this store
at 5.00 p.m. on Thursday

Don't miss this opportunity to meet the author

GILES BARRINGTON

1941

16

GILES HAD NO IDEA where the regiment was going. For days he seemed to be perpetually on the move, never able to sleep for more than a couple of hours at a time. First he boarded a train, followed by a truck, before he climbed up the gangway of a troop carrier that ploughed through the ocean waves at its own pace, until it finally disgorged 1,000 soldiers from the Wessex at the Egyptian port of Alexandria on the North African coast.

During the voyage, Giles had been reunited with his chums from Ypres camp on Dartmoor, who he had to accept were now under his command. One or two of them, Bates in particular, didn't find it easy to call him sir, and found it even more difficult to salute him every time they bumped into each other.

A convoy of army vehicles awaited the Wessex Regiment as they disembarked from the ship. Giles had never experienced such intense heat and his fresh khaki shirt was soaked in sweat within moments of him stepping on foreign soil. He quickly organized his men into three groups before they climbed on board the waiting trucks. The convoy progressed slowly along a narrow, dusty coastal road, not stopping for several hours until they finally reached the outskirts of a badly bombed town that Bates announced in a loud voice, 'Tobruk! Told you so,' and money began to change hands.

Once they'd entered the town, the convoy dropped the men at various points. Giles and the other officers jumped off outside the Majestic Hotel, which had been requisitioned by the Wessex as their company HQ. Giles pushed his way through the revolving doors and quickly discovered there wasn't much majestic about the hotel. Makeshift offices had been crammed into every available space. Charts and maps were pinned on walls where paintings had once hung, and the plush red carpet that welcomed VIPs from all over the world had worn thin with the continual tramping of studded boots.

The reception area was the only feature to remind them this might once have been a hotel. A duty corporal checked off Second Lieutenant Barrington's name on a long list of new arrivals.

'Room two-one-nine,' he said, handing him an envelope. 'You'll find everything you need in there, sir.'

Giles strode up the wide staircase to the second floor and let himself into the room. He sat on the bed, opened the envelope and read his orders. At seven o'clock he was to report to the ballroom, when the colonel of the regiment would address all officers. Giles unpacked his suitcase, took a shower, put on a clean shirt and went back downstairs. He grabbed a sandwich and a cup of tea from the officers' mess and made his way to the ballroom just before seven.

The large room, with its high imperial ceiling and magnificent chandeliers, was already filled with boisterous officers, who were being reunited with old friends and introduced to new ones as they waited to find out which square on the chessboard they would be moved to. Giles caught a glimpse of a young lieutenant on the far side of the room whom he thought he recognized, but then lost sight of him.

At one minute to seven, Lieutenant Colonel Robertson marched up on to the stage, and everyone else in the room quickly fell silent and sprang to attention. He stopped in the centre of the stage and waved the men down. Feet apart, hands on hips, he began to address them.

'Gentlemen, it must seem strange to you to have travelled from all parts of the empire to do battle with the Germans in North Africa. However, Field Marshal Rommel and his Afrika Korps are also here, with the purpose of maintaining a supply of oil for their troops in Europe. It is our responsibility to send him back to Berlin with a bloody nose, long before their last tank has run out of petrol.'

Cheers erupted around the hall, accompanied by the stamping of feet.

'General Wavell has granted the Wessex the privilege of defending Tobruk, and I have told him that we will all sacrifice our lives before Rommel books a suite at the Majestic Hotel.'

This was greeted with even louder cheers and more stamping of feet.

'Now I want you all to report to your company commanders, who will brief you on our overall plan to defend the town, and the responsibilities each of you will be expected to carry out. Gentlemen, we haven't a moment to waste. Good luck, and happy hunting.'

The officers all sprang to attention again as the colonel left the stage. Giles checked his orders once more. He'd been allocated to 7 Platoon, C company, which was to meet in the hotel library following the colonel's address for a briefing by Major Richards.

'You must be Barrington,' said the major when Giles walked into the library a few minutes later. Giles saluted. 'It was good of you to join us so soon after being commissioned. I've put you in charge of seven platoon as understudy to your old friend. You will have three sections of twelve men, and your responsibility will be to patrol the west perimeter of the city. You will have a sergeant and three corporals to assist you. The lieutenant will brief you on the finer details. As you were at school together, you won't have to spend too much time getting to know each other.'

Giles wondered who it could be. And then he recalled the familiar lone figure on the other side of the ballroom.

—◦—

Second Lieutentant Giles Barrington would have liked to give Lieutenant Fisher the benefit of the doubt, although he would never be able to erase the memory of him as a prefect at St Bede's, when he thrashed Harry every night during his first week for no reason other than that he was a docker's son.

'It's good to catch up with you, Barrington, after such a long time,' said Fisher. 'I can't see any reason why we shouldn't work well together, can you?' He obviously also recalled his treatment of Harry Clifton. Giles managed a weak smile.

'We've got over thirty men under our command,

along with three corporals and a sergeant. Some of them you'll remember from your days at training camp. In fact, I've already put Corporal Bates in charge of number one section.'

'Terry Bates?'

'Corporal Bates,' repeated Fisher. 'Never use a Christian name when you're referring to the other ranks. In the mess, and when we're on our own, Giles, you can call me Alex, but never in front of the men. I'm sure you understand.'

You always were an arrogant little shit, and clearly nothing has changed, thought Giles. This time he didn't smile.

'Now, it's our responsibility to patrol the western perimeter of the town in four-hour watches. Don't underestimate the importance of our task, because if Rommel does attack Tobruk, intelligence is that he'll try and enter the city from the west. So we have to remain vigilant at all times. I'll leave it to you to fix the rotas. I usually manage a couple of shifts a day, but I can't do a lot more because of my other responsibilities.'

Like what, Giles wanted to ask him.

Giles enjoyed patrolling the west side of the town with his men, and quickly got to know all thirty-six of them, not least because Corporal Bates kept him so well informed. And although he tried to keep them on perpetual alert following Fisher's warning, as the weeks passed without incident, he began to wonder if they'd ever come face to face with the enemy.

◄○►

It was on a hazy evening in early April, when all three of Giles's patrols were out on an exercise, that a volley of bullets came from nowhere. The men instantly hit the ground, and quickly crawled to the nearest building to find whatever cover they could.

Giles had been with the leading section when the Germans presented their calling card, then fired off a second volley. The bullets fell nowhere near their target, but he knew it wouldn't be long before the enemy identified his position.

'Don't fire until I say so,' he ordered as he slowly scanned the horizon with his binoculars. He decided to brief Fisher before he made a move. He picked up the field phone and got an immediate response.

'How many of them are there, do you think?' Fisher asked.

'I'd guess no more than seventy, at most eighty. If you bring forward number two and three sections, that should be more than enough to hold them off until reinforcements arrive.'

A third volley followed, but after Giles had scanned the horizon, he once again gave the order, 'Hold your fire.'

'I'll send up Two Section under Sergeant Harris to support you,' said Fisher, 'and if you keep me briefed, I'll decide whether to join you with Three Section.' The phone went dead.

A fourth volley quickly followed the third, and this time when Giles focused his binoculars, he could see a dozen men crawling across the open ground towards them.

'Take aim, but don't fire until the target is in range, and make sure every bullet counts.'

Bates was the first to squeeze his trigger. 'Got you,' he said as a German collapsed into the desert sand. As he reloaded, he added, 'That'll teach you to bomb Broad Street.'

'Shut up, Bates, and concentrate,' said Giles.

'Sorry, sir.'

Giles continued to scan the horizon. He could see two, possibly three men who'd been hit and were lying face down in the sand a few yards from their dugouts. He gave the order to fire another volley and Giles watched as several more Germans scampered back to safety, like ants scurrying down a hole.

'Cease fire!' shouted Giles, aware that they couldn't afford to waste precious ammunition. He looked to his left and could see 2 Section already in position under Sergeant Harris, awaiting their orders.

He picked up the field phone and Fisher came back on the line. 'My ammunition won't last much longer, sir. My left flank's now covered by Sergeant Harris, but my right flank's exposed. If you were able to come forward, we'd have a better chance of holding them off.'

'Now that you've got Two Section to strengthen your position, Barrington, I'd better stay back and cover you, in case they break through.'

Another volley of bullets flew in their direction. The Germans had clearly worked out exactly where they were positioned, but Giles still instructed his two sections to hold fire. He cursed, put down the phone and ran across the open gap to join Sergeant Harris. A volley followed his trouble.

'What do you think, sergeant?'

'It's a half-company, sir, about eighty men in all. But I think they're just a reconnaissance party, so all we have to do is bed down and be patient.'

'I agree,' said Giles. 'What do you think they'll do?'

'The Krauts will know that they outnumber us, so they'll want to mount an attack before any reinforcements arrive. If Lieutenant Fisher brought up Three Section to cover our right flank, it would strengthen our position.'

'I agree,' repeated Giles as another volley greeted them. 'I'll go back and speak to Fisher. Await my orders.'

Giles zigzagged across the open terrain. This time the bullets were a little too close to risk that trick again. He was just about to call Fisher when the field phone rang. He grabbed it.

'Barrington,' said Fisher. 'I believe the time has come for us to take the initiative.'

Giles needed to repeat Fisher's words to be sure he'd heard them correctly. 'You want me to lead an attack on the Germans' position, while you bring forward Three Section to cover me.'

'If we do that,' said Bates, 'we'd be like sitting ducks on a rifle range.'

'Shut up, Bates.'

'Yes, sir.'

'Sergeant Harris thinks, and I agree with him,' continued Giles, 'that if you bring up Three Section to cover our right flank, the Germans will have to mount an attack, and then we could—'

'I'm not interested in what Sergeant Harris thinks,' said Fisher. 'I give the orders and you'll carry them out. Is that clear?'

'Yes, sir,' Giles said as he slammed down the phone.

'I could always kill him, sir,' said Bates.

Giles ignored him as he loaded his pistol and attached six hand grenades to his webbed belt. He stood up so that both platoons could see him, and said in a loud voice, 'Fix bayonets and prepare to advance.' He then stepped out from behind his cover and shouted, 'Follow me!'

As Giles began to run across the deep scorching sand with Sergeant Harris and Corporal Bates only a stride behind him, he was greeted with yet another volley of bullets and wondered how long he would survive against such overwhelming odds. With forty yards still to cover, he could see exactly where the three enemy dugouts were situated. He snatched a hand grenade from his belt, removed the pin and tossed it towards the centre dugout, as if he was returning a cricket ball from the deep boundary into the wicket-keeper's gloves. It landed just above the stumps. Giles saw two men fly into the air, while another fell back.

He swung round and hurled a second grenade to his left, a definite run-out, because the enemy's firepower suddenly dried up. The third grenade took out a machine gun. As Giles charged on, he could see the men who had him in their sights. He took his pistol out of its holster and began to fire as if he was on a shooting range but this time the bullseyes were human beings. One, two, three went down, and then Giles saw a German officer lining him up in his sights. The German pulled the trigger just a moment too late, and collapsed on the ground in front of him. Giles felt sick.

When he was only a yard from the dugout, a young German dropped his rifle on the ground, while another threw his arms high into the air. Giles stared into the desperate eyes of the defeated men. He didn't need to speak German to know they didn't want to die.

'Cease fire!' screamed Giles, as what was left of

1 and 2 sections quickly overwhelmed the enemy positions. 'Round them up and disarm them, Sergeant Harris,' he added, then turned back to see Harris, head down in the sand, blood trickling out of his mouth, only yards from the dugout.

Giles stared back across the open terrain they had crossed and tried not to count the number of soldiers who had sacrificed their lives because of one man's weak decision. Stretcher bearers were already removing the dead bodies from the battlefield.

'Corporal Bates, line up the enemy prisoners in threes, and march them back to camp.'

'Yes, sir,' said Bates, sounding as if he meant it.

A few minutes later, Giles and his depleted band headed back across the open ground. They had covered about fifty yards when Giles saw Fisher running towards him, with 3 Section following in his wake.

'Right, Barrington, I'll take over,' he shouted. 'You bring up the rear. Follow me,' he ordered as he led the captured German soldiers triumphantly back towards the town.

By the time they reached the Majestic Hotel, a small crowd had gathered to cheer them. Fisher returned the salutes of his brother officers.

'Barrington, see that the prisoners are interned, then take the lads off to the canteen for a drink; they've earned it. Meanwhile, I'll report to Major Richards.'

'Can I kill him, sir?' asked Bates.

17

WHEN GILES came down for breakfast the following morning, several officers, some of whom he'd never spoken to before, went out of their way to shake hands with him.

As he strolled into the mess, several heads turned and smiled in his direction, which he found slightly embarrassing. He grabbed a bowl of porridge, two boiled eggs and an out-of-date copy of *Punch*. He sat alone, hoping to be left in peace, but a few moments later three Australian officers he didn't recognize joined him. He turned a page of *Punch*, and laughed at an E.H. Shepard cartoon of Hitler retreating from Calais on a penny farthing.

'An incredible act of courage,' said the Australian on his right.

Giles could feel himself turning red.

'I agree,' said a voice from the other side of the table. 'Quite remarkable.'

Giles wanted to leave before they . . .

'What did you say the fellow's name was?'

Giles took a spoonful of porridge.

'Fisher.'

Giles nearly choked.

'It seems that Fisher, against all odds, led his platoon over open terrain and, with only hand grenades and a pistol, took out three dugouts full of German soldiers.'

'Unbelievable!' said another voice.

At least Giles could agree with that.

'And is it true that he killed a Hun officer and then took fifty of the bastards prisoner, with only twelve men to back him up?'

Giles removed the top of his first boiled egg. It was hard.

'It must be true,' said another voice, 'because he's been promoted to captain.'

Giles sat and stared at the yolk of his egg.

'I'm told he'll be recommended for a Military Cross.'

'That's the least he deserves.'

The least he deserved, thought Giles, was what Bates had recommended.

'Anyone else involved in the action?' asked the voice from the other side of the table.

'Yes, his second in command, but I'm damned if I can remember his name.'

Giles had heard enough and decided to let Fisher know exactly what he thought of him. Leaving his second egg untouched, he marched out of the mess and headed straight for the ops room. He was so angry that he barged in without knocking. The moment he entered the room, he sprang to attention and saluted. 'I do apologize, sir,' he said. 'I had no idea you were here.'

'This is Mr Barrington, colonel,' said Fisher. 'You'll remember that I told you he assisted me in yesterday's action.'

'Ah, yes. Barrington. Good show. You may not have

seen company orders this morning, but you've been promoted to full lieutenant, and having read Captain Fisher's report, I can tell you that you'll also be mentioned in dispatches.'

'Many congratulations, Giles,' said Fisher. 'Well deserved.'

'Indeed,' said the colonel. 'And while you're here, Barrington, I was just saying to Captain Fisher, now that he's identified Rommel's preferred route into Tobruk, we'll need to double our patrols on the west side of the city and deploy a full squadron of tanks to back you up.' He jabbed the map spread out on the table with his finger. 'Here, here and here. I hope you both agree?'

'I do, sir,' said Fisher. 'I'll set about getting the platoon in place immediately.'

'Can't be too soon,' said the colonel, 'because I have a feeling it won't be long before Rommel returns, and this time he won't be on a reconnaissance mission but leading the full force of the Afrika Korps. We must be lying in wait and be sure that he walks straight into our trap.'

'We'll be ready for him, sir,' said Fisher.

'Good. Because I'm putting you in charge of our new patrols, Fisher. Barrington, you will remain second in command.'

'I'll have my report on your desk by midday, sir,' said Fisher.

'Good show, Fisher. I'll leave you to work out the details.'

'Thank you, sir,' said Fisher, standing to attention and saluting as the colonel left the room.

Giles was about to speak, but Fisher quickly jumped

in. 'I've put in a recommendation that Sergeant Harris should be awarded a posthumous military medal, and Corporal Bates should also be mentioned in dispatches. I hope you'll support me.'

'Am I also to understand that you've been put up for a Military Cross?' asked Giles.

'That's not in my hands, old fellow, but I'm happy to go along with whatever the commanding officer sees fit. Now, let's get down to business. With six patrols now under our command, I propose that we . . .'

—◦—

After what had become known by 1 and 2 sections as 'Fisher's Fantasy', everyone from the colonel downwards was on red alert. Two platoons patrolled the western edge of the town, one on, one off, night and day, no longer wondering if, only when, Rommel would appear over the horizon at the head of his Afrika Korps.

Even Fisher, in his newly elevated state as hero, had to appear occasionally on the outer perimeter, if simply to maintain the myth of his heroic deed, but only long enough to be sure everyone had seen him. He would then report back to the tank squadron commander, three miles to the rear, and set up his field phones.

—◦—

The Desert Fox chose April 11th, 1941 to begin his assault on Tobruk. The British and Australians couldn't have fought more bravely when defending the perimeter against the German onslaught. But as the months passed and supplies of food and ammunition began to run low, few doubted – though it was never voiced –

that it could only be a matter of time before the sheer size of Rommel's army would overwhelm them.

It was a Friday morning, just as the desert haze was clearing, that Lieutenant Barrington scanned the horizon with his binoculars and focused on rows and rows of German tanks.

'Shit,' he said. He grabbed the field phone as a shell hit the building he and his men had selected as their observation post. Fisher came on the other end of the line. 'I can see forty, possibly fifty tanks heading towards us,' Giles told him, 'and what looks like a full regiment of soldiers to back them up. Permission to withdraw my men to a more secure position where we can regroup and take up battle formation?'

'Hold your ground,' said Fisher, 'and once the enemy's within range, engage them.'

'Engage them?' said Giles. 'What with, bows and arrows? This isn't Agincourt, Fisher. I've got barely a hundred men facing a regiment of tanks, with nothing more than rifles to protect ourselves. For God's sake, Fisher, allow me to decide what's best for my men.'

'Hold your ground,' repeated Fisher, 'and engage the enemy when they come within range. That's an order.'

Giles slammed the phone down.

'For some reason best known to himself,' said Bates, 'that man doesn't want you to survive. You should have let me shoot him.'

Another shell hit the building while masonry and rubble began to fall around them. Giles no longer needed binoculars to see just how many tanks were advancing towards them, and to accept that he only had moments left to live.

'Take aim!' He suddenly thought of Sebastian, who would inherit the family title. If the boy turned out to be half as good as Harry had been, the Barrington dynasty need have no fear for its future.

The next shell hit the building behind them, and Giles could clearly see a German soldier returning his stare from the turret of his tank. 'Fire!'

As the building began to collapse around him, Giles thought about Emma, Grace, his father, his mother, his grandfathers, and . . . The next shell brought the entire edifice crashing down. Giles looked up, to see a large piece of masonry falling, falling, falling. He leapt on top of Bates, who was still firing at an advancing tank.

The last image Giles saw was Harry swimming to safety.

EMMA BARRINGTON

1941

18

EMMA SAT ALONE in her hotel room reading *The Diary of a Convict* from cover to cover. She didn't know who Max Lloyd was, but she was sure of one thing: he wasn't the author.

Only one man could have written this book. She recognized so many familiar phrases, and Lloyd hadn't even bothered to change all the names, unless of course he had a girlfriend called Emma whom he still adored.

Emma turned the last page just before midnight, and decided to make a phone call to someone who would still be at work.

'Just one more favour,' she begged when his voice came on the line.

'Try me,' he said.

'I need the name of Max Lloyd's parole officer.'

'Max Lloyd the author?'

'No less.'

'I'm not even going to ask why.'

She began to read the book a second time, making pencil notes in the margin, but long before the new deputy librarian had started, she had fallen asleep. She woke around five the next morning, and didn't stop reading until a prison officer entered the library and said, 'Lloyd, the warden wants to see you.'

Emma took a long, lazy bath, and considered the fact that all the information she'd been trying so hard to discover had been available for a dollar fifty from any bookstore.

Once she was dressed, she went down to breakfast and picked up a copy of the *New York Times*. She was taken by surprise as she turned the pages to come across a review of *The Diary of a Convict*.

> We should be grateful to Mr Lloyd for bring-
> ing to our attention what is happening in our
> prisons today. Lloyd is a gifted writer with
> real talent, and we must hope that now he's
> been released, he will not put down his pen.

He never picked it up in the first place, thought Emma indignantly as she signed her bill.

Before going back up to her room, she asked the receptionist to recommend a good restaurant near Doubleday's bookstore.

'The Brasserie, madam. It has a first-class reputa-tion. Would you like me to book a table for you?'

'Yes, please,' said Emma. 'I'd like a table for one at lunch today, and another for two this evening.'

The receptionist was quickly learning not to be surprised by the lady from England.

Emma returned to her room and settled down to read the diary once more. She was puzzled why the narrative opened with Harry's arrival at Lavenham, despite the fact that there were several references scattered throughout the book which suggested that his previous experiences had also been recorded, even if they hadn't been seen by the publisher, and certainly not the public. In fact, this convinced Emma that there had to be another notebook in existence, which would not only describe Harry's arrest and trial, but might explain why he had put himself through such an ordeal, when a lawyer of Mr Jelks's standing must have known that he was not Tom Bradshaw.

After reading marked pages of the diaries for a third time, Emma decided another long stroll in the park was required. As she walked up Lexington Avenue, she dropped into Bloomingdale's and placed an order that she was assured would be ready for collection by three o'clock. In Bristol, the same order would have taken a fortnight.

As she walked through the park, a plan was beginning to form in her mind, but she needed to return to Doubleday's and take a closer look at the store's layout before she could apply the finishing touches. When she walked into the bookstore, the staff were already preparing for the author signing. A table was in place and a roped-off area showed clearly where the line should form. The poster in the window now had a bold red banner across it declaring, **TODAY**.

Emma selected a gap between two rows of shelves from which she would have a clear view of Lloyd while he was signing, and would be able to observe her prey while setting him a trap.

She left Doubleday's just before 1 p.m., and made her way across Fifth Avenue to the Brasserie. A waiter showed her to a table that would never have been considered acceptable by either of her grandfathers. But the meal was, as promised, first class, and when the bill was presented, she took a deep breath, and left a large tip.

'I've booked a table for this evening,' she said to the waiter. 'Would it be possible to be seated in an alcove?' The waiter looked doubtful, until Emma produced a dollar bill, which seemed to remove any doubt. She was getting the hang of how things worked in America.

'What's your name?' Emma asked as she passed him the note.

'Jimmy,' the waiter replied.

'And another thing, Jimmy.'

'Yes, ma'am?'

'May I keep a copy of the menu?'

'Of course, ma'am.'

On the way back to the Mayflower, Emma called in at Bloomingdale's and picked up her order. She smiled when the clerk showed her an example of the card. 'I hope it's satisfactory, madam.'

'Couldn't be better,' said Emma. Once she was back in her room, she went over her prepared questions again and again, and after deciding on the best possible order, she pencilled them neatly on to the back of the menu. Exhausted, she lay down on the bed and fell into a deep sleep.

When the persistent ringing of the phone woke her, it was already dark outside. She checked her watch: 5.10 p.m.

'Damn,' she said as she picked up the phone.

'I know the feeling,' said a voice on the other end of the line, 'even if that wasn't the four-letter word I would have chosen.' Emma laughed. 'The name you're looking for is Brett Elders . . . I didn't tell you.'

'Thank you,' said Emma. 'I'll try not to bother you again.'

'I wish,' said the detective, and the line went dead.

Emma wrote the name 'Brett Elders' neatly in pencil at the top right-hand corner of the menu. She would have liked to take a quick shower and change her clothes, but she was already running late and she couldn't afford to miss him.

She grabbed the menu and three of the cards. Stuffing them into her bag, she then dashed out of the door and down the staircase, not waiting for the elevator. She hailed a cab and leapt into the back. 'Doubleday's on Fifth,' she said, 'and make it snappy.'

Oh no, Emma thought, as the taxi sped away. What's happening to me?

─◦─

Emma entered the crowded bookstore and took her chosen spot between politics and religion, from where she could observe Max Lloyd at work.

He was signing each book with a flourish, basking in the glow of his adoring fans. Emma knew it should have been Harry sitting there receiving the accolades. Did he even know his work had been published? Would she find out tonight?

As it turned out, she needn't have rushed, because Lloyd went on signing his runaway bestseller for another hour, until the line began to dwindle. He was taking longer and longer with each message, in the hope that it might entice others to join the queue.

As he was chatting expansively to the last customer in the line, Emma deserted her post and strolled across.

'And how is your dear mother?' the customer was asking effusively.

'Very well, thank you,' said Lloyd. 'No longer having to work in a hotel,' he added, 'following the success of my book.'

The customer smiled. 'And Emma, dare I ask?'

'We're going to be married in the fall,' said Lloyd after he'd signed her copy.

Are we indeed? thought Emma.

'Oh, I'm so glad,' said the customer. 'She sacrificed so much for you. Do give her my best wishes.'

Why don't you turn around and do it in person, Emma wanted to say.

'I most certainly will,' said Lloyd, as he handed her the book and gave her his back-cover smile.

Emma stepped forward and handed a card to Lloyd. He studied it for a moment before the same smile reappeared.

'A fellow agent,' he said, standing to greet her.

Emma shook his outstretched hand, and somehow managed to return his smile. 'Yes,' she said, 'and several publishers in London are showing considerable interest in the rights to your book. Of course, if you've already signed a contract, or are represented by another agent in England, I wouldn't want to waste your time.'

'No, no, dear lady, I'm very happy to consider any proposal you might have.'

'Then perhaps you would join me for dinner, so we can talk further?'

'I think they're expecting me to have dinner with them,' whispered Lloyd, waving an expansive hand in the direction of some of the members of the Doubleday staff.

'What a pity,' said Emma. 'I'm flying to LA tomorrow to visit Hemingway.'

'Then I'll have to disappoint them, won't I?' said Lloyd. 'I'm sure they'll understand.'

'Good. Shall we meet at the Brasserie, then, when you've finished signing?'

'You'll do well to get a table at such short notice.'

'I don't think that will be a problem,' said Emma, before one last customer stepped forward, still hoping to get a signature. 'I'll look forward to seeing you later, Mr Lloyd.'

'Max, please.'

Emma made her way out of the bookstore and walked across Fifth Avenue to the Brasserie. This time she wasn't kept waiting.

'Jimmy,' she said as the waiter accompanied her to an alcove table, 'I have a very important client joining me, and I want it to be an evening he won't forget.'

'You can rely on me, madam,' the waiter said as Emma sat down. After he'd gone she opened her bag, took out the menu and went over her list of questions once more. When she saw Jimmy heading towards her with Max Lloyd in his wake, she turned the menu over.

'You're obviously well known here,' said Lloyd as he slipped into the seat opposite her.

'It's my favourite New York restaurant,' said Emma, returning his smile.

'Can I get you a drink, sir?'

'Manhattan, on the rocks.'

'And you, madam?'

'My usual, Jimmy.'

The waiter hurried off. Emma was curious to discover what he would come back with. 'Why don't we order,' said Emma, 'and then we can get down to business.'

'Good idea,' replied Lloyd. 'Although I know exactly what I want,' he added as the waiter reappeared and placed a Manhattan in front of him and a glass of white wine by Emma's side; the drink she'd ordered at lunch. Emma was impressed.

'Jimmy, I think we're ready to order.' The waiter nodded and turned to Emma's guest.

'I'll have one of your juicy sirloin steaks. Make it medium, and don't spare on the trimmings.'

'Certainly, sir.' Turning to Emma, he asked, 'What can I tempt you with this evening, madam?'

'A Caesar salad please, Jimmy, but light on the dressing.'

Once the waiter was out of earshot, she turned her menu back over, although she didn't need to be reminded of the first question. 'The diary only covered eighteen months of your incarceration,' she said. 'But you served more than two years, so I hope we can look forward to another volume.'

'I still have a notebook full of material,' said Lloyd, relaxing for the first time. 'I've been thinking about incorporating some of the more extraordinary events I experienced in a novel that I have planned.'

Because if you ever wrote them as a diary, any publisher would realize you weren't the author, Emma wanted to say.

The sommelier appeared by Lloyd's side, summoned by the demand of an empty glass.

'Would you care to see the wine list, sir? Something to complement the steak, perhaps?'

'Good idea,' said Lloyd, opening the thick, leather-bound book as if he were the host. He ran his finger down a long list of burgundies, and paused near the bottom. 'A bottle of the thirty-seven, I think.'

'An excellent choice, sir.'

Emma presumed that meant it wasn't cheap. But this was not an occasion to quibble over price.

'And what a nasty piece of work Hessler turned out to be,' she said, glancing at her second question. 'I thought that sort of person only existed in trashy novels, or B-movies.'

'No, he was real enough,' said Lloyd. 'But I did get him transferred to another prison, if you remember.'

'I do,' said Emma, as a large steak was placed in front of her guest and a Caesar salad on her side of the table. Lloyd picked up his knife and fork, clearly ready for the challenge.

'So tell me, what sort of proposal do you have in mind?' he asked as he dug into the steak.

'One where you get exactly what you're worth,' said Emma, the tone of her voice changing, 'and not a penny more.' A puzzled look appeared on Lloyd's face, and he put down his knife and fork as he waited for Emma to continue. 'I am well aware, Mr Lloyd, that you didn't write one word of *The Diary of a Convict*, other than to replace the real author's name with your own.' Lloyd opened his mouth, but before he had time to protest, Emma continued, 'If you're foolish enough to keep up the pretence that you wrote the book, my first visit in the morning will be to Mr Brett Elders, your parole officer, and it won't be to discuss how well your rehabilitation is going.'

The sommelier reappeared, uncorked a bottle, and

waited to be told who would be tasting the wine. Lloyd was staring at Emma like a rabbit caught in the glare of headlights, so she gave a slight nod. She took her time swirling the wine around in her glass before taking a sip.

'Excellent,' she eventually said. 'I particularly like the thirty-seven.' The sommelier bowed slightly, poured two glasses and went off in search of another victim.

'You can't prove I didn't write it,' said Lloyd defiantly.

'Yes I can,' said Emma, 'because I represent the man who did.' She took a sip of wine before adding, 'Tom Bradshaw, your deputy librarian.' Lloyd sank back into his seat and lapsed into a sullen silence. 'So let me outline the deal I'm proposing, Mr Lloyd, while at the same time making it clear that there is no room for negotiation, unless, of course, you want to go back to prison on a charge of fraud, as well as theft. Should you end up in Pierpoint, I have a feeling Mr Hessler will be only too happy to escort you to your cell, as he doesn't come out of the book very well.'

Lloyd didn't look as if the idea appealed to him.

Emma took another sip of wine before continuing. 'Mr Bradshaw has generously agreed to allow you to continue the myth that you wrote the diary, and he won't even expect you to give back the advance you were paid, which in any case I suspect you've already spent.' Lloyd pursed his lips. 'However, he wishes to make it clear that should you be foolish enough to attempt to sell the rights in any other country, a writ for copyright theft will be issued against you and the publisher concerned. Is that clear?'

'Yes,' mumbled Lloyd, clutching the arms of his chair.

'Good. Then that's settled,' said Emma, and after taking another sip of wine added, 'I feel sure you'll agree, Mr Lloyd, that there's no purpose in us continuing this conversation, so perhaps the time has come for you to leave.'

Lloyd hesitated.

'We'll meet again at ten o'clock tomorrow morning, at forty-nine Wall Street.'

'Forty-nine Wall Street?'

'The office of Mr Sefton Jelks, Tom Bradshaw's lawyer.'

'So it's Jelks who's behind this. Well that explains everything.'

Emma didn't understand what he meant, but said, 'You will bring every single notebook with you, and hand them over. Should you be even one minute late, I will instruct Mr Jelks to call your probation officer and tell him what you've been up to since you left Lavenham. Stealing a client's earnings is one thing, but claiming you wrote his book . . .' Lloyd continued to grip the arms of his chair, but said nothing. 'You may go now, Mr Lloyd,' said Emma. 'I look forward to seeing you in the lobby of forty-nine Wall Street at ten tomorrow morning. Don't be late, unless you want your next appointment to be with Mr Elders.'

Lloyd rose unsteadily to his feet and made his way slowly across the restaurant, leaving one or two customers wondering if he was drunk. A waiter held the door open for him, then hurried over to Emma's table. Seeing the untouched steak and a full glass of wine, he asked anxiously, 'I hope everything was all right, Miss Barrington?'

'It couldn't have gone better, Jimmy,' she said, pouring herself another glass of wine.

19

ONCE EMMA had returned to her hotel room, she checked the back of her lunch menu, and was delighted to confirm that she'd been able to tick off almost every question. She thought her demand that the notebooks should be handed over in the lobby of 49 Wall Street was inspired, because it must have left Lloyd with the distinct impression that Mr Jelks was her lawyer, which would have put the fear of God into a perfectly innocent man. Although she was still puzzled by what Lloyd had meant when he'd let slip the words *So it's Jelks who's behind this. Well that explains everything.* She switched off the light and slept soundly for the first time since she'd left England.

Emma's morning routine followed much the same pattern as previous days. After a leisurely breakfast, shared only with the *New York Times*, she left the hotel and took a cab to Wall Street. She had planned to be a few minutes early, and the cab dropped her off outside the building at 9.51 a.m. As she handed the driver a quarter, she was relieved that her visit to New York was coming to an end; it had turned out to be far more expensive than she had anticipated. Two meals at the

Brasserie with a five-dollar bottle of wine plus tips didn't help.

However, she wasn't in any doubt that the trip had been worthwhile. Not least because the photographs taken on board the *Kansas Star* had confirmed her belief that Harry was still alive and had, for some reason, assumed Tom Bradshaw's identity. Once she'd got her hands on the missing notebook, the rest of the mystery would unravel, and surely she would now be able to convince Officer Kolowski that Harry should be released. She didn't intend to return to England without him.

Emma joined a stampede of office workers as they made their way into the building. They all headed towards the nearest available elevator, but Emma didn't join them. She placed herself strategically between the reception desk and the bank of twelve lifts, which allowed her an unimpeded view of everyone who entered 49 Wall Street.

She checked her watch: 9.54. No sign of Lloyd. She checked it again at 9.57, 9.58, 9.59, and 10 o'clock. He must have been held up by traffic. 10.02, her eyes rested for a split second on every person who came in. 10.04, had she missed him? 10.06, she glanced towards reception; still no sign of him. 10.08, she tried to stop negative thoughts from entering her mind. 10.11, had he called her bluff? 10.14, would her next appointment have to be with Mr Brett Elders? 10.17, how much longer was she willing to hang about? 10.21, and a voice behind her said, 'Good morning, Miss Barrington.'

Emma swung round and came face to face with Samuel Anscott, who said politely, 'Mr Jelks wonders if you'd be kind enough to join him in his office.'

Without another word, Anscott turned and walked towards a waiting elevator. Emma only just managed to jump in before the doors closed.

Conversation was out of the question as the packed elevator made its slow, interrupted journey to the 22nd floor, where Anscott stepped out and led Emma down a long oak-panelled, thickly carpeted corridor, lined with portraits of previous senior partners and their colleagues on the board, giving an impression of honesty, integrity and propriety.

Emma would have liked to question Anscott before she met Jelks for the first time, but he remained several paces ahead of her. When he reached a door at the end of the corridor, Anscott knocked, and opened it without waiting for a response. He stood aside to allow Emma to enter, then closed the door, but didn't join them.

There, sitting in a comfortable high-backed chair by the window, was Max Lloyd. He was smoking a cigarette, and gave Emma the same smile he'd bestowed on her when they had first met at Doubleday's.

She turned her attention to a tall, elegantly dressed man, who rose slowly from behind his desk. No hint of a smile, or any suggestion that they should shake hands. Behind him was a wall of glass, beyond which skyscrapers towered into the sky, suggesting unfettered power.

'It's kind of you to join us, Miss Barrington,' he said. 'Please have a seat.'

Emma sank into a leather chair so deep that she almost disappeared from sight. She noticed a stack of notebooks on the senior partner's desk.

'My name is Sefton Jelks,' he began, 'and I have the privilege of representing the distinguished and acclaimed author, Mr Max Lloyd. My client visited me earlier this morning, to tell me that he had been approached by someone claiming to be a literary agent from London, who was making an accusation, a slanderous accusation, that he was not the author of *The Diary of a Convict*, which bears his name. It may interest you to know, Miss Barrington,' continued Jelks, 'that I am in possession of the original manuscript, every word of which is written in Mr Lloyd's hand.' He placed a fist firmly on top of the notebooks, and allowed himself the suggestion of a smile.

'May I be allowed to see one?' asked Emma.

'Of course,' replied Jelks. He removed the book on top of the pile and handed it to her.

Emma opened it and began to read. The first thing she saw was that it wasn't written in Harry's bold hand. But it was Harry's voice. She handed the book back to Mr Jelks, who replaced it at the top of the pile. 'May I have a look at one of the others?' she asked.

'No. We've proved our point, Miss Barrington,' said Jelks. 'And my client will take advantage of every remedy the law provides should you be foolish enough to repeat your slander.' Emma kept her eyes on the pile of notebooks, while Jelks continued in full flow. 'I also felt it appropriate to have a word with Mr Elders to warn him you might be in touch, and to let him know that should he agree to see you, he would undoubtedly be called as a witness, were this matter to end up in court. Mr Elders felt, on balance, that his best course of action would be to avoid meeting you. A sensible man.'

Emma continued to look at the pile of notebooks.

'Miss Barrington, it didn't take a lot of research to discover that you are the granddaughter of Lord Harvey and Sir Walter Barrington, which would account for your misplaced confidence when dealing with Americans. Allow me to suggest that if you intend to continue trying to pass yourself off as a literary agent, perhaps I can offer you some free advice, which is a matter of public record. Ernest Hemingway left America to live in Cuba in 1939—'

'How very generous of you, Mr Jelks,' interrupted Emma, before he could continue. 'Allow me to offer you some free advice in return. I know perfectly well that it was Harry Clifton' – Jelks's eyes narrowed – 'and not your client, who wrote *The Diary of a Convict*. If you were foolish enough, Mr Jelks, to issue a writ for slander against me, you might well find yourself in court having to explain why you defended a man on a charge of murder who you knew wasn't Lieutenant Tom Bradshaw.'

Jelks began frantically pressing a button underneath his desk. Emma rose from her chair, smiled sweetly at both of them, and left the room without another word. She marched quickly down the corridor towards the elevator, as Mr Anscott and a security guard hurried past her on their way to Mr Jelks's office. At least she'd avoided the humiliation of being escorted off the premises.

When she stepped into the lift, the attendant enquired, 'Which floor, miss?'

'Ground, please.'

The attendant chuckled. 'You must be English.'

'Why do you say that?'

'In America, we call it the first floor.'

'Of course you do,' said Emma, giving him a smile as she stepped out of the elevator. She walked across the lobby, pushed through the revolving doors and ran down the steps and out on to the pavement, quite clear what she had to do next. There was only one person left she could turn to. After all, any sister of Lord Harvey had to be a formidable ally. Or would Great-aunt Phyllis turn out to be a close friend of Sefton Jelks, in which case Emma would be taking the next boat back to England.

She hailed a cab, but when she jumped in, she almost had to shout to make herself heard above the blare of the radio.

'Sixty-fourth and Park,' she said, working out how she might explain to her great-aunt why she hadn't visited her earlier. She leant forward and would have asked the driver to turn the volume down, if she hadn't heard the words, 'President Roosevelt will address the nation at twelve thirty this afternoon, Eastern Time'.

GILES BARRINGTON

1941–1942

20

THE FIRST THING Giles saw was his right leg hitched to a pulley and encased in plaster.

He could dimly remember a long journey, during which the pain had become almost unbearable, and he had assumed he would die long before they got him to a hospital. And he would never forget the operation, but then how could he, when they'd run out of anaesthetic moments before the doctor made the first incision?

He turned his head very slowly to the left and saw a window with three bars across it, then to the right; that's when he saw him.

'No, not you,' Giles said. 'For a moment I thought I'd escaped and gone to heaven.'

'Not yet,' said Bates. 'First you have to do a spell in purgatory.'

'For how long?'

'At least until your leg's mended, possibly longer.'

'Are we back in England?' Giles asked hopefully.

'I wish,' said Bates. 'No, we're in Germany, Weinsberg PoW camp, which is where we all ended up after being taken prisoner.'

Giles tried to sit up, but could only just raise his head off the pillow; enough to see a framed picture on the wall of Adolf Hitler giving him a Nazi salute.

'How many of our boys survived?'

'Only a handful. The lads took the colonel's words to heart. "We will all sacrifice our lives before Rommel books a suite at the Majestic Hotel".'

'Did anyone else from our platoon make it?'

'You, me and—'

'Don't tell me, Fisher?'

'No. Because if they'd sent him to Weinsberg, I'd have asked for a transfer to Colditz.'

Giles lay still, staring up at the ceiling. 'So how do we escape?'

'I wondered how long it would be before you asked that.'

'And what's the answer?'

'Not a chance while your leg's still in plaster, and even after that it won't be easy, but I've got a plan.'

'Of course you have.'

'The plan's not the problem,' said Bates. 'The problem is the escape committee. They control the waiting list, and you're at the back of the queue.'

'How do I get to the front?'

'It's like any queue in England, you just have to wait your turn . . . unless—'

'Unless?'

'Unless Brigadier Turnbull, the senior ranking officer, thinks there's a good reason why you should be moved up the queue.'

'Like what?'

'If you can speak fluent German, it's a bonus.'

'I picked up a bit when I was at OTS – just wish I'd concentrated more.'

'Well, there are lessons twice a day, so someone of your intelligence shouldn't find that too difficult. Unfortunately even that list is still fairly long.'

'So what else can I do to get bumped up the escape-list faster?'

'Find yourself the right job. That's what got me moved up three places in the past month.'

'How did you manage that?'

'As soon as the Krauts found out I was a butcher, they offered me a job in the officers' mess. I told them to fuck off, excuse my French, but the brigadier insisted I took the job.'

'Why would he want you to work for the Germans?'

'Because occasionally I can manage to steal some food from the kitchen, but more important, I pick up the odd piece of information that's useful to the escape committee. That's why I'm near the front of the queue, and you're still at the back. You're going to have to get both feet on the ground if you're still hoping to make it to the washroom before me.'

'Any idea how long it will be before I can do that?' asked Giles.

'The prison doc says it'll be at least another month, possibly six weeks before they can remove the plaster.'

Giles settled back on the pillow. 'But even when I do get up, how can I hope to be offered a job in the officers' mess? Unlike you, I don't have the right qualifications.'

'But you do,' said Bates. 'In fact, you can go one better than me, and get yourself a job in the camp commandant's dining room, because I know they're looking for a wine waiter.'

'And what makes you think I'm qualified to be a wine waiter?' asked Giles, making no attempt to hide the sarcasm in his voice.

'If I remember correctly,' said Bates, 'you used to have a butler called Jenkins working for you at the Manor House.'

'Still do, but that hardly qualifies me—'

'And your grandfather, Lord Harvey, is in the wine trade. Frankly, you're over-qualified.'

'So what are you suggesting?'

'Once you get out of here, they'll make you fill in a labour form, listing your previous employment. I've already told them you were a wine waiter at the Grand Hotel, Bristol.'

'Thanks. But they'll know within minutes—'

'Believe me, they don't have a clue. All you have to do is get your German up to scratch, and try to remember what Jenkins did. Then if we can come up with a decent plan to present to the escape committee, we'll march to the front of the queue in no time. Mind you, there's a catch.'

'There has to be, if you're involved.'

'But I've found a way round it.'

'What's the catch?'

'You can't get a job workin' for the Krauts if you take German lessons, because they're not that stupid. They make a list of everyone who attends the classes, because they don't want no one eavesdropping on their private conversations.'

'You said you'd found a way around that?'

'You'll have to do what all toffs do to keep ahead of

people like me. Take private lessons. I've even found you a tutor; a bloke who taught German at Solihull Grammar School. It's only his English you'll find difficult to understand.' Giles laughed. 'And since you'll be locked up in here for another six weeks, and haven't anything better to do, you can start straight away. You'll find a German–English dictionary under your pillow.'

'I'm in your debt, Terry,' said Giles, grasping his friend by the hand.

'No, I owe you, don't I? On account of the fact that you saved my life.'

21

By the time Giles was released from the sick bay five weeks later, he knew a thousand German words but he hadn't been able to work on his pronunciation.

He'd also spent countless hours lying in bed, trying to recall how Jenkins had gone about his job. He practised saying *Good morning, sir*, with a deferential nod of the head, and *Would you care to sample this wine, colonel*, while pouring a jug of water into a specimen bottle.

'Always appear modest, never interrupt and don't speak till you're spoken to,' Bates reminded him. 'In fact, do exactly the opposite of everythin' you've always done in the past.'

Giles would have hit him, but he knew he was right.

Although Bates was only allowed to visit Giles twice a week for thirty minutes, he used every one of those minutes to brief him about the day-to-day workings of the commandant's private dining room. He taught him the names and ranks of each officer, their particular likes and dislikes, and warned him that Major Müller of the SS, who was in charge of camp security, was not a gentleman, and was certainly not susceptible to charm, especially old-school.

Another visitor was Brigadier Turnbull, who listened with interest to what Giles told him he had in mind for when he was moved out of the sick bay and into the camp. The brigadier went away impressed, and returned a few days later with some thoughts of his own.

'The escape committee aren't in any doubt that the Krauts will never allow you to work in the commandant's dining room if they think you're an officer,' he told Giles. 'For your plan to have any chance of succeeding, you'll need to be a private soldier. Since Bates is the only man to have served under you, he's the only one who'll have to keep his mouth shut.'

'He'll do what I tell him,' said Giles.

'Not any longer he won't,' warned the brigadier.

--◦--

When Giles finally emerged from the sick bay and moved into camp, he was surprised to find how disciplined the life was, especially for a private soldier.

It brought back memories of his days at Ypres training camp on Dartmoor – feet on the floor at six every morning, with a sergeant major who certainly didn't treat him like an officer.

Bates still beat him to the washroom and to breakfast every morning. There was full parade on the square at seven, when the salute was taken by the brigadier. Once the sergeant major had screamed, 'Parade dismissed!' everyone became engaged in frantic activity for the rest of the day.

Giles never missed the five-mile run, twenty-five times around the perimeter of the camp, or an hour's quiet conversation in German with his private tutor while sitting in the latrines.

He quickly discovered that the Weinsberg PoW camp had a lot of other things in common with Ypres barracks: cold, bleak, barren terrain, and dozens of huts with wooden bunks, horsehair mattresses and no heating other than the sun, which, like the Red Cross, only made rare visits to Weinsberg. They also had their own sergeant major who endlessly referred to Giles as an idle little sod.

As on Dartmoor, there was a high wire fence surrounding the compound, and only one way in and out. The problem was that there were no weekend passes, and the guards, armed with rifles, certainly didn't salute as you drove out of the gates in your yellow MG.

When Giles was asked to fill in the camp labour form, under 'name', he wrote Private Giles Barrington, and under 'previous occupation', sommelier.

'What the hell's that when it's at home?' asked Bates.

'Wine waiter,' said Giles in a superior tone.

'Then why not bloody well say so?' Bates said as he tore up the form. 'Unless of course you were hoping to get a job at the Ritz. You'll have to fill in another one of these,' he added, sounding exasperated.

Once Giles had handed in the second form, he waited impatiently to be interviewed by someone in the commandant's office. He used the endless hours to keep fit in both mind and body. *'Mens sana in corpore sano'* was about the only Latin he could still remember from his schooldays.

Bates kept him informed about what was happening on the other side of the fence, and even managed to smuggle out the odd potato or crust of bread, and on one occasion half an orange.

'Can't overdo it,' he explained. 'The last thing I need is to lose my job.'

◄○►

It was about a month later that they were both invited to appear before the escape committee and present the Bates/Barrington plan, which quickly became known as the bed and breakfast plan – bed in Weinsberg, breakfast in Zurich.

Their clandestine presentation went well, and the committee agreed that they should be allowed to climb a few more places up the order, but no one was yet suggesting that they should open the batting. In fact, the brigadier told them bluntly that until Private Barrington had landed a job in the commandant's dining room, they were not to bother the committee again.

'Why is it taking so long, Terry?' asked Giles after they'd left the meeting.

Corporal Bates grinned. 'I'm quite happy for you to call me Terry,' he said, 'that is, when we're on our own, but never in front of the men, you understand?' he added, giving a passable imitation of Fisher.

Giles punched him on the arm.

'Court martial offence, that,' Bates reminded him, 'a private soldier attacking a non-commissioned officer.'

Giles punched him again. 'Now answer my question,' he demanded.

'Nothing moves quickly in this place. You'll just have to be patient, Giles.'

'You can't call me Giles until we're sitting down for breakfast in Zurich.'

'Suits me, if you're payin'.'

Everything changed the day the camp commandant had to host lunch for a group of visiting Red Cross officials, and needed an extra waiter.

—<o>—

'Don't forget you're a private soldier,' said Bates when Giles was escorted to the other side of the wire for his interview with Major Müller. 'You have to try to think like a servant, not someone who's used to being served. If Müller suspects, even for a moment, that you're an officer, we'll both be out on our arses, and you'll go back to the bottom of the snakes and ladders board. I can promise you one thing, the brigadier won't ever invite us to throw the dice again. So act like a servant, and never even hint that you understand a word of German. Got it?'

'Yes, sir,' said Giles.

Giles returned an hour later with a large grin on his face.

'You got the job?' asked Bates.

'I got lucky,' said Giles. 'The commandant interviewed me, not Müller. I start tomorrow.'

'And he never suspected you were an officer and a gentleman?'

'Not after I told him I was a friend of yours.'

—<o>—

Before the lunch for the visiting Red Cross officials was served, Giles uncorked six bottles of merlot to allow them to breathe. Once the guests were seated, he poured half an inch of wine into the commandant's glass and waited for his approval. After a nod, he served the guests, always pouring from the right. He then moved on to the officers, according to rank, finally returning to the commandant, as host.

During the meal he made sure no one's glass was ever empty, but he never served anyone while they were speaking. Like Jenkins, he was rarely seen and never heard. Everything went as planned, although Giles was well aware that Major Müller's suspicious eyes rarely left him, even when he tried to melt into the background.

After the two of them had been escorted back to the camp later that afternoon, Bates said, 'The commandant was impressed.'

'What makes you say that?' asked Giles, fishing.

'He told the head chef that you must have worked for a grand household, because although you were obviously from the lower classes, you'd been well taught by a consummate professional.'

'Thank you, Jenkins,' said Giles.

'So what does consummate mean?' asked Bates.

◄o►

Giles became so skilled in his new vocation that the camp commandant insisted on being served by him even when he dined alone. This allowed Giles to study his mannerisms, the inflections in his voice, his laugh, even his slight stutter.

Within weeks, Private Barrington had been handed the keys to the wine cellar, and allowed to select which wines would be served at dinner. And after a few months, Bates overheard the commandant telling the chef that Barrington was *erstklassig*.

Whenever the commandant held a dinner party, Giles quickly assessed which tongues could be loosened by the regular topping up of glasses, and how to make himself invisible whenever one of those tongues began to wag. He passed on any useful information he'd picked up the previous evening to the brigadier's batman while they were out on the communal five-mile run. These titbits included where the commandant lived, the fact that he'd been elected to the town council at the age of thirty-two, and been appointed mayor in 1938. He couldn't drive, but he had visited England three or four times before the war and spoke fluent English. In return, Giles learnt that he and Bates had climbed several more rungs up the escape committee's ladder.

Giles's main activity during the day was to spend an hour chatting to his tutor. Never a word of English was spoken, and the man from Solihull even told the brigadier that Private Barrington was beginning to sound more and more like the commandant.

◀◦▶

On December 3rd, 1941, Corporal Bates and Private Barrington made their final presentation to the escape committee. The brigadier and his team listened to the bed and breakfast plan with considerable interest, and agreed that it had a far better chance of succeeding than most of the half-baked schemes that were put before them.

'When would you consider the best time to carry out your plan?' asked the brigadier.

'New Year's Eve, sir,' said Giles without hesitation. 'All the officers will be joining the commandant for dinner to welcome in the New Year.'

'And as Private Barrington will be pouring the

drinks,' added Bates, 'there shouldn't be too many of them who are still sober by the time midnight strikes.'

'Except for Müller,' the brigadier reminded Bates, 'who doesn't drink.'

'True, but he never fails to toast the Fatherland, the Führer and the Third Reich. If you add in the New Year, and his host, I have a feeling he'll be pretty sleepy by the time he's driven home.'

'What time are you usually escorted back to camp after one of the commandant's dinner parties?' asked a young lieutenant who had recently joined the committee.

'Around eleven,' said Bates, 'but as it's New Year's Eve, it won't be before midnight.'

'Don't forget, gentlemen,' Giles chipped in, 'I have the keys to the wine cellar, so I can assure you several bottles will find their way to the guard house during the evening. We wouldn't want them to miss out on the celebrations.'

'That's all very well,' said a wing commander who rarely spoke, 'but how do you plan to get past them?'

'By driving out through the front gate in the commandant's car,' said Giles. 'He's always a dutiful host and never leaves before his last guest, which should give us at least a couple of hours' start.'

'Even if you are able to steal his car,' said the brigadier, 'however drunk the guards are, they'll still be able to tell the difference between a wine waiter and their commanding officer.'

'Not if I'm wearing his greatcoat, hat, scarf and gloves, and holding his baton,' said Giles.

The young lieutenant clearly wasn't convinced. 'And is it part of your plan for the commandant to meekly hand all his clothes over to you, Private Barrington?'

'No, sir,' said Giles to an officer he outranked. 'The commandant always leaves his coat, cap and gloves in the cloakroom.'

'But what about Bates?' said the same officer. 'They'll spot him a mile off.'

'Not if I'm in the boot of the car, they won't,' said Bates.

'What about the commandant's driver, who we must assume will be stone-cold sober?' said the brigadier.

'We're working on it,' said Giles.

'And if you do manage to overcome the problem of the driver and get past the guards, how far is it to the Swiss border?' The young lieutenant again.

'One hundred and seventy-three kilometres,' said Bates. 'At a hundred kilometres an hour, we should reach the border in just under two hours.'

'That's assuming there are no hold-ups on the way.'

'No escape plan can ever be foolproof,' interjected the brigadier. 'In the end, it all comes down to how you cope with the unforeseen.'

Both Giles and Bates nodded their agreement.

'Thank you, gentlemen,' said the brigadier. 'The committee will consider your plan, and we'll let you know our decision in the morning.'

'What's that young sprog got against us?' asked Bates once they'd left the meeting.

'Nothing,' said Giles. 'On the contrary, I suspect he wishes he was the third member of our team.'

◄○►

On December 6th, the brigadier's batman told Giles during the five-mile run that their plan had been given the green light, and the committee wished them bon voyage. Giles quickly caught up with Corporal Bates and passed on the news.

Barrington and Bates went over their B&B plan again and again, until, like Olympic athletes, they became bored with the endless hours of preparation and longed to hear the starter's pistol.

At six o'clock on December 31st, 1941, Corporal Terry Bates and Private Giles Barrington reported for duty in the commandant's quarters, aware that if their plan failed, at best they would have to wait for another year, but if they were caught red-handed . . .

22

'YOU-COME-BACK-at-six-thirty,' Terry almost shouted at the German corporal who had escorted them from the camp to the commandant's quarters.

The blank look on the corporal's face left Giles in little doubt that he was never going to make sergeant.

'Come-back-at-six-thirty,' repeated Terry, enunciating each word slowly. He grabbed the corporal's wrist and pointed to the six on his watch. Giles only wished he could say to the corporal, in his own language, 'If you return at six-thirty, corporal, there'll be a crate of beer for you and your friends in the guard house.' But he knew that if he did, he would be arrested and be spending New Year's Eve in solitary confinement.

Terry once again pointed to the corporal's watch, and imitated a man drinking. This time the corporal smiled and mimicked the same action.

'I think he's finally got the message,' said Giles as they made their way into the commandant's quarters.

'We still have to make sure he picks the beer up before the first officer arrives. So we'd better get a move on.'

'Yes, sir,' said Terry as he headed off in the direction of the kitchen. Natural order restored.

Giles went to the cloakroom, removed the waiter's uniform from its peg and changed into the white shirt, black tie, black trousers and white linen jacket. He spotted a pair of black leather gloves on the bench that an officer must have left behind on some previous occasion, and tucked them into his pocket thinking they might prove useful later. He closed the cloakroom door and made his way to the dining room. Three waitresses from the town – including Greta, the only one he'd ever been tempted to flirt with, but he knew Jenkins wouldn't have approved – were laying a table for sixteen.

He checked his watch: 6.12 p.m. He left the dining room and went downstairs to the wine cellar. A single bulb lit a room that had once stored filing cabinets full of archives. Since Giles's arrival, they had been replaced by wine racks.

Giles had already decided he would need at least three cases of wine for the dinner that night, as well as a crate of beer for the thirsty corporal and his comrades in the guard house. He studied the racks carefully before selecting a couple of bottles of sherry, a dozen bottles of Italian pinot grigio, two cases of French burgundy and a crate of German beer. Just as he was leaving, his eyes settled on three bottles of Johnnie Walker Red Label, two bottles of Russian vodka, half a dozen bottles of Rémy Martin and a flagon of vintage port. Giles felt that a visitor might be forgiven for not being sure who was at war with whom.

For the next fifteen minutes he lugged the cases of wine and beer up the stairs, constantly stopping to check his watch, and at 6.29 he opened the back door to find the German corporal jumping up and down and slapping his sides in an effort to keep warm. Giles raised the palms of both hands to indicate that he should stay put for a moment. He then moved swiftly back down the corridor – Jenkins never ran – picked up the crate of beer, returned and handed it to him.

Greta, who was clearly running late, watched the handover and grinned at Giles. He returned her smile, before she disappeared into the dining room.

'The guard house,' said Giles firmly, pointing towards the outer perimeter. The corporal nodded, and headed off in the right direction. Terry had asked Giles earlier if he should smuggle some food from the kitchen for the corporal and his friends in the guard house.

'Certainly not,' Giles had replied firmly. 'We want them drinking all night on an empty stomach.'

Giles closed the door and returned to the dining room, where the waitresses had almost finished laying the table.

He uncorked the dozen bottles of merlot, but only placed four on the sideboard, discreetly hiding the other eight underneath it. He didn't need Müller to work out what he was up to. He also put a bottle of whisky and two of sherry at one end of the sideboard, before lining up, like soldiers on parade, a dozen tumblers and half a dozen sherry glasses. Everything was in place.

Giles was polishing a tumbler when Colonel Schabacker walked in. The commandant checked the table, made one or two adjustments to the seating plan, then turned his attention to the array of bottles on the sideboard. Giles wondered if he might comment, but he simply smiled and said, 'I'm expecting the guests to arrive around seven-thirty, and I have told the chef we will sit down for dinner at eight.'

Giles could only hope that in a few hours' time, his German would prove as fluent as Colonel Schabacker's English.

The next person to enter the dining room was a young lieutenant who had recently joined the officers' mess and was attending his first commandant's dinner. Giles noticed him eyeing the whisky and stepped forward to serve him, pouring him half a glass. He then handed the commandant his usual sherry.

The second officer to make an appearance was Captain Henkel, the camp's adjutant. Giles handed him his usual glass of vodka, and spent the next thirty minutes serving each new guest, always having their favourite tipple to hand.

By the time the guests sat down for dinner, several empty bottles had been replaced by the reserves Giles had secreted under the sideboard.

Moments later waitresses appeared carrying plates of borscht, while the commandant sampled the white wine.

'Italian,' said Giles, showing him the label.

'Excellent,' he murmured.

Giles then filled every glass except that of Major Müller, who continued to sip his water.

Some of the guests drank more quickly than others, which kept Giles moving around the table, always making sure that no one had an empty glass. Once the soup bowls had been whisked away, Giles melted into the background because Terry had warned him what would happen next. With a flourish, the double doors opened and the chef entered carrying a large boar's head on a silver salver. The waitresses followed and placed dishes of vegetables and potatoes, along with jugs of thick gravy, in the centre of the table.

As the chef began to carve, Colonel Schabacker sampled the burgundy, which caused another smile to appear on his face. Giles returned to the task of topping up any half-empty glasses, with one exception. He'd noticed that the young lieutenant hadn't spoken for some time, so he left his glass untouched. One or two of the other officers were beginning to slur their words, and he needed them to stay awake until at least midnight.

The chef returned later to serve second helpings, and Giles obliged when Colonel Schabacker demanded that everyone's glasses should be replenished. By the time Terry made his first appearance to remove what was left of the boar's head, Major Müller was the only officer still sober.

A few minutes later, the chef made a third entrance, this time carrying a black forest gateau, which he placed on the table in front of the commandant. The host plunged a knife into the cake several times, and the waitresses distributed generous portions to each of the guests. Giles continued topping up their glasses, until he was down to the last bottle.

As the waitresses cleared the dessert plates, Giles removed the wine glasses from the table, replacing them with brandy balloons and port glasses.

'Gentlemen,' announced Colonel Schabacker just after eleven, 'please charge your glasses, as I would like to propose a toast.' He rose from his place, held his glass high in the air and said, 'The Fatherland!'

Fifteen officers rose at various speeds, and repeated,

'The Fatherland!' Müller glanced towards Giles, and tapped his glass to indicate that he would require something for the toast.

'Not wine, you idiot,' said Müller. 'I want some brandy.' Giles smiled, and filled his glass with burgundy. Müller had failed to trap him.

Loud, convivial chatter continued as Giles carried a humidor around the table and invited the guests to select a cigar. The young lieutenant was now resting his head on the table, and Giles thought he detected a snore.

When the commandant rose a second time, to drink the health of the Führer, Giles poured Müller some more red wine. He raised his glass, clicked his heels together and gave a Nazi salute. A toast to Frederick the Great followed, and this time Giles made sure Müller's glass had been topped up long before he rose.

At five minutes to midnight, Giles checked that every glass was full. When the clock on the wall began to chime, fifteen officers cried almost in unison, 10, 9, 8, 7, 6, 5, 4, 3, 2, 1, and then broke into 'Deutschland, Deutschland über alles', slapping each other on the back as they welcomed in the New Year.

It was some time before they resumed their places. The commandant remained standing and tapped his glass with a spoon. Everyone fell silent in anticipation of his annual speech.

He began by thanking his colleagues for their loyalty and dedication during a difficult year. He then spoke for some time about the destiny of the Fatherland. Giles remembered that Schabacker had been the local mayor before he took over as commandant of the camp. He ended by declaring that he hoped the right side would have won the war by this time next year. Giles wanted to scream, Hear, Hear! in any language, but Müller swung round to see if the colonel's words had evoked any reaction. Giles stared blankly ahead, as if he hadn't understood a word. He had passed another of Müller's tests.

23

IT WAS A FEW MINUTES after 1.00 a.m. when the first guest rose to leave. 'I'm on duty at six in the morning, colonel,' he explained. This was greeted with mock applause, as the officer bowed low and left without another word.

Several other guests departed during the next hour, but Giles knew he couldn't consider executing his own well-rehearsed exit while Müller was still on the premises. He became a little anxious when the waitresses started to clear away the coffee cups, a sign that their evening was coming to an end and he might be ordered back to the camp. Giles kept himself busy, continuing to serve those officers who didn't seem in any hurry to leave.

Müller finally rose as the last waitress left the room and bade goodnight to his colleagues, but not before clicking his heels and giving his comrades another Nazi salute. Giles and Terry had agreed that their plan couldn't be put into motion until at least fifteen minutes after Müller had departed and they had checked that his car was no longer in its usual place.

Giles refilled the glasses of the six officers who

remained seated around the table. They were all close friends of the commandant. Two of them had been at school with him, another three had served on the town council, and only the camp adjutant was a more recent acquaintance; information Giles had picked up during the past few months.

It must have been about twenty past two when the commandant beckoned Giles over. 'It's been a long day,' he said in English. 'Go and join your friend in the kitchen, and take a bottle of wine with you.'

'Thank you, sir,' said Giles, placing a bottle of brandy and a decanter of port in the centre of the table.

The last words he heard the commandant say before he left were to the adjutant, who was seated on his right. 'When we've finally won this war, Franz, I intend to offer that man a job. I can't imagine he'll want to return to England while a Swastika flies over Buckingham Palace.'

Giles removed the only bottle of wine still on the sideboard, left the room and closed the door quietly behind him. He could feel the adrenaline pumping through his body, and was well aware that the next fifteen minutes would decide their fate. He took the back stairs down to the kitchen where he found Terry chatting to the chef, a half-empty bottle of cooking sherry by his side.

'Happy New Year, chef,' said Terry as he rose from his chair. 'Got to dash, otherwise I'll be late for breakfast in Zurich.'

Giles tried to keep a straight face as the chef just about raised a hand in acknowledgement.

They ran up the stairs, the only two sober people in the building. Giles passed the bottle of wine to Terry and said, 'Two minutes, no more.'

Terry walked down the corridor and slipped out of the back door. Giles withdrew into the shadows at the top of the stairs, just as an officer came out of the dining room and headed for the lavatory.

Moments later, the back door reopened and a head appeared. Giles waved furiously at Terry and pointed to the lavatory. Terry ran over to join him in the shadows, just before the officer emerged to make his way unsteadily back to the dining room. Once the door had closed behind him, Giles asked, 'How's our tame German, corporal?'

'Half asleep. I gave him the bottle of wine and warned him we could be at least another hour.'

'Do you think he understood?'

'I don't think he cared.'

'Good enough. Your turn to act as lookout,' said Giles as he stepped back out into the corridor. He clenched his fists to stop his hands trembling, and was just about to open the cloakroom door when he thought he heard a voice coming from inside. He froze, put his ear to the door and listened. It only took him a moment to realize who it must be. For the first time, he broke Jenkins's golden rule and charged back down the corridor to rejoin Terry in the shadows at the top of the stairs.

'What's the problem?'

Giles put a finger up to his lips, as the cloakroom door opened and out stepped Major Müller, doing up his fly buttons. Once he'd pulled on his greatcoat, he glanced up and down the corridor to make sure no one had spotted him, then slipped through the front door and out into the night.

'Which girl?' asked Giles.

'Probably Greta. I've had her a couple of times, but never in the cloakroom.'

'Isn't that fraternizing?' whispered Giles.

'Only if you're an officer,' said Terry.

They only had to wait for a few moments before the door opened again and Greta appeared, looking a little flushed. She walked calmly out of the front door without bothering to check if anyone had seen her.

'Second attempt,' said Giles, who moved swiftly back down the corridor, opened the cloakroom door and disappeared inside just as another officer came out of the dining room.

Don't turn right, don't turn right, Terry begged silently. The officer turned left and headed for the lavatory. Terry prayed for the longest pee in history. He began counting the seconds, but then the cloakroom door opened and out stepped the commandant in all but name. Get back inside, Terry waved frantically. Giles ducked back into the cloakroom and pulled the door closed.

When the adjutant reappeared, Terry feared he would go to the cloakroom to collect his cap and coat, and find Giles dressed as the commandant, in which case the game would be up before it had even begun. Terry followed each step, fearing the worst, but the adjutant stopped at the dining room door, opened it and disappeared inside. Once the door had closed, Terry bolted down the corridor and opened the cloakroom door to find Giles dressed in a greatcoat, scarf, gloves and peaked cap and carrying a baton, beads of sweat on his forehead.

'Let's get out of here before one of us has a heart attack,' said Terry.

Terry and Giles left the building even more quickly than Müller or Greta had.

'Relax,' said Giles once they were outside. 'Don't forget we're the only two people who are sober.' He tucked the scarf around his neck so that it covered his chin, pulled down his cap, gripped the baton firmly and stooped slightly, as he was a couple of inches taller than the commandant.

As soon as the driver heard Giles approaching, he leapt out of the car and opened the back door for him. Giles had rehearsed a sentence he'd heard the colonel say to his driver many times, and as he fell into the back seat, he pulled his cap even further down and slurred, 'Take me home, Hans.'

Hans returned to the driver's seat, but when he heard a click that sounded like the boot closing, he looked back suspiciously, only to see the commandant tapping his baton on the window.

'What's holding you up, Hans?' Giles asked with a slight stutter.

Hans switched on the ignition, put the car into first gear and drove slowly towards the guard house. A sergeant emerged from the sentry box when he heard the vehicle approaching. He tried to open the barrier and salute at the same time. Giles raised his baton in acknowledgement, and nearly burst out laughing when he noticed that the top two buttons of the sentry's tunic were undone. Colonel Schabacker would never have let that pass without comment, even on New Year's Eve.

Major Forsdyke, the escape committee's intelligence officer, had told Giles that the commandant's house was approximately two miles from the compound, and the last two hundred yards were down a narrow, unlit lane.

Giles remained slumped into the corner of the back seat, where he couldn't be seen in the rear-view mirror, but the moment the car swung into the lane, he sat bolt upright, tapped the driver on the shoulder with his baton and ordered him to stop.

'I can't wait,' he said, before jumping out of the car and pretending to undo his fly buttons.

Hans watched as the colonel disappeared into the bushes. He looked puzzled; after all, they were only a hundred metres from his front door. He stepped out of the car and waited by the back door. When he thought he heard his master coming back, he turned around just in time to see a clenched fist, an instant before it broke his nose. He slumped to the ground.

Giles ran to the back of the car and opened the boot. Terry leapt out, walked across to Hans's prostrate body and began to unbutton the driver's uniform, before pulling off his own clothes. Once Bates had finished putting on his new uniform, it became clear just how much shorter and fatter Hans was.

'It won't matter,' said Giles, reading his thoughts. 'When you're behind the wheel, no one will give you a second look.'

They dragged Hans to the back of the car and bundled him into the boot.

'I doubt if he'll wake up before we sit down for breakfast in Zurich,' said Terry as he tied a handkerchief around Hans's mouth.

The commandant's new driver took his place behind the wheel, and neither of them spoke again until they were back on the main road. Terry didn't need to stop and check any signposts, as he'd studied the route to the border every day for the past month.

'Stay on the right-hand side of the road,' said Giles, unnecessarily, 'and don't drive too fast. The last thing we need is to be pulled over.'

'I think we've made it,' Terry said as they passed a signpost for Schaffhausen.

'I won't believe we've made it until we're being shown to our table at the Imperial Hotel and a waiter hands me the breakfast menu.'

'I won't need a menu,' said Terry. 'Eggs, bacon, beans, sausage and tomato, and a pint of beer. That's my usual down at the meat market every morning. How about you?'

'A kipper, lightly poached, a slice of buttered toast, a spoonful of Oxford marmalade and a pot of Earl Grey tea.'

'It didn't take you long to go back from butler to toff.'

Giles smiled. He checked his watch. There were few cars on the road that New Year's morning, so they continued to make good progress. That was, until Terry spotted the convoy ahead of them.

'What do I do now?' he said.

'Overtake them. We can't afford to waste any time. They'll have no reason to be suspicious – you're driving a senior officer who wouldn't expect to be held up.'

Once Terry caught up with the rear vehicle, he eased out into the centre of the road and began to overtake a long line of armoured trucks and motorcycles. As Giles had predicted, no one took any interest in a passing Mercedes that was clearly going about official business. When Terry overtook the leading vehicle, he breathed a sigh of relief, but he didn't fully relax until he swept round a corner and could no longer see any headlights in his rear-view mirror.

Giles continued to check his watch every few minutes. The next signpost confirmed they were making good time, but Giles knew they had no control over when the commandant's last guest would leave and Colonel Schabacker would go in search of his car and driver.

It was another forty minutes before they reached the outskirts of Schaffhausen. They were both so nervous that hardly a word had passed between them. Giles was exhausted just sitting in the back seat, doing nothing, but he knew they couldn't afford to relax until they had crossed the Swiss border.

When they entered the town, the locals were just beginning to wake up; the occasional tram, the odd car, a few bicycles ferrying people who were expected to work on New Year's Day. Terry didn't need to look for signs to the border, as he could see the Swiss Alps dominating the skyline. Freedom felt as if it was touching distance away.

'Bloody hell!' said Terry as he slammed on the brakes.

'What's the problem?' said Giles, leaning forward.

'Look at that queue.'

Giles stuck his head out of the window to see a line of about forty vehicles, bumper to bumper, ahead of them, all waiting to cross the border. He checked to see if any of them were official cars. When he was sure there were none, he said, 'Drive straight to the front. That's what they'd expect us to do. If we don't, we'll only draw attention to ourselves.'

Terry drove slowly forward, only stopping when he reached the barrier.

'Get out and open the door for me, but don't say anything.'

Terry turned off the engine, got out and opened the back door. Giles marched up to the customs post.

A young officer leapt up from behind his desk and saluted when he saw the colonel enter the room. Giles handed over two sets of papers that the camp forger had assured him would pass muster at any border post in Germany. He was about to find out if he'd exaggerated. As the officer flicked through the documents, Giles tapped the side of his leg with his baton and glanced repeatedly at his watch.

'I have an important meeting in Zurich,' he snapped, 'and I'm running late.'

'I'm sorry, colonel. I'll get you on your way as soon as possible. It should only take me a few moments.'

The officer checked the photograph of Giles on his papers, and looked puzzled. Giles wondered if he'd have the nerve to ask him to remove his scarf, because if he did, he would immediately realize that he was too young to be a colonel.

Giles stared defiantly at the young man, who must have been weighing up the possible consequences of holding up a senior officer by asking him unnecessary questions. The scales came down in Giles's favour. The officer nodded his head, stamped the papers and said, 'I hope you won't be late for your meeting, sir.'

'Thank you,' said Giles. He put the documents back in an inside pocket and was walking towards the door when the young officer stopped him in his tracks.

'Heil Hitler!' he shouted.

Giles hesitated, turned slowly around and said, 'Heil

Hitler,' giving a perfect Nazi salute. As he walked out of the building, he had to suppress his laughter when he noticed that Terry was holding open the back door with one hand, and holding up his trousers with the other.

'Thank you, Hans,' said Giles as he slumped into the back seat.

That was when they heard a banging noise coming from the boot.

'Oh my God,' said Terry. 'Hans.'

The brigadier's words came back to haunt them; no escape plan can ever be foolproof. In the end, it all comes down to how you cope with the unforeseen.

Terry closed the back door and returned to his place behind the wheel as quickly as he could, as he feared the guards would hear the banging. He tried to remain calm as the barrier rose inch by inch, and the banging became louder and louder.

'Drive slowly,' said Giles. 'Don't give them any reason to become suspicious.'

Terry eased the gear lever into first and drove slowly under the barrier. Giles glanced out of the side window as they passed the customs post. The young officer was speaking on the phone. He looked out of the window, stared directly at Giles, jumped up from his desk and ran out on to the road.

Giles estimated that the Swiss border post was no more than a couple of hundred yards away. He looked out of the back window to see the young officer waving frantically, as guards carrying rifles poured out of the customs post.

'Change of plan,' said Giles. 'Step on the accelerator,' he shouted as the first bullets hit the back of the car.

Terry was changing gear when the tyre burst. He tried desperately to keep the car on the road, but it swerved from side to side, careered into the side railings and came to a standstill midway between the two border posts. Another volley of shots quickly followed.

'My turn to beat you to the washroom,' said Giles.

'Not a hope,' said Terry, who had both feet on the ground before Giles had dived out of the back door.

They both began running flat out towards the Swiss border. If either of them was ever going to run a ten-second hundred, it would be today. Although they were dodging and changing direction in their attempt to avoid the bullets, Giles still felt confident that he would cross the finishing line first. The Swiss border guards were cheering them on, and when Giles dipped at the tape, he raised his arms in triumph, having finally defeated his greatest rival.

He turned around to gloat, and saw Terry lying in the middle of the road about thirty yards away, a bullet wound in the back of his head and blood trickling from his mouth.

Giles fell on his knees and began to crawl towards his friend. More shots rang out as two Swiss border guards grabbed him by the ankles and pulled him back to safety.

He wanted to explain to them that he didn't care to have breakfast alone.

HUGO BARRINGTON

1939–1942

24

HUGO BARRINGTON COULDN'T remove the smile from his face when he read in the *Bristol Evening News* that Harry Clifton had been buried at sea within hours of war being declared.

At last the Germans had done something worthwhile. A U-boat commander had single-handedly solved his biggest problem. Hugo began to believe it might even be possible that, given time, he could return to Bristol and resume his place as deputy chairman of the Barrington Shipping Line. He would begin to work on his mother with regular phone calls to Barrington Hall, but only after his father had left for work each day. That night he went out to celebrate, and arrived home as drunk as a lord.

When Hugo first migrated to London following his daughter's aborted wedding, he rented a basement flat in Cadogan Gardens for a pound a week. The only good thing about the three-roomed accommodation was the address, which created the impression that he was a man of means.

Although he still had a few bob in the bank, it soon

dwindled, while he had time on his hands and no regular source of income. It wasn't long before he had to let go of the Bugatti, which kept him solvent for a few more weeks, but only until the first cheque bounced. He couldn't turn to his father for help, because he'd cut him off, and frankly Sir Walter would have given Maisie Clifton a helping hand before he'd lift a finger to assist his son.

After a fruitless few months in London, Hugo tried to find a job. But it wasn't easy; if any potential employer knew his father, he never even got an interview, and when he did, his new boss expected him to work hours he hadn't realized existed, and for a wage that wouldn't have covered his bar bill at the club.

Hugo began to dabble what little he had left on the stock exchange. He listened to too many old school chums telling him about deals that couldn't fail, and even got involved in one or two more shady enterprises that brought him into contact with what the press described as spivs, and his father would have considered crooks.

Within a year, Hugo had resorted to borrowing money from friends, and even friends of friends. But when you don't have any means of repaying your debts, you are quickly dropped from most dinner-party guest lists, and are no longer invited to join country-house shooting parties at the weekend.

Whenever he was desperate, Hugo would ring his mother, but not until he was sure his father was at the office. Mama could always be relied on for a tenner, just as she'd been for ten bob when he was at school.

An old school chum, Archie Fenwick, was also good for the occasional lunch at his club or an invitation to one of his fashionable Chelsea cocktail parties. And that was where Hugo first met Olga. It wasn't her face or figure that immediately attracted his attention, but the pearls, three rows of them, that were draped around her neck. Hugo cornered Archie and asked if they were real.

'They most certainly are,' he said. 'But be warned, you're not the only person hoping to dip your paw into that honey pot.'

Olga Piotrovska, Archie told him, had recently arrived in London, having escaped from Poland after the German invasion. Her parents had been taken away by the Gestapo, for no other reason than that they were Jewish. Hugo frowned. Archie wasn't able to tell Hugo much more about her, except that she lived in a magnificent townhouse on Lowndes Square and possessed a fine art collection. Hugo had never taken a great deal of interest in art, but even he'd heard of Picasso and Matisse.

Hugo strolled across the room and introduced himself to Miss Piotrovska. When Olga told him why she'd had to leave Germany, he expressed outrage and assured her that his family had been proud to do business with the Jews for over a hundred years. After all, his father, Sir Walter Barrington, was a friend of the Rothschilds and the Hambros. Long before the party was over, he had invited Olga to join him for lunch at the Ritz the following day, but as he was no longer allowed to sign the bill, he had to cadge another fiver from Archie.

The lunch went well, and for the next few weeks Hugo courted Olga assiduously, within the limits of his resources. He told her that he'd left his wife after she'd admitted having an affair with his best friend, and he'd asked his lawyer to instigate divorce proceedings. In fact, Elizabeth had already divorced him, and the judge had awarded her the Manor House, and everything Hugo hadn't removed after he'd left in such a hurry.

Olga was very understanding, and Hugo promised her that the moment he was free, he would ask her to marry him. He never stopped telling her how beautiful she was and how her rather lifeless efforts in bed were so exciting compared to Elizabeth. He continually reminded her that when his father died, she would become Lady Barrington, and his temporary financial difficulties would be resolved when he inherited the Barrington estate. He may have given her the impression that his father was a lot older and less robust than he actually was. 'Fading fast' was the expression he used.

◂◦▸

A few weeks later Hugo moved into Lowndes Square, and over the next few months he returned to a lifestyle he assumed was his by right. Several chums commented on how lucky he was to have the company of such a charming and beautiful woman, and some of them couldn't resist adding, 'And she's not short of a bob or two.'

Hugo had almost forgotten what it was like to eat three meals a day, wear new clothes and be chauffeured around town. He paid off most of his debts, and it wasn't too long before doors began to reopen that had until recently been slammed in his face. However, he was beginning to wonder how long it could last, because he certainly had no intention of marrying a Jewish refugee from Warsaw.

—◄o►—

Derek Mitchell climbed on board the express train from Temple Meads to Paddington. The private detective was back working full time for his old employer, now that his stipend was once again paid on the first day of the month, and his expenses were redeemed on presentation. Hugo expected Mitchell to report to him once a month on what the Barrington family were up to. In particular, Hugo was interested in the comings and goings of his father, his ex-wife, Giles, Emma and even Grace, but he was still paranoid about Maisie Clifton, and expected Mitchell to brief him on everything she got up to, and he meant everything.

Mitchell would travel to London by train, and the two of them would meet in the waiting room opposite platform seven at Paddington Station. An hour later Mitchell would take the train back to Temple Meads.

That was how Hugo knew that Elizabeth continued to live at the Manor House, while Grace rarely came home since she'd won a scholarship to Cambridge. Emma had given birth to a son, whom she'd christened Sebastian Arthur. Giles had enlisted in the Wessex Regiment as a private soldier, and after completing a twelve-week basic training course, had been sent to Mons Officer Cadet Training Unit.

This came as a surprise to Hugo, as he knew Giles had been passed unfit for active service by the Gloucesters shortly after the outbreak of war, because, like him and his father, he was colour-blind. Hugo had used the same excuse to avoid being called up in 1915.

—◁◦▷—

As the months passed, Olga began to ask more and more frequently when Hugo's divorce would be finalized. He always tried to make it sound as if it were imminent, but it wasn't until she suggested he move back into his flat in Cadogan Square until he could confirm that papers had been lodged with the court that he decided to do something about it. He waited another week before he told her his lawyers had begun proceedings.

A few more months of domestic harmony followed. What he hadn't told Olga was that he'd given his landlord in Cadogan Square a month's notice on the day he moved in with her. If she threw him out, he would have nowhere to live.

—◁◦▷—

It was about a month later that Mitchell phoned Hugo and said he needed to see him urgently, a most unusual request. They agreed to meet at four o'clock the following afternoon at their usual rendezvous.

When Mitchell walked into the station waiting room, Hugo was already sitting on a bench, hidden behind a copy of the London *Evening News*. He was reading about Rommel's sacking of Tobruk, not that he could have placed Tobruk on a map. He continued reading when Mitchell sat down beside him. The private detective spoke softly and never once looked in Hugo's direction.

'I thought you'd want to know that your eldest

daughter took a job as a waitress at the Grand Hotel, using the name Miss Dickens.'

'Isn't that where Maisie Clifton works?'

'Yes, she's the restaurant's manageress, and was your daughter's boss.'

Hugo couldn't imagine why Emma could possibly want to work as a waitress. 'Does her mother know?'

'She must, because Hudson dropped her a hundred yards from the hotel every morning at five forty-five. But that isn't the reason I needed to see you.'

Hugo turned the page of his newspaper to see a photograph of General Auchinleck standing outside his tent in the desert, addressing the troops.

'Your daughter took a taxi to the docks yesterday morning. She was carrying a suitcase, when she boarded a passenger ship called the *Kansas Star*, where she was given a job in reception. She told her mother she was going to New York to visit her great-aunt Phyllis, who I believe is Lord Harvey's sister.'

Hugo would have been fascinated to know how Mitchell had picked up that particular piece of information, but he was still trying to work out why Emma would want to take a job on the ship Harry Clifton had died on. None of this made any sense. He instructed Mitchell to dig deeper and let him know immediately he picked up any more information about what Emma was up to.

Just before Mitchell left to catch the train back to Temple Meads, he told Hugo that German bombers had razed Broad Street to the ground. Hugo couldn't imagine why this would be of any interest to him, until Mitchell reminded him that it was the street on which Tilly's tea shop had stood. He thought Mr Barrington ought to know that some developers were taking an interest in Mrs Clifton's old site. Hugo thanked Mitchell for the information, without suggesting that it was of any real interest to him.

◄○►

Hugo telephoned Mr Prendergast at the National Provincial Bank the moment he got back to Lowndes Square.

'I expect you're calling about Broad Street,' were the bank manager's opening words.

'Yes, I heard the site of Tilly's tea shop might be up for sale.'

'The whole street's up for sale following the bombing,' said Prendergast. 'Most of the shopkeepers have lost their livelihoods, and because it was an act of war, they can't claim insurance.'

'So could I pick up the Tilly's site for a reasonable price?'

'Frankly, you could pick up the whole street for next to nothing. In fact, if you have any spare cash, Mr Barrington, I would recommend it as a shrewd investment.'

'That's assuming we're going to win the war,' Hugo reminded him.

'I admit it's a gamble, but it could show a handsome return.'

'How much are we talking about?'

'For Mrs Clifton's site, I think I could talk her into accepting two hundred pounds. In fact, as half the traders in that street bank with me, I suspect you could pick up the whole shooting match for around three thousand. It's like playing Monopoly with loaded dice.'

'I'll look into it,' Hugo said before putting the phone down. What he couldn't tell Prendergast was that he didn't even have Monopoly money.

He tried to think of some way of raising that amount, when all his usual contacts were unwilling to lend him even a fiver. He couldn't ask Olga for any more money, unless he was willing to walk down the aisle with her, and that was out of the question.

He wouldn't have given the matter another thought if he hadn't bumped into Toby Dunstable at one of Archie's parties.

Toby and Hugo had been contemporaries at Eton. Hugo couldn't remember much about Dunstable, except that he regularly helped himself to the younger boys' tuck. When he was finally caught removing a ten-shilling note from one of the boys' lockers, everyone assumed he would be expelled, and possibly he would have been, if he hadn't been the second son of the Earl of Dunstable.

When Hugo asked Toby what he was up to nowadays, he said rather vaguely that he dabbled in property. Hugo told him about the investment opportunity Broad Street presented, but he didn't seem that interested. In fact, Hugo couldn't help noticing that Toby didn't take his eyes off the diamond necklace that sparkled around Olga's neck.

Toby handed Hugo his card, saying, 'If you're ever in need of some ready cash, it shouldn't prove too difficult, if you get my drift, old fellow.'

Hugo got his drift, but didn't take his hinted proposal at all seriously, until Olga asked him over breakfast one morning if a date had been fixed for the decree nisi. Hugo assured her it was imminent.

He left the house, went straight to his club, checked Toby's card and gave him a call. They agreed to meet at a pub in Fulham, where they sat alone in a corner, drinking double gins and chatting about how our lads were faring in the Middle East. They only changed the subject when they were certain they couldn't be overheard.

'All I'll need is a key to the flat,' said Toby, 'and the exact location of her jewellery.'

'That shouldn't prove difficult,' Hugo assured him.

'The only thing you'll have to do, old chum, is make sure you're both off the premises long enough for me to carry out the job.'

When Olga suggested over breakfast that she would like to see a production of *Rigoletto* at Sadler's Wells, Hugo agreed to book a couple of tickets. He would usually have made some excuse, but on this occasion he readily agreed, and even suggested that they have dinner at the Savoy afterwards to celebrate.

'Celebrate what?' she asked.

'My decree nisi has been granted,' he said casually. She threw her arms around him. 'Just another six months, my darling, and you'll be Mrs Barrington.'

Hugo took a small leather box out of his pocket and presented her with an engagement ring he'd bought on approval in Burlington Arcade the previous day. She approved. He intended to return it in six months' time.

The opera seemed to last for three months, rather than the three hours suggested in the programme. However, Hugo didn't complain, as he knew Toby would be making good use of the time.

Over dinner in the River Room, Hugo and Olga

discussed where they might spend their honeymoon, as they couldn't travel abroad. Olga favoured Bath, which was a little too close to Bristol for Hugo's liking, but as it was never going to happen, he happily went along with her suggestion.

In the taxi on the way back to Lowndes Square, Hugo wondered how long it would be before Olga discovered that her diamonds were missing. Sooner than he'd bargained for, because when they opened the front door, they found the whole place had been ransacked. All that was left on the walls where the paintings had once hung were clear outlines to show what size they had been.

While Olga broke down in hysterics, Hugo picked up the phone and dialled 999. It took the police several hours to complete an inventory of everything that was missing, because Olga couldn't remain calm enough to answer their questions for more than a few moments at a time. The chief inspector in charge of the case assured them that the details of the stolen items would be circulated to all the leading diamond merchants and art dealers in London within forty-eight hours.

Hugo hit the roof when he caught up with Toby Dunstable in Fulham the following afternoon. His old school chum calmly took it on the chin like a heavyweight boxer. When Hugo was finally spent, Toby pushed a shoebox across the table.

'I don't need a new pair of shoes,' Hugo snapped.

'Perhaps not, but you'll be able to buy a shoe shop with what's inside there,' he said tapping the box.

Hugo lifted the lid and stared into the box, which contained no shoes, but was packed with five-pound notes.

'You needn't bother to count them,' said Toby. 'You'll find there's ten thousand pounds in readies.'

Hugo smiled, suddenly calm again. 'You're a good fellow,' he said as he placed the lid back and ordered another two double gin-and-tonics.

As the weeks passed, and the police failed to come up with any suspects, the chief inspector didn't leave Hugo in much doubt that he thought it was an inside job, an expression he used again and again whenever they met. However, Toby reassured him that they would never consider arresting the son of Sir Walter Barrington, unless they had cast-iron proof of his guilt that would convince a jury beyond reasonable doubt.

Olga asked Hugo where his new suits had come from and how he could possibly afford a Bugatti. He showed her the car's logbook, which confirmed that he'd owned it before they met. What he didn't tell her was how fortunate he'd been that the dealer he'd reluctantly sold it to still had it on his books.

As the end of the period after which the decree absolute would be granted was fast approaching, Hugo began to prepare for what they call in military circles an exit strategy. That was when Olga announced that she had some wonderful news to share with him.

Wellington once told a junior officer that timing was everything in life, and who was Hugo to disagree with the victor of Waterloo, especially when the great man's prophecy was about to apply to him?

He was reading *The Times* over breakfast, when he turned to the obituaries and saw a picture of his father staring out at him. He tried to read it without Olga discovering that both their lives were about to change.

In Hugo's opinion, the Thunderer had given the old

man a good send-off, but it was the last paragraph of his record that most interested him. *Sir Walter Barrington is succeeded by his only surviving son, Hugo, who will inherit the title.*

However, what *The Times* didn't add was, *and all that therein is.*

MAISIE CLIFTON

1939–1942

25

MAISIE COULD STILL REMEMBER the pain she'd experienced when her husband didn't come home at the end of his evening shift. She knew Arthur was dead, even though it would be years before her brother Stan was willing to tell her the truth about how her husband had died at the dockyard that afternoon.

But that pain was nothing compared to being told that her only son had been buried at sea after the *Devonian* had been struck by a German torpedo, hours after war had been declared.

Maisie could still recall the last time she'd seen Harry. He'd come to visit her at the Grand Hotel that Thursday morning. The restaurant was packed, with a long queue of customers waiting to be seated. He'd stood in line, but when he saw his mother bustling in and out of the kitchen without a moment to spare, he slipped away, assuming she hadn't noticed him. He was always a thoughtful boy, and he knew she didn't approve of being interrupted at work, and, if the truth be told, he also knew she wouldn't have wanted to hear that he'd left Oxford to join the navy.

Sir Walter Barrington dropped by the next day to let

Maisie know that Harry had sailed on the morning tide as fourth officer on the SS *Devonian*, and would be back within the month to join the crew of HMS *Resolution* as an ordinary seaman, as he intended to go off in search of German U-boats in the Atlantic. What he didn't realize was that they were already searching for him.

Maisie planned to take the day off when Harry returned, but it was not to be. Knowing how many other mothers had lost their offspring because of this evil and barbaric war didn't help.

Dr Wallace, the senior medical officer on the SS *Kansas Star*, was waiting by her front door in Still House Lane when she returned home after work that October evening. He didn't need to tell her why he was there. It was etched on his face.

They sat in the kitchen, and the doctor told her he'd been responsible for the welfare of those sailors who'd been dragged from the ocean following the sinking of the *Devonian*. He assured her that he'd done everything in his power to save Harry's life, but unhappily he'd never regained consciousness. In fact, of the nine sailors he tended to that night, only one had survived, a Tom Bradshaw, the *Devonian*'s third officer, who was evidently a friend of Harry's. Bradshaw had written a letter of condolence which Dr Wallace had promised to deliver to Mrs Clifton as soon as the *Kansas Star* returned to Bristol. He had kept his word. Maisie felt guilty the moment the doctor had left to return to his ship. She hadn't even offered him a cup of tea.

She placed Tom Bradshaw's letter on the mantelpiece next to her favourite photograph of Harry singing in the school choir.

When she returned to work the following day, her colleagues at the hotel were kind and solicitous, and Mr Hurst, the hotel manager, suggested she took a few days off. She told him that was the last thing she needed. Instead she took on as much overtime as she could handle, in the hope that it might dull the pain.

It didn't.

—◦—

Many of the young men who worked at the hotel were leaving to join the armed forces, and their places were being taken by women. It was no longer considered a stigma for a young lady to work, and Maisie found herself taking on more and more responsibility as the number of male staff dwindled.

The restaurant manager was due to retire on his sixtieth birthday, but Maisie assumed that Mr Hurst would ask him to stay on until the end of the war. It came as a shock when he called her into his office and offered her the job.

'You've earned it, Maisie,' he said, 'and head office agrees with me.'

'I'd like a couple of days to think about it,' she replied before leaving the office.

Mr Hurst didn't raise the subject for another week, and when he did, Maisie suggested that perhaps she should be put on a month's trial. He laughed.

'It's usual,' he reminded her, 'for the employer, not the employee, to insist on a month's trial.'

Within a week, they'd both forgotten about the trial period, because although the hours were long and her new responsibilities were onerous, Maisie had never felt more fulfilled. She knew that when the war was over and the lads returned from the front, she'd go back to being a waitress. She'd have gone back to being a prostitute, if it had meant Harry would be among those who came home.

◄○►

Maisie didn't need to be able to read a newspaper to know that the Japanese air force had destroyed the American fleet at Pearl Harbor, and the citizens of the United States had risen as one against a common enemy and joined the Allies, because for days it was the only subject on everyone's lips.

It wasn't long before Maisie met her first American.

Thousands of Yanks found their way to the West Country over the next couple of years, and many of them were billeted in an army camp on the outskirts of Bristol. Some of the officers began to dine in the hotel restaurant, but no sooner had they become regulars than they would disappear, never to be seen again. Maisie was continually, painfully, reminded that some of them were no older than Harry.

But that changed when one of them did return. Maisie didn't immediately recognize him when he wheeled himself into the restaurant and asked for his usual table. She had always thought she was good at remembering names, and even better when it came to faces – you have to be when you can't really read and write. But the moment she heard that Southern drawl, the penny dropped. 'It's Lieutenant Mulholland, isn't it?'

'No, Mrs Clifton. It's Major Mulholland now. I've been sent back here to recuperate before they pack me off home to North Carolina.'

She smiled and showed him to his usual table, although he wouldn't allow her to assist him with his wheelchair. Mike, as he insisted Maisie call him, did become a regular, turning up twice, even three times a week.

Maisie laughed when Mr Hurst whispered, 'You know he's sweet on you.'

'I think you'll find my courting days are over,' she replied.

'Don't kid yourself,' he countered. 'You're in your prime, Maisie. I can tell you, Major Mulholland's not the first man who's asked me if you're walking out with anyone.'

'Try not to forget, Mr Hurst, that I'm a grandmother.'

'I wouldn't tell him that if I was you,' said the manager.

Maisie failed to recognize the major a second time when he came in one evening on crutches, the wheelchair clearly having been abandoned. Another month, and the crutches were replaced by sticks, and it wasn't much longer before they too became relics of the past.

One evening, Major Mulholland telephoned to book a table for eight; he had something to celebrate, he told Maisie. She assumed he must be returning to North Carolina, and for the first time she realized how much she would miss him.

She didn't consider Mike a handsome man, but he had the warmest smile and the manners of an English gentleman, or, as he once pointed out, a Southern gentleman. It had become fashionable to bad-mouth the Americans since they'd taken up residence on bases in Britain, and the oft-repeated jibe that they were oversexed, over-paid and over here could be heard on the lips of many Bristolians who'd never even met an American; not least, Maisie's brother Stan, and nothing she could say would change his mind.

By the time the major's celebration dinner had come to an end, the restaurant was almost empty. On the stroke of ten, a fellow officer rose to toast Mike's health and congratulate him.

As the party was about to leave and return to camp before curfew, Maisie told him, on behalf of the whole staff, how pleased they all were that he had fully recovered and was well enough to go home.

'I'm not going home, Maisie,' he said, laughing. 'We were celebrating my promotion to deputy commander of the base. I'm afraid you're stuck with me until this war is over.' Maisie was delighted by the news, and was taken by surprise when he added, 'It's the regimental dance next Saturday, and I wonder if you would do me the honour of being my guest.'

Maisie was speechless. She couldn't remember the last time she'd been asked out on a date. She wasn't sure how long he stood there waiting for her to respond, but before she could do so he said, 'I'm afraid it will be the first time I've stepped on to a dance floor for several years.'

'Me too,' Maisie admitted.

26

MAISIE ALWAYS deposited her wages and her tips in the bank on Friday afternoon.

She didn't take any money home, because she didn't want Stan to find out she was earning more than he was. Her two accounts were always in credit, and every time the current account showed a balance of ten pounds, five would be transferred to her savings account – her little nest egg, as she described it, just in case something went wrong. After her financial setback with Hugo Barrington, she always assumed that something would go wrong.

That Friday she emptied her purse out on to the counter, and the teller began to sort the coins into neat little piles, as he did every week.

'That's four shillings and nine pence, Mrs Clifton,' he said, filling in her account book.

'Thank you,' said Maisie, as he slid the book under the grille. She was putting it back in her purse when he added, 'Mr Prendergast wondered if he could have a word with you.'

Maisie's heart sank. She considered bank managers and rent collectors a breed who only ever dispensed bad news, and she had good cause in Mr Prendergast's case, because the last time he'd asked to see her, it was to remind her there were insufficient funds in her account to cover Harry's fees for his last term at Bristol Grammar School. She reluctantly headed off in the direction of the manager's office.

'Good morning, Mrs Clifton,' said Mr Prendergast, rising from behind his desk as Maisie entered his office. He motioned her to a seat. 'I wanted to speak to you about a private matter.'

Maisie felt even more apprehensive. She tried to recall if she'd written any cheques during the past couple of weeks that might have caused her account to be overdrawn. She had bought a smart dress for the dance Mike Mulholland had invited her to on the American base, but it was second-hand, and well within her budget.

'A valued client of the bank,' Mr Prendergast began, 'has enquired about your plot of land in Broad Street, where Tilly's tea shop once stood.'

'But I assumed I'd lost everything when the building was bombed.'

'Not everything,' said Prendergast. 'The deeds of the land remain in your name.'

'But what could it possibly be worth,' said Maisie, 'now that the Germans have flattened most of the neighbourhood? When I last walked down Chapel Street, it was nothing more than a bomb site.'

'That may well be the case,' replied Mr Prendergast, 'but my client is still willing to offer you two hundred pounds for the freehold.'

'Two hundred pounds?' repeated Maisie as if she'd won the pools.

'That is the sum he is willing to pay,' confirmed Prendergast.

'How much do you think the land is worth?' asked Maisie, taking the bank manager by surprise.

'I've no idea, madam,' he replied. 'I'm a banker, not a property speculator.'

Maisie remained silent for a few moments. 'Please tell your client that I'd like a few days to think about it.'

'Yes, of course,' said Prendergast. 'But you ought to be aware that my client has instructed me to leave the offer on the table for one week only.'

'Then I'll have to make my decision by next Friday, won't I?' said Maisie defiantly.

'As you wish, madam,' said Prendergast, when Maisie rose to leave. 'I'll look forward to seeing you next Friday.'

When Maisie left the bank, she couldn't help thinking that the manager had never addressed her as madam before. During her walk home past black-curtained houses – she only ever took the bus when it was raining – she started to think about how she might spend two hundred pounds, but these thoughts were soon replaced by wondering who could advise her as to whether it was a fair price.

Mr Prendergast had made it sound like a reasonable offer, but which side was he on? Perhaps she'd have a word with Mr Hurst, but long before she reached Still House Lane she decided that it would be unprofessional to involve her boss in a personal matter. Mike Mulholland seemed a shrewd, intelligent man, but what would he know about the value of land in Bristol? As for her brother Stan, there would be absolutely no point in seeking his opinion, as he'd be sure to say, 'Take the money and run, girl.' And come to think about it, the last person she wanted to know about her potential windfall was Stan.

By the time Maisie had turned into Merrywood Lane, darkness was falling and the residents were preparing for blackout. She was no closer to resolving the problem. As she passed the gates of Harry's old primary school, a flood of happy memories returned, and she silently thanked Mr Holcombe for all he'd done for her son while he was growing up. She stopped on the spot. Mr Holcombe was a clever man; after all he'd been to Bristol University and got a degree. Surely he could advise her?

Maisie turned back and walked towards the school gates, but when she entered the playground there was no one to be seen. She checked her watch; a few minutes past five. All the children would have gone home some time ago, so Mr Holcombe had probably already left for the day.

She walked across the playground, opened the school door and stepped into a familiar corridor. It was as if time had stood still; the same red brick walls, just a few more initials etched into them, the same colourful paintings pinned up on the wall, just by different children, the same football cups, just won by another team. Although, where school caps had once hung, gas masks had taken their place. She recalled the first time she'd come to see Mr Holcombe, to complain about the red marks she'd found on Harry's backside at bath-time. He'd remained calm while she lost her temper, and Maisie had left an hour later in no doubt who the guilty party was.

Maisie noticed a light coming from under the door

of Mr Holcombe's classroom. She hesitated, took a deep breath and knocked softly on the pebbled glass.

'Come on in,' said the cheerful voice she remembered so well.

She entered the room to find Mr Holcombe seated behind a large pile of books, pen scratching across paper. She was about to remind him who she was when he leapt up and said, 'This is a pleasant surprise, Mrs Clifton, especially if it's me you're looking for.'

'Yes it is,' Maisie replied, a little flustered. 'I'm sorry to bother you, Mr Holcombe, but I need some advice, and I didn't know who else to turn to.'

'I'm flattered,' said the schoolmaster, offering her a tiny chair, normally occupied by an eight-year-old. 'How can I help?'

Maisie told him about her meeting with Mr Prendergast, and the offer of £200 for her piece of land on Broad Street. 'Do you think it's a fair price?' she asked.

'I've no idea,' said Mr Holcombe, shaking his head. 'I have no experience of such matters, and I'd be worried about giving you the wrong advice. Actually, I thought it might be another matter you'd come to see me about.'

'Another matter?' repeated Maisie.

'Yes. I hoped you'd seen the notice on the board outside the school, and wanted to apply.'

'Apply for what?' she asked.

'One of the government's new schemes for night classes, designed to help people like you, who are clearly intelligent, but haven't had the opportunity to continue their education.'

Maisie didn't want to admit that even if she'd seen the notice, she would have struggled to read it. 'I'm too overworked to consider taking on anything else at the moment,' she said, 'what with the hotel, and . . . and—'

'I'm sorry to hear that,' said Mr Holcombe, 'because I think you'd be an ideal candidate. I'll be taking most of the classes myself and it would have given me particular pleasure to teach the mother of Harry Clifton.'

'It's just that—'

'It would only be for an hour, twice a week,' he continued, refusing to give up. 'The classes are in the evenings, and there's nothing to stop you dropping out if you decided they weren't for you.'

'It was kind of you to think of me, Mr Holcombe. Perhaps when I haven't got quite so much on my plate.' She stood up and shook hands with the schoolmaster.

'I'm sorry I couldn't help you with your problem, Mrs Clifton,' he said as he accompanied her to the door. 'Mind you, it's a nice problem to have.'

'It was good of you to spare the time, Mr Holcombe,' she replied before leaving. Maisie walked back down the corridor, across the playground and out through the school gates. She stood on the pavement and stared at the notice board. How she wished she could read.

27

MAISIE HAD ONLY taken a taxi a couple of times in her life: once to Harry's wedding in Oxford, and then only from the local station, and on a second occasion, quite recently, when she'd attended her father's funeral. So when an American staff car drew up outside 27 Still House Lane, she felt a little embarrassed, and only hoped the neighbours had their curtains drawn.

As she came down the staircase wearing her new red silk dress with padded shoulders and belted at the waist – very fashionable before the war – she spotted her mother and Stan staring out of the window.

The driver got out of the car and knocked on the front door. He looked unsure that he'd come to the right address. But when Maisie opened the door, he understood immediately why the major had invited this particular belle to the regimental dance. He gave Maisie a smart salute and opened the back door of the car.

'Thank you,' she said, 'but I'd prefer to sit in the front.'

Once the driver had found his way back on to the main road, Maisie asked him how long he'd been working for Major Mulholland.

'All my life, ma'am. Man and boy.'

'I'm not sure I understand,' said Maisie.

'We both come from Raleigh, North Carolina. Once this war's over, I'll be goin' home to my old job in the major's factory.'

'I didn't know the major owned a factory.'

'Several, ma'am. In Raleigh, he's known as the Corn-on-the-Cob King.'

'Corn on the cob?' queried Maisie.

'You ain't seen nothin' like it in Bristol, ma'am. To truly appreciate corn on the cob, it has to be boiled, covered in melting butter and eaten straight after it's picked – and preferably in North Carolina.'

'So who's running the factories while the Corn-on-the-Cob King is away fighting the Germans?'

'Young Joey, his second son, with a little help from his sister Sandy, would be my guess.'

'He has a son and a daughter back home?'

'Had two sons and a daughter, ma'am, but sadly Mike Junior was shot down over the Philippines.'

Maisie wanted to ask the corporal about Mike senior's wife, but felt that the young man might have been embarrassed by questions on that subject, so she moved on to safer ground and asked about his home state. 'Finest in the forty-eight,' he replied, and didn't stop talking about North Carolina until they reached the camp gate.

When the guard spotted the car, he immediately raised the barrier and gave Maisie a smart salute as they drove on into the compound. 'The major asked me to take you straight to his quarters, ma'am, so you can have a drink before going across to the dance.'

The car drew up outside a small prefabricated house

and she spotted Mike standing on the doorstep waiting to greet her. She jumped out of the car before the driver could open the door, and walked quickly up the path to join him. He bent down, kissed her on the cheek and said, 'Come on in, honey, I'd like you to meet some of my colleagues.' He took her coat and added, 'You look just swell.'

'Like one of your corn on the cobs?' suggested Maisie.

'More like one of our North Carolina peaches,' he said as he guided her towards a noisy room, full of laughter and animated voices. 'Now let's make everyone jealous, because they're about to find out that I'm escorting the belle of the ball.'

Maisie entered a room filled with officers and their dates. She couldn't have been made to feel more welcome. She couldn't help wondering, if she'd been the guest of an English major a few miles up the road at the Wessex regimental HQ, would they also have treated her as their equal?

Mike guided her around the room, introducing her to all his colleagues, including the camp commander, who clearly approved. As she moved from group to group, she couldn't help noticing several photographs scattered around the room, on tables, bookshelves and the mantelpiece, of what could only have been Mike's wife and children.

Just after nine o'clock, the guests made their way to the gymnasium, where the dance was being held, but not before the dutiful host had helped all the ladies on with their coats. This gave Maisie the opportunity to look more closely at one of the photographs of a beautiful young woman.

'My wife Abigail,' said Mike when he came back into the room. 'A great beauty, like you. I still miss her. She died of cancer almost five years ago. Now that's something all of us should be declaring war on.'

'I'm so sorry,' said Maisie. 'I didn't mean . . .'

'No. Now you've discovered just how much we have in common. I understand exactly how you feel, having lost a husband and a son. But hell, this is an evening to celebrate, not to feel sorry for ourselves, so come on, honey, now you've made all the officers jealous, let's go and make the other ranks sore.'

Maisie laughed as she took his arm. They left the house and joined a stream of boisterous young people who were all heading in the same direction.

Once she was on the dance floor, the youthful and exuberant Americans made Maisie feel as if she'd known them all her life. During the evening, several of the officers asked her for a dance, but Mike rarely let her out of his sight. When the band struck up the last waltz, she couldn't believe how quickly the evening had flown by.

Once the applause had died down, everyone remained on the floor. The band played a number unfamiliar to Maisie, but which served to remind everyone else in the room that their country was at war. Many of the young men who stood to attention with hand on heart, lustily singing 'The Star-Spangled Banner', would not live to celebrate their next birthday. Like Harry. What an unnecessary waste of life, Maisie thought.

As they walked off the dance floor, Mike suggested that they return to his quarters and enjoy a glass of Southern Comfort before the corporal drove her home.

It was the first bourbon Maisie had ever drunk, and it quickly loosened her tongue.

'Mike, I have a problem,' she said once she'd settled on the sofa and her glass had been refilled. 'And as I've only got a week to solve it, I could do with a dollop of your Southern common sense.'

'Fire away, honey,' said Mike. 'But I ought to warn you that if limeys are involved, I've never been able to get on their wavelength. In fact, you're the first one I've been able to relax with. Are you sure you're not an American?'

Maisie laughed. 'That's sweet of you, Mike.' She took another swig of bourbon, by which time she felt ready to do far more than just tell him her immediate problems. 'It all began many years ago, when I owned a tea shop in Broad Street called Tilly's. It's now nothing more than a derelict bomb site, but someone is offering me two hundred pounds for it.'

'So what's the problem?' asked Mike.

'I have no idea what it's really worth.'

'Well, one thing's for certain, as long as there's a chance the Germans might return and continue their bombing raids, no one is going to be rebuilding anything on that site, at least not until the war is over.'

'Mr Prendergast described his client as a property speculator.'

'Sounds more like a profiteer to me,' said Mike, 'someone who buys derelict land on the cheap, so when the war is over they'll be able to make a quick killing. Frankly, that sort of spiv will do anything to make a fast buck, and ought to be strung up.'

'But isn't it just possible that two hundred pounds is a fair price?'

'Depends on your marriage value.'

Maisie sat bolt upright, not sure she'd heard him correctly. 'I don't understand what you mean.'

'You say the whole of Broad Street was bombed, and not one building survived?'

'Yes, but why would that make my little plot any more valuable?'

'If this speculator guy has already got his hands on every other bit of land in the street, you're in a strong position to strike a bargain. In fact, you should demand a dowry, because your plot may be the one piece of land that, withheld, will prevent him from rebuilding the entire block, although that's the last thing he'd want you to find out.'

'So how do I discover if my little site has marriage value?'

'Tell your bank manager that you won't settle for less than four hundred pounds, and you'll find out soon enough.'

'Thank you, Mike,' said Maisie, 'that's good advice.' She smiled, took another swig of Southern Comfort, and passed out in his arms.

28

When Maisie came down for breakfast the following morning, she couldn't remember who'd driven her home, or how she'd got upstairs to her room.

'I put you to bed,' said her mother as she poured her a cup of tea. 'A nice young corporal drove you home. He even helped me get you up the stairs.'

Maisie sank into a chair, before taking her mother slowly through the evening, leaving her in no doubt how much she'd enjoyed Mike's company.

'And you're sure he's not married?' asked her mother.

'Hold your horses, Mum, it was only our first date.'

'Did he seem keen?'

'I think he asked me to the theatre next week, but I'm not sure which day, or which theatre,' she said as her brother Stan came into the room.

Stan plonked himself down at the end of the table and waited for a bowl of porridge to be placed in front of him, before gulping down the contents like a dog drinking water on a hot day. When he'd finished, he flicked off the top of a bottle of Bass and drank it in one draught. 'I'll have another,' he said. 'As it's Sunday,' he added, burping loudly.

Maisie never spoke during Stan's morning ritual, and she usually slipped off to work before he had time to air his opinions on anything that crossed his mind. She rose from her place and was just about to leave for the morning service at St Mary's, when he bellowed, 'Sit down, woman! I want a word with you before you go to church.'

Maisie would have liked to walk out without responding, but Stan wasn't beyond dragging her back and giving her a black eye if the mood took him. She sat back down.

'So what are you doin' about that two hundred nicker you're in line for?' he demanded.

'How did you find out?'

'Mum told me all about it last night when you were out on the town getting laid by your American fancy man.'

Maisie frowned at her mother, who looked embarrassed, but said nothing. 'For your information, Stan, Major Mulholland is a gentleman, and what I do in my spare time is none of your business.'

'If he's an American, you stupid bitch, let me warn you – they don't wait to be asked, they think everythin's theirs by right.'

'You speak with your usual first-hand knowledge on the subject, no doubt,' said Maisie, trying to remain calm.

'Yanks are all the same,' said Stan. 'They only want one thing, and once they've got it, they bugger off back home and leave us to finish the job, just like they did in the first war.'

Maisie realized there was no point in continuing the

conversation, so she just sat there, hoping this particular storm would blow over quickly.

'You still haven't told me what you're doin' about the two hundred quid,' said Stan.

'I haven't made up my mind yet,' said Maisie. 'In any case, how I spend my money has got nothing to do with you.'

'It's got everything to do with me,' said Stan, 'because half of it's mine.'

'And how do you work that out?' asked Maisie.

'On account of the fact that you're livin' in my house for a start, so I'm entitled. And let me warn you, girl, in case you're thinkin' of double-crossin' me, if I don't get my fair share, I'll beat you so black and blue, even an American negro won't give you a second look.'

'You make me sick, Stan,' said Maisie.

'Not half as sick as I'll make you if you don't cough up, because then I'll—'

Maisie stood up, marched out of the kitchen, ran down the hall, grabbed her coat and was out of the front door before Stan had come to the end of his tirade.

—◇—

When she checked the lunch bookings that Sunday, Maisie quickly realized she'd have to make sure that two of her customers were seated as far away from each other as possible. She put Mike Mulholland on his usual table, and Patrick Casey on the far side of the room, so there wasn't any chance of them bumping into each other.

She hadn't set eyes on Patrick for nearly three years, and wondered if he'd changed. Did he still have those irresistible good looks and Irish charm that had so captivated her when they'd first met?

One of her questions was answered the moment he entered the room.

'How nice to see you after all this time, Mr Casey,' she said before accompanying him to his table. Several middle-aged women took a second look at the handsome Irishman as he crossed the room. 'Will you be staying with us for long this time, Mr Casey?' Maisie asked as she passed him a menu.

'That depends on you,' said Patrick. He opened the menu, but didn't study its contents.

Maisie hoped that no one noticed her blush. She turned, to see Mike Mulholland waiting by reception; he would never allow anyone but Maisie to show him to his table. She hurried across and whispered, 'Hello, Mike. I've reserved your usual table. Would you like to follow me?'

'I sure would.'

Once Mike had turned his attention to the menu – although he always had the same two dishes every Sunday, soup of the day followed by boiled beef and Yorkshire pudding – she walked back across the room to take Patrick's order.

During the next two hours, Maisie kept a close eye on both men, while at the same time trying to supervise a hundred other customers. When the dining-room clock struck three, there were only two people left in the room; John Wayne and Gary Cooper, thought Maisie, waiting to see who would draw first at the OK Corral. She folded Mike's bill, put it on a plate and took it across to him. He paid it without checking.

'Another great meal,' he said, before adding in a

whisper, 'I hope we're still on for the theatre Tuesday night?'

'We sure are, honey,' said Maisie, teasing him.

'Then I'll see you at the Old Vic at eight,' he said as a waitress passed by his table.

'I'll look forward to that, sir, and you can be sure I'll pass on your compliments to the chef.'

Mike stifled a laugh, before leaving the table and strolling out of the dining room. He looked back at Maisie and smiled.

Once he was out of sight, Maisie took Patrick's bill across to him. He checked every item and left a large tip. 'Are you doing anything special tomorrow evening?' he asked, giving Maisie that smile she remembered so well.

'Yes, I'm attending an evening class.'

'You're kidding me,' said Patrick.

'No, and I mustn't be late, because it's the first lesson of a twelve-week course.' She didn't tell him that she hadn't finally decided whether to go through with it or not.

'Then it will have to be Tuesday,' said Patrick.

'I already have a date on Tuesday.'

'Do you really, or are you just saying that to get rid of me?'

'No, I'm going to the theatre.'

'Then what about Wednesday, or is that your night for algebraic equations?'

'No, composition and reading out loud.'

'Thursday?' said Patrick, trying not to sound exasperated.

'Yes, I'm free on Thursday,' said Maisie, as another waitress passed by their table.

'That's a relief,' said Patrick. 'I was beginning to think

I'd have to book in for a second week, just to get an appointment.'

Maisie laughed. 'So what do you have in mind?'

'I thought we'd start by going to—'

'Mrs Clifton.' Maisie swung round to find the hotel manager, Mr Hurst, standing behind her. 'When you've finished with this customer,' he said, 'perhaps you'd be kind enough to join me in my office?'

Maisie thought she'd been discreet, but now she feared she might even get the sack, because it was against company policy for members of staff to fraternize with the customers. That was how she'd lost her previous job, and Pat Casey had been the customer in question on that occasion.

She was grateful that Patrick slipped out of the restaurant without another word, and once she'd checked the till, she reported to Mr Hurst's office.

'Take a seat, Mrs Clifton. I have a rather serious matter to discuss with you.' Maisie sat down and gripped the arms of the chair to stop herself shaking. 'I could see you were having another busy day.'

'A hundred and forty-two covers,' said Maisie. 'Almost a record.'

'I don't know how I'm going to replace you,' he said before adding, 'but management make these decisions, not me, you understand. It's out of my hands.'

'But I enjoy my job,' said Maisie.

'That may well be the case, but I have to tell you that on this occasion I agree with head office.' Maisie sat back, ready to accept her fate. 'They have made it clear,' continued Mr Hurst, 'that they no longer want you to work in the dining room, and have asked me to replace you as soon as possible.'

'But why?'

'Because they're keen for you to go into management. Frankly, Maisie, if you were a man, you'd already be running one of our hotels. Congratulations!'

'Thank you,' said Maisie, as she began to think about the implications.

'Let's get the formalities out of the way, shall we?' said Mr Hurst as he pulled open his desk drawer and extracted a letter. 'You'll need to study this carefully,' he said. 'It details your new terms of employment. Once you've read it, sign it, return it to me, and I'll send it back to head office.'

That was when she made the decision.

29

MAISIE WAS FEARFUL of making a fool of herself.

When she reached the school gate, she nearly turned back, and would have done, if she hadn't seen another woman older than herself entering the building. She followed her through the front door and along the corridor, stopping when she reached the classroom. She peeped inside, hoping to find the room so full that no one would notice her. But there were only seven other people present: two men and five women.

She crept to the back of the classroom and took a seat behind the two men, hoping she couldn't be seen. Maisie immediately regretted her decision, because if she'd taken a seat by the door, she could have escaped more easily.

She bowed her head when the door opened and Mr Holcombe swept into the room. He took his place behind the desk in front of the blackboard, tugged the lapels of his long black gown and peered down at his pupils. He smiled when he spotted Mrs Clifton seated near the back.

'I'm going to start by writing out all twenty-six letters of the alphabet,' he began, 'and I want you to call them out as I write them down.' He picked up a piece of chalk and turned his back on the class. He wrote the letter A on the blackboard, and several voices could be heard in unison, B, a veritable chorus, C, everyone except Maisie. When he came to Z, Maisie mouthed the letter.

'I'm now going to point to a letter at random and see if you can still identify it.' The second time round, Maisie called out over half of them, and on her third attempt she was leading the chorus. When the hour was up, only Mr Holcombe would have realized it was her first lesson in twenty years and Maisie wasn't in any hurry to go home.

'By the time we meet again on Wednesday,' said Mr Holcombe, 'you must all be able to write the twenty-six letters of the alphabet, in their correct order.'

Maisie intended to have the alphabet mastered by Tuesday, so there would be no possibility of her making a mistake.

'To those of you who are unable to join me in the pub for a drink, I'll see you on Wednesday.'

Maisie assumed you had to be invited to join Mr Holcombe, so she slipped out of her chair and headed for the door, while the others surrounded the school-master's desk with a dozen questions.

'Will you be coming to the pub, Mrs Clifton?' asked the schoolmaster just as Maisie reached the door.

'Thank you, Mr Holcombe. I'd like that,' she heard herself saying, and joined the others as they left the room and strolled across the road to the Ship Inn.

One by one, the other pupils drifted off, until only the two of them were seated at the bar.

'Do you have any idea just how bright you are?'

asked Mr Holcombe after he'd bought her another orange juice.

'But I left school at twelve, and I still can't read or write.'

'You may have left school too early, but you've never stopped learning. And as you're Harry Clifton's mother, you'll probably end up teaching me.'

'Harry taught you?'

'Daily, without realizing it. But then, I knew very early on that he was brighter than me. I only hoped I could get him to Bristol Grammar School before he found it out for himself.'

'And did you?' asked Maisie, smiling.

'It was a damn close-run thing,' admitted Holcombe.

'Last orders!' shouted the barman.

Maisie looked at the clock behind the bar. She couldn't believe it was already 9.30, and blackout regulations had to be adhered to.

It seemed natural that Mr Holcombe should walk her home; after all, they'd known each other for so many years. On the way through the unlit streets, he told her many more stories about Harry, which made her both happy and sad. It was clear that Mr Holcombe also missed him, and she felt guilty for not thanking him many years before.

When they reached the front door of her home in Still House Lane, Maisie said, 'I don't know your first name.'

'Arnold,' he said shyly.

'It suits you,' she said. 'May I call you Arnold?'

'Yes, of course.'

'And you must call me Maisie.' She took out her

front-door key and placed it in the lock. 'Goodnight, Arnold. See you on Wednesday.'

―◦―

An evening at the theatre brought back many happy memories for Maisie of the days when Patrick Casey would take her to the Old Vic whenever he visited Bristol. But just as the memory of Patrick had faded and she'd begun to spend time with another man with whom she felt there might be a future, the damned leprechaun bounced back into her life. He'd already told her that there was a reason he wanted to see her, and she wasn't in much doubt what that reason was. She didn't need him to throw her life into turmoil yet again. She thought about Mike, one of the kindest and most decent men she'd ever come across, and guileless in his attempts to hide his feelings for her.

One thing Patrick had instilled in her was never to be late for the theatre. He felt there was nothing more embarrassing than treading on people's toes as you made your way in darkness to the inevitable centre seats after the curtain had risen.

Mike was already standing in the foyer holding a programme when Maisie walked into the theatre ten minutes before the curtain was due to rise. As soon as she saw him she smiled, and couldn't help thinking how he always raised her spirits. He returned her smile, and gave her a gentle kiss on the cheek.

'I don't know a lot about Noël Coward,' he admitted as he handed her the programme, 'but I've just been reading a synopsis of the play, and it turns out to be about a man and a woman who can't make up their mind who they should marry.'

Maisie said nothing as they entered the stalls. She began to follow the letters of the alphabet backwards until she reached H. When they made their way to the centre of the row, she wondered how Mike had managed to get such superb seats for a sold-out show.

Once the lights faded and the curtain rose, he took her hand. He only let go when Owen Nares made his entrance, and the audience burst into applause. Maisie became entranced by the story, even if it was a little too close for comfort. But the spell was broken when the loud whine of a siren drowned out Mr Nares's words. An audible groan went up around the auditorium, as the actors hurried off stage to be replaced by the theatre manager, who efficiently organized an exit strategy that would have gladdened the heart of a regimental sergeant major. Bristolians had long been familiar with flying visits from Germans who had no intention of paying for their theatre tickets.

Mike and Maisie made their way out of the theatre and down the steps to a bleak but familiar shelter that had become a home from home for regular theatregoers. The audience grabbed any place that was available for the unticketed performance. The great social equalizer, as Clement Attlee had described life in an air-raid shelter.

'Not my idea of a date,' said Mike, placing his jacket on the stone floor.

'When I was young,' said Maisie, as she sat down on the jacket, 'many a young fellow tried to get me down here, but you're the first one who's succeeded.' Mike laughed, as she began to scribble something on the cover of the programme.

'I'm flattered,' he said, placing an arm gently around her shoulder as the ground started to shake with bombs that sounded perilously close. 'You've never been to America, have you, Maisie?' he asked, trying to take her mind off the air raid.

'I've never been to London,' admitted Maisie. 'In fact, the furthest I've ever travelled is to Weston-super-Mare and Oxford, and as both trips turned out to be disastrous, I'd be perhaps better off staying at home.'

Mike laughed. 'I'd love to show you America,' he said, 'particularly the south.'

'I think we'd have to ask the Germans to take a few nights off before we could consider doing that,' said Maisie as the all-clear sounded.

A ripple of applause burst out in the shelter, and everyone emerged from the unscheduled interval and made their way back into the theatre.

Once they'd taken their seats, the theatre manager walked on to the stage. 'The performance will continue with no interval,' he announced. 'But should the Germans decide to pay us another visit, it will have to be cancelled. I'm sorry to say there will be no refunds. German regulations,' he announced. A few people laughed.

Within moments of the curtain going back up, Maisie once again lost herself in the story, and when the actors finally took their bows, the whole audience rose in appreciation, not only for the performance, but for another small victory over the Luftwaffe, as Mike described it.

'Harvey's or the Pantry?' asked Mike as he picked up the programme, on which each letter of the play's title had been crossed out and rewritten below, arranged in alphabetical order, A E E I I L P R S T V V.

'The Pantry,' said Maisie, not wanting to admit that on the one occasion she'd been to Harvey's with Patrick, she'd spent the entire evening glancing around the tables, dreading the thought that Lord Harvey's daughter Elizabeth might be dining there with Hugo Barrington.

Mike took a long time studying the menu, which surprised Maisie, because the choice of dishes was so limited. He usually chatted about what was taking place back at camp, or the fort as he liked to call it, but not tonight; not even the oft-repeated grumbles about limeys not understanding baseball. She began to wonder if he wasn't feeling well.

'Is everything all right, Mike?' she asked.

He looked up. 'They're sending me back to the States,' he said as a waiter appeared by their side and asked if they would like to order. Great timing, thought Maisie, but at least it gave her a little time to think, and not about what she wanted to eat. Once they'd ordered and the waiter had left them, Mike tried again.

'I've been assigned to a desk job in Washington.'

Maisie leaned across the table and took his hand.

'I pressed them to let me stay for another six months . . . so I could be with you, but they turned my request down.'

'I'm sorry to hear that,' said Maisie, 'but—'

'Please don't say anything, Maisie, because I'm finding this difficult enough already. Though God knows

I've given it enough thought.' This was followed by another long silence. 'I realize we've only known each other for a short time, but my feelings haven't changed since the first day I set eyes on you.' Maisie smiled. 'And I wondered,' he continued, 'hoped, prayed, that you might consider coming back to America with me . . . as my wife.'

Maisie was speechless. 'I'm so very flattered,' she eventually managed, but couldn't think of anything else to say.

'Of course, I realize you'll need time to think it over. I'm sorry that the ravages of war don't allow for the niceties of a long courtship.'

'When do you go home?'

'At the end of the month. So if you did say yes, we could get married at the base and fly back together as man and wife.' He leant forward and took her hand. 'I've never felt more certain about anything in my whole life,' he said as the waiter reappeared by their side.

'So which one of you is the chopped liver?'

◄o►

Maisie didn't sleep that night, and when she came down to breakfast the following morning, she told her mother that Mike had proposed to her.

'Jump at it,' was Mrs Tancock's immediate response. 'You'll never get a better chance to begin a new life. And, let's face it,' she added, glancing sadly at the photograph of Harry on the mantelpiece, 'there's no longer any reason for you to stay here.'

Maisie was about to express her one reservation when Stan burst into the room. She got up from the table. 'I'd better get a move on if I'm not going to be late for work.'

'Don't think I've forgotten about that 'undred quid you owe me!' he shouted as she left the room.

<o>

Maisie was sitting on the edge of her seat in the front row when Mr Holcombe entered the classroom at seven that evening.

Her hand shot up several times during the next hour, like a tiresome schoolgirl who knows all the answers and wants teacher to notice her. If he did, he didn't let on.

'Could you start coming in on Tuesdays and Thursdays in future, Maisie?' Mr Holcombe asked as they strolled across to the pub with the rest of the class.

'Why?' asked Maisie. 'Aren't I good enough?'

'Am I not good enough,' corrected the schoolmaster without thinking. 'On the contrary,' he added, 'I've decided to put you into the intermediate class, before this lot,' he said, indicating her fellow classmates with the sweep of an arm, 'become overwhelmed.'

'But won't I be out of my depth, Arnold?'

'I do hope so, but no doubt you'll have caught up by the end of the month, by which time I'll have to put you into the advanced class.'

Maisie didn't respond, as she knew it wouldn't be too long before she would have to tell Arnold that she'd made other plans for the end of the month.

Once again, they ended up sitting alone together at the bar, and once again he accompanied her back to Still House Lane, only this time, when Maisie took the front-door key out of her bag, she thought he looked as if he might be trying to summon up the courage to kiss her. Surely not. Hadn't she got enough problems to cope with?

'I was just wondering,' he said, 'which book you ought to read first.'

'It won't be a book,' said Maisie as she placed the key in the lock. 'It will be a letter.'

30

PATRICK CASEY had breakfast, lunch and dinner in the hotel restaurant on Monday, Tuesday and Wednesday.

Maisie assumed that he would take her to dinner at the Plimsoll Line in the hope that it might evoke past memories. In fact, she hadn't been back to the restaurant since Patrick had disappeared off to Ireland. She was right, and it did.

Maisie was determined that she would not be seduced once again by Patrick's charm and good looks, and she intended to tell him about Mike and their plans for the future. But as the evening progressed, she found it more and more difficult to raise the subject.

'So, what have you been up to since I was last in Bristol?' Patrick asked her over a pre-dinner drink in the lounge bar. 'Not that anyone could miss the fact that you're running the best hotel restaurant in the city while somehow managing to fit in evening classes at the same time.'

'Yes, I shall miss all that when . . .' she began wistfully.

'When what?' asked Patrick.

'It's only a twelve-week course,' said Maisie, trying to recover.

'In twelve weeks' time,' said Patrick, 'my bet is you'll be the one who's giving the classes.'

'What about you? What have you been up to?' she asked as the head waiter came over to tell them their table was ready.

Patrick didn't answer the question until they'd sat down at a quiet table in the corner of the room.

'You may remember I was promoted to deputy manager of the company about three years ago, which is why I had to go back to Dublin.'

'I haven't forgotten why you had to go back to Dublin,' said Maisie with some feeling.

'I tried to return to Bristol several times, but once war broke out, it proved almost impossible, and it didn't help that I couldn't even write to you.'

'Well, that problem may well be solved in the near future.'

'Then you can read to me in bed.'

'And how has your company fared during these hard times?' asked Maisie, steering the conversation back on to safer ground.

'Actually, a lot of Irish companies have done rather well out of the war. Because of the country's neutrality, we've been able to deal with both sides.'

'You're willing to do business with the Germans?' said Maisie in disbelief.

'No, as a company we've always made it clear where our allegiances lie, but you won't be surprised to know that quite a few of my countrymen are happy to do business with the Germans. Because of that, we had a couple of tough years, but once the Americans entered the war, even the Irish began to believe the Allies might end up on the winning side.'

That was her chance to tell Patrick about one American in particular, but she didn't take it. 'So what brings you to Bristol now?' she asked.

'The simple answer is, you.'

'Me?' Maisie quickly tried to think of a convincing way of bringing the conversation back on to a less personal footing.

'Yes. Our managing director will be retiring at the end of the year, and the chairman has asked me to take his place.'

'Congratulations,' said Maisie, relieved to be back on safer ground. 'And you want me to take over as your deputy,' she added, trying to make light of it.

'No, I want you to be my wife.'

Maisie's tone changed. 'Didn't it cross your mind, Patrick, just for one moment during the past three years, that someone else might have come into my life?'

'Daily,' said Patrick, 'which is why I came over to find out if there was someone else.'

Maisie hesitated. 'Yes, there is.'

'And has he asked you to marry him?'

'Yes,' she whispered.

'Have you accepted his proposal?'

'No, but I've promised to let him have my answer before he returns to America at the end of the month,' she said more firmly.

'Does that mean I'm still in with a chance?'

'Frankly, Patrick, the odds are stacked against you. You haven't been in touch for nearly three years, and suddenly you turn up out of the blue as if nothing's changed.'

Patrick made no attempt to defend himself, while a waiter served their main courses. 'I wish it was that easy,' he said.

'Patrick, it was always that easy. If you'd asked me to marry you three years ago, I would have happily jumped on the first boat to Ireland.'

'I couldn't ask you then.'

Maisie put down her knife and fork without taking a bite. 'I always wondered if you were married.'

'Why didn't you say something at the time?'

'I was so much in love with you, Patrick, I was even willing to suffer that indignity.'

'And to think I only returned to Ireland because I couldn't ask you to be my wife.'

'And has that changed?'

'Yes. Bryony left me over a year ago. She met someone who took more interest in her than I did, which wouldn't have been difficult.'

'Oh my God,' said Maisie, 'why is my life always so complicated?'

Patrick smiled. 'I'm sorry if I've disrupted your life again, but I won't give in so easily this time, not while I still believe there's even the slightest chance.' He leant across the table and took her hand. A moment later the waiter reappeared by their side, an anxious look on his face as he looked at the two untouched plates of food that had been allowed to go cold.

'Is everything all right, sir?' he asked.

'No,' said Maisie. 'It's not.'

<o>

Maisie lay awake and thought about the two men in her life. Mike, so reliable, so kind, who she knew would be faithful until his dying day, and Patrick, so exciting, so alive, with whom there would never be a dull moment. She changed her mind several times during the night, and it didn't help that she had so little time to make her decision.

When she came down to breakfast the following morning, her mother didn't mince her words when Maisie asked her, if given the choice, which of the two men she should marry.

'Mike,' she said without hesitation. 'He'll be far more reliable in the long run, and marriage is for the long run. In any case,' she added, 'I've never trusted the Irish.'

Maisie considered her mother's words, and was about to ask another question when Stan barged into the room. Once he'd gulped down his porridge, he barged into her thoughts.

'Aren't you seeing the bank manager today?'

Maisie didn't reply.

'I thought so. Just make sure you come straight home with my 'undred quid. If you don't, my girl, I'll come looking for you.'

◂○▸

'How nice to see you again, madam,' said Mr Prendergast as he ushered Maisie into a chair just after four o'clock that afternoon. He waited for Maisie to settle before he ventured, 'Have you been able to give my client's generous offer some thought?'

Maisie smiled. With one word, Mr Prendergast had given away whose interests he was looking after.

'I most certainly have,' Maisie replied, 'and I would be obliged if you would tell your client that I wouldn't consider accepting a penny less than four hundred pounds.'

Mr Prendergast's mouth opened.

'And as it's possible that I might be leaving Bristol at the end of the month, perhaps you'd also be kind enough to tell your client that my *generous* offer will only remain on the table for one week.'

Mr Prendergast closed his mouth.

'I'll try to drop by again at the same time next week, Mr Prendergast, when you can let me know your client's decision.' Maisie rose from her place and gave the manager a sweet smile, before adding, 'I do hope you have a pleasant weekend, Mr Prendergast.'

—◦—

Maisie was finding it difficult to concentrate on Mr Holcombe's words, and not just because the intermediate class was proving far more demanding than the beginners, which she already regretted forsaking. When her hand did go up, it was more often to ask a question than to answer one.

Arnold's enthusiasm for his subject was contagious, and he had a real gift for making everyone feel equal and the most insignificant contribution seem important.

After twenty minutes of going back over what he called the basics he invited the class to turn to page 72 of *Little Women*. Numbers weren't a problem for Maisie, and she quickly turned to the correct page. He then invited a woman in the third row to stand and read the first paragraph, while the rest of the class followed each sentence word for word. Maisie placed a finger at the top of the page and tried desperately to follow the narrative, but she soon lost her place.

When the schoolmaster asked an elderly man in the front row to read the same passage a second time, Maisie was able to identify some of the words, but she was praying that Arnold wouldn't ask her to be next. She breathed a sigh of relief when someone else was invited to read the paragraph again. When the new reader sat down, Maisie bowed her head, but she didn't escape.

'And finally, I'm going to ask Mrs Clifton to stand up and read us the same passage.'

Maisie rose uncertainly from her place and tried to concentrate. She recited the entire paragraph almost word for word, without once looking down at the page. But then, she had spent so many years having to remember long, complicated restaurant orders.

Mr Holcombe gave her a warm smile as she sat down. 'What a remarkable memory you have, Mrs Clifton.' No one else seemed to pick up the significance of his words. 'I would now like to move on and discuss the meaning of certain words in that paragraph. In the second line, for example, you'll see the word betrothal, an old-fashioned word. Can anyone give me a more modern example that has the same meaning?'

Several hands shot up, and Maisie's would have been among them if she hadn't recognized a familiar heavy step heading towards the classroom door.

'Miss Wilson,' said the schoolmaster.

'Marriage,' said Miss Wilson as the door burst open and Maisie's brother barged into the room. He stopped in front of the blackboard, his eyes darting from person to person.

'Can I help you?' asked Mr Holcombe politely.

'No,' said Stan. 'I've come to collect what's rightfully

mine, so keep your mouth shut, schoolmaster, if you know what's good for you, and mind your own business.' His eyes settled on Maisie.

Maisie had intended to tell him at breakfast that it would be another week before she found out if Mr Prendergast's valued customer had accepted her counter-offer. But as Stan walked purposefully towards her, she knew she wasn't going to be able to convince him that she didn't have the money.

'Where's my cash?' he demanded long before he'd reached her desk.

'I haven't got it yet,' said Maisie. 'You're going to have to wait another week.'

'Like hell I am,' said Stan, who grabbed her by the hair and began to drag her, screaming, out from behind her desk. As he moved towards the door, the rest of the class sat mesmerized. Only one man stood in his path.

'Get out of my way, schoolmaster.'

'I suggest you let go of your sister, Mr Tancock, if you don't want to be in even more trouble than you already are.'

'From you and whose army?' laughed Stan. 'If you don't fuck off, mate, I'll knock your teeth right down your throat, and I promise you, that won't be a pretty sight.'

Stan didn't see the first punch coming, and when it landed in his solar plexus, he bent double, so he could be excused for not recovering before the second blow landed on his chin. The third sent him sprawling to the ground like a felled oak.

Stan lay on the floor, clutching his stomach, expecting a boot to be put in. The schoolmaster towered over him, and waited for him to recover. When he finally did, Stan rose unsteadily to his feet, never once taking his eyes off the schoolmaster as he edged slowly towards the door. When he thought he was at a safe distance, he looked back at Maisie, who was still lying on the floor, curled up in a ball, sobbing quietly.

'You'd better not come home till you've got my money, my girl,' he growled, 'if you know what's good for you!' Without another word he stormed out into the corridor.

Even after Maisie heard the door slam, she was still too frightened to move. The rest of the class gathered up their books and slipped quietly out of the room. No one would be visiting the pub that night.

Mr Holcombe walked quickly across the room, knelt down beside his charge and gathered her trembling body in his arms. It was some time before he said, 'You'd better come home with me tonight, Maisie. I'll make up a bed in the spare room. You can stay for as long as you want to.'

EMMA BARRINGTON

1941–1942

31

'SIXTY-FOURTH AND PARK,' said Emma as she jumped into a taxi outside Sefton Jelks's Wall Street office.

She sat in the back of the cab and tried to think about what she would say to Great-aunt Phyllis when, or if, she got past her front door, but the car radio was so loud that she couldn't concentrate. She thought about asking the driver to turn the volume down, but she had already learnt that New York cabbies are deaf when it suits them, although rarely dumb and never mute.

While listening to the commentator describe in an excited voice what had taken place at somewhere called Pearl Harbor, Emma accepted that her great-aunt's first question was bound to be, what brings you to New York, young lady, followed by, how long have you been here, and then, why has it taken you so long to come and see me? To none of these questions did she have a plausible answer, unless she was willing to tell Great-aunt Phyllis everything – something she wanted to avoid because she hadn't even told her own mother *every-thing*.

She might not even realize she has a great-niece,

thought Emma. And was it possible there was a long-standing family feud that Emma didn't know about? Or perhaps her great-aunt was a recluse, divorced, remarried, or insane?

All Emma could remember was once seeing a Christmas card signed Phyllis, Gordon and Alistair. Was one a husband and the other a son? To make matters worse, Emma didn't have any proof that she really was Phyllis's great-niece.

Emma was even less confident about facing her by the time the cab drew up outside the front door and she'd handed over another quarter.

Emma stepped out of the cab, looked up at the imposing, four-storey brownstone and changed her mind several times about knocking on the door. She finally decided to walk round the block, in the hope that she would feel more confident by the time she returned. As she walked down 64th Street, Emma couldn't help noticing that New Yorkers were scurrying back and forth at an unusually frantic pace, with shocked and anxious looks on their faces. Some were looking up at the sky. Surely they didn't believe the next Japanese air raid would be on Manhattan?

A paperboy standing on the corner of Park kept shouting out the same headline, 'America declares war! Read the latest!'

By the time Emma arrived back outside the front door, she had decided she couldn't have picked a worse day to call on her great-aunt. Perhaps it might be wise to return to her hotel and leave it until tomorrow. But why would tomorrow be any different? Her money had almost run out, and if America was now at war, how would she get back to England and, more important, to Sebastian, whom she'd never intended to be apart from for more than a couple of weeks?

She found herself climbing the five steps to face a shiny black door with a large, highly polished brass knocker. Perhaps Great-aunt Phyllis was out. Perhaps she'd moved. Emma was about to knock when she noticed a bell in the wall with the word 'Tradesmen' printed underneath. She pressed the bell, took a pace back and waited, far happier to face the person who dealt with tradesmen.

A few moments later a tall, elegantly dressed man, wearing a black jacket, striped trousers, a white shirt and grey tie, opened the door.

'How may I help you, ma'am?' he enquired, clearly having decided that Emma wasn't a tradesman.

'My name is Emma Barrington,' she told him. 'I wondered if my great-aunt Phyllis is at home.'

'She is indeed, Miss Barrington, Monday being her bridge afternoon. If you'll be kind enough to step inside, I'll let Mrs Stuart know you're here.'

'I could always come back tomorrow, if it isn't convenient,' stammered Emma, but he'd closed the door behind her and was already halfway down the corridor.

As Emma stood waiting in the hall, she couldn't have missed which country the Stuarts hailed from: a portrait of Bonnie Prince Charlie above crossed swords and a Stuart Clan shield hung on the wall at the far end of the hall. Emma walked slowly up and down, admiring paintings by Peploe, Fergusson, McTaggart and Raeburn. She remembered that her grandfather Lord

Harvey owned a Lawrence that hung in the drawing room of Mulgelrie Castle. She had no idea what her great-uncle did for a living, but he clearly did it well.

The butler returned a few minutes later, the same impassive look on his face. Perhaps he hadn't heard the news about Pearl Harbor.

'Madam will receive you in the drawing room,' he said.

How like Jenkins he was: no surplus words, an even pace that never varied, and somehow he managed to display deference without being deferential. Emma wanted to ask him which part of England he came from, but knew he would consider that an intrusion, so she followed him along the corridor without another word.

She was about to start climbing the stairs when the butler stopped, pulled back a lift grille and stood aside to allow her to step in. A lift in a private house? Emma wondered if Great-aunt Phyllis was an invalid. The lift shuddered as it reached the third floor and she stepped out into a beautifully furnished drawing room. If it were not for the noise of traffic, blaring horns and police sirens coming from the street below, one might have been in Edinburgh.

'If you'll wait here please, madam.'

Emma remained by the door while the butler walked across the room to join four elderly ladies who were seated around a log fire, enjoying tea and crumpets while listening intently to a radio that had never blared.

When the butler announced, 'Miss Emma Barrington,' they all turned and looked in Emma's direction. She couldn't mistake which one of them was Lord Harvey's sister, long before she rose to greet her: the flaming-red hair, the impish smile and the unmistakable air of someone who isn't first generation.

'It surely can't be little Emma,' she declared, as she left the group and sailed across to her great-niece, the hint of a Highland lilt still in her voice. 'The last time I saw you, dear girl, you were wearing a gymslip, short white socks and daps and carrying a hockey stick. I felt quite concerned for the little boys playing in the opposing team.' Emma smiled; the same sense of humour as her grandfather. 'And now look at you. You've blossomed into such a beautiful creature.' Emma blushed. 'So what brings you to New York, my dear?'

'I'm sorry to intrude like this, Great-aunt,' Emma began, glancing nervously towards the other three ladies.

'Don't worry about them,' she whispered. 'After the President's announcement, they've got more than enough to keep themselves occupied. Now, where are your bags?'

'My bag is at the Mayflower Hotel,' Emma told her.

'Parker,' she said, turning to the butler, 'send someone round to pick up Miss Emma's things from the Mayflower, and then prepare the main guest bedroom because, after today's news, I have a feeling my great-niece is going to be with us for quite some time.' The butler melted away.

'But, Great-aunt—'

'No buts,' she said, raising a hand. 'And I must insist that you stop calling me Great-aunt, it makes me sound like an old battleaxe. Now it's quite possible that I am an old battleaxe, but I do not wish to be reminded of it on a regular basis, so, please, call me Phyllis.'

'Thank you, Great-aunt Phyllis,' Emma said.

Phyllis laughed. 'I do so love the English,' she said. 'Now come and say hello to my friends. They will be fascinated to meet such an independent young lady. So frightfully modern.'

◄○►

'Quite some time' turned out to be more than a year, and as each day passed, Emma was more and more desperate to be reunited with Sebastian, but was only able to follow her son's progress from letters sent by her mother, and occasionally Grace. Emma wept when she learned of the death of 'Gramps', because she'd thought he'd live for ever. She tried not to think about who would take over the company, and assumed her father wouldn't have the nerve to show his face in Bristol.

Phyllis couldn't have made Emma feel more at home if she'd been her own mother. Emma quickly discovered that her great-aunt was a typical Harvey, generous to a fault, and the page defining the words impossible, implausible and impractical must have been torn out of her dictionary at an early age. The main guest bedroom, as Phyllis called it, was a suite of rooms overlooking Central Park, which came as a pleasant surprise after Emma's cramped single room at the Mayflower.

Emma's second surprise was when she came down for dinner on her first evening and found her great-aunt dressed in a flaming-red gown, drinking a glass of whiskey and smoking a cigarette in a long holder. She smiled at the thought of being described as modern by this woman.

'My son Alistair will be joining us for dinner,' she announced before Parker had been given a chance to pour Emma a glass of Harvey's Bristol Cream. 'He's a lawyer and a bachelor,' she added. 'Two disadvantages from which he's most unlikely to recover. But at times he can be quite amusing, if somewhat dry.'

Cousin Alistair arrived a few minutes later, dressed in a dinner jacket for a meal with his mother, thus embodying 'the British abroad'.

Emma guessed that he was around fifty, and a good tailor had disguised the fact that he was carrying a few surplus pounds. His humour may have been a little dry, but he was unquestionably bright, fun and well informed, even if he did go on a bit about the case he was currently working on. It came as no surprise when his proud mother told Emma over dinner that Alistair was the youngest partner in his law firm, since the death of her husband. Emma assumed that Phyllis knew why he wasn't married.

She couldn't be sure if it was the delicious food, the excellent wine or simply American hospitality that caused her to relax so much that she ended up telling them everything that had happened to her since Great-aunt Phyllis had last seen her on a hockey field at Red Maids' School.

By the time Emma had explained why she crossed the Atlantic despite the risks involved, they were both staring at her as if she'd just landed from another planet.

Once Alistair had devoured the last morsel of his fruit tart and turned his attention to a large brandy, he spent the next thirty minutes cross-examining their unexpected guest, as if he were opposing counsel and she a hostile witness.

'Well, I must say, Mother,' he said as he folded his napkin, 'this case looks far more promising than Amalgamated Wire versus New York Electric. I can't wait to cross swords with Sefton Jelks.'

'What's the point of wasting our time on Jelks,' Emma said, 'when it's far more important to find Harry and clear his name?'

'I couldn't agree more,' said Alistair. 'But I have a feeling that one will lead to the other.' He picked up Emma's copy of *The Diary of a Convict*, but didn't open it, just studied the spine.

'Who's the publisher?' asked Phyllis.

'Viking Press,' said Alistair, removing his glasses. 'Harold Guinzburg, no less.'

'Do you think he and Max Lloyd might have collaborated in this deception?' Alistair asked, turning to his mother.

'Certainly not,' she replied. 'Your father once told me he'd come up against Guinzburg in court. I remember he described him as a formidable adversary, but a man who would never consider bending the law, let alone breaking it.'

'Then we're in with a chance,' said Alistair, 'because if that's the case, he won't be pleased to discover what's been perpetrated in his name. However, I'll need to read the book before I arrange a meeting with the publisher.' Alistair looked across the table and smiled at Emma. 'I shall be fascinated to discover what Mr Guinzburg makes of you, young lady.'

'And I,' said Phyllis, 'will be equally fascinated to discover what Emma makes of Harold Guinzburg.'

'Touché, Mama,' Alistair conceded.

After Parker had poured Alistair a second brandy

and relit his cigar, Emma ventured to ask him what he thought her chances were of being allowed to visit Harry in Lavenham.

'I'll make an application on your behalf tomorrow,' he promised between puffs. 'Let's see if I can't do a little better than your helpful detective.'

'My helpful detective?' repeated Emma.

'Unusually helpful,' said Alistair. 'Once he realized Jelks was involved, I'm amazed Detective Kolowski even agreed to see you.'

'I'm not at all surprised that he was helpful,' said Phyllis, winking at Emma.

32

'AND YOU SAY your husband wrote this book?'

'No, Mr Guinzburg,' said Emma. 'Harry Clifton and I are not married, although I am the mother of his child. But yes, Harry did write *The Diary of a Convict* while he was incarcerated at Lavenham.'

Harold Guinzburg removed the half-moon spectacles from the end of his nose and took a closer look at the young woman seated on the opposite side of his desk. 'I do have a slight problem with your claim,' he said, 'and I feel I should point out that every sentence of the diary was written in Mr Lloyd's hand.'

'He copied Harry's manuscript word for word.'

'For that to be possible, Mr Lloyd would have had to share a cell with Tom Bradshaw, which shouldn't be difficult to check.'

'Or they could have worked together in the library,' suggested Alistair.

'If you were able to prove this,' said Guinzburg, 'it would place my company, and by that I mean me, in an invidious position to say the least, and in the circumstances, I might be wise to seek legal advice.'

'We would like to make it clear from the start,'

interjected Alistair, who was sitting on Emma's right, 'that we came here in a spirit of goodwill, as we felt you would wish to be acquainted with my cousin's story.'

'It was the only reason I agreed to see you,' said Guinzburg, 'as I was a great admirer of your late father.'

'I didn't realize you knew him.'

'I didn't,' said Guinzburg. 'He appeared for the other side in a dispute my company was involved in, and I left the courtroom wishing he'd been on my side. However, if I am to accept your cousin's story,' he continued, 'I hope you won't mind if I ask Miss Barrington one or two questions.'

'I'm happy to answer any questions you might have, Mr Guinzburg,' said Emma. 'But may I ask if you've read Harry's book?'

'I make a point of reading every book we publish, Miss Barrington. I can't pretend I find all of them enjoyable, or even finish every one, but in the case of *The Diary of a Convict*, I knew the moment I'd finished the first chapter that it would be a bestseller. I also made a note in the margin on page two-eleven.' Guinzburg picked up the book and flicked through its pages before beginning to read. *'I've always wanted to be an author, and am currently working on an outline plot for the first in a series of detective novels based in Bristol.'*

'Bristol,' said Emma, interrupting the old man. 'How could Max Lloyd possibly know anything about Bristol?'

'There is a Bristol in Mr Lloyd's home state of Illinois, Miss Barrington,' said Guinzburg, 'as Max pointed out when I told him I'd be interested in reading the first in the series.'

'You never will,' Emma promised him.

'He's already submitted the opening chapters of

Mistaken Identity,' said Guinzburg, 'and I have to say, they're rather good.'

'And were those chapters written in the same style as the diary?'

'Yes. And before you ask, Miss Barrington, they are also written in the same hand, unless you're suggesting that they were also copied.'

'He's got away with it once. Why wouldn't he try it on a second time?'

'But do you have any real proof that Mr Lloyd didn't write *The Diary of a Convict*?' said Guinzburg, beginning to sound a little irritated.

'Yes, sir. I am the "Emma" in the book.'

'If that is the case, Miss Barrington, I agree with the author's judgement that you are indeed a great beauty, and you have already proved, to quote him, to be both spirited and combative.'

Emma smiled. 'And you're an old flatterer, Mr Guinzburg.'

'As he wrote, spirited and combative,' said Guinzburg, placing his half-moon spectacles back on his nose. 'Nevertheless, I doubt your claim would stand up in a court of law. Sefton Jelks could put half a dozen Emmas on the witness stand who would swear blind they had known Lloyd all their lives. I need something more substantial.'

'Don't you find it a little too much of a coincidence, Mr Guinzburg, that the day Thomas Bradshaw arrives at Lavenham just happens to be the first day of the diary?'

'Mr Lloyd explained that he didn't start writing the diary until he became the prison librarian, when he had more time on his hands.'

'But how do you explain there being no mention of his last night in prison, or the morning he's released? He just has breakfast in the canteen, and reports to the library for another day's work.'

'What explanation do you have?' asked Guinzburg, peering at her over the top of his glasses.

'Whoever wrote the diary is still in Lavenham, and probably working on the next volume.'

'That shouldn't be difficult for you to verify,' said Guinzburg, raising an eyebrow.

'I agree,' said Alistair, 'and I've already submitted an application for Miss Barrington to visit Mr Bradshaw on compassionate grounds, and am waiting for the warden of Lavenham to give his approval.'

'May I be allowed to ask a few more questions, Miss Barrington, in the hope of removing any lingering doubts?' asked Guinzburg.

'Yes, of course,' said Emma.

The old man smiled, pulled his waistcoat down, pushed up his spectacles and studied a list of questions on a notepad in front of him. 'Who is Captain Jack Tarrant, sometimes known as Old Jack?'

'My grandfather's oldest friend. They served in the Boer War together.'

'Which grandfather?'

'Sir Walter Barrington.'

The publisher nodded. 'And did you consider Mr Tarrant to be an honourable man?'

'Like Caesar's wife, he was beyond reproach. He was probably the single biggest influence in Harry's life.'

'But isn't he to blame for the fact that you and Harry are not married?'

'Is that question relevant?' asked Alistair, jumping in.

'I suspect we're about to find out,' said Guinzburg, not taking his eyes off Emma.

'Jack felt it was his duty to alert the vicar to the possibility that my father, Hugo Barrington, might also be Harry's father,' said Emma, her voice breaking.

'Was that necessary, Mr Guinzburg?' snapped Alistair.

'Oh yes,' said the publisher, picking up the copy of *The Diary of a Convict* from his desk. 'I am now convinced that it was Harry Clifton, and not Max Lloyd, who wrote this book.'

Emma smiled. 'Thank you,' she said, 'even if I'm not sure what I can do about it.'

'I know exactly what I'm going to do about it,' said Guinzburg. 'To start with, I shall release a revised edition as quickly as the presses can print it, with two major changes: Harry Clifton's name will replace Max Lloyd's on the front cover, and his photograph will appear on the back cover, assuming you have one, Miss Barrington.'

'Several,' said Emma, 'including one of him on the *Kansas Star* as it sailed into New York harbour.'

'Ah, that would also explain—' began Guinzburg.

'But if you were to do that,' interrupted Alistair, 'all hell will break loose. Jelks will issue a writ on behalf of his client for defamation, and claim punitive damages.'

'Let's hope so,' said Guinzburg, 'because if he does, the book will undoubtedly go back to number one on the bestseller lists, and remain there for several months. However, if he does nothing, as I suspect will be the case, it will show that he believes he's the only person who has seen the missing exercise book Harry Clifton wrote about ending up in Lavenham.'

'I knew there was another one,' said Emma.

'There certainly is,' said Guinzburg, 'and it was your mention of the *Kansas Star* that made me realize the manuscript Mr Lloyd submitted as the opening chapters of *Mistaken Identity* is nothing more than an account of what happened to Harry Clifton before he was sentenced for a crime he didn't commit.'

'May I be allowed to read it?' said Emma.

—◦—

The moment Emma walked into Alistair's office, she knew something had gone badly wrong. The familiar warm welcome and gracious smile had been replaced by a furrowed brow.

'They're not going to let me visit Harry, are they,' she said.

'No,' said Alistair. 'Your application was turned down.'

'But why? You told me I was well within my rights.'

'I phoned the warden earlier this morning and asked him exactly the same question.'

'And what reason did he give?'

'You can hear for yourself,' said Alistair, 'because I made a tape recording of our conversation. Listen carefully, because it gives us three very important clues.' Without another word, he leant forward and pressed the play button on his Grundig. Two spools began to whirl.

'Lavenham Correctional Facility.'

'I'd like to speak to the warden.'

'Who's calling?'

'Alistair Stuart. I'm a New York attorney.'

Silence, followed by another ringing tone. A longer silence, then, 'I'll put you through, sir.'

Emma was sitting on the edge of her seat when the warden came on the line.

'Good morning, Mr Stuart. This is Warden Swanson. How can I help you?'

'Good morning, Mr Swanson. I made an application ten days ago on behalf of my client, Miss Emma Barrington, requesting a visit on compassionate grounds to an inmate, Thomas Bradshaw, at the earliest possible opportunity. I received a letter from your office this morning saying the application has been turned down. I can find no legal reason for—'

'Mr Stuart, your application was processed in the usual way, but I was unable to grant your request because Mr Bradshaw is no longer being held at this establishment.'

Another long silence followed, although Emma could see that the tape was still turning. Alistair eventually said, 'And which institution has he been transferred to?'

'I am not at liberty to disclose that information, Mr Stuart.'

'But under the law, my client has the right to—'

'The prisoner has signed a document waiving his rights, a copy of which I'd be happy to send to you.'

'But why would he do that?' said Alistair, casting a line into the water.

'I am not at liberty to disclose that information,' repeated the warden, not rising to the bait.

'Are you at liberty to divulge anything at all concerning Thomas Bradshaw?' asked Alistair, trying not to sound exasperated.

Another long silence followed and, although the tape was still running, Emma wondered if the warden had put his phone down. Alistair placed a finger to his lips, and suddenly the voice was back on the line.

'Harry Clifton was released from prison, but continued to serve his sentence.' Another long pause. 'And I lost the best librarian this prison's ever had.'

The phone went dead.

Alistair pressed the stop button before he spoke. 'The warden went as far as he could to assist us.'

'By mentioning Harry by name?' said Emma.

'Yes, but also by letting us know he served in the prison library until very recently. That explains how Lloyd got his hands on the diaries.'

Emma nodded. 'But you said there were *three* important clues,' she reminded him. 'What was the third?'

'That Harry was released from Lavenham, but continues to serve his sentence.'

'Then he must be in another prison,' said Emma.

'I don't think so,' said Alistair. 'Now we're at war, my bet is that Tom Bradshaw will be serving the rest of his sentence in the navy.'

'What makes you think that?'

'It's all in the diaries,' said Alistair. He picked up a copy of *The Diary of a Convict* from his desk, turned to a page marked by a bookmark and read: *'The first thing I'll do when I get back to Bristol is join the navy and fight the Germans.'*

'But they'd never have allowed him to return to England before he'd completed his sentence.'

'I didn't say he'd joined the British Navy.'

'Oh God,' said Emma as the significance of Alistair's words sank in.

'At least we know Harry's still alive,' said Alistair cheerfully.

'I wish he was still in prison.'

HUGO BARRINGTON

1942–1943

33

SIR WALTER'S FUNERAL was held at St Mary's Redcliffe, and the late chairman of Barrington's Shipping Line would surely have been proud to see such a packed congregation and to hear the heartfelt eulogy delivered by the Bishop of Bristol.

After the service, the mourners lined up to offer their condolences to Sir Hugo as he stood at the north door of the church, alongside his mother. He was able to explain to those who asked that his daughter Emma was marooned in New York, although he couldn't tell them why she'd gone there in the first place, and his son Giles, of whom he was inordinately proud, was interned in a German PoW camp in Weinsberg; information his mother had passed on to him the previous evening.

During the service, Lord and Lady Harvey, Hugo's ex-wife Elizabeth and their daughter Grace had all been seated in the front row of the church, on the opposite side of the aisle from Hugo. All of them had paid their respects to the grieving widow, and had then pointedly left without acknowledging his presence.

Maisie Clifton had sat at the back of the church, her

head bowed throughout the service, and left moments after the bishop had delivered the final blessing.

When Bill Lockwood, the managing director of Barrington's, stepped forward to shake hands with his new chairman and to express his condolences, all Hugo had to say was, 'I expect to see you in my office at nine o'clock tomorrow morning.'

Mr Lockwood gave a slight bow.

A reception was held at Barrington Hall after the funeral, and Hugo mingled among the mourners, several of whom were about to discover that they no longer had a job with Barrington's. When the last guest had departed, Hugo went up to his bedroom and changed for dinner.

He entered the dining room with his mother on his arm. Once she was seated, he took his father's place at the head of the table. During the meal, while there were no servants in attendance, he told his mother that, despite his father's misgivings, he was a reformed character.

He went on to assure her that the company was in safe hands, and that he had exciting plans for its future.

◄o►

Hugo drove his Bugatti through the gates of Barrington's shipyard for the first time in over two years, at 9.23 the following morning. He parked in the chairman's space before making his way up to his father's old office.

As he stepped out of the lift on the fifth floor, he saw Bill Lockwood pacing up and down the corridor outside his office, a red folder under his arm. But then Hugo had always intended to keep him waiting.

'Good morning, Hugo,' said Lockwood, stepping forward.

Hugo strolled past him without responding. 'Good morning, Miss Potts,' he said to his old secretary, as if he'd never been away. 'I'll let you know when I'm ready to see Mr Lockwood,' he added, before walking through to his new office.

He sat down at his father's desk – that was how he still thought of it, and he wondered how long that feeling would last – and began to read *The Times*. Once the Americans and Russians had entered the war, far more people were beginning to believe in an Allied victory. He put down the paper.

'I'll see Mr Lockwood now, Miss Potts.'

The managing director entered the chairman's office with a smile on his face. 'Welcome back, Hugo,' he said.

Hugo gave him a fixed stare and said, 'Chairman.'

'I'm sorry, chairman,' said a man who had served on the board of Barrington's when Hugo was in short trousers.

'I'd like you to bring me up to date on the company's financial position.'

'Of course, chairman.' Lockwood opened the red folder he'd been carrying under his arm.

As the chairman hadn't invited him to sit, he remained standing. 'Your father,' he began, 'managed to guide the company prudently through troubled times, and despite several setbacks, not least the Germans continually targeting the docks during their nightly bombing raids in the early part of the war, with the help of government contracts, we have managed to weather the storm, so we should be in good shape once this dreadful war is over.'

'Cut the waffle,' said Hugo, 'and get to the bottom line.'

'Last year,' continued the managing director turning a page, 'the company made a profit of thirty-seven thousand, four hundred pounds and ten shillings.'

'Wouldn't want to forget the ten shillings, would we?' said Hugo.

'That was always your father's attitude,' said Lockwood, missing the sarcasm.

'And this year?'

'Our half yearly results suggest that we're well placed to equal, possibly even surpass, last year's results.' Lockwood turned another page.

'How many places are currently available on the board?' asked Hugo.

The change of subject took Lockwood by surprise, and he had to turn several pages before he could respond. 'Three, as unfortunately Lord Harvey, Sir Derek Sinclair and Captain Havens all resigned following your father's death.'

'I'm glad to hear that,' said Hugo. 'It will save me the trouble of sacking them.'

'I presume, chairman, you would not wish me to record those sentiments in my minutes of this meeting?'

'I don't give a damn if you do or don't,' Hugo said.

The managing director bowed his head.

'And when are you due to retire?' was Hugo's next question.

'I'll be sixty in a couple of months' time, but if you felt, chairman, given the circumstances—'

'What circumstances?'

'As you will only just have got your feet under the

table, so to speak, I could be persuaded to stay on for a couple more years.'

'That's good of you,' said Hugo, and the managing director smiled for the second time that morning. 'But please don't put yourself out on my account. Two months will be just fine by me. So what's the biggest challenge we're facing at the moment?'

'We have recently applied for a major government contract to lease out our merchant fleet to the navy,' said Lockwood once he'd recovered. 'We're not the favourites, but I think your father gave a good account of himself when the inspectors visited the company earlier this year, so we should be taken seriously.'

'When will we find out?'

'Not for some time, I fear. Civil servants aren't built for speed,' he added, laughing at his own joke. 'I have also prepared several discussion papers for your consideration, chairman, so that you will be well briefed before you chair your first board meeting.'

'I don't anticipate holding that many board meetings in the future,' said Hugo. 'I believe in leading from the front, making decisions and standing by them. But you can leave your briefing papers with my secretary, and I'll get round to them when I find the time.'

'As you wish, chairman.'

Within moments of Lockwood leaving his office, Hugo was on the move. 'I'm going to visit my bank,' he said as he passed Miss Potts's desk.

'Shall I call Mr Prendergast and let him know you'd like to see him?' Miss Potts asked as she hurried after him down the corridor.

'Certainly not,' said Hugo. 'I want to take him by surprise.'

'Is there anything you need me to do before you return, Sir Hugo?' Miss Potts enquired as he stepped into the lift.

'Yes, see that the name on my door is changed before I get back.'

Miss Potts turned round to look at the office door. *Sir Walter Barrington, Chairman* was displayed in gold leaf.

The lift door closed.

As Hugo drove into the centre of Bristol, he felt that his first few hours as chairman could not have gone better. All was finally right with the world. He parked his Bugatti outside the National Provincial Bank in Corn Street, leant across and picked up a packet he'd left under the passenger seat.

He strolled into the bank, past the reception desk and headed straight for the manager's office, giving a little tap on the door before marching in. A startled Mr Prendergast leapt up as Hugo placed a shoebox on his desk and sank into the chair opposite him.

'I hope I'm not interrupting anything important,' said Hugo.

'Of course not, Sir Hugo,' said Prendergast, staring at the shoebox. 'I'm available for you at any time.'

'That's good to know, Prendergast. Why don't you begin by bringing me up to date on Broad Street?'

The bank manager scurried across the room, pulled open the drawer of a filing cabinet and extracted a thick folder, which he placed on the table. He sorted through some papers before he spoke again.

'Ah yes,' he said eventually. 'Here's what I was looking for.'

Hugo was tapping the arm of his chair impatiently.

'Of the twenty-two businesses which have ceased to trade in Broad Street since the bombing began, seventeen have already accepted your offer of two hundred pounds or less for their freehold, namely Roland the florist, Bates the butcher, Makepeace—'

'What about Mrs Clifton? Has she accepted my offer?'

'I'm afraid not, Sir Hugo. Mrs Clifton said she wouldn't settle for less than four hundred pounds, and has only given you until next Friday to accept her offer.'

'Has she, be damned. Well, you can tell her that two hundred pounds is my final offer. That woman has never had a brass farthing to her name, so I don't expect we'll have to wait too much longer before she comes to her senses.'

Prendergast gave a slight cough that Hugo remembered well.

'If you succeed in purchasing every property in the street except Mrs Clifton's, four hundred pounds might turn out to be quite reasonable.'

'She's bluffing. All we have to do is bide our time.'

'If you say so.'

'I do say so. And in any case, I know exactly the right man to convince the Clifton woman that she'd be wise to settle for two hundred pounds.'

Prendergast didn't look convinced, but satisfied himself by asking, 'Is there anything else I can do to assist you?'

'Yes,' said Hugo, removing the lid from the shoebox. 'You can deposit this money into my personal account and issue me with a new cheque book.'

'Of course, Sir Hugo,' said Prendergast, looking into

the box. 'I'll count it and issue you with a receipt and a cheque book.'

'But I'll need to make an immediate withdrawal, as I have my eye on a Lagonda V12.'

'Winner of Le Mans,' said Prendergast, 'but then, you've always been a pioneer in that particular field.'

Hugo smiled as he rose from his chair.

'Give me a call the moment Mrs Clifton realizes that two hundred pounds is all she's going to get.'

—◆—

'Do we still employ Stan Tancock, Miss Potts?' Hugo asked as he marched back into the office.

'Yes, Sir Hugo,' replied his secretary, following him into the room. 'He works as a loader in the stock yard.'

'I want to see him immediately,' said the chairman, as he slumped down behind his desk.

Miss Potts hurried out of the room.

Hugo stared at the files piled on his desk which he was supposed to have read before the next board meeting. He flicked open the cover of the top one: a list of the union's demands following their last meeting with management. He had reached number four on the list, two weeks' paid holiday each year, when there was a tap on the door.

'Tancock to see you, chairman.'

'Thank you, Miss Potts. Send him in.'

Stan Tancock walked into the room, removed his cloth cap and stood in front of the chairman's desk.

'You wanted to see me, guv?' he said, looking a little nervous.

Hugo glanced up at the squat, unshaven docker,

whose beer belly didn't leave much doubt where most of his wage packet went on a Friday night.

'I've got a job for you, Tancock.'

'Yes, guv,' said Stan looking more hopeful.

'It concerns your sister, Maisie Clifton, and the plot of land she owns on Broad Street, where Tilly's tea shop used to stand. Do you know anything about it?'

'Yes, guv, some geezer offered her two hundred quid for it.'

'Is that right?' said Hugo, removing his wallet from an inside pocket. He extracted a crisp five-pound note and laid it on the desk. Hugo remembered the same licking of the lips and the same piggy eyes the last time he'd bribed the man. 'I want you to make sure, Tancock, that your sister accepts the offer, without the suggestion that I'm in any way involved.'

He slid the five-pound note across the desk.

'No problem,' said Stan, no longer looking at the chairman, only at the five-pound note.

'There will be another of those,' Hugo said, tapping his wallet, 'the day she signs the contract.'

'Consider it done, guv.'

Hugo added casually, 'I was sorry to hear about your nephew.'

'Don't make much odds to me,' said Stan. 'Got far too big for his boots, in my opinion.'

'Buried at sea, I was told.'

'Yeah, more'n two years back.'

'How did you find out?'

'Ship's doctor came to visit me sister, didn't he.'

'And was he able to confirm that young Clifton was buried at sea?'

'Sure did. Even brought a letter from some mate who was on board the ship when Harry died.'

'A letter?' said Hugo leaning forward. 'What did this letter say?'

'No idea, guv. Maisie never opened it.'

'So what did she do with the letter?'

'Still on the mantelpiece, isn't it?'

Hugo extracted another five-pound note.

'I'd like to see that letter.'

34

HUGO THREW ON the brakes of his new Lagonda when he heard a paperboy shouting his name from a street corner.

'Sir Hugo Barrington's son decorated for gallantry at Tobruk. Read all about it!'

Hugo leapt out of his car, handed the paperboy a halfpenny and looked at a photograph of his son when he was school captain of Bristol Grammar that dominated the front page. He climbed back into his car, turned off the ignition and read all about it.

> Second Lieutenant Giles Barrington of the 1st Battalion, the Wessex, son of Sir Hugo Barrington Bt, has been awarded the Military Cross following action in Tobruk. Lt Barrington led a platoon across eighty yards of open desert, killing a German officer and five other soldiers, before over-running an enemy dugout and capturing 63 German infantry men from Rommel's crack Afrika Korps. Lt/Col. Robertson of the Wessex described Lt Barrington's action as displaying remarkable leadership and selfless courage in the face of overwhelming odds.

2/Lt Barrington's platoon commander, Captain Alex Fisher, also an Old Bristolian, was involved in the same action, and mentioned in dispatches, as was Corporal Terry Bates, a local butcher from Broad Street. Lt Giles Barrington MC was later captured by the Germans when Rommel sacked Tobruk. Neither Barrington, nor Bates, is aware of their award for gallantry, because both of them are currently prisoners of war in Germany. Captain Fisher has been reported as missing in action. Full story pages 6 & 7.

Hugo sped home to share the news with his mother.

'How proud Walter would have been,' she said once she'd finished reading the report. 'I must call Elizabeth immediately, in case she hasn't heard the news.'

It was the first time anyone had mentioned his former wife's name for a long while.

—◦—

'I thought you'd be interested to know,' said Mitchell, 'that Mrs Clifton is wearing an engagement ring.'

'Who would want to marry that bitch?'

'A Mr Arnold Holcombe, it seems.'

'Who's he?'

'A schoolmaster. Teaches English at Merrywood Elementary. In fact, he used to teach Harry Clifton before he went to St Bede's.'

'But that was years ago. Why haven't you mentioned his name before?'

'They've only recently met up again, when Mrs Clifton began attending evening classes.'

'Evening classes?' repeated Hugo.

'Yes,' said Mitchell. 'She's been learning to read and write. Seems she's a chip off the young block.'

'What do you mean?' snapped Hugo.

'When the class took their final exam at the end of the course, she came top.'

'Did she now?' said Hugo. 'Perhaps I should visit Mr Holcombe and let him know exactly what his fiancée was up to during the years he lost touch with her.'

'Perhaps I should mention that Holcombe boxed for Bristol University, as Stan Tancock found to his cost.'

'I can handle myself,' said Hugo. 'Meanwhile I want you to keep an eye on another woman, who just might prove every bit as dangerous for my future as Maisie Clifton.'

Mitchell removed a tiny notebook and pencil from an inside pocket.

'Her name is Olga Piotrovska, and she lives in London, at number forty-two Lowndes Square. I need to know everyone she comes into contact with, particularly if she's ever interviewed by any members of your former profession. Spare no details, however trivial or unpleasant you may consider them.'

Once Hugo had finished speaking, the notebook and pencil disappeared. He then handed Mitchell an envelope, a sign that the meeting was over. Mitchell slipped his pay packet into his jacket pocket, stood up and limped away.

◄o►

Hugo was surprised how quickly he became bored with being chairman of Barrington's. Endless meetings to attend, countless papers to read, minutes to be circulated, memos to be considered, and a stack of mail that should have been replied to by return of post. And on top of that, before he left every evening, Miss Potts would hand him a briefcase bulging with even more papers that had to be gone over by the time he was back behind his desk at eight the following morning.

Hugo invited three chums to join the board, including Archie Fenwick and Toby Dunstable, in the hope that they would lessen his load. They rarely showed up for meetings, but still expected to receive their stipend.

As the weeks passed, Hugo began turning up at the office later and later, and after Bill Lockwood reminded the chairman that it was only a few days to his sixtieth birthday, when he would be retiring, Hugo capitulated and said that he'd decided Lockwood could stay on for another couple of years.

'How kind of you to reconsider my position, chairman,' said Lockwood. 'But I feel that, having served the company for almost forty years, the time has come for me to make way for a younger man.'

Hugo cancelled Lockwood's farewell party.

That younger man was Ray Compton, Lockwood's deputy, who had only been with the company for a few months, and certainly hadn't got his feet under the table. When he presented Barrington's year results to the board, Hugo accepted for the first time that the company was only just breaking even, and agreed with Compton that the time had come to start laying off some of the dock labourers before the company couldn't afford to pay their wages.

As Barrington's fortunes dwindled, the nation's future looked more hopeful.

With the German army retreating from Stalingrad, the British people began to believe for the first time that the Allies could win the war. Confidence in the future started to seep back into the nation's psyche as theatres, clubs and restaurants began to reopen all over the country.

Hugo longed to be back in town and to rejoin his social set, but Mitchell's reports continued to make it clear that London was one city he'd be wise to steer clear of.

◄○►

The year 1943 didn't begin well for Barrington's.

There were several cancelled contracts from customers who became exasperated when the chairman couldn't be bothered to answer their letters, and several creditors began demanding payment, one or two of them even threatening writs. And then one morning, a ray of sunlight appeared that Hugo believed would solve all of the immediate cash-flow problems.

It was a call from Prendergast that raised Hugo's hopes.

The bank manager had been approached by the United Dominion Real Estate Company, who were showing an interest in purchasing the Broad Street site.

'I think, Sir Hugo, it would be prudent not to mention the figure over the phone,' Prendergast intoned slightly pompously.

Hugo was sitting in Prendergast's office forty minutes later, and even he gasped when he heard how much they were willing to offer.

'Twenty-four thousand pounds?' repeated Hugo.

'Yes,' said Prendergast, 'and I'm confident that's their opening bid, and I can push them up to nearer thirty. Remembering that your original outlay was less than three thousand pounds, I think we can consider it a shrewd investment. But there's a fly in the ointment.'

'A fly?' said Hugo, sounding anxious.

'In the form of Mrs Clifton,' said Prendergast. 'The offer is conditional on you obtaining the freehold for the entire site, including her plot.'

'Offer her eight hundred,' Hugo barked.

The Prendergast cough followed, although he didn't remind his client that had he taken his advice, they could have closed a deal with Mrs Clifton for four hundred pounds some months ago, and if she were ever to find out about United Dominion's offer . . .

'I'll let you know the moment I've heard from her,' was all Prendergast said.

'Do that,' said Hugo, 'and while I'm here, I need to withdraw a little cash from my private account.'

'I'm sorry, Sir Hugo, but that account is overdrawn at the present time . . .'

◄○►

Hugo was sitting in the front seat of his sleek royal blue Lagonda when Holcombe pushed through the school door and began to walk across the playground. He stopped to speak to a handyman who was giving the front gates a fresh coat of lilac and green paint, the Merrywood school colours.

'That's a fine job you're doing, Alf.'

'Thank you, Mr Holcombe,' Hugo heard the handyman say.

'But I still expect you to concentrate more on your verbs, and do try not to be late on Wednesday.'

Alf touched his cap.

Holcombe began walking along the pavement and

pretended not to see Hugo sitting behind the wheel of his car. Hugo allowed himself a smirk; everyone gave his Lagonda V12 a second look. Three young lads loitering on the pavement opposite hadn't been able to take their eyes off it for the past half hour.

Hugo stepped out of the car and stood in the middle of the pavement, but Holcombe still ignored him. He couldn't have been more than a stride away when Hugo said, 'I wonder if we could have a word, Mr Holcombe. My name is—'

'I'm well aware of who you are,' said Holcombe, and walked straight past him.

Hugo chased after the schoolmaster. 'It's just that I felt you ought to know—'

'Know what?' said Holcombe, stopping in his tracks and turning to face him.

'What your fiancée did for a living, not so very long ago.'

'She was forced into prostitution because you wouldn't pay for her son's –' he looked Hugo straight in the eye – '*your* son's school fees, when he was in his last two years at Bristol Grammar School.'

'There's no proof that Harry Clifton is my son,' said Hugo defiantly.

'There was enough proof for a vicar to refuse to allow Harry to marry your daughter.'

'How would you know? You weren't there.'

'How would you know? You ran away.'

'Then let me tell you something you certainly don't know,' said Hugo, almost shouting. 'This paragon of virtue that you're planning to spend the rest of your life with has swindled me out of a piece of land I owned in Broad Street.'

'Let me tell you something you do know,' said Holcombe. 'Maisie paid off every penny of your loan, with interest, and all you left her with was less than ten pounds to her name.'

'That land's now worth four hundred pounds,' said Hugo, immediately regretting his words, 'and it belongs to me.'

'If it belonged to you,' said Holcombe, 'you wouldn't be trying to buy the site for twice that amount.'

Hugo was livid that he had allowed himself to reveal the extent of his interest in the site, but he wasn't finished. 'So when you have sex with Maisie Clifton, do you have to pay for it, schoolmaster, because I certainly didn't.'

Holcombe raised a fist.

'Go on, hit me,' goaded Hugo. 'Unlike Stan Tancock, I'd sue you for every penny you're worth.'

Holcombe lowered his fist and marched off, annoyed with himself for having allowed Barrington to rile him.

Hugo smiled. He felt he had delivered the knockout blow.

He turned round to see the lads on the other side of the road sniggering. But then they'd never seen a lilac and green Lagonda before.

35

WHEN THE FIRST cheque bounced, Hugo simply ignored it and waited a few days before he presented it a second time. When it came back again, stamped 'Refer to Drawer', he began to accept the inevitable.

For the next few weeks, Hugo found several different ways of getting around the immediate cash problem.

He first raided the office safe and removed the £100 that his father always kept for a rainy day. This was a thunderstorm, and the old man had certainly never had to resort to the cash reserve to pay his secretary's wages. Once that had run out, he reluctantly let go of the Lagonda. However, the dealer politely pointed out that lilac and green weren't this year's colours, and as Sir Hugo required cash, he could only offer him half the original purchase price, because the bodywork would have to be stripped and repainted.

Hugo survived for another month.

With no other available assets to dispose of, he began to steal from his mother. First, any loose change left lying about the house, followed by coins in purses and then notes in bags.

It wasn't long before he bagged a small silver pheasant that had graced the centre of the dining-room table for years, followed by its parents, all of which flew to the nearest pawn shop.

Hugo then moved on to his mother's jewellery. He started with items she wouldn't notice. A hat pin and a Victorian brooch were quickly followed by an amber necklace she rarely wore, and a diamond tiara which had been in the family for over a century and was only worn at weddings or ceremonial occasions. He didn't anticipate there being many of those in the near future.

He finally turned to his father's art collection, first taking off the wall a portrait of his grandfather by a young John Singer Sargent, but not before the housekeeper and the cook had handed in their notice, having received no wages for over three months. Jenkins conveniently died a month later.

His grandfather's Constable (*The Mill at Dunning Lock*) was followed by his great-grandfather's Turner (*Swans on the Avon*), both of which had been in the family for over a century.

Hugo was able to convince himself that it wasn't theft. After all, his father's will had stated *and all that therein is*.

This irregular source of funds ensured that the company survived and only showed a small loss for the first quarter of the year, that is, if you didn't count the resignation of three more directors and several other senior members of staff who hadn't received their pay cheques on the last day of the month. When asked, Hugo blamed the temporary setbacks on the war. One elderly director's parting words were, 'Your father never found it necessary to use that as an excuse.'

Soon, even the removable assets began to dwindle.

Hugo knew that if he were to put Barrington Hall and its 72 acres of parkland on the market, it would announce to the world that a company that had declared a profit for over a hundred years was insolvent.

His mother continued to accept Hugo's assurances that the problem was only temporary, and that given time everything would sort itself out. After a time, he started to believe his own propaganda. When the cheques started to bounce again, Mr Prendergast reminded him that there was an offer of £3,500 on the table for his properties in Broad Street, which, Prendergast pointed out, would still show him a profit of £600.

'What about the thirty thousand I was promised?' Hugo shouted down the phone.

'That offer is also still on the table, Sir Hugo, but it remains subject to your purchasing Mrs Clifton's freehold.'

'Offer her a thousand,' he barked.

'As you wish, Sir Hugo.'

Hugo slammed the phone down and wondered what else could go wrong. The phone rang again.

—◦—

Hugo was hidden away in a corner alcove of the Railway Arms, a hotel he'd never frequented before, and never would again. He nervously checked his watch every few minutes, while he waited for Mitchell to arrive.

The private detective joined him at 11.34 a.m., only minutes after the Paddington express had pulled into

Temple Meads station. Mitchell slipped into the chair opposite his only client, although he hadn't received any remuneration for several months.

'What is so urgent that it couldn't wait?' demanded Hugo, once a half pint of beer had been placed in front of the private detective.

'I'm sorry to report, sir,' Mitchell began after taking a sip, 'that the police have arrested your friend Toby Dunstable.' Hugo felt a shiver shoot through his body. 'They've charged him with the theft of the Piotrovska diamonds along with several paintings, including a Picasso and a Monet, that he tried to offload on Agnew's, the Mayfair art dealer.'

'Toby will keep his mouth shut,' said Hugo.

'I fear not, sir. I am reliably informed that he has turned King's evidence in exchange for a lighter sentence. It seems Scotland Yard are more interested in arresting the man behind the crime.'

Hugo's beer went flat while he tried to take in the significance of Mitchell's words. After a long silence, the private detective continued. 'I thought you'd also want to know that Miss Piotrovska has hired Sir Francis Mayhew KC to represent her.'

'Why doesn't she just leave the police to deal with the case?'

'She did not seek Sir Francis's advice on the burglary, but on two other matters.'

'Two other matters?' repeated Hugo.

'Yes. I understand a writ is about to be served on you for breach of promise, and Miss Piotrovska is also lodging a paternity suit, naming you as the father of her daughter.'

'She'll never be able to prove it.'

'Among the evidence that will be presented to the court is the receipt for an engagement ring purchased from a Burlington Arcade jeweller, and both her resident housekeeper and her lady's maid have signed affidavits confirming that you resided at forty-two Lowndes Square for over a year.'

For the first time in ten years, Hugo asked Mitchell for his advice. 'What do you think I should do?' he almost whispered.

'If I found myself in your position, sir, I'd leave the country as soon as possible.'

'How long do you think I've got?'

'A week, ten days at the most.'

A waiter appeared by their side. 'That will be one shilling and nine pence, sir.'

As Hugo didn't move, Mitchell handed the waiter a florin and said, 'Keep the change.'

Once the private detective had left to return to London, Hugo sat alone for some time, considering his options. The waiter came over again and asked if he'd like another drink, but Hugo didn't even bother to reply. Eventually he heaved himself up from his chair and made his way out of the bar.

Hugo headed towards the city centre, slower and slower with each pace, until he'd finally worked out what he had to do next. He marched into the bank a few minutes later.

'Can I help you, sir?' asked the young man on reception. But Hugo was halfway across the hall before he'd had time to call the manager and warn him that Sir Hugo Barrington was heading towards his office.

Prendergast was no longer surprised that Sir Hugo always assumed he would be available at a moment's notice, but he was shocked to see that the chairman of Barrington's hadn't bothered to shave that morning.

'I have a problem that needs to be dealt with urgently,' Hugo said as he sank into the chair opposite the manager.

'Yes of course, Sir Hugo. How can I be of assistance?'

'What's the most you could hope to raise for my properties on Broad Street?'

'But only last week I sent a letter advising you that Mrs Clifton has rejected your latest offer.'

'I'm well aware of that,' said Hugo. 'I meant without her site.'

'There is still an offer on the table of three thousand five hundred, but I have reason to believe that were you to offer Mrs Clifton a little more, she would release her site and the thirty-thousand-pound bid would still be valid.'

'I don't have any more time,' said Hugo without explanation.

'If that is the case, I'm confident that I could press my client to raise his bid to four thousand, which would still show you a handsome profit.'

'If I were to accept that offer, I would need your assurance on one thing.' Mr Prendergast allowed himself a raised eyebrow. 'That your client does not have, and never has had, any connection with Mrs Clifton.'

'I am able to give you that assurance, Sir Hugo.'

'If your client was to pay me four thousand, how much would that leave in my current account?'

Mr Prendergast opened Sir Hugo's file and checked the balance sheet. 'Eight hundred and twenty-two pounds and ten shillings,' he said.

Hugo no longer joked about the ten shillings. 'In which case, I require eight hundred pounds in cash immediately. And I'll instruct you later where to send the proceeds of the sale.'

'The proceeds of the sale?' repeated Prendergast.

'Yes,' replied Hugo. 'I've decided to place Barrington Hall on the market.'

36

No one saw him leave the house.

He was carrying a suitcase and was dressed in a warm tweed suit, a pair of stout brown shoes that had been made to last, a heavy topcoat and a brown felt hat. A casual glance, and you would have taken him for a commercial traveller.

He walked to the nearest bus stop, which was just over a mile away, most of it his own land. Forty minutes later he boarded a green single-decker bus – a mode of transport he'd never used before. He sat in the back seat, not letting the suitcase out of his sight. He handed the clippie a ten-shilling note, despite the fact that he was only asked for thruppence; his first mistake if he hoped to avoid drawing attention to himself.

The bus continued on its way into Bristol, a journey he would normally cover in about twelve minutes in the Lagonda, but today it took over an hour before they finally pulled into the bus station. Hugo was neither the first nor the last passenger to get off. He checked his watch: 2.38 p.m. He'd left himself enough time.

He walked up the slope to Temple Meads station – he'd never noticed the slope, but then he'd never had to carry his own suitcase before – where he joined a long queue and purchased a third-class single to Fishguard. He asked which platform the train would be leaving from, and once he'd found it, stood at the far end, under an unlit gas light.

When the train eventually pulled in, he climbed aboard and found a seat in the middle of a third-class compartment, which quickly filled up. He placed his suitcase on the rack opposite him, and rarely took his eyes off it. A woman pulled open the carriage door and glanced into the crowded compartment, but he didn't offer her his seat.

As the train pulled out of the station, he let out a sigh of relief, delighted to see Bristol disappearing into the distance. He sat back and thought about the decision he'd made. By this time tomorrow, he'd be in Cork. He wouldn't feel safe until his feet were treading on Irish soil. But they had to arrive in Swansea on schedule if he hoped to link up with the train for Fishguard.

The train pulled into Swansea with half an hour to spare; time for a cup of tea and a Chelsea bun in the station buffet. It wasn't Earl Grey or Carwardine's, but he was too tired to care. As soon as he'd finished, he exchanged the buffet for another dimly lit platform and waited for the Fishguard train to appear.

The train was late, but he was confident that the ferry wouldn't leave the harbour before all the passengers were on board. After an overnight stay in Cork, he would book a passage on a ship, any ship, that was sailing to America. There he would begin a new life, with the money he made from the sale of Barrington Hall.

The idea of his ancestral home going under the hammer made him think about his mother for the first time. Where would she live, once the house had been sold? She could always join Elizabeth at the Manor House. After all, it had more than enough room. Failing that, she could move in with the Harveys, who had three houses, not to mention numerous cottages on their estates.

His thoughts then turned to the Barrington Shipping Line – a business that had been built up by two generations of the family, while the third had managed to bring it to its knees quicker than a bishop's blessing.

For a moment, he thought about Olga Piotrovska, thankful that he would never see her again. He even spared a passing thought for Toby Dunstable, who had been the cause of all his trouble.

Emma and Grace crossed his mind, but not for very long: he'd never seen the point of daughters. And then he thought about Giles, who had avoided him after escaping from Weinsberg PoW camp and returning to Bristol. People regularly asked after his war hero son, and Hugo had to make up some new story every time. That would no longer be necessary, because once he was in America the umbilical cord would finally be severed, although in time – and Hugo was still determined it would be some considerable time – Giles would inherit the family title, even if *all that therein is* was no longer worth the paper it was written on.

But most of the time he thought about himself, an indulgence that was only interrupted when the train arrived at Fishguard. He waited for everyone else to leave the carriage before he took his suitcase down from the rack and stepped out on to the platform.

He followed the megaphone directions, 'Buses to the harbour. Buses to the harbour!' There were four. He chose the third. This time it was only a short journey, and he couldn't miss the terminal, despite the blackout; another long third-class queue, this time for the Cork ferry.

After buying a one-way ticket, he walked up the gangway, stepped on board and found a nook that no self-respecting cat would have curled up in. He didn't feel safe until he heard two blasts on the foghorn and, in the gentle swell, felt the ship drifting away from the quayside.

Once the ferry had passed the harbour wall, he relaxed for the first time, and was so exhausted he rested his head on the suitcase and fell into a deep sleep.

Hugo couldn't be sure how long he'd been asleep when he felt a tap on his shoulder. He looked up to see two men towering over him.

'Sir Hugo Barrington?' one of them asked.

There didn't seem much point in denying it. They yanked him up by the shoulders and told him he was under arrest. They took their time reading out a long list of the charges.

'But I'm on my way to Cork,' he protested. 'Surely we must be beyond the twelve-mile limit?'

'No, sir,' said the second officer, 'you're on your way back to Fishguard.'

Several passengers leaned over the ship's railings to get a closer view of the handcuffed man being escorted down the gangway, who had been the cause of them being delayed.

Hugo was bundled into the back of a black Wolseley car, and moments later he began the long journey back to Bristol.

–<o>–

When the cell door opened a uniformed man brought in some breakfast on a tray – not the kind of breakfast, not the kind of tray and certainly not the kind of uniformed man Sir Hugo was accustomed to seeing first thing in the morning. One look at the fried bread and tomatoes bathed in oil, and he pushed the tray to one side. He wondered how long it would be before this became part of his staple diet. The constable returned a few minutes later, took away the tray and slammed the cell door closed.

The next time the door opened, two officers entered the cell and escorted Hugo up the stone steps to the charge room on the first floor. Ben Winshaw, the Barrington Shipping Line's company solicitor, was waiting for him.

'I'm so very sorry, chairman,' he said.

Hugo shook his head, a look of resignation on his face. 'What happens next?' he asked.

'The superintendent told me they'll be charging you in the next few minutes. You'll then be taken to court, where you'll appear before a magistrate. All you have to do is plead not guilty. The superintendent made it clear that they would oppose any request for bail, and would point out to the magistrate that you were arrested while trying to leave the country in possession of a suitcase containing eight hundred pounds. The press, I fear, are going to have a field day.'

Hugo and his solicitor sat alone in the charge room and waited for the superintendent to appear. The solicitor warned Hugo that he should be prepared to spend several weeks in prison before the trial opened. He suggested the names of four KCs who might be retained to defend him. They had just settled on Sir Gilbert Gray, when the door opened and a sergeant walked in.

'You are free to leave, sir,' he said, as if Hugo had committed some minor traffic offence.

It was some time before Winshaw recovered enough to ask, 'Will my client be expected to return later in the day?'

'Not that I'm aware of, sir.'

Hugo walked out of the police station a free man.

◄○►

The story only made a small paragraph on page 9 of the *Bristol Evening News. The Hon Toby Dunstable, second son of the eleventh Earl of Dunstable, died of a heart attack, while in custody at Wimbledon Police Station.*

It was Derek Mitchell who later filled in the details behind the story.

He reported that the earl had visited his son in his cell, just a couple of hours before Toby took his own life. The officer on duty overheard several sharp exchanges between father and son, during which honour, the family's reputation and the decent thing to do in the circumstances were repeated again and again by the earl. At the inquest held a fortnight later at Wimbledon Crown Court, the magistrate asked the officer in question if he'd seen any pills pass between the two men during the earl's visit.

'No, sir,' he replied, 'I did not.'

Death by natural causes was the verdict delivered by the magistrate's panel at Wimbledon Crown Court later that afternoon.

37

'MR PRENDERGAST has telephoned several times this morning, chairman,' said Miss Potts as she followed Sir Hugo into his office, 'and on the last occasion he emphasized that it was urgent.' If she was surprised to see the chairman unshaven and wearing a tweed suit that looked as if he'd slept in it, she said nothing.

Hugo's first thought on hearing that Prendergast wanted to speak to him urgently was that the Broad Street deal must have fallen through and the bank would expect him to return its £800 forthwith. Prendergast could think again.

'And Tancock,' said Miss Potts, checking her notepad, 'says he has some news that you'll want to hear.' The chairman didn't comment. 'But the most important thing,' she continued, 'is the letter I've left on your desk. I have a feeling you'll want to read it immediately.'

Hugo began reading the letter even before he'd sat down. He then read it a second time, but still couldn't believe it. He looked up at his secretary.

'Many congratulations, sir.'

'Get Prendergast on the phone,' barked Hugo, 'and

then I want to see the managing director, followed by Tancock, in that order.'

'Yes, chairman,' said Miss Potts, and hurried out of the room.

While Hugo waited for Prendergast to come on the line, he read the Minister of Shipping's letter a third time.

Dear Sir Hugo,

I am delighted to inform you that Barrington Shipping has been awarded the contract for . . .

The phone on Hugo's desk rang. 'Mr Prendergast on the line,' announced Miss Potts.

'Good morning, Sir Hugo.' The deference was back in the voice. 'I thought you'd want to know that Mrs Clifton has finally agreed to sell her site on Broad Street, for a thousand pounds.'

'But I've already signed a contract to sell the rest of my property in the street to United Dominion for four thousand.'

'And that contract is still on my desk,' said Prendergast. 'Unfortunately for them, and more fortunately for you, the earliest time they could make an appointment to see me was at ten o'clock this morning.'

'Did you exchange contracts?'

'Yes, Sir Hugo, I most certainly did.'

Hugo's heart sank.

'For forty thousand pounds.'

'I don't understand.'

'Once I was able to assure United Dominion that you were in possession of Mrs Clifton's plot, as well as the deeds for every other freehold in the street, they wrote out a cheque for the full amount.'

'Well done, Prendergast. I knew I could rely on you.'

'Thank you, sir. All you need to do now is countersign Mrs Clifton's agreement, and then I can bank United Dominion's cheque.'

Hugo glanced at his watch. 'As it's already gone four, I'll drop in to the bank first thing tomorrow morning.'

The Prendergast cough. 'First thing, Sir Hugo, is nine o'clock. And may I ask if you still have the eight hundred pounds I advanced to you in cash yesterday?'

'Yes I do. But how can that still be of any significance?'

'I do consider it would be prudent, Sir Hugo, to pay Mrs Clifton her thousand pounds before we bank United Dominion's cheque for forty thousand. We wouldn't want any embarrassing questions from head office at a later date.'

'Quite so,' said Hugo as he looked at his suitcase, relieved that he hadn't spent one penny of the £800.

'There's nothing more for me to say,' said Prendergast, 'other than to congratulate you on closing a most successful contract.'

'How do you know about the contract?'

'I beg your pardon, Sir Hugo?' said Prendergast sounding a little puzzled.

'Oh, I thought you were referring to something else,' said Hugo. 'It's of no importance, Prendergast. Forget I mentioned it,' he added as he put the phone down.

Miss Potts came back into the room. 'The managing director is waiting to see you, chairman.'

'Send him straight in.'

'You've heard the good news, Ray?' said Hugo as Compton entered the room.

'I have indeed, chairman, and it couldn't have come at a better time.'

'I'm not sure I understand,' said Hugo.

'You're due to present the company's annual results at next month's board meeting, and although we'll still have to declare a heavy loss this year, the new contract will guarantee that we go into profit next year.'

'And for five years after that,' Hugo reminded him, waving the minister's letter triumphantly. 'Why don't you prepare the agenda for the board meeting, but don't include the news about the government contract. I'd rather like to make that announcement myself.'

'As you wish, chairman. I'll see that all the relevant papers are on your desk by noon tomorrow,' Compton added before leaving the room.

Hugo read the minister's letter a fourth time. 'Thirty thousand a year,' he said out loud, just as the phone on his desk rang again.

'A Mr Foster from Savills, the estate agency, is on the line,' said Miss Potts.

'Put him through.'

'Good morning, Sir Hugo. My name is Foster. I'm the senior partner of Savills. I thought perhaps we ought to get together to discuss your instructions to sell Barrington Hall. Perhaps a spot of lunch at my club?'

'No need to bother, Foster. I've changed my mind. Barrington Hall is no longer on the market,' Hugo said, and put the phone down.

He spent the rest of the afternoon signing a stack of letters and cheques his secretary put in front of him, and it was just after six o'clock when he finally screwed the cap back on his pen.

When Miss Potts returned to collect all the correspondence, Hugo said, 'I'll see Tancock now.'

'Yes, sir,' said Miss Potts with a hint of disapproval.

While Hugo waited for Tancock to appear, he fell on his knees and opened the suitcase. He stared at the £800 that would have made it possible for him to survive in America while he waited for the funds raised by the sale of Barrington Hall. Now, that same £800 would be used to make him a fortune on Broad Street.

When he heard a knock on the door, he snapped the lid of the suitcase closed and quickly returned to his desk.

'Tancock to see you,' said Miss Potts before closing the door behind her.

The docker marched confidently into the room and approached the chairman's desk.

'So what's this news that can't wait?' asked Hugo.

'I've come to collect the other five quid what you owe me,' Tancock said, with a look of triumph in his eyes.

'I owe you nothing,' said Hugo.

'But I talked my sister into selling that land you wanted, didn't I?'

'We agreed on two hundred pounds, and I ended up having to pay five times that amount, so as I said, I owe you nothing. Get out of my office, and go back to work.'

Stan didn't budge. 'And I've got that letter you said you wanted.'

'What letter?'

'The letter what our Maisie got from that doctor off the American ship.'

Hugo had completely forgotten about the letter of condolence from Harry Clifton's shipmate, and couldn't imagine that it would be of any significance now Maisie had agreed to the sale. 'I'll give you a pound for it.'

'You said you'd give me a fiver.'

'I suggest you leave my office while you've still got a job, Tancock.'

'OK, OK,' said Stan, backing down, 'you can have it for a quid. What's it to me?' He took a crumpled envelope out of his back pocket and handed it over to the chairman. Hugo extracted a ten-shilling note from his wallet and placed it on the desk in front of him.

Stan stood his ground as Hugo put his wallet back in an inside pocket and stared defiantly at him.

'You can have the letter or the ten-bob note. Take your choice.'

Stan grabbed the ten-bob note and left the room grumbling under his breath.

Hugo put the envelope to one side, leant back in his chair and thought about how he would spend some of the profit he'd made on the Broad Street deal. Once he'd been to the bank and signed all the necessary documents, he would walk across the road to the car saleroom. He had his eye on a 1937 2-litre 4-seater Aston Martin. He would then drive it across town and visit his tailor – he hadn't had a suit made for longer than he cared to remember – and after the fitting, lunch at the club, where he would settle his outstanding bar bill. During the afternoon, he would set about replenishing the wine cellar at Barrington Hall, and might even consider redeeming from the pawnbroker some of the jewellery his mother seemed to miss so much. In the evening— there was a tap at the door.

'I'm just leaving,' said Miss Potts. 'I want to get to the post office before seven to catch the last delivery. Do you need anything else, sir?'

'No, Miss Potts. But I may be in a little late tomorrow, as I have an appointment with Mr Prendergast at nine o'clock.'

'Of course, chairman,' said Miss Potts.

As the door closed behind her, his eyes settled on the crumpled envelope. He picked up a silver letter opener, slit the envelope open and pulled out a single sheet of paper. His eyes impatiently scanned the page, searching for relevant phrases.

> *New York,*
> *September*
> *8th, 1939*

My dearest mother,

. . . I did not die when the Devonian *was sunk . . . I was plucked out of the sea . . . the vain hope that at some time in the future I might be able to prove that Arthur Clifton and not Hugo Barrington was my father . . . I must beg you to keep my secret as steadfastly as you kept your own for so many years.*

> *Your loving son,*

> *Harry*

Hugo's blood ran cold. All the triumphs of the day evaporated in an instant. This was not a letter he wanted to read a second time or, more important, that he wished anyone else to become aware of.

He pulled open the top drawer of his desk and took out a box of Swan Vestas. He lit a match, held the letter over the wastepaper basket and didn't let it go until the frail black cinders had evaporated into dust. The best ten shillings he'd ever spent.

Hugo was confident that he was the only person who knew Clifton was still alive, and he intended it to remain that way. After all, if Clifton kept his word and continued to go by the name of Tom Bradshaw, how could anyone else find out the truth?

He suddenly felt sick when he remembered that Emma was still in America. Had she somehow discovered that Clifton was alive? But surely that wasn't possible if she hadn't read the letter. He needed to find out why she'd gone to America.

He had picked up the phone and begun to dial Mitchell's number when he thought he heard footsteps in the corridor. He replaced the receiver, assuming it must be the night watchman checking to see why his light was still on.

The door opened, and he stared at a woman he had hoped never to see again.

'How did you get past the guard on the gate?' he demanded.

'I told him we had an appointment to see the chairman; a long overdue appointment.'

'We?' said Hugo.

'Yes, I've brought you a little present. Not that you can give something to someone when it's already theirs.' She placed a wicker basket on Hugo's desk, and removed a thin muslin cloth to reveal a sleeping baby. 'I felt it was about time you were introduced to your daughter,' Olga said, standing aside to allow Hugo to admire her.

'What makes you think I would have the slightest interest in your bastard?'

'Because she's also your bastard,' said Olga calmly, 'so I will assume you want to give her the same start in life you gave Emma and Grace.'

'Why would I even consider making such a ridiculous gesture?'

'Because Hugo,' she said, 'you bled me dry, and now it's your turn to face up to your responsibility. You can't assume you will always get away with it.'

'The only thing I got away from was you,' said Hugo with a smirk. 'So you can bugger off and take that basket with you, because I won't be lifting a finger to help her.'

'Then perhaps I'll have to turn to someone who just might be willing to lift a finger to help her.'

'Like who?' snapped Hugo.

'Your mother might be a good place to start, although she's probably the last person on earth who still believes a word you say.'

Hugo leapt up from his seat, but Olga didn't flinch. 'And if I can't convince her,' she continued, 'my next stop would be the Manor House, where I would take afternoon tea with your ex-wife, and we could talk about the fact that she'd already divorced you long before we even met.'

Hugo stepped out from behind his desk, but it didn't stop Olga continuing. 'And if Elizabeth is not at home,

335

I can always pay a visit to Mulgelrie Castle and introduce Lord and Lady Harvey to yet another of your offspring.'

'What makes you think they'd believe you?'

'What makes you think they wouldn't?'

Hugo moved towards her, only stopping when they were a few inches apart, but Olga still hadn't finished.

'And then finally, I'd feel I owe it to myself to visit Maisie Clifton, a woman I greatly admire, because if all I've heard about her—'

Hugo grabbed Olga by the shoulders and began to shake her. He was only surprised that she made no attempt to defend herself.

'Now you listen to me, you Yid,' he shouted. 'If you so much as hint to anyone that I'm the father of that child, I'll make your life so miserable that you'll wish you'd been dragged off by the Gestapo with your parents.'

'You don't frighten me any longer, Hugo,' said Olga, with an air of resignation. 'I only have one interest left in life, and that's to make sure you don't get away with it a second time.'

'A second time?' repeated Hugo.

'You think I don't know about Harry Clifton, and his claim to the family title?'

Hugo let go of her and took a step back, clearly shaken. 'Clifton is dead. Buried at sea. Everyone knows that.'

'You know he's still alive, Hugo, however much you want everyone else to believe he isn't.'

'But how can you possibly know—'

'Because I've learnt to think like you, behave like

you, and more important, act like you, which is why I decided to hire my own private detective.'

'But it would have taken you years—' began Hugo.

'Not if you come across someone who's out of work, whose only client has run away a second time and who hasn't been paid for six months.' Olga smiled when Hugo clenched his fists, a sure sign that her words had hit home. Even when he raised his arm she didn't flinch, just stood her ground.

When the first blow came crashing into her face, she toppled back, clutching her broken nose, just as a second punch landed in her stomach, causing her to double up.

Hugo stood back and laughed while she swayed from side to side, trying to stay on her feet. He was about to hit her a third time when her legs crumpled and she collapsed to the ground in a heap, like a puppet whose strings have been cut.

'Now you know what you can expect if you're ever foolish enough to bother me again,' shouted Hugo, as he towered over her. 'And if you don't want more of the same, you'll get out while you've still got the chance. Just be sure to take that bastard with you back to London.'

Olga slowly pushed herself up off the floor and on to her knees, blood still pouring from her nose. She attempted to stand, but was so weak that she stumbled forward, only breaking her fall by clinging on to the edge of the desk. She paused for a moment and took several deep breaths as she tried to recover. When she finally raised her head, she was distracted by a long, thin silver object that glistened in a circle of light thrown out by the desk lamp.

'Didn't you hear what I said?' Hugo hollered as he stepped forward, grabbed her by the hair and yanked her head back.

With all the force she could muster, Olga jerked her leg back and rammed the heel of her shoe into his groin.

'You bitch,' screamed Hugo as he let go of her hair and fell back, allowing Olga a split second to grab the letter opener and conceal it inside the sleeve of her dress. She turned to face her tormentor. When Hugo had caught his breath, he once again moved towards her. As he passed a side table, he grabbed a heavy glass ashtray and raised it high above his head, determined to deliver a blow from which she would not so easily recover.

When he was only a pace away, she pulled up her sleeve, gripped the letter opener with both hands and pointed the blade towards his heart. Just as he was about to bring the ashtray crashing down on her head, he spotted the blade for the first time, tried to swerve to one side, tripped and lost his balance, falling heavily on top of her.

There was a moment's silence before he sank slowly to his knees and let out a scream that would have woken all Hades. Olga watched as he grabbed at the handle of the letter opener. She stood mesmerized, as if she was watching a slow-motion clip from a film. It must have been only a moment, although it felt interminable to Olga, before Hugo finally collapsed and slumped to the floor at her feet.

She stared down at the blade of the letter opener. The tip was sticking out of the back of his neck and blood was spurting in every direction, like an out-of-control fire hydrant.

'Help me,' Hugo whimpered, trying to raise a hand.

Olga knelt by his side and took the hand of a man she'd once loved. 'There is nothing I can do to help you, my darling,' she said, 'but then there never was.'

His breathing was becoming less regular, although he still gripped her hand tightly. She bent down to be sure that he could hear her every word. 'You only have a few more moments to live,' she whispered, 'and I wouldn't want you to go to your grave without knowing the details of Mitchell's latest report.'

Hugo made one last effort to speak. His lips moved, but no words came out.

'Emma has found Harry,' said Olga, 'and I know you'll be pleased to hear he's alive and well.' Hugo's eyes never left her as she leant even closer, until her lips were almost touching his ear. 'And he's on his way back to England to claim his rightful inheritance.'

It wasn't until Hugo's hand went limp that she added, 'Ah, but I forgot to tell you, I've also learnt how to lie like you.'

◄○►

The *Bristol Evening Post* and the *Bristol Evening News* ran different headlines on the first editions of their papers the following day.

SIR HUGO BARRINGTON
STABBED TO DEATH

was the banner headline in the *Post*, while the *News* preferred to lead with

UNKNOWN WOMAN THROWS HERSELF
IN FRONT OF LONDON EXPRESS

Only Detective Chief Inspector Blakemore, the head of the local CID, worked out the connection between the two.

EMMA BARRINGTON

1942

38

'GOOD MORNING, MR GUINZBURG,' said Sefton Jelks as he rose from behind his desk. 'It is indeed an honour to meet the man who publishes Dorothy Parker and Graham Greene.'

Guinzburg gave a slight bow, before shaking hands with Jelks.

'And Miss Barrington,' said Jelks, turning to Emma. 'How nice to see you again. As I am no longer representing Mr Lloyd, I hope we can be friends.'

Emma frowned, and sat down without shaking Jelks's outstretched hand.

Once the three of them were settled, Jelks continued. 'Perhaps I might open this meeting by saying I thought it would be worthwhile for the three of us to get together and have a frank and open discussion, and see if it were possible to come up with a solution to our problem.'

'Your problem,' interjected Emma.

Mr Guinzburg pursed his lips, but said nothing.

'I am sure,' continued Jelks, focusing his attention on Guinzburg, 'that you will want to do what is best for all concerned.'

'And will that include Harry Clifton this time?' asked Emma.

Guinzburg turned to Emma and gave her a disapproving grimace.

'Yes, Miss Barrington,' said Jelks, 'any agreement we might reach would certainly include Mr Clifton.'

'Just as it did last time, Mr Jelks, when you walked away at the time he most needed you?'

'Emma,' said Guinzburg reproachfully.

'I should point out, Miss Barrington, that I was doing no more than carrying out my client's instructions. Mr and Mrs Bradshaw both assured me that the man I was representing was their son, and I had no reason to believe otherwise. And of course I did prevent Tom from being tried for—'

'And then you left Harry to fend for himself.'

'In my defence, Miss Barrington, when I finally discovered that Tom Bradshaw was in fact Harry Clifton, he begged me to keep my counsel, as he didn't want *you* to discover that he was still alive.'

'That's not Harry's version of what happened,' said Emma, who appeared to regret her words the moment she'd said them.

Guinzburg made no attempt to mask his displeasure. He looked like a man who realizes his trump card has been played too soon.

'I see,' said Jelks. 'From that little outburst, I must assume you have both read the earlier notebook?'

'Every word,' said Emma. 'So you can stop pretending you only did what was in Harry's best interests.'

'Emma,' said Guinzburg firmly, 'you must learn not to take things so personally, and try to consider the bigger picture.'

'Is that the one where a leading New York lawyer ends up in jail for falsifying evidence and perverting the course of justice?' said Emma, her eyes never leaving Jelks.

'I apologize, Mr Jelks,' said Guinzburg. 'My young friend gets quite carried away when it comes to—'

'You bet I do,' said Emma, now almost shouting, 'because I can tell you exactly what this man –' she pointed at Jelks – 'would have done if Harry had been sent to the electric chair. He would have pulled the lever himself if he thought it would save his own skin.'

'That is outrageous,' said Jelks, jumping up from his seat. 'I had already prepared an appeal that would have left the jury in no doubt that the police had arrested the wrong man.'

'So you did know it was Harry all along,' said Emma, sitting back in her chair.

Jelks was momentarily stunned by Emma's rebuke. She took advantage of his silence.

'Let me tell you what's going to happen, Mr Jelks. When Viking publishes Harry's first notebook in the spring, not only will your reputation be shattered and your career in ruins, but, like Harry, you'll discover at first hand what life is like at Lavenham.'

Jelks turned to Guinzburg in desperation. 'I would have thought it in both our interests to reach an amicable settlement before this whole affair gets out of hand.'

'What do you have in mind, Mr Jelks?' asked Guinzburg, trying to sound conciliatory.

'You're not going to give this crook a lifeline, are you?' said Emma.

Guinzburg raised a hand. 'The least we can do, Emma, is hear him out.'

'Just as he heard Harry out?'

Jelks turned to Guinzburg. 'If you felt able *not* to publish the earlier notebook, I can assure you I would make it worth your while.'

'I can't believe you're taking this seriously,' said Emma.

Jelks continued to address Guinzburg as if Emma wasn't in the room. 'Of course, I realize that you stand to lose a considerable amount of money if you decide not to go ahead.'

'If *The Diary of a Convict* is anything to go by,' said Guinzburg, 'over a hundred thousand dollars.'

The figure must have taken Jelks by surprise, because he didn't respond.

'And there's also the twenty-thousand-dollar advance that was paid to Lloyd,' continued Guinzburg. 'That will have to be reimbursed to Mr Clifton.'

'If Harry were here, he'd be the first to tell you that he's not interested in the money, Mr Guinzburg, only in making sure that this man ends up in jail.'

Guinzburg looked appalled. 'My company has not built its reputation on scandal-mongering, Emma, so before I make a final decision on whether or not to publish the notebook, I have to consider how my more distinguished authors might react to a publication of that kind.'

'How right you are, Mr Guinzburg. Reputation is everything.'

'How would you know?' demanded Emma.

'While we're on the subject of distinguished authors,' continued Jelks a little pompously, ignoring the interruption, 'you may be aware that my firm has the privilege of representing the F. Scott Fitzgerald estate.' He leaned back in his chair. 'I remember so well Scotty telling me that if he were to change publishers, he would want to move to Viking.'

'You're not going to fall for that line, are you?' said Emma.

'Emma, my dear, there are times when it is wise to take the long view.'

'How long have you got in mind? Six years?'

'Emma, I'm only doing what is in everyone's best interests.'

'It sounds to me as if what you're doing will end up in your best interests. Because the reality is that once money becomes involved, you're no better than him,' she said, pointing at Jelks.

Guinzburg appeared wounded by Emma's accusation, but quickly recovered. He turned to the lawyer and asked, 'What do you have in mind, Mr Jelks?'

'If you'll agree not to publish the first notebook in any form, I would be happy to pay compensation, equivalent to the sum you have earned for *The Diary of a Convict* and, on top of that, I would repay in full the twenty thousand dollars you advanced to Mr Lloyd.'

'Why don't you just kiss me on the cheek, Mr Guinzburg,' said Emma, 'and then he'll know who to give the thirty pieces of silver to.'

'And Fitzgerald?' said Guinzburg, ignoring her.

'I will grant you the publishing rights of the F. Scott Fitzgerald estate for a period of fifty years, on the same terms as his current publisher.'

Guinzburg smiled. 'Draw up a contract, Mr Jelks, and I'll be happy to sign it.'

'And what pseudonym will you use when you sign the contract?' asked Emma. 'Judas?'

Guinzburg shrugged his shoulders. 'Business is business, my dear. And you and Harry won't go un-rewarded.'

'I'm glad you mention that, Mr Guinzburg,' said Jelks, 'because I've been holding a cheque for ten thousand dollars made payable to Harry Clifton's mother for some time, but because of the outbreak of war I had no way of getting it to her. Perhaps, Miss Barrington, you would be kind enough to give it to Mrs Clifton when you return to England.' He slid the cheque across the table.

Emma ignored it. 'You would never have mentioned that cheque if I hadn't read about it in the first note-book, when you gave Harry your word that you'd send Mrs Clifton ten thousand dollars once he agreed to take the place of Tom Bradshaw.' Emma stood up, before adding, 'You both disgust me, and I only hope I never come across either of you again in my life.'

She stormed out of the office without another word, leaving the cheque on the desk.

'Headstrong girl,' said Guinzburg, 'but I'm sure, given time, I'll be able to convince her we made the right decision.'

'I feel confident, Harold,' said Jelks, 'that you'll handle this minor incident with all the skill and diplo-macy that have become the hallmark of your distin-guished company.'

'That's kind of you to say so, Sefton,' said Guinzburg as he rose from his chair and picked up the cheque. 'And I'll make sure that Mrs Clifton gets this,' he added, placing it in his wallet.

'I knew I could rely on you, Harold.'

'You most certainly can, Sefton, and I look forward to seeing you again, once the contract has been drawn up.'

'I'll have it ready by the end of the week,' Jelks said as they left the room together and walked down the corridor. 'Surprising we haven't done any business before.'

'I agree,' said Guinzburg, 'but I have a feeling this is just the beginning of a long and fruitful relationship.'

'Let's hope so,' said Jelks when they reached the lift. 'I'll be in touch as soon as the contract is ready to sign,' he added as he pressed the down button.

'I'll look forward to that, Sefton,' said Guinzburg, and shook Jelks warmly by the hand before stepping into the lift.

When the lift reached the ground floor, Guinzburg stepped out, and the first thing he saw was Emma heading straight for him.

'You were brilliant, my dear,' he said. 'I confess that for a moment I wondered if you'd gone a little too far with your comment about the electric chair, but no, you'd got the measure of the man,' he added as they strolled out of the building arm in arm.

◄○►

Emma spent most of the afternoon sitting alone in her room rereading the first exercise book, in which Harry had written about the time before he was sent to Lavenham.

As she turned each page and was made aware once again what he had been willing to put himself through in order to release her from any obligation she might feel she owed him, Emma resolved that if she ever found the idiotic man again, she wouldn't let him out of her sight.

With Mr Guinzburg's blessing, Emma became involved with every aspect of publishing the revised edition of *The Diary of a Convict*, or the first edition, as she always referred to it. She attended editorial meetings, discussed the cover lettering with the head of the art department, chose the photograph that would go on the back cover, wrote the blurb about Harry for the inside flap and even addressed a sales conference.

Six weeks later, boxes of books were transported from the printer by rail, truck and plane to depositories all across America.

On publication day, Emma was standing on the pavement outside Doubleday's waiting for the doors of the bookstore to open. She was able to report to Great-aunt Phyllis and Cousin Alistair that evening that the book had been running out of the shop. Confirmation of this came in the form of the *New York Times* bestseller list the following Sunday, when the revised edition of *The Diary of a Convict* appeared in the top ten after only a week's sales.

Journalists and magazine editors from all over the country were desperate to interview Harry Clifton and Max Lloyd. But Harry couldn't be found in any penal establishment in America, while Lloyd, to quote *The Times*, was unavailable for comment. The *New York News* was less prosaic when it ran the headline, **LLOYD ON THE LAM**.

On the day of publication, Sefton Jelks's office issued a formal statement making it clear that the company no longer represented Max Lloyd. Although

The Diary of a Convict hit the number one spot on the *New York Times* bestseller list for the next five weeks, Guinzburg kept to his agreement with Jelks and did not publish any extracts from the earlier notebook.

However, Jelks did sign a contract giving Viking the exclusive right to publish all of F. Scott Fitzgerald's works for the next fifty years. Jelks considered that he'd honoured his side of the bargain and that, given time, the press would become bored with the story and move on. And he might have been right if *Time* magazine hadn't run a full-page interview with the recently retired Detective Karl Kolowski of the New York Police Department.

'And I can tell you,' Kolowski was quoted as saying, 'that so far they've only published the boring bits. Just wait until you read what happened to Harry Clifton before he arrived at Lavenham.'

The story hit the wires around 6 p.m. Eastern Time, and Mr Guinzburg had received over a hundred calls by the time he walked into his office the following morning.

Jelks read the article in *Time* as he was driven to Wall Street. When he stepped out of the lift on the twenty-second floor, he found three of his partners waiting outside his office.

39

'WHICH DO YOU want first?' asked Phyllis, holding up two letters. 'The good news or the bad news?'

'The good news,' said Emma without hesitation, as she buttered another piece of toast.

Phyllis placed one letter back on the table, adjusted her pince-nez and began to read the other.

Dear Mrs Stuart,

I've just finished reading The Diary of a Convict *by Harry Clifton. There was an excellent review of the book in the* Washington Post *today, which towards the end posed a question about what happened to Mr Clifton after he left Lavenham Correctional Facility seven months ago, having completed only a third of his sentence.*

For reasons of national security, which I am sure you will appreciate, I am unable to go into any great detail in this letter.

If Miss Barrington, who I understand is staying with you, would like any further information concerning Lieutenant Clifton, she is welcome to

*contact this office, and I will be happy to make an
appointment to see her.*

*As it does not breach the Espionage Act, may I
add how much I enjoyed Lieutenant Clifton's diary.
If the rumours in today's* New York Post *are to be
believed, I can't wait to find out what happened to
him before he was shipped off to Lavenham.*

Yours sincerely,

John Cleverdon (Col.)

Great-aunt Phyllis looked across to see Emma bouncing up and down like a bobby-soxer at a Sinatra concert.
Parker poured Mrs Stuart a second cup of coffee, as
if nothing unusual was taking place a few feet behind
him.

Emma suddenly stood still. 'So what's the bad
news?' she asked, sitting back down at the table.

Phyllis picked up the other letter. 'This one is from
Rupert Harvey,' she declared. 'A second cousin, once
removed.' Emma stifled a laugh. Phyllis observed her
critically over her pince-nez. 'Don't mock, child,' she
said. 'Being a member of a large clan can have its
advantages, as you're about to discover.' She turned her
attention back to the letter.

Dear cousin Phyllis,

*How nice to hear from you after all this time. It
was kind of you to draw my attention to* The Diary
of a Convict *by Harry Clifton, which I thoroughly
enjoyed. What a formidable young lady cousin
Emma must be.*

Phyllis looked up.

'Twice removed in your case,' she said before returning to the letter.

I'd be delighted to assist Emma in her current dilemma. To that end: the Embassy has an aircraft that will be flying to London next Thursday, and the Ambassador has agreed that Miss Barrington can join him and his staff on the flight.

If Emma would be kind enough to drop by my office on Thursday morning, I will make sure that all the necessary paperwork is completed. Do remind her to bring her passport with her.

Yours affectionately,

Rupert

PS. Is cousin Emma half as beautiful as Mr Clifton suggests in his book?

Phyllis folded the letter and placed it back in the envelope.

'So what's the bad news?' demanded Emma.

Phyllis bowed her head, as she did not approve of displays of emotion, and said quietly, 'You have no idea, child, how much I shall miss you. You are the daughter I never had.'

◄○►

'I signed the contract this morning,' said Guinzburg, raising his glass.

'Congratulations,' said Alistair, as everyone else around the dinner table raised their glasses.

'Do forgive me,' said Phyllis, 'if I appear to be the

only one among us who doesn't fully understand. If you signed a contract that prevents your company from publishing Harry Clifton's earlier work, what exactly are we celebrating?'

'The fact that I put one hundred thousand dollars of Sefton Jelks's money into my company's bank account this morning,' Guinzburg replied.

'And I,' said Emma, 'have received a cheque for twenty thousand dollars from the same source. Lloyd's original advance for Harry's book.'

'And don't forget the cheque for ten thousand you failed to pick up for Mrs Clifton, which I retrieved,' said Guinzburg. 'Frankly, we've all done very well out of it, and now the contract has been signed, there will be even more to come, for the next fifty years.'

'Possibly,' said Phyllis, taking the high ground, 'but I'm more than a little irked that you've allowed Jelks to get away with murder.'

'I think you'll find he's still on Death Row, Mrs Stuart,' said Guinzburg, 'though I accept we've granted him a three-month stay of execution.'

'I'm even more confused,' said Phyllis.

'Then allow me to explain,' said Guinzburg. 'You see, the contract I signed this morning wasn't with Jelks, but with Pocket Books, a company who have bought the rights to publish all Harry's diaries in softback.'

'And what, may I ask, is a softback?' said Phyllis.

'Mama,' said Alistair, 'softbacks have been around for years now.'

'So have ten-thousand-dollar bills, but I've never seen one.'

'Your mother makes a fair point,' said Guinzburg. 'In fact, it could explain why Jelks was taken in, because

Mrs Stuart represents an entire generation who will never come to terms with books being published in softback, and would only ever consider reading a hardback.'

'What made you realize that Jelks was not fully acquainted with the concept of a softback?' asked Phyllis.

'F. Scott Fitzgerald was the clincher,' said Alistair.

'I do wish you wouldn't use slang at the dinner table,' said Phyllis.

'It was Alistair who advised us,' said Emma, 'that if Jelks was willing to hold a meeting in his office without his legal assistant present, it must mean he hadn't alerted his partners to the fact there was a missing notebook, and that if it were published it would be even more damning to the firm's reputation than *The Diary of a Convict.*'

'Then why didn't Alistair attend the meeting,' said Phyllis, 'and make a record of everything Jelks said? After all, that man is one of the slipperiest lawyers in New York.'

'Which is precisely why I didn't attend the meeting, Mother. We didn't want anything on the record, and I was convinced that Jelks would be arrogant enough to think that all he was up against was a slip of a girl from England and a publisher he was sure he could bribe, which meant we had him by the short and curlies.'

'Alistair.'

'However,' Alistair continued, now in full flow, 'it was just after Emma had stormed out of the meeting that Mr Guinzburg displayed a moment of true genius.' Emma looked puzzled. 'He told Jelks, "I look forward to seeing you again, once the contract has been drawn up."'

'And that's exactly what Jelks did,' said Guinzburg, 'because once I'd gone over his contract, I realized it was modelled on one that had originally been drawn up for F. Scott Fitzgerald, a man who was only ever published in hardback. There was nothing in that contract to suggest that we couldn't publish in softback. So the sub-contract I signed this morning will allow Pocket Books to publish Harry's earlier diary, without breaking my agreement with Jelks.' Guinzburg allowed Parker to refill his glass with champagne.

'How much did you make?' demanded Emma.

'There are times, young lady, when you push your luck.'

'How much did you make?' asked Phyllis.

'Two hundred thousand dollars,' admitted Guinzburg.

'You'll need every penny of it,' said Phyllis, 'because once that book goes on sale, you and Alistair will be spending the next couple of years in court defending yourself against half a dozen libel writs.'

'I don't think so,' said Alistair after Parker had poured him a brandy. 'In fact, I'd be willing to bet that ten-thousand-dollar bill you've never seen, Mama, that Sefton Jelks is now spending his last three months as the senior partner of Jelks, Myers and Abernathy.'

'What makes you so sure of yourself?'

'I have a feeling Jelks didn't tell his partners about the first notebook, so when Pocket Books publish the earlier diary, he will be left with no choice but to hand in his resignation.'

'And if he doesn't?'

'Then they'll throw him out,' said Alistair. 'A firm which is that ruthless with its clients won't suddenly become humane with its partners. And don't forget, there's always someone else who wants to be senior partner . . . So, I'm bound to admit, Emma, you're far more interesting than Amalgamated Wire—'

'—versus New York Electric,' said the others in unison, as they raised their glasses to Emma.

'And should you ever change your mind about staying in New York, young lady,' said Guinzburg, 'there'll always be a job for you at Viking.'

'Thank you, Mr Guinzburg,' said Emma. 'But the only reason I came to America was to find Harry, and now I discover that he's in Europe while I'm stranded in New York. So once I've had my meeting with Colonel Cleverdon, I'll be flying home to be with our son.'

'Harry Clifton's a damn lucky man to have you in his corner,' said Alistair wistfully.

'If you ever meet either of them, Alistair, you'll realize that I'm the lucky one.'

40

EMMA WOKE EARLY the following morning and chatted happily to Phyllis over breakfast about how much she was looking forward to being reunited with Sebastian and her family. Phyllis nodded, but said very little.

Parker collected Emma's bags from her room, took them down in the lift and left them in the hall. She'd acquired another two since arriving in New York. Does anyone ever go home with less than they started out with? she wondered.

'I'll not come downstairs,' said Phyllis after several attempts to say goodbye. 'I'll only make a fool of myself. It's better that you simply remember an old battleaxe who didn't like to be disturbed during her bridge parties. When you visit us next time, my dear, bring Harry and Sebastian with you. I want to meet the man who captured your heart.'

A taxi blasted its horn in the street below.

'Time to go,' said Phyllis. 'Go quickly.'

Emma gave her one last hug and then she didn't look back.

When she stepped out of the lift Parker was standing by the front door waiting for her, the bags already stowed away in the boot of the taxi. The moment he saw her, he walked out on to the pavement and opened the back door of the cab.

'Goodbye, Parker,' said Emma, 'and thank you for everything.'

'My pleasure, ma'am,' he replied. Just as she was about to step into the taxi, he added, 'If it's not inappropriate, ma'am, I wondered if I might be allowed to make an observation?'

Emma stepped back, trying to mask her surprise. 'Of course, please do.'

'I so enjoyed Mr Clifton's diary,' he said, 'that I hope it will not be too long before you return to New York accompanied by your husband.'

—◦—

It wasn't long before the train was speeding through the countryside and New York was no more, as they headed towards the capital. Emma found she couldn't read or sleep for more than a few minutes at a time. Great-aunt Phyllis, Mr Guinzburg, Cousin Alistair, Mr Jelks, Detective Kolowski and Parker all made their exits and entrances.

She thought about what needed to be done once she arrived in Washington. First, she had to go to the British Embassy and sign some forms so she could join the ambassador on his flight to London, as arranged by Rupert Harvey, a second cousin twice removed. 'Don't mock, child,' she could hear her great-aunt remonstrating, and then she fell asleep. Harry entered her dreams, this time in uniform, smiling, laughing, and then she woke with a jolt, quite expecting him to be in the carriage with her.

When the train pulled into Union Station five hours later, Emma had trouble lugging her suitcases on to the platform, until a porter, an ex-serviceman with one arm, came to her rescue. He found a taxi for her, thanked her for the tip and gave her a salute with the wrong arm. Someone else whose destiny had been decided by a war he didn't declare.

'The British Embassy,' Emma said as she climbed into the cab.

She was dropped on Massachusetts Avenue, outside a pair of ornate iron gates displaying the Royal Standard. Two young soldiers ran across to help Emma with her bags.

'Who are you visiting, ma'am?' An English accent, an American word.

'Mr Rupert Harvey,' she said.

'Commander Harvey. Certainly,' said the corporal, who picked up her bags and guided Emma to an office at the rear of the building.

Emma entered a large room in which the staff, most dressed in uniform, scurried about in every direction. No one walked. A figure appeared out of the melee and greeted her with a huge smile.

'I'm Rupert Harvey,' he said. 'Sorry about the organized chaos, but it's always like this when the ambassador is returning to England. It's even worse this time, because we've had a visiting cabinet minister with us for the past week. All your paperwork has been prepared,' he added, returning to his desk. 'I just need to see your passport.'

Once he'd flicked through the pages, he asked her to sign here, here and here. 'A bus will be leaving from the front of the embassy for the airport at six this evening. Please make sure you're on time as everyone's expected to be on board the plane before the ambassador arrives.'

'I'll be on time,' said Emma. 'Would it be possible to leave my bags here while I go sightseeing?'

'That won't be a problem,' said Rupert. 'I'll have someone put them on the bus for you.'

'Thank you,' said Emma.

She was about to leave when he added, 'By the way, I loved the book. And just to warn you, the minister is hoping to have a private word with you when we're on the plane. I think he was a publisher before he went into politics.'

'What's his name?' Emma asked.

'Harold Macmillan.'

Emma recalled some of Mr Guinzburg's sage advice. 'Everyone is going to want this book,' he'd told her. 'There isn't a publisher who won't open their doors for you, so don't be easily flattered. Try and see Billy Collins and Allen Lane of Penguin.' He'd made no mention of a Harold Macmillan.

'Then I'll see you on the bus around six,' said her second cousin twice removed, before he disappeared back into the melee.

Emma left the embassy, walked out on to Massachusetts Avenue and checked her watch. Just over two hours to spare before her appointment with Colonel Cleverdon. She hailed a cab.

'Where to, miss?'

'I want to see everything the city has to offer,' she said.

'How long have you got, a couple of years?'

'No,' Emma replied, 'a couple of hours. So let's get moving.'

The taxi sped away from the kerb. First stop: the White House – 15 minutes. On to the Capitol – 20 minutes. Circling the Washington, Jefferson and Lincoln Memorials – 25 minutes. Dashing into the National Gallery – another 25 minutes. Ending up at the Smithsonian – but there was only 30 minutes left until her appointment, so she didn't make it past the first floor.

When she jumped back into the cab, the driver asked, 'Where to now, miss?'

Emma checked the address on Colonel Cleverdon's letter. '3022 Adams Street,' she replied, 'and I'm cutting it fine.'

When the cab drew up outside a large white marble building that occupied the entire block, Emma handed the cabbie her last five-dollar note. She would have to walk back to the embassy after her meeting. 'Worth every cent,' she told him.

He touched the rim of his cap. 'I thought it was only us Americans who did that sort of thing,' he said with a grin.

Emma walked up the steps, past two guards who stared right through her, and on into the building. She noticed that almost everyone was dressed in different shades of khaki, although few of them wore battle ribbons. A young woman behind the reception desk directed her to room 9197. Emma joined a mass of khaki uniforms as they headed towards the lifts, and when she stepped out on the ninth floor, she found Colonel Cleverdon's secretary waiting to greet her.

'I'm afraid the colonel has got caught up in a

meeting, but he should be with you in a few minutes,' she said as they walked along the corridor.

Emma was shown into the colonel's office. Once she had sat down, she stared at a thick file on the centre of the desk. As with the letter on Maisie's mantelpiece and the notebooks on Jelks's desk, she wondered how long she would have to wait before its contents were revealed.

The answer was twenty minutes. When the door eventually swung open, a tall, athletic man, around the same age as her father, burst into the room, a cigar bobbing up and down in his mouth.

'So sorry to have kept you,' he said, shaking hands, 'but there just aren't enough hours in the day.' He sat down behind his desk and smiled at her. 'John Cleverdon, and I would have recognized you anywhere.' Emma looked surprised, until he explained. 'You're exactly as Harry described you in his book. Would you like coffee?'

'No, thank you,' said Emma, trying not to sound impatient as she glanced at the file on the colonel's desk.

'I don't even have to open this,' he said, tapping the file. 'I wrote most of it myself, so I can tell you everything Harry's been up to since he left Lavenham. And now, thanks to his diaries, we all know he should never have been there in the first place. I can't wait to read the next instalment and find out what happened to him before he was sent to Lavenham.'

'And I can't wait to find out what happened to him after he left Lavenham,' Emma said, hoping she didn't sound impatient.

'Then let's get on with it,' said the colonel. 'Harry volunteered to join a special services unit, which I have the privilege of commanding, in exchange for his prison sentence being commuted. Having begun his life in the United States Army as a GI, he was recently commissioned in the field, and is currently serving as a lieutenant. He's been behind enemy lines now for several months,' he continued. 'He's been working with resistance groups in occupied countries and helping to prepare for our eventual landing in Europe.'

Emma didn't like the sound of that. 'What does behind enemy lines actually mean?'

'I can't tell you exactly, because it's not always easy to track him down when he's on a mission. He often cuts off communication with the outside world for days on end. But what I can tell you is that he and his driver, Corporal Pat Quinn, another Lavenham graduate, have turned out to be two of the most effective operatives to come out of my group. They're like two schoolboys who've been given a giant chemistry set and told they can go and experiment on the enemy's communications network. They spend most of their time blowing up bridges, dismantling railway lines and bringing down electricity pylons. Harry's specialty is disrupting German troop movements, and on one or two occasions the Krauts have nearly caught up with him. But so far he's managed to stay a step ahead of them. In fact, he's proved such a thorn in their flesh that they've put a price on his head, which seems to go up every month. Thirty thousand francs when I last checked.'

The colonel noticed that Emma's face had gone as white as a sheet.

'I'm so sorry,' he said. 'I didn't mean to alarm you but I sometimes forget, when I'm sitting behind a desk, just how much danger my boys face every day.'

'When will Harry be released?' asked Emma quietly.

'I'm afraid he's expected to serve out his sentence,' said the colonel.

'But now that you know he's innocent, can't you at least send him back to England?'

'I don't think that would make a great deal of difference, Miss Barrington, because if I know Harry, the moment he set foot in his homeland he'd only swap one uniform for another.'

'Not if I have anything to do with it.'

The colonel smiled. 'I'll see what I can do to help,' he promised as he rose from behind his desk. He opened the door and saluted her. 'Have a safe journey back to England, Miss Barrington. I hope it won't be long before the two of you end up in the same place, at the same time.'

HARRY CLIFTON

1945

41

'I'LL REPORT BACK, SIR, as soon as I've located them,' said Harry, before putting the field phone down.

'Located who?' asked Quinn.

'Kertel's army. Colonel Benson seems to think they could be in the valley on the other side of that ridge,' he said, pointing to the top of the hill.

'There's only one way we're going to find out,' said Quinn, shifting the Jeep noisily into first gear.

'Take it easy,' Harry told him, 'if the Hun are there, we don't need to alert them.'

Quinn remained in first as they crept slowly up the hill.

'That's far enough,' said Harry when they were less than fifty yards from the brow of the hill. Quinn put the handbrake on and turned the ignition off, and they jumped out and ran on up the incline. When they were only a few yards from the top, they fell flat on their stomachs, then, like two crabs scurrying back into the sea, they crawled until they stopped just below the crest.

Harry peeped over the top and caught his breath. He didn't need a pair of binoculars to see what they were up against. Field Marshal Kertel's legendary Nineteenth Armoured Corps was clearly preparing for battle in the valley below. Tanks were lined up as far as the eye could see, and the support troops would have filled a football stadium. Harry estimated that the Second Division of the Texas Rangers would be outnumbered by at least three to one.

'If we get the hell out of here,' whispered Quinn, 'we might just have enough time to prevent Custer's second-to-last stand.'

'Not so fast,' said Harry. 'We might be able to turn this to our advantage.'

'Don't you think we've used up enough of our nine lives during the past year?'

'I've counted eight so far,' said Harry. 'So I think we can risk just one more.' He began to crawl back down the hill before Quinn could offer an opinion. 'Have you got a handkerchief?' Harry asked as Quinn climbed behind the wheel.

'Yes, sir,' he said, taking one out of his pocket and passing it to Harry, who tied it to the Jeep's radio mast.

'You're not going to—'

'—surrender? Yes, it's our one chance,' said Harry. 'So drive slowly to the top of the ridge, corporal, and then on down into the valley.' Harry only ever called Pat 'corporal' when he didn't want to prolong the discussion.

'Into the valley of death,' suggested Quinn.

'Not a fair comparison,' said Harry. 'There were six hundred in the Light Brigade, and we are but two. So I see myself more like Horatius than Lord Cardigan.'

'I see myself more like a sitting duck.'

'That's because you're Irish,' said Harry, as they

crested the ridge and began the slow journey down the other side. 'Don't exceed the speed limit,' he said, trying to make light of it. He was expecting a hail of bullets to greet their impudent intrusion, but clearly curiosity got the better of the Germans.

'Whatever you do, Pat,' Harry said firmly, 'don't open your mouth. And try to look as if this has all been planned in advance.'

If Quinn had an opinion, he didn't express it, which was most unlike him. The corporal drove at a steady pace, and didn't touch the brake until they reached the front line of tanks.

Kertel's men stared at the occupants of the Jeep in disbelief, but no one moved until a major pushed his way through the ranks and headed straight for them. Harry leapt out of the Jeep, stood to attention and saluted, hoping his German would be up to it.

'What in God's name do you imagine you're doing?' asked the major.

Harry thought that was the gist of it. He maintained a calm exterior.

'I have a message for Field Marshal Kertel, from General Eisenhower, Supreme Commander of the Allied Forces in Europe.' Harry knew that when the major heard the name Eisenhower, he couldn't risk not taking it to a higher level.

Without another word the major climbed into the back of the Jeep, tapped Quinn on the shoulder with his baton and pointed in the direction of a large, well-camouflaged tent that stood to one side of the assembled troops.

When they reached the tent, the major leapt out. 'Wait here,' he ordered, before going inside.

Quinn and Harry sat there, surrounded by thousands of wary eyes.

'If looks could kill . . .' whispered Quinn. Harry ignored him.

It was several minutes before the major returned.

'What's it going to be, sir,' mumbled Quinn, 'the firing squad, or will he ask you to join him for a glass of schnapps?'

'The field marshal has agreed to see you,' said the major, not attempting to hide his surprise.

'Thank you, sir,' Harry said as he got out of the Jeep and followed him into the tent.

Field Marshal Kertel rose from behind a long table that was covered in a map that Harry recognized immediately, but this one had models of tanks and soldiers all heading in his direction. He was surrounded by a dozen field officers, none below the rank of colonel.

Harry stood rigidly to attention and saluted.

'Name and rank?' the field marshal asked after he had returned Harry's salute.

'Clifton, sir, Lieutenant Clifton. I am General Eisenhower's ADC.' Harry spotted a Bible on a small folding table by the field marshal's bed. A German flag covered the canvas of one side of the tent. Something was missing.

'And why would General Eisenhower send his ADC to see me?'

Harry observed the man carefully before answering his question. Unlike Goebbels's or Goering's, Kertel's battle-worn face confirmed that he had seen frontline action many times. The only medal he wore was an Iron Cross with oakleaf cluster, which Harry knew he'd won as a lieutenant at the Battle of the Marne in 1918.

'General Eisenhower wishes you to know that on the far side of Clemenceau, he has three full battalions of thirty thousand men, along with twenty-two thousand tanks. On his right flank is the Second Division of the Texas Rangers, in the centre, the Third Battalion of the Green Jackets, and on their left flank, a battalion of the Australian Light Infantry.'

The field marshal would have made an excellent poker player, because he gave nothing away. He would have known that the numbers were accurate, assuming those three regiments were actually in place.

'Then it should prove a most interesting battle, lieutenant. But if your purpose was to alarm me, you have failed.'

'That is no part of my brief, sir,' Harry said, glancing down at the map, 'because I suspect I haven't told you anything you didn't already know, including the fact that the Allies have recently taken control of the airfield at Wilhelmsberg.' A fact that was confirmed by a small American flag pinned on the airport on the map. 'What you may not know, sir, is that lined up on the runway is a squadron of Lancaster bombers, awaiting an order from General Eisenhower to destroy your tanks, while his battalions advance in battle formation.'

What Harry knew was that the only planes at the airfield were a couple of reconnaissance aircraft stranded because they'd run out of fuel.

'Get to the point, lieutenant,' said Kertel. 'Why did General Eisenhower send you to see me?'

'I will try to recall the general's exact words, sir.' Harry attempted to sound as if he were reciting a message. 'There can be no doubt that this dreadful war is fast drawing to a close, and only a deluded man with a limited experience of warfare could still believe victory is possible.'

The allusion to Hitler did not go unnoticed by the officers who surrounded their field marshal. That was when Harry realized what was missing. There was no Nazi flag or picture of the Führer in the field marshal's tent.

'General Eisenhower holds you and the Nineteenth Corps in the highest regard,' Harry continued. 'He has no doubt that your men would lay down their lives for you, whatever the odds. But in the name of God, he asks, for what purpose? This engagement will end with your troops being decimated, while we will undoubtedly lose vast numbers of men. Everyone knows that the end of the war can only be a matter of weeks away, so what can be gained by such unnecessary carnage? General Eisenhower read your book, *The Professional Soldier*, when he was at West Point, sir, and one sentence in particular has remained indelibly fixed in his memory throughout his military career.'

Harry had read Kertel's memoirs a fortnight before, when he realized they might be up against him, so he was able to recite the sentence almost word for word.

'"Sending young men to an unnecessary death is not an act of leadership, but of vainglory, and unworthy of a professional soldier." That, sir, is something you share with General Eisenhower, and to that end, he guarantees that if you lay down your arms, your men will be treated with the utmost dignity and respect, as set out in the Third Geneva Convention.'

Harry expected the field marshal's response to be, 'Good try, young man, but you can tell whoever it is commanding your puny brigade on the other side of that hill that I am about to wipe them off the face of the earth.' But what Kertel actually said, was, 'I will discuss the general's proposal with my officers. Perhaps you would be kind enough to wait outside.'

'Of course, sir.' Harry saluted, left the tent and returned to the Jeep. Quinn didn't speak when he climbed back into the front seat and sat beside him.

It was clear that Kertel's officers were not of one opinion, as raised voices could be heard from inside the tent. Harry could imagine the words, honour, common-sense, duty, realism, humiliation and sacrifice being bandied about. But the two he feared most were 'he's bluffing'.

It was almost an hour before the major summoned Harry back into the tent. Kertel was standing apart from his most trusted advisers, a world-weary look on his face. He had made his decision, and even if some of his officers didn't agree with it, once he had given the order they would never question him. He didn't need to tell Harry what that decision was.

'Do I have your permission, sir, to contact General Eisenhower and inform him of your decision?'

The field marshal gave a curt nod, and his officers quickly left the tent to see that his orders were carried out.

Harry returned to his Jeep accompanied by the major, and watched 23,000 men lay down their arms, climb out of their tanks and line up in columns of three as they prepared to surrender. His only fear was that having bluffed the field marshal, he wouldn't be able to pull off the same trick with his area commander. He picked up his field phone and only had to wait a few moments before Colonel Benson came on the line.

Harry hoped the major hadn't noticed the bead of sweat that was trickling down his nose.

'Have you discovered how many of them we're up against, Clifton?' were the colonel's first words.

'Could you put me through to General Eisenhower, colonel? This is Lieutenant Clifton, his ADC.'

'Have you gone out of your mind, Clifton?'

'Yes, I will hold on, sir, while you go and look for him.' His heart couldn't have beaten faster if he'd just run a hundred yards, and he began to wonder how long it would be before the colonel worked out what he was up to. He nodded at the major, but the major didn't respond. Was he standing there hoping to find a chink in his armour? As he waited, Harry watched thousands of fighting men, some perplexed, while others looked relieved, joining the ranks of those who had already abandoned their tanks and laid down their arms.

'It's General Eisenhower here. Is that you, Clifton?' said Colonel Benson when he came back on the line.

'Yes, sir. I'm with Field Marshal Kertel, and he has accepted your proposal that the Nineteenth Corps lay down their arms and surrender under the terms of the Geneva Convention, in order to avoid, if I remember your words correctly, sir, unnecessary carnage. If you bring forward one of our five battalions, they should be able to carry out the operation in an orderly fashion. I anticipate coming over Clemenceau ridge, accompanied by the Nineteenth Corps –' he looked at his watch – 'at approximately 1700 hours.'

'We'll be waiting for you, lieutenant.'

'Thank you, sir.'

Fifty minutes later Harry crossed the Clemenceau ridge for the second time that day, the German battalion following him as if he were the Pied Piper, over the hill and into the arms of the Texas Rangers. As the 700 men and 214 tanks surrounded the Nineteenth Corps, Kertel realized he had been duped by an Englishman and an Irishman, whose only weapons were a Jeep and a handkerchief.

The field marshal pulled a pistol from inside his tunic, and Harry thought for a moment that he was going to shoot him. Kertel stood to attention, saluted, placed the pistol to his temple and pulled the trigger.

Harry felt no pleasure in his death.

Once the Germans had been rounded up, Colonel Benson invited Harry to lead the nineteenth un-armoured corps in triumph to the compound. As they drove at the head of the column, even Pat Quinn had a smile on his face.

They must have been about a mile away when the Jeep passed over a German landmine. Harry heard a loud explosion, and remembered Pat's prophetic words, *Don't you think we've used up enough of our nine lives during the past year?*, as the Jeep cartwheeled into the air before bursting into flames.

And then, nothing.

42

DO YOU KNOW when you're dead?

Does it happen in an instant, and then suddenly you're no longer there?

All Harry could be sure of was the images that appeared before him were like actors in a Shakespearian play, each making their exits and entrances. But he couldn't be sure if it was a comedy, a tragedy or a history.

The central character never changed, and was played by a woman who gave a remarkable perform- ance, while others seemed to flit on and off the stage at her bidding. And then his eyes opened, and Emma was standing by his side.

When Harry smiled, her whole face lit up. She bent down and kissed him gently on the lips. 'Welcome home,' she said.

That was the moment when he realized not only how much he loved her, but also that now nothing would ever keep them apart. He took her gently by the hand. 'You're going to have to help me,' he began. 'Where am I? And how long have I been here?'

'Bristol General, and just over a month. It was touch and go for a while, but I wasn't going to lose you a second time.'

Harry gripped her hand firmly and smiled. He felt exhausted, and drifted back into a deep sleep.

—◦—

When he woke again it was dark, and he sensed that he was alone. He tried to imagine what might have happened to all those characters during the past five years, because, as in *Twelfth Night*, they must have believed he'd died at sea.

Had his mother read the letter he wrote to her? Had Giles used his colour-blindness as an excuse not to be called up? Had Hugo returned to Bristol once he was convinced Harry was no longer a threat? Were Sir Walter Barrington and Lord Harvey still alive? And one other thought kept returning again and again. Was Emma waiting for the right moment to tell him there was someone else in her life?

Suddenly, the door to his room was thrown open and a little boy came running in, shouting, 'Daddy, Daddy, Daddy!' before leaping on to his bed and throwing his arms around him.

Emma appeared moments later and watched as the two men in her life met for the first time.

Harry was reminded of the photograph of himself as a boy that his mother kept on the mantelpiece in Still House Lane. He didn't have to be told that this was his child and he felt a thrill he couldn't have begun to imagine before. He studied the boy more closely as he leapt up and down on the bed – his fair hair, blue eyes and square jaw, just like Harry's father.

'Oh my God,' said Harry, and fell into a deep sleep.

◄o►

When he woke again, Emma was sitting on the bed beside him. He smiled and took her hand.

'Now I've met my son, any other surprises?' he asked. Emma hesitated, before adding with a sheepish grin, 'I'm not sure where to start.'

'At the beginning possibly,' said Harry, 'like any good story. Just remember that the last time I saw you was on our wedding day.'

Emma began with her trip to Scotland and the birth of their son Sebastian. She'd just pressed the doorbell of Kristin's apartment in Manhattan, when Harry fell asleep.

◄o►

When he woke again, she was still with him.

Harry liked the sound of Great-aunt Phyllis and her cousin Alistair, and although he could only just remember Detective Kolowski, he would never forget Sefton Jelks. When Emma came to the end of her story she was on a plane crossing the Atlantic back to England, sitting next to Mr Harold Macmillan.

Emma presented Harry with a copy of *The Diary of a Convict*. All Harry said was, 'I must try and find out what happened to Pat Quinn.'

Emma found it difficult to find the right words.

'Was he killed by the landmine?' Harry asked quietly.

Emma bowed her head. Harry didn't speak again that night.

◄o►

Each day produced new surprises because, inevitably, everyone's life had moved on in the five years since Harry had seen them.

When his mother came to visit him the following day, she was on her own. He was so proud to learn that she was excelling at reading and writing, and was deputy manager of the hotel, but was saddened when she admitted she had never opened the letter delivered by Dr Wallace before it disappeared.

'I thought it was from a Tom Bradshaw,' she explained.

Harry changed the subject. 'I see you're wearing an engagement ring, as well as a wedding ring.'

His mother blushed. 'Yes, I wanted to see you on my own, before you met your stepfather.'

'My stepfather?' said Harry. 'Anyone I know?'

'Oh yes,' she said, and would have told him who she'd married, if he hadn't fallen asleep.

◄○►

The next time Harry woke it was the middle of the night. He switched on the bedside light and began to read *The Diary of a Convict*. He smiled several times before he reached the last page.

Nothing Emma told him about Max Lloyd came as a surprise, especially after Sefton Jelks had made a reappearance. However, he was surprised when Emma told him that the book had been an instant bestseller, and that the follow-up was doing even better.

'The follow-up?' enquired Harry.

'The first diary you wrote, about what happened to you before you were sent to Lavenham, has just been published in England. It's racing up the charts here, as it did in America. That reminds me, Mr Guinzburg keeps asking when he can expect your first novel, the one you hinted at in *The Diary of a Convict*?'

'I've got enough ideas for half a dozen,' Harry said.

'Then why don't you get started?' asked Emma.

◄O►

When Harry woke that afternoon, his mother and Mr Holcombe were standing by his side, holding hands as if they were on their second date. He'd never seen his mother looking so happy.

'You can't be my stepfather,' Harry protested, as the two shook hands.

'I most certainly am,' said Mr Holcombe. 'Truth is, I should have asked your mother to be my wife twenty years ago, but I simply didn't think I was good enough for her.'

'And you're still not good enough, sir,' said Harry with a grin. 'But then, neither of us ever will be.'

'Truth be known, I married your mother for her money.'

'What money?' said Harry.

'The ten thousand dollars Mr Jelks sent, which made it possible for us to buy a cottage in the country.'

'For which we will be eternally grateful,' chipped in Maisie.

'Don't thank me,' said Harry. 'Thank Emma.'

If Harry was taken by surprise when he discovered that his mother had married Mr Holcombe, it was nothing compared to the shock when Giles walked into the room, dressed in the uniform of a lieutenant in the Wessex Regiment. If that wasn't enough, his chest was covered in combat medals, including the Military Cross.

But when Harry asked how he'd won it, Giles changed the subject.

'I'm planning to stand for Parliament at the next election,' he announced.

'To which seat have you granted this honour?' asked Harry.

'Bristol Docklands,' Giles replied.

'But that's a safe Labour seat.'

'And I intend to be the Labour candidate.'

Harry made no attempt to hide his surprise. 'What caused this Saint Paul-like conversion?' he asked.

'A corporal I served with on the frontline called Bates—'

'Not Terry Bates?' said Harry.

'Yes, did you know him?'

'Sure did. The brightest kid in my class at Merry-wood Elementary, and the best sportsman. He left school at twelve to work in his father's business: Bates and Son, butchers.'

'That's why I'm standing as a Labour candidate,' said Giles. 'Terry had just as much right to be at Oxford as you or me.'

—◦—

The following day, Emma and Sebastian returned, armed with pens, pencils, pads and an India rubber. She told Harry the time had come for him to stop thinking and start writing.

During the long hours when he couldn't sleep, or was simply alone, Harry's thoughts turned to the novel he had intended to write if he hadn't escaped from Lavenham.

He began to make outline notes of the characters

that must turn the page. His detective would have to be a one-off, an original, who he hoped would become part of his readers' everyday lives, like Poirot, Holmes or Maigret.

He finally settled on the name William Warwick. The Hon. William would be the second son of the Earl of Warwick, and have turned down the opportunity to go to Oxford, much to his father's disgust, because he wanted to join the police force. His character would be loosely based on his friend Giles. After three years on the beat, walking the streets of Bristol, Bill, as he was known to his colleagues, would become a detective constable, and be assigned to Chief Inspector Blakemore, the man who'd intervened when Harry's uncle Stan had been arrested and wrongly charged with stealing money from Hugo Barrington's safe.

Lady Warwick, Bill's mother, would be modelled on Elizabeth Barrington; Bill would have a girlfriend called Emma, and his grandfathers Lord Harvey and Sir Walter Barrington would make the occasional entrance on the page but only to offer sage advice.

Every night, Harry would read over the pages he'd written that day, and every morning his wastepaper basket needed emptying.

◄o►

Harry always looked forward to Sebastian's visits. His young son was so full of energy, so inquisitive and so good-looking, just like his mother, as everyone teased him.

Sebastian often asked questions no one else would have dared to: what's it like being in prison? How many

Germans did you kill? Why aren't you and Mama married? Harry sidestepped most of them, but he knew Sebastian was far too bright not to work out what his father was up to, and feared it wouldn't be long before the boy trapped him.

—◄○►—

Whenever Harry was alone he continued to work on the outline plot for his novel.

He'd read over a hundred detective novels while he was working as deputy librarian at Lavenham, and he felt that some of the characters he'd come across in prison and in the army could provide material for a dozen novels: Max Lloyd, Sefton Jelks, Warden Swanson, Officer Hessler, Colonel Cleverdon, Captain Havens, Tom Bradshaw and Pat Quinn – especially Pat Quinn.

During the next few weeks, Harry became lost in his own world, but he had to admit that the way some of his visitors had spent the last five years had also turned out to be stranger than fiction.

—◄○►—

When Emma's sister Grace paid him a visit, Harry didn't comment on the fact that she looked so much older than when he'd last seen her, but then she'd only been a schoolgirl at the time. Now Grace was in her final year at Cambridge and about to sit her exams. She told him with pride that for a couple of years she'd worked on a farm, not going back up to Cambridge until she was convinced the war was won.

It was with sadness that Harry learnt from Lady

Barrington that her husband, Sir Walter, had passed away, a man Harry had admired second only to Old Jack.

His uncle Stan never visited him.

As the days went by, Harry thought about raising the subject of Emma's father, but he sensed that even the mention of his name was off-limits.

And then one evening, after Harry's doctor had told him that it wouldn't be too long before they re-leased him, Emma lay down next to him on the bed and told him that her father was dead.

When she came to the end of her story, Harry said, 'You've never been good at dissembling, my darling, so perhaps the time has come to tell me why the whole family is so on edge.'

43

HARRY WOKE the next morning to find his mother, along with the whole Barrington family, seated around his bed.

The only absentees were Sebastian and his uncle Stan, neither of whom it was felt would have made a serious contribution.

'The doctor has said you can go home,' said Emma.

'Great news,' said Harry. 'But where's home? If it means going back to Still House Lane and living with Uncle Stan, I'd prefer to stay in hospital – even go back to prison.' No one laughed.

'I'm now living at Barrington Hall,' said Giles, 'so why don't you move in with me? Heaven knows there are enough rooms.'

'Including a library,' said Emma. 'So you'll have no excuse not to continue working on your novel.'

'And you can come and visit Emma and Sebastian whenever you want to,' added Elizabeth Barrington.

Harry didn't respond for some time.

'You're all being very kind,' he eventually managed, 'and please don't think I'm not grateful, but I can't believe it needed the whole family to decide where I'm going to live.'

'There's another reason we wanted to talk to you,' said Lord Harvey, 'and the family have asked me to speak on their behalf.'

Harry sat bolt upright, and gave Emma's grandfather his full attention.

'A serious issue has arisen concerning the future of the Barrington estate,' began Lord Harvey. 'The terms of Joshua Barrington's will have turned out to be a legal nightmare, rivalled only by Jarndyce and Jarndyce, and could end up being just as financially crippling.'

'But I have no interest in either the title or the estate,' said Harry. 'My only desire is to prove that Hugo Barrington was not my father, so I can marry Emma.'

'Amen to that,' said Lord Harvey. 'However, complications have arisen that I must acquaint you with.'

'Please do, sir, because I can't see that there's any problem.'

'I'll try to explain. Following Hugo's untimely death, I advised Lady Barrington that as she had recently suffered two onerous demands for death duties, and remembering that I am over seventy, it might be wise for our two companies, Barrington's and Harvey's, to join forces. This, you understand, was at a time when we still believed you were dead. Therefore, it seemed that any dispute over who would inherit the title and the estate had, however unhappily, been resolved, making it possible for Giles to take his place as head of the family.'

'And he still can, as far as I'm concerned,' said Harry.